EVERYONE LOVES THE BOYS OF BRIGHTON

"I loved this book and I love this town. I hope there's going to be more."
—Melissa Lemons on *Gabe*

"An amazing read that was filled with lust, love, crazy hot sex, danger, action and so much more This is the first book I have read in this series but I will definitely be reading more in the future."
—Gay Book Reviews on *Sam's Soldiers*

"I was crazy impressed that the author made me teary over the ending of a relationship that I shouldn't have even been invested in. I didn't yet know these characters yet the author made me hurt for them. That takes some mad writing skills!"
—Love Bytes Reviews

"Jesse and Royce together have my heart. Jesse has it all by himself."
—The Book Junkie Reads on *Jesse*

"So much action, intrigue, drama and angst for the long awaited story of Grady and Ben. This was worth the wait. Sexy and sweet. I can't wait for the next."
—SamD on *Grady*

"I knew this one would be my favorite to date! There was something about Vincent that said awesome then came Tristan."
—Booky on *Vincent*

"This installment of the Boys of Brighton was so good! I loved Shadow and Randy 's story I was hooked from the first page to the last. This book was definitely worth the wait!"
—AG on *Shadow*

"I have loved this series from the very first story and this holiday novella is simply perfect. We get a glimpse of all our couples and what is happening in their lives while the holidays explode around them. I cannot wait for more!"

—bookobsessed on *The Holidays*

BOYS OF BRIGHTON
VOLUME 2

M. TASIA

www.BOROUGHSPUBLISHINGGROUP.com

PUBLISHER'S NOTE: This is a work of fiction. Names, characters, places and incidents either are the product of the author's imagination or are used fictitiously. Any resemblance to actual events, locales, business establishments or persons, living or dead, is coincidental. Boroughs Publishing Group does not have any control over and does not assume responsibility for author or third-party websites, blogs or critiques or their content.

BOYS OF BRIGHTON VOLUME 2
Travis, Grady, Vincent, Shadow, The Holidays

ISBN: 978-1-957295-45-9

To my family for their unwavering support.
I love all of you to the moon and back.

TRAVIS

Chapter One

The heat from the flames moved like waves slowly burning his hair and skin. The pain was excruciating, but he held on. He heard people screaming, but he didn't dare look down. He somehow knew the fire was getting closer, and no matter what he did, the firemen would never reach him in time. The flames shot upward, licking at his feet and legs. The screams ringing in his ears were now his own. The smoke sucked the air out of his lungs as he began to gasp and cough. His fingers slipped slightly, and he knew it would all be over soon.

Travis jackknifed out of bed so fast he slipped on the hardwood and fell flat on his back. His heart was racing. He drew in a ragged breath while he tried to clear his brain, but he could still feel the flames on his skin, and the smell of burning flesh still clogged his nose. He blinked to clear his vision and looked around his tiny apartment.

Safe. He was safe.

He sat up and rubbed his bruised back, feeling raised scars through the fabric. To this day, even when he was in bed, he remained covered in a shirt and sleeping pants, as if he could hide away the past.

Slowly, he stood then made his way over to his small kitchenette where he placed the kettle on his one-burner hotplate. He grabbed his one mug from the cupboard, along with his packages of tea and sugar. His little place might not have looked like much to someone else, but it was perfect for him. Considering mere months ago he was living out of his car, this was an upgrade. It was clean and safe, and that was all that mattered.

Still unsteady on his feet, he leaned against the tiny counter as he pulled his long hair into a ponytail and then took a deep breath to try to clear his mind. The nightmares were getting worse, and the room seemed quieter and emptier than ever before. In the past, Travis wouldn't have minded so much if it weren't for one persistent person who had become a constant presence in his life since moving to Brighton. Officer Bo Mason had turned Travis's solitary life upside down with his kind brown eyes and gentle touch. In contrast to his manner, the man was physically intimidating, standing over six and a half feet tall. Any sane gay man would have perked right up at the first sign of interest. *But not me, of course.* Travis knew once the truth came out, Bo would never look at him the same way again.

When the kettle whistled, Travis turned off the burner and poured the steaming water over the teabag in his mug. The aroma of chamomile wafted up, soothing Travis's jumpy nerves. He looked around his room again, and for the first time in a long time, he felt lonely. *I wouldn't be alone if I weren't screwed up. I should have accepted Bo's offer.*

Travis had fallen from scaffolding at work and wound up in the hospital. The police had come to the scene—Officer Bo Mason to be exact, who had become a guardian angel of sorts. After endless cajoling, Travis had agreed to spend his recovery at Bo's house while trying to get a handle on the relentless nightmares. At the last minute, Travis had backed out and returned to his room above the diner where he worked. Alone and in pain, but his scars and secrets remained protected.

He knew he was quiet and held people at arm's length, but nonetheless, he was dismayed that people viewed him as incapable of caring for himself. He knew he had issues but he wasn't an invalid.

Now it was four in the morning, so there was no use trying to go back to sleep. He needed to open the diner in a couple of hours anyway. Sarah would be in by six, and another busy day would begin again. But today would be a little different—it was payday and Travis had something special planned. Just the thought of it made him smile.

Travis cleaned his cup, made his bed, showered, and headed downstairs to the diner. The dining room was dark, the solo light from the kitchen spilling out into the area, casting a dim glow. He loved this time of day. Everything was fresh and new; anything was possible. Since the diner faced east, he'd soon be graced with a beautiful sunrise filled with reds and yellows. Someday, he would capture that sight on a canvas.

He turned from the window and headed for the kitchen. He'd get a tray of biscuits on before he started the coffee, knowing he'd have company soon enough. Since he'd decided to come back to his apartment from the hospital, Bo had been showing up every morning before the diner opened to have coffee with Travis. Then throughout the day into the evening, Bo would stop by until Travis was done with work. If he were honest with himself, he looked forward to their time together. And that was all he could allow. Nothing closer and certainly nothing more. Aside from the hospital staff and physical therapists at the rehab facility, no one willingly had or would ever touch him.

Within twenty minutes, Travis had a tray of biscuits ready for the oven. He set the timer and went to turn on the coffee when he heard a knock on the front door. *Bo.*

"Just a minute," Travis yelled as he poured the remaining water into the coffee makers and headed for the door.

He rounded the booths and saw Bo's police cruiser in the parking lot, and the man's large body filling the front door's frame. Bo stood there smiling wide as if he had good reason. Travis felt his body heat up, and he knew he was blushing. Life had made him tough; he was a loner, and he didn't blush, dammit. But the sight of Bo turned Travis's brain into tapioca pudding.

Quickly, he unlocked the door and let in the man of his dreams.

He could look but never touch.

"Good morning." Bo's deep voice resonated throughout Travis's body like a caress. He reminded himself to remain unaffected; he could never allow himself to slip.

"Good morning, Bo. I just put the coffee on. It should be ready any minute."

"Great. Will you be joining me this morning?" Bo's brown eyes were so warm and inviting.

Travis had already put on the biscuits, so he had a few minutes to spare. *But should he?*

Bo being a cop meant he could read people well. "A couple minutes is all I'm asking for, promise."

Oh, what the hell, why not?

"Okay, I'll get the coffee."

Bo sat his large body on a stool at the counter. With only the light from the kitchen illuminating the area, this familiar scene felt almost intimate. Travis's hands shook slightly with equal parts excitement and trepidation. Though there could be nothing physical between them, maybe they could be friends. That way he wouldn't lose Bo completely once the man realized Travis was a lost cause and Bo moved onto someone who could be what he needed.

Carefully, Travis added sugar and cream to Bo's coffee, and then walked to the opposite side of the counter across from Bo, making sure a physical barrier remained between them. Bo smiled when Travis returned with his black coffee, and if Bo noticed Travis was keeping his distance, the cop gave no indication.

"How was your night? More nightmares?" Bo cradled the coffee mug between his large hands.

Travis had tried to keep his nightmares to himself, but Bo had seen the effects they had on him in the hospital, so there was no use in pretending they didn't exist.

"It wasn't so bad. Only one last night." Travis played off how shaken he'd been and attempted a smile.

Bo reached over and took Travis's hand, holding it gently. Travis froze, unable to pull his hand away. The big man's warmth moved up Travis's arm, and excitement filled his body. Bo reached into his pocket and pulled something out before placing it into Travis's open palm.

"I want you to have this." Bo removed his hand, leaving a shiny, black cell phone behind. "Please accept it."

Travis never had enough extra money to buy a cell phone—a roof over his head and food in his stomach took precedence over any creature comforts. He looked at the phone's shiny screen and its sleek body and had no clue what to do with it. Of course, he knew there was a button to turn it on, but that was as far as his knowledge base went.

"I…I've never…I can't take this."

"Yes, you can. I bought it for you."

"But why?" Travis asked, truly confused.

Travis could have sworn Bo's cheeks pinked. *Why would he be embarrassed? I'm the one who doesn't know how to use the damn thing.*

"You should have one for safety in case you need help, or if you just want to talk to someone. I programmed my number into it, but you can add as many people as you like. Here is your new phone number." Bo handed Travis a slip of paper then took the phone from his hand and said, "I'll show you how it works," saving him the embarrassment of admitting he was clueless. He figured Bo must have noticed Travis didn't have much by way of possessions, particularly a phone.

Bo spent the next ten minutes explaining all the features. The only things that registered with Travis were how to text and make a call. He had no idea what he'd use the Bluetooth for. There was even a little picture of Bo on the screen Travis could push if he wanted to call him. Bo smiled wide, handed the phone back to Travis then stood while placing his money for the coffee on the counter.

"I'll drop in later today for lunch."

"But I didn't say I'd take it," Travis called out as Bo headed for the door.

"Try it out. See if you like it," Bo replied. "Have a good day." The door swung shut, and he was gone.

Travis stood at the counter for a few minutes, trying to figure out what to do with the phone. In the end, he shoved it into his pocket before returning to the kitchen.

Soon Sarah arrived to get the dining room ready for the breakfast rush. She kept glancing at him then finally came out and asked, "Why do you look especially happy this morning?"

Travis froze. Was it wrong to want to keep this private—at least for now? "Just having a good morning, and it's payday."

Sarah looked like she wasn't buying it. "Okay, you keep it to yourself. But I gotta say, it's nice to see you smile."

With that the day began as it always did, in a flurry of faces and food. The kitchen of the only diner in town was fast-paced most of the time; they had a few small lulls between the breakfast, lunch, and dinner crowds, but for the most part, time moved quickly.

When noon came and went without any sign of Bo, Travis began to worry. Surely someone would know if there'd been an incident and would tell him, right? Or maybe Bo decided he'd leave Travis with the phone for a while to get used to it. In any case, Travis had to admit not seeing Bo was disappointing.

Jesse, the diner's manager, came in around four in the afternoon to prepare for the evening shift, which gave Travis the opportunity to go to the bank, deposit his check, and pop by a place he'd been dreaming of visiting since he started working at the diner. "I'll be back in an hour to help with the dinner rush," Travis told Jesse while taking off his apron.

"No hurry, you've already stocked the kitchen, so there won't be much to do for prep. I don't know what I did before you got here," Jesse muttered as he rifled through the fridge. "You even filled all the sauces. Thank you, man."

"It's my job," Travis replied, unsure what he'd done to deserve the praise. He'd always worked hard. Like his dad used to say: If you're going to do it, you better make damn sure it's done right.

"Well then thank you for doing your job so well." Jesse smiled before reaching into his apron pocket to hand Travis his weekly check.

"No problem. I like my job." And he truly did. This had been the first time in a long time that he'd felt welcomed and accepted. Jesse, Sarah, Bo, and Brighton had given him that.

Travis walked down the spotless sidewalk and wondered if there was a person who cleaned the general areas of the town, or did the people clean up as they walked, or didn't they litter? It was the cleanest town he'd ever lived in.

As he made his way to the bank, he waved at Mrs. Wollart who was leading her children by the hand across the crosswalk. There were overflowing flower baskets hanging from the lamp posts, and brightly painted signs announced each store. Travis couldn't help but smile at how the town looked like it made him feel.

He turned when he heard something hit the ground and saw Mrs. Wollart's grocery bag had spilled across the sidewalk. Immediately, he went to her side and started gathering the cans. The bag was still useable, so he began to fill it.

"Thank you. Geesh, the bag slid right out of my hands." Mrs. Wollart fussed as she gathered her two sniffling toddlers to her side. The little girl looked to be about five, while the boy seemed to be around three.

"How far do you have to go?" Travis asked.

"Our home is a few houses down the street," she answered.

"I'll carry it for you, ma'am."

"Oh, I couldn't ask you to do that." She smiled as she lifted her sleepy little boy into her arms.

"You've got your hands full. I don't mind," Travis assured her.

Mrs. Wollart grabbed her daughter's hand and led the way to their house. She walked up to a modest ranch with a large American flag displayed out front, which fit; Sarah had told Travis that Mr. Wollart had been deployed to Afghanistan on his third tour of duty with the Army.

When Mrs. Wollart opened the door, Travis followed her through a house strewn with children's toys. He deposited her bag of groceries on the kitchen table and noticed colorful paintings on the fridge.

"Thank you, Travis."

"No problem, ma'am. Have a good day." He headed out of the house and with one final glance back he saw the little girl waving at him through the big picture window. He waved back and was on his way.

His stop at the bank only took a few moments; there was only one other person in line. Then he was off to his final destination, Brighton Stationery and Art Supply. He stopped to look at the beautiful artwork displayed in their front window. The paintings and graphics were breathtaking. The bell tinkled as he opened the clear glass door. The moment he stepped inside, his heart lightened at the sight of all the paper choices and canvases. Paint tubes shone in the late afternoon sunlight and called to him.

Places like this one were what he missed most. Since being out on his own he'd never had the ability to continue drawing, let alone paint anything. Today was a special day. He'd finally had enough money in his budget to buy a new sketchbook and pencils. It wasn't that Jesse paid poorly; Travis was saving the bulk of his money for a newer car. His fingers itched to touch the various paints until he saw a set of well-priced sable brushes displayed at the end of one of the aisles. They were beautiful but not in his budget this time.

"Can I help you, Travis?" A young man asked as he joined Travis, who was debating his purchases. The man's smile was warm and genuine. Sometimes Travis's tattoos made people nervous and kept them away though he thought his ink was beautiful.

"I'm sorry, have we met?" Travis wracked his brain for a name.

"Not formally. I'm Bo's cousin, Keith." The clerk offered his hand in greeting. Keith was shorter than Travis, had black hair and a full beard, and looked nothing like Bo.

"It's nice to meet you." Travis shook the man's hand; he had a strong handshake.

"They're well priced, aren't they? I have a set of them at home. Would you like me to take them out from the case?"

"I wish. No, I'm looking for a sketchbook and pencils."

"Right this way." Keith led Travis across the store, past the clay and molds, and up to intricately carved wooden shelves.

"I'll leave you to browse," Keith said as he handed over a piece of paper with all the weekly specials. "Yell if you need anything." Then he turned and walked back to the shelf he had been stocking.

Travis scanned the supplies, shocked and pleased that a small-town store had such an extensive selection. He had walked past the store many times since his arrival in Brighton but had never stepped inside. He wasn't a glutton for punishment; he wouldn't set foot in a store if he didn't intend to buy something.

At seeing all the different sketchpad options, Travis couldn't wipe the smile off of his face if he'd tried. It'd been years since he'd allowed himself to even dream of drawing again. After *that* night, there was no longer time for dreaming. But now, he knew exactly what he wanted and picked it off the shelf. This pad had a high paper weight so it wouldn't crumple under stress, as well as spiral bindings with perforated pages, which could be torn out easily. Once he had his new book, he went in search of the perfect pencils, or, more specifically, the best he could afford. He found a set of four graphite pencils on sale, half price. *Sold.*

He held his treasures to his chest as he approached the cash register. Though it wasn't much, it felt like a triumph.

Halfway back to the diner his worry that he hadn't seen Bo since early that morning returned. Travis couldn't help but think of all the terrible things that could have happened to him. Bo was a cop after all. Travis reached into his pocket and pulled out the cell phone.

Would he think I'm prying or be happy to hear from me?

Travis looked down at the dark screen and turned it on. His finger hovered over the little picture of Bo on the display as Travis weighed his choices. He stopped walking and leaned against the brick wall of the flower shop. He took a deep breath and tapped the screen. Before he had the chance to rethink it, Bo's voice came across the line.

"Travis, are you okay?"

"I was wondering the same about you. You didn't come in like you normally do for lunch," Travis said in a rush.

There was silence for a moment before Bo spoke, his voice deeper than before. "You were worried about me."

"Are you okay?"

"I'm fine. We had a six-car pileup on the interstate north of town. That's been tying me up all day, but I'll be in for dinner," Bo explained. "I'm sorry I worried you."

"Sorry to have interrupted you. I wasn't worried, just curious," Travis lied, not wanting to seem clingy.

"You're not interrupting. I'm back at the station finishing paperwork. I want you to call me. If I don't answer, I'll call you back as soon as I can." Bo's voice was low and did strange things to Travis's stomach. His heart was skipping beats.

God, I'm doomed.

But...Bo sounded happy to hear from him. Travis hadn't felt that in a long time; he hadn't realized how much he'd missed being close to anyone, even just having friends. Moving around so much, coupled with not trusting anyone, didn't help.

"Travis? Are you still there?"

"Yeah, sorry." Travis fumbled the phone. "I should let you go so you can finish your work."

"But I'll see you tonight."

"I'll be at the diner until nine."

"Then I'll be there," Bo said. "I'm glad you called."

Travis had no idea how to respond, so he went with the safest reply. “Bye, Bo.”

“See you soon.”

Travis pushed the disconnect button and leaned more heavily against the wall for support.

What am I doing?

I can’t lead him on when it’s all going to end in disaster.

***

Bo placed his cell in his pocket and tried to go back to his paperwork, but his mind was focused on the beautiful man across town. From his silky black hair to his multiple intricate tattoos, Travis was breathtaking. His pale blue eyes revealed his every emotion and gave Bo insight into the amazing man. He could see Travis’s doubts, and the guilt he carried. When Bo found out that Travis had been living in his car before being renting the apartment above the diner, Bo’s heart went out to the man. He would have offered to help, but he’d found out after the fact.

Within weeks of coming to Brighton, Bo learned Travis had volunteered his time at the new youth center. Bo wasn’t surprised; it was easy to see the man had a caring heart. But Travis was hiding something, something painful that made him hold himself apart from everyone. Bo wasn’t easily dissuaded or pushed away, and in Travis’s case, Bo was more determined than usual to get closer to the elusive man. The cell phone was the first step. Bo would get the man used to talking with him, even if it was only over the phone. If it hadn’t been for the scaffolding accident, Travis would have never talked to Bo. And, until a few weeks ago, Travis barely said a word when Bo went into the diner.

From the day he’d first set eyes on Travis, Bo was attracted to the man. The pull had grown stronger ever since.

"Should I guess who put that smile on your face?" Chief David Graham asked as he sat in the chair opposite Bo's desk. "How is Travis doing?"

"He's still having nightmares like the ones he had in the hospital." Bo chewed his bottom lip as he thought about what Travis was reliving every night. In the hospital, he would call out names as he screamed in what had to be horrific pain. The anguish had made Bo want to gather Travis in his arms and fix whatever was wrong.

"Is he getting any therapy?" Dave grilled. He couldn't help but sound like a cop. He and Bo had been friends since childhood and they'd been working together for years at the Brighton PD. Dave was married to Bo's cousin Kate, and he went to Dave and Kate's house once a week for dinner. He was godfather to their daughter, Kimmy.

"He's supposed to, but he hasn't gone yet. Dr. Green set up everything from the hospital," Bo explained. "I just have to get Travis to go."

"You'll have to take him if he doesn't go on his own," Dave advised.

"I don't know if he'll let me. I did manage to get him to keep a cell phone though." Bo had shared his feelings and concerns with his best friend.

"You sure you don't want to take a look into his past?" Dave pointed at the computer screen.

"No, he'll tell me when he's ready." Bo didn't want to break Travis's trust, but he understood Dave was trying to protect Bo. Truth be told, he had been fighting his natural urge to check up on Travis, but held strong. For how much longer, Bo had no idea.

"Okay, buddy. But, I don't want to see you getting hurt."

"I know what I'm doing," Bo assured.

"I hope you do," Dave replied. "Why don't you invite him to come to dinner at our house next week?"

"I don't think he's ready for that. How about a rain check?"

"Anytime you want, bring him along."

"Thanks, Dave."

The chief got up and went into his office, closing the door behind him. Bo refocused on his computer screen, eager to get the work done so he could head over to the diner. No one had been seriously injured in the traffic accident, but the fact that there were multiple vehicles involved made for a truckload of word processing.

One hour later Bo sat on his favorite stool at the diner's counter, eager to see Travis after such a long day. The place was fairly busy, and Sarah had two high school girls waitressing with her. Bo knew what he was hungry for—food wise. Travis made a phenomenal fried chicken, which Bo had every Friday night when he was on shift, or lately whenever a certain cook was working.

"Hey, Bo. Fried chicken for you tonight?" Sarah asked as she placed a full cup of coffee in front of him.

"Yes, ma'am. That would be perfect. Thank you."

Sarah smiled and wrote out his order on her pad before sticking it to the railing above the pass-through to the kitchen. Bo could see Jesse working over the grill, but there was no sign of Travis. Bo hoped he hadn't missed him. Jesse looked up, saw Bo, nodded his head in greeting, and did the one thing Bo wished he could have done—called Travis's name.

Within moments, Travis's head popped into view, and Jesse pointed to Bo's order. Travis immediately looked over at Bo and smiled. His heartbeat sped up, and his palms began to sweat. It was crazy. He'd dated plenty in the past, but one smile from Travis had Bo behaving like a kid with his first crush, like when he'd made a fool of himself fawning over Billy Fallan in the third grade. Bo picked up the glass of water sitting in front of him and took a big gulp in an attempt to calm his racing heart. He'd never had someone affect him like this.

Minutes later, the swinging door to the back opened and Travis came walking out with a plate of fried chicken, mashed potatoes, gravy, and corn—everything a growing boy needed, as Bo's mother would say. He sat a bit straighter as Travis approached; this was the first time he'd hand-delivered Bo's food.

"Hey." Bo couldn't keep the smile off his face.

"Hi, Bo." Travis placed the plate on the counter. "How are you?"

"Better now." Bo knew that was a cheesy response, but it made Travis smile all the same. "How was your day?"

"Good. I met your cousin Keith today."

"Oh? Where?"

"At the store he works at." Travis looked away as he answered.

"The art store. He owns that. He's quite the artist. What were you getting there?"

"Um, some art supplies."

"Supplies. Are you an artist, too?"

"I draw. I don't know if you'd consider me an artist." Travis stopped and looked around the diner. "Huh, I haven't shared that with anyone in a long time. It's my hobby."

"Would you show me your work sometime?" Bo knew he was pushing the secretive man, but if it meant spending more time with Travis, Bo would try anything.

"I'd like that."

"So would I." Their eyes met and neither looked away. In that moment, Bo got the same feeling he had every morning when he had Travis all to himself—lucky.

"Travis," Jesse hollered from the kitchen, breaking the spell. "We need more mashed potatoes."

"I should be heading back," Travis muttered, but he didn't make a move to turn away.

"Okay, I'll see you in the morning. Remember to call me anytime," Bo urged. "For any reason."

"Are you sure about me using your cell phone?"

"It's your cell phone, and you can do whatever you like with it."

Travis looked like he wanted to argue, but instead he began picking at his shirt. Bo had learned that was one of Travis's *tells* when he was nervous.

"Is something wrong?"

Travis dipped his head. "Why are you doing all this for me?"

"Why wouldn't I? I like you. I want to get to know you better, and I thought talking on the phone was a good place to start. Besides, you don't have one and you need a cell in case of an emergency," Bo explained.

Travis smiled and muttered, "Are you sure?"

"Positive."

Bo had never been surer about anything or anyone.

Chapter Two

Travis sat staring at the cell phone in his hand. It'd been three days since Bo had given it to him, and he had yet to call him again. But he sure could use him right about now. Travis had woken up covered in flames—well, that had been what he thought when he jumped from his bed, yet again. Another nightmare—worse than the night before. Was five in the morning too early to call Bo? Would he be up getting ready for work? Travis felt like a fool for even considering it.

But his hands were shaking, and he couldn't seem to calm down. Tears continued to stream down his face, which made him angrier. *Such a damaged sap.*

Travis had never asked for help before, but he knew he was losing the battle, and that his nightmares were bleeding over into reality. Bo knew about the nightmares; he'd understand. *I hope.* Travis pushed the button, and the phone began to ring on the other end.

"Travis, what's wrong?" Bo didn't sound groggy. Maybe he'd been awake.

"I just…I just…"

"Are you hurt?"

"No," Travis gasped out between breaths. He knew he was hyperventilating but couldn't stop himself.

"Another nightmare?"

"Yes, I just…I needed to talk."

"I'll do you one better. I'll be there in two minutes. I started my shift at five."

Travis was so freaked out by his nightmare he didn't argue. Holding the phone tight against his ear, he started down the stairs, still in his sleeping clothes, and went to the back door. "I'm sorry to bother you."

"You are never a bother. I'm pulling into the back parking lot." When Travis saw the police cruiser, he opened the door. He knew he'd regret this later, but right now he couldn't stand to be alone.

He watched as Bo parked, jumped out of his car and seemed to get to Travis's side in the work of a moment. "Let's go inside and talk, sweetheart."

Travis caught the endearment. It was the first time Bo had said it, or anything like it. Travis decided to let it slide; he didn't want to draw any attention to it, or get used to it. He led Bo up to the apartment. Travis knew it was small, but when Bo stood in the center, it became unbelievably tiny. Instead of sitting, Bo walked over and stood directly in front of Travis. He raised his big hand and gently wiped Travis's cheek.

"Do you want to tell me what the nightmare was about?" Bo asked softly.

"I can't."

"You can't remember or you're not able to tell me?"

"I can't. I can't tell you."

"You need to talk to someone about what's bothering you. If not me, the therapist Dr. Green suggested before you left the hospital. I still have the therapist's business card."

Travis began to back away. He wasn't crazy; he didn't need therapy. Before he could take another step, Bo gathered him in his arms and held Travis tight. "Easy. Therapy is a good thing. It's a safe place for you to talk about these nightmares."

"I'm not crazy," Travis insisted as he tried to break free of Bo's hold.

"Of course you're not crazy. Why would you think that?"

"You want me to see a therapist."

"That doesn't make you crazy." Bo shook his head. "Hell, sweetheart. I've seen a therapist before, and you don't think I'm crazy, do you?"

"No, of course not," Travis mumbled.

"But I was in therapy. I needed someone's help to get through a tough time in my life."

"Why did you have to have therapy?" Travis wanted to know everything about this man but realized too late that might be a sensitive question.

Bo gathered him closer and buried his face in Travis's hair. He leaned into Bo and was about to tell him he didn't have to say a word when Bo began to speak.

"I didn't start out my career on the Brighton Police Force. For the first five years, I was posted in Houston. I had the same partner for all those years, and we'd become friends. I would go over for Sunday dinner at Roy's house with his wife and son. The couple had been high school sweethearts."

"Had been?" Travis had a bad feeling about this.

"We got a call out to a domestic, and when we arrived, the house was dark. We waited for backup before we went in, did everything by the book. Once we cleared the living room, Roy and I headed down the hallway toward the bedrooms. The suspect burst out of a closet with a shotgun in his hands, pumping out rounds at us. I fired my gun, but I was hit in the chest and thrown back into the living room. If it hadn't been for my bulletproof vest, I wouldn't be standing here. By the time I regained consciousness, the suspect was dead, and so was Roy."

"I'm so sorry," Travis whispered, and his heart ached as he tried to comfort the big man holding him. The thought of Bo being hurt, or worse, made Travis's throat close and his heart rattle against his ribs.

Bo held him closer and began rubbing Travis's back. "Thank you, it was a long time ago, but I needed help getting through it. I went to therapy for a little over a year. It was the best decision I ever made."

Travis stood there quietly taking it all in. Bo's rhythmic rubbing was hypnotizing, and Travis almost forgot why touching was such a bad idea. Bo had to be able to feel the raised flesh and jagged scars through Travis's thin T-shirt. He stiffened and began to pull away, but Bo held on tighter and continued to rub softly.

"Easy, sweetheart, it's okay." Bo voice was deep and comforting.

"No, it's not. You don't know." Travis was tired of people saying it was okay, because it never was.

"Yes, I do." Bo said gently as he trailed his finger across Travis's chin, lifting it so that he was looking into Bo's eyes. "You were pretty out of it at the hospital, and the gown they gave you really didn't hide much."

Travis froze. Holy shit. Bo had seen his body. He'd seen the puckered skin covering Travis's back, butt, and legs. In some places, they had used skin grafts for more serious of the wounds. It took years for the skin to stretch enough for Travis to regain most of his flexibility. But worst of all were the burns to his genitals. He was hideous, and Bo knew his secret—and had known for weeks. Why did he continue to come around? He should have hightailed it to another county by now.

"Are you in any pain?"

"Not really, not anymore. Unless I reach a certain way," Travis admitted.

"Do you want to talk about it?"

"I need to get ready to open the diner." Travis freed himself from Bo's embrace, taking a few steps back. He wasn't ready to discuss his past; he didn't know if he ever would be.

"Okay, but we're not finished with our conversation about you going into therapy. What time are you done working today?"

"Four."

"I'll pick you up after work, and we'll finish this over dinner. I'll cook."

"But...," Travis began; he didn't know if he should protest, cut Bo off, or throw himself into the strong man's arms. Travis wanted to spend more time with Bo, but he knew how hideous Travis was, and no matter how wonderful Bo seemed, no one wanted to be with someone as damaged as Travis. "I can't."

"Then I'll come back here and we'll talk. We can bring dinner up from the diner. Either way, we're going to get this therapy issue worked out." Bo leaned forward and grabbed Travis's hand. "I care about you. I want to help you. You can't keep brushing these nightmares aside."

Sure I can.

Travis had never talked to anyone about what happened. Sure, he'd answered medical questions at the hospital and during his long recovery at the rehab facility, but he never talked about the fire. Not to the social workers. Not to the shrinks they sent to clear him for release. Never. He didn't know if he could. From the moment he regained consciousness and knew he was a disfigured mess, he'd wanted to bury that horrible day as deep as possible. But bastard that it was, it was seeping to the surface again. And he was suffering. He could at least admit that to himself.

It couldn't hurt to discuss the possibility of therapy, right?

"I guess we could talk about it," Travis agreed.

Bo's smile was breathtaking. "Thank you."

"I haven't agreed to go yet." Travis wanted to be clear.

"I understand, but you'll hear me out. That's all I ask. I'll pick you up at four."

"Okay." Travis was in shock he'd agreed to discuss it.

"I'll go downstairs and let you get ready. Meet you down there for coffee." Bo squeezed Travis's hand once then left the apartment.

Travis stood rooted to the spot. Shit. *Bo knows.* He'd seen how damaged Travis's body was, and Bo hadn't turned away. If the years had taught Travis anything, he knew that could, and likely would, happen at any time.

But…he'd lived a solitary existence for so long that letting someone in was probably impossible. Perhaps this was a first step.

Stop it. His imagination was running away with him. Bo was trying to help. Nothing more. He didn't want to become part of Travis's life. Who would?

His world had taken a strange turn this morning, and he wasn't going to think past getting to work or he'd never leave the apartment.

He put himself on autopilot and got ready for his day.

***

Bo sat at the counter flipping the business card for the therapist through his fingers. Dr. Gordon was supposed to be one of the best. He'd checked the guy out before recommending that Travis see him. Gordon had treated many first responders in the area; he'd be perfect for Travis. Bo wished he could help, but he knew a professional would be the best option.

He heard Travis's footsteps on the stairs before he saw the beautiful man come around the corner. His gorgeous pale blue eyes looked apprehensive, but there was a small smile creasing his face, which gave Bo hope.

"I've started the coffee," Bo told Travis as he went behind the counter.

"Thanks. I have to put on the bread and biscuits, so I won't be able to have a coffee with you this morning, but I'll get you one. Do you want it to go?"

"Yeah, if you don't mind."

Once Bo had his coffee and was on his way out the door of the diner, he couldn't help but smile. He was having dinner with Travis and he was going to insist they have dinner at Bo's place. But what was he going to make? He couldn't cook. Of course, he was never going to admit that when he'd suggested it to Travis. Bo knew what he had to do. Time to call in reinforcements.

It was early, but his parents would be up. Henry and Dot Mason never slept in. They were up at five every day. Bo took out his cell to call them. After a few rings, his dad picked up the phone.

"Are you okay?" His father's deep voice came across the line.

"Yeah. I'm fine."

The other phone in the house clicked, and his mother came on the line. "Robert, is something wrong?"

"Yeah. I can't cook, and I'm having dinner with Travis tonight." His family already knew Bo was attracted to Travis. Christ, half the town did, the way he was mooning over the man. Only Travis seemed oblivious.

"That's wonderful, son, but you'll give him food poisoning if you try to cook for the boy."

"So, it's an emergency." His mom laughed.

"Yes, what am I going to do? I'm picking him up at four."

"Buy a cookbook," his dad suggested, and Bo could tell he was fighting back his laughter.

"Not helpful."

"Don't you worry, son. I'll whip something special up for your man," Mom assured.

"Thank you. You're a lifesaver." Bo knew he was lucky to be so close with his family, which included three sets of aunts and uncles and over a dozen cousins, as well as Grandma Rose, who was the matriarch of the family. Though his family had their share of not-so-perfect situations—his cousin being arrested by the FBI came to mind—they were a tight bunch. Of course, they argued like cats in a barrel, but they always loved each other. He wondered about Travis's family; he never spoke of them.

"Now what would you like to serve him for dinner?" Mom asked.

Bo already had an idea of what would be perfect. "Would you make your four-cheese lasagna with Caesar salad and garlic bread?"

"Perfect, and it doesn't hurt that that's your favorite meal as well." Dad laughed.

"Travis will love it. I can't thank you enough."

"We'll have everything at the house before four. You'll have to put the lasagna into the oven to finish cooking it, but I'll leave instructions."

They said their goodbyes, and Bo pulled out of the parking lot as Sarah was pulling in to start her shift. He waved before turning the cruiser toward the station. The chief had planned a staff meeting for this morning. There were seven full-time officers on the Brighton police force and three part-timers. All were dedicated to protecting the people of Brighton, even if that meant Bo had to give his friends and family tickets on occasion. Grandma Rose had a bit of a lead foot.

He parked out front, alongside two other cruisers, and walked into the old two-story brick building that had been the police station ever since Bo was a child. Behind the front desk was their dispatcher, Joanne, an older lady who was only a few years away from retirement. She treated each of the officers like they were her children, and there was always a plate of sweets on her desk. Sadly, she'd lost her only child in a car accident over a decade earlier.

"Hey, Joanne. You're in early today." Another dispatcher worked the night shift and weekends.

"Good morning, Bo. Chief Graham wanted me to attend this morning's meeting. I brought breakfast sandwiches. They're in the breakroom." Joanne tilted her head back. "You go in there and get yourself one before they're all gone."

"Yes, ma'am." Bo headed straight for the sandwiches. Joanne was an excellent cook.

Bo walked into the breakroom and found three other officers helping themselves to the breakfast treats.

"Morning," Bo greeted as he took one, and after a round of "good mornings," they all sat down and ate in silence.

Conversation started up as soon as the last bites had been devoured. By then, the room was filled with officers who knew each other well. With such a small force, they were close. They had monthly barbeques, a softball team, and everyone knew each other's families. This was one of the many reasons why Bo liked living in a small town—the sense of community.

Chief Graham walked in and the room quieted. "Good morning, everyone. We'll meet in five minutes in the boardroom," Dave said, before grabbing a sandwich and walking out.

Bo stood and started for his desk when Grady, a new officer who had come from Dallas, stopped him in the hallway. "Hey, Bo, can I talk to you for a minute?"

"Sure. What's up?"

"I wanted to ask you about the new guy who started a few months back over at the diner. You've talked to him?" Grady asked, and immediately Bo gave Grady his full attention.

"His name is Travis. What about him?"

"Do you know if he's seeing anyone?"

Bo's face must have said it all because Grady took a step back before holding his hands up in surrender, "I didn't know, man. I would never poach."

"No harm done. He's a wonderful man, and I don't blame you for noticing, but yeah, I'm interested."

"Enough said, I understand. No hard feelings." Grady held out his hand. They shook, and Bo patted Grady on the back.

No doubt Travis attracted attention from men and women, but he hadn't been prepared for it to hit so close to home. If he hadn't already, Travis was going to get other offers from men attracted to him. But Travis was special; a man had to earn his trust before he would ever consider letting anyone get close. Bo had firsthand experience in that department.

Bo's heart hurt every time he thought about the pain Travis must have gone through to sustain burns like that. Knowing what Travis endured and the resulting scarring didn't change the desire Bo had for Travis. If anything, Travis's strength to go on day after day, clearly alone, made him even more attractive. The man was beauty and strength wrapped up in a kindhearted bundle, and Bo was head over heels. He needed Travis to give Bo a chance to show how good they could be together.

Bo walked into the boardroom, joining the chief and the rest of the team. There was a map on the wall with a number of red push-pins in it. Something was up.

The chief stood at the front of the room waiting for everyone's attention. The room quieted.

"There's a situation that could be heading our way. Over the last month, there have been five armed robberies in small towns along the interstate." The chief turned and pointed at the map. "It's been the same male suspect in every case. He's targeting general stores and small businesses, and he's getting closer to Brighton. We need to be prepared in case his next stop is our town. I'll be handing out a description of the suspect and the reports on each robbery. We need to stay vigilant. He's already shot and killed two innocent bystanders."

Questions began to fly from around the room as each officer took a copy of the file.

"How far away was the last robbery?" Grady asked.

"Are there other agencies involved?" a voice asked from the back.

"The last holdup was roughly one hundred and twenty miles away. It's been two weeks since the last incident. We think he's laying low. There is a manhunt, and all area agencies have been informed, but as of yet, no one has been able to catch him. There's been plenty of false reports, and people are scared. That's why we need to be on the lookout for anything out of the ordinary until he's captured. Most of us know or have seen every person in this community so an unknown male traveling alone would stand out. Check abandoned properties across the county in case that's where he's hiding. Stay safe and alert at all times. We know he has no compunction about using the weapons he's carrying."

After answering a few more questions, the chief called the meeting to an end and the team left. By the time Bo reached his patrol vehicle all the information on the crimes and the suspect were already downloaded to his mobile data terminal. He knew his unease wouldn't leave until the suspect was caught; after all, everyone he cared about was in Brighton.

His family, friends, and Travis could be at risk.

Nothing could be more terrifying.

Chapter Three

Jesse came in early for the night shift, allowing Travis the time to run upstairs and have a shower before Bo arrived. Bear, the owner, had been into the diner today with his man, Rick, and their nephew, Joshua. They'd come in for lunch, and to give Travis some good news—he was getting more hours.

He'd delivered their lunch and been shocked by the news. "Thank you."

"You deserve it. You run that kitchen like a dream," Bear had stated before he cut up his nephew's chicken strips into tiny pieces so the boisterous—and apparently hungry—toddler could eat.

When Bear had asked Travis to deliver the food to the table, he thought he was being let go. Again. He'd broken out in a cold sweat even though Jesse had told him he was doing a good job. Travis's previous positions around Texas hadn't turned out so well. He'd been fired for his speed, his lack of attention, or the fact that he wasn't a team player because he wouldn't go out with the manager. But more often than not, the cause was simply because he was different. He didn't want to hang out or go for drinks. He didn't need friends, or to socialize. He needed to save money and survive. Once, a busboy accused him of being gay and of coming onto him in the back of the kitchen. He didn't deny that he was gay but did deny the busboy's claim. It didn't stop him from being on the receiving end of the staff's disgusted looks. He was fired within the week for job performance issues. Of course the real reason went unsaid; after all, it was illegal.

Now, taking in what he called his Brighton luck, Travis fixed his shirt for the tenth time and wiped his sweaty palms on his jeans. Earlier, Bo had texted that dinner was at his house—no more diner food for Travis. And while he was excited to have been asked, he was nervous as all hell. He hadn't been invited to someone's house for dinner in a long time. And while he understood that this was set up so they could talk about him going to therapy, he was still thrilled he would be spending more time with Bo. Why, when he knew nothing would come of it? Maybe he was counting on his Brighton luck.

Travis rolled his shoulders and felt his skin pull slightly. Sometimes it felt like his damaged flesh was too tight for his body. He was immediately reminded of Bo's gentle touch that morning. Bo knew the awful truth—Travis was damaged and heavily scarred. Over fifty percent of his body had been burned on that awful day, and there was nothing he could do to change his condition, no matter how much he wished it.

There was a soft knock on his door, making Travis jump up from his chair. He took a deep breath and opened the door. Bo stood there in his dark blue police uniform, his badge shining in the sunlight, exuding a self-confidence that Travis only dreamed of having. Bo was breathtaking, and Travis would have his undivided attention for the next couple hours.

No pressure. Yeah, right.

"Hey, are you ready?"

"Yup."

Bo smiled and held out his hand, and god help him, Travis took it. The moment their hands touched, electricity shot up his arm, jolting Travis's heartbeat into overdrive. He prayed his palms weren't sweaty, and that Bo couldn't hear Travis's heart knocking against his ribs. Bo stood there holding Travis's hand as their eyes locked, and Travis found himself falling into those deep brown depths. His body moved on its own accord, and he found himself closer, and then closer again to Bo.

Travis was close enough to feel Bo's breath tickle his face.

A shrill sound broke the moment, and Travis quickly pulled back and released Bo's hand. Bo's cell phone rang again, and with a sigh, he reached into his pants pocket, pulled it out, and answered.

"Bo here."

Travis backed away to put distance between them, and then turned so he could catch his breath and clear the fog from his mind. How could he be so stupid? *Hell, I almost threw myself at him.*

After a few silent moments, Bo said, "Okay. Thanks, Mom," before disconnecting the call and placing the phone back in his pocket.

Travis turned back around to find Bo watching him closely. He didn't know what to say to explain his behavior. Bo crossed the room and stopped in front of Travis. He placed a large hand under Travis's chin and gently lifted his head so they were again looking eye to eye.

"I'm sorry," was all Travis could think of to say.

"Sorry? What are you sorry for?" Bo's eyes squinted, as if he were trying to see inside Travis's mind to find the answer.

"For almost..." Travis tried to talk, but the words were coming out as whispered gasps.

"Kissing me?" Bo asked softly. "Because I want to kiss you."

Travis stood stock-still, unsure if he'd heard Bo correctly. Slowly, Bo leaned down, giving Travis the opportunity to pull back, but he wasn't going anywhere. He watched as Bo's full lips inched closer. Travis closed his eyes as Bo's soft lips met his mouth. The rush was instantaneous as Bo's tongue teased the seam of Travis's lips. Excitement filled him as he stepped closer to Bo, who slid his hand behind Travis's head and held him tight.

After a moment Bo slowly pulled back. Travis had never felt anything like that kiss, which was on him; he hadn't permitted anyone to get close enough to kiss him before. He'd never had a physical relationship with anyone. Travis would never allow himself to be put in that situation.

“Was that okay? Me kissing you I mean? I don’t want to push you, but God I’ve wanted to do that for so long.” Bo’s eyes shone with sincerity, and it astounded Travis that Bo had wanted to kiss him even after knowing part of his secret.

“Ah, yeah, sure, I liked the kiss.” *Considering it’s my first.*

“Good. So did I.” Bo’s smile seemed genuine, and Travis chose to believe it was. Holy hell. Bo wanted him. Amazed and flattered as Travis felt, he wasn’t anywhere near ready for anything more than kissing. “How about we get outta here?”

Travis smiled wide and nodded. “Okay.”

Bo stepped back, took Travis’s hand, and led him through the door. After he shut and locked it, his hand still clasped in Bo’s, Travis followed Bo out to his truck, which was parked at the front of the diner. Travis didn’t miss the curious looks from customers, but there wasn’t a single disgusted sneer in the bunch. Travis held Bo’s hand a little tighter, and being able to do so without fear of reprisal was so novel it was heady.

Travis had never been to Bo’s house; he didn’t even know where it was, but he looked forward to gleaning insight into Bo’s personal world. Bo drove only five minutes from the diner into a cozy neighborhood lined with large, mature trees. Ranch-style houses sat on either side of the road. Flowerbeds filled with colorful blooms brought a smile to Travis’s face.

“It’s so beautiful here,” he muttered.

“I think so. I’ve lived in this neighborhood all my life. My parents’ house is down the street from mine.”

“You’re close with your family?”

“Yeah. There’s a lot of Masons living here in Brighton.” Bo smiled and winked, causing the butterflies in Travis’s stomach to begin aerial maneuvers. Bo’s short hair shone in the sunlight and his dark brown eyes seemed to sparkle as he looked at Travis.

The truck slowed and Bo turned into the driveway of a red brick ranch-style house with a large bay window and full flowerbeds. It was stunning with its bright white double doors, hanging baskets, manicured trees and green grass. Travis sat transfixed. This was a home, not just a house. He was beginning to wonder if he'd fallen into Mayberry or perhaps an episode of *The Twilight Zone*. Everything in Brighton was so different than his life until now.

"Do you like it?" Bo's voice sounded uncertain.

"Like it? Your home is stunning," Travis answered, and it wasn't a lie. "Are you the one with the green thumb?"

Bo smiled. "It's my hobby. The way I deal with stress from work."

"It's beautiful."

"Thanks. Let's go in so I can get out of my uniform."

"Pardon?" Travis teased. He knew what Bo meant but couldn't help himself.

"I mean I'll get changed into something more comfortable."

Travis continued to look at him stone-faced.

"And by comfortable I mean jeans and a t-shirt—not the other comfortable," Bo mumbled in a rush.

Travis started laughing. "I know what you meant."

Bo shook his head, cut Travis a look, and then began laughing as well. They got out of the truck and Bo came around and took Travis's hand before leading him to the front door. Travis took a deep breath; he knew after tonight he would probably be going to therapy. He had no doubt Bo could be persuasive. The real question was, could Travis follow through?

***

Bo's heart was racing. He was about to open his private world to the man he dreamed of sharing it with. He thought back to the kiss they'd shared and nearly groaned. Travis's soft lips begged to be kissed again, but Bo knew he had to take things slow. He redirected his wayward thoughts so the pull in his groin wouldn't become a bulge he couldn't hide. He pushed the front door open and ushered Travis inside.

From the foyer you could see through to the living room, and down the hall was the kitchen. When he'd first bought the house the rooms were all separated by walls, which he had torn down. He was forced to leave the hallway because it was loadbearing. Every day he walked in and still loved how open his house was now. He'd bought comfortable furniture, wanting his home to be designed for relaxation, not style. After a few years, his home had become well-loved and lived in.

Bo watched Travis closely, hoping he liked what he saw because Bo had decorated the place all on his own. Of course, his parents wanted to help, but they understood that this was a labor of love for Bo. It had taken over four years to get the house the way he wanted, and Bo had enjoyed every minute of the renovation. Being a police officer came with a great deal of stress, and working with his hands was Bo's way of releasing it.

"Bo, it's perfect." Travis commented as he ran his hand across the oak dining room table, which Bo felt like a physical touch. He'd made that table after the death of his friend in Houston; a lot of emotion had gone into it.

"Thanks. How about I go get changed and you have a look around?"

Travis smiled wide, lifting Bo's spirits even higher. He had the man he'd wanted to get close to in his home. What more could he ask for?

"Okay, is there anything I can do to help with dinner?"

Bo knew it was time to come clean. "About that—I have to tell you the truth. I can't cook. But don't worry, we have lasagna with all the fixings for dinner, thanks to my mom."

"You don't know how to cook?"

"Well, I know the basics to survive. But to put together a whole meal without giving someone food poisoning is a bit of a stretch for me," Bo admitted.

"It's a good thing I know how to cook," Travis replied. Then his eyes opened wide as he realized what he'd said. "I didn't mean to insinuate that I would be cooking for us on a regular basis, I just…um."

"I know what you meant, and I agree it's a good thing one of us knows his way around a kitchen. But I'm a pro at doing dishes." Bo spoke nonchalantly, but deep down he was overjoyed that Travis seemed to be thinking of a future that included him. Even if Travis didn't realize it or wouldn't admit it.

Bo couldn't help himself; he closed the distance between them. "You've got to know that tonight isn't only about discussing therapy—it's about us."

"Us?"

"Yes."

"What if I can't offer you more than friendship?" Travis looked panicked. "What if I'm too broken?"

"You're not broken and I'll take whatever you're willing to give." *For now.* "You're not alone anymore." Bo swore every single word was true. "Now I'm going to get changed and we'll put mom's lasagna in the oven." He trailed his thumb across Travis's jaw, memorizing every inch of his beautiful face before leaning down and capturing his soft lips in another tender kiss. Travis responded in kind and inched closer to Bo's body, and Travis's hand rested on Bo's chest.

Bo slowed the kiss and pulled away. Travis's eyes were still closed and his lips were slightly parted. Bo wanted to dive back in for another taste but knew better. Travis was skittish and unsure. Bo wanted Travis's trust. Rushing things was not the way to earn it.

"I'll be right back." Bo released Travis and headed down the hall to his bedroom. He took off his duty belt and locked his gun in the safe beside the bed, then he quickly changed into his comfortable, worn jeans and put on an old t-shirt.

When he returned to the living room, Travis was gone and Bo's heart fell. He walked into the kitchen and found the meal already in the oven. *Why would he put the food on and leave?* He slowly sat down on one of the barstools beside the kitchen island and buried his head in his hands. Had he come on too strong? What did he do now?

Bo stood and was about to head for the front door to find Travis—he couldn't have gotten far—when the sliding doors to the backyard opened.

"The back is as beautiful as the front. Can we eat outside tonight?" Travis asked as he walked in.

Bo was up and out of his chair before he even realized what he was doing. He gathered Travis into his arms and held him tight. "I thought you'd left." Bo hadn't even had the chance to process that he'd spoke without a filter.

Travis's brows went up. "Why would I leave?" Bo held him even tighter. "What's wrong?"

Bo released Travis before saying, "I thought you'd left because I came on pretty strong."

Travis wrapped his arms around Bo, shocking him, but he held Travis to his chest.

"I wouldn't leave you," Travis murmured. "I want to be here and I wanted to kiss you."

Bo could breathe again, but now that his panic had passed, he felt embarrassed and pulled away. "I'm sorry. I shouldn't have acted like that."

"It's okay. It's kind of nice to know I'm wanted." Travis smiled. "I put the lasagna in the oven. Your mom left instructions. It should be about an hour. Also, the rain gutters at your parents' house are stuffed full of leaves again. You need to clean them out before your dad tries, falls off the ladder, and ends up in the hospital. It was in the instruction letter. I didn't mean to snoop."

"No worries. My dad is as uncoordinated as they come. Whether he's up five feet or fifty he'd manage to fall off," Bo said with a chuckle. "Okay, that might be a bit of an exaggeration but you get the point."

"So we have an hour. What do you want to do?" Travis asked innocently, but of course Bo's mind raced in only one direction.

Bo put his libido in check, intent that their evening would be on track. "Let's sit in the living room and discuss the possibility of you going to therapy."

Travis took a deep breath, squared his shoulders, and raised his head before nodding his agreement. Bo held Travis's hand and led the suddenly quiet man to the large sectional couch. They sat down side by side and Bo pulled out Dr. Gordon's business card. Travis was fidgeting with his shirt; clearly this was not a discussion he wanted to have.

Bo laced his fingers with Travis's. "What scares you about going into therapy?"

Travis was quiet for a moment before answering. "I don't want to have to relive it again."

"But you are reliving it every night in your nightmares."

Travis mumbled, "I know. I wish they would stop."

"Dr. Gordon can help you with that. I relived Roy's death every time I closed my eyes. Even though I didn't see him get shot, in my dreams it played out as if I did. Over and over and over again."

Travis squeezed Bo's hand and said, "I'm so sorry."

"Thank you," Bo replied. "I want you to get the same help that I did."

"What if it doesn't work? What if the nightmares never end?" Bo could feel Travis's body tense.

"Dr. Gordon can help you with that, I swear he can. He does a lot of work with first responders who go through all sorts of stressful and horrific situations. He has a great reputation. But most of all I trust him to help you."

Travis was quiet and Bo waited patiently. He knew that this was a hard decision for Travis to make and Bo swore to stand by his side either way Travis decided to go.

"I can't take time off work. Jesse would have to pick up the slack. It wouldn't be fair to him."

Bo knew Travis was scared and trying to come up with excuses not to go. "I'm sure Dr. Gordon could work around your schedule. I can take you since your car isn't running."

"What if it doesn't help?"

"Then we try something else. I'll be there every step of the way…if you want me to be."

"Why do you care so much? No one has ever cared."

The dejection broke Bo's heart. "Because you are important to me. From the first time I met you, I knew you were special and I wanted to get to know you better. As I did I realized how amazing you are, and the more time I spent with you the harder I fell. I know you don't reciprocate those feelings now, but that doesn't change my affection for you. I want to be part of your life in any way possible. If that turns out to be just friends, in the end I'll accept that. But you need to understand I only have your best interests at heart, and I honestly believe therapy will help you." Bo hadn't meant to lay it all on the line, but it was out there now and he didn't want to take it back.

Travis looked down and was silent for a long time. Bo started to worry. For the most part, cops weren't subtle. They didn't have time to be. And while he wasn't a bull in a china shop, Bo could be too forceful sometimes. He'd done his level best to rein that in around Travis, but now, he feared he had overstepped.

When Travis lifted his head and faced Bo, the pain in Travis's eyes was heartbreaking. Bo leaned forward and held out his arms then wrapped them around Travis, who buried his face in Bo's chest. After a few moments Travis mumbled something Bo couldn't quite understand. "I couldn't hear you. What did you say?"

Travis raised his head and looked Bo in the eye. "I'll go, but I can't promise you anything."

Bo's heart lifted with hope. "Are you sure?"

"I'm sure." Travis nodded.

"Good. Good for you."

Travis resumed his position against Bo's chest and they sat in silence until the quiet was broken by deep snores. Travis had fallen asleep. Bo knew Travis's fitful nights had to leave him sleep deprived, so Bo decided to let Travis rest. Dinner could wait. Bo eased Travis onto the couch. He grabbed the blanket hanging over the arm of the sofa and covered Travis with it.

Bo took the lasagna out of the oven and left it on the stovetop to cool. They could always reheat it later. He'd set the second plate on the table when he heard a low, pain-filled whine coming from the living room. Bo looked up to see Travis squirming on the couch; his arms began to flail and a horrifying scream left his mouth. Bo ran around the kitchen island and quickly scooped Travis off the couch and into his arms.

Travis's arms were still thrashing about and one caught Bo in the side of the nose. He shook it off and held Travis closer. "Travis, wake up. Wake up, Travis. Come on, wake up babe."

Suddenly the struggling stopped and the room was silent again except for Travis's heavy breathing, his body limp in Bo's arms.

"Are you all right?"

"I'm sorry," Travis whispered.

"You have nothing to be sorry for."

Travis looked up and gasped. "Bo, your nose is bleeding."

Bo ran the back of his hand under his nose and it came away bloody. "It was an accident. You didn't mean to do it."

"Oh my god. I'm so sorry." Travis looked horrified.

"Stop saying you're sorry. None of this is your fault," Bo replied a bit more sternly then he'd intended.

"But you're bleeding?"

"Not much."

"Bo."

"Travis."

Bo wasn't going to allow Travis to take any of the blame for the horrors that plagued him, and he held him closer. When Travis's shaking stopped, Bo loosened his grip, allowing Travis to move away if he wanted. Travis didn't move. "I can't believe I fell asleep with you in the room. Normally that would never be possible."

"How about you go to the bathroom and clean up while I get our dinner reheated?" Bo hoped that acting as natural as possible would help relax Travis.

Travis took a deep breath before saying, "Okay."

They stood and Travis headed down the hall while Bo returned to the kitchen. As soon as he put the lasagna in the oven to warm he headed to his en-suite bathroom to wash the dried blood from his face. Travis had gotten in a lucky shot, but honestly Bo didn't feel much pain. He washed up and came back to the kitchen to find Travis taking their dinner out of the oven. Bo thought it best not to bring up the nightmare and to act as if continuing on with their plans was all they had on their mind.

"I thought we could fill up our plates and head out back. The sun should be setting soon," Bo suggested.

Travis set the lasagna on the stove, turned and gave Bo a small smile. "I'd like that."

Bo noticed that Travis looked relieved and Bo knew he'd made the right choice. They loaded their plates with Dot Mason's thick, cheesy lasagna and the all the fixings before heading out the back door.

Bo couldn't help but smile. They'd made it past several hurdles so far this evening. But he wasn't so naive as to think there wouldn't be more to come, or that they wouldn't be getting worse.

Chapter Four

Travis couldn't have been more confused if he tried. By all rights he should be running—no, flying—out of Bo's place and heading back home. Hell, how had he fallen asleep in front of Bo in the first place? And then, in the middle of another embarrassing nightmare, he had to go and hit Bo. The man who was trying to help him. But Bo acted as if it was nothing and he wasn't bringing up the nightmare, so maybe it wasn't as bad as Travis thought. Which was why he agreed to go out back and eat Bo's mother's lasagna.

The back deck had patio chairs, a table, and loungers with comfortable-looking cushions. He imagined what it would be like to lie out here in the sun, something that wasn't going to happen anytime soon. If he kept hitting Bo it might never happen. Bo placed Travis's plate on the table and pulled out a chair for him to sit on. Once Bo sat down across from Travis, he reached for his fork.

"Dig in. You're going to love this," Bo said as he lifted a piece of lasagna to his mouth.

Travis stuck his fork into the gooey goodness and took a bite. Rich tomato sauce, spicy meat, stringy cheese, and tender noodles exploded across his taste buds, making him moan. It was one of the best lasagnas he'd eaten in a long time. "They should put this on the menu at the diner," he suggested.

He looked up to see Bo watching him closely, his hooded eyes smoldering. "So you like the lasagna?"

"It's excellent. Do you think your mom will give me the recipe?"

Bo nodded. "Definitely."

"I'll be happy to trade recipes. I have a great chili or maybe pierogis," Travis offered.

"Fried chicken. God, I love your fried chicken."

"I know," Travis said. "You order it every chance you get."

"You've been keeping track of what I order."

"Yes, and you need to get more vegetables into your diet."

"More vegetables, no."

"Yes. The next meal you order at the diner, there will be a salad coming with it." Travis had no idea where this was coming from but he had to acknowledge he'd never felt more comfortable with anyone else.

"Fine, I'll eat your salad."

"Damn straight you will."

Bo dropped his fork onto his plate and broke out laughing. "I knew you'd be tough."

Travis lifted his head high. "I'm not a wimp."

"No, you're not. You're one of the strongest people I know."

Travis smiled to himself—that someone saw that in him was a gift. To be seen as strong, not a victim, for who he was and not what happened to him was a first. Lost in thought, they went back to their meals in companionable silence.

Afraid to break the spell, but needing to know, Travis asked, "You're not planning on coming into Dr. Gordon's sessions with me, are you?" There was no way he was ready to share his past and deepest, darkest secrets with Bo. Let alone the guilt he felt for his part in all of it.

"I would never invade your privacy like that. I'll stay in the reception area."

Travis was relieved. He still didn't know if he'd ever be able to tell Bo everything let alone a therapist, but he'd try.

Bo smiled warmly and reached across the table, taking Travis's hand in a gentle hold. "Someday, we'll get to a point where you trust me enough to share anything. Either way, I'm staying right here."

Travis thought it would be best to change the subject. He was tired of talking about his problems. "Obviously, you're close to your parents. What are they like?"

Bo leaned back in his chair and rubbed his muscled stomach before answering. "Henry and Dot Mason are one of a kind. I grew up here in Brighton along with my younger brother, Ben. He's a fireman with the Brighton FD. My dad's a psychiatrist and mom is the co-owner of Hidden Treasures here in town with my five aunts. They sell various crafts and artwork from local artists in their store and online. I also have over a dozen cousins. You've met Keith already."

"Your dad's a psychiatrist? Is he the one you saw after Roy's death?"

"God, no. He wouldn't have treated me, and I didn't want him to. Never mind the ethical dilemmas, that was mine to work out on my own. What about your family?"

Travis figured he might as well get this part over with. "My dad is deceased and my mom is remarried."

Bo reached over and squeezed Travis's hand. "I'm sorry to hear about your father."

"It was a long time ago."

"Are you close to your mother and her new husband?"

"No. Everything changed after the fire."

Bo seemed to see straight through to Travis's soul, which made him fidget. Ever perceptive, Bo changed the subject. "How about we take these dirty dishes inside and get comfortable on the couch? Maybe watch a little television."

"Okay, I'd like that." Relieved, Travis cleared the table while Bo loaded the dishwasher.

After the kitchen was cleaned, Travis and Bo were sitting together on the couch, and Bo grabbed the remote. He turned on the large television then his arm snaked behind Travis's shoulders and pulled him close to Bo's side. Travis melted into Bo, who had made it easy to relax—a concept that was foreign to Travis.

"What would you like to watch?" Bo asked.

"Can we watch the Space channel? They have a sci-fi movie marathon starting tonight." Travis figured if Bo wanted to learn more about him, this was as good a place as any to start.

"Great. I've been looking forward to that all week," Bo half-shouted. Travis couldn't tell if he was teasing or not.

"Are you joking or…"

"No, I'm serious. I love sci-fi movies and television shows. I could show you my DVD collection. I have *Star Trek* from the original series up to the final show from *Enterprise* in 2005."

"Really? You're hiding your inner geek in this handsome package."

"You think I'm handsome?" Bo grinned.

"I don't know what you're talking about."

"Suuure," Bo laughed before turning on the television and flipping to the Space channel.

Up on the screen the young captain of a spaceship strode in and struck a pose in front of his chair, making Travis sigh. This evening could have gone wrong in so many ways, but they'd made it through so far.

"Bo?"

"Yeah?"

"Thanks again for tonight," Travis muttered. He quickly threw in, "Are we planning to do it again?"

Bo's eyes softened and he pulled Travis closer while continuing to rub his back. "Definitely."

Travis was enjoying the contact, something he would have never allowed before moving to this town and meeting this man. Travis had spent his entire life avoiding contact with anyone, too ashamed to share his body with another human being.

For the next couple hours they sat watching one of their favorite movies while Travis relaxed further into Bo's chest. Neither spoke, caught up with the story and seemingly content in each other's arms. When the wall clock chimed ten, Travis sat up and yawned.

"It's getting late and we need to be up early," Travis announced even though he wanted to curl back up.

"When can we do this again?" Bo asked as he sat up.

Travis didn't even have to think about it. "I'm on days all this week."

"Perfect, so am I." Bo inched closer to Travis's lips. This time Travis didn't wait. He met Bo halfway and kissed him back. Travis could become addicted to Bo's soft lips and sinful mouth. Travis's hands shook as he rubbed Bo's muscled chest. He wanted to explore a bit more, so he opened his mouth and welcomed Bo's tongue in.

Bo responded immediately, delving deep into Travis's mouth as if mapping it. He joined in, his tongue dueling with Bo's as sensations flooded Travis's body and headed straight to his groin. His cock began to thicken and push against the zipper of his pants, and that little extra bite brought him back to reality. Holy shit. He was about to come in his pants.

Travis pulled back from a confused looking Bo. Both were breathing heavily.

"Is something wrong?"

Travis couldn't possibly explain that he hadn't had a hard-on or even successfully pleasured himself since *that* day. "No, no nothing's wrong," Travis responded before looking down at the bulge in his pants. Even though the flames had left his cock burned and misshapen, apparently he still could manage to get hard. This was a true victory. He knew for every normal man, this was an everyday occurrence, but to him this was a step forward.

When he looked up, Bo's eyes were hooded and burning with desire. *He really wants me.* But Travis still wasn't ready for anything more than these delicious kisses. He had a few things to work out.

Bo cleared his throat before saying, "I should take you home."

Travis stood to walk toward the front door when he found himself lifted off the floor and spun in circles. Travis started laughing, which broke the tension hanging between them.

"So which day can we do this again? I'm off at four on Wednesday." Travis smiled.

"Will you check to see if you can get an appointment with Dr. Gordon? Then we can come back here and relax over dinner and a movie. I still have a lot of movies for you to look through."

"Okay, I'll go if you can get an appointment. If you leave it to me I might never call." Travis doubted Bo would be able to get one when it was only days away.

They drove back to the diner holding hands, surrounded by the quiet downtown. When they arrived the diner was still open, so Bo went around to the back parking lot. Travis pulled out his keys, one for the back door and the other key to the door on his apartment. He didn't carry his car key because the poor old thing had died in a parking spot out back months ago. It was bound for the junkyard, even though it was the last piece of his father he had.

"Thank you for dinner and everything else." He knew he didn't have to explain to Bo what he meant.

"You're welcome. Thank you for trusting me. I'll see you in the morning for coffee," Bo said and then kissed Travis's palm. "Call me if you need anything."

Travis undid his seatbelt and decided to be bold and do exactly what he'd been thinking. He leaned over and kissed Bo. This was the first kiss he'd ever initiated and he planned to do it more often—with Bo of course. Decision made to see where this attraction would lead, Travis ended the kiss and got out of the truck. Bo stepped out and walked Travis to the back door. The romantic gesture made him smile.

"G'night, Bo."

"Good night, Travis."

Travis went directly up to his apartment. He knew the moment Jesse saw him there'd be questions and he wasn't willing to share yet. He locked his door and took a deep breath; he'd had a date with Bo and there would be more. Then his mood took a bit of a dive. He was going to therapy. He'd never talked to anyone about what happened. His mother refused to talk about the fire and carried on with her own life, while Travis, alone and trying to deal with his pain, needed—desperately needed—an anchor in his emotional and physical storm.

Ultimately she left him alone, completely.

He shook his head, trying to dislodge the troubling thoughts, and began unbuttoning his shirt to get ready to go to sleep. It wasn't long before he was standing naked beside his bed, staring at the mirror in front of him on the wall. Travis took a deep breath, grabbed the hand mirror from his dresser and turned around. It had been a long time since he really looked at himself.

His back, butt, and legs were covered in discolored red patches interlaced with lighter skin that looked stretched. He reached around and felt his warm, leathery skin. His hand found the thicker patches that appeared in spots on his lower back and he cringed. Other areas had contractures, scar tissue over his burns that tightened his skin, making certain movements difficult in varying degrees.

He looked down at his cock with its darkened, shriveled skin that made it point to the right. Scars spider-webbed across the surface gave his sensitive skin an almost shiny plastic sheen. Travis had been lucky; his face and the front of his torso weren't burned, giving him the opportunity to hide the damage from most people.

As he stared at himself his mind drifted to one night over eight years ago. He had decided to stay in a men's shelter because he couldn't keep running the car for heat and using up his precious gas. He woke to the feel of someone pressing their hand over his mouth and a sharp edge being held to his throat. He had assumed it was a knife at the time but it turned out to be a sharpened metal pen casing. He remembered every detail. His attacker's hot breath across Travis's ear as he whispered his promise to kill Travis if he made a sound. The way the man's bony hands bit into his arms when he dragged Travis to a small, dark room away from everybody else. No one was coming to his aid even if they were awake. Probably thankful it wasn't them.

The only light coming into the room was from the full moon through the dirty window. Recalling the violation, Travis felt like he was choking on the same fear and helplessness he'd had when his attacker ripped the clothes from his body. But that's when things had changed. His attacker's dirty hands pulled away from his body and the man backed toward the door. The look of disgust on his face was highlighted by the moonlight. His final words before leaving echoed in Travis's head to this day: "You disgusting freak."

Travis knew he shouldn't be comparing an attempted rape to what he could have with Bo, but the words haunted him. Would Bo still desire him when he got a closer look at the scars or the disfigurement to his cock? Sure, he may have seen the scars in the hospital but that wasn't the same as having Travis naked in Bo's arms.

Would Bo change his mind if their relationship ever became physical? Travis turned away from the mirror and pulled on his comfortable sleep pants and soft t-shirt.

With a deep sigh he climbed into bed. He knew he was creating problems that weren't even there, but he had to think ahead. He pulled his comforter up to his chest and closed his eyes.

His mind was full of visions of Bo.

He hoped to have one night free of his nightmares but knew better.

***

The days had flown by, and before Travis knew it, Wednesday was upon him. Bo had managed to get him an appointment with Dr. Gordon. Now he was pacing the kitchen of the diner waiting for Bo to arrive and take him for his first therapy session.

"It'll be okay, Travis," Jesse said from the counter while carving one of the turkeys for that day's special.

Travis had shared only the basics with Jesse—that he'd been having nightmares and needed to see a therapist, nothing more. His boss didn't push and told Travis he'd make sure he had the time off to go.

"I hope so," was all Travis could think to say. He adjusted his shirt again.

The bell over the front door jingled. Travis turned and locked eyes with Bo. He had continued to visit Travis multiple times a day, and tonight after therapy was their second official date. He'd let down his guard with Bo and prayed he didn't regret it. He honestly didn't believe Bo would hurt him but Travis had lived a long time on his own, unable to allow anyone in. It was a habit that would be hard to break.

"I'll see you later, Jesse."

"Good luck."

Travis walked out of the kitchen and up to Bo, who was waiting patiently by the door.

"How are you?"

"Nervous."

"I won't be far if you need me for anything."

"Thanks." Knowing Bo would be in a nearby room helped calm Travis but he was still apprehensive over the whole therapy thing.

Bo took his hand and led him out to the truck. In what felt like the blink of an eye they pulled into the Brighton Medical Center, even though Travis knew it was a few miles out from the center of town. He wished it had taken a bit longer to get to his appointment. Was he ready for this?

His side door opened and he jumped back. He hadn't even heard or felt Bo getting out of the truck.

"Easy, Travis. It's only me."

I can do this, I can do this. He kept chanting over and over again in his mind. "I can do this."

"Yes, you can." Bo sounded so confident it gave Travis some strength.

Travis straightened his spine and stepped from the truck. *I can do this.* He took Bo's hand and followed him into the building and up to

Dr. Gordon's office. The reception area was empty so Travis sat in the first available seat after checking in.

"Hey, look at me," Bo demanded softly. Travis looked up. "You're stronger than you think. Do you trust me?"

"Yes."

"Then believe me when I tell you this is nothing to be scared of. Everything goes at your pace," Bo assured.

"Mr. Boone," the receptionist called from an open doorway. Travis's heart began to race. He attempted to give Bo a smile when he stood but he was sure it came out as a grimace, and he followed the young woman down a long, brightly colored hall. If the yellow was meant to be cheerful it missed the mark. He could feel a headache forming in the back of his head.

The receptionist stopped outside a closed door and smiled warmly. "The doctor will be here in a moment."

"Thank you." Travis walked into what appeared to be a living room, complete with a couch, chairs, drapes, and a coffee table in the center of the grouping. The walls were covered in stunning paintings. Travis couldn't help himself; he had to get a better look. He'd been working on a few sketches for the past couple days but they were nowhere near the perfection in front of him. Confident brush strokes and bold colors graced a large canvas that caught his eye the moment he stepped into the room. It was spectacular.

"Beautiful, isn't it?" a deep voice said from the other side of the room. Travis spun around and brought his arms up to protect himself. Living on the streets had taught him always to be on guard. But nothing happened. Travis lowered his arms and looked up to see a large, dark-haired man standing on the other side of the room. He hadn't moved and Travis realized that this must be Dr. Gordon. Great first impression.

"I'm sorry. I startle easily."

"Not a problem. I knocked but you must not have heard me," the man noted with a smile. "The painting—it's beautiful, isn't it?"

"Yes," Travis responded, not turning his back on the man. He had no idea why he was acting this cautious—after all, he'd come to this man for help.

"I'm Dr. Gordon."

"Travis Boone."

"It's nice to meet you, Travis," Dr. Gordon said as he took a seat in one of the many comfortable-looking chairs.

He had yet to ask Travis to sit and he wondered if he should stay standing. He'd feel a lot better standing. *I can do this.*

"The artist is from Brighton. His name is Keith Mason."

"Keith painted this? I met him at his shop. He's Bo's cousin."

"So you're an artist as well. I'll bring in a few more pieces I have of Keith's for you to see on your next visit."

That excited Travis, but he didn't miss the fact there would be more visits. He wasn't naïve; he knew his kind of problem would take more than one visit to solve.

"Would you like something to drink? Water, juice, coffee?" Dr. Gordon asked.

"I'd love a coffee." He'd been up late last night; between nightmares and thinking about therapy, he couldn't find any peace.

"How do you take it?"

"Black, please."

Dr. Gordon stood and walked over to a screened-in area where Travis assumed the fridge and coffee pots were hiding. Looking around the room he wouldn't have guessed he was in a doctor's office. He assumed this was intended to make patients more comfortable. It was working. A few moments later the doctor returned with two steaming cups. He placed one on the table in front of the chair Travis was standing behind, before going back to his original seat.

Travis was beginning to feel like an idiot for standing while the doctor sat, so he walked around to the front of the chair and sat down. Immediately, he lifted the coffee cup into his hands to keep them busy.

“I want you to know you’re safe here. What we discuss will be kept between us unless you authorize me to share with a significant other. The only time I would alert anyone was if yours or someone else’s life were in danger.”

“I understand. Bo’s the only person I’m close with. He’s bringing me to my appointments. He’s my friend, so I can authorize him if you need someone as a sort of next of kin. But maybe I should ask him first. He may not want that kind of responsibility.”

“When we meet next you can let me know and I’ll have the authorization paperwork drawn up.”

“Okay.”

“So Travis, do you want to tell me what has brought you in to see me?” Dr. Gordon asked.

“I’m having nightmares.” *Straight and to the point. I can do this.*

“Every night?”

“Yes, but recently on odd nights it happens more than once.” Those nights were hell.

“Do you remember what’s happened in your nightmare when you wake up?”

“Unfortunately, yes. It feels like they follow me back into the real world after I open my eyes.”

“Do you want to tell me a little bit about them?”

“I’m not sure I can. I’ve never talked about them or my past before.”

“How about we break it up into portions you can handle, a little bit at a time. How’s that sound?”

Travis thought about it as he took a gulp of his cooling coffee. Maybe if he started small he could get through this. His nightmares were now disrupting his sleep to the extent that he was afraid he’d fall asleep standing up. He took another swig of his coffee. He’d had these dreams since the explosion, but recently they’d become more *real* to him.

He needed help.

“Okay, we can try.”

"That's all I'm asking for. I'm not here to judge you for your feelings or the events in your life. I'm here to help you deal with things in a healthy way so that you can lead a happy life."

"I'd like that," Travis muttered before taking a deep breath and jumping right in. "I grew up in a suburb of Dallas. You know, a normal enough life, two parents, both worked. We were comfortable middle-class America. My dad and I were really close; he coached my baseball team and helped with every science fair project. He taught me important things. Like when I was thirteen, my dad took me to a soup kitchen on a Saturday.

"I thought we were going to the park. I spent all afternoon fuming over a tub of dirty dishes and my dad knew it. I couldn't understand why we were making food for people we didn't even know. Later that night we loaded up the van and my dad made me hand out sandwiches to homeless people. Halfway through the night we came across a family living under a broken-down bridge, a mother and father with two kids. One of the little girls was about my age. She had nothing. I had a room full of toys at home and she didn't even have a home. After that day, I went with him every Saturday to make the sandwiches and deliver them. It was our thing."

"He sounds like a wonderful man," Dr. Gordon commented.

"He was the best dad. He died when I was sixteen." Travis got that familiar squeeze to his stomach.

"I'm sorry." Dr. Gordon looked as genuine as his words sounded. "How about your mom? You haven't mentioned her."

Travis looked away from the doctor before saying, "She wasn't around much when I was growing up. She was away a lot for work."

"How was your relationship with her?"

"What relationship? She wasn't there and was never really a mom. But that was okay. I still had my dad until the fire." Travis's eyes began to blur slightly and he knew he was seconds away from crying. He fought it back with everything he had and managed to shed only one. He was stronger than this.

"This is a safe place, Travis. You'll learn that over time. And crying is not a sign of weakness. It takes a great deal of strength to allow your emotions out."

"Then why do I feel so bad if I do?"

"Because men have been taught to keep their emotions bottled up. That they weren't strong if they cried or even spoke about their emotions. Which is a lie. This is a safe place for you to let those emotions out in a healthy way."

Travis nodded but refused to look up as he wiped his eye. Travis hadn't thought of his mother in a long time. He'd tried to bury that time in his life along with his dad.

"How about we end here today? That was a great start. I want to see you twice a week for now and I'm going to prescribe some medication to help you sleep. You mentioned Bo was driving you here. Do you mind if we discuss the schedule with him as well?"

"That's probably a good idea. And I have to talk to my boss to get the time off."

"Let's say Mondays and Thursdays at four p.m.?"

"If you think it's that important." Travis didn't believe he needed to come that often.

"You are that important, Travis. Now let's go talk to Bo."

Travis was ready to leave. He'd brought up enough old memories for one day. All he wanted now was a quiet night with Bo.

Chapter Five

Bo drove to his house after stopping at the pharmacy to pick up Travis's new prescription. He was happily surprised when Dr. Gordon introduced himself and wanted to discuss the schedule with him. It made him feel as though he was part of Travis's life, exactly where he wanted to be. He would find a way to make Monday and Thursday work.

Travis had been quiet since his appointment and Bo wished he could do something to make this easier for him. But in truth all he could do was stand by him and wait until Travis was ready to tell him. If he ever would.

"I've gotten us steaks for dinner. I can barbeque like a pro, but not cook on a stove or oven. I also picked up fixings for salad and baked potatoes. I figured I couldn't ruin that."

Travis seemed to come out of his thoughts and smiled. "I should cook something special for you but my kitchen isn't big enough to handle that."

"My kitchen is at your disposal anytime you wish." Bo wanted Travis to feel comfortable in Bo's world.

"Okay, I may take you up on that someday. I love trying new recipes. You could be my guinea pig." Travis smiled.

"I'm perfectly fine with that." Bo smiled back. "And before I put this off any longer, I don't want you to be worried, but there's something you need to know. There's been a rash of armed robberies in towns bordering the interstate and they've come close to Brighton. I need you to stay safe. I want you to keep your eyes open for anything out of the ordinary. Like a person you've never seen before. We're a small town, you should be able to recognize a stranger."

"I will. I promise," Travis replied quickly. "But I'm sort of still new and I'm sure I don't know even a tenth of the people that live here. I'd be calling you all the time."

"Good point. Okay, how about this? If someone comes in and Sarah doesn't know him and you think he poses a threat, either by his body language or verbally, call the station." Sarah had grown up in Brighton and had lived there for over sixty years. Bo knew she'd notice anything even slightly out of the ordinary.

They pulled into Bo's driveway and he went around the front of the truck and waited for Travis. Bo took hold of Travis's hand and, thankfully, he held Bo's hand just as tightly.

"How about I help get the baked potatoes ready and we get those on before we make the salad and put the steaks on?" Travis suggested as he walked through the front door. Bo noticed how much more comfortable Travis was now compared to the first time he'd come over, and Bo liked that.

Travis headed straight for the kitchen and Bo happily followed. The bag of potatoes sat on one of the back pantry shelves and Travis immediately brought it over to the sink.

"How hungry are you?" Travis asked.

"Famished," Bo replied before rounding the corner of the kitchen island, taking Travis into his arms and claiming the beautiful man's lips in a deep, wet kiss. He'd been waiting days to do that. Of course, he kissed Travis every morning when he left the diner, but he'd kept it PG. Not tonight, though. Tonight he wanted to taste the man he'd been hungering for. His tongue explored Travis's willing lips and mouth until he heard Travis whimpering softly. Bo pulled back to look down at Travis's dilated eyes and kiss-swollen lips.

"You are so beautiful," Bo whispered while caressing Travis's stubble-covered cheek.

"No, I'm not," Travis mumbled as he attempted to pull away.

Bo would never allow Travis to feel less because of his scars. He was beautiful and it was time he heard it more often. "You are beautiful, and that's a fact that I'll be happy to remind you of repeatedly."

Travis stared at Bo. Travis's pale blue eyes seemed to pierce straight through Bo's chest directly into his heart. He didn't flinch under Travis's gaze, willing him to see the truth of his statement.

Bo knew he'd succeeded when Travis's body relaxed into Bo's and Travis tucked his head under Bo's chin. He marveled at how well they fit together and wrapped his arms even further around Travis's body.

"As long as I'm beautiful to you, I can live with that," Travis whispered.

"Always beautiful, and not only to me."

Travis's blue eyes looked up at him in confusion. "Not only you?"

Bo had to be honest and tell him about Grady. "There's this guy at work that asked about you."

"Me?"

"Yes, you." Bo looked at the ground before he continued. "I kind of warned him off."

"Warned him off, why?"

Bo looked at Travis and said his piece. "Because I want to be the man you look to. I want to be the one who holds you, kisses you. I want to be your boyfriend." And there it was, out in the open.

Travis's eyes went wide and his mouth opened and closed several times without making a sound. Bo hoped he hadn't blown it already but he was trying to be honest.

"Me?"

"Yes."

"But what if I can't be physical with you? What if I can't get over this? I've never been with anyone." Bo was sure Travis hadn't meant to add that last part but it was too late to take it back.

“I’d still want you. The question is, do you want me? Do you want to find out where these feelings are leading? Are you willing to take a chance on me?” Bo had laid himself out to be crushed, but he could wait for an answer, he could be patient.

***

Boyfriend. He wants to be my boyfriend. The words kept playing over and over again in Travis’s mind. Bo wanted a committed relationship with him. Travis couldn’t think of anything he wanted more, but was that fair to Bo? He didn’t know if he could give Bo everything a normal relationship had. But he’d never know if he didn’t give this a chance. Of all the people Travis had met since that night, Bo was the kindest, the most steadfast, and the most open. That he saw something in Travis that was good and true was a miracle. And no doubt, Travis was attracted to Bo both physically and emotionally. If Travis didn’t give this a shot he’d regret it for the rest of his life, and he already had enough regrets.

“Yes.”

“Yes?”

“I would like to be your boyfriend. But I can’t promise anything but to try.”

Bo looked so happy, and Travis knew he’d made the right choice. Bo lowered his lips for a kiss that Travis was all too willing to give. Bo met him halfway, bringing his mouth to Travis’s for a kiss more impassioned than any they’d shared. Emboldened by Bo’s eager response, Travis explored that tantalizing mouth with his tongue. Bo was quick to capture it and began sucking on it. Travis felt the pull all the way down to his cock, which was hardening by the second. Bo had to be able to feel it against his leg.

Slowly Travis pulled back, not wanting to get too carried away. His body had other ideas, and his hips flexed against Bo’s thick leg while they were parting.

"So how about we get these potatoes ready?" Bo asked as he released Travis.

Travis licked his lips and gained Bo's laser focus, his eyes dark. "Yes, we should get dinner started."

Bo smiled, caressed Travis's cheek before turning toward the counter. Travis's heart was racing and his cock was rock hard. That was two hard-ons in one week, compared to nothing over ten years. It was thrilling, but he needed to calm down. He concentrated on dinner and over the next hour and a half he was able to slow his racing heart and hold a meaningful conversation. Bo talked about his family with such love that Travis felt as though he knew them himself. He found it funny that in ninety minutes he knew more about Dot Mason than his own mother over his lifetime.

"You okay?" Bo asked as they were getting comfortable on the couch. Obviously Travis hadn't been able to keep all the thoughts and feelings that had been stirred up in his session with Dr. Gordon under wraps. How bad would it be to share a little of his past with Bo? Bo had shared with Travis after all.

"I'm not close to what remains of my family. Honestly, I have no idea where my mother is living." Bo held onto Travis's hand but remained silent, allowing him the time he needed to organize his thoughts. "We were never close and after the…the accident, I became a constant memory of what happened. She couldn't live with that. I was recovering from my last surgery when she left me to fend for myself." Travis looked down at his inked arms before saying, "I used to get a new tattoo to commemorate each surgery. I think they're beautiful."

"They are beautiful," Bo agreed.

"Thanks. I haven't gotten a new one in a long time."

"How did you pick the designs?"

"I drew them."

"I can't wait to see one of your sketches. You're still going to show me, right?" Bo asked, while tracing the outline of one particularly intricate tattoo.

Travis smiled. It'd been ages since someone asked to see one of his sketches. Since before his father's death. "Sure. I'll show you soon."

"I'm holding you to that," Bo insisted before changing the subject. "Um…there's something that I'd like to ask you. This Saturday my parents are having a barbeque for family and friends and I wanted to take you with me."

Immediately doubts crept into Travis brain. *What if I make a fool of myself? What if they take one look at me and disapprove?* Travis knew he was panicking, but he hadn't been invited to anything in a while, let alone a family barbeque. At work in his kitchen he felt safe and secure, and in his apartment the same, but now he was being asked to a social gathering with strangers. He liked the anonymity of the streets; no one noticed the homeless guy, but at this party he knew he's be a star attraction. He could see it now—*Bo's new boyfriend.*

"I promise if you're uncomfortable we'll leave. I would really like you to come. Even if it's for only a little while," Bo assured.

Travis could tell this was important to Bo. And if Travis wanted to get better, wanted to enter the land of the living, how could he refuse? "Okay, I'll come for a bit, but I work until four that afternoon."

"I'll pick you up after your shift," Bo was quick to reply.

"Since we're at it, I have a favor to ask." Travis figured now was a good a time as any. "Dr. Gordon needs a next of kin of sorts for me and I thought that maybe you would be okay with being mine."

"You want me to stand in as your next of kin?"

Travis scratched at his shirt before answering. "Yes."

"I'd be honored."

"Thanks. Really." He wasn't sure of it being much of an honor for Bo, but Travis would take it. He cuddled close as the television came to life. He still couldn't quite believe that he was somebody's boyfriend. He'd never expected to be anything close to that, ever. He wasn't ready to jump into bed with Bo but he was willing to see where all these changes and feelings were leading.

***

Saturday

Travis sat in Bo's big black truck as it rumbled toward doom. *Okay, that is a little dramatic, even for me. It's not like the Masons are going to tie me to the spit and barbeque me. Okay, not a good example. How bad could it be?* Travis looked over at Bo in his button-down shirt and jeans. The man made everything look good. His blond hair shone in the afternoon sunlight streaming through the driver's window. *God, he's so handsome, and he's mine...for now.* Travis wasn't all that sure if he was going to be able to keep him.

"Sweetheart, everything is going to be fine," Bo reassured. He reached across the seat and took Travis's hand. Bo was a constant source of strength, and Travis knew he could easily get used to it.

He had learned to be apprehensive of all unknown situations because they usually led to him being beaten, robbed, or losing his spot to sleep for the night. Living on the street or even in shelters could be dangerous. He was constantly on guard. He had trusted people who said they wanted to help him, at least in the beginning. But every offer had strings attached. They turned out to be drug dealers or pimps, and even the odd cult masquerading as a church group wandered through.

That was one of the many reasons Travis volunteered at the site for Brighton's new youth center and halfway house. He wanted to support his boss, Jesse, who was building and donating it to the town. It was geared toward homeless youths living on the street, a lot of whom identified as LGBTQ.

"I'd really like to continue volunteering at the youth center, but will there be enough time with the therapy?" Travis asked. Considering Bo was his ride to therapy twice a week, that didn't leave a lot of extra time when he included work and everything else that came with having a life.

"Your appointments are what's important right now. But we should be able to work something out, okay?"

"Yup. I don't want to stop going to the site and pitching in." This was important to him. If he'd had a safe place to go, who knows how his life would have changed? Then he looked over at Bo. He would have never met him. Travis's stomach began to roll at that thought. Over the months since they'd first met, Bo had become a part of Travis's life, from his multiple visits during the day to their private times. Bo had wormed his way into Travis's heart and that's exactly where he'd stay.

Bo slowed the truck and Travis saw all the vehicles lining the street. He took a deep breath. He could do this. This was stepping way out of his comfort zone, but that was what he needed to do to get better. He wanted to be part of this community. Bo pulled up to the driveway and into a spot that looked to be waiting for him. Luck or planning, Travis didn't know. All too soon he found himself outside a light tan brick house similar to Bo's. There was no turning back now.

He slid out of the truck and met Bo at the front of his vehicle. Travis reached for him. He knew he was acting like a child, but even though he'd seen most of these people through his window from the kitchen of the diner, he hadn't socialized with them.

Bo kissed the back of Travis's hand. "I'll be right by your side, I promise." Bo smiled. "Trust me, this is the safest place you could ever want to be."

"I'll have to take your word for that."

"You'll see."

Bo led the way to the side gate of the fenced backyard and Travis heard the hum of voices echo all the way to the front. It sounded like the party was bigger than he'd presumed. As they rounded the corner and the huge yard opened up Travis knew he was in trouble.

The backyard was crawling with people—talking, eating, laughing people. *What if they take one look at my tattoos and decide I'm a freak?* Travis wished he was back in his kitchen.

"Bo, Travis, you're here," a short, plump woman yelled from across the yard, and everyone stopped to look straight at him. *Shit.*

"Mom." Bo shook his head and the lady smiled as she started walking toward them.

"Sorry, sorry. Everyone go back to what you were doing," she announced as she got closer.

She had a wide smile much like her son's, the same brown eyes and blonde hair. When she was less than two feet away she opened her arms wide and Bo leaned down and hugged her. Then she turned to Travis and did the same, and he had no other choice but to hug her as well.

"It's so nice to finally meet you in person. We've come into the diner but you're always back in the kitchen. I'm Dot Mason, Bo's mom," she stated proudly.

"It's nice to meet you, ma'am," Travis replied.

"Call me Dot."

"Okay. Dot."

"Come with me. I have so many people to introduce you to." Dot grabbed both their hands and began leading them over to the grouping of barbeques.

"Mom, remember what I told you."

"Yes, and I am taking things slow. If I weren't, your aunts would be huddling around him already planning the wedding."

Wedding?

"Mom, please. I want Travis to have a good time."

"He will, come along," she insisted, still pulling them forward. For such a short lady she had a serious grip.

Travis couldn't help but smile. This was what a mother was supposed to be. Loud, embarrassing, unapologetic, and filled with love for her child. He liked the woman from the start.

Bo looked over at him and mouthed, "I'm sorry." Travis smiled and decided to roll with it. What's the worst that could happen? Dot seemed to like him. They came to a stop beside a group of men, a few he recognized from the diner.

A tall man stepped forward and stuck out his hand. "Henry Mason, Bo's dad. Good to meet you, Travis."

Travis wondered how many people already knew who he was. He took Henry's hand and said, "Nice to meet you, sir."

"Son, call everyone by their first names. We don't stand much on ceremony here," Henry chided with a smile. "And don't worry about all these people. They're mainly family."

"Wow. That's a lot of family," Travis noted.

"That's what I thought when I first met them all," a man with curly blond hair interjected. He was standing beside a huge guy with a Brighton Fire Department shirt on. "I'm Johnny and this is Gabe, my fiancé."

"Nice to meet you," Travis muttered as he reached for the security of Bo's hand. Dot had moved to stand beside her husband.

"Gabe is my cousin," Bo explained. "He and Johnny are getting married in the spring."

"Congratulations."

"Thank you." Gabe smiled as he pulled Johnny close and kissed the top of his head. It was easy to tell they were in love. Travis could feel it.

"How about we take a walk around and I'll introduce you to a few family members?" Johnny asked. "I promise to never leave your side."

But Travis already had that deal with Bo, who he could see was about to clarify until Travis spoke up. "It's okay, Bo. I'd like that." Travis had no idea why he was changing the plan, but there was something about Johnny that made him want to trust the guy. Which was even weirder given Travis's trust issues.

Bo smiled, leaned down, and whispered, "You are so strong," before kissing him deeply in front of everyone in the yard. Travis's cheeks began to heat up but he held his head high. He was allowed to kiss his boyfriend anytime he wanted.

It was a freeing feeling.

***

Bo watched as Travis and Johnny walked off, straight toward the White Hair Crew. *They might as well start at the top.* He was mesmerized by Travis's strength. He had been thrown into an unknown situation and dived right in even though he'd had apprehensions.

"He's a cutie," Gabe commented.

"He's stunning," Bo countered. Gabe laughed.

"Someone's got it bad."

"Oh, like you were any different when you met Johnny. You brought him home straight from the hospital without even knowing him but for a minute before that."

"I just knew. Johnny was meant for me."

"I feel the same way about Travis," Bo admitted within earshot of his parents, aunts, and uncles. Big Mistake. He swore getting all the cousins married off was their favorite pastime and he'd added fuel to the fire.

"You feel that strongly about him, son?" Henry asked.

"Yes, I do. He's an amazing man," Bo answered honestly.

His mother smiled wide, gathering Bo's five aunts around her, and it had begun. The Mason women meant well. They did everything with love in their hearts, but Bo knew he still had to get Travis on board with the idea. That might be one of the toughest challenges ahead of him. There was no doubt Travis was attracted to him and that he trusted Bo, but he had to make it through Travis's layers. That would start tonight.

Ben, Bo's brother and a Brighton firefighter, brought over a beer and handed it to him. "So you managed to get him to come out. Good job, big brother."

"Thanks. I'm glad he's here." Bo couldn't help but watch Travis working his way through the mass of family and friends.

"You can't take your eyes off of him, Bo," Ben said before laughing at him.

"Wait until you find your soulmate. You'll act the exact same way."

"Soulmate. Don't get me wrong, I'm happy for you. But there is no such thing as a soulmate. You're lucky if you can find someone willing to put up with your shit."

Bo knew where this was all coming from. Ben went through a rather nasty breakup a few years back. An eight-year relationship came to an abrupt end when his partner was offered his dream position across the country in New York and didn't want Ben to come along. It had broken his heart and the entire family was still concerned.

Bo turned away from watching Travis and gave his brother his full attention. "How are you doing?"

"I'm fine, big bro, just a cynic about love, that's all." Ben's eyes shifted to something over Bo's right shoulder.

Bo turned to find Grady standing inside the back gate, still in uniform. Bo had invited him to come over after his shift. Grady was new to the area and Bo had wanted him to feel welcome and to make a few friends.

"Hey Grady, come on in," Bo called out, but Grady's eyes were locked on Ben and nobody else. As it turns out, Ben was laser focused on Grady. This was interesting.

Grady seemed to come out of it and walked over to where Bo and his brother were standing. "Hey Bo, thanks for inviting me."

"You're welcome," Bo replied, but he noticed his fellow officer kept glancing over at Ben. "This is my brother, Ben."

Ben stuck out his hand and Grady shook it but neither released the other quickly. Bo had a great idea.

"Grady, I have to go collect my boyfriend. Do you mind if Ben shows you around and introduces you to the family?"

Grady answered but never looked away from Ben. "Sure, if that's okay with your brother."

"All good. I'll take care of him." Ben barely acknowledged Bo was still beside him.

As the two men walked off to a private corner instead of into the party Bo knew Ben wanted Grady to himself. Bo scanned the crowd for his beauty and found him surrounded by the aunts. *Shit.* He began to weave his way over to the group to save Travis but stopped short when he heard Travis's laughter. Bo took a few steps back and watched as Travis charmed his mother and aunts by simply being himself. His father came over and stood beside Bo with a metal spatula in his hand. After all, he was manning the grill.

"Travis seems to be having fun, son."

"It's good to see him happy. He hasn't had an easy life."

"Anything I can help with?" his dad asked, always ready to step in.

"Not this time, Dad. He's already in therapy."

"Good, as long as he's getting the help he needs."

"Dr. Gordon comes highly recommended."

"He's a good man. Hey, where did your brother go?" His dad turned, looking side to side through the throng in the yard.

Bo turned around and scanned the assemblage. Yep, no Ben or Grady. "He's showing Grady around."

"The new deputy?"

"That's the one, and by the looks they were giving each other I wouldn't be surprised if we don't see them again tonight." Which was fine considering they had these barbeques monthly at various family members' houses.

"Really? He hasn't shown interest in anyone in a long time."

"Oh, there was interest. Now if you'll excuse me, I need a little Travis time." Bo slapped his dad on the shoulder before heading toward the women surrounding his boyfriend. As he picked his way through the group he was stopped for quick conversations along the way. Eventually he made it to Travis who was smiling wide and discussing fried chicken with his Aunt Ellen, Gabe's mom.

"Hey there, are you hungry, sweetheart?" Bo asked.

Travis looked up and Bo sank into those striking blue eyes. He looked so happy. "I could eat," he answered.

Bo held out his hand and Travis took it. Once away from everyone, Bo asked, "How are you doing? Is this too overwhelming?"

"Better than I thought, and everyone has been so welcoming I began to calm down almost immediately. You really have a nice family." Travis seemed wistful.

"They're available whenever you need a little family time," Bo offered. "They'd be happy to have you around. They really like you."

Travis nodded but didn't look up. It would take time but Bo would make sure Travis knew how much he was wanted. For the next few hours, they ate and talked. Bo introduced Travis to people as they passed by. It turned out to be a wonderful evening and they left around ten p.m., much later than Bo had expected.

He pulled into his driveway and turned off the engine. "I have something to ask you, and if you're not comfortable with it, tell me."

"Okay."

"I want you to spend the night, and it has nothing to do with sex. I wouldn't betray your trust like that. I want to hold you. Maybe give you a bit of peace from the nightmares, at least for one night."

Travis sat quietly, making Bo a nervous wreck. "I don't have my clothes or medication."

"We could go over and pick all that up. It would only take a few minutes. We both are on afternoons tomorrow so we can sleep in and have a late breakfast. But you may have to help me with that."

Travis smiled, as Bo had hoped he would. "Yes, I'll stay with you tonight."

Before Travis could change his mind, Bo reversed the truck out of the driveway and headed toward the diner. Fifteen minutes later they were back inside Bo's house getting ready for bed. He led Travis down the hallway and into the master suite.

Bo walked up to one of his dressers. "You can put your clothes in here whenever you stay over." Stating clearly he hoped there would be more sleepovers.

Travis didn't deny him, so Bo took that as a good sign.

"Do you mind if I take a shower?"

"Of course you can. There should be extra towels in there. I'll take a shower in the guest bathroom and meet you back here," Bo instructed before leaning down and taking Travis's lips in a tender kiss. "Thank you for saying yes and trusting me." Bo knew how much it took for Travis to agree to this.

"I wanted to spend more time with you. I don't know where this is going to lead, but never doubt that I want to be with you." Travis stood up on his tiptoes for another kiss before turning and walking into the bathroom.

I'm a lucky man. Bo hurried down the hallway and into the guest bathroom. He quickly stripped and jumped under the stream of hot water. Bo grabbed his bar of soap and began building up a lather on his chest hair. He was excited at the prospect of spending the night with Travis. Even though they had no plans to become intimate, Bo's body had a mind of its own and his dick was growing hard from having Travis in his master suite. A simple thump to his cock was not going to make this go away and the last thing he wanted was to sport wood while holding Travis tonight. He had to get this out of his system.

Bo reached down with his soapy hand and took hold of his hard cock in a firm grip. He leaned his back against the tiled wall, spread his legs and flexed his hips with every stroke. The pleasure was escalating as images of Travis flashed through his mind. He bit his lip to stop himself from moaning or crying out loud. The last thing he wanted was for Travis to hear him. His cock was rock hard and dripping with precum as his one hand began to pump faster and his other massaged his balls. He felt the rush as he pushed his thumb nail into his slit and his balls pulled up tight. Fire raced down his back and through his balls as he came. Bo leaned heavily against the wall, his spent cock in his hand as he tried to catch his breath. That had been one of the hardest orgasms he'd had in a long time, no doubt because of the man in the next room.

Bo slowly came back to himself and continued to wash up. By the time he was done, his breathing had evened out. He was quick to dry off and put on his sleeping pants. Typically he slept naked but he knew Travis wasn't ready for that, so he'd stay in his loose-fitting cotton pants. By the time he returned to his bedroom Travis was sitting in one of the chairs by the window. He looked nervous. That wouldn't do.

Bo reached out to Travis and waited. Slowly Travis stood and walked the few feet over to take Bo's hand. The moment they touched Bo felt his body relax. Travis had that effect on him.

"Did you take your medication?"

"Yes."

Bo gathered Travis close to his bare chest. The smell of soap and Travis filled Bo's senses and he held him even tighter. "Good. Ready for bed?"

Travis smiled and nodded. Bo didn't believe Travis allowed anyone close enough to do this since he was burned. Bo swore never to break the trust Travis was giving him.

"Then let's get you in bed." Bo reached out and turned off the overhead light. The bedside lamps still provided muted light for them to see by.

Bo led him over to the right side of the bed, pulled back the covers, and waited for Travis to jump in. Once he did Travis slid over to the middle, allowing Bo to follow him in. Bo hadn't had anyone in his bed in a long time and the mere sight of his gorgeous boyfriend lying there made his cock twitch. He had to get himself under control all over again.

Bo crawled in, settled beside Travis and gathered him close. Bo could have purred when Travis laid his head on his chest and settled in. Bo ran his hand up and down Travis's back and for the first time Travis didn't tense. Bo'd take that as a victory.

"Comfortable, babe?"

Travis tilted his head back and looked up at him. Bo's heart squeezed tight and he knew then and there that he was definitely in love with Travis. The realization wasn't a shock. Travis was so easy to love.

"Much more comfortable than I thought I would be. I was afraid I wouldn't be able to do this but I'm actually calm. Listen, if I have a nightmare, stay back. I don't want to hit you again." Bo could hear the guilt in his voice.

"It's not your fault. I don't want you to feel bad about that."

"But I hit you."

"Did you mean to hit me?"

"No, of course not."

"Then you shouldn't accept responsibility. You were asleep after all."

Travis didn't look convinced but nodded and lay down onto Bo's chest. His slim fingers ran through Bo's chest hair, leaving a trail of heat in their wake. If Travis wanted to explore his body, Bo had no problems lying still for him. He wanted nothing more than to feel his love's hands on him.

Travis's hand travelled down Bo's abs, stopping at the edge of the covers before working their way back up to his pecs. Travis's nail grazed Bo's nipple before carrying on to his shoulder and bicep. Bo wanted to moan in pleasure but held back, not wanting Travis to stop. After a couple minutes Travis's hand began to slow and finally stopped altogether as his breathing evened out.

Bo ran his fingers through Travis's ebony hair. It was so soft. He wrapped it around his fingers and he couldn't help but imagine holding that hair as he made love to Travis. Bo hoped someday Travis would feel safe enough to show him his scars willingly. Of course, Bo had already seen them in the hospital, but for Travis to trust Bo enough to bare them to him would be a completely different thing.

Bo wouldn't make a move unless Travis initiated it, and then he doubted either of them would stop.

Bo would wait for that day, no matter how long it took.

Chapter Six

The sound of birds chirping was the first thing Travis noticed as he slowly woke up. The second was the muscled body lying beside him. Deep snores broke the silence as he carefully shifted his weight onto his elbow so that he could look at the man he desired more than anything or anyone. *Bo.*

He looked so relaxed in sleep, younger than his thirty-one years. The smile lines in the corners of his full lips stood as testament to the happiness Bo embraced. His broad shoulders and strong arms, one wrapped around Travis's waist, the other over Bo's head, made Travis feel so safe. Lightly he rubbed his fingers across Bo's wide chest, amazed at how soft his skin was compared to his hard body.

"Like what you see?" Bo's sleep-filled voice sounded husky. That combined with the gorgeous body he was touching had a definite effect on Travis, and he was getting hard.

"Yes, you have a beautiful body."

"I'm glad you like it because it's all yours to explore." Bo smiled before reaching over and pulling Travis closer so that they were now face to face. He could feel Bo's erection pushing into his stomach. Bo was large everywhere. But he didn't make a move, didn't try for more, allowing Travis to just lie there. He weighed his options: he could do nothing and remain in a sort of stasis, never going forward, never really living, or he could take a chance.

Bo lifted his head off the bed and Travis made his choice. Their lips met. Their kiss started out slow and relaxed but soon turned into something much more heated. Bo's tongue explored Travis's mouth thoroughly before he moved on to trail kisses down Travis's chin and neck. Teasing little nibbles had Travis flexing his hips into Bo's thigh, desperate for some friction.

"Are you sure about this?"

"This is the first thing I've been sure about in a long time. I want to explore and experience life with you."

"Anything you want." Bo's deep voice spurred Travis on.

Bo's lips continued down until he reached the spot where Travis's shoulder met his neck and began sucking deeply. He was going to leave a mark and Travis was completely on board with that. Travis could feel each pull down to his throbbing cock.

"Can I touch you, Travis?" Bo asked after releasing his neck.

Travis refused to let his fear win out, not this time. "God, yes."

Bo's big hand slid between their bodies and into Travis's pants. It was a good thing they were loose and allowed Bo to move around easily. Without stopping Bo wrapped his hand around Travis's cock and began pumping. Travis had a moment's trepidation then their eyes locked on one another as Travis experienced the pleasure of the first touch. Sure, he'd jerked himself off but that was before the burns turned him into this *freak*. The word crashed into him like a wave and he immediately pulled away.

Bo released his cock but not Travis's body, which he held gently. "What is it? Do you want us to stop?"

Travis thought about it—did he really want Bo to stop? *No*. Bo wasn't doing anything Travis didn't want. This was his issue and he needed to start facing it.

"I don't want you to stop. It's just an old memory I'm working on excising from my life. But I was thinking we could slow down a bit?"

"Anything you need, babe, you tell me. That way I won't accidentally do something you don't like or that's painful." Bo stopped as if afraid to say any more.

"What is it?"

"I wanted to ask if it hurt anywhere when I touched you. I don't want to cause you pain."

"My back and legs are healed but there's a bit of nerve damage that causes me pain occasionally. Um…and my dick is also healed. In fact, the other day with you was the first time I've had a hard-on since the fire burned me. I didn't think it was possible. It had been so long." Travis spread his legs wide before saying, "Please touch me."

Bo took his lips in a desperate kiss before sliding his hand back into Travis's pants and taking hold of his cock. Travis couldn't hold back the moan that escaped his lips as he leaned his forehead against Bo's chest and closed his eyes. Pleasure shot through his body, taking his breath away as he dug his fingers into Bo's shoulders.

Travis felt Bo's hard cock and desperately wanted to touch him and give Bo as much pleasure as he was receiving. But he was laying on top of Bo. He'd never get his hand between them from the top especially with Bo's hand already between them.

"Bo, please I need to touch you."

Bo pushed Travis's body into a sitting position so he was now straddling Bo's body with his cock jutting out in front of him and engulfed in Bo's hand. He had no time to feel embarrassed about his scars being seen as Bo reached down with his free hand, pulled the elastic hem of his sleep pants down, and exposed himself to Travis who was quick to take hold of Bo's thick cock. Any doubts quickly dissolved and were replaced by the overwhelming feeling of power and freedom. Travis pumped his hand in time with Bo's. They still hadn't looked away from one another and Travis began to moan softly as Bo increased the speed of his hand and asked. "Do you trust me?"

"Yes."

Bo slowly slid his hand to Travis's hip while he continued stroking him. Bo's hand didn't stop at his hip, it continued on around to Travis's ass cheek. Travis began to pull away. He knew the burns were horrific and they felt bumpy and patchy; it took a lot for him to have already exposed himself this much.

"Trust me, Travis. I would never hurt you," Bo whispered.

It was true. Travis felt safe and desired in Bo's arms. He looked deep into Bo's eyes and saw love shining back. *Love—when did that happen?* Sure, he had feelings for Bo, strong feelings. Is that love? Travis had to admit he'd been falling for the big guy for a while now.

Travis's hand slid over the soft skin of Bo's rigid cock before he nodded his head and said, "I trust you." Bo slowly slid his hand a little further until his entire cheek was covered. Bo squeezed Travis's ass while he continued to work his cock. Travis knew he was going to come soon and when he felt Bo's fingers circling his hole there was nothing he could do to stop it. With a final jerk of his hips Travis cried out and came all over Bo's stomach. Moments later Bo moaned deeply as warm cum covered Travis's hand.

Travis collapsed down onto Bo's chest, gasping for breath as Bo reached his arm around Travis and held him close. Both took their time coming down. Travis rested his head on Bo's chest and his eyes grew heavy. He decided to close them for just a minute.

***

Travis opened his eyes to find himself alone in the bed. He must have fallen asleep. He reached down, expecting a dried mess to be covering him, but there was nothing but clean skin. Even his hand had been cleaned. *Bo must have cleaned me up.* But where was his boyfriend?

The smell of bacon came drifting into the room and Travis's mouth began to water. He loved bacon. He rolled over onto his back and stretched his body before sitting up. He could hear pots clanging in the kitchen and suddenly remembered Bo couldn't cook. Travis jumped out of bed and hurried to the kitchen to save breakfast.

When he got there, smoke was pouring out of the toaster and what looked like every pan in the house covered the counters. The fire alarm started to sound and Bo ran over to wave a tea towel below it to stop the screeching. In a flash Travis was dragged back in time, smoke surrounding him, choking every breath he took. His body was charred black and he was screaming in pain but all he could hear was the thunderous roar of the fire.

"Travis. Travis, look at me. Please come back to me. You're safe." Bo commanded until eventually Travis started hearing the words coming through the fog of his mind. "There you are."

Travis looked around him, trying to figure out where he was. The walls weren't glowing with the light from the flames and his world hadn't just been ripped from him. Bo was standing in front of him, worry written all over his face. Travis realized he'd must have had a flashback. He hadn't had one of those in years. It made him angry that something as simple as the toaster and smoke alarm could do that to him. He didn't want to talk about it so he chose to carry on as if the last few minutes never happened.

"Looks like breakfast is another meal you can't cook," Travis mumbled before hugging Bo tight and taking a deep breath. Travis pulled back and looked at the man he was falling in love with and couldn't think of a single reason why he shouldn't.

"We're a team. We can make breakfast together." Bo smiled wide. It seemed as though he was taking Travis's lead and not talking about what happened. For the next hour Travis instructed Bo on how to make the perfect omelet and how to turn down the temperature on his toaster. In the end they had ham and cheese omelets with home fries, bacon, and toast. The extra pots and pans Bo had pulled out were back where they belonged. Travis took the last bite of his omelet and thought about his next question carefully. He was afraid of the answer considering what happened to him this morning.

"Did I have a nightmare last night?"

"You became agitated once but I rubbed your back and you stayed asleep. It didn't take long," Bo explained.

"Thank you, and I'm sorry I woke you."

"That was nothing to be sorry about. I would gladly take having you in my bed with your nightmares then not having you at all," Bo explained. "And that brings me to my next topic. I want to make these sleepovers a regular occurrence, maybe a couple times a week. What do you think?"

Travis knew that would only bring him closer to Bo and solidify his place in Travis's life. Did he really want to remain alone? Did he want to push Bo away? Hell no. "I'd like that."

"Thank god. If you'd said no, I was going to suggest your place but I couldn't picture both of us trying to fit into your bed." Bo looked relieved.

"Yeah, I can't see that working out so well." Travis laughed. He was so happy that neither one of them felt strange about what they'd shared that morning. Bo was behaving as he would any other day, and that made all of Travis's nerves melt away.

He felt his cheeks getting warm as he thought about it. He stood, collected the plates, and turned toward the kitchen, hoping Bo hadn't seen the effect that one thought had on him. He should have known better.

"Why are you blushing?" Bo asked as he came up behind Travis.

"I was thinking about earlier this morning, in bed."

"About this morning? Good, because I can't get it out of my head either. I loved every minute, from waking with you in my arms to getting you off," Bo rasped as he held Travis. "How about you? Did you enjoy our time together?"

"Oh, yeah," Travis rushed out as though he'd been holding his breath.

"Good, because I intend for it to happen again and again."

Travis was all for that plan, just as long as he didn't have to expose more of his body yet.

He wasn't ready for that.

Chapter Seven

It had been four weeks since his first therapy session with Dr. Gordon and Travis had worked through some of his abandonment issues and anger toward his mother. Now they would be moving on to discussing the fire. He was not looking forward to this but he had to face it head on if he was to ever have a life. He'd made his choice to see this through. He looked at the bright white walls of Dr. Gordon's waiting room. Didn't they know how to use a muted color around here?

Travis thought back to the last several weeks and realized he and Bo had gotten into a routine of sorts. Monday and Thursday—therapy. Monday, Thursday, and Saturday—sleepovers. Travis began to find himself looking forward to it and finding it all the lonelier at his apartment. Johnny, whom he met at the barbeque, had become his friend. He'd seen the raised white scars on Johnny's hands, and knew all too well the pain he must have suffered. Travis hadn't asked what happened; he didn't want to make Johnny relive it if he didn't want to. But it made him wonder what it would be like if a few people knew about his scars. He already had Bo who knew. How bad would it be?

"Travis. Babe, they're calling your name," Bo's voice brought Travis back to the here and now. He looked at the clock on the wall, and sure enough it was four p.m.

"Mr. Boone," the receptionist called out.

Travis quickly stood and looked at Bo. "I'm going to tell him about the accident today and a few other things I've been holding onto. I don't know how that will work out. Do you want to come in with me?" If he was going to relive these things he was only doing it once. There wouldn't be a repeat performance so Bo might as well be involved.

Bo stood and held Travis's hand. He was still dressed in his uniform. "Yes, of course I'll come in with you. Whatever you need."

Travis turned and led the way down the bright yellow hallway and into the fake living room where he typically had his sessions. They sat down on the couch and waited for Dr. Gordon to come in. Travis's nerves were shot but he knew this was the right path to take. He was one hundred percent positive it was time to get the burden of what happened off of his shoulders and out of his head.

Bo didn't try to engage him in conversation, for which Travis was thankful. He needed to concentrate on getting it out. Then they could work on the nightmares he continued to have. Even though some nights at Bo's had passed without one, they hadn't left Travis completely and he seriously doubted they ever would.

Dr. Gordon walked in, and if he was surprised by Bo's presence he didn't let on. "Good afternoon, Travis, Bo."

"Hi, Dr. Gordon," Travis said.

"Dr. Gordon," Bo replied.

"How are you feeling today, Travis?" the doctor asked.

"Nervous, unsure." *Might as well be honest.*

"Why are you feeling this way?" Dr. Gordon's eyebrows creased as he talked.

"Because I have to relive a portion of my life I'd sooner forget." *But never will.*

"You know you are safe here. We can work through anything without fear," Dr. Gordon reassured him.

"Nothing could change the way I feel about you," Bo stated in a strong, sure voice.

Travis wished he had that kind of confidence, but he wasn't going to turn back. He needed to do this. He'd lived alone with these memories for far too long.

“I thought I could spit this out all in one shot then we can work on them later,” Travis suggested.

“Whatever way you need it to be, is absolutely fine,” Dr. Gordon gave the therapist answer Travis was used to hearing.

Here we go. “When I was sixteen, my life as I knew it ended, and I lost the one person I knew loved me, my dad. It was just any normal day for me and my dad. We’d gotten home from our soup kitchen deliveries and Dad was on the phone with my mother. She was away on another business trip. I…I heard a hissing sound…right before….” He was hyperventilating. *Shit, when did that happen?*

“Breathe, Travis. That’s it, take a deep breath for me.” Bo was crouched down in front of him and Dr. Gordon set a glass of water on the coffee table for him. “You don’t have to do this, babe, if you’re not ready.”

“I have to get this out…I HAVE to.” *Take a breath. Then another.* “The hissing sound happened before the dining room floor exploded.” Travis stopped to sort through his memories and calm himself. Bo took the opportunity to sit down on the couch. “I was standing maybe a foot away from the hole when the fire started. It happened so fast. Before I had a chance to move the floor underneath me gave way. I don’t know how, but I managed to grab the edge of a two-by-four sticking up out of the hole. But my body was still hanging over the hole to the basement directly in the path of the flames. I c-could feel the heat…singeing my clothes, but there was nothing I could do to stop it…the flames burned through my clothing…”

Even now the flames felt real to him. Bo squeezed his hand, giving him his silent support. “I could hear my own skin sizzling. I’d had enough and was about to let go. I couldn’t take it anymore. Then my dad grabbed my hands and dragged me out of the hole. As I was crawling away the floor opened up and my dad was gone. He didn’t even scream. The next thing I knew I was in the back of an ambulance. My mother didn’t arrive at the hospital for two days. She said she had been getting everything prepared for my dad’s funeral.”

"What? She left you in the hospital alone?" Bo asked, his voice higher than normal.

Travis nodded before continuing. "The nurses assured me that my mom was always in contact with the doctors. I didn't get to go to my dad's funeral. That hurt more than the physical pain. Later I found out the explosion and fire were caused by a gas leak. For the next four months I was in the hospital and I saw her once a week, at most. When I got out, my mother had moved us into a two-bedroom condo and all my father's belongings were gone."

Travis had to stop and take a deep breath. He couldn't meet their eyes but he needed to finish. "It's because of me that my dad died. It's all my fault." He couldn't hold back his tears any longer and they streamed down his face. His secret was out. He was guilty of his father's death.

"Why do you feel it's your fault?" Dr. Gordon asked.

"If my dad hadn't had to save me he'd still be alive. My mother couldn't help but remind me of that fact every day. When I turned eighteen I was given my walking papers. She said she couldn't stand to live with me anymore after what I'd done. She handed me five hundred dollars and the keys to my dad's old car."

"Travis, did you start the fire?" Dr. Gordon questioned softly.

"No."

"Did you intentionally stand close to the edge of the hole?"

"No, it opened up beside me."

"Did you force your dad to come over and save you?"

"No, but he's my dad. Of course he would help me."

"Exactly. Any decent father would do the same thing for their child. Does that make the child responsible?"

"There's more." Travis was choking on the thought and how to get it out quickly before he lost his nerve. No one knew about this; he'd never spoken the words out loud. "I knew about the gas leak and didn't tell my dad."

"How did you know about the gas leak?" Travis was thankful Bo was still holding his hand.

"Before we left for the soup kitchen, I heard a small hissing sound when I was downstairs in the rec room."

"At the time did you know what it was?" Dr. Gordon questioned.

"No. I was sixteen and oblivious. But I intended to tell him when I went upstairs."

"Why didn't you?"

"Friends of my dad's stopped by and then we ran out the door because we were late. By then I completely forgot about it. I was… just a stupid kid."

"It's not your fault," Bo said as he gathered Travis close.

Of course Bo wouldn't see him as guilty, but it still didn't make it the truth. His dad was dead and he could have stopped it. "I wish I could believe that."

"We'll have to work on that, Travis," Dr. Gordon stated. "Tell me how the events of that evening have impacted your life."

"What hasn't it impacted? I can't sleep without being covered in clothing, I've never been intimate with someone before Bo, and I still haven't taken all my clothes off in front of him. The scars are disgusting and I'm only half a man with half a dick. You already know about the nightmares. Sometimes I'm so tired after a particularly bad night that I'm surprised I can still stand. It's affected everything. I can't reach the top shelves of the diner without pulling on the scars and causing myself pain. I'm half a man."

Travis was exhausted.

He knew he'd never be free of this no matter how long he was in therapy.

***

Bo held Travis close, his tears soaking into Bo's uniform shirt. He had been reliving that horrible experience and the overwhelming guilt during sleep, over and over again for ten years. No doubt he was tired. Bo listened to every word as the doctor continued to ask questions. And Bo's heart broke. It was bad enough that Travis had lost his father, but to be so extensively burned. Then to have the only parent he had left abandon him. Travis had been through hell.

"Do you want to be intimate with Bo?" Dr. Gordon asked.

Bo sat frozen waiting for Travis's reply. Their relationship wasn't dependent on his answer but Bo was curious if he saw them heading that way. Bo could wait as long as it took for Travis to become comfortable with that thought.

"Yes. He's the first one I'm willing to risk having an intimate relationship with. But hell, my attacker didn't want anything to do with me after he saw my scars."

"Attacker? How did he see your scars?" Bo wanted to kill this guy.

"Do I really have to answer that? Living on the street isn't safe," Travis replied and Bo's suspicions were confirmed. "Let's just say he didn't take what he was after once he saw the whole me. I know it's insane to even take that into account, considering what he tried to do to me, but there it is. In all its fucked-up glory."

Bo sat silently, unsure what to say. After everything Travis had been through, what could Bo say? But his anger was through the roof. He wanted to find that asshole and grind him into the ground. No jail, no judge, just him. And that was a dangerous thought for a cop to have.

"Travis, I can't tell you there's a quick way to fix this. You'll always have some effects from the trauma you've suffered. But together we can work to make living with it easier so that you can lead a happy and fulfilled life. I know I could try to convince you that your father's death wasn't your fault, but at this moment you wouldn't believe me. Over time we'll work through that, among other things. You're doing well so far," Dr. Gordon assured before leaning forward in his chair.

"I hope you're right. I want a normal life." Travis sighed before looking at Bo. "Especially now that I have Bo in it."

Those words were like a caress to Bo's heart and the anger he felt slipped away, if only temporarily.

"Then you need to make steps toward that goal. Go at whatever pace feels comfortable to you," Dr. Gordon explained. "Each step you take brings you closer to the life you say you want. But be careful not to push yourself too hard in an attempt to get where you think you need to go."

Travis nodded but remained quiet. To Bo he seemed to be deep in thought.

"I think that's enough for one day. We'll continue this on Thursday. How is the medication working? Any side effects?"

"I haven't noticed any and I am sleeping more now than before."

"Good. Let me know if you have any questions."

"I will," Travis said as he stood. Bo did the same before shaking Dr. Gordon's hand.

They exited the building and shockingly Travis had a smile on his face. Bo didn't know whether they should talk about what Travis had said or let it rest. But there were a few things he had to make clear.

When they reached the truck, Bo stopped Travis and spun him around. "You are not responsible for your dad's death and you are definitely not half a man. You're all man."

Travis tried to look away but Bo held him gently and waited until he looked back. "I'm trying, Bo, but I think it will be a long time before I accept that."

"I'll be happy to remind you anytime you ask. Probably even when you don't."

Bo leaned down and Travis clung to him as they kissed deeply. It wasn't until a horn sounded that Bo pulled away and looked up to see Grady driving by and waving. Bo waved back and smiled. He really liked the new addition to the Brighton force and wondered if Grady and Ben had hit it off. He'd have to remember to ask.

"Let's go home," Travis hiccupped as he climbed into the truck. Bo loved the sound of that request. He wanted Travis to consider the house Bo had renovated as a home for Travis as well.

"I'm sorry, and I know this is not the night to have to tell you this, but I have to run back to the station to finish some paperwork. I don't want to leave you but I won't be long. Maximum one hour." Bo felt horrible for leaving Travis and hoped he would agree to stay at the house while he was gone. He hadn't had time to finish everything he had to do at work before picking Travis up for his appointment. His years on the force and his dedication demanded Bo return to finish the reports.

"If you don't mind me being in your house alone."

"Of course I don't mind. I trust you completely. Please feel free to look around if you'd like. I want you to be comfortable there."

"Okay, I'll start dinner," Travis replied. He looked happier to Bo, like he'd had a great weight lifted off of his shoulders. Which Bo guessed was true.

"The house is stocked up for you, chef." Bo had been paying more attention when he went grocery shopping. Now he had fixings for dinner and spices he'd never heard of. Travis had given him a list. They'd been enjoying their times cooking together, or rather Travis cooked while Bo tried not to get in the way.

"I'll surprise you with something new we haven't tried yet."

"Perfect," Bo agreed as he lifted Travis's hand and kissed his palm. He dug into his duty belt and pulled out a surprise—hopefully a good one. "I'd like you to have this."

Bo placed it in Travis's open palm. He looked down and asked, "A key?"

"Yes. When we get home I'll show you how to disarm the alarm as well."

"You're giving me a key to your house?"

"I want you to feel free to come and go as you please. I want you in every aspect of my life, Travis," Bo stated, not wanting there to be any confusion.

Travis flipped the key around between his fingers and then took Bo out of his misery. "I'll accept the key to your house but I want to give you one to mine."

"Deal," Bo said happily.

Twenty minutes later Bo walked in the front doors of the station house. He settled in behind his desk, unlocked his computer, and clicked open two files. The first was for a fender bender, nothing too complicated there, but the second involved an assault. Even a town as amazing as Brighton had its crimes. He pulled out his notepad where he kept a record of the day's activities and got to work.

"Hey, Bo," Grady called out as he sat his big body behind a desk a few seats over. The man was honestly the size of two people but he was a gentle bear. Bo looked up at the clock on his computer screen and realized it had already been forty minutes since he'd left Travis.

"Hey Grady, how's your evening going?"

"Calm. It's pretty quiet out there."

"That's good," Bo muttered as he laid his notepad on the desk and hit Save on his report. "So when are you going to tell me what's going on between you and my brother?"

Grady looked down at his computer keyboard before saying, "We're friends."

"Friends, huh?"

A sad look crossed Grady's face before he answered. "Yep, just friends."

Before Bo had a chance to ask him another question, Chief Graham walked in carrying a red file folder. "Grady, Bo, our armed and dangerous suspect has struck again over in Marshall. The state police are tracking his movements but have not been able to get close to him. It's like the bastard disappears into thin air. This time it was a diner but thankfully no one was hurt. He hit it at closing time."

"Marshall—that's only a couple counties over." Bo's mind began racing with ugly scenarios. That was too close to Brighton. Bo worried about the people of the community, his family and Travis's safety, particularly since he worked a few late-night shifts at the only diner in town.

"We need to up patrols until this guy is caught. I'll be adding more shifts but I'll keep you on the same nights off Bo. This is the sixth armed robbery this guy has committed and they're no closer to finding him. He must stay on the move because I can't see him having that many places across the state to hole up in."

"Let me know which shifts I can pick up or if anything else comes across about this guy. I'm surprised with all the eyewitness reports he still hasn't been caught," Bo stated.

"So am I. Hey, why are you even here?" Dave asked. "Shouldn't you be home with Travis?"

"I had some paperwork to finish up. I'm almost done. Travis is home making dinner."

"Really. So everything is going well?"

"Yes, and I couldn't be happier. Travis is amazing. He's really brought joy and purpose into my life."

Dave, his boss and best friend, regarded him for a moment before saying, "You do look different. I'm happy for you buddy."

"Thanks, Dave."

"Okay, back to work Grady. Bo, finish up and get your ass home, it's already past six-thirty."

Grady stood and headed out to his cruiser and Bo finished his entries and put his notes in his drawer before relocking it. Time to go home to Travis. Bo liked the sound of that.

He pulled into the driveway and the first thing he noticed were the windows all lit up. Usually when he came home it was dark and empty inside. That fact alone made a warm feeling spread through his body. *Home.* The thought of Travis making this his home had Bo three shades of happy. He walked to his front porch and unlocked the door. The aroma hit him the moment he stepped into the hall. The smell of garlic, peppers, and chili powder filled his senses. Chili. He loved chili. He walked in and heard the music playing from the kitchen, dance music. Bo rounded the corner and stopped in his tracks.

There, in the middle of the kitchen was Travis with his back to Bo, swaying his hips to the music. The sight was so captivating he couldn't look away. There was no doubt he wanted Travis, and moments like this drove that fact home in spades. Travis's ass bounced in time with the music and Bo groaned out his appreciation.

Travis spun around and dropped the ladle he was holding, splashing red sauce all over the bottom cabinets. "Babe, it's just me. It's just me," Bo said as he lifted his hands in a nonthreatening way.

Bo inched his way forward and then he engulfed Travis in his arms. "I'm so sorry I scared you. I should have made myself known sooner."

"It's okay." Travis's muffled voice came from Bo's chest and he quickly loosened his hold. "We're working on this, right, and maybe in time Dr. Gordon will get me to a place where I don't startle so easily."

"I should be more conscious of it," Bo apologized. "But honestly, I got distracted by your beautiful ass swaying back and forth."

Travis laughed as Bo had hoped. There had been enough sadness and memories for one day. Travis bent over to retrieve the ladle from the floor and Bo grabbed some paper towels and began cleaning the mess left behind. Once done, Bo looked over Travis's shoulder at the pot bubbling on the stove. "That is a lot of chili."

"I made enough so that you had leftovers for when I'm not here," Travis explained. He'd often said he was worried that Bo had no good food when he wasn't staying over. Bo had the greatest boyfriend.

"Thank you, babe. I appreciate everything you do for me," Bo rasped and Travis stretched up for a kiss.

"You're welcome," he mumbled while nibbling Bo's bottom lip.

Bo cupped Travis's cheek before kissing him again and saying, "You are so important to me. I want you to know that."

Travis reached up and held Bo tight. "You mean a lot to me, Bo."

Bo rubbed the side of Travis's head with his chin. He loved Travis, and knew in that moment that he wanted him to move in. But Bo would have to keep it to himself for the moment until he thought

Travis was ready to hear it. The last thing he wanted to do was move too fast and risk losing his love.

"I have to go get out of these clothes. I'll be right back," Bo said, releasing Travis.

Travis kissed him quickly and returned to stirring the pot as Bo headed for the bedroom. He secured his duty belt and gun before changing out of his uniform and put on loose-fitting track pants and a t-shirt. He heard plates being placed on the table. He hurried back to the dining room to find Travis waiting for him at the table with bowls full of chili.

It was all so normal and exactly what Bo had dreamed of.

Chapter Eight

Travis stepped out of the shower and began drying his body. He ran the soft towel over his uneven back then slowly turned to look at himself in the full-length mirror. Travis ran his fingers over his mangled flesh. It was warm and soft in some places, hard in others. Would Bo even want to touch him when he got the full picture?

Travis sighed. He turned himself back around and looked at his patchy legs and disfigured cock. Would Bo still desire the complete package? *I have to try if I'm ever going to know.* Travis could hear Bo moving around in the bedroom. He waited until he heard the bed squeak before taking a deep breath and opening the door wearing nothing more than his towel. As he thought, Bo was in bed lying on his side facing Travis. When he saw Travis in only a towel his jaw dropped but he said nothing. Travis was good with that. He had no idea what to say or what to reply if Bo'd had any questions.

Bo's gaze roamed over Travis's body and the evident desire reassured Travis that he'd made the right choice. If he wanted a real relationship with Bo, Travis knew he had to try even if the exposure made him feel like monster on display.

Travis approached the bed, and when he was less than a foot away he removed his towel. He waited a moment before crawling onto the bed and settling on his stomach beside Bo, which gave him an unobstructed view of the rest of Travis's mangled flesh. He closed his eyes and waited for the fallout. After a moment he felt Bo's big hand ghosting over Travis's back and down to his butt. The next touch was a little bit firmer.

"You're sure it doesn't hurt you for me to touch your skin?"

"Doesn't hurt," Travis replied softly. "It feels good." Which it did. No one had ever touched him unless it was clinically required by doctors, therapists, or from an attempted assault. Having someone touch him for no other reason than to feel him as a person, not a patient or victim, was thrilling.

Bo's fingers traced the edges of Travis's ragged skin in a slow exploration that left him breathless. Inch by inch, not a spot was missed. Then Bo moved his attention to Travis's ass and legs. His touch was tender but firm, exactly what Travis needed and wanted. He didn't want to be treated like an invalid. He wanted to be treated like a whole man.

The bed dipped as Bo shifted his body, and then to Travis's surprise Bo's soft lips kissed his shoulder. Bo worked his way lower, taking his time until he came to Travis's ass, where he stopped to kiss each cheek thoroughly. Travis wasn't being rejected; he was being loved. His heart felt like it burst open. Emotions were flooding him and he couldn't hold back the sob that found its way out of his throat.

Travis was flipped onto his back and then found himself crushed against Bo's wide chest. *Not a bad turn of events.* Happy tears seemed to wash away some of the stains of his past and he held Bo tighter.

"I'm never letting you go. Do you understand what I'm saying? I want you to be with me, and I want us to build a life together," Bo murmured against Travis's skin as he kissed Travis's neck and face.

Travis looked up and he saw warmth and sincerity in Bo's eyes. "You want me permanently? But we haven't even made love yet. I could be terrible at it."

Bo smiled and brushed the hair out of Travis's face. "We don't need to make love for me to know I want you in my life. I'm willing to wait as long as it takes."

"Bo, do you love me?" Travis asked with a racing heart.

"I can't lie," Bo answered quickly. "I've loved you for a while. But I don't want to pressure you. I know you have things to work through. We have lots of time to figure everything out."

Holy shit. Bo loved him. Travis had strong feelings for Bo, but the only love Travis had ever known was a father's love. As he thought of the months he'd spent getting to know Bo, Travis tallied their time together: he loved being with Bo, loved their private times, and trusted him with his past. But Travis knew he wasn't ready to jump into the deep end even though he wanted to.

"Bo, I want to tell you that I feel the same way, but I'm not ready." Travis felt horrible that he couldn't reciprocate Bo's feelings.

"We have time. There's no rush. I couldn't lie to you when you asked. I'll never lie to you," Bo swore.

Travis dipped his head. "I have strong feelings for you and I want to be with you. There's so much happening right now and I want to be on solid ground," Travis tried to explain.

"I completely understand," Bo soothed. "I love you and I'm not going anywhere."

"Thank you," Travis murmured as he wrapped his arms around Bo's neck and leaned forward. Bo angled his body over Travis and nibbled his bottom lip.

Bo laid Travis down and plundered his mouth. Strong arms held him securely as Bo's hand worked its way down to Travis's ass and grabbed hold of one cheek. Bo's hips began to grind against Travis's hard cock and he was reveling in the friction when Bo suddenly stopped and stood to the side of the bed.

Travis was about to ask what made him stop, when Bo spoke. "Babe, can I get rid of my pants?"

He was touched Bo asked him. It gave Travis the control he needed after years of having none. "Naked is good."

Bo hooked his thumbs in the band of his sleeping pants and slowly lowered them. Until now, they'd given each other hand jobs, but not once had they been completely naked together. Bo was stunning, from his broad shoulders and muscled chest and arms to his strong legs and long, thick cock. He was a perfect specimen of the male body, and Travis wanted to sketch him naked.

Travis was ready to take this next step forward in their relationship, having no barriers between them. He'd already stepped out of the clothes he'd worn as armor and wanted to feel Bo's naked body against his. Bo crawled back onto the bed and over Travis's trembling body. Bo's eyes seemed incredibly dark, and his muscles flexed as he moved. Travis could feel Bo's body ghosting over his until they were face to face once again.

"You're so beautiful," Bo said as he bent down and claimed Travis's lips.

Travis knew that Bo believed it to be true, and Travis could live with that. Deep, drugging kisses left him breathless and he wanted more, but apparently Bo had other plans. He began to work his way down Travis's neck and to his chest. He stopped at a nipple, licking it into a hard peak before sucking it into his mouth. Travis cried out as the pleasure raced through his body.

Bo released one sensitive nub before he lapped the other with the same vigor. Travis moaned in response and arched his back to get closer to Bo's talented mouth. It didn't take long before Bo was kissing his way down Travis's abdomen but stopped above Travis's throbbing cock. Bo looked up at Travis in question and all he could do was groan in need. He held his breath as Bo's head lowered and he licked Travis's cock from root to tip before sucking him down.

Travis found himself gasping for air as the warmth of Bo's mouth enveloped him. His hips flexed every time he felt Bo's tongue swirling around the end of his cock and dipping into his slit. Bo pushed Travis's legs further apart, baring him fully to Bo's perusal and touch. Travis clawed at the sheets as Bo released his cock and began licking and sucking his sensitive balls. If this kept up he was going to come; he wouldn't be able to stop it. Bo continued to torture Travis as if he wasn't going to explode at any second.

Travis reached down, grabbed his cock and squeezed hard, trying to stave off his orgasm, but the moment Bo's tongue touched Travis's hole it was all over. His cock pulsed in his hand as he came in wave after wave until his balls emptied. Travis felt the bed shift and opened his eyes to see Bo leaning over him, pumping his own cock at a furious pace. Seconds later he came all over Travis's abdomen and groin before collapsing on top of him.

Bo rolled them onto their sides, allowing Travis to breathe. The big lug was heavy. They lay silently, both coming down from the rush. Travis opened his eyes and found Bo staring at him intently and smiling.

"What are you smiling at?" Travis teased.

"The man of my dreams," Bo answered breathily.

Travis had no reply to that so he simply slid over and kissed Bo.

"Do you want to have a shower together?"

"Sounds great." Travis had nothing to hide from Bo any longer. He was safe in these four walls.

It was first safe place he'd had in over ten years.

***

Bo sat behind the counter of the diner watching his love through the kitchen pass-through. Earlier Travis had brought out a juicy steak with a gigantic salad. He'd been forcing the salads for weeks now. Bo was growing accustomed to having green, leafy things in his diet. Travis looked so confident and sure in the kitchen that it was like a well-orchestrated performance as plate after plate was filled with delicious food.

It was Saturday night and Travis worked until nine. They'd hired a third cook, giving everyone a break from being scheduled six to seven days straight. After work, Bo and Travis had a quiet night in planned and Bo was looking forward to a little alone time with his man. Travis was spending more of his off hours at Bo's house—four, five nights a week and Bo couldn't have been happier. Travis had yet to use his new key and go to the house when Bo wasn't there, but that would happen sooner or later.

Bo thought back to the night when he'd been shocked when he first saw Travis come out of the bathroom wearing only a towel. He thought it would have taken longer before Travis felt comfortable enough to walk around naked. No complaints, just surprise. Their relationship was moving forward at a pace Bo had dreamt about.

Travis came through the kitchen's swinging doors carrying his backpack and wearing an adorable smile. That right there was the man that owned Bo's heart.

"Hey sweetheart, all done?"

"Yep, and ready to go."

Bo took Travis's hand and led him out to his truck. The sun had set and the quiet streets seemed almost ethereal in the twilight. Bo shook his head, wondering where the hell that came from. Then he looked at the man beside him and knew it was because he was seeing the world differently now. Their ride home was quick and it took no time for them to settle onto the couch. A bowl of popcorn—with no melted butter because Travis wouldn't allow it—sat in Bo's lap. He was about to turn on the television when Travis stopped him.

"I brought over something you've been asking to see." Travis stood and walked over to his backpack. He reached in and pulled out a sketchpad.

"Your sketches." Bo's voice came out an octave higher then he'd intended. He was excited, after all. He wiped his hands of the little oil the popcorn had been made in.

"Listen, it's rough and not quite perfect but you asked, so…," Travis handed the book over.

"Thank you for trusting me with this," Bo whispered.

Travis leaned against Bo and he could feel Travis's muscles tense. Bo lifted the cover of the sketchpad and was face to face with himself. It looked so lifelike that he was momentarily stunned. Of all things Travis could have done this rendering solidified Bo's belief that Travis loved him but wasn't ready to admit it.

"It's beautiful. It really is. So lifelike." Bo couldn't take his eyes off of the drawing. "That's some serious talent you have there, love."

"You really think so?"

"Yeah. I'm not flattering you. For real, you're talented."

"Thanks," Travis replied softly.

Bo was blown away by his boyfriend's raw talent, and couldn't wait to see what he could in color. "Do you paint?"

"I do. Soon as I can afford to, I'll buy some supplies."

Bo understood. He'd seen the prices of art supplies in Keith's store. "I can't wait to see more of your work."

"Now that I have a solid job and a place to live, I hope to have more time to sketch and paint."

Bo was already putting plans in place to ensure that happened. He set the pad on the coffee table and gathered Travis into his arms.

They watched television as Bo started to make a mental checklist of everything he needed, and he knew the perfect person to call.

Chapter Nine

Travis closed the front door and punched in the security code. Even though Bo had given Travis a key, it felt weird. This was the first time he'd used it and Bo didn't know Travis was there. It was a surprise. Bo worked until seven and Travis planned on having an incredible dinner ready for him. Travis rounded the corner and walked into the kitchen. He felt at home here. Which was an odd yet settling feeling after years of living like a nomad.

He dug the ingredients out of the pantry for his homemade manicotti: olive oil, garlic, onion, tomatoes, basil, sugar, and salt for the sauce; fresh ricotta, eggs, parmigiana reggiano, mozzarella, and spinach for the filling. He had everything he needed, including the noodles.

Bo was going to love this.

Travis turned on the CD player. He knew Bo would announce himself when he got home so there'd be no chance of surprising Travis. He hummed along with whatever song was playing. He didn't care what it was as long as it had a good beat. He pulled out the big pot and filled it with water before setting it on the stove, and then pulled out a cutting board. While the noodles were boiling he'd cut everything else up.

Travis was busy cutting tomatoes when he accidentally hit the edge of the plastic board with his hand and covered the front of his shirt, pants and floor with diced tomato. *Shit.* He took a deep breath before cleaning up the mess but his clothes needed more than a wipe with a cloth so he took them off and headed for the washer. He felt comfortable enough in the house to remain in his boxers; after all, the blinds were closed.

Another little step.

Finally he had everything back in order and pulled out a new tomato and went back to chopping. Once done he turned to the stove, which faced the beautiful yard, and began humming again. He was happy for the first time since his father's death. Truly happy.

That all faded away when he heard the creak of a floorboard. He had set the volume low enough on the stereo so that he could hear when Bo arrived. But it wasn't time for him to be home yet. The sound had come from the foyer down the hall from the kitchen.

It could have been his imagination. That thought lasted a few seconds until Travis heard another small, barely audible scrape of a shoe on the floor. He had no idea how Bo had managed to sneak up on him the other day since his hearing had become attuned to the world around him. That didn't matter now; someone was in the house. He'd locked the door but somehow they got in.

Travis reached for one of the knives out of the butcher block before squatting down behind the kitchen island to hide. It was too late when he realized he'd left the stove on and the pot boiling because whoever it was had just entered the kitchen. A shoe squeaked on the tiled floor and his head began to pound as fear spiked through his body. He wasn't a fighter. Though he would stick up for others, he was more of the head-for-the-hills kind of guy. The footsteps got closer to his hiding spot and his heart was pounding its way out of his chest. He felt the panic attack coming on but he fought it back as best he could. His breathing was getting shallow and he could barely hold the knife.

Visions of being dragged back into that dark room at the shelter flashed though his mind. The air ripe with the body odor of over fifty homeless men. Sharp nails grabbing at Travis's skin and clothes as he prayed for help that would never come.

"I know you're in here," a man's voice said from somewhere close to Travis's right. For a moment he thought he recognized the voice.

The last thing he saw was the barrel of a gun inching over the top of the island above his head. Then his world went dark.

***

When Travis woke he was disoriented. He was lying down and he could hear hushed voices coming from not too far away. He tried pushing himself up on his elbows but his head began to swim again.

"Don't sit up, Travis." Bo's voice reached him before his body came around the corner of the couch.

"Bo?"

"It's okay, you're safe," Bo assured as he cupped the side of Travis's face.

"But someone was in the house, I swear. I saw his gun."

A noise in the corner alerted Travis to another person in the room. He turned to see Police Chief David Graham and Grady standing off to the side. "What's going on?" He looked down and for the first time he noticed he now had his sleeping pants and shirt on. "What happened?"

Grady looked uncomfortable and Chief Graham looked furious, but Bo remained calm. That had to be a good sign.

"Travis, there *was* someone in the house." He looked up at Grady, indicating it had been him.

"Grady? Why would he have been in the house? Wait, I locked the door."

"I gave Grady a key several months ago when he first moved here. He hadn't found a place to rent yet so I let him stay in the guest room," Bo explained.

"That explains the how. What about the why?"

Grady stepped forward at this point but he still wouldn't look Travis in the eye. "I'd left work and knew Bo was still at the station for another hour. I'd told him earlier this week that I'd drop in and pick up the rest of my belongings."

"I didn't even think to say anything to you." Bo shook his head, guilt written all over his face.

"I opened the door and heard movement inside. I called it in and went to investigate. There wasn't supposed to be anyone here."

"So you immediately thought I was an intruder and pulled out your gun." Travis knew he was angry but the lethal tone of his voice surprised him. "I was cooking dinner. You could have called out from the door when you realized someone was here. Hell, when does an intruder turn on music?"

"Yes, I realize that now," Grady agreed. "I'm sorry."

Travis wasn't ready to accept the apology quite yet—he was still furious. After everything he'd lived through, to have his safe place taken away was just a step too far. "What happened after I had a gun pointed at me?" He didn't remember the rest.

"Your eyes rolled to the back of your head and you passed out," Grady answered before stepping back beside Chief Graham, who remained silent.

"Dave and I arrived right after that," Bo said. "I tried to raise Grady on his radio to tell him that it might be you, but he'd turned the volume down when he entered."

Great. Travis had passed out in front of all of them. *Grow a pair of balls much?* Even though anyone would be scared facing a gun, they all didn't pass out. But he did. He could picture himself on the floor in his boxers—boxers. The room had gotten really quiet as he realized what had happened.

"They saw?"

"Yes," he replied softly.

"They helped you dress me?" God, could this get any worse?

"No. I would never allow anyone to touch you when you're unconscious other than medical professionals. They waited in the foyer until I had you dressed and laying on the couch."

Travis glanced up at the two officers who were now looking anywhere but at him. He'd seen that reaction many times before: doctors, nurses, his mother, and it never got easier.

"I don't know how to deal with that right now. Can you please leave? Or I could go."

"No, Travis. I don't want you to leave," Bo insisted. Travis tried to stand, but like the idiot he felt he looked, he was caught up in the blankets.

"We'll go. I'm sorry this happened," Dave stated and for the first time Travis noticed Dave was holding a duty belt and Grady had none. The two men walked out the front door before Travis had a chance to ask why.

Bo came to sit beside Travis on the couch but he needed to move. Sitting still would mean more time to think and he didn't want that right now. He unraveled his legs from the blankets and got up.

"I'm going to clean up the kitchen," he announced.

Bo followed him. "You don't have to do that. I'll take care of it."

Travis turned to face Bo. "I need to keep moving right now. I want to save dinner. I'll have to boil fresh noodles but everything else should be fine."

He knew Bo understood when he asked, "What were you making?"

"Manicotti."

Bo smiled and said, "Oh yeah, we're definitely saving that."

"Thank you."

Bo held Travis close. "Any time, my love."

"I'll go see what I can salvage of dinner." Travis sighed. "Can you tell me why the police chief was carrying Grady's belt?"

At the mention of Grady, Bo's eyes turned hard. "He'll be suspended until there can be a hearing."

"What? Dave suspended him?"

"He got off lucky. I would have fired him outright. He's still on probation for god's sake. He should have waited or announced himself before entering our house. He pointed a gun at you in *our* house."

"He thought I was an intruder." Wait, how did Travis manage to be the one defending Grady?

"He should have waited for us to arrive. If he had followed department policy of waiting for backup none of this would have happened. You wouldn't have been pushed into a situation like this. You could have been killed."

"All valid reasons, but he's not some horrible person. He made a mistake."

"Travis, I know you have a big heart and I'm not saying he's a bad person, but he might be a bad cop."

"You liked him. He hasn't changed."

"That was before he pointed a loaded gun at my partner."

Travis knew it was no use talking about this right now; it wouldn't fix anything. In truth it surprised him that he was defending Grady and hadn't broken down. In the past he would have been a mess by now. Hell, he'd passed out at the sight of a gun less than an hour ago. But now he was standing having a conversation with no difficulty. Progress?

"I'm gonna get changed." Bo kissed Travis loudly on the lips. "I love you, Travis Boone."

Travis wished he could say it in return, but something kept holding him back. Instead he hugged Bo close before turning to walk into the kitchen while wondering if he'd ever be ready or able to face Dave and Grady again.

Chapter Ten

Travis waited quietly in Dr. Gordon's office for the doctor to arrive. Bo sat out in the reception area. Over the past two weeks, especially after the Grady event, Travis had grown even closer to Bo, but Travis still hadn't said he loved him. He knew he felt it. He knew he loved Bo, but he hadn't been able to say it out loud. Travis needed to know why.

Dr. Gordon walked in with his usual smile and sat in the chair opposite Travis. He wondered if Gordon was really happy or it was a show for his patients. "Good afternoon, Travis."

"Hello, Dr. Gordon."

"What would you like to discuss today?"

No time like the present. "I need you to help me figure out why I can't tell Bo that I love him."

Dr. Gordon leaned forward in his seat and asked, "Do you love him?"

"Yes," Travis answered easily.

"You have no doubts?"

"None. But I can't get the words out. It feels almost paralyzing to try," he explained.

Dr. Gordon was silent for a moment. Perhaps the doctor didn't have an answer either, which depressed the hell out of Travis.

The doc shifted in his seat before saying, "I want you to answer me honestly. How many people have you told you loved them in your life?"

"That's easy—two."

"And who were those two people?"

Travis got that same queasy feeling in his stomach he had when he tried to say he loved Bo. "My dad and mother."

"And one died and the other abandoned you. You're living with a lot of loss, Travis. Have you ever thought that maybe that's the reason why you're so terrified to express your love to someone?"

Nausea rose in Travis's throat and for a moment the world spun. He closed his eyes and breathed through the fear. Then, as he quieted his mind, the pieces fell into place. How had he not seen that himself? It made sense that he'd been unable to say the words. Everyone he'd ever loved had either died or left him. Did that mean he'd never be able to express his love?

"What if I can never say it? That's not fair to Bo."

"The way I see him look at you and the way you look at him, I think he might already know you love him."

"I should be able to say the words," Travis argued.

"I know lots of people who can say the words but never actually show anyone real love. You aren't able to say it, but you feel it and show it. That's what's important."

"Maybe."

"Travis, I noticed you call your father 'dad' but your mom is 'mother.' Is there a reason for that?"

"My mother was never a mom. Once she gave birth to me she left me for my dad to raise. Even when she was home she was unapproachable. But I loved her because she was my mother. That ended the day she abandoned me."

"It's understandable you feel that way, but holding onto so much anger isn't good for you. It eats away at you. You deserve to have a life without fear and anger. You need to release it."

"I don't know how to do that."

"We'll get there."

The rest of the hour was spent discussing Travis's mother, a topic he had tried to avoid at all costs his entire life but couldn't run from anymore.

***

Travis and Bo walked out of the doctor's office hand in hand, Travis's mind replaying everything he and Dr. Gordon had discussed.

"Do you want to drive, sweetheart?" Bo asked.

"Me? Drive your truck?" Travis wasn't sure he'd heard correctly.

"Sure. You haven't been able to drive since your car gave out. I thought you might like to."

Travis looked at the beautiful Ford F250, black with shiny chrome, sitting in the parking lot. Hell yeah, he wanted to drive it.

"Okay, I'd like that," Travis replied calmly. Inside he was fist pumping.

Bo handed over the keys and opened the driver's door for Travis to climb in. He was so excited to drive this big beautiful beast. Bo got in the passenger side and Travis couldn't contain himself or the smile on his face. He put the key in the ignition and brought the rumbling V8 to life. This was nothing like his old rusted car. This was power.

When he pulled out onto the roadway he couldn't believe how different it felt to drive the truck compared to driving his car. Obviously, it was bigger and taller, which made Travis feel like he could see everything, but the purring engine begging to be let loose was what jazzed him. He'd never driven a vehicle with such power. Unfortunately, they were only a few minutes away from the house so there'd be no chance he'd be able to give into his fantasies.

Carefully, he navigated the traffic and soon pulled into the driveway. He put the truck in park and turned off the engine before letting out a deep breath. He'd enjoyed that. Since his mother had kicked him out, driving had always meant freedom. It was exhilarating.

"Enjoyed that, did you?" Bo grinned.

"Oh, yeah, I love to drive. It's freedom." Travis held out the keys.

"Well, feel free to drive us around town when we're together."

"Are you serious?"

"Of course. I don't mind in the least. Considering I drive around all day in a cruiser it'd be nice not to drive on my down time."

"Deal." Travis laughed. He wouldn't refuse such a generous offer.

"Come on, sweetheart, let's go start dinner."

Travis followed Bo into the house and as he was about to turn toward the kitchen he grabbed Travis around the waist and kissed his back and neck. Bo tended to be spontaneous when he was especially happy or horny.

Travis looked over his shoulder. "What's with you tonight?"

Bo turned Travis around. "I can't wait until after dinner to show you so it's going to have to be now. Come with me. I have a surprise for you."

Bo tugged Travis down the hall to the bedrooms.

"If you wanted to take advantage of me I'm more than willing. You didn't have to drag me there," Travis teased. He received a light tap on his ass in answer.

Bo stopped in front of the door to the spare bedroom and turned Travis to face the door as Bo reached around and opened it. At first Travis didn't know what he was looking at. The bed had been moved to the far corner of the room, and in its place, in front of the large bank of windows, was an easel and full bags from Keith's art store.

Travis took a tentative step into the room, not sure if this was real or if he was seeing things. "Bo?"

Bo followed Travis into the room, wrapped his arms around him from behind, and said, "It's all for you. I thought there'd be a lot of light in here so you could work."

"Bo, I—"

"Before you say it's too much, remember you get the family discount now. So it's not as expensive as it seems, and really it's for my benefit."

"Your own benefit, how?"

"Well ever since you showed me that sketch I've wanted to see it in color. So it was necessary for me to get what I want."

"To get what *you* want." This guy.

"Yes, of course. I can be selfish when I want to be."

"You bought me all these art supplies because you're selfish?"

"Absolutely."

Travis stepped forward and peeked inside the full bags to find paints—oil, acrylic, watercolors, and the sable paintbrush set he'd drooled over when he'd visited Keith's store.

"How did you know what to get?"

"Honestly, I didn't. But Keith did," Bo admitted.

Travis's emotions ranged from anger to gratitude. He knew the anger came from his pride at not being able to afford the supplies. He looked at Bo and saw the uncertainty in his eyes and his anger dissipated. The man he loved had bought him a gift. How could he be anything but grateful? Travis turned and walked into Bo's arms, hugging him close.

"It's too much, but it's perfect. Thank you."

"You're welcome, sweetheart. I wasn't sure how you'd react. For real, I want to see more of your work. You have true talent."

This would be the perfect moment to say it, to tell Bo that he loved him, but the words wouldn't come out. He was so damn frustrated.

"What's wrong?"

"You know how I feel about you, don't you?"

Bo's warm smile immediately put Travis at ease. "Yes, sweetheart, I know you love me. It's in your eyes when you look at me."

"I do. But for the life of me, I can't say it. I talked to Dr. Gordon about it today."

"Good. He'll help you."

Bo never asked Travis what was discussed in his sessions. He was always willing to listen, but Bo never pried.

"I thought we could start dinner and while it's in the oven I could bring in a few tables from the garage and you could set everything up tonight. Then tomorrow we're both off work—you can spend the day painting or drawing, whatever you want."

"How did I end up with someone as amazing as you?" Travis thought it was a legitimate question considering he still hadn't figured it out.

"I feel the same way about you. I love you and want you to be happy."

"I am happy. You make me happy."

"Then I'm doing a good job." Bo laughed and led them down the hall into the kitchen.

The rest of the evening was spent chopping, cooking, and laughing. Travis hadn't felt this light since he was a child.

As he looked across the dining table at the man he never expected to find, he prayed to whoever would listen that they would remain this way.

He couldn't handle any more loss.

Chapter Eleven

Bo stretched his body across the bed and reached for his love but came up empty. He moved his hand around and still nothing. Bo opened his eyes and cleared his vision but he didn't see Travis anywhere. He listened for him in the kitchen but the house was silent. Travis wouldn't have left. A thread of fear raced through Bo but he quickly pushed it away.

He reached for his sleep pants and put them on. They'd been sleeping naked since the night Travis had come out of the bathroom in only a towel. Bo loved the fact that Travis felt comfortable being naked, especially after what happened with Grady and Dave. Bo felt badly about that whole situation and was trying to find a way to work out getting his best friend, Dave, and the love of Bo's life in the same room under friendly circumstances. Dave's wife had been sending out invitations to dinner since Bo had started dating Travis, and to date, Bo had declined every invitation. Dave felt guilty for what one of his officers had done. And Travis wouldn't look Dave in the eye anymore when he went into the diner. What a mess.

The hallway was filled with light coming in from the guest bedroom, exactly where he thought he'd find Travis. Bo stood outside the doorway and watched as Travis spread the paint over the canvas. His graceful fingers held the brush almost delicately. Bo was mesmerized by the strokes of blue in varying shades blending perfectly together.

He watched for a long time unnoticed. Travis was lost in his own world. It was worth any cost to see him like this. Bo decided to give

Travis some privacy and headed toward the kitchen. He flipped the switch on the coffee maker then walked to the front door to retrieve the newspaper.

With a cup of coffee steaming in front of him, Bo sat at the kitchen island and opened the paper. The first thing he saw on the front page was the headline "Interstate Bandit Strikes Again." He took a moment to wonder why the media always had to sensationalize criminals before he grabbed the phone and dialed Dave's number.

"Graham here."

"It's Bo. I saw the headline."

"Yeah, you weren't scheduled to be in today and I thought I'd give you a day off without having to hear about another robbery."

"Where was it?"

"Two counties to the west of us. It seems like he's passed us by again."

"Do you think it'll stay that way?"

"We can only hope," Dave answered, the sound of exhaustion heavy in his voice.

"You okay?"

"Yeah, Kimmy's been up at all hours of the night for the past couple days."

"Something wrong? Is she sick?"

"Nope. She wants to get out of her crib and visit every couple hours."

"Ouch."

"Enjoy your day off with your man, Bo. I won't be calling you unless we need the National Guard." Dave laughed at his own joke. In other words, Dave wouldn't be calling him.

"Thanks. By the way, this might be a bad time, but was that dinner invite still open for me and Travis?"

"Of course. But are you sure he'll want to come?"

"You let me worry about that."

"Okay, buddy. You let me know when and I'll tell Kate."

They said their goodbyes and Bo turned back to the table to find Travis standing. His face glowed. He looked so happy.

"Hey babe, having fun?"

With a huge smile Travis declared, "God, yes." Then he proceeded to round the island, climb onto Bo's chair, and lean into his arms. "Thank you for everything."

"Any time, sweetheart. What did you want to do today?" Bo ran his finger over one of Travis's nipples. "I was thinking of doing a bit of gardening."

"Do you mind if I keep working in the studio?"

"The studio. You've already named the room."

Travis looked away "Uh, yes?"

Bo hugged him close. "I like the sound of that. We have a studio in our home."

"Your home," Travis corrected.

"I'd like it to be ours," Bo stated. He'd been thinking about it for quite a while.

"You want me to move in with you?"

"Yeah. You already stay here four to five days a week."

Travis's mouth opened and closed a few times before he said, "Can I think about it?"

"Definitely. As long as you want. No pressure. I want you any way I can get you."

Bo could see the love in Travis's expressive blue eyes. There was no doubt in Bo's mind. Travis loved him. Bo didn't need the words. Some people threw them around so carelessly. But the love he felt coming from Travis was strong and real. Their relationship was solid. Travis spun around on his lap and straddled his thighs. It seemed to be a position he liked.

"Would you agree I'm thinking clearly?"

"Yeah, why?" Bo asked suspiciously.

"Then you won't question me when I say I want us to make love." Travis's smile remained firmly in place.

Bo sat stunned for a moment. "You want to make love?"

"Yup. I'm ready and I want to share this with you."

Something clicked inside Bo and he dove in for a kiss full of tongues and teeth. His need went from smoldering to wildfire in nanoseconds. He'd dreamed of this day for months and he wasn't going to waste it.

Bo stood and Travis wrapped his legs around Bo's waist, still kissing. They remained glued together as Bo walked down the hallway, ping-ponging off the walls all the way to their bedroom.

Bo crawled onto the bed and laid Travis down on his back. Bo sat on his heels and quickly pulled Travis's sleeping pants from his body and shed his own. Travis's swollen, jutting cock was too much of a temptation as Bo leaned down and sucked it to the back of his throat. Travis cried out and Bo redoubled his efforts until he was forced to hold Travis's hips down to stop him from jerking upward.

Bo released his prize and recaptured Travis's lips in a deep, drugging kiss that left him craving more. He hovered over Travis, only inches away, but he had to ask one more time to make sure.

"Ready?"

Travis winked. "Definitely."

Bo reached across the bed to the nightstand and pulled out a new bottle of lube and a piece of paper and handed it to Travis. He knew it was a mood killer but he had to make sure Travis was fully informed.

"I went to the medical center and had a blood test done. The results show I'm clean. Since you've never had sex before, we know you're clean. Do you want me to wear a condom? I'll do whatever you decide."

Travis looked at the paper and then at Bo. "I don't want any barriers between us any longer."

Bo hands itched to touch his lover, to make sure this was real and that he wasn't still sleeping. He felt a hunger so intense that he had to take a deep breath and slow down. With Travis's scarred but beautiful body beneath Bo, it felt like flames were licking through his veins. He turned his attention back to Travis's throbbing cock and wrapped his lips around it again. He had to make sure Travis was mindless with passion before Bo attempted to stretch him.

When Travis began moaning Bo's name he knew he'd accomplished his goal and reached over for the bottle of lube. With his finger he began circling Travis's hole, causing him to cry out. Bo pressed firmly with his slick finger until the muscle slowly gave way.

"Have you ever used toys on yourself?" Bo asked. He'd never brought it up before because he thought sex was off the table. Now would be a good time to know.

"Yes, but I was trying to see if I could give myself a hard-on after the accident. It never worked and eventually I gave up." Bo breathed a sigh of relief; Travis wouldn't be unfamiliar with the stretch. He never wanted to hurt his lover.

"You certainly don't have that problem any longer." Bo bent to lick Travis's hard cock as Bo slid his finger in as far as his second knuckle without much resistance. But when he added a second finger he felt Travis's body tense.

"Try to relax your body and let me in."

His love took a deep breath and Bo wrapped his fingers around Travis's cock and began pumping in time with the thrusts of his fingers. Travis's bent legs fell open even farther and Bo added a third finger. He pushed in deep in search of the tiny gland that would set Travis's world on fire. Within a few moments Bo found what he was looking for and began pegging Travis's prostate mercilessly.

Travis screamed his pleasure as he came in long lines across his abdomen. Bo wasn't worried about him coming so soon; he didn't plan on giving Travis a chance to calm down. Bo shifted his body up, lifted Travis's legs to Bo's shoulders and then pressed his hard, aching cock to Travis's hole. Bo looked down and locked eyes with Travis as Bo pushed forward slowly. Travis's tight channel rippled as the crown of Bo's cock breached him.

"I love you, Travis."

"Ditto," Travis moaned out.

Pure pleasure flooded him as he sank deep in one slow push. Travis was panting and moaning, begging Bo to move faster, but he knew better. He would take it slow until Travis became accustomed to the feeling of Bo's cock inside of him.

They didn't break eye contact until Bo hips met Travis's ass and Bo closed his eyes and concentrated on staving off coming. Travis's hole squeezed Bo tight in its warm, silky embrace and Bo sizzled with pleasure.

He caressed the side of Travis's face and his beautiful blue eyes opened. His pupils were dilated, and his face flushed. *Stunning, absolutely stunning*. Bo drew out slowly to make sure Travis was ready, and when he groaned in pleasure Bo knew it was time. His thrusts slowly increased in strength until he found himself slamming into Travis.

Bo felt Travis's nails biting in Bo's biceps, which made his body burn hotter. He pulled free of Travis and in one fluid motion flipped Travis onto his stomach, raised his hips and dove right back in. Bo blanketed Travis's body as his lover's pleasure-filled cries and moans permeated the room. Bo was completely lost in a world of intense pleasure and instinct.

He was close to coming and he knew there'd be no way he could stop himself. He took hold of Travis's stiff cock and began pumping as Bo laid his head on Travis's back in complete surrender to the pleasure racing through his body. He felt Travis's body tense and his cock pulse seconds before he came all over Bo's hand. That was all it took Bo as fire raced through his body and straight to his balls. He buried himself deep and came inside the man he loved.

Heavy breathing was the only sound in the room as Bo gently lowered them to their sides, pulled out and held Travis close. After a few more moments of silence Bo became worried, Travis hadn't said a word. Had Bo been too rough? Had Travis been really ready?

"Sweetheart, are you okay?"

Travis rolled over to his back, a satisfied smile on his face. "Oh, yeah. I didn't know what to expect, but that blew away anything I have imagined. Can we do it again? Well, once the tenderness goes away?"

Bo laughed and hugged Travis close. "I've unleashed a sex addict."

They cuddled close and Bo pulled up the covers as they settled in. Soon he heard Travis's soft snores and Bo closed his eyes to rest because by the sounds of things it was going to be a busy day.

And he had no intention of them leaving this bed.

Chapter Twelve

Travis poured the gravy over the hot beef sandwich and put the plate up into the pass-through window of the diner for Sarah to pick up. It'd been a long week and he was looking forward to his days off. He had two in a row and he was going to make the best of them in his studio and with Bo.

Right now, Bo sat at the counter. He'd finished work and was the diner to pick up Travis who was off in ten minutes. Bo looked so handsome in his uniform and Travis couldn't help but get a little hard from the sight of him. Since the first time they'd made love it'd become one of Travis's favorite pastimes, beating out painting by a nose. What could he say? He was an artist after all.

Travis had completed two canvases, the one of Bo and another of flowers from the garden. Bo had hung both in the living room. They'd had Bo's parents over for dinner, and with Dot's unfiltered comments and Henry's good-natured chiding every time she said something off color, the evening had been filled with laughter. They were good people who had welcomed Travis with open arms.

He was still considering whether or not to move in with Bo, which seemed stupid since Travis had been at the house all week as it was. It would be a matter of moving the rest of his few belongings over there. But he was cautious of that final step; he'd be dependent on Bo for a place to live, and while he didn't believe they'd break up, no one knew the future. Travis had lost his security the day his dad died, and he was just starting to gain some of that back.

Would it be a foolish risk if he moved in with Bo?

Bear, the diner's owner, walked into the kitchen to take over for Travis. He liked his boss. He like Jesse, and he enjoyed the hell out of his work. He never felt stressed at the diner; it was another safe place for him.

"So, Travis, you've finished your probation period a while ago and I think it's time to discuss your performance while there's a break in customers."

Okay, now I'm stressed.

Travis looked out the window at Bo and his boyfriend immediately sensed his distress and went on alert. Travis smiled to calm him before he decided to come marching into the kitchen. That wouldn't do wonders for his review.

"Tell me how you think you did," Bear ordered.

Travis almost froze but with a last look at Bo he began to list off his accomplishments. "I work quickly and efficiently. I keep the kitchen clean and tidy. I always make sure prep is done before I leave, and the people seem to like my cooking."

Bear stood silently, driving Travis crazy.

"I agree," Bear huffed.

What?

Bear continued, "I've been hearing wonderful things about you, and I've seen how hard you work. When I upped your hours, you rose to the challenge and your work didn't suffer. Taking all that into consideration I believe it's time for a raise."

"A raise?" Travis's voice squeaked.

"Yes, a raise. You'll see it on your next paycheck," Bear stated.

"Thank you, boss. I don't know what to say."

"Just keep up the good work and go home already before Bo has a fit worrying about what's happening in here," Bear ordered while looking over Travis's shoulder.

Travis looked out front to find Bo standing with his legs spread and his arms crossed over his chest. Total cop. Travis waved at him and mouthed he'd be right out to ensure Bo retook his seat. He was overprotective, and Travis loved him for it.

“Thanks, really. I’ll see you in a couple days, Bear.” Travis walked to the back to collect his backpack and then joined Bo up front.

Bo looked worried. “Are you okay? What was all that about?”

Travis took his hand and led him out the front door. “It was my review.”

“Review. You work hard and your food is amazing, what could be the problem?” Bo looked ready to go back inside.

Travis couldn’t help himself; he smirked and began bouncing in place. “I got a raise.” This was a first.

“Congratulations, sweetheart. You deserve every penny of it.” Bo gave Travis a hug.

“Thank you, honey.”

Bo handed Travis the keys to the truck, but they weren’t the keys he normally used. This one had a shiny blue keychain. “New keys?”

“Yeah. They’re yours.”

“Mine?”

Bo nodded.

Mine. I have my own keys to his house and now his truck. Bo had given Travis so much, and he felt bad that he had no way of reciprocating Bo’s generosity. Travis climbed into the driver’s seat but didn’t put the keys in the ignition. They needed to talk about this.

“I can’t take one more thing from you, Bo. I have nothing to give to you in return.”

Bo turned in his seat. He took hold of Travis’s hands and brushed his thumbs across his fingers. “You have no idea how much you’ve given me. Before you came into my life I was alone. Sure, I have family and friends, but I didn’t have someone to share my life with. The love and strength you give me is far more than anything I could give you. Honestly, it was getting to the point that the only time I felt any real joy was when I was in my gardens. Now I’m happy, truly happy. You gave that to me.”

Travis sat speechless, staring at Bo and seeing a new side of the man. Travis would have never guessed Bo felt so strongly about the impact on his life Travis had. Bo came across so confident and sure that Travis would have never though Bo had problems and doubts. Travis felt honored to know the whole man. Instead of saying anything, Travis smiled, took his new keys, and started the truck. Bo looked content as he buckled in.

Travis would look at things a little bit differently from this point on.

Later that evening as they sat on the couch watching the news Bo hit him with a question he didn't expect. "How do you feel about going over to Dave and Kate's for dinner?"

Before Travis could say a word, Bo continued, "I know this will be difficult for you, but I'd really like to try to have the man I love get along with my oldest friend. But if you're not ready or simply don't want to go, then we won't."

Travis knew how important this was to Bo, and it was Travis's embarrassment that was holding him back. He'd accepted what Grady had done and why, but couldn't get past the way they had reacted. Neither of them could look at him that night, so he had stopped looking at either of them when they came into the diner.

Travis looked up at Bo, and after seeing the hope in his eyes, Travis knew he would agree.

"Okay."

Bo held Travis's gaze. "Are you sure?"

Travis ran his hand across Bo's cheek, his stubble scratching Travis's palm. "I'm sure."

"Thank you," Bo said and Travis could feel the tension leaving his lover's body. Now all that remained was for Travis to face Dave. *No problem.*

***

Sunday came too quickly. While he waited for Bo to finish dressing, Travis picked at his new polo shirt. It felt like his day of reckoning for some inexplicable reason. He'd been told a couple times that

Dave felt badly for what had happened, and it wasn't his fault. And Travis hadn't actually tried to approach Dave to discuss this like adults.

"All ready?" Bo asked as he joined Travis in the kitchen.

Travis managed a smile and said, "Yep."

Bo looked at him closely. Travis tried to keep up the façade, but he must not have done a good enough job. "Tell me the truth."

"I'm nervous, that's all." Travis left out how nervous he was because that wouldn't help.

"Are you sure you're up for this? I don't want to pressure you into it."

Travis wasn't turning back; he had to face this for Bo. "Yes, I want to go over for dinner. It'll be fine." He didn't know if he was trying to reassure Bo or himself.

The drive over to the Grahams' house didn't take as long as Travis had hoped. They pulled in front of a two-story Victorian, complete with its steeply pitched roofs and wrap-around porch. Its beautiful asymmetrical exterior was highlighted by a turret, bay windows, and trim everywhere.

"It would be hell to paint this," Travis said. "Don't get me wrong, it's a stunning house, but wow."

"Trust me, it's hell. I learned that the hard way." Travis raised a brow. "Conscripted." Bo shrugged.

Bo led the way down the stone walkway and to the front door. *Here we go.* Bo knocked and the door was opened almost immediately. Dave stood in the doorway, a friendly smile on his face and an infant sleeping peacefully in his arms. Her blonde curls fell over her chubby face and Travis smiled at the sight.

"Hey guys, good to see you." Dave welcomed them into his home.

"Thanks for having us." Bo put his hand on Travis's back, urging him forward, but he was stuck to the spot. "Travis?"

“What an amazing piece.” Travis stared at a breathtaking stained-glass window hanging in the foyer. It depicted a sunrise over the very house they were standing in.

“Bo told me you were an artist. I’m glad you like it.” Dave seemed pleased.

“Does the artist live in Brighton?”

“He does. It’s one of mine.”

“You work with stained glass? I’ve always wanted to try the art but never had the opportunity.”

“Well you do now. I can show you the ropes.”

“Really? You’d do that for me?”

“Sure. And maybe you could show me some of your work.”

“We have a few hanging in the house if you’d like to come over.” Saying that reminded Travis of what happened the last time Dave was at the house and his mood soured. It didn’t go unnoticed.

“Come into the kitchen. Kate’s working on dinner,” Dave coaxed before leading them out of the foyer. Travis’s eyes lingered on the window even as he was being ushered forward. It was truly stunning.

They walked down a long hallway with closed doors on either side until they came into a brightly lit kitchen. A small woman wearing a “Kiss the Cook” apron was dashing around looking a bit harried.

“Kate. Travis and Bo are here.”

The woman spun around and smiled wide. “Bo, good to see you again and it’s about time you brought Travis over to formally meet us. Of course we’ve seen you at the diner, but I’ve never had a chance to introduce myself.”

“It’s nice to meet you, Kate.” Travis smiled.

“Oh, and the little one sleeping in her daddy’s arms is Kimmy.” Kate went back to stirring a pot on the stove before saying, “I got dinner started a little late. Hope you don’t mind.”

“Of course not,” Bo replied.

“Do you want some help? I know my way around a kitchen,” Travis suggested as he approached the counter.

"I couldn't ask you to do that. You work in a kitchen all day."

"You didn't ask, I'm offering."

Travis joined Kate and threw himself into being her sous chef.

"Dave and I are going to go sit in the living room." Bo stood in the doorway waiting for Travis's response.

It was sweet Bo was concerned about Travis being left alone with Kate, but he had this. He was secure in a kitchen. "I'm good, honey."

Bo's smile spoke volumes and Travis was glad he could concentrate on something other than the conversation he was likely going to have with Dave. Travis and Kate quickly got a routine down and worked together in sync. The roast was almost done, the gravy was perfect, the potatoes fluffy, and the vegetables steaming. All in all, everything was back under control.

"So tell me, how nervous were you coming here today?"

Travis was so thrown by the question that he stuttered. "W-w-what?"

"Well, I assume you have to be nervous because I know Dave is."

"You know?" Travis cringed. His worst fears were coming true. Dave hadn't kept it a secret.

"No. Not all of it. He only said that Grady and he had scared you badly by going into the house. They should have never gone in."

Dave hadn't revealed anything as Bo had predicted. Travis's heart slowed considerably as he thought how to answer that. He went with the truth.

"I was beyond nervous. Somewhere in the *lock your doors, hide under the bed* category."

Kate laughed softly and placed her small hand on Travis's arm. "You have nothing to be nervous about. He's so sorry for what he did, Travis."

"He's sorry? He did nothing wrong."

"I don't understand."

"It wasn't his fault. It was a mistake. I understand why he has a hard time looking at me."

Kate grabbed Travis's hand and led him into the living room. Bo and Dave immediately stopped talking and stood.

"Is something wrong?" Dave asked as he placed Kimmy on the couch and covered her with a baby blanket.

"You two need to talk because I'm not going through dinner with the two of you side-stepping each other. Get it out," Kate ordered while crossing her arms.

"Are you always this upfront about things?" Travis asked Kate. It was Dave who answered.

"You mean pushy." He rolled his eyes. "You have no idea."

Kate huffed. "I live with a police chief. You define the word pushy."

Travis looked at Bo and then Dave before saying, "I'm sorry."

"You're sorry for what?" Dave looked incredulous. "That was all on me. I'm the one that needs to apologize."

"But you came in with good intentions. You were checking on Bo's house," Travis explained.

"I shouldn't have assumed that Grady would wait for backup. He shouldn't have walked in on you like that and he's my responsibility. I'm truly sorry for everything that happened."

Travis had to know the truth. "Why wouldn't you look at me that night?"

"I was ashamed."

"Of me?" *Ouch.*

"No. God no. Of what we had done to you. We took away your feeling of security and invaded your privacy."

"I feel like there's something I'm missing. That there's more to this." Kate put her hands on her hips as she looked shrewdly at her husband. "What didn't you tell me? Why would he think you'd be ashamed to look at him?"

Oh shit. Now he was going to cause a rift between a married couple. He couldn't have that. "He kept the secret for my benefit."

"Secret, what secret?" she asked, taking a step away from Travis, as if he might be a threat.

"Travis, you don't have to do this," Bo promised.

"Yes, I do. I've got to be able to face it head on. No more hiding in the shadows hoping no one will see me. I'm tired of that life. I'm tired of hiding."

"You can face anything, sweetheart." Bo's reassurance meant the world to Travis in that moment.

He looked at Kate and explained, "Your husband didn't mention that I was in my boxers."

"But you're both men. Are you shy?" Kate looked more confused than ever.

Travis turned his back to Kate and pulled his shirt over his head. "Because he saw this and I freaked out."

Travis heard the same intake of breath he'd expected to hear from someone who's shocked. Slowly he put his shirt back on and walked over to Bo. "He was only keeping the secret out of respect for me."

"How did it happen?" Kate whispered.

"Kate, don't pry," Dave warned.

"When I was younger I was in a house fire. I have burns over fifty percent of my body and I lost my dad that night." Travis gave her the condensed version of events.

"I'm so sorry that you had to go through such a horrible thing." Kate was the picture of compassion.

Bo put his arm around Travis's shoulder and nuzzled the side of his head. "So strong."

"Can we consider this whole thing to be worked out? Everyone's good." Kate carried on like it was no big deal, and Travis liked her even more for it.

"Yup," Travis said.

"Yes," Dave agreed.

"Good. So let's go get everything on the table before it's ruined." Kate grabbed Travis's hand and dragged him back to the kitchen. She was a powerhouse.

The rest of the evening went by in a blur of great food and laughter. Travis had a wonderful time and could easily see why Bo and Dave were best friends. They acted like brothers. Well, they were cousins-in-law, considering Kate was formerly a Mason.

Bo was helping with the dishes while Travis was with Dave on the front porch enjoying the warm night. They sat in two of the rocking chairs that lined the porch, enjoying a comfortable silence while sipping on coffee.

"You know you've changed him," Dave said out of nowhere.

"Changed who?" Travis asked but he had a pretty good idea.

"Bo. He's changed. He has that old spark in his eyes again. Believe me when I say after he came home from Houston, Bo was reserved and becoming a bit of a loner. If he wasn't working he was at home in his gardens. But now he has life in him again and you gave him that," Dave explained.

"I can't take the credit for that."

"You should because it's the truth."

Travis thought it through and secretly hoped he'd been able to give Bo anything close to what Dave was describing. He remembered what Bo had said to him in the truck, that Travis had made Bo's life whole again. Maybe there was more truth to that then Travis realized.

"I wanted to thank you for that."

"I'm still not entirely sure I did that much, but I'm happy if I helped in any way."

"You did. Trust me," Dave replied.

The screen door opened and Bo and Kate walked onto the porch to join them. Bo came over to Travis and ran his fingers through Travis's hair. He leaned his head into Bo's hand and nuzzled it out of habit before he realized he was in front of his friends. Immediately, he pulled back.

"Don't worry about showing affection in front of us. You guys are so cute together," Kate bid from her perch on top of Dave's lap. She was one of a kind.

Travis had been waiting for the right time all evening and needed to know before they left. "What's happening with Grady?"

Bo and Dave looked at each other before Dave answered. "His hearing is scheduled for next month."

"You said it's a hearing, right? People can testify?" Travis asked.

Dave got a strange look on his face. "We already have all the evidence and statements necessary. You won't need to testify against him."

"Why would I testify against him? I want to say something in his defense."

"What?" Dave and Bo said in unison, making Kate laugh.

"Oh, honey," she chuckled. "You are truly one of a kind, and take that as a compliment. We're going to get along just fine."

"Thank you for dinner but we should get going. We both have to get to work early in the morning," Bo said in a rush before taking Travis's arm and gently ushering him out of his chair.

"You're welcome. Come back anytime. We really enjoyed tonight," Dave responded, while still regarding Travis with a confused look on his face.

"At first you won't look at me and now you're staring. Have I done something wrong?" Travis had no idea where his ballsy behavior was coming from, but he liked it.

Dave shook his head and answered, "No, nothing's wrong. I'm trying to understand. You want to testify in defense of the officer that could have shot you?"

"Sure. I don't believe he's a bad person or a bad cop. I think he made a mistake and has learned from it. I agree he should stay on probation and be overseen until he can prove himself again. But I don't think he should be fired."

Dave's face was a picture of confusion, but Kate was smiling ear to ear.

They said their goodbyes, shook hands, and headed home. *Home.* Travis was beginning to associate Bo's house as home. Travis was still on the fence about whether that was a good thing or not.

During the ride home, Bo didn't mention anything about what Travis had said regarding Grady's hearing, and Travis decided to let it go. He knew Bo was still angry with Grady for putting Travis in danger. He hoped in time Bo would see things differently, but if his behavior were any indication, the road to forgiveness would be pitted with potholes.

When they got home, Travis headed straight for the shower while Bo returned a few phone calls. Travis stripped down and had barely gotten into the oversized shower when he heard the bathroom door open. Travis turned to see Bo shedding his clothes, revealing all that gorgeous skin, and he began to harden right before Travis's eyes. There was no longer any doubt in his mind that Bo found him attractive and sexy. Two things he never thought anyone would feel about him.

Bo joined Travis in the shower wearing that salty grin before Bo gathered Travis into an embrace. "Now what do we have here? A hot, wet, soapy man begging for help with his shower."

"I don't remember begging for anything." Travis laughed and wrapped his soapy arm around Bo.

"Don't worry, I'll have you begging soon enough."

Travis went from partially hard to rock solid so fast he was a little dizzy. Bo leaned down and took Travis's lips in a crushing kiss that left him gasping for breath. His hands slid over the plains and valleys of Bo's muscles—Travis's personal playground, and boy did he want to play.

Travis went to his knees and wrapped his lips around Bo's hard cock. Even though he was a novice at giving blowjobs, Bo's moans increased his confidence immeasurably. Travis swirled his tongue around the crown of Bo's magnificent cock before taking it as far as he could into his mouth. Travis wasn't quite to the point where he could take Bo down his throat, but he was happily working on it. Bo groaned and leaned his back against the tiled wall, his hips thrusting forward in time with Travis's mouth.

Travis was completely lost in the moment. The noises Bo was making and the taste of him on Travis's tongue drove him on. Bo moved slightly and soon his hands were under Travis's arms lifting him off the ground and bringing them face to face.

"I love you, Travis."

"Ditto."

Bo kissed him again and Travis wrapped himself around his lover, their wet bodies tangled together. He began to grind himself against Bo's hard abdomen, desperate to get any friction to his aching cock. Bo spun Travis around so that he faced the shower wall. The steam from the shower blanketed them in mist. He heard Bo squirting what he assumed was the waterproof lube and opened his legs wider desperate for his lover's touch.

Travis didn't have long to wait because seconds later Bo's slick fingers circled his hole. He thrust his ass back further, desperate for Bo to breach him. The warmth from Bo's body blanketed his back as the first finger slid in deep, quickly followed by a second. Travis liked the stretch and burn and Bo knew it. Travis's moans turned to whimpers as Bo pegged his prostate with every thrust.

"Please Bo, I need more."

Bo inserted a third finger and began driving them in and out of Travis. Bo increased his speed, and Travis was out of his mind with need from the extraordinary sensations suffusing his body. Bo reached around and took hold of Travis's cock. He couldn't stop his pleasure-filled cries if he tried; they bounced off the tiled walls echoing throughout the bathroom. Bo removed his fingers, and Travis felt the head of Bo's cock a moment before he slowly pushed into Travis's body. He was completely at Bo's mercy and couldn't be happier or more turned on.

"God babe, you feel so right," Bo gasped before he started sucking up marks on the back of Travis's neck.

Waves of heat raced through Travis's bloodstream and he knew he'd be coming soon. "Close."

Bo sped up and Travis's hold on the wall slipped but he didn't teeter forward or fall. Bo had a secure hold on him as he continued to thrust until Travis couldn't hold his orgasm at bay any longer. His balls pulled up tight to his body and his cock pulsed as he came against the shower wall. Bo's rhythm faltered and he growled as he drove deep into Travis and came.

Slowly Bo pulled out but he didn't release Travis right away. When Travis turned to face Bo he was engulfed by his lover's big frame and held tight.

"You okay, babe?"

"Perfect."

"Told you I'd make you beg," Bo teased before grabbing the soap and lathering it up on a washcloth. Travis hummed in appreciation as Bo ran his hands over Travis's chest and began gently washing him. Travis knew he was home. This was his home and it was time to accept that and take another step forward.

"I'll move in with you."

Bo's hands stopped rubbing as he stared at Travis for a moment. "I was that good, huh?"

Travis laughed. "Smug much?" In his heart, Travis knew this was right.

Bo picked him up and hugged him tight. Travis loved his amazing boyfriend and planned on making him happy every single day.

Chapter Thirteen

Bo drove his cruiser down Main Street, as he had a thousand times before. The night was quiet and there were only a few people out walking. They waved as he passed by. That was Brighton, a small, nosy, tight-knit community. Finally, last week, Travis had made it official and moved in with Bo. He had never been happier. Waking every morning of every day with his love in his arms was a feeling he couldn't describe, but the peace it gave him was life altering.

Bo was on his way to pick up Travis and take him home; Bo was working the overnight shift and wanted a few minutes with his man. The diner was still lit up, though it was past closing time. Bo figured they were busy cleaning up. He pulled his cruiser into a nearby parking spot, same as he'd done on any other day, but the hairs on the back of his neck stood on end. He scanned the area and saw nothing out of place, but kept up his guard when he walked through the front door of the diner.

Silence. Not the sound of the grill being scraped or dishes being washed and no sign of Travis or Sarah. Immediately Bo knew something was wrong. After working in law enforcement for so many years, he had a sixth sense about these things.

He pushed his radio and whispered, "I need units at the diner."

"Copy," the dispatcher replied.

Bo turned his radio down and inched further into the building. He heard an angry unknown male shout, "Get down. Put your face on the floor."

Bo pulled his gun from his holster and put his back to the wall between the dining room and kitchen. His heart was racing, Travis and Sarah were in there. He heard the unmistakable sound of a fist hitting flesh and then his love cried out.

"Open the safe," the voice yelled.

"Leave him alone," Sarah screamed.

"You shut it or I'll put a bullet in it. Don't think I won't. I've done it before."

Bo suspected that the unidentified male was the robbery suspect. The bastard had backtracked from his last known location. Slowly, Bo sidestepped his way to the saloon-style doors leading to the kitchen and took a quick peek around the corner. Sarah was lying on her stomach on the floor and a disheveled, dark-haired man held Travis by his throat a few feet away. Bo had to do something; he couldn't wait for backup, it would come too late.

Bo pushed off the wall and burst into the kitchen, aiming his gun directly at the stranger. "Let him go and drop the gun."

The man spun around and pulled Travis in front of him like a shield, his gun pointed at Travis's head. "Try it, cop, and his brain will be painting the wall."

Bo's world came to a dead stop. He watched his terrified partner gasping for air as the man continued to hold him by his throat. Travis looked at Bo with pleading eyes. Then he noticed his love's eyes kept flicking downward towards the kitchen floor as if trying to tell Bo something. Moments later Travis went limp in his attacker's arms. The man couldn't hold the extra weight and Travis dropped down and out of harm's way.

"Put the gun down," Bo ordered. He could hear the sirens in the distance getting closer.

Instead of following direction the man immediately turned his gun on Bo. He heard the shot milliseconds before he pulled the trigger on his own gun. Burning pain ripped through his right shoulder and threw him to the ground. Quickly, he turned onto his side and kept his gun trained on the shooter, who was lying unmoving on the floor.

Bo heard Travis's scratchy voice as he knelt in front of him. "Bo. Oh, god, you've been shot."

Bo saw Sarah knock the gun away from the stranger a moment before the kitchen was flooded with officers. Travis pushed a towel to Bo's shoulder and he yelled out in pain.

"I'm sorry, honey, but I have to slow the bleeding," Travis explained as he continued to apply pressure to the wound.

"Paramedics are on their way, Bo. You hold on," Dave ordered as he crouched down beside Bo.

He couldn't help but notice the pool of blood around him growing no matter how many towels or amount of pressure they used. *Shit, not like this. I just found my soulmate.*

Travis's face was covered in tears, his eye already swelling from where he'd been punched earlier. Bo raised his hand and gently touched one of the bruised spots on his love's face. He didn't like seeing the worry in his Travis's eyes, but Bo didn't have the strength to do anything about it.

"Keep your eyes open, Bo," Travis demanded. Bo tried to concentrate, but everything was getting a little fuzzy around the edges.

He looked up at Travis, desperate to hold him in his arms, but Bo couldn't move. "Love you," was all he managed to get out before his world went dark.

***

Travis sat in the waiting room with most of the Brighton police force and the entire Mason family. They'd all been waiting for word on Bo's condition for over three hours and Travis was at his wit's end. His right eye had swollen shut but he hardly noticed as all his attention and concern was on Bo and what they were doing to him behind those locked doors.

“He’ll be okay, Travis. He’s strong,” Dot, Bo’s mom, assured as she held Travis’s hand even tighter.

“He has to be,” Travis sobbed, praying that someone was listening to him. His mind kept replaying the sight of Bo’s limp body lying in a pool of blood. Travis would never be able to wipe that from his memories.

Across the waiting room Travis could see Grady consoling Ben, Bo’s brother. Grady ran his hands up and down Ben’s arms while talking to him quietly. The automatic doors opened and Dr. Green walked out and came up to Travis, Dot, and Henry.

“He’s in recovery. We were able to remove the bullet and stop the bleeding. The brachial artery was nicked, which is why we had to give him a blood transfusion halfway through the surgery. He’s stable and should make a full recovery.”

Travis almost collapsed to the floor with relief as tears filled his eyes. Dot, Henry, and Ben formed a knot, hugging him and each other close. When they unknotted, Travis grabbed Dr. Green’s hands. “Thank you. Thank you for everything you did.”

Dr. Green smiled and informed Travis, “He’s been asking for you.”

“Really?” He assumed Bo’s family would be first.

“Of course, sweetie.” Dot patted his shoulder. “You’re the most important person in his life. As it should be.”

Travis looked around the waiting room at all the happy faces before he turned to follow Dr. Green through the security doors. Travis always felt antsy in hospitals. Too many bad memories, but he shoved his shit aside. All that mattered was Bo.

Dr. Green stopped outside a curtained room and smiled at Travis. “I’ll make sure a chair is brought in so that you can sit with him.”

“Thank you again for saving Bo’s life.”

“You’re welcome, Travis.” Dr. Green ushered Travis forward.

Travis walked up to the curtain then stopped. He could hear the beeping monitors, a familiar sound considering he’d spent years in and out of hospitals. Carefully, he pushed the drape open and stepped inside. The sight that greeting him made his stomach drop. Bo lay motionless and pale on the hospital bed, wires running from his arms to various machines. Travis stared at Bo's chest and waited until he saw him breathe before sighing in relief. Travis believed Bo would be fine, but in this moment, all Travis could see was the devastation the bullet had caused.

Travis approached the bed and saw the bandages covering Bo's shoulder and part of his chest. His heart ached at the pain Bo would have to go through as he healed, but at least he would heal. Travis reached out to softly touch Bo's warm hand, and the moment he did Bo's eyes opened.

Bo turned his head, locked onto Travis, and smiled. "Hi, sweetheart."

Tears filled Travis's eyes all over again. "Hi."

"Don't cry. I'm going to be fine."

"You better be." Travis felt a strange anger bubbling up. "You can't leave me. We're supposed to have a long life together. I just found you and you go and get yourself shot."

Bo smiled and Travis could see the amusement in his tired eyes.

"Don't you lay there and smile at me, you could have died. I love you and I need you in my life, dammit." Travis pointed his finger accusingly at Bo.

"You love me," Bo smiled even wider. "I knew it all along."

Travis had said it. Finally, he got out what he thought would be trapped inside of him forever. "I do love you." And in the work of a moment, Travis felt a weight lift from his soul.

"I know." Bo's smile was wide but his eyes were closing.

"Rest, love. I'll be here when you wake up," Travis promised while he ran his fingers through Bo's short hair.

Bo closed his eyes and drifted off. Not long afterward, a nurse brought in a chair and Travis took his post at Bo's side. He didn't plan on leaving it until he was forced to, and even then it would take a great deal of force. The rest of the family filtered in and out a few at a time, but Bo never woke up again that night.

On the third day of Bo's hospitalization he ordered Travis to go home and rest. Bo had his mom and dad take Travis out of the room and drive him home to make sure it happened. Travis wandered through the empty house for a long time before finally crawling into bed. He hugged Bo's pillow to his chest and fell asleep with tears in his eyes.

***

Three weeks later...

Bo sat in the lounge chair on the back patio enjoying the morning sunshine as he watched Travis run around weeding the gardens. Since his arm was in a sling Bo wouldn't be gardening for a while. But he thoroughly enjoyed watching his love's butt sticking up in the air as he bent over to pull the weeds.

Travis had taken responsibility for everything after Bo was released from the hospital. Now, no matter what he said, Travis wouldn't slow down or relinquish any household chores back to Bo. This was becoming a serious problem because Travis was wearing himself down, but Bo had a plan to get him to rest for a few days. He'd been cleared by his doctors to leave town and he intended to take full advantage of it.

"Travis, could you come here please?" Time to put the plan into motion.

His beautiful lover stood and came to his side. "Do you need something, honey?"

"Do you trust me?" Bo asked.

Travis got this adorably confused look on his face before saying, "You keep asking me that but you already know I do."

"Then I want you to go inside and pack for a few days. You'll need walking around the city clothes and that suit we got you last month."

"Away? But I have to work, and your shoulder. You have doctors' appointments," Travis said in a rush. "And why the suit?"

"I've already cleared it with Bear and my doctors. So go pack."

"Where are we going?"

Bo stood. "It's a surprise. Now let's go pack."

He followed Travis into the house and to their bedroom. Bo had the suitcase out and sitting ready on the bed.

"Seems you have everything planned." Travis eyed him suspiciously.

"I like to be thoroughly prepared," Bo teased.

"So do I," Travis replied with a saucy look on his face. Bo figured they weren't talking about the suitcase any longer.

"I'll take care of that later, I promise." Bo laughed on the way to his dresser before grabbing socks and underwear and throwing them into the suitcase.

"I'll hold you to that," Travis warned, and began sorting through his clothing in the dresser.

"Now, you'll have to drive because it's a few hours away. Do you mind driving in the city?" Bo knew some people hated driving in heavy traffic.

"City? Where exactly are we going?"

"I'll navigate, all you'll have to do is follow my directions," Bo explained before walking into their closet to grab his suit. Travis would have to wait to see where they were going because Bo was keeping his lips sealed.

Travis packed in a huff, clearly not enjoying being kept out of the loop. He loaded up the truck, ushered Bo in like he was an invalid, and then backed out of their driveway, squinting at Bo every few minutes.

After a three-hour drive they reached the outskirts of Houston. Its shiny towers filled the skyline. Bo was happy it was early afternoon, that way they could check into their hotel and go for lunch.

“Why are we in Houston?” Bo had learned quickly that Travis was organized and responsible. Even though his dad had raised Travis until he was sixteen, he’d done a great job.

“I’ll direct you to our hotel,” was all Bo shared.

“Still not going to give me a hint?”

“Nope. Turn left at the next intersection.”

Travis grumbled but followed directions. They checked into their hotel and within an hour were at a restaurant a block away, having drinks while sitting on the patio. Considering he was still on a few medications for his shoulder Bo stuck to iced tea while Travis had a beer. They’d placed their orders for lunch, not forgetting Bo’s mandatory salad, and sat relaxing in the shade of the umbrella that was swaying over the table.

“See, now aren’t we relaxing?” Bo asked as he reached across the table to hold Travis’s hand. His love immediately glanced around at the patrons. “It’s okay for us to show affection outside of Brighton, Travis.”

“I know, but old worries die hard,” Travis explained. Bo knew how far his love had come since moving to Brighton and working with Dr. Gordon. Still, Travis had nightmares, but they weren’t as common, and seemed less intense. He didn’t startle as easily anymore, but Bo was always conscious of letting Travis know when Bo entered the room, especially when Travis’s back was turned.

In other ways, Travis was blooming. He hung one of his paintings in Keith’s storefront and had been receiving positive feedback, which encouraged him. Slowly, Travis was finding his footing in a world that had been cruel to him for far too long.

“You let me worry and you enjoy the next three days.”

“Three days? What are we going to do for three days? I’m not complaining, honey, but we could have gone out to lunch at home.”

Travis could be an interrogation specialist with his persistence. “Okay. We are here to relax and get away, but there’s another reason we need to be in Houston.”

“Enough with the suspense, Bo. Tell me.”

“Grady’s hearing is being held in the city tomorrow.” Bo watched as the emotions on Travis’s face went from excited to confused in a heartbeat.

“The hearing is here? Tomorrow? Why did you bring me? I sent my letter with Dave to read at the hearing.”

“About that,” Bo said as he pulled a sealed envelope from the inside of his sling. “I thought it might sound better coming from you.” He hoped he’d done the right thing because it was too late to turn back now. He supposed he could always arrange with Dave to get the letter back to him but…

His thoughts were cut short by the squirming body of his lover as he sat on Bo’s lap and hugged him tight. Guess he wasn’t worried about what people thought anymore. “You’re amazing. Thank you for this. I love you so much.” Travis had been saying those three words for weeks now and even though they weren’t necessary, it warmed Bo’s heart to hear them. Travis slowly released him and returned to his chair. “I thought you were against this.”

“I wasn’t completely against it. I’ll admit I was angry with Grady because he could have hurt you. But I concede your point about learning from your mistakes. I don’t think he’ll make this one twice,” Bo stated before taking a more serious tone. “When I heard you cry out from the kitchen of the diner that night, and I knew that bastard had you, nothing else mattered to me. Not code or policy. Only you. I wouldn’t change what I did because you and Sarah are safe, but let’s say I learned something that day as well.”

“What did you learn?” Travis held tight to Bo’s hand.

“That anybody can go off script under the right circumstances. I’m not saying what Grady did wasn’t wrong, but I am saying that it’s worth giving him another chance.”

Travis looked at Bo like he’d hung the moon just for him. “I love you, Bo Mason.”

“Ditto, Travis Boone.”

Epilogue

Grady sat in his rusting truck behind the Brighton police station. Today marked his first night back on the force, at least on a probationary basis. He wouldn't be here if it weren't for Travis and Chief Graham speaking on his behalf. Grady swore he'd prove he was a capable officer and regain everyone's trust.

His cell phone rang and he answered it without looking at the screen. "Hello." As soon as he heard the voice he cursed himself for not checking.

"Hello, Grady."

"Ben." Definitely not a person he wanted to talk to right now. Grady was nervous enough.

"I thought I'd call and wish you good luck on your first night back." Ben's deep, rumbling voice that never failed to send chills through Grady's body echoed through the phone.

"Thank you." Short and sweet.

"Did you want to meet up after your shift?" Ben's voice purred across the line.

And there it was. The reason for the call. Damn if he wasn't tempted. "I don't know, Ben."

"I miss you, Grady. I need to see you." Ben spoke softly. His voice sounded sincere and Grady knew he'd cave.

"I'm off at six in the morning. Meet me at my apartment." The moment the words left his mouth, he regretted them. How many times was he going to punish himself with the impossible? How long could he hold out while Ben made his decision? It'd been months already.

"I'll be there." Ben disconnected the call.

Grady sat staring at the screen. He'd promised himself that the last time they were together would be the last time. It wouldn't happen again. And yeah, he'd said that the time before, and the time before that.

How many more times would he put himself directly in the path of the wrecking ball that was Ben Mason?

The Boys of Brighton continue with ***Grady***

GRADY

Chapter One

Grady sat in his rusting truck behind the Brighton police station. Today marked his first night back on the force, at least on a probationary basis. He wouldn't be here if it weren't for Travis and Chief Graham speaking on his behalf. Grady swore he'd prove he was a capable officer and regain everyone's trust.

His cell phone rang and he answered it without looking at the screen. "Hello." As soon as he heard the voice on the other end, he cursed himself for not checking.

"Hello, Grady."

"Ben." Definitely not a person he wanted to talk to right now. Grady was nervous enough.

"I thought I'd call and wish you good luck on your first night back." Ben's deep, rumbling voice that never failed to send chills through Grady's body echoed through the phone.

"Thank you." *Short and sweet.*

"Did you want to meet up after your shift?" Ben's voice purred across the line.

And there it was. The reason for the call. Damn if he wasn't tempted. "I don't know."

"I miss you. I need to see you," Ben spoke softly. He sounded sincere, and dammit, Grady knew he'd cave.

"I'm off at six in the morning. Meet me at my apartment." The moment the words left his mouth, he regretted them. How many times was he going to punish himself with the impossible? How long could he hold out while Ben made his decision? It'd been months already.

"I'll be there." Ben disconnected the call.

Grady sat staring at the screen. He'd promised himself that the last time they were together would be the last time. It wouldn't happen again. And yeah, he'd said that the time before, and the time before that.

How many more times would he put himself directly in the path of the wrecking ball that was Ben Mason?

Okay. Time to get your head on straight and concentrate on getting back to the police officer you're meant to be. Grady reprimanded himself for being so easily distracted today of all days.

He sat in his truck for a few more minutes to clear his thoughts. So much had happened since he'd moved to Brighton, Texas. His father, Detective Richard Reynolds, would say Grady had gotten what he deserved. Perhaps. But he'd sworn to himself he would make this work. He didn't plan on going back to Dallas. Not now. Not ever.

Grady looked at himself in his rearview mirror, steeling his nerve. The sun hung low in the sky and shined onto his reflection, making him seem almost golden. Yeah, the "Golden Boy." He was so far away from those days. He grabbed his lunch and opened his door, the familiar creak comforting him. It was one constant in his turnstile life, considering the truck, along with his clothing, were the only things he'd left Dallas with.

He didn't bother locking the door; it didn't work, and he had nothing to steal. His father would flip his lid if he realized Grady wasn't adhering to basic safety practices, and that made him smile. Since he'd moved here Grady had let a few of his demons go, but that ended when he met Ben, and shortly after that, Grady had gotten himself suspended from the force. Now, he stood right back at the start of his journey. Well, except for Ben. That story should have ended a while ago.

The police department's old brick building stood proud. Its wide stone steps and banisters always reminded Grady of arms welcoming people. It brought back memories of the station his father worked in when Grady was only a small child. Detective Reynolds had been a patrol officer back then and brought young Grady into the station for visits. He had loved every minute of being around a police department, and still did. Every time he walked through those doors his purpose renewed, and his conviction strengthened. He would be the best officer he could and protect the people of this community.

Grady huffed; that was the reason he found himself suspended: overzealous in his duty. So intent on doing his job he didn't take a second to think through his actions before going into his fellow officer Bo's home. If he'd stopped to wait for backup, he wouldn't have pulled his gun on Bo's boyfriend, Travis.

That'd been months ago; now Grady had the chance to redeem himself. He sucked in a deep breath and took the first step back onto the road of what he hoped would be the future he'd given up so much to have.

The station bustled with activity, officers arriving for shift and others finishing reports before leaving for the night. Grady had a few minutes before roll call so he stowed his lunch in his locker and left in search of that heavenly brew, coffee.

He walked into the small kitchenette area where they kept the fridge, coffeepots, and vending machines. Grady filled his mug, added sugar and cream before making his way back to the bullpen. As he sat down, Officer Bo Mason came walking through the front door. It'd been Bo's boyfriend whom Grady had pulled his gun on by mistake. He doubted he and Bo would restart their friendship, but he'd try. They were a small department, and bad blood between officers hung over everyone.

"Evening, Bo," Grady greeted.

Bo looked up and gave Grady a curt nod before walking by him toward the break room. Grady took that as a good sign. At least Bo hadn't ignored him. Chief Graham came out of his office and headed to the conference room; time for roll call. Grady took a seat at the back of the room, cupped his hands around his warm coffee mug, and waited for everyone else to arrive. The chief handed out the briefing sheets. Any ongoing investigations, warrants, incident reports would be available in their mobile data terminal at a push of a button.

"All right, quiet down. This won't take long," the chief ordered. He read through the sheets, making announcements, and reminded everyone of the charity dinner coming up in a few weeks, which they would be expected to attend, in suits.

A few officers came over and shook Grady's hand, welcoming him back, while others nodded in greeting. So far so good. The chief finished his announcements before looking at Grady.

"Officer Reynolds, meet me in my office. Everyone else, you're dismissed. Be safe out there."

Everyone stood and headed for the door. Grady waited and followed the chief out of the conference room and into his office. "Have a seat."

"Yes, sir." He sat and watched as Chief Graham pulled Grady's duty belt and service revolver from a locked drawer and laid them on the table between them. He knew better than to reach for them; this would not be that easy.

"So, here we are, Grady," the chief sighed. "I don't assume I need to remind you what's at stake."

"No, sir."

"Good. I'm sending you out to the cutoff leading from the interstate. We've had a rash of speeders coming through there," Chief Graham explained as he slid Grady's duty belt and gun across the table toward him. "Check your new shift schedule before you leave and stay safe."

"Thank you, Chief," Grady said before standing and gathering his belongings. He let out the breath he hadn't realized he'd been holding. "Thanks, boss. I'm thankful to be here." With a nod, Grady left the office and returned to the bullpen.

He took a long moment to look over his service revolver, confirming the chief had someone clean and lubricate the slide, barrel, and frame for him. After loading a magazine into it and checking his Glock 22 once again, he put his service belt on, its weight reassuring. He'd missed this. He grabbed his lunch and walked out to his cruiser. It took only ten minutes for Grady to reach his post and park the cruiser on a nearby side road. He set up his radar, adjusted his communications radio, and got comfortable.

Working a roadside speed trap wasn't glamorous, but it was necessary to slow speeding motorists down on this stretch of the highway leading into Brighton. The night ended up being clear and warm. Stars flooded the sky as he sat alone with his thoughts.

It'd been slightly over a year since he'd come out to his family. He'd been twenty-eight and tired of living only half a life, always hiding his true self. At the time he'd been in a two-year relationship with a man named Tony, and was so in love. After he came out to his family, and they'd thrown him off the property, he'd sped past his apartment and raced to Tony's house only to find him in bed with an unknown woman. Bisexual and a cheater—Grady's heart tore wide open.

Things got worse after that; his father smeared him at every turn. Right until the day Grady resigned his position with the Dallas PD. Working in the same building as his detective father, who had contacts all over Texas, became too much. Grady's applications to other departments had been rejected, and the Dallas PD had turned against him. Finally, Grady had an offer from the Brighton PD. Apparently Chief Graham didn't care about the good detective's reach or Grady's sexual orientation. Now here he sat on the side of the road in small town America and loved it. It'd been a big change for him, but this life suited him better. He now had the freedom to be the man he wanted to be. No more hiding. No more lies.

Well, that'd been the plan until the day he met Ben Mason, a firefighter with the Brighton FD. The mouthwatering man wore his light blond hair short, and his green eyes zeroed in on Grady the moment he set foot in the backyard of the barbeque Bo had invited him to. Ben took charge from the first moment he touched Grady; dominant, and sexy as hell, Ben was all kinds of wrong for Grady.

He'd become someone else's secret, as Tony had been for him. A twist of fate or karma, either way his eyes had been opened.

Maybe it wasn't exactly the same because everyone understood and accepted that the two of them were gay, but Grady remained forbidden from mentioning they were lovers, and public affection was out of the question. He'd agreed to those conditions the second night they spent together because it seemed so important to Ben. But as time wore on it became painful to keep the promise.

It felt as if Grady had been shoved back into the closet. Not quite the one he came out of last year, but still a box. Ben made it clear if Grady broke that promise the relationship would be over. Sanity dictated he should tell Ben to get gone, but Grady had inexplicably fallen for the secretive man in the short time they'd been together.

So there he sat, trapped yet again in a cage of his own making.

His ten-hour shift had been quiet. Only two speeders who received tickets, and a loose cow wandering down the road. Grady corralled the escapee back into the pasture through the hole in the fence. The land belonged to the Fraser family. Grady had contacted them about the fence problem, and they came right out to repair it. That'd been the excitement for the evening, cow wrangling. He laughed to himself when he considered what his father would say.

Detective Richard Reynolds would be shocked to learn that Grady had given up chasing drug dealers in Dallas to chase livestock in Brighton, but Grady loved it. This policing allowed him to be hands-on with the community.

Grady hadn't seen his father since the day he'd left Dallas, but the vindictive bastard showed up at Grady's disciplinary hearing after he'd messed up in Brighton. The man he used to look up to sat in the back of the room, his disapproval easy to see as he glared at Grady when he entered and left the hearing. Being gay had become a black spot on the family's strong policing heritage. This hearing must have confirmed his father's belief that Grady had somehow weakened the bloodline.

To cap off his humiliation, Tony had the nerve to show up at the hearing. How he'd found out was still a mystery. He'd said he came to support Grady and that he wanted a few minutes of his time. Tony spent those few minutes trying to convince Grady to take him back. It was a short conversation.

Ben hadn't shown up, and Grady hadn't expected him too, but he'd hoped.

The man Grady used to love wanted him back while the man Grady loved hadn't even touched him in public. It stung, and as he looked out his truck window he saw the lights were on in his apartment. Ben was waiting for him.

In the beginning, Grady had been in the *glow* of a new relationship when he'd given Ben a key, but now he considered taking it back. Ben had never offered Grady a key to his house, and Grady wasn't holding his breath he'd see one soon.

How had he fallen in love with a man who refused to acknowledge him in public? It would've been easy to walk away if Ben was as cold as his request, but underneath it all he was one of the kindest, most caring men Grady had ever met. Ben volunteered his time all over Brighton: at the youth center the city was building, the sanctuary for LGBTQ youths at risk, and at any community event the fire department held or participated in.

Ben was passionate about serving this community and the two of them had lain awake in bed talking about what more needed to be done. Ben talked about his family with such love it had brought Grady to tears over the loss of his own. And knowing his background, Ben had held him close and soothed his pain. Inside the walls of his apartment they were free to share themselves with each other. But eventually they had to return to the real world, a place where Ben continued to behave as if they were nothing more than friends.

Grady sighed, opened the door, and stepped out of his truck. He climbed the stairs to his second-story apartment. He wondered if Ben planned to stick around or run out the door after they made love, same as last time. Grady reached for the door handle to his apartment but the door flew open before he'd grasped it. He was pulled into the apartment and the door slammed shut. Grady found himself pressed against the wall right there in his hallway.

"Damn, I've missed you," Ben growled before claiming Grady's mouth, his tongue diving deep as he demanded Grady's submission. Though they were both the same height, Grady weighed at least sixty pounds more than Ben. While Grady was more heavily muscled, Ben was long and lean; a runner's body with subtly sculpted muscles, which never failed to excite Grady every time they got together.

"I've missed you, too," Grady said when they came up for air.

Ben unbuttoned Grady's shirt and worked his way down to his duty belt.

"Hold on, I have to put my belt and gun in the safe." He skirted around Ben on his way to his bedroom. He removed his gear and locked it away in the floor safe. Grady had barely gotten to his feet when Ben tackled him onto the bed. Ben straddled him and continued stripping off Grady's clothes while managing to get out of his at the same time. In a matter of moments Grady found himself naked and writhing beneath Ben's hard body as Grady sucked and licked his salty skin, inhaling the woodsy masculine scent that was all Ben.

"I have to see you more than once a week," Ben whispered before nibbling his sensitive ear. Ben explored all the spots that turned Grady on.

"You're the one who decided that once a week was enough time together," he reminded Ben. "I'd like to see more of you."

Ben stopped trailing kisses down Grady's neck and looked at him. He was quiet before nodding his head as if coming to some sort of decision. "We'll try twice a week from now on."

Grady's heart skipped a beat. Ben wanted to spend more time with him. Maybe he was warming up to coming out as a couple. Grady could only hope. Ben doubled his efforts to torture him. His strong hands roamed over Grady's chest, pinching his nipples as he went. The small bite of pain raced through Grady's body and to his throbbing cock, making his balls pull up tight. No way in hell would he come this soon, so he reached between his legs and squeezed the base of his cock until his orgasm receded.

Ben's soft lips ghosted over his heated skin; his wicked tongue flicked out and circled Grady's left nipple before sucking it into his hot mouth. Grady's back bowed off the bed as he groaned his approval. Ben's thick cock left trails of pre-cum along Grady's thighs, making him desperate to have that gorgeous piece of flesh stretch him wide. His lover continued his slow, methodical exploration of Grady's body as if trying to memorize every inch of him.

Grady couldn't help but reach for Ben and drag him back up his body for a kiss. He had to taste Ben. The kiss lasted until they needed to breathe and they separated, both gasping for air. The passion between them was electrifying, snapping through the air, and Grady held on tight for as long as he could.

Ben slid over Grady's body and hovered over his aching cock. Grady needed his lover to do something, anything to take the ache away. He didn't have to wait long as Ben leaned forward and licked him from root to tip.

"Please," was all Grady could get out before his cock was sucked down Ben's throat. Grady's legs fell open, giving Ben complete access and control.

Being a cop required concentration and control, and Grady loved that he could release his tight control to let someone else lead, at least for a little while. Before he'd come out, he'd held rigid control of himself. He could never relax. He could never disappoint his father.

Grady didn't like the direction his thoughts were heading and concentrated on the sensation running through his overheated body as Ben's tongue lapped at his shaft and dipped into his slit. If he didn't stop, Grady knew he would come any second. He fought to stop it. Fire raced through his body as he lay, arms thrown wide, palms up, and rode the wave of pleasure that overtook him causing him to cry out as he came.

Ben took every drop before rearing up and flipping Grady onto his stomach in one fluid motion. While he lay recovering from his orgasm, he felt two lubed fingers breach his hole. Ben knew Grady liked the burn and made quick work of preparing him. By the time he heard the tear of the condom wrapper, his cock was rock-hard again and throbbing. Grady felt the bed dip as Ben lined his cock up with Grady's hole and pushed through the tight ring of muscle before burying himself deep.

Ben moaned out words of affection that Grady never took as sincere as they waited for his body to relax. Ben ran his lips across Grady's shoulder blade and sucked up marks before he pumped in and out of him at an ever-increasing pace. Ben pegged Grady's prostate with every thrust until Grady's arms gave out and he rested his head on the bed. This position always brought out the wild side in Ben as his lover's hips snapped faster and faster.

"Oh baby, I need you in my life," Ben moaned as he draped his hard body over Grady's back, pushed deep and groaned out his orgasm. Warmth filled the end of the condom sending Grady over the edge for a second time. He came all over his sheets before collapsing and taking Ben down to the bed with him.

The only sound in the room was their heavy breathing. Ben ran his hand across Grady's back in a comforting, loving way. Grady had learned not to read too much into what Ben said or how he behaved in the moments after they'd made love. This might only be a hookup for Ben, but for Grady it was making love.

But slivers of hope sprang eternal that Ben meant what he said in the throes of passion.

After a few moments Ben pulled away from Grady and got out of bed. He listened as the water ran in the bathroom sink before he heard Ben's footsteps approach the bed. He kept his eyes closed as the man he was in love with used a warm washcloth to clean him and a towel to dry. In those moments Grady believed Ben loved him, at least in some way.

Grady rolled over as Ben reached for his pile of clothing on the floor. He watched as Ben dressed and came to sit at the head of the bed beside Grady. It had been weeks since Ben stayed and held him until he fell asleep. Those days were nothing but distant memories now, and Grady had to accept that if he chose to continue this…whatever they were doing.

Ben cupped the side of Grady's cheek and ran his thumb over his stubbled jaw. "We'll talk soon." Ben's deep voice traveled through Grady's body as those words confirmed there would be no more time spent with him today.

"Sure. Lock the door on your way out," Grady muttered before he slid out of bed and walked to the bathroom without looking back.

Grady heard the door shut and the lock snick then he turned on the water and stepped into the large shower as soon as the water warmed. He let the hot water pound on the tight muscles in his neck and shoulders. He knew he had no right to be upset; he'd agreed to this. Frustrated and disappointed in himself for allowing this arrangement to affect him to this extent, Grady tried to wipe it from his mind. He preferred to concentrate on the fact he'd made it through the first day back at work without incident.

He finished washing and turned the water off before grabbing a towel and drying himself off in the steam-filled bathroom. He wrapped the towel around his waist and stepped out into his empty bedroom. *What did I expect? Ben to be lying in the bed waiting for me to crawl into his arms and fall asleep? Yeah, that won't be happening.*

He walked into his living room, checked the front door to confirm it was indeed locked, and turned to open his fridge when he noticed a note on the kitchen island. He abandoned his need for a drink and picked up the piece of paper. At first he wasn't sure what he held but he soon realized it was Ben's schedule for the next month at the fire station. This was the first time Grady had received any insight into Ben's schedule and life.

A few personal dates were listed; a family barbeque, a birthday party, and poker night between the firehouse and the police station. The event raised money to feed the less fortunate and to purchase more Christmas lights to decorate downtown. Grady planned on attending at the end of the month. He wasn't sure if Ben realized that, but it didn't matter. They wouldn't acknowledge each other, anyway.

But the note was a step in the right direction.

Grady could accept that much for now.

***

Ben drove his truck to the end of Main Street on his way to the firehouse. His shift started at eight so he had a little time for a pit stop at the diner for coffee. He should have stayed at Grady's and made coffee, but he didn't want to keep him up considering he got off shift. *Yeah right, I ran out of there like the fires of hell were on my heels.* He felt sick about the way he was treating Grady, but he had no choice. It must be this way.

He parked out front of the diner and took a deep breath before shutting off the truck. His thoughts wandered to the gorgeous man he'd walked out on, again. Grady, with his short, dark hair, deep brown eyes, and a body that should be carved in marble, meant everything to Ben. He didn't want to break that kind man's heart, but remained powerless to stop it. When they began their relationship he'd been cautious, not wanting to reveal their relationship to everyone. Now, he was being forced to keep it a secret and hurt the man he loved. If he were a decent man, he'd have walked away by now, but he couldn't bring himself to do it. Not yet.

Ben opened his eyes, not remembering closing them, and released the tight grip he had on the steering wheel. These stolen moments he and Grady shared were all he had to offer until he figured out what to do. None of this was fair to Grady. Ben realized the man loved him back but how long would that last?

The knock on his driver's side window startled Ben. He looked up to see his brother, Bo, standing only a foot away from his truck. Ben opened his door and stepped out.

"Morning. Here to visit with Travis?" Ben asked as the two walked toward the diner entrance.

"No, not this time. I saw you sitting out here in your truck and thought we should have a coffee together." Bo tilted his head toward the diner, and Ben could tell there would be more than coffee involved.

"I have ten minutes, then I need to head to the firehouse."

"Perfect," Bo replied and held the door open for him to walk through. Bo led him to a booth far away from the counter, raising Ben's suspicions further. The team from Sentinel, former military personnel who created a private group to aid those in need, sat at a far table. From what Ben understood, they still took contracts from the government, and he'd learned their reach was global. Sarah came over with two coffees; neither wanted to order anything else. The moment Sarah walked away Bo began.

"Ben, you know we love you, right?"

Not a good way to start a sentence but Ben nodded his agreement. This should be interesting.

"It's been years, and you still refuse to give anyone a chance. You can't be alone for the rest of your life."

"I'm fine, Bo, you don't need to worry." Ben had heard the same thing over and over, but of late the family had taken an even bigger interest in his love life.

"Prove you're fine," Bo challenged.

"How would you like me to do that?" Ben asked.

"Go out on a double date with me and Travis."

"W-what?"

"Dave Graham's cousin is in town visiting, and we thought this might be a great way to get your feet wet again."

"Bo, I don't need your help with my love life."

"Don't worry, the guy knows there's not a chance for a love match, but thought it would be fun to go out as friends for the evening. If you are fine and ready to move on, prove it. Then I'll stop worrying."

Ben felt trapped. If he said no to Bo, the entire Mason clan wouldn't believe he wasn't still recovering from his bastard ex, and their "help" might never end. If he agreed, there was a possibility they'd leave him alone for a while, but what about Grady? Maybe he need not find out. The chance of him falling for the guy was zero because he loved Grady. If he was told about it, there was a possibility of only hurting him more even if Ben explained why he had to do it.

He'd caused Grady enough pain.

"Okay, when?" Ben blurted out before he changed his mind.

"Next Friday night. We'll come here to the diner so that it's a comfortable night." Bo looked so happy that Ben understood he couldn't back out of it.

He took a long last drink of coffee before setting it on the table and standing. He needed to get out of here. "I'll see you later, big brother." Ben dropped money on the table and left the diner as quickly as he could without looking like he was running.

He drove to the firehouse with his mind racing. What had he done? If Grady found out, he risked losing him. Maybe that's what he should do. If he ended it with Grady, he'd be out of danger.

The firehouse was quiet as he entered through one of the open bay doors. A few men kept busy rolling up one of the cross-lay hoses while others watched television in the common room or were eating in the kitchen. Ben waved and said hello as he passed on the way to his locker; he wasn't ready to put on his "nothing's wrong" face yet.

He opened his locker and hung up his jacket before returning to the kitchen and putting his lunch in the fridge. Somebody would be on cooking duty tonight, but he wasn't sure who, so he brought food in case of an impending cooking disaster. Not every firefighter could cook, and they should never be permitted to try again.

"Hey, Ben," Gabe called out as he walked into the room. "This came for you."

Gabe handed Ben a plain white envelope with his name and the mailing address for the firehouse on it. His heart sped up and his hands shook from seeing the envelope. "Thanks, Gabe. I'll be right back."

Ben took the missive back to the empty locker room. He opened his locker, using it as a shield, and ripped into the thick paper. His heart dropped as he looked at the three Polaroid pictures of Grady, two in uniform, one out grocery shopping. The same words written on a scrap of paper that haunted him day and night.

"Remember, he'll be the first to die."

Chapter Two

Grady pushed hard on his accelerator as he joined the pursuit in progress. A lone officer from the highway patrol had radioed for assistance with an armed carjacking. The subject was attempting to outrun the highway patrol officer, and considering Grady was the closest unit to the interstate, he joined in the chase.

He called out their location over the radio for the other officers heading in their direction. The subject drove a newer model, four-door sedan in the far right lane at eighty miles per hour. Highway patrol took the center lane so Grady stayed behind the sedan. Speeds reduced to sixty-five and the lead car requested permission to PIT the sedan. This tactic forced the fleeing car to turn sideways, causing the subject to lose control and stop.

Clearance came back and the other patrol officer pulled his cruiser alongside the sedan, lining up the front quarter of his car with the back quarter of the subject's vehicle. At the last second Grady heard gunshots and the patrol officer's front passenger tire blew out.

"Shots fired," Grady announced across the radio. The highway patrol officer slowed and Grady watched as he pulled into the grass on the side of the road. "Officer Gimble's vehicle has been disabled."

This guy needs to be stopped.

He saw the flashing lights behind him at a distance, and he knew he had to wait until they got closer before he tried to PIT the sedan. The lights from the overhead lampposts reflected off the sedan's rear window seconds before it shattered and a bullet ricocheted off

Grady's push bumper and over his car. The next bullet smashed through the passenger side window. Grady swerved out of the line of fire and reached for his radio to call it in when Bo's voice came across the radio announcing that more shots had been fired.

Grady looked in his rearview mirror and saw two Brighton cruisers pulling up fast. Another shot came through the front window of his cruiser, covering him in glass, but he held steady to the wheel. This dangerous asshole wasn't getting away only to hurt another innocent person. But, remembering what one more misstep would cost him, Grady wanted to do this by the book.

"Requesting PIT maneuver," he sent out over the radio.

Seconds later Chief Dave Graham's voice came over the radio. "Cleared to PIT when safe."

Speeds increased to seventy miles per hour and the road ahead was clear with grass on either side. Conditions didn't get better than this. Grady brought his cruiser up alongside the sedan, lined his quarter panel up with the rear of the vehicle, and tapped it. The back of the sedan broke free, and the subject lost control as his vehicle and spun off to Grady's left.

He drove straight through and brought his cruiser to a stop over two hundred feet away. Grady turned his vehicle around and pulled up to the smoking sedan. Bo and Stan leapt out of their vehicles, guns drawn, using the engine blocks of their cruisers as cover. Grady got out, drew his weapon, and crouched behind his vehicle, his body braced against the open door. He registered pain as a second thought, adrenaline still running high in his body.

Bo issued commands to the suspect, ordering him out of the car and onto the ground. Stan moved forward, handcuffs at the ready as Grady came around his vehicle and kept his gun trained on the suspect. The moment they had him cuffed, Grady holstered his weapon.

The suspect screamed at them, promising to kill each of them. It wasn't the first time he'd heard that. Stan shut him in the back of his cruiser and joined Bo and Grady at the front of his car. It was smoking as badly as the suspect's vehicle. Grady figured one of the stray bullets must have hit his radiator. He looked up at the holes in his window and sent a silent prayer of thanks to whoever was watching out for him.

"Good job." Bo clapped Grady on the back before he turned away from the busted cruiser and looked straight at him. His expression changed from smiling to a frown in a heartbeat and Grady figured he must still be in the doghouse with Bo until he said, "You're hurt."

"What?" Grady replied, his brain not connecting the dots fast enough.

"You're bleeding from your right arm. You have cuts across your neck and jaw." Bo reached for his arm, and Grady finally registered the pain radiating from his bicep. He watched as Stan brought over a towel from his trunk and pressed it against the wound. *Shit, now it hurt.*

"Take your shirt off so we can get a better look at the damage," Bo ordered. Grady heard the sirens in the background. Fire and ambulance had been called in.

Grady undid the buttons on his uniform shirt with his left hand as Stan kept pressure on the wound. Bo helped get the shirt the rest of the way off until Grady stood in his bloody white undershirt and his bulletproof vest. Bo lifted the corner of the cloth and took a peek.

"Can't tell if the bullet's still in there, we'll have the paramedics handle it." Bo's voice was filled with concern.

"It's far from the heart. I think I'll be okay," Grady said, trying to calm his fellow officers though he felt anything but. Bo smiled, and Grady knew he understood.

A fire engine came to a stop behind Bo and Stan's cruisers and Stan took off at a run toward it. Grady leaned back against the door of his cruiser, trying not to curse with pain.

"They're coming, buddy," Bo assured, and Grady looked up to see Stan, Gabe, and Chief Mason headed his way with a large, red first aid bag. Grady looked for Ben, who was on shift tonight, but didn't see him. Grady glanced at his arm and became more alarmed when he saw the towel covered in his blood. *Maybe that asshole got me worse than I thought.*

Tires squealed as Police Chief Graham pulled up. *Now we have a party.* Grady huffed, not enjoying being the center of so many people's attention. Though the one man Grady wanted attention from was busy lifting the hood of the suspect's sedan along with a few other firefighters. That moment of hurt stabbed more deeply at Grady than a bullet ever could.

"Let's see what we've got here," Gabe said as he removed the cloth and cleaned the wound. "The bullet is still in there. We'll bandage you up and get you to the hospital so they can dig it out."

"Dig it out, you have one hell of a bedside manner." Grady laughed, trying his best not to show how Ben's lack of concern affected him. He hadn't seen Ben privately since Grady's first night back on the force. That had been a week ago. *God, what am I doing?*

The men surrounding him laughed along with him, and then dispersed while Gabe went to work on the wound.

"You okay?" Chief Graham asked, his voice low enough so as not to travel far.

"Yeah, boss. I'll be up and back out there before you know it."

"Well, depending on what the doctor says, you will be off for a few days at least," Chief Graham confirmed.

"But I started back only a week ago, I can't take time off," Grady argued before groaning in pain as Gabe wrapped his arm. The ambulance arrived and paramedics readied to take over and get him to Brighton General.

"This isn't a punishment, Grady. You've been shot in the line of duty. You have to have time to heal," the chief explained.

Grady nodded before looking off toward the fire engine where Ben now stood. Their eyes met but Ben made no move to acknowledge him. Grady looked away from the man he loved and straight at Bo, Ben's brother. Bo looked back and forth between Grady and Ben, but said nothing. For that Grady was thankful. They escorted him to the back of the ambulance and whisked him off to have his arm stitched up. Shame he couldn't do the same with his heart.

Dr. Green performed a minor surgery to remove the bullet, and fifteen stitches later Grady was as good as new. After that he spent hours at the station filling out reports and answering the chief's questions. By the time he'd finished, Grady was in no position to drive his truck home so Bo gave him a ride. Their conversation was short and perfunctory. Grady wasn't willing to answer any more questions. His arm throbbed in time with his heartbeat.

The sun had risen by the time he made it back to his apartment. As the lock on his front door clicked behind him Grady stripped out of his bloody uniform. The only thing he had on his mind was making it to his bed before he passed out. He dropped his boxer briefs on his bedroom floor, crawled into his king-size bed, and fell asleep before he pulled the covers over himself.

***

Ben unlocked the door and let himself into Grady's apartment. He was never more thankful to have a key of his own than today. He needed to see and hold his injured lover to confirm he was safe. A trail of bloody clothing ran through the living room and into the bedroom. Ben's heart clenched tight seeing them. He'd almost lost Grady last night, and Ben had never even told him he loved him.

It gutted him when he couldn't run to Grady at the scene, but he still had someone stalking him. Threatening to kill Grady first before killing Ben if he didn't stay away from Grady. With no idea who kept sending him the notes and pictures, Ben had to stay on alert. He parked two blocks over, behind the old movie theatre, walking through the alley to Grady's apartment. Keeping his distance out in public helped make Grady safe.

Ben leaned against the bedroom wall and watched his love sleeping soundly in the middle of the bed. Each rise and fall of his muscled chest allowed Ben to breathe easier. His eyes roamed over Grady's sculpted body until he reached the large bandage wrapped around his bicep. He'd called the hospital from the firehouse to check on Grady's condition. Ben was sick when he found out Grady had gone through surgery to remove the bullet. If that bullet had been any closer to the driver's side, Grady might have been severely injured or even killed.

His stomach had clenched when they got the call about an officer-involved shooting. Ben could no more stay away than he could stop breathing. Once his shift ended, he'd come straight from work to Grady's apartment.

Ben removed his boots, took off his uniform, and slid into bed beside the first man he'd ever trusted after his ex took off to New York. He gathered the man he loved, and had to protect, close to him before giving in to his exhaustion.

"Ben?" Grady's sleep-roughened voice always made him want to snuggle in and never leave.

"Yes, love. Go back to sleep," Ben assured as he ran his fingers through Grady's short dark hair.

"Will you be here when I wake up?" The despair in his voice was crushing. Ben was to blame for instilling that uncertainty.

"I'll be right here beside you," he confirmed as Grady turned over and laid his head on Ben's chest. Within moments his body relaxed and his eyes closed. Ben pulled Grady closer and gave up the fight to stay awake.

At 4:00 pm Ben laid a note on Grady's bedside table. He'd cleaned up his love's bloody clothes and tidied for him but he had to go. He had a promise to keep, and a plan to make. Dante from the Sentinels would be his first call.

Ben didn't want to leave Grady, but the man needed his rest so he could heal. Ben refused to wake him when sleep was truly the best medicine. With one last kiss to his love's stubbled cheek, Ben pulled himself away. He locked the door, his mind filled with what and who he'd need to make his plan work.

Ben swore that someday soon he'd never have to leave Grady again.

***

Grady held the piece of paper in his hand as he read it over for a second time. *My Love, I'm sorry I had to leave. Someday soon I'll explain everything and we'll never have to be apart again. It will be forever. Ben xo.*

Barely breathing, afraid he might still be asleep, Grady sat in bed, stunned. His throbbing arm confirmed he was awake. *Never have to be apart again.* The words kept replaying through his mind as excitement grew in his heart. Grady hoped this meant that their relationship could be brought out into the open. No more hiding. He'd no longer be a secret.

Knowing the possibility existed for a normal relationship made up for some of the pain he was in.

Grady left the note on his side table and went in search of an over-the-counter painkiller. He'd refused Dr. Green's offer to give him a prescription for something stronger. He didn't want to mess with medication. The bathroom light seemed so bright when he turned it on but it didn't stop him from stepping in and opening his medicine cabinet. After taking a couple pills he climbed into the shower, hoping that might help his muscles relax, and it had.

By the time he'd dried off, changed his bandages, and dressed, Grady felt more like himself. Before he left the bedroom, he grabbed Ben's note, folded it, and slid it into his pocket. He didn't know why, but it calmed him to have the note in his possession. The promise of a future for the two of them together. Grady noticed that his ruined clothing had been cleaned up off the floor and his apartment looked tidy. Even with the day's crappy beginning, this was turning out to be a stellar Friday.

His search for food came up empty. Since he'd missed breakfast and lunch, his stomach was making loud complaints. He was not cooking, which meant he had to go out whether or not he wanted to. Then he remembered his truck was at the station, so he figured he could pop in at the diner. Grady called Jesse and put his order in. By the time he walked over to the station and drove back to the diner, his food should be ready.

Plan in place, Grady grabbed his keys and walked out the door. He felt lighter than he had in months though he was on medical leave for the next week. *Love.* Ben had used that word in the note, confirming Grady meant more to him than a hookup. He walked into the back parking lot of the police station and received a few pats on the back from his fellow officers as he walked by. Their acceptance meant a lot.

A few minutes later he pulled into the diner parking lot to pick up his supper. He walked through the doors, not even trying to hide the smile on his face. He was happy and looking forward to his future here in Brighton. It amazed Grady how one event managed to change his view. Moments later that thought came back to haunt him.

He stood frozen inside the diner's front door staring at a table in the corner. Four people were sitting there; Bo, Travis, Ben, and an unknown male who practically sat in Ben's lap. In that instant he realized the pain he suffered by the twin betrayals of his father and Tony were nothing compared to this.

Love, he'd said love...why, if he was leaving me to do this?

Grady snapped out of it the moment his eyes met Ben's and he walked up to the counter where Sarah greeted him. "Good evening, honey. I hear you had a bit of excitement last night. How you holding up?"

"Hey, Sarah. I'm holding up okay. I called in an order. Spoke to Jesse." He needed to get out of here. *Don't look over. Don't breathe too fast. Shit, am I shaking?*

"I'll go get it for you, dear. I'm glad you're okay." Sarah looked like she wanted to ask more questions, but she walked away.

Grady smiled, hoping to make it out of there with his dignity. He should've known that wouldn't happen. He tried to pretend he couldn't hear Bo call his name until the man was close to hollering and Grady had to turn and acknowledge them.

"Grady, come on over, buddy." Buddy? Since when did he rate "buddy"? He remembered Bo saying the same thing to him last night as they waited for the paramedics.

Grady had no other choice but to walk toward the man he loved, who'd finally put the last nail in the coffin of their secret relationship. He reached the table and stood to the side before saying, "Hi, guys. Having a nice dinner?"

"Why don't you join us?" Travis asked, as always, thinking of others.

Grady glanced over at Ben, who revealed nothing, not shame or guilt, nothing. He had his answer. The stranger reached for Ben's hand and spoke up. "No, we're on a date. I'm sure he wouldn't want to ruin that." He had to admit the guy was a beautiful man. Slender body, shoulder-length blond hair, blue eyes, and pouty lips. Nothing like the plain oaf Grady thought himself to be.

He stepped farther away from Ben and turned to Travis. "That's nice of you, Travis, but I think I'll go back to my apartment."

"How's your arm?" Bo asked, his eyes flicking between Ben and Grady.

"Sore, but on the mend. I'll be good as new in no time," he answered.

"That was a real brave thing you did," Travis praised with a hint of awe in his voice. "I'm glad you aren't more seriously hurt."

"Grady," Sarah hollered from the counter. "Your food is ready."

Hallelujah, Sarah. I've got to get out of here before I lose my shit.

"Well, you have a good night." Grady turned and walked away. He dared to take one more glance at Ben, and at that moment, his date took the opportunity to kiss Ben right on the lips. Grady had to admit, Ben looked surprised, but that didn't change anything. He hightailed it to the counter where Sarah waited with his food.

"Thank you," Grady said as he placed his money on the counter and reached for his to-go container with his right hand. He hissed in pain and pulled his arm in close to his side. He wouldn't be using that arm at full strength for a while.

"Are you okay?" Sarah asked; her voice filled with concern. "Do you need anything?"

Grady was about to answer when Bo appeared at his side. "Heard your hiss all the way over there. You okay?"

"Yep. I have to remember to use my left arm for a while." Grady smiled, trying to steer Bo from continuing this conversation. Grady needed to get his ass out of here.

Bo looked at him for a long moment before asking, "Are you sure everything's okay?" Grady got the impression Bo was no longer talking about his arm. Bo glanced back to his table and they both watched as Ben's date wrapped his arms around him.

Grady took a deep breath, picked up his dinner with his left hand, turned to Bo, and stated with all the positive cheer he could muster, "It will be in time. Good night, Bo." Then with his head held high, he left the diner and drove the few minutes it took to get to the hardware store.

After purchasing what he needed to make sure he had no uninvited guests showing up in his apartment, he returned home. It only took ten minutes to change the lock on his front door, which surprised him given his injured arm, but he was motivated. Once he completed the task, he sat on the couch to calm himself and think things through.

His mind raced in a million directions. Should he confront Ben? Why did he lie and say he wasn't ready to make their relationship public when that date was public as hell? Should Grady say nothing and carry on as if it didn't happen? He was confident which one Ben would choose, but Grady had enough self-worth to realize he deserved better.

He deserved love and respect, and he refused to be anyone's dirty little secret. What had he been thinking allowing this to carry on so long? Was he that desperate for love? This wasn't the type of man he wanted to be. Today was the day that that behavior ended.

He picked up his cell phone and called Chief Graham to inform him he'd be out of town for a few days. He was on leave, but he didn't want something to come up and for no one to know where he'd gone. Then he called his best friend Tristan, who'd been his buddy since they met in fourth grade. Grady could always count on him.

Tristan was one of the most beautiful men Grady had ever met on the inside and out. With short wavy red hair, chiselled features, and striking green eyes that revealed his every emotion, Tristan was a keeper. He might be only five-foot-four but his outrageous personality made him appear bigger. While they'd never been intimate together, they were as close as any two people could be.

On the second ring Tristan's excited voice rushed over the line. "Hey, I haven't talked to you in months. You left me behind here in Dallas to fend for myself."

"Leave you behind? Never, it's been a hectic couple months here."

"Don't worry, I'll always forgive you. Now tell me why your voice sounds as if somebody shot your dog." Tristan's uncanny ability to sense when something was up was spot-on and why would this time be any different?

For the next forty-five minutes Grady laid out everything for Tristan: Tony, his father, the job, the screw-up at Bo's house, the disciplinary hearing, returning to work, and the shooting. But most importantly, he told his friend about Ben. Tristan was the first and only person Grady had ever told, and it felt good to get it out in the open, as if a weight had been lifted.

His friend was silent and Grady imagined him biting his fingernails as he thought through everything he'd been told.

"So, any pearls of wisdom?" Grady asked.

"Have you packed?" Tristan asked back; he knew Grady so well.

"Not yet."

"Well, get a move on. I'll get the spare bedroom ready for you," Tristan declared as if it was a forgone conclusion Grady would be going to his house. "You'll get through this. You're stronger than you think. I promise you."

And that's why Grady loved Tristan: he never let him down.

Grady had sworn he'd never return to Dallas, but it was that or beating the shit out of Ben for playing him like a fool.

Grady packed a bag for a few days. He needed this distance to clear his head. He'd come back to Brighton with a new attitude and game plan.

Ben Mason was no longer his concern and never would be again.

Chapter Three

Hours later Ben raced to Grady's apartment; he ran up the stairs and put his key in the lock, but nothing happened. It didn't turn. He tried again, but it didn't budge. Then he noticed that the door handle was silver and not gold. He'd been locked out. Ben knocked but there was no answer. Fear, so deep his bones were cold, like nothing he'd ever felt before, flooded his body from head to toe. He'd lost Grady.

He kept trying for over ten minutes until old Mrs. Elmer came out of her apartment. "He's not there."

Ben stopped and asked, "Did he say where he went?"

"Saw him leave about an hour ago with a bag in his hand," she answered.

Gone? Grady couldn't be, could he? Shit. Ben had lost the man he loved.

As he absently thanked Mrs. Elmer, a familiar truck rumbled into the parking lot. Bo. His brother sat in his vehicle and waited for Ben to come over to the open driver's window.

"Whatcha doing here?" Ben asked in as calm a voice as he could muster.

"I thought this was where I'd find you. Get in." Bo's face appeared drawn and tight. Ben decided not to mess with his big brother when he was in this kind of mood.

Ben walked around the back of the truck and climbed into the passenger seat. Bo put the truck into drive and rolled through the alley. With unerring accuracy he followed the route Ben had always taken after he'd hid his truck and walked to Grady's. As if to confirm his suspicion that Bo knew something, his brother pulled in beside Ben's truck and parked. *Shit.*

"You want to tell me what's going on?" Bo asked.

"What do you mean?" The moment the words came out of his mouth he regretted them. Playing dumb with his cop older brother never worked well for Ben.

Bo took a deep breath and sighed. "Want to play it this way, do you?"

"No, but I'm not sure it's safe to tell you." Ben admitted as he straightened his back, squared his shoulders, and prepared to tell someone his secret.

Bo looked worried. "What's wrong? Is Grady leading you on? Is he pressuring you for a relationship?" It didn't surprise him that his brother didn't think this was his fault.

"No. Grady's innocent in all this. He's done nothing wrong." Ben swore he'd let none of the blame fall onto Grady.

"All of this? All of what? Talk, Ben, or I'll call the family in," Bo ordered, and Ben took it as a serious threat. If clan Mason got involved, whoever was stalking him and Grady might find out that Ben had talked, and kill his love.

Ben turned to face his brother. "This is important, Bo. Swear not to say a word until I figure out what to do. Lives are at stake."

Bo's face changed from concerned to stern; he was in his official cop mode. "Tell me everything."

Ben began with the best day he'd had in over three years, the day he met Grady Reynolds at his family barbeque. He didn't stop until he brought Bo to the moment Ben began pounding on Grady's door. Ben left nothing out: not his love, the fear when he received the first letter a few days after the barbeque, or the first night they'd made love. He revealed his desperate longing to be with Grady and to make everything right for the pain he'd caused the man.

Bo sat listening, his face inscrutable. By the end of his story, Ben was emotionally drained, and he buried his aching head in his hands, groaning. How was he going to fix this? How was he going to keep Grady safe if he couldn't stay away from him?

Bo's heavy hand came to rest on Ben's shoulder before he said, "We'll figure this out, brother. Then Grady can hand you your ass for not telling him, and putting him through this hell. Now let's go to your house and you can show me those letters and pictures. Then we call in reinforcements."

"But I don't know who's stalking us. If whoever is behind this finds out I've said something, they'll go after Grady. I can't risk that." He refused to put Grady in any more danger than he was in already.

"We'll only bring in people who we can be certain aren't involved. Now let's get going."

"But what about Grady?" Ben asked. "I have no idea where he went."

"He's out of town for a few days. Dave told me when I popped in to have a chat, you know, cop to chief. Maybe it's good Grady's out of town. It'll give him a chance to calm a bit. Christ, you should have told me. I would have never insisted you go out with Mr. Handsy."

"It's not like I don't already understand I'm a complete asshole. I don't need you to confirm it," Ben grumbled as he glared at his brother.

"I call 'em like I see 'em, little bro. You should have told Grady, he's a police officer. He's not defenseless, and he'll find it offensive that you assumed he was."

"Hindsight is twenty-twenty. It was the only thing I could think to do to protect him. I haven't felt this way in so long, never thought I'd be able to again."

"I understand the pain you went through, Ben. It's time this bastard found out what it feels like to mess with a Mason."

***

Hours later, Ben's small living room was overtaken by a group of people he trusted with this sensitive information. His dad, Police Chief Dave Graham, his uncle, Fire Chief Roger Mason, his cousin Gabe, his brother Bo, and the members of the Sentinel team. The only reason he didn't include his uncles and aunts in the meeting was to keep it as low-key as possible. Soon enough, they'd find out through the family members in attendance. Once again, Ben recounted everything that had happened to the group, and he hoped to hell he hadn't made a deadly mistake. The important thing was for them to keep this knowledge as quiet as possible until they could figure out who was threatening them.

"I wish I knew why this person is so against Grady and me being together," Ben questioned out loud, not to anyone in particular.

"Brother, I hate to break it to you, but after everything, I'm sure you're not together now."

Ben shot Bo a dirty look, not needing reminding of the shit he'd caused. "Can you do or say something productive?"

"Well, it's obvious this is personal. Someone has a personal stake in this," Bo said as he leaned back in his chair.

"Any exes we should be aware of?" Dante asked. Shannon worked away on her laptop; Vincent, Shadow, Spider, and Coop stood along the far wall.

"I haven't heard from mine in over three years," Ben explained.

"Date anyone since then?" Spider asked.

"No one." And how depressing was that?

"And Grady?" Spider asked.

"He dated a guy back in Dallas. They broke up when Grady found him in bed with someone else." Ben understood Grady had told him that in confidence, but if it helped find out who was behind this, he'd apologize later.

"Tony," Chief Graham stated, surprising Ben.

"How do you know his name?" Ben asked in shock.

"The guy came to Grady's disciplinary hearing. He said he was there to support Grady," Dave answered.

"Shit, and I couldn't show my face in case I was being watched. Grady must've thought I didn't care." Ben stood and paced. Christ, Grady had his ex sniffing around.

"Easy, little brother," Bo said as he squeezed Ben's shoulder. "He'll understand once he knows the truth. Grady doesn't strike me as a person who wouldn't give someone a second chance."

"I thought you said he'd hand me my ass?"

"Oh, he will. Then after he cools off and thinks it through, I'm sure he'll realize why you did what you did."

Ben prayed his brother had some sort of insight because if Ben lost Grady he didn't know what he'd do. He loved him, and he couldn't picture a future without Grady in it.

"His father screwed him over," Shannon announced, never looking away from her screen. "Detective Reynolds appears to have made life difficult for his son. Denied transfers by supervisors in Detective Reynolds's bowling league to start."

"How do you know that?" Ben asked.

Shannon looked up for a split second. "It's what I do." Then she spun her laptop around so Ben could see a group of older men standing in matching bowling shirts with a trophy being held high. "This dark-haired man in the center is Grady's father."

"Reynolds had the nerve to contact me and warn me away from hiring Grady," Dave stated with a slight growl. "I looked through Grady's file and everything looked fine, nothing suspicious in his history. So I thanked the detective and called Grady to let him know he had the position. I never liked being told what to do."

"His father wasn't too happy that Grady came out, and did everything in his power to hurt him," Ben explained. Another tidbit he hoped Grady forgave him for sharing.

"Hard-core nasty shit," Shannon grumbled but kept typing.

Ben wasn't sure of the extent of gay bashing Grady had gone through; Ben had learned what Grady chose to share. Now Ben felt as if there were a lot of things he wasn't aware of or hadn't bothered to ask. He swore if Grady forgave him he'd learn everything about the amazing man.

"We will set up surveillance around Grady's apartment. See who's hanging around. It will be more difficult when's he's working considering he'll be in his cruiser," Vincent commented from his spot against the back wall.

"When he returns from medical leave, I can have him team up with another officer," Dave suggested.

"Team him up with me," Bo offered. "I can keep an eye on him."

"I'll take the letters and photos back to the compound and have Matthew take a crack at them. See if we can get something off the paper," Shannon said as she packed up her laptop, gathered the information into an evidence bag, and then stood.

"We'll have Vincent and Shadow do surveillance. Shannon and Matthew will dig through everything from both of your pasts, and Grady's family. Coop and I will go over any leads, and Spider will keep an eye out for anyone new showing up in town," Dante explained.

"We'll probably have to draw whoever's doing this out into the open," Coop stated.

"We aren't putting Grady in any danger. If you need bait, you can use me, but not him." Ben's voice came out a lot harsher than he'd intended, but he was adamant.

"We must use the both of you. If the subject gets rattled by seeing the two of you together, that's exactly what might bring him out into the open." Spider explained, as if this was no big deal. Ben understood that this was what they did for a living, and that this was considered normal to them.

"How long will Grady be out of town?" Spider asked.

"He said he'd be back on Friday sometime," Dave answered.

"Okay, that gives us three days to come up with a plan. I want everything in place by then," Dante ordered before heading for Ben's front door. "We'll meet at the compound at eight tomorrow morning to put a plan into place."

"Just so we're clear. Protect Grady at all times." Ben's voice shook but he wanted to make sure everyone understood that there was never a question of who came first. "If there is ever a situation where you have to decide between covering me or Grady, you go with Grady."

Ben's father, Henry, stood and crossed the room toward him. Ben was falling apart. The man he loved hated him, someone was stalking them, and Grady had taken off to god knows where. Now this team was planning an all-out defense to protect the one person in this world who had the ability to destroy him.

His dad wrapped his arms around Ben and hugged him close. "This will work out, son."

"I hope you're right, Dad. I'm not sure I can survive another loss," Ben muttered. It had taken over three years and an amazing man to bring Ben back to the land of the living; he doubted he could do it again.

***

Grady leaned back in his chair staring at the piece of paper in his hand. He'd crumpled it into a ball and then flattened it back out four times. Love…never have to be apart…bullshit! Anger and pain raced through his body yet again. And when he thought he'd calmed the deep sense of betrayal, it came crashing back and tore at his heart.

Tristan's apartment represented a safe harbor, and he was thankful for his best friend's generosity. Grady planned on lying low for a few days, and considering he was back in Dallas, he had no intention of wandering the streets and chance running into members of his family. He missed his younger brother but couldn't risk visiting him. That was all Grady needed, a run-in with his father.

Grady folded Ben's note and shoved it back into his wallet. He didn't understand why he was keeping it, but he couldn't bring himself to throw it away.

"Here we go. Tea for two and two for tea." Tristan sang as he set the tray on the flowered coffee table. Grady loved Tristan and his over-the-top personality and behavior. From his bright, red toenails and colorful clothing to his curly red hair and deep blue guyliner, Tristan was one of a kind, always caring for others, loyal beyond question, and fearless to a fault when defending others.

Grady turned his chair to face his friend, who sat on the couch before picking up his mug of tea. Grady brought his tea to his lips and let the chamomile filled his senses then took a sip of the sweet goodness. He took a deep breath and let the peace in the room settle over him.

"Better?" Tristan asked, his usual smile in place. The man made you comfortable without even trying.

"Getting there, but I doubt I'll be anywhere near normal again for some time," Grady admitted and he could hear the defeat in his own voice. This was not the person he wanted to be.

"Love sucks, plain and simple. The moment you think everything is perfect it blows up. That's why I'll always be single." Tristan used his normal overdramatic tone. Grady appreciated that Tristan was trying to cheer him up, but he doubted that was possible. "There are many gorgeous fish in the sea, and now you get to explore them. Free to explore your sexuality and be no one's secret."

"Yeah, I should call Tony to apologize for the way I treated him when we were dating," Grady lamented.

"Nothing excuses Tony's messing around on you," Tristan was quick to say.

"No, nothing excuses that. But forcing him to be a secret before I came out. It wasn't fair to him." Grady now understood what it felt like, and it sucked.

"You deserve better than to be someone's secret after everything you've been through to break free of your family. But are you sure there's not an explanation for this?" Tristan asked, a look of hope on his face.

Grady smiled at his friend. Tristan always tried to find the good, but there wasn't one in this situation. "What can explain the games he played with me? Leading me on, saying he wasn't ready to have our relationship out in the open when he was dating other guys the entire time."

"Guy. It was only one guy."

"That we're aware of."

"True. But I see the love shining in your eyes when you talk about him. Any chance of working things out?"

"I love him. I will for a long time, but I can't live with his betrayal. My family and Tony betraying me was enough." Grady voice cracked. He'd been taught a long time ago to keep your emotions to yourself.

Tristan picked up his tea and took a sip. Grady could see the wheels turning in his friend's mind. He was deep in thought and that worried Grady. You never knew what Tristan might come up with.

"We have three days to come up with a game plan."

"We?"

"You think I'm letting you go back to that town without me, you're crazy. You still have that extra room in your apartment. I'll stay there," Tristan announced as if it was normal.

"But there's no furniture."

"I'll get that, I don't need much."

Grady looked at Tristan's coifed hair and waxed legs and wanted to disagree, but he needed his best friend by his side. "You want to come to small town America? I thought you liked the big city life."

"It's getting old. Besides, after everything you've told me, how can I not check Brighton out?" Tristan's face became serious, and he stared into his tea before continuing. "I think we both need our best friends around us right now."

Grady sat forward in his chair and inspected Tristan. "What's wrong?"

Tristan's head snapped up as if for a moment there he forgot he wasn't alone. His glowing smile went back into place, but Grady had seen enough; something was wrong. “It’s nothing. I need some time with my best friend.”

“Tristan?”

He took a deep breath and mumbled, “Stavros has been dropping by.”

Every alarm bell Grady had rang in warning, Stavros was the last person he wanted around Tristan. The man wouldn’t take no for an answer. “How long has this been going on?”

“Since you left town.”

Shit. “Why didn’t you call me?”

“You were concentrating on starting your new life. I didn’t want to bother you.”

“Bother me, we’ve been best friends since childhood. Nothing you could say or do would bother me. We swore to take care of each other. Whether I’m in Dallas or Brighton makes no difference.” Grady stood and joined Tristan on the couch, then wrapped his arms around the smaller man, who was shaking. “Let’s get you packed up. We can spend a few days relaxing in Galveston before heading back to Brighton.”

Grady had no doubt Tristan would take his work with him. After all, Tristan Thomas was a well-known author of romance novels and was able to work anywhere as long as he had a connection to the Internet.

“By the Gulf?” Tristan asked.

“We’ll unwind on the beach. What do you say?”

Tristan’s face brightened to its usual happy state, and he nodded his head. “Sounds perfect.”

***

The warm sand slid in between his toes as Grady lounged back in his beach chair and watched Tristan bouncing through the waves. His exuberance for life was contagious. Galveston Island would be the perfect place to disappear for a few days. If Grady didn’t think too hard, he could imagine he was on a holiday, instead of forced medical leave coupled with unbearable heartbreak.

For what had to be the hundredth time today, Grady thought about Ben. Was Ben looking for him? Did he miss Grady? Did he care about what happened? Questions he'd never have the answers to considering he never intended to have a personal conversation with Ben again. But, they would have to deal with each other on a professional level since cops and firefighters crossed paths regularly.

Grady was loath to admit how much he missed Ben. Though they only had the opportunity to be together a short time, he felt the loss though he never truly had him in the first place. His thoughts kept circling back to the same conclusion: the man he loved had used him and tossed him aside.

His arm throbbed as he reached for his iced tea on the table between his and Tristan's chairs. Grady pulled his arm back and rubbed his bandaged bicep. His injury was healing but much too slowly for his liking. He had a follow-up appointment with Dr. Green scheduled for Friday afternoon. He hoped the doc intended to give him good news, and he'd be able to go back to work soon. Grady couldn't help but be nervous that he'd only returned to work for one week before being shot and forced to take time off again. Would he lose his position?

Emerald green eyes flashed through Grady's memory, causing him to groan in frustration. Visions of Ben popped into his mind unbidden, and no matter how hard he tried he couldn't wipe the memory of the man away.

"What was that deep groan for?" Tristan asked as he approached, water dripping everywhere.

Grady grabbed a towel from the back of his chair and threw it at his friend. "Just thinking."

"I thought we agreed not to think for the next two days?" Tristan questioned with a grin before sitting in the lounge chair across from him. "So tell me what's bothering you, or should I try to guess."

"I can't get him out of my mind."

"It will take time, Grady. You love him."

"Loved," Grady argued.

"Oh, I doubt that." Tristan grinned as he leaned over the table toward Grady. "I'm not saying what Ben did can ever be excused, but I'm also aware how hard it is to find love. Real love."

"This wasn't real love for him. He used me," Grady argued.

"Okay, okay. I will only say this once, and I'll never bother you again about it."

"I doubt that." Grady laughed.

"Yeah, you're right, but I will still say it. After everything you've told me and after reading that note he left you, I believe he loves you. You need to find out what he's hiding."

"Hello. Me. He's hiding me from the entire town of Brighton. Maybe he's embarrassed of me. Maybe he doesn't do relationships. Whatever, it doesn't matter anymore. I'm done."

"Ben loves you. Give him a chance to explain."

"How can you be sticking up for someone you've never met? I'm your friend, you should be backing me up." Grady realized he wasn't mad at Tristan, but his anger over the entire mess was bubbling over.

"I'm not sticking up for him. What I want is for you to be happy. That's all I've ever wanted for you." Tristan's eyes misted over.

Grady's anger slipped away. Tristan always wanted the best for him. And even though it sometimes annoyed him, he always saw the good in people.

"I'll think it over," he acquiesced before hugging his friend.

"Thank you. I love you. You're my brother."

"I love you too, Tristan. Now, why don't you tell me everything Stavros has done since I've been gone?" Grady needed to get the facts if he was to protect his best friend.

Grady saw Tristan cringe at the mere mention of the man's name and felt his anger return. Stavros and Tristan had dated for a short time over a year ago and the man had become possessive and obsessed with Tristan. When his friend realized this, he broke up with the guy but Stavros didn't take it well. Grady couldn't prove the bastard had something to do with the attack that put Tristan in the hospital, but he swore the man had been involved.

"It hasn't been so bad."

"Tristan." Grady drew out his friend's name as he reached for his hand. "Tell me."

"I've seen him at the places I go to write. The park, that coffee shop off John Street that we used to go to, the library downtown, and that bookstore by my home."

"Did he come by your apartment?"

"Yes, but I didn't answer the door." Tristan sighed and lowered his head. "I'm such a coward."

"No you're not. You did the smart thing. He's twice your size and is known to be violent. I never want you to face him alone." Grady worried what Stavros might do if he ever got a hold of Tristan.

"Trust me, I won't ever put myself in that position," Tristan swore before picking up his glass of fruit juice and taking a long drink.

"You'll be safe in Brighton. I'll put out the word to keep an eye out for Stavros."

"Why would anyone else care?" Tristan asked, looking confused.

"You'll understand when I get you there. It's a special place. They look after each other."

"I hope you're right because Stavros has more money than brains. I think he believes I belong to him. Christ, I didn't even sleep with him," Tristan grumbled. "Now let's get back to this mini vacation and forget about the outside world, at least until we have to leave Friday morning."

"Deal," Grady agreed before leaning back in his chair and turning his face toward the bright sun. "Reality will come crashing in soon enough."

Chapter Four

They were almost back to Brighton. The last two days had been exactly what Grady needed: rest and relaxation. His arm continued to heal, and the pain was subsiding, so he hoped to be back on duty soon. Ben had called him over the past three days, but Grady never answered and refused to listen to his messages. Chief Graham had called to confirm that Grady planned on returning today, and that Dr. Green's receptionist confirmed his afternoon appointment.

Tristan's head swiveled left and right as they drove down Main Street. If he kept it up, he'd give himself whiplash. Grady had to admit Brighton was a beautiful town. The shops on Main Street featured carved masonry, tall pillars, grand entrances, outdoor eateries, large window displays, mature trees, and a park covered in flowers with a gazebo at its center. Brighton was the quintessential small town.

Tristan wiggled around in the passenger's seat like a puppy on his ride home from the shelter. "This place is amazing," Tristan gushed from the passenger seat. "Is that the police station?"

Grady looked over at the familiar brick building and smiled. "Yeah, it is."

"Is that the firehouse where Ben works?"

He didn't bother to look; Grady knew the firehouse was across the street from the police station. "Yup."

If Tristan noticed the brisk answers, he gave no sign and continued staring at the firehouse. "Um, remind me what Ben looks like."

"Why?"

"'Cause I think he's standing out front staring at us."

Grady couldn't stop himself from looking, no matter how hard he tried. Sure enough, the man invading his dreams every night stood in his uniform, blond hair shining in the sun. He tracked Grady as he drove by. Neither waved nor acknowledged the other, and Grady carried on as if his heart wasn't breaking all over again. He wondered how long it would take before the sight of the man didn't gut him.

"Yep, that's him."

"Wow, he's fiiine."

"Not helping, Tristan." Grady's voice came out sharp and hard.

"Sorry," Tristan mumbled.

Grady took a deep breath. "I'm the one who's sorry. I shouldn't take my anger out on you. It will be rough for the next little while."

Tristan smiled wide, reached over, and took Grady's hand. "No matter what, I'm here to help you through this. I love you and you're stuck with me. Never ever would I abandon my brother." Tristan had the knack for calming people, and his touch helped Grady regain his control. Grady accepted he'd be seeing Ben, it's not that big of a town, but that didn't make it any easier.

"Here we are, home sweet home," Grady said as he pulled into the parking lot behind his building. Tristan looked as though he was going to burst out of the truck, his excitement was that palpable. One of a kind.

"Oh, it's a stately old building. How many apartments? Does it have high ceilings and wood floors?" Tristan asked.

"Six. And you know it. Wainscoting and trim everywhere," Grady confirmed.

As soon as he parked, Tristan was out of the truck and spinning in a circle looking at everything. Grady laughed and pulled their bags out of the back of the truck. Tristan raced back to the truck and grabbed his messenger bag before following Grady up the stairs to his apartment. He saw the envelope lying on the floor the moment he opened the door.

"What's this?" Tristan asked as he leaned over and picked up the envelope. "It has your name on it."

Grady set the bags on the floor and took the envelope from his friend. Sure enough, in fancy, black script was his name. Grady threw it on the coffee table; he'd get to it after he unpacked.

"There's the spare bedroom," Grady said as he pointed to the door across the room.

"Sweet," Tristan cheered before grabbing his bag and disappearing into the spare bedroom.

Having the guy around lifted Grady's spirits. He went to his bedroom and unpacked, then he stepped in the bathroom to put his shaving kit away when he noticed the second razor lying on the vanity. Ben's razor; he'd left it when they first started seeing each other. Grady picked it up, examined it, unsure what he was looking for, but as strange as it sounded, he couldn't bear to throw it away. Instead, he placed it on the top shelf of his medicine cabinet, feeling like a complete idiot the entire time.

He let out a deep breath and walked back into his bedroom to put his dirty clothes in the hamper. It didn't take long and soon he found himself staring out of the bedroom window, seeing nothing.

"Grady?" Tristan whispered from across the room. "You okay?"

Grady turned from the window and looked at his friend through blurry vision. He lifted his hand and wiped the wetness from his cheek. When had he started to cry? Seconds later he found his arms full of a squirming Tristan.

"It will be okay, I promise. I'll do whatever it takes to help you through this."

Grady held his best friend tight; he could always count on Tristan. Sometimes he thought life played a joke on them because it would have been easier if they were physically attracted to each other. Then neither of them would have to go through all this relationship bullshit.

"Everything will work out. One way or another." Grady knew it was a platitude, but he figured, fake it 'til you make it.

"Well, you'll always have me."

"And I'm thankful for that," Grady said as he let Tristan go and wiped his face. *Keep this up and they'll pull my man card.* "Now, let's get furniture and fixings for your new room. Do you need a special place for your writing?"

"I think I'll invest in a small desk for over by the bay window that looks out on Main Street. It gets lots of light and I can open the windows to catch the breeze."

"Sounds like a plan. My doctor's appointment isn't until four this afternoon. So that will give us enough time to find most of what you'll need, and get to my appointment. After, we'll stop off at the diner for supper."

"Perfect, give me a second to put on my new jeans, they're purple," Tristan gushed before racing into his bedroom. Grady couldn't help but smile. He was thankful. He doubted that he'd have made it through the last couple days without his friend, but the time had come to stand on his own two feet. He wouldn't allow his true feelings to come to the surface; he had to carry on as if his heart were still in one piece.

***

Vincent watched as Grady and his new companion left the apartment. The small man's flaming red

hair was only surpassed by his bright purple jeans encasing his tight ass. Vincent couldn't make out the little cutie's eye color but Vincent imagined they'd be green. His smooth pale skin seemed to shine in the sunlight and stood in such contrast with Vincent's coloring of his Navajo ancestors. He imagined how soft that guy's skin would be, and what it'd feel like under Vincent's work-roughened hands.

He pulled the binoculars away from his face and watched as Shadow stepped out of the van they'd parked across the street from Grady's apartment building. Shadow blended into the crowd as he followed the two along the street. Vincent informed Dante, his team leader, that they now had an extra person of interest to watch over. Matthew and Shannon, the two tech experts of the team, had already tried to identify him by the pictures they'd sent when Grady had arrived home.

Vincent ran his fingers through his hair and pulled it into a ponytail at the base of head. This new guy might be a problem. For all they knew, he could be the one sending the letters. Vincent hoped not; he had plans for the little sparrow.

***

Ben watched as the man he needed to hold walked across the street with another man. They'd walked into Harold's Furniture Store over a half hour ago and were still in there. *What did Grady need with new furniture?* Then it hit Ben right in the stomach; the unidentified man was moving in with Grady. It might be Grady's ex Tony. Ben couldn't breathe. He stepped back through the bay doors leading into the fire station. He made it to his locker before crashing hard on the bench and lowering his head in between his knees. He'd heard Tony had been there for Grady throughout his discipline hearing. Yet another thing Ben had been forced to miss because of their stalker.

He'd lost Grady. Plain and simple.

"I guess you've seen them then." Gabe's voice broke the silence in the room, making Ben jump. "Sorry, buddy. I didn't mean to scare you."

"It's okay. And yes, I've seen Grady's friend." Ben tried to keep the anger out of his voice, but he wasn't successful.

Gabe sat beside him and wrapped his big arm around Ben's shoulder. "His name is Tristan, and he's visiting from Dallas."

Ben's head snapped up to look at Gabe. "How do you know that?"

"I met them walking across the street on my way here. I know you don't want to hear it, but he seems nice. Strange, but nice all the same."

"Great, he has a new guy living with him and he's *nice*." At least it wasn't Tony. Grady deserved better. Question was, was he better than Tony?

"Yeah, said they picked out a mattress, sheet sets, and dressers."

"I don't care what they bought him. Don't you see? I've lost him." Why would Gabe rub this in? He understood how much Grady meant to him.

"Oh, I don't think you should be jumping to any conclusions, considering they ordered all of it for Grady's spare bedroom." Gabe looked at Ben with a smirk on his face.

"The spare bedroom?" Ben's voice was hushed as he thought through the possibility he'd been wrong in his assumption.

"Yes."

"They aren't sharing a bed?" It made Ben sick to think it, let alone say it out loud.

"They aren't. Grady introduced Tristan as being his best friend since childhood. They appear to be close but not in a romantic way."

Thank God.

Ben swore a weight had been lifted off his shoulders. Grady hadn't replaced him, at least not yet. Ben still had a chance to explain why he did what he did, and then pray that Grady forgave him.

"I thought that bit of information might make you calm down," Gabe said with a hint of humor in his voice.

"You wait, once I get everything worked out, there will be payback," Ben groused before he stood and shut his locker.

"When are you planning to tell Grady the truth?" Gabe asked.

"Once he gets back to work. It will be easier to get Grady over to Bo's house without somebody noticing. The hell of it is, he may find out the truth and not forgive me either way."

Gabe was quiet, deep in thought for a moment before he answered. "I don't think it'll be easy, but I believe the two of you will end up together."

"How can you be so sure?" Ben asked.

"I've seen the way Grady looks at you before any of this came to light. There was love in his eyes, and need. I wondered if there was something between you two. You seemed to be attuned to each other in a room. Saw it happen a few times at the diner."

"I haven't been keeping my emotions hidden. Considering what's at stake, I should've tried harder." Ben huffed as he ran his fingers through his hair in agitation. "I've received another letter, it had more pictures of Grady with it."

"When did you get the letter?" Gabe asked.

"This morning. Found it lying on my front porch when I left for work. I dropped it off at Police Chief Graham's office before I came to work."

"What did it say?" Gabe asked.

Ben sat on the bench and took a deep breath. "That he knew Grady and I were seeing each other, and that I must be punished."

"Shit, what's the chief suggesting we do now?"

Before Ben could answer, the fire bells rang, bringing both men running from the lockers and into the truck bays. They donned their gear and jumped up onto the truck and into the backseat. Moments later they were on their way out of the bay, sirens wailing their warning. They didn't have to drive far as they pulled up in front of a three-story apartment building. Smoke billowed from one of the third-story apartment's windows. The moment the fire truck came to a stop Ben jumped off and strapped on his self-contained breathing apparatus.

Chief Mason gathered his team around him and spoke. “I want Ben, Gabe, and Roy to check for any trapped people while the rest of us get the hoses set.”

Without giving a second thought to their own safety, the three ran into the burning building. The smoke clawed at him the moment he stepped into the building’s foyer. Ben knew if he wasn’t wearing his breathing apparatus he’d soon be overcome by the carbon monoxide. Countless people perished every year from smoke inhalation, not the flames of the fire.

Ben took the stairs to his left up to the second level, where he saw the fire was fully engaged. Gabe radioed from the third floor that the fire was working its way down the hall, and Roy radioed that the first floor had minimal fire but was smoke-filled. The entire time they remained in radio contact to make sure the three of them remained safe. Ben could barely see his hands out in front of his face as he used them to follow the wall leading him forward. He noticed the glow from the flames at the far end of the hallway. He stopped in front of apartment 2A and laid his palm on the door. It was cool to the touch, so he tried to open it but the door was locked. Ben took a few steps back and kicked the door open; the sound of crashing wood was swallowed up by the roar of the flames.

After a quick search he found the apartment was empty and went on to apartment 2C. The fire appeared to be contained in that apartment, but he didn’t know for how long. He moved down the hall and found the door to 2B was unlocked. When he stepped inside, thick smoke filled the room much the same as the other apartments, but this time there was a glaring difference. A tall man stood in the center of the small living room, his face obscured by the oxygen mask covering his features.

That should’ve been Ben’s first clue that something wasn’t right. But he was so determined to make sure the rooms were clear and everyone had been brought to safety that he didn’t stop to process why the guy had on an oxygen mask and was standing there like he was waiting.

Calmly, Ben went up to the man to check if he was okay and to lead him out of the apartment building only to find himself being shoved to the ground, breaking a coffee table on his way down. Before he could regain his footing the man kicked Ben viciously. Every time he fought to get up he was beaten back down until soon Ben stopped moving. The stranger ripped Ben's mask off his face and then leaned over to whisper in Ben's ear. "I warned you," he hissed before storming out of the room and leaving Ben to his fate.

Ben tried to push himself up with his arms as he spit blood out onto the floor, but the shooting pain from his ribs made it slow going. He was positive he had a few broken ribs, at minimum, but that was the least of his concerns if he couldn't get out of the apartment. Ben didn't have time to puzzle out how their stalker had found him, or how he knew Ben was working this fire. He had to make it out of here alive.

He reached for his oxygen mask but it was of no use to him, the rigging had been cut. On his hands and knees, he began the painful journey to the front door. Ben made it halfway across the floor before his arms gave way and he fell yet again. He struggled for every breath he took. His world was dimming with each passing second. He couldn't call for help because his communication device was in pieces, crushed under his attacker's feet.

As Ben lay on the floor, his breaths becoming shallow, he knew he didn't have long before he succumbed to the smoke. His throat and lungs burned with every hard-fought breath. He envisioned Grady, and wished for so many things to be different, but knew he'd lost his chance.

A single tear escaped as Ben gave in to the darkness.

***

Gabe came barreling up the stairs in search of Ben, Roy at his side. They were outside with the survivors they'd found in the building when Ben stopped communicating with them. Brighton FD hadn't lost a single firefighter in its many years; no way in hell they were starting now. The smoke was thick and Gabe swore he saw someone run past him, but whoever it was they were gone. The first apartment had already had its door kicked open. Nonetheless, they searched all the rooms, but came up empty. Flames were climbing up the walls and onto the ceiling at the far end of the hallway. They were running out of time.

"The fire's moving fast, Gabe," Roy radioed, mirroring what Gabe had thought.

Both turned their attention to the next apartment over, where the door was closed. Gabe felt the wood, and it was cool so he opened the door, and what he saw inside sent a chill through his body. Ben was lying unconscious on the floor, blood dripping from his mouth into a larger puddle under his head. Both of them knew Ben's injuries weren't caused by the fire, but they didn't have time to stick around to try to figure out what happened.

Gabe knelt and lifted Ben's lifeless form over his shoulders with Roy's help. As gently as possible they carried Ben down the smoke-filled stairs and out into the fresh air. Four steps away from the building, Gabe was relieved of his load as paramedics laid Ben on a waiting gurney. Royce, a paramedic, began CPR on Ben while Jamar, the other paramedic, attached tubes and wires to Ben's body.

Gabe knew he had to get back to the fire but he couldn't make himself leave his cousin's side. With one final look and more willpower than he thought he possessed, Gabe turned and resumed fighting the fire that was engulfing the entire apartment complex.

***

Grady watched as the fire trucks raced away, and he sent up a prayer that Ben stayed safe. He couldn't turn off his emotions when it came to Ben; it was going to take a long time to get over the man.

Earlier, Grady and Tristan had visited pretty much every shop in Brighton to get Tristan settled into his new bedroom. It appeared as though his friend planned on staying for the long haul, which Grady didn't mind in the least.

He hadn't come face-to-face with his former lover, but he knew it was inevitable in a small town such as Brighton. Grady wasn't one hundred percent sure what he'd say or do when it happened, and hoped he had more time to work it out in his own head first.

An ambulance came speeding down Main Street in the same direction the fire trucks had gone. Grady's chest tightened at the thought of something happening to Ben. Instead of listening to his instincts to follow the ambulance, Grady turned and walked into the diner with Tristan at his side.

"Do you want to check on him?" Tristan asked as they sat at a table by the bank of windows covering the front of the diner.

Grady ran the silk petals of the daisies decorating their table through his fingers, buying more time before answering. "I know that I shouldn't still love him or care, but I do. It'll take time to get over him, and I might as well start now. Let's eat."

Tristan looked at him and Grady could see the doubt in his eyes—surely, they mirrored his own—but he sat and opened the menu. Grady didn't bother opening the menu; he knew today's special was fried chicken and Travis made the best.

As he scanned the dining room, he noticed more than one person watching them. Coop and Matthew sat at a booth in the corner and both turned their heads in another direction when Grady looked their way. Bear, the owner of the diner, didn't even bother turning away; he continued to stare at Grady while taking in the entire area.

Sarah worked her way over to take their order and he was in the middle of giving it when Police Chief David Graham walked in and came straight up to their table. He looked pissed.

"Grady, I need you and your friend to come with me," Dave said with authority.

Tristan's face paled and Grady reached over and took his hand. "It'll be okay, Tristan. Chief, is there a problem?"

"Yes, I'm afraid there is. I need the two of you to come with me. I will explain everything. Give me a little of your faith for now, Grady."

Grady thought it over; the chief had never acted this way toward him before, ensuring this must be important. Dave had given him his faith when he went before the disciplinary committee, and stood up for him having a second chance. There was no reason not to put his faith in Dave.

"Okay, Chief, we'll come with you," Grady responded before he stood. Tristan was quick to follow suit and the three of them were out the diner door and in Dave's cruiser in the next few moments. The steel mesh cage was disconcerting for Grady; his place was in the front seat of these cars.

Dave was silent as they drove to the police station, causing Grady's nerves to spike. Tristan's eyes were wide, and Grady felt his friend trembling. He put his arm around Tristan to calm him.

Something was wrong, and it somehow involved him.

But what?

Chapter Five

"Are we being arrested?" Tristan asked as he paced from one end of the conference room to the other. "Because I'll get my lawyer here so fast it'd make heads spin." And the feisty man Grady knew and loved was back.

"The cells are out back. If we were being arrested, that's where we'd be, not here. No, this is something different," Grady answered as he crossed his arms over his chest and sat waiting for Dave to return. The minute they had walked into the police station they were both ushered into the conference room. That had been over thirty minutes ago and Grady was at the point where he was ready to storm out and demand answers.

Moments later, Dave walked back in along with Fire Chief Mason, Dante, Spider, and Vincent. *What the hell is going on?* Tristan came to sit beside Grady as the rest of the men sat in chairs around the long conference table. The expression on their faces was grim, which dashed any last hope he had that it wasn't as serious as it seemed.

Grady leaned forward, resting his arms on the tabletop, and looked straight at Dave. "What exactly is going on?"

Dave opened the file he carried in his hands, took a deep breath, and fifteen minutes later Grady's world had been turned upside down. He couldn't form words as he sat staring at the men across the table from him. A stalker, they had a stalker, and this was the reason Ben had kept his distance. Could it be true? He looked at the multiple pictures and letters Dave showed him, copies of the ones that had been delivered to Ben. *Why didn't he tell me? I'm not the one who needs protecting; I'm the one who does the protecting. Didn't Ben understand that?*

"I need to talk to Ben." He stood to leave the room and head over to the fire station.

"You can't talk to him, Grady," Fire Chief Mason said.

"What do you mean? Why can't I talk to him?"

"There's been an accident or an attack, we're not sure yet."

Grady's ears were ringing, and he slid back into his chair as they explained the events that ended with Ben being in the ICU of Brighton General. How had things taken such a bad turn? He needed to uncover who their stalker was and why they were so adamant that Grady and Ben not be together. But first the most pressing thing was to get to Ben.

Grady stood and started for the door; there'd be no stopping him this time. "I'm going to the hospital with or without you."

"At least let me drive you. It's safer to have someone with you at all times since we don't know when he might attack again," Dave explained. "Dante, will you make sure Tristan gets back to your apartment and that he's guarded well?"

"Sure thing, Dave."

Grady hung his head in guilt; in that moment, he hadn't thought of his best friend. He turned to check on Tristan but his friend was locked on to Vincent, who was staring right back. Looked as though his friend would be in good hands so Grady continued to the door. Dave caught up with him at his cruiser, and Grady jumped into the passenger seat this time for the ride over to the hospital.

Neither man talked, which gave Grady time to think. Ben had been beaten and left for dead in an apartment fire. He had three broken ribs, a collapsed lung, and severe smoke inhalation. He was on a ventilator to keep him stable while he healed, and had yet to wake up. Why hadn't he trusted Grady with what was going on? It could've saved them both so much pain. He wasn't sure how to deal with everything, but he'd wait until Ben was on the mend before they broached the subject. They had so much to work through.

"Why didn't he tell me?" Grady hadn't meant to speak out loud.

"Because he was so worried you'd get hurt he wasn't thinking straight," Dave answered.

"I'm a cop. I'm capable of defending myself. And why the hell did he go on that date? If he was trying to protect me, there was no need to go out on a date."

Dave cringed before he answered. "You have to ask Ben on that one. It was my cousin he took to dinner."

"Your cousin?"

"It was before I had been informed what was going on. And I can honestly tell you that Ben clarified that they were only going out as friends."

"Well, your cousin must have not gotten the message because he was sitting on Ben's lap in the diner. His hands and lips were all over Ben." Grady should've known it was for his benefit that the little twit was pawing Ben. But he was so shocked that he never thought of it until now.

"I'm sorry that happened, Grady. I truly am."

"None of this is your fault, Chief, you have nothing to be sorry for." Grady didn't want there to be any hard feelings between himself and Dave. He was Grady's boss, but he was his friend first.

The lights coming from the hospital were like a beacon; he needed to get to Ben. Once he healed, Grady intended to hand him his ass for not telling him the truth. Trust was a hard thing to give anyone after his family's and Tony's betrayals, and he didn't know if Ben had a chance of gaining it back. But for now everything was on hold, and all his energy was now focused on helping Ben heal.

Dave pulled up to the ER entrance and angled in one of the police personnel spots. Grady was out of the vehicle and across the parking lot before Dave could put the car in park. An overwhelming need to get to Ben drove Grady forward. He might be mad at the man, but he still loved him.

Grady rushed through the automatic doors and up to the intake desk. Sam was on duty and stood at Grady's approach.

"Where is he, Sam?" Grady demanded, his voice coming out harsher than he had intended.

Sam seemed to know who he was asking for. "I'll take you to the ICU." Sam came around the desk and walked toward the far left hallway. By now Dave had caught up and walked by his side.

"Someone has to be with you at all times, remember," Police Chief Graham reminded Grady. Dave was back in his police chief persona, fully in charge of the situation.

"Then you better keep up," Grady huffed as he followed a few feet behind Sam through a set of doors. "How did Sam know?"

"Sam's Ben's cousin."

"I realize he's Ben's cousin, but how did he know I was looking for Ben?"

"He's family, he would know," Dave answered.

"Ben told the whole family about me? I thought he wanted to keep me a secret."

Sam turned around and looked at Grady. "He didn't want to keep you a secret, he was forced to. There's a difference."

"I'm sorry, Sam, but I'm the one who was kept in the dark. So it's going to take a while for me to accept this new reality I've stepped into the middle of. All I'm concerned about right now is Ben's recovery."

Sam lowered his head and rubbed his temples. "Yeah, I get it. It's difficult all around. We're all worried about Ben."

"It's okay, Sam, I understand." Grady would be there for Ben's family if they needed him. Sam gave a small smile, turned, and continued down the hall; Grady and Dave followed.

Grady's nerves were fried, first finding out about their stalker, and then Ben being attacked and placed in ICU. With what had gone wrong over the last couple of months, Grady figured he deserved good news soon. He was sick and tired of being fate's joke.

Sam stopped in front of a phone hanging on the wall outside another set of locked doors. He said a few words into the handset before the locks released on the door. Grady was happy to see the security in place; Ben would be safe here. As they passed through the double set of security doors, he was happier to see his fellow officer Stan standing outside the doorway Grady presumed was Ben's room.

Stan patted him on the back as Grady walked through the door. He heard his own heartbeat as he kept putting one foot in front of the other. He reached for the drape surrounding Ben's bed and crushed the fabric in the palm of his hand. The machines beeping set him on edge even more than he had been. Grady took a deep breath and pulled the curtain aside.

The first thing he noticed was how small Ben's usually strong body looked in the middle of his hospital bed where wires and tubes ran between him and the machines helping him remain stable. Grady sensed there were other people in the room with him, but they all faded into the background as he neared the bed and took Ben's hand. He felt a chair being pushed up behind him and he sat slowly; his body was on autopilot. He couldn't look away from the man he loved.

Slowly the world started seeping in, and Grady realized that Dot and Henry Mason, Ben's parents, sat on the far side of the room, giving him a small wedge of privacy with Ben. They didn't seem offended he was there and actually smiled when he brought Ben's hand to his mouth and kissed it. Then one of the machines began to beep louder than the others. Grady understood the basics of first aid but that was all; he had no idea what all these machines were responsible for.

A nurse came in and pushed a few buttons, checked Ben's vital signs, and stepped back out of the room. He assumed that meant Ben was fine. Grady saw the edges of a bruise running along Ben's jaw and under the straps holding the ventilator in place. He stood and ran his fingers over Ben's swollen jaw.

“The doctors say that his jaw isn’t broken, only bruised. I guess that’s one fortunate thing.” Dot Mason approached the bed.

“I’m so sorry this happened, Mrs. Mason. I promise to find the person responsible for this. Dave told me about Ben’s broken ribs and smoke inhalation. Is there anything else that I need to know?” Grady asked quietly as tears gathered in his eyes. Soon they spilled over and ran down his face. He didn’t bother trying to hide his emotions from Ben’s parents; they would understand.

Dot gently stroked Ben’s hair; her face was red and tear-stained. “No, those are his main injuries. Did Dave tell you that Ben called out your name?”

“He called out for me?” Grady asked as he tried to absorb how much he meant to Ben. Perhaps this knowledge would help chip away at the anger he held since finding out he’d been lied to.

“It’s true, son. They had to sedate him before making Dave promise to find and protect you,” Henry said as he joined them.

Grady brushed his hand up and down Ben’s arm, wishing he would wake up. But considering the pain he would be suffering, being unconscious might be for the best until he had healed a bit. Whatever it took, Grady would stay by Ben’s side. “Whoever did this will be found and pay for what they’ve done,” Grady growled.

“We have no doubt that you and your fellow officers will be able to find who’s responsible for hurting our son,” Dot said as she walked around the bed and took Grady into her arms, hugging him close. At first the move surprised him, but he soon returned the caring gesture.

“Now, Henry and I are going to take the opportunity to step out and contact the rest of the family to give them an update. They all weren’t allowed to come in to the ICU, only when he’s in a normal hospital room. We’ll inform the nursing staff that you are Ben’s partner and to extend you that courtesy of being able to see him anytime you wish.”

“Thank you for understanding,” Grady said. “I’m still on medical leave so I’ll be here as much as I’m allowed.”

"We understand how hard this has been for you. Ben loves you. It's easy for the rest of the family to see. Please give him a chance to explain because all of us know that Ben is too strong and stubborn to die," Henry said as he took Dot's hand and led her from the room.

Grady stared at their retreating figures. That's the way parents were supposed to act, loving their children no matter what. Too bad his parents hadn't gotten the memo. He turned back to look at the man he loved, then leaned over to whisper into Ben's ear. "You promised me we wouldn't have to be apart anymore. I expect you to stand by your word." Grady wiped away his tears and kissed Ben's forehead before saying, "I love you, and you don't even know it." He caressed Ben's face before sitting down in the chair beside the bed to begin his vigil over the man he loved.

Grady swore he would find the person responsible for all this pain and make him pay for the damage he'd done.

***

Ben was stuck in a thick fog-like soup floating in the middle of darkness. No matter how hard he tried he couldn't make his body move. It was as if he was being suspended without choice. Then he heard it, the voice he'd heard before. Something about this voice kept drawing him forward out of the fog, but not quite far enough to surface. He tried to get closer to that voice; the deep timbre and soothing tone seemed to call to him on every level. He wanted to hold on to that voice and wrapped it around him when the pain became too much.

He floated as the softly spoken words comforted him. He recognized that voice but he couldn't place it. Although he seemed to know innately that the person was important to him. Ben wanted to get closer to the voice, but there seemed to be some sort of wall between them. He didn't know how long he'd been like this or why, but he remembered a fire. He'd been in a building fire, then nothing;

a blank. He pushed hard to try to remember what had happened, but it wouldn't come to him.

"You have to wake up soon, baby, you're scaring me. It's been over a week now, and it's time you came back to me." The beautiful voice sounded sad and Ben wanted to comfort the person with that wonderful voice. So Ben struggled against his invisible bonds, desperate to get to the man behind the voice.

"That's it, Ben, come back to me. Fight to wake up, baby." The voice cheered him on but Ben quickly grew tired and soon ran out of strength. The fog got thicker and began closing in on him until he simply surrendered and rested.

In the background the voice became softer and softer until he couldn't make out the words being said, and the darkness took over once again.

***

Grady stood and took a deep calming breath. Ben had come close to waking up this time, which gave him hope. Over the last week and a half he had stayed by Ben's side. Thankfully, Grady was still on medical leave from his gunshot wound and had the opportunity to spend this time at the hospital. He regretted having to leave his best friend, Tristan, alone though the Sentinels had sworn to take good care of him. All the furniture Tristan had ordered had been delivered and set up. Tristan took video and sent it to Grady. As with everything Tristan, the room looked fantastic. He had converted a dull space into a sparkling jewel. Now he was working on his latest book and told Grady that he didn't mind having the apartment to himself.

The Mason family had been in and out on a daily basis, with Dot remaining for the entire day alongside Grady. He'd gone home late at night only to shower and change clothes before coming back to the hospital and taking up his post at Ben's side. A Sentinel stayed with Grady whenever he left the hospital since the person responsible for Ben's injuries hadn't been found yet.

Between Ben's mother and Grady, Ben received constant family updates and encouragement to wake up. His ventilator had been removed three days ago and he was healing well according to Dr. Green. But Ben wouldn't wake up. The longer it took the more worried Grady became that the smoke inhalation had done more damage than they'd originally thought.

It was close to one in the morning, and the hospital was eerily quiet. Grady paced over to the window and stared out at the park across the street. Dark and empty, the only light coming from the overhead streetlamps gave everything a bluish tinge. It was fitting, and seemed to mirror how he felt.

He refused to give up hope that Ben would return to him soon. There would be no more hiding, no more quick hook-ups, no more burying his feelings. They would find whoever was responsible for stalking them and hurting Ben. Grady would make sure of it.

He turned away from the window and settled down in the chair he kept close to the side of Ben's bed. He looked down at his love and noted that he needed a shave, and promised Ben he would get one tomorrow.

Before long, Grady lowered his head onto his arms lying on the edge of the bed and closed his eyes. He'd try to get a few hours' sleep before the nurses came in on their early morning rounds.

The last thing he did before sleep claimed him was to slide his hand into Ben's and hold on tight, like he intended to do for the rest of his life.

***

This time Ben fought with all the strength he had to surface from the fog, and he opened his eyes. It took a few moments for everything to come into focus, but once they did he realized he was in a hospital room. Slowly, he turned his head to take in all the machines surrounding him. He wondered how badly he was hurt, then realized he wasn't alone in the room.

Ben turned his head to the other side and smiled at the sight of his love, Grady. He was asleep and leaning his head on the edge of the bed. Ben didn't know how long he'd been unconscious, but he imagined by now someone had told Grady the truth. Ben wondered how the man had reacted to the news that they had a stalker, and that Ben had kept the truth from Grady. Would he forgive Ben? Did their relationship have a chance? Funny how priorities change. Ben should be worried about his injuries, but instead all he could think about was how Grady would react to him.

He tried to turn his body at an angle so he could get a better look at a sleeping Grady, but pain shot through his ribs and took his breath away. He must have made a noise because the next thing he knew he was wrapped in Grady's large arms while he said soothing words over and over again softly into Ben's ear. Once the pain began to subside Ben relaxed against Grady, enjoying having the man so close. Too soon Grady gently laid Ben back against the mattress and fixed his sheets.

"I have to run and tell the nurse that you've woken up. It should only take me a few seconds," Grady whispered with a huge smile on his face.

"No," Ben rasped.

Grady leaned down to look Ben straight on. "Why, what's wrong?"

Ben had to tell him before the world broke in and took over. "Grady, I love you." It came out scratchy and low, but by the look on Grady's face he'd heard what Ben had said.

Grady's smiling face moved closer until their lips were almost touching, the only sound in the room coming from the machines and Ben's raspy breathing. So many emotions seemed to flit across Grady's face: surprise, confusion, joy and finally the emotion he'd been waiting for, love.

"I love you too, Ben," Grady whispered before closing the gap between their lips and kissing Ben gently. Grady's lips were soft and Ben missed them and the rest of the man so much.

Grady loved Ben, which was the most important thing to remember; at least until the pain started to kick in. His love must have noticed the change in his body and slowly pulled away. "You're in pain." It was a statement, not a question. "We can talk later, right now you need the nurse. I'll be right back, love."

Before Ben could argue Grady was out the door. He figured it was for the best because the pain was getting severe. He slid his hands under the sheets and felt bandages wrapped around his chest and abdomen. Ben finally remembered why he was here; he'd been kicked several times by what had to've been steel toe boots, and then without his respirator he'd succumbed to the carbon monoxide in the smoke. Which explained why his lungs and throat felt raw and he was having trouble taking a deep breath.

Grady came back followed by two excited nurses. He took Ben's hand and stayed by his side as the nurses checked him over and injected something into his IV. They explained his injuries to him, and soon his pain faded away. The nurses left with a promise to contact his family and the doctor.

As soon as the nurses stepped out the door, Grady bent over the bed and began kissing Ben again. He reached out and threaded his fingers through Grady's short, dark hair. He never thought he'd have the opportunity to hold the man he loved again, and Ben swore to never take it for granted.

"Don't ever scare me like that again." Grady's voice cracked as he spoke.

"I'll do my best," Ben replied, and then broached the subject he wished he could ignore. "Do you want to talk about everything? I assume you've been informed of what's been going on."

Grady stayed silent for more than a moment, taking his time answering, and driving Ben crazy. If his love wanted to hash this out right now, he would do it no matter how tired he became.

After dropping his head, Grady looked over at Ben and said, “No. I want you to concentrate on healing and not worrying about anything. I’m not going anywhere.”

Ben let out a deep breath. “I like the sound of that.” His eyes began to droop and he fought to keep them open but it was a losing battle. “I think I need to take a nap. Will you stay with me?” He honestly didn’t want to be without Grady any longer.

“I’ve been by your side for the past week and a half, I’m not planning on leaving you now.” Grady caressed Ben’s stubbled cheek. “You rest, I’ll be here when you wake up.”

With one final kiss Ben drifted off, safe in the knowledge that Grady would be there when he woke.

Chapter Six

Three days later

Every day seemed to bring on a new battery of tests. Thankfully, all coming back either passed or Ben's responses were in the normal range. They tested his cognitive functions in case of brain damage from the lack of oxygen when he was unconscious in the fire. Physically, he couldn't do much due to his healing ribs and damaged lungs. But he was able to stay awake for longer periods during the day, which in itself was an improvement.

Once he remembered everything that had happened, Police Chief Graham came over and had taken his account of the attack in the apartment building during the fire. Unfortunately, his attacker had worn an oxygen mask, which hid his identity. Ben didn't recognize the voice with only the few words his attacker had spoken, and there were no leads. It had seemed that the guy had vanished in the chaos of the fire because nobody remembered seeing him leave the building.

Grady had stayed by Ben's side throughout all the tests. His mother spent most of the day with them in the hospital until his father came at suppertime to visit and pick her up. Other family members had been in and out often now that he'd been moved to a regular hospital room. His room was doubling as a jungle from all the flowers and cards he had received. Brighton always rallied around one of their own.

Sure enough Grady walked into his room carrying a plant with yellow and orange flowers. "This one is from Mr. and Mrs. Williamson from the bakery." He laughed before placing the colorful plant among the others.

"I have no idea where I'm going to put them all when I get to go home. My house is only so big." Ben laughed as well but he noticed Grady had yet to look him in the eye. A sure sign something's up. "What's wrong?"

His love turned and looked at him. "Dr. Green thinks that you can be released at the beginning of the week."

"That's great news. Why do you seem so upset about it?" Ben asked, confused by Grady's response.

Grady walked over and stood looking out the window. "Well, I've been thinking, with all that has happened and the threat still present that maybe…"

Ben waited for him to continue, but after a moment when it didn't seem like Grady was going to continue Ben asked, "That maybe, what?"

Grady walked over from the window and stood beside Ben's bed and took his hand. "I thought that maybe it would be best if I came home with you to your house. You need someone to take care of you and it would be easier for the Sentinels to keep an eye on us if we're in the same place. Well, at least until he's caught."

That Grady was still unsure of how he fit into Ben's life upset and surprised him. He'd done that, and he needed to fix that right now. "Babe, I love you. I want you with me wherever that might be. I'm sorry that I ever made you doubt that, and I'll do my best to let you know how I feel and what's going on so you never are unsure again."

Grady squeezed Ben's hand and the tension lines on his handsome face seemed to disappear almost immediately. Ben felt terrible for making the man he loved uncertain about their relationship. Logically, he knew he'd tried to protect Grady, but in the end it had almost cost him everything. From here on out, they would face this danger together with the help of their friends and family.

"Besides, you're part of the Mason family now," Ben added as reassurance. "You have so many family members now they'll drive you crazy."

"Considering my parents disowned me when I came out, I'll accept yours, no problem." Grady chuckled before leaning over and capturing Ben's lips in a needy kiss. Ben couldn't do much given his injuries, but it never stopped his body from reacting to the gorgeous man.

The sound of someone clearing their throat interrupted the kiss and had both men lifting their heads. Grady pulled away and gave Ben a magnificent smile before turning toward the open doorway. The man who had come back with Grady and moved in to his apartment stood staring at them. His flaming red hair and bright yellow T-shirt were enough to blind a person, but it matched his happy smile.

"Tristan, come in," Grady urged before crossing the room and leading his best friend over to Ben's bedside. Vincent came through the door and stood in one of the corners, his eyes scanning like a machine. "I see you have your own bodyguard following you around."

"Yeah, this one won't let me do anything by myself. Literally," Tristan complained and rolled his eyes as he looked toward Vincent, who appeared to not be listening. Ben highly doubted that.

"Ben, I would like you to meet one of my oldest and dearest friends. He's like a brother to me. This is Tristan." Tristan stepped forward and held out his hand to shake.

Ben knew he'd overreacted when he first saw Tristan and Grady together. Since he'd woken up, Grady had explained who Tristan was and what he meant to him. "You're the famous Tristan. I've read a few of your books. Loved them. You're talented. It's great to meet you." Ben reached out, took Tristan's hand, and shook it.

"I'm so happy to meet you and that you're healing. I brought you a few of my latest novels to help occupy you while you heal." At that Tristan handed over a bag of books to Grady, who set them on a nearby chair.

They spent the next couple of hours talking and laughing, sometimes causing Ben to have to clutch at his side because of the pain. But he couldn't help it; Tristan was a funny, likable man and Ben understood why his love held him as a dear friend. He was outrageous and unapologetic, and the man seemed to exude happiness. Tristan was certainly one of a kind, and thankfully he'd been around to help Grady through the tough time after he had come out, and his family disowned him.

All in all, Ben couldn't help but like the guy.

Chapter Seven

After another week in the hospital, Ben was released to go home. Grady had brought over clothing so that he could stay near Ben while he recovered. After a couple days he began to notice Ben becoming less talkative and more drawn into himself. By the fifth day Grady was worried; it was after one in the afternoon and Ben hadn't even gotten out of bed.

Grady walked into the master bedroom to find Ben sitting up in a chair looking out the large window into the backyard. He hadn't come out of his room when he woke up. This was getting out of hand. Grady sat in the chair opposite Ben and reached for his lover's hand. Ben never turned his head, his gaze locked on the backyard.

"Babe, you have to tell me what's wrong." Grady kept his voice even, though he wanted to scream his frustrations.

"Will you ever forgive me?" Ben asked, his voice monotone.

And there it was, the one conversation Grady had been avoiding since they'd come home to Ben's house. He'd already forgiven him for keeping the information about their stalker, which explained why Ben kept Grady a secret. But what about the date with Ryan? There was no reason Ben could give for going; that had been a betrayal Grady didn't know how to forgive.

"I don't want to talk about this, Ben," Grady muttered, but even he could hear the anger in his voice.

"When? When will you want to talk about it?"

Grady stood and paced to the other side of the bedroom. Ben stayed seated and Grady figured that had to be the pain; Ben hadn't taken his medication yet. "I don't know when or even if I'll ever want to talk about it."

"So you're biding your time until I'm healed to leave me," Ben concluded.

"Leave you?" Grady asked. "I didn't say anything about that."

"Well, it only stands to reason. You don't want to talk about it, and you can't forgive me. We can't build a relationship on that," Ben explained. "If that's the case I'd prefer you go now before you're hurt or worse. There's no need to risk your life if you mean to leave me."

It was like a sucker punch to the stomach. Was Grady simply helping Ben heal, then leave because forgiveness wasn't on the horizon? Grady wasn't consciously preparing for that inevitability, but he knew it could look that way.

Suck it up. If Ben wanted to hash this out now, it was on.

"You intentionally cheated on me. How do you explain that? There isn't a logical reason to take some guy out and let him climb you like a tree in front of me."

"I didn't have a choice. I had to make it look good for the stalker." Ben's voice was calm but his eyes were turbulent.

"Oh you made it look good all right. But ya know, you didn't have to cheat. You were keeping me at arm's length anyway. No one knew about us."

"The stalker seemed to. No matter how hard I tried to stay away from you, those damn pictures kept arriving. I had to throw him off the trail. I thought by taking Ryan out to dinner it would keep you safer."

"Safer? You went on a date to make me safer. Hate to see what you do to make me safer now that I'm staying here."

Ben flinched. Could Grady allow petty jealousy to ruin what could be between them? He didn't doubt that Ben loved him, but trust and love were entirely different things.

Ben tried to stand but he ended up wrapping his arms around his ribs and groaning instead. Grady helped Ben sit back down. "I'll get your medication."

"No. I need to call my parents. They'll come and help me," Ben stated, his tone flat.

"Help you? I'm here."

"Why drag it out? It'll only hurt more the longer we stay together."

"'Cause I love you, you idiot."

"But you can't forgive me?"

"At this moment, no. But jealousy fades. I may not like what you did, but I can try to understand why you did it."

"You understand?"

"Sort of. I have to process it. In the meantime, I don't want to leave you."

"Are you sure? 'Cause I don't think I could take it if you stayed for now, only to leave later."

"I'm not going anywhere. I love you and you love me. Together we can work anything out. Now let's get you fed and medicated before you get worse," Grady ordered as he helped Ben get out of his chair and walk to the kitchen.

Grady knew he'd have to try harder to get over it; he loved Ben and wasn't going to lose him over this.

***

Two days after "the talk," Grady returned to duty with his new partner, Bo, at his side. Another safety precaution. When Grady was out policing, Tristan or Dot—sometimes both—would come over and help Ben. One or more Sentinels were stationed either inside the house or somewhere on the property—always.

Currently, Grady was on patrol with Bo. The town was quiet, and they'd had only one service call so far this evening. Getting used to having a partner again after so many years of working alone would take time, but because of the reason he and Bo were riding together, Grady would be happy for the day it was over.

Ben and Grady were waiting in limbo for the stalker to attack again, and he was getting tired of the two of them being targeted by some faceless lunatic. Grady couldn't wait for them to begin their future together, but right now that seemed like only a dream.

Yet, a few good things had come out of this mess; finally, he and Ben had solidified their love, and Bo and Travis had forgiven Grady for the day he'd scared Travis with a gun. That day seemed like forever ago with everything else that had happened recently. At least his injured arm had healed; he got the occasional twinge when he overused it.

Bo was finishing a report on his tablet when dispatch requested they respond to a disturbance at the same building where Grady's apartment was located. This couldn't be a coincidence. Grady switched on the lights and headed to the other side of town. When they arrived, the police chief's personal vehicle sat there along with an SUV belonging to the Sentinels. Grady parked the cruiser, and he and Bo made their way through the vehicles to the back of the building. What they found there was confusing.

Shadow stood in the center of a group consisting of Police Chief Graham, Dante, and Spider, holding on to a terrified-looking teenage boy. As Bo and Grady got closer, he noticed the white envelope in Dante's hand and immediately realized what was going on. The group must have heard them approach and turned to greet them.

"Is that another envelope from the stalker?" Grady asked Dante.

"Yep. Shadow here caught this boy trying to slide it under the door of your apartment." Dante held the sealed envelope by the tip of one corner.

"Our stalker is a teenage boy?" Grady found that hard to believe.

"No, we don't think so. The boy claims an older man paid him to deliver it. We haven't opened it yet. We're waiting on Shannon and Matthew to show up with gloves and the materials needed to lift a fingerprint from somewhere on that paper," Dante explained. "Or even DNA from licking the envelope."

"Let's move this back to the station. I want answers," Police Chief Graham ordered before placing the teenager in handcuffs and leading him to his cruiser. They didn't know with certainty whether the boy was involved or not. Until he could be cleared, he'd have to stay in custody. But Grady knew that Dave would call the boy's parents and allow them to be with the teenager during questioning. The boy looked familiar to Grady but he couldn't place the family.

"What's the boy's name?" Grady asked.

"Joey Whiteman. He lives with his parents over on Gerrard Street. His father works for one of the ranches outside of town. Good, honest folk," Bo explained as they walked back to the cruiser and headed over to the station.

Once everyone had gotten to the station, they gathered in the conference room and waited for the boy's parents to arrive. Considering he was only sixteen years old, he needed to have his parents present. Shannon and Matthew came in a few minutes after everyone else, and were followed by Joey's parents. Dave explained the situation to them and they swore their complete cooperation in finding the man who had paid their son to deliver the envelope.

Unfortunately, Joey couldn't give them an exact description of the man because he wore glasses and a baseball cap. But he did notice the man's hair was mostly gray with a few dark brown streaks. He also stated that the man had a crooked nose like he'd been in some sort of fight. Joey went on to explain that the man was slightly taller than him, making the stalker over six feet tall with a bit of a belly. Police Chief Graham allowed the Whitemans to take Joey home. The kid had learned a hard lesson about taking money from strangers.

Shannon stretched a piece of white fabric on the conference table and placed the envelope in the middle of it. There wasn't any writing on the outside of the envelope. Matthew, one of the Sentinel computer experts, believed there was more than one thing in the envelope. Shannon and Matthew wore white gloves and used what looked like long tweezers, one with a sharp edge, to cut a slit in the top of the envelope. Anxiety growing in the pit of his stomach, Grady wondered what the hell this note would say. Who would be threatened this time?

Matthew took another set of tweezers and pulled a folded note and picture out of the envelope. The moment he saw the picture his stomach dropped. It was of him and Tristan walking out of the hospital together after visiting with Ben. In red marker, crosshairs were placed over Tristan's head. They carefully unfolded the note, allowing him to see the words written there. "You brought someone else into this, now he'll pay the price. You should have listened to me."

"Where's Tristan right now?" Dave asked.

Grady began walking away from the conference table and said, "He's at Ben's house keeping him company while I'm working. Someone get on the phone with Vincent and tell him what's going on. We need that house on lockdown now." Grady's heart raced as he ran to his cruiser followed by Bo, Dave, Dante, and Spider.

He prayed that they made it in time.

***

Ben sat on the couch watching *Big Bang Theory* reruns with Tristan. He enjoyed the company and he knew Vincent was nearby, but that man was not particularly talkative—much more the silent but deadly type. Even with everything that had been hanging over their heads, Ben had been enjoying his time with Grady and couldn't see his life without the man in it. So he had come to a decision: Once everything had calmed down, he would ask Grady to move in with him permanently. Tristan could always take over the apartment if he decided to stay.

It was 11:30 in the evening and they'd finished the second season when a cell phone rang in a nearby room; he assumed it must be Vincent's. Tristan stood up from the couch and stretched. That's when Ben saw the bright red dot in the middle of Tristan's chest. He didn't even think, Ben flung himself at the smaller man and took him to the ground as the front bay window shattered and a bullet slammed through his flat-screen TV on the opposite wall.

"Are you okay?" Tristan asked as he huddled under Ben's body. But before he answered Vincent came running into the room, his gun drawn as he took a protective position over both of them. Ben was equal parts afraid to move because someone was shooting at them and because his ribs throbbed in excruciating pain every time he tried. He wasn't completely healed, and boy was he going to pay for the quick movements that took Tristan to the floor. But Ben was damn happy that he had; Tristan wouldn't have survived a shot through the heart.

"I'm okay. Stay down until they can clear the house and area," Ben explained.

"Trust me, I'm not going anywhere." Tristan seemed to make himself as small as possible underneath Ben. "That bullet was meant for me?"

Ben could hear the sirens coming in the distance; help was on the way. He had to tell Tristan the truth. "Yes."

Soon his living room filled with police officers and Sentinels. Grady immediately came over and gently helped Ben back onto the couch. Vincent lifted Tristan like he weighed nothing and sat with him in a chair in the corner. It didn't seem as though Vincent was going to be far away from Tristan from now on.

Grady sat down next to Ben and gathered him into his arms while the rest of the officers checked the apartment, the building, and the surrounding areas. One by one voices came through their radios: "Clear." "Clear." "Clear." Whoever had tried to kill Tristan was gone. Frustrated but determined, the Sentinels and the police were collecting all the evidence and continued to search for the shooter.

"Why would somebody try to shoot Tristan?" Ben asked, comfortable in Grady's arms.

Police Chief Dave Graham explained about the latest letter. Apparently their stalker had decided Tristan was another target simply because he left the hospital with Grady after visiting Ben.

"Up until now I've been working under the assumption that whoever this person is was fixated on Ben," Dante addressed everyone in the room. "All the letters before this one had gone to Ben, and Ben was the person attacked first. But now that we have this new one, I'm not so sure anymore. Obviously, whoever this is knows Grady is living here with Ben, so why deliver the letter to Grady's apartment? And if the nutjob knew we were watching the apartment, why bother sending the envelope by third party?" Dante mused before he answered his ringing cell phone.

"Wait a minute. With everything else that's been going on, I forgot that the day we came back from Galveston we found an envelope when we came home. It had my name on it," Grady told the group.

"Did you open it?" Vincent asked.

"Do you know where it is now?" the chief questioned.

"No, I didn't open it. I forgot about it. It should still be on my coffee table," Grady answered and looked at Tristan for confirmation.

"I haven't touched it," Tristan responded in a small voice.

"We'll retrieve it," Spider confirmed.

"Who the hell hates us this much?" Grady shook his head before burying his face in Ben's hair and taking a deep breath. It seemed to calm him.

Ben, on the other hand, raged on the inside at what could have happened if he'd been one second slower. He liked Tristan, and he didn't want to see anything bad happen to the man. Grady would have blamed himself if his friend had so much as a scratch on him.

"He has to know that there's surveillance all over Grady's apartment and bodyguards in this house. That we would stop the kid from going anywhere near Grady's door," Vincent muttered.

Spider continued with. "He was here readying to take a shot at Tristan while Joey was delivering the envelope. A diversion to draw as many of us away from Ben's house and over to Grady's apartment."

"I think it's best if we move the three of you to the Mason cottage. Not only can we protect the area better, there won't be any chance of an innocent bystander getting caught in the crossfire," Bo suggested as he looked down at his brother, Ben.

"The Mason cottage?" Grady asked.

Ben laid his head back on Grady's shoulder and looked up into Grady's deep brown eyes. "Yes, the family owns a cottage on Little Bear Lake about a good hour from Brighton. Members of the family use it to get away for a few days in the forest that surrounds the cottage. Over the years it's been updated. It has two bedrooms, open living and kitchen area, and a beautiful deck that overlooks the water. There's no television and cell service is spotty."

"We'll bring a mobile satellite to boost the reception out there," Spider stated.

"Good idea. If we can lure the stalker out of Brighton it would not only prevent others from getting hurt, but it will increase our chances of catching the guy. It seems he doesn't mind bringing innocent people like Joey into this," Dante added. And with the move to the lake decided, Spider and Vincent nailed a couple of pieces of plywood over the broken window while Ben and Grady packed for the trip to the lake, hoping that this would be the end of this nightmare.

***

It was almost daylight when they reached the property and Ben was wired on adrenaline and coffee. It had been a long night but he doubted he would be able to sleep anytime soon. Flashes of that red dot on Tristan's chest kept replaying in his mind.

"Christ, if I had been half a second slower, he would have shot Tristan."

"But he didn't. You saved Tristan. You've been protecting everybody else for so long; now it's my turn to protect you," Grady declared, causing some of the tightness in Ben's chest to loosen.

"I'm good with that as long as you don't get hurt. I know I keep saying it, but I am sorry for keeping the truth from you. I know you're able to protect yourself and me from the stalker."

When they stopped beside the cottage, Grady opened the door of the SUV and scanned the area before allowing Ben or Tristan out. Ben attempted to lift his bag but hissed in pain as the movement hurt his ribs.

"Don't you dare try to lift anything. I've got all the bags, you get inside the cottage and relax," Grady ordered and Ben sighed, but agreed he was in no shape to argue. The pain had worsened and he needed to lie down. "When was the last time you took one of your pain pills the doctor gave you?"

"About eight hours ago, give or take." Ben figured he was about due for another but he didn't like the way it made him feel fuzzy, like he wasn't himself. He had to stay alert, especially now that they were drawing out their stalker, hoping he would follow them to the cottage.

"We'll get you comfortable lying down on the couch and give you one of those pills."

"I don't want to take them now; they make me groggy. I can make it without them." Ben was lying through his teeth, the pain was becoming unbearable, but given the choice of taking the pill and dulling the pain or staying alert to protect his family, he'd stay alert.

"Not a choice. You'll get one when you lie down, which will be soon," Grady announced as he lowered the four bags to the floor and gathered Ben into his arms. "Remember, it's my turn to protect you."

Ben acquiesced and followed Grady over to one of the couches in front of the fireplace. Carefully Ben lowered himself onto the cushions and laid his head back on the pillow, all done with Grady's help. As soon as Ben was in a comfortable position, Grady left him for the kitchen. Soon enough he came back with a glass of water and Ben's prescription bottle. "Here you go, now take your pill while I get us settled in one of the bedrooms."

Until now, Grady had slept on a rollaway bed. He didn't want to cause Ben any pain by rolling in his sleep or chance moving Ben. But now there wasn't a spare rollaway, which made Ben happy. This would be the first time they shared a bed since Grady had been shot in the arm. Even though they had spent time together, the last few weeks had been about healing.

Ben took his medication and downed the glass of water Grady had given him. It wouldn't be long before the pill kicked in and exhaustion took over. He heard Grady moving things in one of the bedrooms, and if he tried really hard, he could pretend that they'd come up here to get away together and weren't running for their lives.

His head was getting heavier as he sank deeper into the pillow. The knit blanket was tucked up close to his neck, but he didn't know who'd done it because his eyelids wouldn't open. That was the last thing Ben remembered as the breeze from the open windows floated, in bringing with it the scent of citrus from the few hop trees scattered around the property.

***

Grady watched as Ben fell into a deep sleep before leaving him and joining the rest of the men outside. Vincent still had a tight hold on Tristan, who wasn't attempting to get away. They stood beside Dante, Shadow, Bo, Coop, and Matthew. Shannon and Spider were already gone looking around the property for the best places to set up motion sensors.

Vincent looked down at Tristan and asked, "Would you go inside, little sparrow, and keep an eye on Ben for us?" Tristan nodded his head and quietly walked away. Last night had rattled him; he didn't even tell Vincent off for the "little" comment.

Grady grabbed hold of his best friend and hugged him tight. "I'm so sorry you got dragged into this."

He hugged Grady back and smiled weakly. "I don't blame you. None of this is your fault or Ben's." He continued on into the cottage and slowly closed the door behind him.

Grady looked over and stared at Vincent. An understanding passed between the two where it concerned Tristan. Grady would always be Tristan's "brother," and would make sure that the man in Tristan's life kept him happy.

"You two got that worked out?" Dante asked, looking between them.

Vincent smiled and answered on behalf of the both of them. "Yeah, we're good."

"Okay, now let's get to work," Dante said as he unrolled blueprints of the cottage and a topographical survey of the land.

"How the hell did you get all this stuff in such a short period of time?" Grady asked, both impressed and a little worried.

"You'd be amazed by what my team is capable of getting accomplished when push comes to shove," Dante explained with a healthy dose of pride. "These will help us map out the best places to set traps and sensors as well as hiding spots around the cottage that could be used against us."

Spider and Shannon returned from the forest, and the group went ahead to secure the cottage and surrounding area. Matthew set up the portable satellite dish and terminal on the back deck, which would provide reliable satellite communications as well as access the multiple cameras set up throughout the forest. Then, multiple laptops and other electronics were set up on the dining room table. Coop, Matthew's boyfriend, stayed behind to guard the cottage, while the rest of the team set up cameras, trip wires, and sensors.

Grady had set his last sensor and took a moment as he stood on the front lawn and looked at the Masons' cottage. It was perfect, like Grady had always imagined a family retreat would be. His parents never had time for vacations. They were too busy keeping up with their social engagements, always climbing the social ladder on their quest to be part of the upper crust of society. There was no such thing as family vacations or a family getaway cottage in Grady's childhood.

The Masons' cottage had a board and batten exterior, which was painted light blue. The trim and filigree around the roof, porch, and windows were white. Small flowering bushes planted around the porch smelled amazing, and the sparkling lake was less than one hundred feet from the deck off the kitchen in the back. Grady hoped Ben and he would be able to come back after all of this was over and make new, better memories.

Grady stretched out his sore back and slowly walked onto the porch and into the cottage. The first thing he noticed was Ben was no longer on the couch. "Where did Ben go?" he asked Spider before walking into the kitchen to grab a bottle of water.

"He moved to the bedroom, it's quieter in there. Why don't you go in and lie down with him and get some rest?" Spider suggested as he grabbed the package of Oreos off the counter, taking out an entire sleeve for himself. "We'll wake you if anything comes up."

Grady thought about it for a moment. He was exhausted and he desperately wanted to be near Ben. *Why not?* "That sounds like a great idea, thanks."

The big man waved an Oreo at Grady but didn't say a word; difficult since he had two Oreos stuffed in his mouth. Grady laughed and turned toward the bedroom he would be sharing with Ben. It felt good being able to share a bed and show affection toward the man he loved without having to hide it from anyone. The freedom of it was exhilarating.

Grady carefully opened their bedroom door, trying his best not to wake Ben. As soon as the door shut, Ben's eyes opened and zeroed in on him. "Sorry, sweetheart, I tried not to wake you."

"That's okay. Are you coming to bed?" Grady didn't miss the hopeful expression on Ben's face.

"Yeah, babe, I'm exhausted. How are you feeling? Are you in any pain?" Grady began stripping out of his clothes. He hadn't taken off his uniform since he'd gone on duty yesterday. He stowed his duty belt and service weapon in the top drawer of the dresser. His sidearm looked like a toy compared to all the weapons Sentinel had brought along, but nonetheless, he would keep it close just in case.

With Ben lying on the left side of the old canopy bed, Grady walked over to the right, stripped down to his boxer briefs. If something happened, he didn't plan on running out of the bedroom to take on a madman while naked. He slid under the blankets, trying his best not to jostle the mattress and cause Ben any extra pain.

Grady let out a deep breath as he melted into the mattress, more tired than he had thought. He wished he could take up his usual position, laying his head on Ben's chest, but with his love's injuries it would be some time before he had that opportunity.

"Lie on your side, babe. I'd like to spoon you. I need to feel you in my arms," Ben requested as he rolled over.

Grady was all for cuddling, and did as he was asked. Though he was slightly larger than Ben, this had been one of the many positions that Grady had loved during their short interludes. He had always felt protected and loved whenever Ben had his arms around him. It was strange, a large, capable man whose job it was to protect others felt safer in Ben's arms than anywhere else.

"I'll be here when you wake up, babe." He wasn't sure if Ben was trying to assuage his own fear or Grady's. This would be the first time they were sharing the same bed since the day he had found Ben on that date with Dave's cousin.

"I know." Grady leaned back slightly and gave Ben a soft kiss on the lips before laying his head down, and almost instantly fell asleep.

Chapter Eight

Ben sifted his fingers through Grady's soft brown hair. It was barely long enough for him to get a hold of. He'd rested while Grady slept. Their bedroom was on the west side of the cottage, and the sun was shining through their window. Ben guessed it must be early evening, but he didn't hear anyone about. He shoved away the momentary panic, knowing it would take a tank to get through what the Sentinels had intended to set up.

His ribs ached but he was finally able to take a fairly deep breath without buckling over in pain. He still looked and felt like he had been in a car wreck, but the bruising had finally begun to fade. Grady's tanned skin was warm underneath his hands and Ben couldn't help but move closer to his love.

They still had quite a bit to work through, and Ben understood he wasn't getting a free pass from the mistakes he'd made. But at least Grady had stayed and heard him out. It was more than he'd expected after everything that had gone down in the diner that day. The hurt he'd seen in Grady's eyes would never be erased from Ben's memory.

Grady's breathing changed and his body tensed for a second before he relaxed back into Ben's arms. "You awake?"

"Hhmmm," Grady mumbled before rolling over and facing Ben. "Hi, babe."

Grady looked up at him, and Ben was lost in the warm depths of Grady's beautiful eyes. Ben knew he'd never loved his ex like this. This feeling was all-encompassing and out of control.

"Hi, Grady."

Grady reached up and cupped Ben's cheek, and he melted into his lover's touch. "Love you," he murmured, still amazed he was free to speak those words out loud.

Grady's handsome face broke into a wide smile. "I love you too. How are you feeling?"

"Better. But again I haven't tried to get up so that may change," Ben joked before turning to kiss the palm of Grady's hand.

His dark eyes turned hot and needy, drawing Ben in. Grady's large hands gently pushed him onto his back. "Are you comfortable?" Grady was leaning over Ben, his hands on both sides of his head. He wanted to feel that large, muscled body pressed against his, but he hadn't healed enough for that to happen.

"Yes. What do you have planned?" Ben asked, excitement starting to course through his veins; his dick was already hard.

"I plan on relieving a little tension for the both of us," Grady's voice rumbled through Ben's body and settled right in his aching balls, making him shudder. "Easy, Ben, I don't want you to reinjure yourself." The need to feel the man he loved in the throes of passion was so strong that he'd almost tried to sit up. "So here's the deal, as long as you promise not to move, I'll give you exactly what you need. But if you move I'll have to stop."

"But what about you?" Ben wanted to bring Grady the same pleasure.

"Don't worry, sweetheart, I'll be fine," Grady replied before leaning forward and taking Ben's lips in a demanding, take-no-prisoners kiss.

Grady's soft lips devoured Ben's, driving him to moan out his approval. As his hands explored the dips and valleys of Grady's hard body, he did his best not to move anything else, but he so wanted to flex his hips in search of friction for his throbbing cock.

"I've missed you so much, babe. Never wanted to be without you, and I don't plan on ever being again," Ben gasped once Grady had released his lips.

"I'll hold you to that, Ben Mason," Grady stated. Ben could see a sliver of doubt, and knew he'd caused Grady to doubt him. He promised himself to never be the cause of his love's pain again.

Ben caressed the side of Grady's handsome face. "I swear to you on my life I didn't want to do it the first time. But I honestly had to protect you and that was the only way I thought to do it. I'll never lie to you or cause you pain ever again."

"You can't promise to never cause me pain again. No one's perfect. I'm sure there'll be a day when I'll unintentionally hurt you. What matters is that we work it out together and that we're always honest with each other."

The earnest look on Grady's face brought Ben to his knees. He swore then and there that someday he was going to marry this man. "I'll do everything in my power to make sure that happens. I'll never risk losing you again."

"Good, because I don't want to be lost." Grady smiled, that roguish grin of his driving Ben to want to dip his tongue into those handsome dimples.

Grady dove in for another kiss, his tongue mapping the inside of Ben's mouth, then Grady began working his way down Ben's body, stopping to nibble and suck his hard nipples. Ben could hardly catch his breath as Grady gently kissed the fading bruising on his chest and abdomen, evidence of where Ben had been kicked.

He felt the love Grady showered on him and he soaked it up. Before today, neither of them had allowed their true emotions to be set free when they'd made love; now that'd changed. Every touch seemed new, uninhibited—they had nothing to hide anymore. Of course there was still a madman out there, but any restraint Ben had held on to was now gone. He shared every bit of himself with the man he intended to spend the rest of his life with.

Ben almost came when his hands were pinned to the mattress. "Keep these here, love," Grady rasped.

A chill ran down Ben's spine as Grady licked and kissed his way down to Ben's boxers. He dug his fingers into the bedding when

Grady began mouthing and licking his hard cock through the fabric. He'd give anything to have that thin piece of fabric out of the way, but it seemed Grady had other ideas, which seemed to include driving Ben out of his mind with need.

"Baby, please." Ben heard the desperation in his own voice. His ribs gave a little twinge of pain but there was no way in hell he was stopping.

Grady's fingers slid under the waist of Ben's boxers and mercifully pulled the fabric down and over his hard cock. Trails of precum crossed over the hair on his stomach.

"That's what I wanted to see," Grady whispered as he wrapped his calloused hand around Ben's shaft, making his balls pull up tight. "You desperate for my touch."

Ben couldn't speak; a deep groan was his only response as he concentrated on not moving or coming. Grady pumped his hand up and down at a leisurely pace, rubbing his thumb over the sensitive head of Ben's cock.

"God, I want to be balls deep inside of you, love," Ben groaned, digging his fingers farther into the mattress and spreading his legs, giving Grady more room. The warm evening breeze gently scattered the thin white drapes of their bedroom window and caressed Ben's overheated body.

Before he had a chance to recover from Grady's touch, Ben's cock was surrounded in a warm, wet heaven before he was swallowed down his lover's throat. Ben cried out before he had a chance to stop himself from alerting anyone within hearing distance to what they were doing.

He didn't care. The only person who mattered was in this bed with him. The late-day sun bathed Grady's muscled body in a golden glow as his head bobbed up and down, bringing Ben to the brink. Grady's tongue swirled around the sensitive head of his dick and dipped into the slit, almost sending Ben off the bed. If it weren't for his lover's hands on his hips, he would surely have broken his promise of not moving. Grady's muffled moans drove Ben higher past the point of being able to stop himself.

"Babe, babe, I'm going to come," Ben gasped.

That seemed to spur Grady on as he doubled his efforts, sucking him down over and over again. Lightning shot down Ben's spine and into his balls seconds before he came with a shout that echoed off the walls. Grady reared up, pulled down his boxers with one hand as he jerked himself off with the other and came all over Ben's cock and balls before collapsing down beside him.

Their chests rose and fell as they fought to catch their breaths. Ben was thoroughly enjoying the blissful afterglow when someone started knocking on the door. He jerked and hissed in pain; he'd moved too fast. Grady helped him to lie down and covered him with a blanket, then Grady pulled on a pair of loose-fitting sleeping pants, retrieved his Glock from the dresser drawer, and went to answer the door.

Ben hated the fact that he was injured and could do nothing but lie there. He was no help, which only added to his stress. Grady came back into the room and put his gun in the dresser before joining him on the bed.

"What's wrong?" Ben asked as Grady wrapped his strong arms around him.

"Nothing, babe. Supper's ready and Dante wants to discuss a few things."

"Discuss a few things?"

"Yeah, they've set up a perimeter and picked up the envelope from my apartment that I received the day I came back from Galveston."

"Have they opened it?"

"No, they're waiting for us to join them," Grady said as he cuddled closer. Ben welcomed his love into his arms and Grady carefully set his head on Ben's shoulder. In their relationship Ben had always been the dominant one. Now he had to take a backseat—definitely a new perspective.

Ben wasn't looking forward to whatever they would find in that envelope. So far every time he'd received one it had made things worse, but this letter had been for Grady and was the first. There couldn't be anything good in it.

"I guess we should get cleaned up."

"Let me help you into the shower, it's big enough for both of us, and that way I can keep an eye on you." Grady nodded before sliding to the end of the bed and standing.

Ben didn't know what it was. Maybe the tone, maybe he was reading more into it, but it hit him in the gut. "I'm completely capable of taking care of myself."

Grady turned around so quickly that he almost slipped on the hardwood floor. "I've never said that you couldn't. Of course you're able to take care of yourself."

Ben shifted as best he could to his side of the bed and, using the bedpost, he pulled himself into a standing position. Slowly, he walked around the bed and headed for the en suite. This was the only bedroom that had an en suite; the remaining guests had to use the full bath at the end of the hall. He looked up at Grady and saw the confusion.

Ben felt like an asshole. The fact that he was useless and unable to protect the people he loved was no reason to take his anger out on Grady. "I'm sorry. I should never have said that. You love me and you're only trying to help, but I'm not capable of protecting you. That's all I've ever wanted to do from the beginning, and now I'm useless."

Grady walked over and pulled Ben into his arms. His body relaxed into his love's touch. "No you're not. You saved Tristan, and you protected me for so long. It's my turn to do the same for you. That's what a loving and healthy relationship is based on, taking care of each other."

Grady was right. Ben had overreacted. He looked up into Grady's dark eyes and smiled. "I would love your help in the shower."

"Of course, sweetheart. I'd do anything for you." Grady smiled and held Ben a moment longer before leading him to the bathroom.

Ben was thankful for his partner's understanding and love. They went in to the en suite and to the large walk-in shower. Grady bent and slid Ben's underwear from his hips then stepped out of the sleeping pants. Ben's ribs weren't taped. The doctor had said it impeded deep breathing, which could cause pneumonia. He'd been told it would be a one- to two-month healing period before he began to feel better, and the pain would lessen. Way too long as far as Ben was concerned.

Grady reached in and turned on the shower, protecting Ben from the initial cold blast of water with his own body. A hard lesson, but Ben now knew, he didn't need to be the protector all the time; it wasn't all on him. He had a partner in life and love, and he could share every bit of that life with Grady.

Once the water had warmed, Grady turned and placed Ben under the stream and massaged the muscles on his shoulders. Ben looked up at Grady and sank into his lover's dark eyes. "Do you know how much I love you?"

"Yeah, I do," Grady replied as he buried his face in Ben's blond hair.

Ben held on to the most important person in his life and thanked any and all gods listening for the second chance he'd been given. Grady leaned out to grab a fresh washcloth from the vanity and began cleaning Ben as he clasped onto his lover's shoulders. He couldn't stand up for long periods of time without a great deal of pain. Grady knew this. It didn't take long before a clean Ben found himself wrapped in a towel sitting on the side of the bed.

Ben unzipped the bag Grady had placed on the bed for him. He pulled out a pair of sweatpants, a T-shirt, along with a clean pair of underwear and placed them on the bed. Grady had already dressed in jeans and a T-shirt and came over to help Ben dress. Once they were ready Ben walked toward their bedroom door ready to rejoin the real world.

They walked out into the open living room and kitchen area to find Dante, Coop, Matthew, Sam, Vincent, and Tristan around the large island in the kitchen. Spider, Shadow, and Shannon were missing, and presumably were out keeping watch on the area surrounding the cottage. Ben also noted that his brother, Bo, was gone. Probably on duty patrolling Brighton.

Ben slowly sank down onto one of the stools surrounding the kitchen island and addressed the group. "Good evening. Thank you for everything you've done for Grady and myself. We don't know how to repay you."

Dante looked at his team before turning to Ben. "It's what we do."

"I don't buy it. I don't believe you have to do this. You choose to. I'm thankful for that." Ben had the feeling that none of the Sentinel team had done this for the money. It was a choice.

The rest of the Sentinels went back to their dinner of roast beef, mashed potatoes, and corn, but Dante held Ben's gaze. "You're right, you know. None of us are required to do this for a living, and half the jobs we do for individual clients of lesser means we do for free. Though I would like that to remain private," Dante answered with his usual calm demeanor.

"The last thing I'd do is say anything." Ben nodded as he reached for the bottle of water Grady had placed on the island in front of him along with his medication. "But I wanted to let you know how much I appreciate everything you've done for us."

"Same here. You don't know me since I'm new to Brighton, but thank you for everything you've all done. You've gone above and beyond." Grady's voice came out deep, a sure sign of his emotions.

Grady sat down beside Ben and began dishing out food for the both of them. It was weird to be the person cared for. In his previous relationships Ben had always been the protector, the top, the man in charge. Ben had always been forced into the position of protector and provider. But Grady had changed the ground rules; they were equals, both responsible for and to each other, no one more than the other.

The group finished their supper and cleared the dishes. Grady handed Ben another bottle of water as the team spread maps and files across the large kitchen island. The sealed envelope from Grady's apartment sat on top of the pile in a small plastic bag. Ben knew what was coming, and it made his stomach turn.

"Let's get this out of the way, then we can move on and come up with a game plan to take this asshole out," Dante said before he picked up the plastic bag and unzipped it.

Matthew took over from there much the same as he and Shannon had done with the last envelope. With those same tweezers he carefully opened the envelope and pulled out two pictures. He took care to separate them before placing them in front of the group.

Ben's heart stopped. He couldn't breathe.

***

Grady felt Ben's body go from relaxed too rigid in a heartbeat. He wrapped his arms around his boyfriend in comfort. Ben looked over at him with tortured eyes and Grady finally looked down at the pictures.

There, in living color, were two pictures of Ben and his "date" in the diner on the night after Grady had been shot. Close-ups of the guy basically mauling Ben. Grady looked at Ben and saw the guilt written all over his face—and could understand why. But everything had been explained, and Grady knew that Ben had only been trying to protect him by keeping him a secret.

Ben turned in his chair and Grady saw him wince in pain. "I'm sorry, babe. I wish I could change the past, but I can't. I hope you forgive me for handling everything so badly."

Grady held Ben tight and looked him straight in the eye. "I've already forgiven you. Besides I was there when this happened; you weren't exactly a willing participant."

At first Ben looked shocked but quickly recovered and buried his face in the crook of Grady's neck. "I love you."

Matthew took the envelope and pictures over to the desk he'd set up as his makeshift lab. Grady knew from having watched and waited that Matthew would be analyzing the photos for hours. If there was one speck of evidence they could use to identify the stalker, he'd find it.

Dante looked at Ben and Grady with sympathy before saying something neither of them wanted to hear. "We'll have to bring the police chief's cousin up here for his own protection."

"Couldn't this be the stalker rubbing it in to upset them?" Tristan asked as he waved his hand toward Ben and Grady. A good friend was trying to do anything to keep the handsy man away from the cottage. "Hell, the envelope's been sitting in the apartment for weeks. Wouldn't the stalker have already tried to attack whatshisname? He came after me fast enough."

"We can't be sure what the stalker intended. You're right, it could be an attempt to hurt Grady because it was in his apartment when he returned from Galveston. Or this man could be in danger. We don't have enough information to make that decision, and we will not risk a life based on supposition," Dante explained.

"What is his name anyway?" Grady asked. He couldn't walk around calling the guy dickhead. Well, not out loud anyway.

"Ryan Graham," Ben answered in a monotone voice.

"Someone call Dave and let him know what's going on. See if Ryan is still at his house. If he's returned to his own home, we need to know where that is," Dante ordered.

Coop pulled out his cell phone and made the call. The satellite dish Matthew had set up made communications reliable this far into the woods. Dante continued to explain all the measures they had taken outside the cottage to ensure their safety, and the patrols that would be running twenty-four seven. The entire time Grady knew that Ben was barely listening. The fact that Ryan might be coming up here had thrown his lover into a tailspin.

Grady was curious what this Ryan would try to pull if and when he got there, considering he'd refused to keep his hands to himself at the diner. But honestly, Grady didn't feel any jealousy or anger toward the man. He was fully aware of what Ben had done and why. Grady would never risk what he and Ben had—finally—over some random guy that Ben had used as a smokescreen. But that didn't mean he was going to let the twink close enough to his boyfriend to give him another chance.

"Do you want to go sit down on the couch and rest?" Grady asked. They'd been up for a few hours and he knew between healing and the medication, Ben required a lot of rest.

"Okay," Ben agreed and stood, using the kitchen island for balance.

Grady held him under his arm and saw Ben drooping. Everyone had to be more conscious of Ben's physical needs; he'd been severely injured. They got to the couch, which was a large U-shaped sectional facing a stone fireplace. On the wall above a flat-screen television was mounted, and on either side stood two sets of garden doors leading out to the deck.

Grady helped Ben lower himself onto the couch and grabbed a pillow and blanket from the other end. Placing the pillow under his love's head, Grady then covered him with the blanket.

Ben's eyes had almost closed when he whispered, "I'm sorry, babe. I never wanted to hurt you."

Grady wished he could take away Ben's guilt, but it would take time before he accepted the fact that Grady no longer blamed him for any of this. He also knew that Ryan had purposefully instigated all the physical contact in the diner for Grady's benefit. The little twit had read the situation and made sure the show was memorable.

"I know, sweetheart. If they bring him up here, it's not an ideal situation, but I know you love me and I love you. Nothing is going to tear us apart ever again."

"Promise?" Ben asked.

Grady nodded. "I swear it to you. Now rest so you can heal. Once we get this over with, we have a lot of time to make up for, and plans to discuss about starting our life together."

"I like the sound of that, baby," Ben said softly before closing his eyes and falling asleep.

Grady sat there silently brushing his fingers through Ben's blond hair. He didn't want to live in the past, and didn't want to hold any of this against Ben. The bastard at fault was still out there, hunting them. Looking up, Grady noticed Sam trying to get his attention. With one final glance at Ben, Grady stood and followed Sam out onto the front porch.

Sam—also a Mason, Ben's cousin and a nurse at Brighton General—was partnered with Dante and Spider. When Grady had first heard about their triad family, he had been a little surprised. After having been all but drawn and quartered by his family for being gay, he had a hard time wrapping his mind around how easy-going everyone in Brighton was about all types of family arrangements. After he'd met the three of them, it was easy to see how much love they all had for each other, and couldn't imagine why anyone would have a problem with that.

"Is something wrong?" Grady asked.

They sat down in a pair of red Adirondack chairs and he waited for Sam to speak. "I know you might think that none of this is any of my business, but please hear me out."

"Okay." He drew out the word.

"So, about Ben."

"What about Ben?"

Sam traced one of the many colorful tattoos on his arm before saying, "Ben's a good man. And I'm not saying that because he's my cousin. I mean it because it's true. It makes complete sense that he would only think to protect you. But I wanted to give you a little insight into why he probably agreed to go on that date."

"Sam, it's okay."

"Please let me finish." He nodded and Sam continued, "The Mason family are close, as in c-l-o-s-e, and there's a lot of us. Ever since he went through that horrible breakup, the family has rallied around him whether Ben liked it or not. Bo, being Bo, put Ben in a no-win situation. If he didn't agree to go on that date and prove that he'd indeed moved on, the family would've surely come in full force.

"They mean well, but that opened up the possibility that they might have found out about you; he couldn't risk it. He didn't know who his stalker was, only that it was somebody in town keeping an eye on the both of you. The family would've accidentally put you in danger. Please don't hold this against Ben, he loves you so much."

Sam echoed some of what Ben had confessed, but Sam's spin filled out the picture. Over the months Grady had been living in Brighton, he'd met various members of the family, and he could understand why Sam loved his family so much. Ben spoke of them with affection all the time. Grady would've met more of the family, but at the Mason barbeque Ben had whisked him away so quickly that he'd barely met anyone. Their long night of lovemaking had certainly made up for being dragged away.

"It's okay, Sam." Grady placed his hand on Sam's shoulder. "I love him too and nothing or no one is going to change that. I understand why Ben did what he did, though I would've preferred if he had come to me in the first place. But make no mistake, Ben is mine as much as I am his. Nothing will change that."

A brilliant smile broke out on Sam's face as he stood up and hugged Grady. "Welcome to the family, cuz."

That one word, "family," echoed in Grady's head. He'd lost his own parents, brother, sister, aunts, uncles, and cousins when he was disowned for being gay. But now here he had a family welcoming him with open arms and risking their lives, along with their friends and the people of Brighton, to protect them.

Ben had given Grady so much more than he thought he'd ever have after leaving Dallas. Now, he needed to make sure they stayed safe so he could hold on to it for the rest of their lives.

Chapter Nine

Ben felt fingers brushing through his hair, which brought a smile to his face. The blankets were tucked around him, making him feel like he was in a cocoon of warmth and love with his boyfriend at his side. Exactly the place he wanted to be.

The fingers in his hair slowed, then he could hear the soft humming coming from the person beside him. There was no way Grady's voice went that high, and definitely no way that was him humming. Ben tensed, sending an instant jab of pain through his chest and a loud groan of pain up his throat. He opened his eyes and looked up to find Ryan sitting beside him with a smile on his face.

Ben jumped off the couch to get away from Ryan, but his legs tangled up in the blanket and he crashed to the floor between the couch and coffee table. He fought to catch his breath through the pain, when suddenly there were voices and yelling above him. His eyes were squeezed shut as he lay there frozen in pain.

"Get away from him," a deep voice growled. Now that was his man.

Suddenly he felt the coffee table being pulled away from him and he opened his eyes to find Grady lying on the floor beside him. "Sweetheart, we're going to let Sam have a look at your ribs to see if everything's all right before we lift you back up onto the couch. Okay?"

Ben's eyes were watering but he could still see his lover and nodded his head in agreement. His body was rolled until he was lying flat on his back. Sam lifted Ben's shirt and pulled out his stethoscope. He pushed and listened over and over. Ben was beginning to feel nauseous.

"It doesn't appear that anything has been made worse, but I wouldn't try your luck and do that again," Sam advised.

"I didn't intend to do it the first time. I was shocked by who was pawing me when I woke up."

Grady growled again, but said nothing. Instead he and Spider arranged their arms underneath Ben's body and lifted him back onto the couch. He was pretty impressed with himself; he'd yelled in pain only once. Tristan tucked the blanket back around him, and after Ben settled back into the cushions, he had a chance to look around the room.

Tristan sat on the edge of the couch at Ben's feet glaring daggers at Ryan, who was in the kitchen with the police chief. "I only left the room for a few seconds to grab another bag of coffee out of the hallway closet. He must've been waiting for me to leave."

Grady sat down next to Ben and handed him a bottle of water and a painkiller, which Ben gratefully took. His love wrapped his arm around Ben's shoulders, allowing him to lean back onto Grady's chest as he sipped the water. *Much better.*

"Are you okay? Do you need anything else?" Grady asked. His voice may have been soft but his eyes were stormy. Spider stood between the living room and kitchen while Vincent stood behind the couch where Tristan was sitting. They were both still scowling at Ryan, who silently stood off to the side with a smirk on his face. Chief Dave was looking at his cousin like he'd never seen him before. Which seemed weird to Ben.

"I'm okay. Idiot move. I got tangled in the blankets, slipped, and fell." He needed to help downgrade this situation from a hurricane to a tropical depression.

"You would have never jumped up in the first place and felt the need to get away if that twit over there hadn't been running his fingers through your hair," Tristan yelled and got to his feet as if to attack Ryan. Vincent quickly scooped Tristan into his arms and took a few steps behind the couch.

Ben's head spun. Clearly Ryan had been brought to the cottage to be protected, but who the hell was going to protect him from Ryan? It would seem that Dave's cousin had no intention of keeping his distance.

Ben's blood started to boil. He'd told this idiot that there could be nothing between the two of them, and there never would be, but obviously Ryan didn't listen. "Yo, dude. Dense much? I've told you more than once we were going out only as friends. You knew from the get-go there could never be anything romantic between us. I told you I loved somebody else."

That got Grady's attention. "You told him you loved me?"

Ben felt his cheeks getting warm but he couldn't look away from those dark eyes. "Yeah, I told him I was in love with another man. Your name remained a secret because of the threat, but numbnuts over there knew I was involved."

Without jostling him, Grady held Ben closer, lowered his head to take his lips in a deep kiss. Ben forgot why he was pissed off, or that they had an audience; all that mattered was Grady. In that moment nothing else existed, only them. Ben couldn't help but take over the kiss. His tongue journeying deep in Grady's mouth, the taste of his delicious man sliding down the back of his throat. This was the man he loved; no one else could compare.

A loud gagging sound came from the kitchen, interrupting their moment. Ben looked up to see Ryan gagging over the sink. The bastard was doing it on purpose, but Ben couldn't figure out why. He'd never lied to the man. Dave immediately grabbed hold of his cousin by his arm and dragged him out of the cottage.

Ben shook his head at the ridiculousness of the situation, then turned his gaze back to Grady. "I'm sorry, babe. I didn't realize it was him until I opened my eyes, and then I tried to get away."

"The only thing I'm upset about is the fact that you were hurt. Nothing else. None of this is your fault. I don't know why Ryan seems to be attached to you, but I never doubted your intentions," Grady assured, allowing Ben to release some of the guilt he had been carrying.

Dave came back into the cottage and stood before everyone in the living room. Ben had known Police Chief Dave Graham for most of his life; he was married to Ben's cousin Kate. He was an honorable man who worked hard to keep Brighton safe, and had Ben's respect.

"I don't know what to say, I've never seen my cousin act this way. Though I haven't seen him in over three years, he'd never behaved like this in the past. I'm sorry for the complications he's causing. I can keep him safe somewhere else. Even if it's in a prisoner's cell at the station." Dave looked apprehensive and furious at the same time.

Ben knew this was the safest place for Ryan. Ben had spent his life protecting people; how could he risk somebody's life just to avoid feeling uncomfortable for a little while? He couldn't, and that was the answer.

"He can stay here, Dave. It's the safest place for him. We don't know why the stalker sent us a picture of Ryan, but we are responsible for keeping him safe." Ben looked up at his partner to confirm they were on the same page, and thankfully they were. "We'll protect him here."

"I can't ask you to do that. He's been here less than half an hour and has already proven he can't be trusted." Dave was giving them every chance to get out of this, but Ben wouldn't be able to live with himself if something happened to the guy.

Ben looked up at his love and Grady took over. "He stays. But he'll have to be watched at all times to make sure he stays honest," Grady ordered and after a moment Dave nodded his head in agreement. He turned and went to collect Ryan from the porch.

Vincent released Tristan, who gave the bigger man a dirty look before storming over to him and Grady. "I am not leaving Ben alone with that handsy asshole for a second."

Ben was a little surprised by Tristan's vehemence; it appeared he'd become Tristan's responsibility. Grady squeezed Ben and looked at his friend. "Thank you, I would appreciate that, and I'm sure Ben would agree."

"Absolutely. Thanks, man." Considering he spent most of his time sleeping and healing, Ben needed a backup.

"Are you hungry, Ben? You didn't eat much for supper," Sam asked as he headed into the kitchen. His cousin had always been a caregiver, one of the main reasons he'd become a nurse.

Ben had always loved the open concept of the cottage, but he didn't like being the center of attention, he never had, and Grady seem to pick up on this. He gathered Ben into his arms, blocking out the rest of the room. Again he felt weak for depending on everyone else, but one look at Grady's loving face had him settling back down.

He had to accept the fact that he was injured and would need his friends' and family's help to heal and stop their stalker from attacking anyone else. Buddy, Sam's golden retriever, came over and sat on the floor in front of Ben. Looked like he'd gained another protector.

"Yeah, I could eat. If you don't mind?" He had to keep his strength up so that he'd heal as quickly as possible.

"I'll make you a plate," Sam replied as he went into the kitchen and got busy putting something together.

"We'll survive having Ryan here." Ben sighed. "We have bigger problems to deal with. Anything new come up while I was sleeping?"

"One of the sensors at the edge of our perimeter went off but by the time we got out there to investigate we found nothing," Spider reported. "Ryan had already arrived."

"That's why we were outside when you woke up. It didn't cross my mind that little twit would try anything or I would have never left you in the same room with him. I'm sorry, sweetheart. It won't happen again." Grady squeezed Ben's hand.

"Not your fault. That asshat doesn't know from boundaries. Now what about that sensor? Could it have been an animal?" Ben asked, steering the conversation back to the more crucial aspect of what had occurred this evening.

Spider grabbed a laptop from the long kitchen counter, then brought it over and set it on the coffee table in front of Ben. With Grady's help, Ben sat up a little straighter and watched as the screen came to life. "This is the feed from the motion-sensing video cameras we have placed throughout the surrounding forest. This particular camera was facing in the direction of the sensor that had been tripped."

The black-and-white image came to life; the trees seemed to glow in contrast to the darkness of the night. After a few seconds the image changed to show a heavyset man dressed in black with a ski mask on his face. What made Ben's heart kick against his aching ribs was the assault rifle in the guy's hands.

"Well, it didn't take long for him to find us again. Kind of hoped we would have had more time before we were shot at again," Ben murmured while shaking his head.

"Dante, Coop, Shadow, and Shannon are scouring the area. Spider, Vincent, and I are watching over the cottage until they get back. We are keeping everybody else inside and out of harm's way," Grady explained as the group broke up and went back to what they were doing before Ben had woken up.

Hell, a lot happened while I was sleeping. What does it matter? I'm of no use to anyone.

Grady looked down at Ben as if he was trying to read his mind, but he kept the smile plastered on his face. Grady didn't need anything else to worry about. Thankfully, Sam walked over and set down a plate with a hot roast beef sandwich on it and Ben's stomach began to growl.

Grady laughed, dispelling the tension and making Ben genuinely smile. He leaned forward slightly for a kiss but ended up hissing in pain instead.

"Easy, love. I'm more than happy to come to you." And Grady did just that. Ben melted at the first touch of Grady's soft lips. This was the way love was supposed to be, like every moment together was a gift. He could feel himself getting hard and didn't care who saw.

Grady pulled back, his eyes hooded. "I have to go finish up the checks before the team gets back, but keep all those wonderfully dirty thoughts of yours for later tonight 'cause I aim to please."

"Love you."

"Love you too, sweetheart." Grady stood and walked out the front door. Ben didn't like Grady being out in the open, but he was right, he could take care of himself. Ben realized now how crazy it was to keep the threat away from his love—a cop who had worked in a big city for years.

Ryan came back into the cottage as Ben began eating his succulent roast beef. Tristan walked from the kitchen to the end of the couch and sat down at Ben's feet while giving Ryan a squinty-eyed stare before opening a book and sitting back. Tristan had taken to protecting Ben with a vengeance. He wasn't exactly sure why, but he was grateful.

Vincent sat at the dining room table watching Ryan like a hawk. Ben would have laughed if he wasn't certain he'd end up back on the floor rolling around in pain. Instead, he smiled and went back to his snack, considering it was well past suppertime; in fact it was approaching midnight.

Ryan sat on one of the cots the Sentinel team had brought with them. Considering how many men were here and the fact that there were only two bedrooms and one couch, the cots were a necessity. He shoved his bag under the cot before lying down and turning his back on them.

Asshole.

***

Days passed and they'd gotten into a routine of sorts. The Sentinel team had easily settled in, and it was clear they were used to adapting to all kinds of situations. They did their jobs with an intensity Ben had never seen.

Things were quiet. Too quiet. There hadn't been another sensor hit since the initial contact, but they all suspected something would happen soon. They didn't know when, or, what the Sentinels had identified as the more pressing concern, what the stalker would do next.

Ben and Grady had grown closer. The fact that they were together twenty-four hours a day had helped, but in truth Ben had found Grady irresistible right from the start. The man had brought him back to the land of the living; ironic now that they were fighting for their lives.

Vincent and Tristan continued their weird dance of sorts; one minute they couldn't keep their eyes off each other, and the next Tristan would storm off, yelling at Vincent for being overbearing. Vincent always had a smile on his face when it came to Tristan; whether he was being yelled at or cuddled with, he smiled at Tristan like the cat who ate the cream. Not at anybody else in the group—the rest of them got the stoic, taciturn version of the man who watched everything.

For the most part Ryan had stayed relatively quiet, he hadn't tried to force himself on Ben again, for which he was grateful. But the man hadn't tried to get along with anyone in their large group, let alone he wouldn't apologize for his behaviour. He watched everything closely, but stayed at a distance. Ben didn't know what Ryan's deal was, but he had enough things to worry about that he didn't waste his energy trying to figure the man out.

The police chief had come out a few times to give them updates and to check on his cousin. But Ryan refused to talk to Dave, and that had him more confused with his cousin's behavior. Apparently the two had been close when they were children, but had grown apart over the years. Dave had hoped to rekindle their friendship, but that didn't seem possible now, and each visit only put one more nail in the coffin lid that closed down their friendship forever.

Dante, Shadow, Coop, and Shannon had left for morning rounds, leaving Spider, Vincent, Grady, Tristan, Matthew, Ryan, and Ben at the cottage. Sam was at the ER on shift. Ben had been up and able to move around the cottage a little easier every day. His pain had started to abate a little, making him even happier, though he still had to stop for breaks and naps.

He was enjoying a peaceful moment in Grady's arms as they sat on the large porch swing. They had decided that being outside was safe, considering all the sensors their stalker would have to go through made it impossible to get close enough to the cottage.

"How are you feeling, sweetheart?" Grady asked as he looked up from Ben's shoulder.

"Perfect, when I have you lying beside me," Ben answered honestly. "I'm so lucky to have you."

"Same here."

Ben had been waiting for the right moment and it wouldn't get any better than this. "Look, Grady, I've been doing some thinking and I was hoping we could talk about something that's important to me."

"That doesn't sound ominous, does it?" Grady joked, but Ben knew there were still some doubts because of what Ben had put him through. He hoped that someday his love would be able to fully trust him.

"It isn't, I promise you," Ben swore. "I wanted to mention this to you so that you will have time to think about it."

"Think about what?"

"When all of this is over, I want you to move in with me." *Now, it's out there.* Ben heard his heart beating as he waited for an answer; he could see the surprise on Grady's face. *Maybe this wasn't such a great idea.*

Grady's mouth opened and closed a couple times like a fish out of water and Ben pretty much had his answer. What could he have expected, pulling something like this on Grady? "I understand. With everything else going on I'm the king of bad timing."

"Wait, no…it's just—" Grady began but was cut short by the screeching of alarms going off on the machines monitoring the sensors.

Tristan came running out onto the porch. "Sensors are going off everywhere."

Grady got up and carefully pulled Ben into a standing position, his arm held protectively over his ribs.

"Let's get inside and see what's going on," Ben suggested, closing the door on any further conversation about living arrangements.

They walked into organized chaos. Guns were being loaded and information relayed to the other half of the team already out in the woods. Spider, Vincent, and Matthew were suiting up and Grady was given his own semiautomatic rifle. Ben claimed a Glock so he could still protect everyone even if he was injured.

"Okay, here's the plan," Spider announced, getting everyone's attention. "Vincent, Matthew, and I are going to scout the area while the rest of the team that are already on patrol work their way back here, but it will be at least a half an hour before they arrive. Sensors are going off in two areas. The ones to the west are where the other team were already headed, and they'll check there before coming here. The sensors going off to the south we're going to take. Grady and Ben, we need you two to watch over the cottage and keep Ryan and Tristan safe."

"Do you know how to operate the sensor system?" Matthew asked as he hovered over his "baby"; the man loved his gadgets.

"Yes, I've been watching you use it over the last couple days. At least I know where the sensors are in relation to the cottage," Ben stated.

"Perfect. If any other sensors sound, get a hold of us immediately," Spider instructed as he headed for the door followed by Matthew. Ben could remember a time when Matthew wasn't coordinated enough to climb a tree.

Vincent was busy hugging Tristan tight, a few feet off the floor. Ben looked away so that they had a moment of privacy. Soon Vincent followed the team out of the door stopping only to give Tristan a soft kiss on his cheek and place a necklace over his head.

Grady locked the door behind them, though they all knew a locked door wouldn't keep out the person stalking them. Ben had wracked his brain trying to figure out who this man was. At this point all he knew was who it wasn't; not the exes, that's for sure, both were happy in their new lives and had no reason to threaten either of them. Honestly, Ben had thought Grady's ex who had attended the hearing might have something to do with it, but he had an alibi according to Dante.

"Well, we might as well get comfortable, this could take a while," Ryan said, which was the most he'd said all day. He went to his cot and pulled open his bag.

Ben turned to Grady and said, "I'll keep an eye on the sensors."

Grady nodded as he walked to the front window and looked through the heavy drapes. Tristan had gone to the kitchen to cook. Ben had noticed whenever Tristan was stressed he cooked. The more stressed, the more elaborate the meal. Ben kept his gaze on the screen but soon learned that that was his first mistake.

"Step away from the window or I'll shoot him."

Ben's head shot up to find Ryan holding a gun to the side of Tristan's head. Tristan's hands were bound in front of him in duct tape and his mouth was covered. Grady turned from the window, and only then did Ben realize that Grady's gun was lying on the dining room table. He immediately put his hands up along with Grady, though that made Ben hiss out in pain from the movement.

"Don't think to grab for that gun. And Ben, put your handgun on the table as well," Ryan ordered as he pushed the muzzle into the side of Tristan's head. The sick bastard was enjoying himself, and poor Tristan looked ready to pass out.

Ben took his Glock and placed it on the table beside Grady's gun. Ben didn't know what to do that wouldn't risk Tristan's life. *Shit.*

"Grady, take a chair and put it in the center of the room." His love did what he was told, always careful to keep them both in view. "Now, sit down," Ryan ordered.

Ben watched as Grady complied. He looked at Tristan but knew he would be no help, having his hands already tied.

"Come here slowly, Ben, and keep your hands where I can see them."

Ben moved toward Ryan and when he got within two feet he was ordered to stop. With his free hand Ryan handed him a large roll of duct tape.

"Tape him securely to the chair." *Dammit. Grady is the only person in the room at full strength and free.*

He walked slowly up to Grady; knowing the teams would be back soon, he thought any delay would buy some time. But Ryan slapped Tristan across his face before pushing the gun into his mouth. "Speed it up or he dies."

Ben had no choice: as he leaned down he locked eyes with Grady, anger and fear clear to see, and then, with his heart cracking, Ben taped him to the chair. There'd be no way Grady could get out without help. Which left Ben alone to make sure Tristan didn't die. He rolled out the last piece of tape, lowered his head, and kissed his love for what could be the last time.

"I love you, babe."

Before Grady had a chance to answer, Ryan coldcocked him with the butt of his gun, knocking him out. Ben raged and turned on Ryan, who quickly placed the gun back to Tristan's head. His eyes were wide as Tristan looked at his unconscious friend and began struggling.

"He'll live, not so sure about everybody else." Ryan laughed and Ben got the first look at the real man. Cold, vicious, and insane.

Ryan attached something to the sensor screen then pointed at the back door that led to the porch and said, "Get moving."

Ben complied with a final caress to Grady's cheek. He knew this might be the last time he saw his love.

They went out the back and into the forest. Without someone there to watch the sensors going off on the screen, no one was coming to help him and Tristan.

About ten minutes into their forest hike, Ben asked, "Why don't you let Tristan go? You don't need him since you have me." As they crested another fairly large hill, his ribs were screamed at him to stop moving. His head was swimming and his stomach rolled.

"Oh no, this is personal. The other guy wants you, but I want to shut this peacock up, permanently." Ryan shoved Tristan forward, the gun still trained on his head. Tristan was busy rubbing the necklace Vincent had given him between his two bound hands.

"What other guy?" Ben asked as a large man in camouflage came out of the forest in front of them.

"Him." Ryan laughed and Ben felt it like nails on a chalkboard.

Ben stared at the man, who looked to be around fifty-five, with graying hair and dark eyes. *Who the hell is this guy?*

"Good job. Now let's get them to the camp," the man ordered before turning and continuing away from the cottage, and farther away from help.

Ben couldn't restrain himself any longer. "Who the hell are you and why are you doing this?"

The stranger laughed and turned to face Ben with a vicious sneer on his face. "I'm Detective Richard Reynolds, you piece of scum, and you'll pay for leading my boy into this kind of life. You're all sick and depraved. You need to be wiped from the face of the earth. We'll see what my son is willing to give up for someone like you."

Shit, Grady's father.

Ben looked over at Ryan, wondering how a gay man was working with homophobic Detective Loco here. Ryan seemed to pick up on his thoughts and smiled. "Hell, a straight man will do about anything for the right price. You disgusting piece of shit."

Det. Loco led them on and Ben, who was dragging, had lost track of time. Every time he made a move to slow down or stop, asshole Ryan shoved him in the back with the barrel of the gun.

Shit. It had been morning when he and Tristan were taken, and it was now hours past sunset.

Chapter Ten

Grady picked at the piece of glue left over on his arm from the duct tape. They'd searched the area but Ben and Tristan were gone. Vincent had gone off the deep end when he found Tristan missing when they'd returned. He'd been outside the cottage ever since. Grady would never forgive himself for this. The love of his life and his best friend were taken from him and he couldn't stop it.

"It's not your fault. We didn't expect Ryan to be working with the stalker," Spider tried to reassure Grady as he sat down beside him at the dining room table.

"They're gone. We can't wait around here and do nothing," Grady ground out as he ran his fingers through his hair to the bump on the back of his head from being coldcocked. "They could be hurt. They need us." *Need me.*

"I understand, but they left a note with the DV5 communication device attached to our system. Matthew and Shannon said that it was a video feed and the note confirmed it." The letter had stated that they would be contacting them with demands. Shannon had attached another device and did something to the system so that she would be able to confirm the specific area from where they were being contacted.

"I can't believe Ryan would do this." Coop shook his head, and Grady noticed the police chief cringe. Dave had raced to the cottage, along with Bo and a few other deputies after the team had arrived, released Grady and got the full story.

Grady's anger and guilt were bubbling close beneath the surface. The only thing keeping him from exploding was the fact that he knew Ben depended on him to keep his shit together. He would find Ben, and Lord help whoever got in his way.

In the end all the sensors had been tripped, making it impossible to follow them through that trail. So far they hadn't been able to pick up their physical trail but Vincent was still at it.

The last thing Ben will remember is that I refused his offer to live together. I'm an idiot. Grady didn't have a chance to explain. *Explain what, that I'm a coward? What did I do?*

He stood up and began pacing from one side of the cottage to the other. The love of his life had been taken from him and he was useless while they waited for their stalker to call. It had been hours since they were taken; the sun had set and with each passing minute Grady got closer to the edge. No one believed Ryan was the mastermind behind this; Grady wished he knew who was pulling the strings.

"I've contacted my aunt and uncle, Ryan's parents. It seems that this little vacation to Brighton was their attempt at saving their son." Dave hung his head and continued, "Apparently, in the last couple years they've been keeping their son's transgressions away from the family out of embarrassment. The rest of the family had no idea what they'd been going through. Ryan's turned to drugs and gambling. From what my uncle says, he owes people money. People you don't want to owe money to."

"So they sent him here to Brighton to straighten him out, but didn't tell you he had big problems that could follow him here?" Dante asked.

"It would seem so," Dave answered, shaking his head. "How they thought I would be able to help Ryan out without knowing what was really going on, I don't know. They are as shocked as I am at what he did today. I'm so sorry that someone from my family had anything to do with this."

"You had no way of knowing." Grady didn't want the man living with the guilt over something he had no power to control. "This was your cousin's decision, not yours. You're a good man and a great police chief."

Dave nodded his head in acknowledgment but didn't say a word.

Matthew walked away from his computer holding a piece of paper and joined the group. He stood directly in front of his boyfriend, Coop, as if he needed his support. "My tests have come back in on the envelopes. I wasn't able to get a complete fingerprint, but the DNA testing on the saliva of your stalker came back with a match of sorts. I had sent in everyone's DNA who had access to the envelopes. That way we could rule people out. One of the results came back…" Matthew stopped and cleared his throat. "With an over ninety-eight percent familial match to you, Grady."

Grady was numb; he refused to believe someone from his own family would have done this. Sure his parents were pissed but that didn't mean*…it couldn't possibly be…Shit!*

Suddenly, the video screen on the dining room table came to life. Matthew and Shannon went to work tracking the signal as everyone else stood in front of the screen; everyone wanted to know who was behind this. The camera turned, bringing his love into focus. Ben was tied to a chair and slouched over, his blond hair streaked with blood. Grady had to try to put aside what had happened to Ben, who had been obviously beaten, and concentrate on the room. It looked like the walls were made of plywood. Like a hut of some sort. But that's all he could make out before his world was rocked to its very core.

"Hello, son," Richard Reynolds said as he stood beside Ben, grabbed his bloody hair, and pulled Ben's face back so everyone would see the damage he'd done. "Do I have your attention now?" He dropped Ben's head, which lolled to the side.

"What the hell are you doing? Christ, you're a cop," Grady yelled as his heart broke at what his love had been through. He had to get to him. He had to think. Grady took in the room once again;

they could be anywhere but he doubted his father chanced taking any of the roads. So walking distance.

"I warned you and you still went ahead with this perversion."

"Richard, I'm not a perversion." Grady refused to call him Father.

"Oh, yes you are, and that sickness infected your younger brother," he sneered.

"Randy's gay?"

"Oh, he might think so now. But I'm sure he'll see the truth once he's done with his therapy." His father's eyes shone with a weird light, and Grady knew he was insane. The way he pulled at his own hair, his quick glances around the room… He was dirty, unshaven, and completely out of his mind.

"What have you done with Randy?" Grady demanded and prayed this had nothing to do with conversion therapy.

"You need to worry a little bit more about your *lover* and not your brother." Richard sneered.

"Where's Ryan, how did you get him to work with you?" Dave asked.

"Work for me, not with me. Your cousin has proven to be useful. He's taken pictures and kept track of my son and his lover. The date was merely icing on the cake." Richard laughed. "And all for the low, low price of twenty-four thousand six hundred dollars. His debt to some unsavory characters, you should thank me. Then it was just a matter of Ryan wanting to reconnect with his cousin in Brighton. Bibbidi-bobbidi-boo."

Dante broke into Richard's rant and asked, "What do you want?"

"I want my life back to the way it used to be. Since I can't have that, I offer you a choice, son. Your life for his. If you truly believe that gay love is as real as a man and a woman's, prove it." Richard flung Ben's head forward, almost tipping him over along the chair he was tied to.

"Done. Where do you want to meet?" Grady agreed without reservation. He would trade his life for the man he loved. No question.

"There's a cell phone in the bag Ryan left. Turn it on and I'll direct you. Of course you'll come alone," Richard explained as he wiped his bloody hand off on Ben's shoulder.

His love hadn't moved this entire time.

A loud voice boomed behind Grady. "Where's Tristan?" Vincent demanded.

Richard seemed to get great satisfaction out of seeing Vincent upset. He didn't resemble the man Grady had admired when he was a child.

"The little mouthy one?" Richard laughed as Vincent began growling, which only made him laugh harder. "He's around here somewhere. Ryan had plans for him. I don't believe you'll want him back after Ryan's done with him."

"Listen, you fucked-up bastard. I will kill you myself," Grady swore. "You've known Tristan has been my friend since we were children. You bowled with his father for Christ sake."

"You can try to kill me but nothing you can do or say will save your *best friend*," his father mocked and disconnected the call.

The rage that ran through Grady was fast and violent. Without a word he walked to the cot Ryan had been using and pulled the bag out from underneath. Sure enough there was a cell phone right on top. He pulled it out and turned it on to wait for instructions.

"Okay, what do we know?" Dante asked as the team gathered around the table.

"I found a trail about twenty feet from the cottage but it disappears over the first ridge," Vincent spat out while walking straight up to Dave. "I will kill your Ryan if there is even a scratch on Tristan."

Dave didn't flinch. "I pray it doesn't come to that and Tristan is unhurt." That seemed to calm Vincent slightly and he nodded his head before walking back to the dining room table where all the maps were located.

"We've got him," Matthew yelled while frantically typing on his computer, pulling up a map of the area on the screen. "There." Matthew pointed at the red area on the screen.

Grady came closer and the moment he saw the screen he knew exactly where Richard was. "That's the Jacksons' hunting camp."

"Suit up. We move in two minutes," Dante ordered. "Find the closest road we can use without alerting them to our presence. Shoot to kill. That crazy bastard won't be reasoned with. Shadow, I need you to go as backup for Grady; you have the best chance of going unnoticed. Make us proud."

Grady walked over to Vincent, placed his hand on Vincent's shoulder, and said, "Bring back my best friend."

"I promise," the large man said, and by the look on his face Grady believed him.

Grady put on his bulletproof vest underneath his jacket, grabbed his Glock, and headed for the door. His father should be contacting him shortly; he'd never been a patient man. As if thinking it made it come true, the phone pinged. Grady had a message.

Burrows Road, mile marker twenty-eight.

And it'd begun. One way or another someone was going to die today.

***

Ben had been conscious throughout the call but he wasn't going to alert Det. Loco. He'd heard Grady agree to give his own life for Ben's, and he couldn't allow that to happen. Ben ached from head to toe. He didn't think the asshole had missed a spot on Ben's body; his ribs were re-broken and more added to the original number, but he wasn't down for the count yet.

Grady's father had left with Ryan immediately after the call ended. Ben raised his head a little and looked over at Tristan. It was true. Ryan did have plans for Tristan, but as of yet Loco hadn't allowed Ryan to do anything to Tristan. He didn't have a scratch on him, but Ben knew that wouldn't remain true when they came back. Tristan was tied to a chair on the opposite side of the room and looked over when he saw Ben's head move.

"How are you?" Tristan whispered softly; neither of them wanted to alert their captors to Ben being conscious.

"Well enough to make sure old Rick there gets what he deserves. How are you?" Ben tried to calm Tristan with a soothing tone.

"Scared out of my mind. But if Ryan thinks I'm going down without a fight, he's sorely mistaken."

"If you get a chance, run. Don't look back, don't worry about me, just run," Ben stated firmly. Tristan's only chance would be if he somehow got out of his bindings. "Swear it to me, Tristan. Please."

Tristan looked ready to fight but after staring at Ben for a moment he acquiesced. "I promise, Ben."

They could hear footsteps outside the small building. Ben took one final look at Tristan and closed his eyes once again. The door opened and he heard two sets of shoes walk in.

"Help me get him to the truck. We have an appointment to keep," Richard ordered, and Ben knew this might be his only chance to get Tristan out of there. The chairs they were tied to were wooden and breakable. Now the only problem was, did he have enough strength to pull it off?

He could feel his bindings being loosened and allowed his arms to flop down to his side as if he was still unconscious. Once he was completely freed, he waited until both men tried to lift him before he attacked. With one arm wrapped around Ryan's neck, he flung the man across the room where he landed in a heap on the floor. Richard was a bit harder to take down.

Ben looked over and saw Tristan wiggling out of his ropes. How he got them free Ben would never know, and he hoped to live to hear the story over a few beers.

Ben and Grady's father traded blows, but Ben knew he only had to keep the asshole occupied until Tristan could make a run for the door.

"You think you can get away?" Richard growled.

Ben looked back at the empty space that had held Tristan, the door open wide. That brave man had done exactly what Ben had hoped: he'd run. "Not really, asshole, but I thought I'd give you something to remember me by." With that Ben threw a vicious uppercut to Richard's jaw, sending the man flying into the wall.

He took the chance and made a run for the door. The searing pain hit him before he heard the shot and he fell to the ground.

Ben grabbed his shoulder to try to slow the bleeding seconds before he was kicked in the back of his head and the world went dark.

***

Tristan ran as hard as he could, but he had no idea where he was going. He didn't know the woods; hell, he didn't frequent them, but he had to figure it out and fast. Thankfully there was a full moon and a clear sky, so that at least he wasn't tripping over roots as he ran.

After roughly half an hour Tristan decided to stop and get his bearings. He'd heard the shot ring out behind him and prayed that Ben was still alive. He knew Ben had attacked Ryan and Richard so Tristan could get away. He had to get help so Ben would survive.

Tristan leaned against a tree that had a trunk three times his size, hoping for some divine inspiration. Instead, he heard running feet and breaking branches heading his way. It had to be Ryan. No one else was going to be that noisy.

There was no way in hell he'd let himself be taken back. Tristan looked around for a place to hide. Someday this would be a great scene in a book he would write, but right now all he wanted was Vincent. He rubbed the medallion of a bird Vincent had placed around his neck, giving him the courage he needed.

The footsteps were getting closer; Tristan was running out of time. He jumped into the thicket of bushes off to his right. They were thick with large leaves, providing perfect camouflage. Tristan made himself as small as possible, hoping Ryan would run past him. The Sentinels had to be on the trail by now, but how were they going to find him if he couldn't keep himself alive?

The steps got closer and stopped roughly ten feet in front of where Tristan was hiding. He peeked through the bushes and recognized Ryan's blue canvas shoes. *Shit.*

"Come out, come out, wherever you are," Ryan sang, making Tristan's skin crawl. "Your trail ends here, so you might as well come out because I'm going to find you. Then you will pay for making me run through this godawful forest. When I'm done with you, you'll be begging me to kill you."

Tristan couldn't get away; he'd have to fight if he wanted to live. He despised fighting even though he'd been trained how. After the whole Stavros debacle, Grady had made Tristan learn how to defend himself. But of course his best friend Grady wouldn't leave it at merely self-defense. He also had Tristan trained in Krav Maga. The classes were brutal, and he bitched each and every day he had to go, but if this worked, it was worth every bit of pain. He would have tried to fight back at the shack, but he had sworn to Ben that he'd run.

First, he had to get the gun Ryan surely had away from him. Ryan walked around the area, coming closer to Tristan with every pass. He knew his time was up; he'd have to fight his way out of this. Sure enough, Ryan began searching through the bushes, using both hands to move the leaves. In one hand was the gun.

With one final look at his medallion, Tristan attacked. Krav Maga had taught him if you couldn't get away to use physical aggression while applying both defensive and offensive moves to bring the attacker to submission. Fast and deadly, as he was taught, Tristan sprang out of the bushes and kicked the gun out of Ryan's hand. He took Ryan's momentary shock and went for his eyes while simultaneously kneeing him in the groin. It might not have been pretty, but it worked.

Ryan fell to the ground and Tristan leapt on him. He'd been taught to not stop until the attacker quit moving. So he kept fighting Ryan, who got in a few shots at his face, but Tristan didn't stop. After Ryan was finally out, Tristan stood, his face and knuckles bloody, but he was alive. He quickly picked up the gun in case his attacker was playing possum.

"You fag piece of shit. You think I'm done with you." Ryan's speech was slurred but it was strong.

Tristan turned as Ryan stood up. Tristan raised the gun and said, "Stay where you are or I'll shoot you."

"Yeah, right. As if you have enough balls to pull the trigger. You pansy-assed fag," Ryan spat out as he moved closer. "You might have gotten a few hits in but this is far from over."

"Stop or I will shoot you," Tristan stated as loudly as he could, but Ryan kept coming.

Could he kill someone? Tristan shot at the ground in front of Ryan to make him stop but he laughed and kept walking. Ryan had to be insane; there was no other answer. A normal person would have stopped, but what the hell about this situation was normal?

"I'm going to make you pay for every time you protected Ben, for every second I had to walk through this fucking forest, and each and every bruise you gave me. Ready to die?" With that Ryan lunged at Tristan.

In that last second, the words Vincent had said to him pulsed through his head. *Protect yourself at all costs until I find you.* Tristan pulled the trigger. The sound seemed so much louder than before and everything seemed to slow down as the bullet hit Ryan in the chest and he collapsed to the ground.

Tristan was frozen to the spot; he could barely breathe. He'd killed a man. He didn't know how to process this but Ryan wasn't getting up, and never would be again. Tristan dropped the gun and took a few steps back. He knew he was in shock but damned if he knew how to handle it. Thankfully, he didn't have to think too long.

Rustling in the brush had him scooping the gun off the ground. He'd survived some crazy shit, but he refused to be taken out by a bear or a wolf...*did they have them here*? Tristan's lack of knowledge about the forest had him bringing the gun up, ready to protect himself.

One by one the members of Sentinel appeared in the small clearing, armed to the teeth, but the only one who mattered was Vincent.

The beautiful man slowly walked across the clearing and carefully removed the gun from Tristan's hand. Everything he'd been through finally came to a head and Tristan collapsed into Vincent's arms.

***

Grady drove like a madman to keep up with his father's texts. He'd gone to the first location only to be rerouted to a second and third. Richard was using every trick in the book to keep him guessing and to confirm no one was following him.

Shadow popped up from the backseat and took out the few small interior light bulbs. "Do you think we'll be heading to a new spot again?"

"Richard is insane. I'm not sure what he has planned, but make sure you're ready," Grady muttered as he took a left down another endless country road. "Fuck. Where the hell are we?"

"Almost to the edge of Brighton. Soon we'll be pushing the county's boundaries," Shadow answered after he checked his GPS.

Grady might be a cop in this county but even he had never taken these old roads. They neared the fourth meeting site and this time they saw headlights. "Shadow, I need you to swear something to me."

"Swear something? What the hell?"

"In case anything happens to me I need to know someone is looking for my brother. He's not like me. He's an artist, a free spirit who won't know how to survive whatever Richard has planned for him." Grady had to make sure his brother was found. "Swear you will find my brother and bring him here to Brighton, to safety."

Shadow seemed to think about it for a moment before he said, "I swear to you that I will find your brother Randy."

Grateful for the promise; he knew Shadow was good to his word. Grady sucked in a harsh breath and with his voice breaking, murmured, "Thank you."

He slowed the SUV and parked on the side of the road fifty feet in front of the other vehicle. "I'll take out Richard. If he gets the best of me then you take him out."

"Agreed."

Grady took a deep breath and opened the driver's door. The night felt colder than normal or it could have been the sight of his father holding a gun on the man Grady loved. Ben was standing head down and swaying from side to side. He could see a large patch of blood covering Ben's shoulder and the hole in his clothing. He'd been shot.

"You bastard, you shot him," Grady yelled and began storming toward them.

A gunshot hit the ground only a few feet ahead of Grady. He pulled the Glock from his side and pointed straight at his father's head. Richard jammed his gun into the side of Ben's head and Grady lowered his weapon.

"No, no, no," his father sang. "See, I have the power here. Not you. You may have ruined my good name, but I'll return the favor by ruining your life."

"I came here like you wanted. Now release Ben."

"You don't give the orders here, I do. Now walk over here like a good boy." Grady was barely holding on to the edge of restraint but he had to remain calm, Ben was depending on him.

Ben's head moved slightly and he looked up at Grady. Instead of seeing pain and defeat, there was determination and strength. That was one amazing man. Grady was sure Ben was planning something. He was waiting for his moment.

"I said, get over here. Do you want to see how many holes I can put into your 'boyfriend' before he dies?" Richard threatened.

By now his father was wildly waving his gun in the air, out of control. Ben took the opportunity to wink one swollen eye at Grady, raise his left leg, and slam his heel into Richard's knee, effectively breaking his kneecap. Richard howled in pain, released Ben, and grabbed for his knee as he crumpled to the ground. Ben stumbled backward against the truck as Grady raced across the distance to get to him.

His father was writhing on the ground in pain and had dropped his gun. Grady quickly grabbed it and went directly to Ben, who was leaning heavily on the hood of the truck.

"Baby, hold on. We'll get you to the hospital," Grady begged as he took Ben into his arms. Shadow came from behind Richard's truck. How he'd managed to get out of Grady's truck and all the way over without being seen was a mystery. The man had skills.

Ben didn't say a word; he was too busy gasping for air and trying to stay standing. Grady was certain Ben's ribs had been reinjured. Blood was still seeping from his gunshot wound and he was weaving on his feet. Grady placed Ben's uninjured arm over his shoulders and began a type of walk-carry back to his truck.

Once he got Ben lying in the back of the SUV, Grady turned to see the road filling up with vehicles. Shadow had handcuffed Richard, who was screaming obscenities. The Sentinels and police chief, with Bo by his side, filled the area. People ran toward Grady but he didn't have time for discussions.

"I have to get Ben to the hospital," Grady hollered as he jumped into the driver's seat. "Did you get to Tristan?"

"Hold on, Shannon's a medic. She should ride in the back with Ben." Dante had his hand up. "Vincent has Tristan back at the compound, he wasn't seriously injured," he explained as neared the truck.

Bo came to the driver's door and opened it. "Get in the back with Ben, my brother needs you. I'll drive."

"I'll clear the way with my cruiser," the chief said before turning back to his car.

Grady got out and walked around to get into the back of the SUV. He crawled in beside Ben and watched as Shannon went to work setting up an IV, cutting off Ben's shirt, and attaching a heart monitor. She mumbled, "The gunshot to his shoulder was a through and through," then continued wrapping it to slow any further bleeding. Grady had been trained in first aid but Shannon was moving so fast he didn't want to get in her way.

Grady held Ben's hand and gently brushed his fingers through his beautiful blond hair. "How is he?"

"The sooner we make it to the hospital the better. I believe he has another collapsed lung," Shannon uttered as she listened to Ben's chest with a stethoscope. Apparently, Sentinel medical bags mimicked EMT bags. Grady figured it was essential considering what they did for a living.

"Bo, speed up," Grady yelled.

He felt the truck change gears as Bo pressed harder on the accelerator. Grady didn't know what to do to help so he laid himself down beside Ben, holding his hand and softly speaking to him.

Tears were streaming down Grady's face as he told Ben how much he loved him and that he wanted to move in with him, and that he wanted to start their lives together. Then he began listing all the things they were going to do. But Ben needed to hold on.

They pulled into the ER at the same time Shannon's machine started to emit a screaming bell that scared the hell out of Grady. "What's wrong?"

"He's crashing." She immediately began CPR as the back doors opened to reveal doctors and nurses with a stretcher.

Grady got out of the way as they loaded Ben onto the gurney and rushed him inside the building while Shannon continued CPR. Grady followed right behind them, but when they pushed Ben through a pair of double doors he was stopped. Grady went around the person and kept going; he wasn't leaving his partner.

Someone grabbed his shoulder and Grady turned to find the chief and Bo standing there with their hands up, taking a few steps backward.

"Easy, Grady. You can't go in there."

Logically he knew they were right, but he couldn't stop himself from trying to get to Ben. "I need to stay with him."

Grady turned around to continue until he heard a commanding female voice: Dot Mason. "Young man, you will come with me." And just like that he deflated.

The chief must have called Ben's family.

Grady walked over to Ben's mom, who took his hand and led him to the waiting room that was packed with Masons and all the Sentinels, except Vincent.

He didn't bother to look anyone in the eye. This was his fault. His father had done this. Grady would never be able to forgive himself.

How could he expect Ben to?

***

Beep…beep…beep. Okay, that's annoying. Ben tried to reach for his alarm clock but the intense pain had him pull back and hiss.

"Easy there, take it slow," a soft feminine voice said, and he knew it was his mother.

Ben opened his eyes, having to blink a few times to clear his vision, and sure enough she was right beside his hospital bed. *Hospital?* Suddenly everything came back to him. Grady's father wanted to kill them.

"Tristan, is he okay? What happened to Grady? Where is he?" Ben became agitated, but he couldn't stop himself.

"Son, son, calm down," Dot whispered and pointed toward the corner of the room.

There he was, his love lying in a reclining chair fast asleep. "Tristan is safe. Ryan is dead, and Grady's father has been transferred to the state penitentiary until his hearing for kidnapping, attempted murder, and quite a few other charges."

"How long have I been unconscious?" Ben asked. By the sound of things it wasn't merely overnight.

"Five days, but you're going to be just fine." She smiled and patted his hand. Ben couldn't help but look over at Grady. He wanted to touch him and console him for everything his father put him through. "I don't want to wake that poor boy up yet."

That got Ben's attention like nothing else would. He looked at the clock on the wall; it was 2:30 am. "He's been here with me all the time, hasn't he?"

"Of course, he refused to leave you. We finally got him to go home to take a shower but other than that he's never left your side. Grady has barely spoken to anyone and steps to the back of the room when family comes in."

"Why?" Ben didn't want Grady in the back. After everything they'd been through to be together, he wanted his love right up front.

"That brave young man of yours believes this is all his fault because it was his father who did all this damage. He can't forgive himself, and he doesn't expect anyone else to either. He needs to be put straight," Dot explained. "Now, I'm going to go let the doctors and nurses know you're awake and to let the family know. Expect to have a room full of people before the day starts if the doctor allows it." His mom bent over and gave Ben a soft kiss on his forehead before walking over to Grady and tapping his leg.

Grady's flew out of the chair. "Mrs. Mason, is something wrong?"

"No, dear, Ben's awake," she answered before turning toward the door.

Grady turned and raced to his side. Their eyes met, both filled with tears. Ben raised his hand to Grady, "Come here, babe."

He took Grady's hand and Ben took a good long look at the man he loved and intended to keep for the rest of his life. Grady had yet to say a word, and Ben could feel the guilt and shame pouring off him. That had to stop.

"Grady, I love you."

"After everything that's happened? After everything my father did to you and the people of Brighton? God, you could have died, and Tristan could've died, but you saved him. You got him free to run." Grady's tears flowed freely. "I should have known Richard was capable of this. I should have thought of him as a suspect," Grady rasped, his voice rough and low as he rambled on nervously.

Ben placed his hand on Grady's cheek. "I have one request." Grady stared at Ben. "Show me what's in your pocket."

Grady looked adorably confused but began digging into his pocket without question. He pulled out his keys, a few dollar bills, his wallet, and exactly what Ben had been looking for: a crumpled piece of paper that had been folded flat repeatedly.

"Read that note to me, please."

Grady carefully unfolded the paper and began reading, "*My Love, I'm sorry I had to leave. Someday soon I'll explain everything and we'll never have to be apart again. It will be forever. Ben xo.*"

Ben knew that Grady had taken to carrying around that note in his pocket every day. He'd have to get a cover for it before it fell apart. "Grady, we are in this together. You stuck with me when we all thought the stalker was mine, and you loved me throughout all of this. 'We'll never have to be apart again' means I'm not going anywhere. Ever. Now that this is behind us I intend to start our lives together."

Grady looked distant. Ben could wait forever, as long as Grady stayed with him. Ben ran his thumb over Grady's knuckles. He loved this man beyond reason and wouldn't know what to do if he left him.

"Then, I just have one question for you, Ben."

Ben didn't miss the smirk on Grady's face. "Yeah?"

"Do you still want me to move in with you?" Grady asked. There was a touch of uncertainty in his voice.

Ben knew where this was going and couldn't wait for them to get there. "Yep, I want you to move in with me. I want to build my life with you."

Grady carefully folded the piece of paper and stuck it in his wallet. "I'll move my things in when you get out of the hospital."

Ben would have cheered if he didn't hurt so much. Grady held his hand a little bit tighter. "I truly love you. I don't ever want to know what it's like to not have you in my life."

"Same here," Grady replied before he leaned down and kissed Ben softly.

The door to the room opened and two nurses and a doctor walked in followed by Ben's mother. He winked at his mom and she smiled knowingly.

Grady was the man who made Ben's life whole.

There would never be another.

Epilogue

Grady parked his old truck in the laneway of the house he and Ben now shared. It had been over a month since Ben was released from the hospital, and he was getting stronger every day. But Ben wouldn't be able to return to work until his shoulder had healed from his latest surgery.

The one thing that kept Grady from accepting his new life and happiness completely was the fact that Shadow hadn't found his younger brother, Randy, yet.

Grady had left for a few days to go back to Dallas only to find his family home sold, and the new owners had no idea where his family had gone. They'd approached Richard's old bowling team, who were varying degrees of helpful. One confirmed Grady's fear that whatever had happened to Randy involved conversion therapy.

Officially, his mother, brother, and sister were missing. Police Chief Graham had reached out to other counties and cities to forward on the missing person's reports. The Sentinels were helping Grady search, especially Shadow, who had taken his promise to heart and had made this his mission.

Chief Graham had taken his cousin's body back to his family for burial. Nothing more was ever said about Ryan's part in all that happened, but Dave took full responsibility for his cousin's actions. It would be a while for Dave to get over his guilt no matter what anyone said to reassure him.

They'd found a few surprises in Richard's truck. He had his old police radio and it was tuned in to Brighton's PD communications.

That was how he'd kept an eye on where Grady and the other officers were working. Also, they'd found a pipe bomb, numerous guns, and an insane amount of ammunition. Grady had learned that Richard had been placed on medical leave months earlier, after Grady left for Brighton, due to increasingly violent behavior. He'd read several Internal Affairs reports of professional misconduct against Detective Richard Reynolds.

The Mason family had welcomed him and never once blamed him for Richard's actions. It would take a long time before Grady saw it the same way.

"Are you going to stare at the house all day or are you coming in?" Ben asked, while laughing from the front porch.

Grady had no idea how long he'd been standing there but it had to have been a few minutes at least. He smiled at his lover and walked up the flagstone pathway to the porch and Ben's waiting arms.

"Smart-ass," Grady said before he wrapped his arms around Ben and kissed him deeply. Ben took control, making Grady moan as he pressed up against his love, his duty belt getting in the way.

"God, I love it when you moan. How about you follow me to the bedroom where we can discuss this smart-ass issue a little bit further. Supper can wait," Ben suggested with a wink and ran his free hand over Grady's chest, causing his heartbeat to speed up.

Grady had no idea how he'd gotten this fortunate to finally have the unconditional love he'd been missing. He'd never take it for granted.

"I'd follow you anywhere," Grady swore. "But first, I've got something for you. Let's go sit down."

"Okay, is something wrong?" Ben asked, his playful flirting gone.

"No, nothing, sweetheart," Grady assured. "I want you to have something."

They walked over to the couch and sat down facing one another. Grady could tell Ben was worried so he quickly pulled out the small, dark gray box and held it in his hands.

Ben looked at it, his eyes wide, but Grady wanted to explain first before he said anything. "Ben, please let me talk, and then you can say what you need to say."

"Okay," Ben said while taking one of Grady's hands.

Here goes everything. "There's a tradition in my family going back before World War One that we were afraid ended with my father. It was my great-great-great-grandpa's ring and it would be handed down from generation to generation. But after Grandpa gave the ring to my father it was lost. No one could find it, and my father didn't seem too broken up about some tradition from my mother's side of the family. He'd gone out the following day and bought himself a new three-diamond, twenty-four-carat gold ring to replace Grandpa's ten-carat band.

"I was devastated because I was the oldest son in the family so the honor was to be mine to inherit after my father. I intended to give it to the man I loved and wanted to spend the rest of my life with. But it was gone."

Ben slid closer and held Grady with his one arm; the other was still in a sling. "I'm sorry, babe."

"Thank you." Grady leaned over and gave Ben a kiss. "Earlier today we received the contents of my father's safety deposit box. We thought we might find a lead to the location of my brother and the rest of my family." Grady took a deep breath. "After believing it was lost for over twenty years, there it was, my grandpa's ring. The bastard had lied."

Grady rubbed his finger over the rough material covering the old ring case. This was it. He opened the lid and held it out for Ben to see. It was a simple, thick, golden band with a few scratches in it from many lifetimes of use. "I know it's not much compared to the fancy rings you can get these days, but I'm hoping you'll want to wear my ring."

For some unknown reason Grady couldn't find it in him to look Ben in the eyes. Maybe he was rushing things. What if he'd read this all wrong?

Ben's shaking fingers took the band out of the box. He looked it over and handed it back to Grady. He could actually hear the door closing in his heart. Ben sat there with his left hand out and it took Grady a moment to catch on. He wasn't being rejected; he was being asked to put the ring on his love's finger.

He took Ben's left hand and slid the ring on without breaking eye contact. Seeing that ring on Ben's hand made everything settle within Grady's heart.

He was home.

In this man's strong arms, he was home.

The Boys of Brighton continues with ***Vincent***

VINCENT

Chapter One

Nizhóní *(Navajo) – Beautiful. Something that's attractive. It also refers to something that is good. The Navajo idea of beauty goes beyond appearances. Beauty is a sense of being, and is comprised of harmony and balance that is felt within.*

The cold mist bit and swirled, surrounding him in its steely grip. He felt the spirits joining him one by one until there could be no mistake. The cry of an eagle pierced the air followed by the yip of a coyote. One the messenger, the other the trickster, a troublemaker, and not what he needed at that moment. Then he heard the one he'd been searching for. The happy chirps were unmistakable: his sparrow.

Vincent pushed forward using all his strength but only managed to move a few inches. He had to get to his sparrow before it was too late. But he already knew all was lost. He felt the blade pierce his palm seconds before the shrill cry of his sparrow ripped him through his heart. Then silence. He knew what was coming next, it always did, and he was powerless to stop it.

The mist started to clear and he felt the weight of the knife with his uninjured hand yet again and couldn't stop himself from looking down. The wound continued to bleed, dripping life-giving blood down his fingers and onto the ground. In his other hand, he held a knife stained in his own blood and that of another. He wanted to throw the blade far away but his hand wouldn't respond to his commands.

What came next he'd repeatedly begged the spirits and creator to take from his view, but they never heard his prayers or had simply chosen to ignore them. Vincent's sparrow lay lifeless on the ground a few feet in front of him, his chest cut open and his heart missing. He wanted to scream and shout at the wind for the injustice of it all, for the life lost and the future withheld from him.

The wind released its hold and Vincent collapsed onto the ground beside his sparrow. He lifted the blade, brought it to his chest, readying to stop his own beating heart. His muscles bunched, preparing to plunge the knife deep, the tip of the blade slicing through his skin from its own weight.

Vincent took a deep breath and in the softest of whispers spoke his sparrow's name before plunging the sharpened steel deep…*Tristan.*

***

Tristan bolted upright in bed, his heart racing as a storm raged outside his window, his hand clutching the silver medallion hanging from his neck. He looked around his room and found no one, but he was positive he'd heard his name being called. The rain pelted the windows in what felt and sounded like anger as he ran his hands through his hair. The apartment was dark so he turned on the light on the side table. He looked at his watch and realized it was only three in the morning. *Damn.*

He'd been burning the candle at both ends recently with his latest book's deadline looming ever closer while completing his move from Dallas to Brighton at the same time. He had one more trip back and then the new owners could take possession of his old condominium. Tristan had decided to take over his best friend's apartment in Brighton. Grady had moved in with his boyfriend, Ben, leaving almost everything in the two-bedroom apartment for Tristan's use.

He'd been busy adding his touches and blending his furniture in with what was already here, like the hot pink loveseat by the bank of windows at the back of the apartment. The front bay window held his desk where he wrote his romance novels and looked out onto the Main Street of Brighton below.

Tristan pulled on his bright blue track pants and white t-shirt, before making his way to the kitchen. He was about to make himself a cup of tea when someone began banging on his door. His heart froze in his chest; the first thought that ran threw his mind was his ex had found him and was out for blood. But Tristan hadn't seen Stavros in months.

Again, his hand found the silver and turquois bird charm at his neck for comfort. He pushed the terrifying thoughts from his mind and walked to the door as any rational person would. Stavros wasn't going to affect his new life in Brighton; Tristan refused to allow it. Glancing through the peephole brought his heart to full speed in an instant. *Vincent.*

His fingers couldn't move fast enough to turn the locks on the door. He had to take a deep breath to calm himself and then tried again. Tristan had always hated how easily he became flustered and often hid it behind an easy smile and misdirection. Carefully, he undid the locks and opened the door to the man who fulfilled every dream Tristan had ever had.

From his long black hair and bronze skin to his light blue eyes, he was a proud Navajo male—stunning and the center of Tristan's attention since they had first met. He couldn't explain the attraction. Whatever the pull, it seemed natural. Even though their first encounter was during a stalking investigation, the moment Tristan's eyes met Vincent's Tristan couldn't look away. Tristan felt as if a part of him "recognized" the stunning man. The best way Tristan could describe it: that feeling when he'd been away for a long time and he walked through the door of apartment, dropped his bags, and melted into his favorite chair. Every part of him knew he was where he was meant to be—home.

Tristan waited for Vincent to come in but he remained standing on the small piece of wood that was called the back porch. Water dripped from his chiseled face and Tristan imagined following the drops with his tongue.

"Vincent, you're soaked. Come in," Tristan directed as he tried to rein in his wayward thoughts.

"I know it's late, or early depending on the way you look at it. I don't want to keep you up but I saw your light was on and thought maybe…."

"Come in. I was already awake, *nizhóní*." He'd been learning a few words in Navajo out of respect for Vincent's culture.

Vincent stepped in; his initial look of pleasure at hearing the endearment was clouded with concern. "Are you sick?"

"No, no. It's…you'll think I'm crazy, but I thought I heard my name being called about a half hour ago. It must have been a dream." Tristan shook his head, trying to rid himself of the memory. "Would you like some tea?"

Vincent looked distracted for a moment before taking off his leather jacket and hanging it on the back of one of the kitchen chairs. His hair was pulled back in a large braid that ran partway down his broad back.

Before Tristan knew what was happening he found himself in the big man's arms. "Can we sit down on the couch for a little while, sparrow?" Vincent asked.

"Sure. Is something wrong?" Tristan found himself being carried across the room as his answer. The nickname never ceased to thrill Tristan and made him feel important to his boyfriend.

Once they sat with him still in Vincent's arms, Tristan tried again. He placed both of his hands on either side of his gorgeous man's face and asked, "What's going on? Why were you out at this hour?" When he noticed hesitation, Tristan added, "Are you my new stalker? Because if you are I'll leave the door unlocked."

Vincent smiled as Tristan had hoped. Typically, Vincent was the quiet one in any group, surpassed only by Shadow, who was near invisible. But when Vincent spoke, people listened. Anyone who thought he wasn't paying attention or could be ignored was sorely mistaken. Not only was he a retired Navy Seal, but a master of many disciplines of martial arts; he never missed a thing that was happening around him. Unfortunately, that meant Tristan couldn't get away with anything as long as Vincent was around.

Vincent lifted Tristan's turquoise and silver sparrow medallion between his fingers and rubbed it gently. He had given it to Tristan while they were holed up in the Masons' cottage trying to protect Ben and Grady from a lunatic who turned out to be Grady's own father. That familiar feeling of panic from that horrible day came rushing back. Tristan had killed a man that day.

Of course, Vincent didn't miss it. "What's wrong?"

"I was thinking about when you gave this to me and what I did." Tristan still couldn't say the word "killed" aloud.

"You had to shoot Ryan or he was going to kill you. You had no other choice. He was as psychotic as Grady's father. You have nothing to feel sorry about. I'm proud of you for protecting yourself," Vincent assured as he held Tristan a bit tighter.

He wished he could accept what Vincent said as true, but the guilt remained and silently he fought daily to keep it at bay, leaving no one the wiser. If anyone knew the extent of his turmoil and guilt, they'd worry, so he kept his emotions and the havoc they wrought to himself. After all, it had been more than a month since the incident; he should be getting over it by now, right?

Tristan nodded his understanding and leaned his head back against Vincent's wide chest. "You still haven't told me why you're out in this storm at three in the morning."

Vincent grunted something before laying his head against the top of Tristan's. He loved the fact that such a strong, war-hardened man loved to cuddle. Their relationship was progressing at a slower pace than what some would consider normal for two healthy men, but that's the way Tristan had wanted it. After his last experience, he was in no hurry to rush into anything. So they had only gone as far as making out. From what Tristan could feel under Vincent's clothing, the man was built like a god, which tested the hell out of Tristan's resolve.

"What'd you say, babe?"

"Just a nightmare."

"A nightmare?" Tristan asked. "What was it about?"

Vincent seemed to take a moment to think about it before answering. "I can't remember."

For the first time since they've known each other Tristan felt as if Vincent was lying to him and it felt like an actual blow. But before he could say a word Vincent continued.

"That's not true. I never want to be dishonest with you, sparrow. I'm not ready to talk about it until I've had time to think over its meaning."

"Its meaning?" he asked. "You believe that the nightmare had a meaning?"

"Yes, sparrow. Sometimes they have a message for us, but we need to take the time to decipher them," Vincent explained as he traced Tristan's bottom lip with his thumb.

Tristan felt the touch like a full-body caress and sank into it. "When you're ready you'll tell me. I can wait."

"You are such a joy to me," Vincent murmured, his eyes turning from affectionate to heated in seconds.

Every fiber of Tristan's being called out to this amazing man, and all he wanted to do was climb him like a tree. He watched in anticipation as Vincent's soft lips lowered to claim his own in a passionate kiss. Tristan moaned as Vincent's tongue explored and dominated his mouth, causing his cock to harden almost instantly. He couldn't help but flex his hips, searching for friction of any kind.

Vincent reached down and cupped Tristan's balls through the fabric of his track pants. They'd never been naked together, but at that moment all he wanted was to feel Vincent's strong hand wrapped around his hard cock.

"Please, touch me," Tristan begged his man.

Vincent lifted his head and looked Tristan in the eye. “Are you sure?”

“Yes, babe. Please, I need to feel you.”

Vincent stood with Tristan still in his arms, so he wrapped his legs around his lover’s waist. Their lips never parted. He needed this amazing man more than his next breath. It was crazy, he felt out of control, but there was no way in hell he was going to stop.

For the first time in his life, Tristan trusted someone else to stop before they went too far. It wasn’t that he didn’t want to make love with his glorious man. In fact, he wanted to share everything with him, but his own fears stood in his way. His boyfriend understood and supported him.

Boyfriend. They’d never discussed what they were to each other. As far as Tristan was concerned, they were in a relationship, but did Vincent feel the same way?

Tristan pulled away from the kiss as they entered his bedroom. “Vincent, what am I to you? Are we exclusive?” *Please say yes.*

Vincent stopped in the center of the bedroom and looked at Tristan with serious, solemn eyes. “You are my sparrow. I want no one else but you.”

Who could argue with that? Tristan had never believed in love at first sight but from the first moment he’d laid eyes on Vincent, Tristan had felt an immediate attraction. He dove in for another kiss, desperate to show his *nizhóní* how much he meant. By his reaction, he already knew.

The second Tristan’s back touched the mattress he unwound his arms from Vincent’s neck and began exploring the valleys and planes of the hard body hovering above him. He didn’t know what it was about this man but Tristan had never been drawn to another human being like he was to Vincent. He was quickly becoming a necessity in Tristan’s world.

Vincent shifted to lie beside him, saving Tristan from being crushed under his weight. Vincent’s large hand ran over Tristan’s body as they continued to kiss as if their lives were at stake.

Tristan's head was spinning with the sensations running through his body. The calluses on Vincent's hands lightly scraped over Tristan's chest, causing him to hiss in pleasure. He could feel the evidence of Vincent's arousal through his pants and was overcome with the need to rub their naked bodies together.

"Naked. I need us to be naked, now," Tristan announced as he began unbuttoning Vincent's shirt. Slowly, more and more bronze skin was revealed to his appreciative gaze until Vincent gently held Tristan's hands, effectively stopping his progress.

"Are you sure?"

Vincent rose even higher in Tristan's estimation, if that was possible. "I know I'm the one who wanted to go slowly, and I still want that, but I'm sure we can be naked together without penetration. I want to feel your body against mine."

Tristan knew he seemed overly cautious to wait when he was so on fire for this man, but after everything he'd been through in the last six months, he had to be sure. But, oh, he needed to feel that beautiful bronze skin against his. He nodded.

Vincent smiled wide and jumped from the bed. His shirt hung open, giving Tristan sexy snippets of the muscled body underneath. Vincent slid out of his shirt and Tristan joined him by removing his own and tossing it across the room. He watched as gorgeous muscles flexed with every move Vincent made. He reached down, undid his belt, and opened his jeans, then pushed them, along with his boxer briefs, to the floor before stepping out of them.

Tristan's breath caught in his throat at the sight before him. Vincent stood in all his six-foot-five-inch naked glory. A large intricate tattoo covered the left half of his chest and down his left arm. Tristan watched as the already sexy-as-hell man reached up and took the tie from his long black hair, releasing the braid, which allowed his hair to fall in silky waves across his chest and back. The sight almost caused Tristan to come in his pants.

"You've got to know how hot you are, right?" Tristan asked.

His boyfriend's returning smile gave him his answer as Vincent stepped forward and reached for the hem of Tristan's track pants. In one swift motion, his pants slid off, joining the growing pile of clothing on the floor.

Vincent stood looking down at Tristan for a few long moments and he was beginning to feel self-conscious. A moment before he was about to pull the covers over his body, Vincent said, "*Nizhóní*, sparrow," before he reached out and ran his fingertips across Tristan's pale skin. The difference in their coloring stood out in alluring contrast as fire raced through his body at Vincent's touch. "I can't help but want you."

"Then jump in here already," Tristan teased as he opened his arms wide in invitation.

Thankfully, Vincent quickly accepted as he crawled back in beside Tristan. The slide of his warm skin elicited a low moan from Tristan's kiss-swollen lips. That familiar feeling of being wrapped in a cocoon of their own began to settle in. No one could reach them here; it was only the two of them. Tristan had noticed the feeling getting stronger every time they were together, making him wonder if it was only him or if Vincent felt it as well.

Tristan ran his hands down Vincent's chest before pushing him onto his back. Tristan quickly straddled his waist and took Vincent's lips in a deep kiss, letting his tongue map out his lover's mouth. He lost himself to the feeling of Vincent's skin against his own and rubbed his aching cock against Vincent's muscled abs.

The sounds of pleasure coming from Vincent spurred Tristan on as his lover's thick cock sat nestled between Tristan's ass cheeks. The heat firing between them should have singed his body as beads of sweat slid down his back. He knew he was going to come soon: his balls had already pulled up tight and a telltale tingling was beginning at the base of his spine.

"Vincent, I'm going to come, babe," Tristan moaned.

Suddenly he felt like he was flying through the air until he was on his back once again. Vincent took his own cock and Tristan's in one of his large hands and began pumping them together. The hot silky skin of Vincent's cock sent fire racing through his veins as he spread his legs wider, desperately flexing his hips in time with Vincent's hand.

His lover began speaking, but too softly for Tristan to understand as he rained kisses across Tristan's neck and chest. Vincent's hand sped up, leaving Tristan gasping for air between moans until he could no longer stave off his orgasm. One more expert slide caused Tristan to cry out his release. His cock throbbed as his balls emptied. A few moments later Vincent followed with a roar before collapsing down beside Tristan, then pulled him into his arms.

Their heavy breathing was the only sound in the room as all the stress of moving to another city, then working furiously to meet deadlines caught up with Tristan. His eyes closed, safe in the knowledge that Vincent was here with him.

Tristan was safe and cared for…for now.

***

Vincent heard the soft beep of his cellphone and knew he had to answer but wasn't pleased at having to leave Tristan in bed alone. He gently slid his arm out from around his sparrow's warm, pale body and stood. After covering Tristan in a thick blanket, Vincent went in search of his phone. Comfortable in his nudity, he walked out into the open-concept living/kitchen area and grabbed his jacket off the back of a chair.

He pulled his phone from the pocket and saw he had one new message from Dante. Never a good sign. It meant the team had another assignment. Vincent typed in his code and listened as his boss confirmed his suspicions: they had a job and Dante needed Vincent back at the compound. He sent off a return text, letting Dante know that Vincent was on his way.

He walked back into the bedroom and ducked into the bathroom, where he quickly cleaned up. Then he gathered his clothing off the bedroom floor and dressed before going to Tristan's side. He wiped the evidence of their need for each other from Tristan's cock and stomach. His sparrow was still asleep and Vincent was unsure whether he should wake him. He knew Tristan had been working long hours recently so Vincent decided to leave his love sleeping. He knew it was far too early to speak of love with Tristan, but it didn't make it any less real to Vincent. He'd seen and done things people couldn't even imagine and he knew his own mind and emotions well. Vincent loved Tristan—a fact that wasn't going to change.

Vincent brought the comforter up from the end of the bed and laid it over Tristan's lean body. His sparrow's red hair stuck out in all directions against the white pillow, making the color even more vibrant. All he needed now was for Tristan's expressive green eyes to open and the handsome picture of his man would be complete. However, he needed his rest.

Quietly Vincent relocked Tristan's door—the key his love had given him came in handy. Vincent left a note explaining he had to leave and soon he was on the road out of town, heading to the Sentinel compound. The Sentinels were a group of retired armed forces specialists who banded together years ago to use their skills to protect those in danger, retrieve kidnapped personnel when the government didn't want to admit any knowledge of them, and a multitude of other assignments that were best executed covertly.

The original team led by Dante and Spider consisted of Shadow, Shannon, Coop, and Vincent. Recently Sam, Dante and Spider's partner, and Matthew, Coop's partner, had joined the team as well. They had purchased a large plot of land outside Brighton and renovated an old three-story Victorian so that each member had their own space. They had added several outbuildings to hold their gear and vehicles. They had a helicopter pad out back, along with various simulation courses and firing ranges.

Often they teamed up with local law enforcement when needed as well as different agencies across the country, and a number of others around the world. In fact, one of the latest cases they'd taken on had brought Tristan into Vincent's life, and he'd be forever grateful for that, even though he'd failed to keep Tristan safe. That thought was enough to make his stomach roll at what his sparrow had to do to protect himself. Vincent shook his head and lowered the driver's-side window to help clear his thoughts. He'd sworn to never fail his love again.

He pulled up to the compound's gated entrance and pressed his thumb to the fingerprint scanner. The monitor turned from red to green and the gates began to open. These security measures were necessary considering the Sentinels had pissed off cartels, a few extremist leaders, and other hateful groups. Some of whom had tried to extract their revenge.

Vincent parked his big truck in his usual spot and jumped out. Considering he was almost six and a half feet tall, he needed a vehicle that fit him. In the early dawn hours, he could see lights on throughout the large house, confirming something was up. His boots echoed on the stairs as he stepped onto the wraparound porch on his way to the front door.

Buddy, Sam's dog, greeted him as he opened the door. "Hey, boy, where is everybody?"

"In the conference room," Sam's voice came from the nearby kitchen, from where Vincent could smell the heavenly aroma of coffee being brewed.

He walked down the hall, passing the office on his way to the larger conference room. He could hear the team's voices the closer he got until he walked through to find everyone waiting on him. *Shit.* Well, everyone except Shadow, who was still searching for Grady's younger brother, Randy.

Grady's psychotic father had taken Randy away to be cured of being gay and no one could find him. Shadow was chasing down the latest lead on Grady's behalf; he'd been unsuccessful in finding his brother so far.

"So, where were you at this hour?" Coop asked with that same smirk on his face. "Could it have anything to do with a certain author?"

Vincent couldn't help but smile. He was proud of his relationship and didn't care who knew. "Yeah, man, I was with Tristan."

"Does he act out any of the scenes from his books?" Shannon asked. "'Cause I gotta tell you they're *hot*!" Vincent knew she was teasing him; they were more of a family than colleagues.

"You'll never know," he shot back. What he and Tristan did in private was no one's business. Tristan's pleasure was for Vincent's ears alone.

"Oh, that's where you're wrong," Matthew kept the ribbing going. "Eventually he'll move in here and get teased as much as I did when Coop and I made a little extra noise."

"A little extra noise? You're kidding right? It sounded like the two of you were performing a trapeze act in there with all the jumping and hollering." Spider laughed as he handed out the information on their latest assignment.

Vincent had thought about moving Tristan in, which was what he wanted to happen, but he also wanted the two of them to have some privacy. The property had acres of land, and maybe he'd be able to build them a home of their own. The more he thought about it, the more Vincent was convinced that was what he wanted to give his sparrow. Tristan would need the peace to write. Vincent started imagining the office he could have built for him. *Whoa, don't rush this. You're likely to scare him off.*

He looked down at the information in front of him, pushed everything else to the back of his mind, and concentrated on their latest assignment. By the looks of things, there would be hot, dry sand in his immediate future and not the good kind that comes with palm trees and fruity drinks.

Chapter Two

Tristan adjusted his sunglasses in the reflection of the bookstore window. He was pleased that the cherries on his shirt matched his red jeans. His yellow messenger bag containing his laptop stood in contrast, making Tristan smile. With a quick check of his eyeliner, which matched his eyes, into the bookstore he went.

The moment he opened the door he felt at home. From the smell of the books to the row after row of colorful covers, this was Tristan's idea of heaven. Jeffrey, the owner, was busy arranging books on a desk in the back while Jesse stood nearby holding a cardboard box.

"Tristan, I'm so happy you have the time to come and do this for us," Jesse said as he placed the box on the end of the table and walked toward Tristan.

"Hey, it's my pleasure to help out," Tristan replied as he shook Jesse's outstretched hand.

"Copies of your single-title books and the five different series arrived yesterday; thanks for the donation." Jeffrey pulled more books from their boxes. "We're so excited to have this promotion."

"As long as all the proceeds go to Jesse's project, I'm in," Tristan stated as he set his bag on the counter.

Jesse worked as a cook at Bear's diner. He and his partner, Royce, were opening a youth and homeless shelter with small apartments, a learning center, and a recreational center. All aimed at providing LGBTQ+ youths living on the streets with a safe place to go. Tristan had an extensive fan base and was somewhat famous; he wanted to use that for good.

They'd decided to sell signed paperback copies of his books in store and sell them online through the bookstore's site. The live book signing held in the store was being advertised far and wide. Any proceeds from books by other authors sold during the promotions went to the bookstore.

"Definitely, all proceeds from the sale of your books will be given to the group home," Jesse assured as Tristan sat in the chair behind the table and reached for a black pen.

Tristan flashed a happy smile at his friends and got to work; he had hundreds of books to sign. He let his mind wander while completing the repetitive task and soon found himself on his favorite subject, Vincent. Two days ago, he had left a note the morning he disappeared from Tristan's bed. He knew Vincent and the rest of the Sentinels were on assignment halfway across the world and Tristan missed his lover.

He didn't know when they'd be back or if he'd be hearing from him anytime soon.

Tristan knew all too well, how dangerous these situations could be. In fact, it was during a scary situation that he first met Vincent. Grady, Tristan's best friend and a Brighton police officer, was being stalked and Tristan wound up in the middle of the drama when the stalker took a shot at Tristan. In the end, to save his life, he'd been forced to shoot and kill Ryan Graham. Tristan brushed those thoughts away, but apparently, not fast enough to go unnoticed.

"Are you okay, Tristan?" Jesse asked as he placed another box of books on the floor beside the table. "Your hand is shaking."

Tristan quickly dropped the pen and rubbed his hand as if it were sore. "Writer's cramp. I'll be fine."

Jesse seemed to look right through him, but he went along with Tristan's explanation. "I'm really grateful for your support. The youth center needs all the friends it can get."

"What you're doing here is an amazing thing. Though my parents were open to the fact that I'm gay, I know a lot of parents like Grady's who threw their own children out. This will be a safe place for them to go," Tristan explained. "And to that end I was hoping you would allow me to hold classes on creative writing in your learning center."

Jesse's mouth opened and closed a few times while Tristan waited patiently for him to get his thoughts together. Tristan understood; he typically thought things out before speaking…well, most of the time.

"We'd be honored to have you, but we might not be able to pay you the salary that you're worth." Jesse looked abashed.

"Well, isn't it a good thing I'm not expecting to be paid." Tristan laughed as he picked up his pen.

Jesse stood frozen for a moment before asking. "Are you sure?"

"Positive. Now how many online orders have we had so far?"

"Over five hundred at last count."

"Well, I'd better get my ass in gear then," Tristan joked as he went back to work.

Vincent was never far from his thoughts, but Tristan needed to focus on the here and now. He was leaving tomorrow for Dallas to pick up the last of his belongings, effectively closing the door on his former life. The funny thing was, he wasn't sad about it, not even a little. His parents were in Houston and the other people he cared about were right here in Brighton.

One of the darker parts of his life in Dallas was most certainly Stavros Menzotto—a man whose mission in life was to own Tristan. They'd gone out on a few dates, but Tristan had broken things off the moment Stavros began telling him Grady was a bad influence. Obviously, Stavros was jealous of the close relationship Tristan and Grady shared. Stavros couldn't accept the friendship, and he didn't walk away when Tristan broke it off. Stavros began stalking Tristan and showing up places that he frequented.

Then one night on his way home, he was attacked and beaten by two men only to be miraculously saved by Stavros. Tristan smelled a setup and called Grady, who investigated the attack and found Stavros's hands all over it. The problem was neither of the men who had attacked him would testify that Stavros had hired them. Further investigation revealed that Stavros's parents had tons of money, and fancy lawyers helped get the two thugs six months' probation after they used the bullshit "gay panic" defense.

Tristan reached for another book to sign, but his hand came back empty: the stacks were gone. He looked at the clock on the wall and realized hours had passed, and it was almost noon. Jesse sat in a chair behind the counter as Jeffrey helped a customer.

"You were sort of in your own world so I thought it best to leave you to it. Would you like to go to the diner for lunch?" Jesse asked. "My treat, my way of thanking you for all this."

Tristan didn't have to be asked twice; an invite to lunch was always welcomed. "You're on."

After a quick stop to ask Jeffrey if he wanted them to bring anything back from the diner, Tristan and Jesse were on their way They made small talk as they went but Tristan had the feeling Jesse had something on his mind. Authors studied human behavior and were great people watchers—inspiration for Tristan's books. His curiosity was peaked but he'd wait Jesse out and see where this went.

As they walked into the diner people hollered out their hellos. Tristan loved this town. He smiled and thanked the day Grady brought him here. Tristan saw the White Hair Crew—Brighton's gang of grandmothers composed of Rose Mason, Mrs. Graham, Betty, Bertha, and Mrs. Walker. Nothing happened in Brighton without their knowledge, and sometimes approval. He thought he would test Jesse's desire for them to be alone so they could talk.

"Oh, there's the Crew, we should sit with them and visit."

Jesse was caught off guard but he quickly recovered. "We need to talk about the center. Maybe we should sit in one of the quieter booths."

Tristan nodded and did a drive-by with the Crew. As he kissed each of them on their cheeks he said, "Grandma Rose, you look lovely today. Grandma Betty, love the new hat. Grandma Bertha, sassy as ever. Grandma Walker, love the new haircut, and Grandma Graham, how are you?"

Grandma Graham was Police Chief Graham's grandmother. Tristan had killed her grandson, Ryan, and Tristan wasn't sure how to deal with that. He'd been avoiding the chief for a month and knew it was just a matter of time before he'd have to face the man.

Grandma Graham's eyes softened as she took Tristan's hand. "I'm doing just fine, honey. Thank you for asking."

Tristan couldn't come up with anything to say…*sorry I killed your grandson.* Not appropriate no matter how sorry he truly was. So he smiled and turned away before any more could be said.

He and Jesse walked to the other side of the restaurant and took a booth. Sarah brought over menus and took their drink orders, but Jesse had yet to speak. *Maybe he needs some help.*

"So, what was it you wanted to talk to me about?" Tristan asked. Jesse was becoming noticeable nervous. "Is something wrong?"

"That's what I've been wondering," Jesse muttered. "I'm sorry if I'm overstepping my bounds but, Tristan, you're hurting. I can see that."

Tristan was caught off guard. No one had said anything to him since the shooting. He knew Vincent understood what having to kill Ryan did to him, but he'd rather keep those facts between the two of them.

"I'm fine. I have a few deadlines hanging over my head, that's all."

Jesse wasn't buying it. "Fear brought me to Brighton and I've never been so happy. I'd run from my parents the moment I had some money saved and ended up floating around for a lot of years. They used to beat me, and I'd always believed they did that because I was gay. As it turns out, it all came down to money. I'd been willed a great deal of property, and my family felt they deserved it. In the end, they came here looking for me to make me disappear. Needless to say, it hit the fan and in the end they took Royce to convince me to sign everything over."

"Holy shit," Tristan blurted out. "I'm sorry."

Jesse simply laughed and continued. "Yeah, that's what hit the fan, but thankfully with the help of the Sentinels and Brighton PD we came through the other side bruised but not broken. What helped me was Royce's support and Dr. Gordon's help."

And the other foot falls. This wasn't the first time he'd heard Dr. Gordon's name. It seemed as though everyone knew this Gordon fellow. "Jesse, I'm fine. I promise." Tristan wasn't sure who he was trying to convince anymore.

"I hear you and I respect your privacy. Think about it, though. I wouldn't recommend him if he wasn't one of the best," Jessie stated as he slid a business card across the table.

"If I take Dr. Gordon's card, will you let this go?" Tristan asked.

"Yes." Jesse smiled wide as if he'd won. Little did he know Tristan would dispose of the card as soon as he had a chance.

"Fine." He took the card and put it in his messenger bag. "Now let's eat."

Jesse raised his hands in surrender. "You got it."

Once they got through that awkwardness Tristan calmed enough to enjoy his lunch. The fried chicken helped. Travis was working so the food was amazing. There was something about that man's ability to cook fried chicken.

Jesse took Jeffrey's to-go bag and Tristan headed back to his apartment to get in some writing time.

Walking down the streets in Brighton, Tristan half thought Andy Griffith should be walking by. The town had every modern amenity, but the stores and houses were about a hundred years old and were well taken care of. Even the more modern houses were built with the neighborhood aesthetic in mind. He loved how it only took him ten minutes to walk anywhere in downtown. He'd brought his lightning blue Ford Fiesta back from Dallas. His beautiful baby sparkled in the sunlight, and anything that sparkled was perfect.

He walked around to the back of his building to climb the back steps. Tristan had a front door but for some reason he never used it.

He stood on his four-by-four deck, rifling through his keys when he felt it. He turned and scanned the area but saw nothing out of place. But he knew better than that. Since his attack he'd been sensitive to his surroundings, noises, and anything that made him feel like things were out of place.

Tristan turned around and stared into the patch of bushes to the right of his car. It was the only area where someone could hide, unless they were in one of the buildings nearby. After a few minutes, the bushes began to move and Matthew came strolling out before waving at him. Tristan let out a loud huff and turned to unlock his door.

He left it open and continued into the kitchen. His yellow bag went flying onto the couch and the books he'd bought at the bookstore were set on his desk. Matthew's footfall announced his arrival so Tristan dug two bottles of water from fridge and met his *stalker* at the island.

Matthew took the water and drank down half the bottle before even speaking.

"How long have you been out there?" Tristan asked.

"Almost four hours. Where the hell have you been?"

"Where the hell have I been? You're the one staking out my back door," Tristan scolded while shaking his head in disbelief. "Did Vincent put you up to this?"

Matthew had the decency to look ashamed. "Well, not exactly. He asked me to check in on you while he was gone. He didn't tell me to hide in the bushes. But I thought I could work on my surveillance skills while checking up on you."

Tristan knew that Matthew's partner was a Sentinel named Coop who had been training Matthew to take care of himself and help with his clumsiness. He'd helped out when Grady was being stalked. The man had the heart of someone twice his five and a half feet, and Tristan had liked him from the start.

"So in other words, Vincent asked you to pop in not lurk in the bushes." Tristan laughed before taking another drink of his water.

"Don't feel bad about me finding you. Ever since the attack in Dallas, I've been hypersensitive to my surroundings. I can feel when someone is looking at me. I get uneasy and the hairs on the back of my neck stand up."

"That's a great gift, but I'm sorry you had to be attacked to get it."

"Yeah, I prefer to look on the bright side of that. Now you may call me Super Senses." Matthew laughed as Tristan had hoped, and stood to leave.

"Okay, so you're doing good, blah, blah, blah."

"Yes, I'm fine while he's away. In fact I'm heading back to Dallas tomorrow to get the rest of my things."

Matthew stopped in the doorway. "Do you need any help with that?"

"No. It's only my grandmother's china and about five boxes of clothing."

"Well, if anything comes up, give me a call. Sam's on shift at the hospital for the next five days."

"I'll keep you in mind just in case," Tristan promised.

"Good. Talk to you later."

"See ya."

Tristan shut the door and locked it before heading for his desk and his deadline.

***

Tristan wandered around his former home, the now empty condo in Dallas, making sure he hadn't forgotten anything. He'd already loaded the last of his things into the car, which he had parked out back in the visitors' parking lot so no one could see his car and know he was there. The condo's new owner already had a key and would be moving in next week.

Tristan felt foolish for still being afraid of Stavros showing up but could do nothing to rid himself of that fear. Maybe Tristan would be free of him now that he lived in Brighton and would, in time, gain control over that fear.

Checking that all the windows were locked was the last thing he had to do when he saw the truck. With its recently waxed shine and those flashy spinning hubcaps, which Tristan hated, the arrival of the one person who enjoyed making his life hell was announced. Stavros.

Tristan's heart sped up so fast it felt like it was beating its way out of his chest. Then the knocking began the same as every time Stavros showed up. It could last for minutes or hours. There was no way Tristan was answering or going out the front door. He may be trained to defend himself, but he wasn't crazy enough to test it. Time for another option.

Tristan ran to his back balcony; his condo was only on the third floor. Maybe he could jump. *Yep, that was a viable option.* However, when he actually looked three stories down, he changed his mind. His neighbors' balconies were within reach, but there was a two-foot gap between them and nothing to hold on to. The pounding on the door was getting louder. Tristan assumed Stavros's ego couldn't stand to be ignored, as Tristan's ex's irate voice could be heard all the way to the back of the condo. He was running out of time before the asshole broke down the door. *How does he know I'm here?*

Old Mrs. Alvarez owned the condominium next to his. Tristan had often gotten her groceries for her and helped her around the house when her children were too busy to come by. He hoped he didn't give the poor woman a heart attack by jumping onto her balcony, but he had no other choice. Later he'd figure out how to make it back to his car.

Tristan pulled over a chair, used it to step up onto the stone railing, and readied himself to jump when Mrs. Alvarez stepped out onto her balcony. She took one look at Tristan as the banging echoed out his patio door. Surprised at her calm, she waved him over but stayed silent. With one last look down, he closed his eyes and jumped. It wasn't until his body hit the other patio that he opened his eyes. If he was going to fall to his death, he wasn't going to watch it coming.

His elderly neighbor ushered him inside in time to hear his front door crashing in. Stavros had gotten tired of waiting. Mrs. A. quickly shut and locked her patio doors and closed the drapes. They could hear things crashing and Tristan wondered what the asshole was breaking since everything had been cleared out.

"I've already called the police, they're on their way. Are you hurt?" she asked before pulling a shotgun from the front closet and setting it on her antique dining table between the china salt and pepper shakers. *Where the hell did an eighty-year-old woman get that?*

She seemed to read him so easily, always had. "The gun is from my daughter, she worries." Grinning she added, "My grandsons paid for the lessons."

Tristan could feel relief rush over him, leaving him an exhausted lump on the floor. Mrs. A. went to her kitchen and came back with a bottle of water. Things were still crashing on the other side of the wall, but he knew he was safe. He looked down at the bloody scrapes on his palms and knees he hadn't noticed until now. The concrete balconies could be rough if you slid across them.

A small red first aid kit was pushed in front of him and he gingerly took it. "Is the man who is over there the one who hurt you before?"

There was no use in lying. "He's the one who had two guys attack me."

She began speaking in Spanish, but Tristan couldn't keep up. He'd taken it in high school, and that was years ago. "You don't need to worry, he won't be getting in here."

The destruction next door suddenly stopped, and then he heard voices. Tristan wondered who'd arrived, but it didn't take long for him to figure it out. The "Fuck you, cop" was clear enough through the wall. More crashing and then silence.

"Mrs. A, the police are going to come over here because you called, but they can't know I'm here. Please give them my phone number to contact me," Tristan explained as he slowly stood and headed for the guest bedroom down the hall.

"Why don't you want them to know you're here?" she asked.

"Because if Stavros finds out, there's no stopping him from coming back and hurting you. Right now all you are is a concerned neighbor calling about noise and I would like to keep it that way. Please," Tristan pleaded. He hoped she understood how serious this was and how dangerous that man could be.

Mrs. A's eyes grew considerably bigger and he hated scaring her, but he had to keep her safe. There was a knock on her front door and thankfully, she waved him away. He limped his way into the spare bedroom and shut the door. Damn, now his right ankle hurt; he must have twisted it when he landed on the balcony. He sat the bed, opened the first aid kit, and began cleaning and bandaging his wounds.

He wasn't worried if the police called his phone; it was on silent so that nothing would give him away. There were people talking in the front room, but he couldn't understand what was being said. His eyes were getting heavy and he knew the adrenaline crash was coming, and that the sleepless nights were catching up with him. The bed felt so welcoming and before he knew it, he was cuddled in and swore to only rest for a short time.

That was the last thing he remembered as he drifted off, feeling safe with Mrs. A and her shotgun.

He missed Vincent even more.

Chapter Three

The blowing sand burned his eyes, but he couldn't look away without missing his target, so Vincent sucked it up and remained perfectly still. He wouldn't get another chance like this and he knew it. The rest of the team were in position, waiting on his word, and at the moment one lone asshole was standing in his way. Either the rebel climbed down from his post the same as he'd done every night since they'd arrived, or Vincent would make sure the guy was out of the way. Honestly, Vincent didn't want to shoot him because any noise might alert the rest of the rebel group to their location, but if needs be, he would.

He watched and waited another few minutes, lined up the rebel in the crosshairs, and was about to pull the trigger when the sentry turned and climbed down the ladder. He'd never know how close he'd come to his death.

"Clear," Vincent whispered into the tiny microphone around his neck.

He climbed down from his perch and took position against the far wall, where they'd noticed several boards missing during their surveillance run. The rest of the team would draw attention to the other side of the compound while Vincent snuck in and relieved the rebels of their prisoner, Captain Nick Campbell.

Campbell had been captured while on a supply mission. The driver he'd been with was found dead alongside the burned-out shell of their truck. They'd tracked the group back here and confirmed Campbell was indeed in their possession. The rebels had brought the captain out to parade around in front of their cameras, which helped the Sentinels judge if he could walk or not. So far, he could.

The sound of gunfire broke out on the other end of the compound, and without reservation, Vincent slipped through the fencing. He stayed to the shadows as much as he could as he picked his way through the bombed-out remains of a building until he came out on the far side where Campbell was being held. He heard boots heading his way and sank back into the shadows as two men ran past, heading toward the gunfight.

Vincent eased his way around the next corner and was less than thirty feet from his target. There was one guard standing outside the front of the tent. Vincent pulled his knife from its sheath on his thigh and stabbed it through the tent fabric until he'd made a big enough slit for him to slip through. Once inside his eyes adjusted to the darkness until he could make out a lone figure lying on the floor.

He sank down beside the still form and searched for a pulse. Once he found it, he covered Campbell's mouth before shaking him awake. The more alert the captain was, the easier it would be for them to get out of this in one piece. He woke up thrashing his arms and legs as much as he could since ropes seemed to bind him wrist to ankles. He screamed a muffled "Fuck you, asshole."

"Captain Campbell, my name is Vincent. The Sentinels are here to get you out."

The thrashing stopped and Campbell muttered, "You've come to save me."

"Yes." Without any further chitchat, Vincent cut the man out of his bonds and led him to the hole in the thick tent lining. He noticed Campbell's legs were shaking. "Are you going to be able to walk?"

"Trust me, I'll keep up," the captain answered in a confident voice.

Vincent nodded but would keep an eye on him anyway in case he'd have to carry him. "Follow me. Do what I do."

He slid through the opening with Campbell on his heels. They moved much the same as Vincent had coming in, keeping to the shadows, stopping only when they heard someone coming. As soon as they cleared the fence, Vincent radioed that they were clear and heading to the rendezvous point over the next ridge where their armored Sand Cats were located.

After an hour trek through the sand, Vincent found himself carrying the exhausted captain across his upper back and shoulders. He met up with the rest of the team and Coop took over the carrying duties until they reached their vehicles. They buckled Campbell into the back, gave him a bottle of water and a helmet while the rest of the team buckled in. Shannon operated the remote turret in one vehicle, which housed their machine guns and missile launchers, while Vincent took the other.

They could hear alarms going off in the distance and knew the rebels had discovered their prisoner was missing. Dante drove the vehicle Vincent was in; Spider drove the other with Coop. Top speed of one of these armored vehicles was roughly seventy-five miles per hour, and he was sure Dante was pushing that now.

Headlights behind them in the distance confirmed they'd been spotted. The closest allied-held territory was over forty-five minutes away going at top speed. They'd have to make sure they stayed ahead of the rebels.

"We'll be good as long as they don't call for help or a helicopter. We'll keep running dark for as long as we can," Dante explained as he seemed to press down even harder on the accelerator.

Vincent used satellite imagery to watch the heat signatures of the vehicles following them and the surrounding area. They didn't need any surprises right now. Almost thirty minutes later, they could see the lights of the allied forces' base in the distance. They radioed and identified themselves so they wouldn't be caught in friendly fire. Captain Campbell remained quiet throughout, giving them the silence to concentrate, or that's what Vincent hoped.

He didn't get to contemplate that thought for long as two large heat signatures appeared on the screen, overtaking the chase vehicles and heading straight for them. "We have two choppers incoming and fast. Does the base know we're coming in hot?"

“Yeah. They’re organizing a surprise party if the rebels cross into allied-controlled space,” Dante confirmed, and Vincent was happy for the backup. Initially, they’d intended to continue on to the American base farther in the safe zone, but right now they needed the help. They could always carry on to the other base after this had been dealt with.

The choppers were only about twenty seconds away and the Sentinels hadn’t reached the border yet so the allied forces couldn’t engage. Vincent brought his machine gun to the ready and zeroed in on the closest chopper. As soon as it was in range, the rebels began raining bullets down on their armored vehicles.

Vincent’s response was swift and deadly, his bullets leaving holes in the metal sides of the lead chopper. The rebels backed off out of range of his machine gun, but he still had a couple missiles that would do the job if they didn’t keep their distance. He hoped that the little exchange was enough to convince the rebels that this was a fight they wouldn’t win. But it wasn’t long before the second chopper took its shot at the second vehicle being driven by Spider.

Vincent couldn’t help but smile when Shannon’s turret turned and fired off her anti-tank guided missile straight into the center of the chopper. No one got a second chance to screw with them. The fireball could be seen for miles and it was enough incentive for the other chopper to turn around and head back. Vincent finally took a deep breath once they drove into the base in one piece.

Their mission had been a success, and as Vincent exited the vehicle, he felt that rush of relief he always received by bringing people back alive. Medical staff were tending to Captain Campbell so Vincent walked over to the bosses and sat on the track of the tank the other two were leaning against. Coop and Shannon soon joined them.

“Nice shooting there, Tex,” Dante joked with Shannon.

“I guess it was okay for a Navy brat,” Coop huffed.

“Shut up, Army. Like you could do any better,” Shannon shot back.

Coop looked at the rest of them for help but Vincent put that to an end. "Don't look at me. Navy Seal, remember, Private?"

"Well, how about my fellow Army brothers?" Coop asked as he looked at both Dante and Spider.

"Hell, don't get us involved. Sure, we're Army proud but we're not getting on the bad side of Shannon," Dante explained. "It's a good thing Shadow's not here."

"Who, the 'modest' marine?" Coop laughed along with the rest of them.

The Sentinels came from various branches of the Armed Forces and liked to take jabs at each other about which was better. They knew their differences only made them stronger. They were a cohesive team and intended to stay that way. Vincent couldn't help but think about his sparrow and the possibility of living together. Would the team still be as close if he wanted to build his own house for Tristan?

"Vincent…yo, man, you with us?" Spider asked as he waved his hand in front of Vincent's face.

Vincent pushed his hand away and asked, "Yeah, what's up?" How long had he been standing there daydreaming about Tristan?

Dante was busy looking at his phone and didn't look up to answer. "Matthew has been trying to reach us." He didn't bother to try to hide his worry; Sam was back in Brighton along with Tristan and Matthew.

All four men went on alert. Vincent felt his heart plummet at the thought of his sparrow needing him while he was on the other side of the world. He held on to the hope that maybe nothing was wrong.

"What did he say?" Shannon asked.

"Nothing, his call was cut short when we lost satellite signal, but he wouldn't have called unless it was important," Dante stated.

The base commander was heading their way. Talk about bad timing. "Good job, team. The captain will be taken care of. We're happy to have him back. I've arranged air transport to a landing strip farther north first thing in the morning. Is there anything else I can do for you?"

"Can you get us a line to call the States?" Spider asked.

"Sure. We'll try to secure one while you and Dante come in for the debriefing," the commander informed them.

"Perfect," Dante responded before he turned to look at Vincent, Coop, and Shannon. "Try to get some rest. I'll let you all know what's going on once I've reached Matthew."

The three of them grabbed their gear and went to find a spot to bed down. They settled on a flat piece of sand outside the med tent. They didn't need much; they could sleep anywhere. Vincent set his gear down on the ground but didn't bother to roll out his sleeping bag; he wouldn't be resting until he knew what was going on at home.

"I'm going to take a walk," Vincent muttered as he grabbed his M4 and hung it over his shoulder. In this area of the desert you never went anywhere without having your weapon on you. Attacks came in all shapes and sizes at any time of the day, and the enemy wasn't going to wait for him to collect his gun.

"Okay, man," Coop said. Vincent knew his teammate and friend wasn't really concentrating on him. He too had a partner to worry about.

The rule had always been, "Don't call unless it's an emergency." The team would reach out to their loved ones when it was safe. Sam, Matthew, and Tristan all knew the protocol and that's what scared him most.

Vincent sat down on a retaining wall made out of sand bags and stared up at the stars. He was doing his best not to overreact; staying calm was key to being able to handle any situation. Still that didn't stop horrible scenarios from racing through his mind.

Reaching deep inside himself, he pulled his calm to the surface kicking and screaming. He pushed out the noise surrounding him and centered himself on the one thing that never failed to ground him: his home. He hadn't been back for a visit in almost a year and he was due. Maybe he'd take Tristan on a trip. His family ranch was located outside Winslow, Arizona in Navajo Country, on the high desert grassland plains.

As a kid, he used to run through snakeweed and prickly pears chasing prairie dogs with his older brother across their property. His *dine* (family) was spread across four states: Arizona, Utah, Colorado and New Mexico, which made up the Navajo Nation. Vincent would take his sparrow to see the petroglyphs and the Painted Desert. He knew Tristan would appreciate the beauty of the land.

The only wild card—he'd never brought anyone home before and wondered what his family might do, but he had a good idea. They'd start planning the wedding ceremony. He loved each and every one of his crazy family members but preferred them in small, controlled doses. They were a bit overbearing when they got together, and he didn't want Tristan to run for the airport. Picturing it made Vincent smile, the first one he'd had since he found out about the missed call.

Of course, that would be the moment Dante, Spider, and the rest of the team rounded the corner and headed straight for him. From the looks on their faces he already knew the call was about his sparrow.

Chapter Four

Tristan woke up and panicked. This wasn't his bed. He pushed himself up and almost screamed at the pain. As he looked at the bandages, it all came back to him: the break-in, jumping balconies, Mrs. A's shotgun, and worst of all, Stavros. That bastard was going to pay for all this. Tristan would press charges this time and Stavros couldn't talk his way out of it.

There was a soft knock on the bedroom door, which made Tristan jump. Shit, he had to pull himself together. He slid his scraped legs to the edge of the bed and slowly stood. It felt like he was walking like a robot, but he was sore and he didn't want to start bleeding again. He turned to the door and called, "Come in."

People he never expected to see here walked through the door. Matthew and Grady stood before him and all Tristan could manage was to ask, "What time is it?"

"You've been asleep most of the day. We thought you needed the rest so we didn't want to wake you until it was necessary," Matthew answered.

Tristan looked at Grady and saw the anger and guilt in his eyes. "This is not your fault. You couldn't have seen this coming or stopped it."

"I should have come with you or sent somebody else. I should have never allowed you to come back here alone. Especially after telling me that Stavros was coming around again. I've been so concerned about Randy and finding him."

Tristan slowly walked over to Grady and gave him the biggest hug he could without using his hands. “Of course you are. It’s understandable. He’s your brother. Anyway, that jerk is in jail, right?” He still had a touch of fear that Stavros was out there waiting for him.

“Yeah. They brought in a doctor who recommended Stavros be placed on a psychiatric hold even though his parents were ready to pay to bail him out,” Grady assured as he gently hugged Travis.

“How are you guys even here?”

“Mrs. A called me after the police left,” Grady explained. “I’d given her my information years ago before I moved, in case something happened to you.”

“And you?” Tristan asked Matthew.

“Grady called me to check when Vincent would be back, and once I found out about the attack, I had to come and help if I could,” Matthew replied, and Tristan noticed his friend’s jacket looked a bit puffy.

“How many gadgets did you bring along?” Everyone knew Matthew was the king of gadgets. Many were used in actual battle situations. He was crazy smart.

Matthew smiled wide and answered, “Ten.”

“Ten. How did you fit them all in there, and should I know if there are any explosives involved?” Tristan asked.

“Rest assured nobody wants to mess with us. Not Stavros or his friends.”

After only knowing the guy for slightly over a month, Matthew was certainly a good friend to have in a bad situation. Tristan had never had anyone other than Grady to come to his rescue. Well, until Vincent, who would come as well…as long as he was in the country. Tristan’s heart began to feel heavy, but he brushed it aside.

“So you guys going to follow my car back to Brighton to make sure all is well?” Tristan asked jokingly, but inside he was grateful to have someone at his back.

"Why don't we go out to the kitchen. You need something to eat before we leave for home," Grady urged as he helped Tristan to the door.

How was he going to drive when he couldn't use his hands?

"Tristan, about your car." Grady hesitated for a moment before saying, "It's not drivable."

"What do you mean? What's wrong with it?" His feisty Fiesta hadn't given him anything to worry about driving here.

Grady raked his hand down his face and looked at the floor before answering. "It's been destroyed."

"Destroyed?" This wasn't making sense; his beautiful blue Fiesta couldn't be destroyed.

"It looks like asswipe took a tire iron to it along with your car's contents," Matthew answered.

Tristan's heart dropped. "My grandmother's china?"

Grady shook his head.

Everything after that seemed to carry on around him but Tristan felt distanced from it all. He ate and thanked Mrs. A repeatedly before leaving. Without her he may not have come out of this with only minor injuries. Police tape covered his doorway and a piece of plywood had been put up to cover his broken door. God, he'd have to call the buyer and tell him about the break-in. Who would want to live where a psycho had lost his mind?

Before he realized it, Tristan was being led through the dark parking lot and up to a big black SUV, obviously from the Sentinels' motor pool. He was loaded into the backseat and was given a blanket by Matthew. Tristan nodded his thanks then eased his seat back and buried himself under the covers. He didn't want to talk anymore. He wanted it all to go away. That china had been the last thing he'd had of his beloved grandmother and it was now gone.

He heard the front doors open and close and the engine begin to rumble, but he didn't care. He'd had enough for one day. Even he had the right to check out on occasion.

Tristan closed his eyes and prayed for sleep to take him once again. With his last conscious thought, he wondered what Vincent was doing at that moment and hoped he was safe.

***

Tristan was being nudged awake by something cold and wet. He reared his head back only to find Buddy, Sam's golden retriever, looking at him as if he was the dog's new best friend. His tail wagged at top speed and thankfully there was nothing on the coffee table or it would have gone flying across the room.

He didn't worry about where he was this time around, knowing he was inside the big Victorian home situated on the Sentinels' compound. Grady must have carried him in, but Tristan wondered where everyone was. Sam and Matthew should surely be home somewhere. Grady might have headed back into the station or gone home. Why hadn't they taken him home instead of here?

Tristan stood on shaky legs, determined to find his friends. First, he checked the kitchen but only found the back door open. He glanced outside but no one was there, and all the lights were off in the out buildings. His injured hands ached as he relocked the door and went down the hallway to the game room. As he passed Vincent's suite of rooms he heard something crash to the floor inside.

His heart sped up. Was Vincent home? He had to be home. Tristan's hand shook as he turned the door handle and entered the room. Movement was coming from the en suite bathroom; the bedroom and separate sitting area were empty.

"Vincent?"

Nothing.

"Vincent…are you—."

The figure in the bathroom came through the door and Tristan tried to scream but nothing came out. Stavros stood in the middle of Vincent's private space, his superior grin firmly in place.

He didn't care how much it hurt; Tristan turned and ran out of the room. He headed straight for Matthew's room. Someone had to be here.

Tristan ran inside his friend's suite and quickly locked the doors. Stavros must have followed him here. He must have found a way out of the hospital. Slowly, Tristan backed into the room and farther away from the locked door. Stavros started pounding on the door and the wood began to splinter.

When Tristan's back touched something, he turned around and a cold, bony hand grabbed him by his throat and pinned him to the wall. Tristan's mouth hung open in another silent scream as he looked down into the milky dead eyes of Ryan Graham.

"No. No. You're dead," Tristan screamed as he shot up and almost out of his seat. If it weren't for the seatbelt, he'd be on the floor right now.

The vehicle swerved, and then Grady got it back under control. Matthew struggled to get out of his seatbelt and into the backseat. "Everything's okay. It was only a dream."

"Nightmare."

"Yeah, right, nightmare," Matthew agreed. "Here's some water."

"Thank you."

"Do you want to tell me what it was about?" Grady asked from the driver's seat.

The last thing Tristan wanted to do was relive that horror or have others try to analyze it. "No, not really. Sorry."

"Not to worry, you will when you're ready." Tristan knew Grady had a good idea already, but at least he hadn't said anything aloud.

"Thanks for understanding. How close are we to home?"

"Thirty minutes. We've been discussing that and decided it might be best if you stayed with the Sentinels until we get this Stavros thing figured out," Grady shared.

Tristan's nightmare came back full force, but he was able to rein it in before screaming "No." He thought about going back to his place and had to admit it made sense for him to stay in the big old

Victorian. He'd be safe from physical harm. Now, if he could only get his subconscious under control.

"That sounds like a plan. Will we be able to stop and pick up a few things from my apartment?" Not for the first time today, Tristan was grateful he'd left his laptop and messenger bag at home because if he'd left it in the Fiesta it would have been destroyed along with everything else.

"Sure, buddy," Grady replied, and Tristan could tell how guilty his best friend was feeling, but he didn't have the strength to cheer anybody up.

Forty-five minutes later Tristan was being ushered into the beautiful old house where Sam met them with a first aid kit on steroids. Honestly, he had to be able to perform surgery with the size of that thing. At this point, Tristan had given up trying lead this *party* back to the "This isn't so bad" reaction from the all-out DEFCON 1 response going on at the moment.

Sam began cleaning Tristan's wounds more thoroughly than he liked. Once they were bandaged, Matthew brought him a cup of chamomile tea and Grady sat stoically on the couch watching everything.

All Tristan wanted was to be alone with Vincent, but at the moment he couldn't have that so he'd take alone. "Thank you for everything, but if it's okay with everyone, I'd like to go to bed."

"But you've been sleeping all day, are you sure you're all right?" Matthew asked.

Grady came to the rescue. "He's been through a lot. I'm sure he needs to decompress."

Tristan stood, gathered his messenger bag, and hobbled to Vincent's rooms. Later, Tristan would apologize for leaving so abruptly, but if he hadn't left when he did, he might have had a breakdown and he couldn't have that. Closing the door behind him, he gathered his courage around him, checked and rechecked every spot of the bathroom, bedroom, and lounge area to make sure he was alone. It embarrassed him to be acting this way, but he couldn't stop himself. He was happy no one was around to see it.

Once he confirmed he was well and truly alone, he set his bag down on the coffee table. Then he sank into one of the two soft leather recliners in the lounge, which could seat two people, before turning on the television. He needed the background noise to help distract him from his troubling thoughts.

Would he ever be free of this stress or would it be simply replaced by another? Vincent throwing himself at danger came to mind.

What am I going to do about Stavros?

Funny, only a day ago Tristan was walking down Main Street thinking his only problem was meeting a deadline. He wished he could turn back time, but that wasn't how the real world worked.

Tristan might be able to control time in his books, but reality was much harsher.

Chapter Five

Two days. It had been two damn days since they'd left base and begun heading home. The team had been grounded due to sandstorms, but he'd at least been able to reach Tristan for a few minutes. Even from that far away he could hear how shaken he was. Now, Vincent sat in the passenger seat of one of their SUVs in the middle of the night only minutes away from his sparrow.

Logically he knew Tristan was okay physically, but his need to hold him and confirm it for himself was overpowering. It seemed like everything was trying to stand in his way as he attempted to make it to the man he loved. First the sand storm, and the layover, then one of the main roads into Brighton was closed due to a seven-car pileup and they had to take a longer route around. After offering assistance, of course. By now, he was so far on edge that no one spoke, trying to keep the truck as calm as possible. This ex of Tristan's pissed off the wrong person and Vincent intended to show the bastard the error of his ways.

Mercifully, they finally drove through the gate and he barely waited for Coop to put the truck in park before Vincent was flying out the door. He ran up the steps and through the front door before Sam even had a chance to open it. All that mattered was getting to Tristan, and he knew exactly where to find him. His sparrow had grown fond of the recliners in his room and Matthew had told them that Tristan barely came out of the one he'd claimed as his own.

Vincent stopped outside his door; he had to calm the hell down or he might end up scaring his boyfriend. He took a couple deep breaths and when he thought he had himself under control, he opened the door. The first thing he noticed was how spotless his entire bedroom was and that it was empty. He walked the ten feet to the opening of his lounge and found his love curled up in the recliner, wrapped in one of the blankets Vincent's mother had sent him.

Tristan's pale skin stood in stark contrast to the vibrant colors on the blanket, and Vincent wondered if his sparrow was even paler than before. After the events of the last few days, he could understand. On the coffee table was Tristan's trusty laptop and a bottle of pills. Vincent had been told that Dr. Green had come out to see Tristan and had prescribed something to sleep. Which explained why he hadn't woken yet.

Vincent slid his hands under Tristan and slowly lifted him into his arms. He buried his face in his love's fiery hair and breathed in his scent, calming him even further. Vincent was sure this was where Tristan had been sleeping the last couple of nights and immediately headed toward the bed.

He laid Tristan down on the side of the bed and began removing his clothing so that he could sleep in comfort. When he finally got all his sparrow's clothes off, he looked up and into a pair of gorgeous green eyes.

"Am I dreaming?" Tristan asked in a small voice.

"No, love. Not a dream. I'm home," Vincent confirmed as he covered Tristan with the comforter. He noticed the bandages on the palms of Tristan's hands and knees. "You rest and I'll be right beside you."

"Promise me if this is a dream you won't wake me up," Tristan begged, breaking Vincent's heart. He knew that the medication Tristan used to fall asleep was affecting his love's thoughts and Vincent simply smiled.

"I promise not to wake you up," Vincent murmured before leaning down and softly kissing the man who'd quickly become an integral part of his life.

Tristan fell back to sleep and Vincent quickly got undressed and took a quick shower to wash off the stink of the last two days; he wanted it nowhere near Tristan. When Vincent came back into the bedroom, Tristan was fast asleep, so Vincent crawled into bed beside him. The first thing he did was gather his sparrow in his arms; the second was coming up with a plan to find this Stavros.

***

Tristan woke up slowly. He didn't like the way the medication made him feel so out of it in the mornings. Maybe he would stop taking it. The first thing he realized was that he wasn't in the chair any longer and he wasn't alone. He turned his head and looked up into a pair of soft blue eyes and felt the events of the last two days fade a bit. Vincent was back.

"Vincent..."

"I'm here, love."

He couldn't stop himself if he wanted too, be damned his pride. Tristan threw himself against Vincent's chest and began to cry. From what he'd been through with Ryan and Stavros to all that he'd lost, it all poured out as his lover held him close. Of course, the first thing out of his mouth wasn't about his grandmother's china or his destroyed condominium or even the sale falling through.

"The bastard killed Feisty."

"I know, sweetheart. But things can be replaced; you can't. We'll get you a new Feisty," assured Vincent as he held him closer. "I don't know what I would have done if he'd gotten his hands on you."

Tristan shivered at the thought. He'd seen pictures of his condominium, or better yet, what's left of his condominium. The drywall had been ripped from the walls and spindles torn out of the stairs. The mirrors were shattered and his appliances had been destroyed from what appeared to have been a baseball bat. That Stavros brought a weapon confirmed he intended to hurt Tristan or maybe worse. Vincent must have felt him tremble because he pulled up the comforter and tucked it around him.

"He'll never get the chance to come near you again," Vincent stated with absolute certainty.

"Hopefully this time he'll go to jail, but I doubt it with his family's money."

"They've been in oil for a couple generations now. Even got a few of the Menzottos in government office," his lover replied without skipping a beat.

"How did you know that?" Tristan asked in shock. They'd never discussed Stavros before, at least not in detail.

"I spent two days trying to get back to you so I did a little investigating with Shannon's help. Found out quite a bit, in fact. Stavros's family has been cleaning up after him for a long time now."

"Really?" Tristan was getting a bad feeling.

Vincent never missed a thing. "I'll give you the file later, but for now you need to heal."

Tristan raised his bandaged hands and said, "I'm not too badly hurt. I'll be fine in no time."

"I don't only mean physically, sparrow," he answered, but before Tristan could get defensive, Vincent continued, "Now is not the time to worry about that. For now, all I want is to be near you, to hold you, and keep you safe in my arms."

Tristan was all for that and maybe a whole lot more. With everything that was going on around them Tristan needed to feel alive and loved. He sat up and straddled Vincent's waist before running his hands across his man's smooth, muscled, bronze chest. His knees ached a little but he didn't care. Vincent's nipples peaked into hard little nubbins that Tristan wanted to taste. The burning in his lover's eyes gave him all the permission he needed and he dove in.

Vincent groaned the moment Tristan's tongue swiped across his chest, making him feel better than he had in days. He explored the dips and valleys of his lover's body while working his way up to

Vincent's soft lips. On the journey, he became distracted by the gorgeous man's Adam's apple and decided to suck on it.

By now, Vincent's hands were travelling up and down Tristan's body, leaving trails of heat wherever he touched. He found himself arching into every caress, desperate for more. In that moment all was right in the world and Tristan knew he loved Vincent. Even if he thought he wasn't ready to admit it openly, the fact that he admitted it to himself was monumental.

Throughout his adult life, Tristan had never felt this way for another man. Sure, he'd dated as much as any other guy, but no matter how hard he'd tried he never felt more than mild affection for the person he was dating. He'd thought it wasn't possible for him, the romance novelist who could write about love but never truly feel it. In all his novels, he'd put his hopes and dreams for what he thought love felt like, but never truly had any of his own. That was until now.

"Make love to me," Tristan moaned as he nibbled his way up Vincent's neck and to his ear.

Vincent gently cupped the side of Tristan's face and looked him in the eyes. "Are you sure? You've been through a lot the last couple days."

If he didn't already love him, that would have done it. He knew Vincent wanted him, the hard shaft between his ass cheeks confirmed it, but Vincent still wanted Tristan to be sure. Who wouldn't love this man?

"Yes, I'm sure," Tristan answered, and he wondered if maybe he should tell Vincent how he felt. "Vincent, I-I…you know how I feel about you, right?" *What the hell chickenshit cop-out was that?*

Vincent smiled wide before answering, "I love you too."

All movement stopped and all Tristan could manage was to stare down at Vincent in wonder. Tristan didn't know what he'd done to deserve this man, but he was definitely keeping him. Vincent pulled him down for a kiss while simultaneously rolling Tristan to his back.

Vincent held most of his weight off Tristan, ensuring he could breathe. At least he would once Vincent was finished kissing him.

When they came up for air, Tristan asked, "How do you say 'I love you' in Navajo?"

"*Ayor anosh'ni,*" Vincent answered, and Tristan watched as the big man's expression softened.

"*Ayor anosh'ni*, Vincent." Tristan had no idea why it was easier for him to say the words in Navajo.

Instantly, they were locked in another all-consuming kiss. Their naked bodies rubbed against each other, heightening Tristan's need to feel his lover slide deep inside him. He'd always been a physical person; he loved showing his affection but had never found "the one." Now, there was nothing holding him back.

"You are gorgeous," Vincent said as he ran his hands down Tristan's chest to his hips but avoiding his hard cock. Vincent's dark hair was free of its braid and fell over his shoulder and onto his chest.

"Please." Tristan wasn't sure what he was begging for, but he was so close to the edge he didn't care.

Vincent raised both of Tristan's arms over his head and pinned them there with one big hand before taking Tristan's cock in the other. His mind went blank as his lover pumped him in long, firm pulls. All too soon, the telltale tingle began and his balls pulled up tight.

"I'm going to come," he warned so Vincent would slow down. Tristan didn't want this to end so soon.

Instead of doing what he'd expected, Vincent sped up, making Tristan's hips buck wildly in response. Fire raced down his spine, his legs fell open, and he pushed into Vincent's hand one last time and came with a loud cry.

"That's it, sparrow. Give me your passion."

Tristan floated in blissful satisfaction, his body too heavy for him to move. Apparently, not for Vincent, who turned him over with ease. His lover reached into the side table and took out a new bottle of lube and a condom. Tristan was still in his post-orgasmic haze when he felt Vincent's finger breaching him. He moaned out his pleasure as he was slowly stretched and opened for his lover's thick cock. His own was getting harder again as Vincent added another finger until Tristan was on his hands and knees rocking back against them. The first brush against his prostate sent him flying and he angled his hips for more.

He felt Vincent reach for the condom and rolled onto his back to watch him slide the latex over his impressive cock. They were both roughly the same length but when it came to girth, Vincent won hands-down. His ass clenched at the thought of that sliding into him.

Tristan spread his legs as Vincent placed them over his shoulders and leaned down to kiss him again. "Love you, sparrow."

He looked at the man above him and saw the emotion in his eyes. "I love you, Vincent." It slipped out as if it were the most natural thing in the world when only moments before he froze and could say it only in Navajo.

Vincent looked so happy that Tristan couldn't stop from saying it again. "I love you."

Their lips met in a deep kiss full of tongues and teeth. Pulling at each other as if trying to get even closer. Tristan could feel the head of Vincent's cock at his hole and did everything in his power to relax as he was filled inch by inch. His moans had turned to needy whimpers when his prostate was rubbed over and over again.

The room was filled with the sounds of their passion and Tristan didn't care if anyone heard them. He watched as Vincent's muscles flexed and beads of sweat slid down his glowing bronze skin as he pushed deep. Words of love passed between them as their bodies joined together as one.

The slightest of tingles began at the base of his spine and he knew time was running out before he came again. "Baby, I'm close."

Those three words seemed to set Vincent off as his hips began driving into him as he bent Tristan in two and hungrily kissed him.

Seconds later, he came screaming Vincent's name, and soon after his lover roared and the condom inside him filled with heat.

Gently, Vincent removed Tristan's legs from Vincent's shoulders as his lover pulled out and disposed of the condom before collapsing on the bed and gathering Tristan into his arms. Their labored breathing broke the silence of the room as both tried to slow their thundering hearts.

Tristan felt a certain peace fall over him as the two lay in the darkened room with sunshine trying to peek through the curtains. He didn't want to face the world yet but knew he couldn't hide out forever. He'd have to go back to his apartment and pull himself together. He had a book to finish and a signing next week. On top of his usual busy schedule, he had to find a contractor to repair his condominium, have his realtor put it on the market again, and then go looking for a new Feisty.

No, he couldn't hide out from the world too much longer; he was an adult and he had to handle all this. Tristan had gotten his life back together after the last attack and he could do the same again.

He hoped he didn't have to keep doing it repeatedly.

***

Vincent left their bedroom in search of food. He and his sparrow had taken a long, hot shower before he bandaged Tristan's wounds. Now he was tucked into a recliner trying to write with his sore hands. It was excruciating to watch as he grimaced when he hit a key. The least Vincent could do was scare them up something to eat.

They'd already missed breakfast and he knew how particular Mrs. Walker could be about showing up on time, so he doubted there'd be anything left. Imagine his surprise when he opened the swinging kitchen door and found the team still eating.

"Wasn't breakfast a couple hours ago?" he asked the group.

"We thought we'd let everyone sleep in this morning," Dante answered.

"Yeah, we decided it last night, but you were already gone. Where's Tristan?" Matthew asked.

"He's busy working on his latest."

"I can't wait to read it. Tristan promised me an ARC," Sam gushed.

"He's taking you on an arc?" Coop asked.

"No an ARC, an Advanced Reader's Copy. I get it before it's released to the public," Sam explained as he sat happily between his two men.

"How is he today?" Spider asked.

"Better. Still freaked out, but his wounds are healing nicely. Thank you for taking care of that for him." Vincent nodded his head toward Sam, who waved his hands as if it was no big deal. "It's good to know if something happens when I'm gone on assignment Tristan will have people looking out for him."

"We're a family. That's what we do," Matthew assured before being pulled into Coop's arms for a kiss.

"Vincent, do you want to take your man some food?" Mrs. Walker asked as she flipped the pancakes.

"Yes please, ma'am."

"Always so polite," Mrs. Walker huffed and looked at Coop. "You could learn something from the man."

"Hey, I'm polite," Coop groused.

Mrs. Walker turned and put her hands on her ample hips and stared Coop down. "Was it polite when I made that peach cobbler for dessert and you ate half of it before dinner was even served? Was it polite when you and Buddy went for a roll in the mud and then traipsed right through the living room?"

"Hey, I cleaned that up." Mrs. Walker stared harder. "Okay, I cleaned that up with Matthew's help." Still nothing. "Fine, Matthew cleaned it up."

All the while Matthew was sitting in his chair trying not to crack up at the scolding his partner was getting from a formidable woman.

Vincent loved his blood family and the family he'd chosen. Would Tristan love them as well?

Mrs. Walker turned back to the stove, but not before saying, "It would do you good, young man, to think of others before yourself."

Coop hung his head and muttered, "Yes, ma'am."

She turned from the stove and plunked two fluffy pancakes onto Coop's plate, bringing that smile back to his face. With a wink, she swatted him with the spatula and went to prepare plates for Vincent and Tristan.

"Dr. Green is coming back out today to check on Tristan," Matthew said.

"Why?" Vincent asked. "His hands and knees are healing up fine."

"That wasn't what the doctor was worried about. He was concerned with Tristan's mental state," Sam explained gently. "You know the whole Ryan thing and now this. He thinks Tristan should see Dr. Gordon."

The sound of something crashing alerted Vincent to someone on the other side of the swinging doors. He opened the door to find his sparrow picking up pieces of broken glass from the floor. *Shit, what did he hear?*

Tristan wouldn't meet Vincent's eyes or anyone else's as he carried the glass to the garbage. His back was rigid and absolutely no one said a word, which wasn't helping.

"Mrs. Walker is making two plates for us. How's the writing going?" Vincent asked, desperate for something to say. Of course Tristan was upset that the whole team was talking about his mental state.

Tristan took Mrs. Walker's hand and said, "Thank you for being so kind to me over the past couple days. I appreciate everything but I won't be eating." Then he turned to Sam and Matthew. "And thank you for everything. You two have been amazing and I'm not sure how to thank you properly, but I will think of something."

Last, he turned his cold gaze on Vincent. "Would you please take me home?" Then he left the kitchen without waiting for an answer.

Of course, he would drive his sparrow anywhere, but he didn't want Tristan to leave. He was safe and loved right where he was. He took a moment to think about it from Tristan's perspective; he would be embarrassed and ashamed that they were all talking about him so openly. *Dammit.*

Before anyone could say a word, Vincent followed his love out of the kitchen and back to their bedroom. He found Tristan trying to pack his clothing, laptop, and jacket into his yellow messenger bag. Frozen to the spot, Vincent didn't know what to do. Then it came to him and he casually walked up to his closet and pulled out a duffle bag. He began filling it with necessities, including his Glock, and it didn't take long for Tristan to notice.

"What are you doing?" Tristan asked.

"Packing."

"Why?"

"Where you go I go." Simple as that. He would follow his sparrow to the ends of the earth.

"But you can't, you live here."

"Are you saying I'm not welcome at your apartment?"

"Of course you're always welcome at my apartment."

"Perfect," Vincent replied as he continued to pack. Once he was done, he set his bag by the bedroom door and went to help his love. Now that they'd declared how they felt and shared their bodies, there was no way he'd be going anywhere without Tristan and vice versa.

Tristan was struggling trying to get his shirts into the bag. "Can I help you?"

"Yeah, would you? I can't get it all in properly." Tristan sighed before handing the bag over to him.

"I have your back, no need to worry," Vincent joked, hoping to make Tristan smile. It didn't. "Tristan, you've got to know—"

"I've got to know…excuse me, but what I know is that my mental state is a breakfast topic. Maybe we should have a vote.

Those who think I'm crazy, raise a pancake. Those that don't, keep eating. Which side are you falling on?"

"You aren't crazy."

"You might be the only one who thinks so."

"No one thinks you're crazy," Vincent said as he took Tristan into his arms and held him tight.

His sparrow struggled and he immediately let go. He would never restrain Tristan unless it was for pleasure or safety. Tristan grabbed his messenger bag, cringing slightly, and turned toward the door.

"I heard them discussing how Dr. Green had to come to check my mental health. Shit. Why does everyone feel the need to mess in my life? I've never forced anyone to live by my beliefs but suddenly everyone has an opinion about my life," Tristan choked out, and Vincent noticed the unshed tears in his love's eyes. "I need peace and to be away from everything and everyone."

Vincent felt that like a knife to his heart, at least until Tristan followed it up with, "You're the only one I feel comfortable with at this point. I want to go home. You're welcome to come but that's it, I'm done when my mental health becomes a round table discussion."

Vincent understood why Tristan was upset; something like this shouldn't have been an open discussion amongst the team, and Vincent was as guilty as the rest of the group. After all, he stood there listening to them talk without saying a word. How could he have betrayed his sparrow so easily?

Tristan must have noticed his change in demeanor because he asked, "What's wrong?"

"I should have never allowed the conversation to carry on. I should have stopped it."

Tristan did the one thing Vincent hadn't expected: he sank into Vincent's arms. He lifted his love and carried him to the lounge and sat in one of the recliners, holding his soul mate close to his heart.

He didn't know how to fix this, but he did know one thing: no matter what, he would stay by his sparrow's side.

Even if it meant leaving the Sentinels.

Chapter Six

A long line of people wound around the block by the time Jeffrey had opened the doors to the bookstore. Having seen the crowd, Tristan had come through the back door. He'd never thought so many readers would show up for this charity book signing, but here they were. He loved his fans; they were always so supportive. Vincent stood off to the side watching everything and everyone. They had agreed to stay in Vincent's room on the Sentinels' compound once everyone swore to stay out of the Dr. Gordon debate. Tristan knew they were trying to be helpful, but he wanted to keep his personal life private. His professional life was open enough.

Matthew and Coop, and Jesse and Royce had come to help out any way they could. It had been a week since the incident at his condominium, and his hands had finally stopped stinging when he used them. Grateful for small mercies, at least the book signing hadn't been painful so far. Tristan had worn his lucky red jeans with a new bright white dress shirt opened far enough so that his sparrow pendent was on display. His outfit was capped off with a pair of shiny black Magnanni Silvio double monk strap shoes. Oh, how he loved shoes.

So far he'd signed over two hundred books and the line still extended outside the store. Every so often, he'd look away from the books and fans to find his love watching him closely. The sense of security helped him focus on the event and enjoy visiting with his fans. Even though he didn't expect Stavros to show up, being watched over by his own personal Sentinel went a long way to giving him the head space to concentrate on the book signing.

During the past week, Tristan had managed to find a contractor to start repairing his condominium, given a statement about Stavros to the police, and had gone car shopping. Tristan hadn't found a replacement for Feisty, but considering Vincent was driving him everywhere, there was no hurry. However, he knew he had to get back to his life; he couldn't allow that awful man dictate how Tristan lived.

Stavros had been released from the hospital and bailed out of jail by his parents. If the doctor released that psycho, Tristan was sure money had exchanged hands. Stavros was restricted to his parents' house until he went to trial. Like that would hold him.

"Hello again, Tristan."

Although his head was down, he didn't need to look up to know who it was. "Hello, Shawn." Tristan noticed Matthew stop beside him and Vincent take a couple steps closer, but he smiled and waved them off. "It's nice to see you again."

"Oh, I'd never miss a signing." And there was the problem. Shawn was too serious a fan and had even started his own fan club. At first Tristan had shrugged it off, but when Shawn kept appearing at every event, no matter where the signing or reading was, Tristan began to notice. Shawn wasn't unattractive; in fact, he was quite handsome in an old Hollywood kind of way. Nevertheless, Tristan wanted a man who wanted him for him and not what they fantasized about.

Vincent hadn't read any of Tristan's books before they met, which had been perfect.

"Which book would you like signed?" Tristan asked, hoping for a different answer than the last signing.

"All of them in all the series." Nope, no different. That was over twenty-five books at ten dollars a pop. Shawn had done the same thing the last three times.

Matthew set the pile of books down beside Tristan and he began signing away; it was for the youths' center after all. When he looked up, Vincent was talking to Coop and both were staring at Shawn. Tristan almost laughed. Shawn was harmless as they came; he was little more than an exuberant fan.

When Tristan was done, Matthew bagged up the books and handed them to Shawn, but the man didn't move. Tristan stared at him for a moment, but Shawn quickly snapped out of it and said, "Could I take you out for coffee? We can talk about your books for my club newsletter."

"I'm sorry, Shawn, I have prior engagements. But if you send questions to my publisher, they'll forward them on, and I'd be happy to answer them for your newsletter. I'll arrange for a few new posters to be sent as well." Tristan was trying to be as diplomatic as possible without leading the guy on or crushing him.

"Of course. I'm sorry, I should have known. I'll send those questions over to your people," Shawn said with a toothy smile, but his eyes looked anything but happy.

Before more could be said, the man turned and walked toward the cash register before disappearing into the crowd. Tristan brushed it off; after all, Shawn had acted far stranger the last time.

The rest of the day went by in a haze of happy fans, pictures, and signatures until they finally locked the doors after the last customer left. Many of the residents of Brighton had come in support of the charity event, which didn't surprise Tristan at all. This was the type of town where neighbors helped their neighbors.

"I'd say that was a success," Jeffrey cheered.

"I can't feel my fingers," Tristan joked as he held up his sore hand.

"We'll put ice on it when we get home," Vincent commented before asking, "Who was that guy Shawn?"

"An avid fan. He's been to a few signings." Best to keep the number to himself or Vincent would worry. "He's no threat."

"How do you know for sure?" Jesse asked as he pulled a chair up to the table.

"He's been following my books from the beginning. If he wanted to do something, he would have done it years ago."

Everyone seemed to think about it before nodding their agreement. Vincent walked over, lifted Tristan out of his chair, and then sat before placing Tristan in his lap. He had to admit it felt good to be held by his lover, and the PDA did a lot to calm him.

"So, you ready to go for supper?" Vincent asked.

After such a long day, all he wanted to do was soak in a hot tub. "If it's okay with you, how about we pick something up to go from the diner and eat at home?"

Tristan realized he'd called Vincent's place home, and he was becoming more comfortable with that thought. Vincent seemed to like the sounds of it as well, if his smile was any indication.

"Sure, sparrow, we'll do take-out."

"Thank you, *nizhóní*."

"*Nizhóní*, what does that mean?" Matthew asked

"Beautiful," Vincent answered. "It means beautiful in Navajo, but not only physical beauty. It's beauty of spirit, harmony with the world around a person, you know, the whole package."

"Vincent is teaching me a little at a time. His culture is so fascinating you can't help but respect the history. I've learned so much. Vincent's great-grandfather was a Navajo Code Talker in the Second World War," Tristan gushed about his partner's strong military background.

"Yeah, wasn't your dad a Ranger at one point?" Coop asked.

"He was," Vincent answered proudly. "And my grandfather was in the Air Force."

"Your family has covered a wide range of the armed services," Jeffrey stated before taking a drink of his coffee.

"Yeah. My older brother helps our father with the ranch now, but he was a Marine during the time of the Twin Towers tragedy," Vincent shared. Tristan could feel his eyes getting heavy, and

Vincent noticed. "I better get this one home before he falls asleep right here."

Everyone laughed including Tristan, who rubbed his tired eyes and stood. "I think it's time to leave. I'm bushed. Thank you for having me here, Jeffrey."

"No, thank you for doing this for the center. I'll let you know what the tally is once I have a chance to add up the receipts."

"Honestly, thank you for everything, man," Jesse said as he extended his hand to Tristan.

They shook and Tristan said, "My pleasure. We'll talk further about the classes when the day gets closer to opening."

"Deal."

Tristan gathered his messenger bag and headed for the front door hand in hand with Vincent. He felt lighter than he had in days and couldn't help but smile.

"It's good to see that smile again," Vincent commented.

"Thank you for being there for me."

Instead of answering, Vincent pulled Tristan under his arm and kissed the top of his head. They hopped into his big black Dodge and headed for the diner. Tristan's stomach growled in agreement. They pulled up outside of the diner and thankfully Vincent went in to get their two orders of the roast beef dinner, leaving Tristan a moment to lean his head back and relax.

He listened to the country singer croon over the radio. He didn't know who it was, considering he was more of a fan of mainstream music, but he was gaining an appreciation. He hummed a few bars before he got that feeling again, the one when he knew he was being watched.

Tristan opened his eyes and looked into the diner. Vincent wasn't watching him, and neither was anyone else. He scanned the street but saw nothing out of the ordinary. It had to be his imagination this time because there was literally no one giving him a second look. Maybe it was the fact that he'd been so tired recently or that he'd been fighting a headache for days that never truly went away. Whatever it was, Tristan decided to lock the doors and keep his eyes open. Vincent was back soon enough and they were on their way home.

The house was quiet when they arrived. Dante, Spider, and Sam had gone away for a few days; Coop and Matthew were still out. Shadow was still searching for Randy, and Shannon was searching for a small arms dealer in South America. Apparently this bad guy had recently moved up to atomic grade weaponry, so they had to find him before something catastrophic happened.

Tristan understood how important the team was in keeping the world safe by targeting the key bad actors, but it still worried him. Vincent spent a large part of his life in a dangerous world and now, thanks to Tristan, there was danger at home. The one place he should be able to relax was now filled with stress over Stavros and whether he'd come after him—again.

Once they got to their room Tristan began to strip; he'd been getting hot flashes for days. Now he knew sometimes he acted like a queen, but he certainly wasn't having any sort of change of life. He figured it had to do with stress. He checked his phone and saw it was after ten in the evening; no wonder he was tired.

"I'll go grab us some plates and cutlery, babe," Vincent said before pulling Tristan into his arms.

Tristan couldn't help but smile and happily kiss his lover. "Maybe we could soak in the tub after we eat?"

"That sounds like the perfect plan to me," Vincent agreed.

"Then hurry back," Tristan teased, and Vincent took off like a shot.

It was so easy to love that man, Tristan thought as he wandered into the lounge. They could eat on the coffee table so he turned on the television and got comfortable in one of the big recliners. He had on his purple boxer briefs so he wouldn't be naked while eating, then he thought about it and slid out of those too. After all, it was only he and Vincent.

Tristan was finally cooling down and was feeling a bit better when Vincent returned. Along with plates and cutlery, Vincent brought in a bottle of red wine. He set the Styrofoam containers containing their roast beef suppers on the table and uncorked the wine. Tristan opened a compartment in the coffee table that held their wineglasses. The two of them had enjoyed sitting and having a glass of wine at the end of the night, giving them time to decompress.

He looked at the bottle but didn't recognize it. "What type of wine are we drinking tonight?"

Vincent smiled and Tristan was struck again by how gorgeous the man really was. "It's a Malbec from Argentina. I thought it would be nice with the beef."

Tristan took a sip and the bold, spicily rich taste slid across his taste buds. He looked at the deeply colored liquid as various notes of fruit blended perfectly to his unsophisticated tastes buds. "It's wonderful." He might not be a sommelier, but he knew what he liked.

"I thought you might. This is one of my mother's favorite wines. My parents taught me an appreciation for great wine," Vincent explained as Tristan dished out supper.

Soon they dug in and all discussion ended once the succulent beef Travis had made today hit their hungry stomachs. For the next twenty minutes, the two ate in comfortable silence. That was another aspect of this relationship that Tristan adored—the fact that they were comfortable being together in silence. They didn't need to fill it with words. This relationship had changed him for the better; now with Vincent as his solid base, maybe Tristan could fly even higher.

While Vincent started filling the tub, Tristan cleaned up then filled one glass with wine so they could share it when they relaxed in the tub. A touch of steam floated in the air as he opened the bathroom door to find Vincent waiting for him stretched out like a Greek god, his arm dangling over the edge. Tristan knew Vincent had put the bubbles in because Tristan liked it. He was so lucky, and he knew it.

After setting the glass on the marbled edge surrounding the tub, Tristan slid into the hot water in front of Vincent. He leaned his back into his boyfriend's wide chest and lounged in the luxury of his gorgeous man.

"When do you think I should go back to my apartment?" Tristan asked. He knew he'd have to leave someday so he thought now was a good time to get that awful thought cleared up.

Vincent didn't say anything for a moment but when he did speak, Tristan was even more confused. "You like your privacy, don't you, love?"

"Well, yes. So much of me is in the public eye already that I tend to embrace my private time. Why do you ask?"

"I've been thinking, and I don't want you to answer now, but I'd like to build us a place of our own on the compound's acreage. Close enough to walk to this house, but far enough to give you the privacy you need."

Tristan sat frozen to the spot. Yeah, he loved Vincent, but was he ready for the two of them to build a home together? True, he liked the idea of them having their own place on the property, but weren't they moving too fast? It had been only a few months since they first met. Didn't that mean they should wait?

Vincent quickly followed up with, "I know it's quick and I don't want you to answer me now, but I also know you are the only man I want by my side. Think about it; nothing needs to be decided now."

"I'll think it over, that's all I can promise. I do love you." Vincent squeezed him tighter, as he did every time Tristan said those words. "I don't want to move too fast and risk this blowing up and me losing you."

"I'm not going anywhere, sparrow. When you're ready, we'll discuss this again." Vincent kissed the back of Tristan's neck, signaling that they were good, and it was all right to table the discussion for later.

The next hour was spent washing one another between kisses and laughter. Tristan couldn't remember ever being this happy and he basked in its warmth like a turtle with a heat lamp. The bubbles were beginning to fade and so was he; the day was catching up with him fast.

"Come on, love, let's get you dry," Vincent murmured as he stood and stepped out of the tub before offering Tristan his hand.

With Vincent's help, he stood on a large comfortable navy bathmat that matched the towels. He took the towel Vincent offered and dried himself before following his lover to the bed. Tristan crawled in and Vincent covered him before walking around to his side. Tristan never thought that little things like having sides in bed would mean so much to him.

Vincent lifted his arm and Tristan sank into his spot on his lover's chest. "*Ayor anosh'ni.* You make me so happy."

"I love you too, sparrow. You are the light in my life."

"I've always wondered why you call me sparrow. I thought it was because of the pendent you gave me," Tristan muttered in a groggy voice while trying not to yawn.

Vincent smiled down at him and said, "Sparrows are social, creative, and have strong spirits. They are resourceful and adaptable no matter the situation."

"That's how you see me?" Tristan asked. He didn't think he could love a nickname more.

"Yes."

"You're an amazing man, Vincent."

"As long as I'm amazing to you, that's all that matters, sparrow."

***

Vincent woke the next morning alone. The sheets were still warm so Tristan couldn't be far. That's when Vincent heard the retching coming from the bathroom. He jumped out of bed and raced into the other room to find Tristan hanging over the toilet vomiting violently.

His body was shaking and his hair was wet from sweat. Vincent grabbed a washcloth and ran it under the cold water before kneeling down behind his love and placing the cloth on the back of Tristan's neck.

Tristan grabbed some toilet paper, wiped his mouth clean, and leaned back into Vincent's arms. He felt hot. Tristan was running a fever. The question was how high. Vincent took the cloth from around Tristan's neck and gently pressed it to his forehead.

"I'm going to carry you back to bed, okay?" Vincent asked, and waited for Tristan's nod before picking him up.

His sparrow looked up at him with glassy eyes and rasped, "I think I have the flu."

Vincent wanted Sam to take a look in case it was something worse than a garden variety bug. There were no taking chances with Tristan.

Vincent covered Tristan's shivering body with the comforter and tucked him in so he could warm up. "I'm going to get you some ginger ale, Gravol, and pain reliever. If Sam is home, I'd like him to come see."

"It's just the flu, but if you want to bring Sam in, that's okay."

Vincent quickly pulled on his track pants and placed a garbage can on the floor beside the bed. "I'll be right back, love. If you feel sick, there's a bucket beside the bed to throw up in."

"Thank you," Tristan mumbled before closing his eyes.

Vincent left the room and headed straight for the kitchen. It was after six in the morning and he hoped Sam was back from his trip. Mrs. Walker was in the kitchen working away on breakfast while Dante sat drinking a coffee at the table and reading the paper.

"You're back, that's great. Is Sam up?" Vincent asked as he collected the ginger ale and a glass.

"Yeah. Why? What's wrong?"

"I woke up to find Tristan vomiting in the bathroom. He has a fever but says it's only the flu. Could Sam come and have a look at him?"

"I'll go get him for you," Dante said as he stood.

"I'll make him some dry toast and tea," Mrs. Walker added.

"Thank you," Vincent said before leaving them and returning to his sick boyfriend.

Tristan hadn't moved an inch since he left so Vincent poured him a glass of ginger ale before heading for his bathroom in search of the medication. He'd set a chair down beside the bed and was about to sit down when there was a knock on the door. He went to answer it and found Sam and Mrs. Walker waiting for him.

"Thank you for coming."

"Of course." Sam nodded as he carried their house first aid kit over to Tristan.

Vincent took the tea and toast from Mrs. Walker and thanked her before she left the room. He joined Sam beside the bed and set Mrs. Walker's offerings on the side table.

Tristan was telling Sam his symptoms and that he'd been not feeling quite right for days. It bothered Vincent that Tristan hadn't told him he'd felt off, but at the moment that wasn't his main concern. Sam took out his thermometer and took Tristan's temperature. Sure enough, it read 100.6 F; he had a fever. Sam listened to Tristan's lungs and heart, and checked his blood pressure as well as his pulse. Everything else was within normal ranges.

"As far as I can see it looks like the flu, but if you have any concern, we should take him to see Dr. Green," Sam stated.

Vincent looked down at Tristan, who was already shaking his head. "It's only the flu. I'll be fine in a couple days."

"The effects of the flu can last from one to two weeks. You need to get lots of liquids and rest. You can take over-the-counter pain relievers for any aches or headache, and Gravol for your nausea. If it gets worse in a few days, then we take you to see a doctor. Agreed?"

"Agreed," Tristan huffed.

Sam smiled and said, "I'll hold you to it."

"So will I," Vincent added. There was no way he'd allow Tristan to worsen and not see a doctor.

Tristan suddenly leaned over the bed, reaching for the garbage can. Vincent grabbed it and barely got it under his sparrow's mouth before he began vomiting again. With every gag and retch, his slender body convulsed and it hurt Vincent to watch. Anyone who'd ever had the flu understood what it took out of you.

"Don't worry, love, I'll be right here to help you get better," Vincent promised as he held Tristan's head while his love continued to vomit.

Chapter Seven

The next three days played out much the same as the first. Only now, Tristan was much weaker than before and unable to keep anything solid down. Sam was checking him over again while they waited for Dr. Green to arrive. Vincent refused to wait any longer to involve a doctor even if his love was convinced the flu would run its course and go away.

"Fever is up over one hundred one now. It keeps inching its way up. There has to be some sort of infection causing this," Sam concluded.

"I'd be great if I could get rid of this headache and joint pain; I'd be good to go," Tristan teased softly. Vincent's brave sparrow was still trying to make everyone else comfortable. "I'll be fine in a few days. My immune system was knocked down from the moving and all the other stuff that's been happening. I need a little time to get back on my feet."

Vincent crawled onto the bed and leaned over Tristan. "Humor me, love. I want to make sure that's all there is to it."

"But I don't want to see Dr. Green," Tristan admitted.

"Why?" Vincent didn't know the doctor well, but from what he'd heard and seen, he was a stand-up guy.

"The last time he came he kept pushing Dr. Gordon on me. I'm not ready for that again."

Vincent understood. It seemed as though a few people had been beating Tristan over the head with recommendations for Dr. Gordon in an attempt to help. "There will be no more talk of therapy unless you bring it up, okay?"

"Promise?" Tristan asked.

"Absolutely," Vincent answered as he pulled Tristan into his arms. Within minutes his love had fallen back asleep on Vincent's chest. Sam remained at a respectful distance doing research on the Internet.

After about fifteen minutes, Sam stood up from the desk and came to them in the bed. "Can you help me check Tristan for any abrasions or marks?"

"Definitely, what are you thinking?"

"I'm not sure yet, but as soon as I know I'll tell you."

Carefully they rolled Tristan from his back to his front; the poor man didn't even wake up. Sam checked his head, neck, chest, and back while Vincent took care of the private areas, which didn't have a mark. Vincent was sure this was a wild-goose chase until Sam looked up and told Vincent, "Found it."

"Found what?" Vincent asked as he joined Sam at Tristan's feet.

Sam held Tristan's right foot up and pointed at the bite mark and the bull's-eye rash. *Shit.* "A tick bite, but he hasn't been out in the woods since the incident with Grady's father. That was seven weeks ago."

"It can take that long for the symptoms of Lyme disease to show up. Tristan even mentioned feeling sick before he ever started throwing up. Dr. Green should be here any minute. He'll be able to do blood tests to try to confirm my diagnosis."

Vincent went to the side of the bed and gently tried to wake Tristan. They had to find out when he was bitten to figure out how long the infection had been in his system.

Slowly Tristan opened his eyes and he looked at Vincent before smiling. "Love you."

"I love you as well, but right now I need you to concentrate on something for me."

"Sure." Tristan gave him as big a smile as he could for being so weak and groggy.

"When did you get bitten on the foot by a tick?"

Tristan cringed before saying, "I found that thing when I took off my socks after being taken hostage by Grady's dad and Ryan. I don't know how long it was on there, but it was huge when I found it. I took a pair of tweezers and pulled it out before flushing it down the toilet. I had to look it up on the Internet since it was the first time I've ever been bitten." He curled onto his side before muttering, "It's okay. It's not even itchy."

Warning bells were going off in Vincent's head and when he turned to Sam, he saw the same look. "It could be Lyme disease, right?"

"Yes, it could," Sam answered before he headed to the door. "I'll see where Dr. Green is."

The room was quiet as Vincent curled beside his sparrow, who had fallen back to sleep. The thought of Tristan having Lyme disease was sickening. Not only would he have to fight the pain and fatigue while going through courses of antibiotics, but the bacteria could have already spread to his heart and brain. Considering his joints were sore, they might be infected already. Lyme disease was so serious that it had been known to cause complications that could carry on for the rest of a person's life. It could also cause death.

Some time had passed before there was a soft knock on the door. Vincent made sure to tuck the comforter around Tristan before he went to answer it. He opened the door to find Dante, Sam, and Dr. Green waiting for him. He let the three in, allowing Sam and Dr. Green to go to Tristan and taking Dante to the lounge.

"We have one of the SUVs being readied to take him in to Brighton General if the doc thinks we need to," Dante explained.

"Thank you. I'm hoping we aren't that far gone yet that we can't treat him here with antibiotics." Vincent knew there was a chance that they'd have to treat Tristan with intravenous antibiotics if the infection had already crossed to his nervous system.

How could he have not thought of this possibility? Hell, Ryan had dragged them through the woods on their way to that shack they were holed up in. Tristan could have picked up a blacklegged tick anywhere. Not all deer ticks were infected with the bacteria that caused Lyme disease, but it was becoming more obvious that the one that had bitten him was infected with the borrelia bacteria.

Vincent knew Lyme disease was serious. He'd spent a lot of time in the bush, trees, and jungles. Part of their training was to look for bites since any and everything that could bite, infect, or poison him lived in all the areas he seemed to be assigned to over the years.

Dr. Green didn't take long and walked over to Vincent and Dante. "I need him to be taken to the hospital immediately so we can start intravenous antibiotics."

"It's crossed over to neurological symptoms?" Dante asked.

"Yes. He's having issues feeling his right hand. Tristan said it has been numb since the book signing," Dr. Green explained.

Dante glanced at Vincent then left the room. Vincent looked over at his sparrow, who couldn't look him in the eye. He walked over to the bed and asked, "Why didn't you tell me about your hand?"

"I honestly thought it was because it had been injured the week before and that I overdid it at the signing."

"I need you to promise to tell me these things. I love you and all I want is for you to feel better."

Tristan's eyes filled with tears before he mumbled, "I'm sorry. I promise."

Vincent felt like an ass. He sat down on the side of the bed and gathered Tristan into his arms. "I'm not mad at you. I'm worried. I'm sorry as well." After all, this was his fault. Tristan had trusted him to do what was best and he'd waited too long.

"Vincent, we need Tristan to get dressed," Sam said as he went to the dresser in search of clothes. "Is this one Tristan's?" he asked as he pointed to the six-drawer dresser. Vincent nodded but didn't let go of his sparrow. Tristan had his arms loosely around Vincent's waist as if he didn't have the strength to hug him.

The heat radiating off Tristan was enough to make Vincent start to perspire. He should have suspected something else was going on with his love. Now he was being rushed to the hospital.

"I'll be fine, Vincent," Tristan said in a soft voice. "We'll go to the hospital and they'll fix me right up."

How was it that the man who was deathly sick was comforting him? Vincent needed to get his shit together. "Of course they will. I hate to see you so sick."

"I agree…I hate it too." Tristan tried to laugh as his green eyes sparkled.

"Here we go. Some comfortable clothes for the drive," Sam said as he brought over a pair of track pants, a tee shirt, and socks.

Vincent helped Tristan dress even though his strong-willed sparrow said he could do it on his own. Vincent wrapped Tristan in a blanket and lifted him from the bed, Sam grabbed the door, and they were on their way. The house was silent. It was late in the evening, but when he turned the corner to the living room, he found everyone waiting. All the members of his team and their partners stood in a loose huddle to see them off with a kind word and encouragement.

Tristan smiled at everyone, but his eyes began to droop as they loaded him into the back of the SUV. They'd placed a soft mattress in the cargo area for Tristan to lie on, knowing how much his joints already hurt. Vincent's sparrow was keeping a brave face for everyone, but Vincent could see the cracks of pain and worry seeping through.

"Don't worry about anything. I'll make sure you have the best care," Vincent promised and he could afford it too. He hadn't explained his financial situation to his love because the time was never right. In truth all the Sentinels were wealthy. The nature of their work was costly, and early on they'd pooled their money and invested well. Now each of them could live a life of luxury if they so desired.

Tristan looked up at him with complete trust.

Vincent wouldn't fail him again.

***

For the next few days, Tristan was awake on and off. It frustrated him how fatigued and weak he felt all from a stupid bug bite. His body ached, but at least his headache was now under control. He'd been attached to an IV since he'd arrived at the hospital, and he was told the IV wouldn't be coming out anytime soon. He noticed that he often found himself in a fog and would lose track of conversations. He worried that the disease had affected his brain.

He was being treated with intravenous antibiotics and had even seen a rheumatologist for his joint pain. Vincent had called in a doctor from Dallas who specialized in Lyme disease and the affect it had on the joints. Tristan had asked several times if he could go home and do the treatment as an outpatient and as many times as he had asked, he'd been told he could once he was stable. No matter how hard he tried to convince Vincent and Dr. Green that he was better, they never bought it. So here he sat or lay, stuck in the hospital. He hated it.

Vincent had been with him night and day since he first became sick. Tristan had finally ordered him to go home and sleep last night in a real bed and not the old recliner the nurses had been kind enough to find for him. Now he missed Vincent's company as he stared at the landscape painting hanging on the far wall. It was breathtaking and he could make out that the artist was a Mason.

He'd had a few visitors: the White Hair Crew had been by, the Sentinel team, and a few friends he'd made around town. Tristan had been out of it for some of the visits, but he managed to stay awake most of the time until the visits were over. Grady had stopped by every day and it took a lot to convince him this wasn't his fault. Vincent had mentioned that Police Chief Dave Graham had stopped in, but Tristan had been asleep at the time. He wasn't sure why Dave had come by. After all, he'd shot and killed the man's cousin. What did they have to say to each other?

"Why do you look so glum, chum?" Matthew asked as he walked through the door carrying two coffees. *Bless him.*

Tristan reached for a cup with his right hand but quickly pulled it back and exchanged it for his left. His hand was still numb and unusable. Even though Vincent thoughtfully brought him his laptop so he could write, Tristan hadn't picked it up, no matter how much he wanted to. The fear that he'd lose the use of his right hand, his dominant hand, permanently was terrifying to him.

"Tristan?"

Tristan concentrated on Matthew. How long had he been lost in his own thoughts that time? "Sorry, Matthew, what did you say?"

"I asked why you looked so down. You okay?"

"Yeah, I'm fine. I don't mean to drift off like that; it just happens. It's maddening." Tristan hated whining. "And now I'm behaving like a child."

"You're not behaving like a child…a tween, definitely," Matthew joked, bringing Tristan out of his malaise.

He took a sip of his coffee and let out a sigh of happiness. "The nectar of the gods."

Both laughed as Matthew took one of the seats beside the bed. "So how are you feeling today? Have you called your parents yet?"

"Better, except I feel like I'm tied to this bed. Freedom, I need freedom," Tristan said while imitated one of his favorite movies. "And, no, I haven't called them yet. They'll worry for nothing. I'm healing. Really. But don't worry, I've given Vincent their number in case I get worse again."

"Okay, as long as there's a plan. You want to go for a walk around the hospital? We can borrow a wheelchair," Matthew suggested.

Tristan perked up at the thought of breaking out of this room. "Sounds great."

"Okay, I'll go get a wheelchair. Be right back."

Tristan slowly brought his legs over the side of the bed and stood. Although it felt uncomfortable and downright painful, it still felt good to get out of his bed for something other than using the bathroom. Vincent had taken to coming into the shower with Tristan to make sure he didn't fall. He liked the company for a whole other reason, but was too weak to act on his imagination.

He reached for his comfy purple bathrobe and wrapped it around himself; the IV line ensured he didn't go any farther. While he waited, Tristan looked out and down the three stories at the street below. He watched cars picking up and dropping off patients, an ambulance at one of the emergency doors, and a group nurses crossing the street on their way to the park. On the opposite side of the street, a tall man with short dark hair and wearing a dark suit stood facing away from the hospital. The closer Tristan looked, the more the man seemed familiar but he was in the wrong direction for him to see his face no matter how hard he tried.

Suddenly, time stopped as the man turned around: *Stavros.* How could that psycho have found him? He needed Vincent and the police. Matthew came back into the room along with a nurse and he turned to look at them. They must have seen the terror on his face because both ran forward.

"Are you okay, Mr. Michaels?" Nurse June asked, and Matthew took his hand.

"It's…" Tristan started and turned to look back out the window, but Stavros was gone. Everything else was exactly the same as he scanned up and down the street.

"Did you see something?" Matthew asked as he too looked out the window.

Did he? Could this be part of that fog he was living in playing tricks on him? How could Stavros have found him? He's confined to his family's estate in Dallas.

"Tristan?"

"It's nothing, I thought I saw someone I knew but it was my imagination. Sorry to worry you." He felt like a fool jumping at ghosts.

"Not to worry." Nurse June smiled wide and went to disconnect his IV bags from the pole attached to the bed to the one on the wheelchair. "That should do it. Have a nice walk, gentlemen."

Tristan sat in the wheelchair and Matthew pushed him out into the hallway. “Which way do you want to go first?”

“Whichever way leads outside to the sun,” Tristan decided, and Matthew quickly agreed.

He was finally feeling excited about something and couldn’t knock the smile off his face. People smiled back at him as Matthew kept up a constant commentary on where everything was and what places they weren’t allowed into. *Odd.*

“How would you know where not to go?” Tristan asked. “Wouldn’t the area be locked anyway?”

“Um, yep they are,” Matthew answered before looking away.

“What did you do?” Tristan knew along with being a computer genius and making all kinds of neat things that could kill you, he watched and inventoried his surroundings like a GPS tracker.

“Well, you see, Coop was getting a few stitches after one assignment and it was late at night. There’d been an accident, so understandably we had been waiting for hours until they had the victims stable. I went for a walk around the ER when I noticed a door open to a long hallway.”

“Here we go.”

“You can’t blame me, they left the door open. Anyway, I went through it and down the hall. It led to what looked like a lab but all the lights were off so I took a look around. Before I knew it, the doors had closed and they wouldn’t open up without a keycard.”

“What happened?” Tristan asked while trying to hold back his laughter.

“A couple hours later Coop found me along with security who made sure to tell me which areas of the hospital were off limits to anyone but staff.”

“Why didn’t you let yourself out?” Along with being super smart, there wasn’t a system or code Matthew couldn’t crack.

“After the incident with Coop’s stereo, I’m not allowed to take anything apart without checking first. So I couldn’t open up the security panel without breaking my promise to Coop, and I'd never do that."

This time Tristan did laugh and so did Matthew. They waited for the elevator to take them down to the ground floor when Matthew asked, "So you going to tell me who you think you saw?"

Tristan should have known better than to assume his friend would let what happened earlier go. "It's not important. It was my imagination going haywire because of this damn Lyme infection."

"Was it Stavros?"

"Yeah."

"The team and the police have been given a photo of the guy. If he sets one foot into Brighton, he'll be identified and arrested. You don't have to worry about anything, promise." Matthew tried to reassure him, but Tristan knew if there was a chance, Stavros would take it. "Have you ever figured out why he's so zeroed in on you?"

"No. We went out on a few dates, he wanted to move faster and I didn't. The final straw was when he showed up when Grady was over visiting and demanded that I choose between the two of them. I chose my best friend and told Stavros to get out. We hadn't even had sex. I don't know why he's so fixated on me. I wanted him to go away, and now I want him in jail for the rest of his life," Tristan explained as they neared the automatic doors leading out to a sunny patio area with flowers and umbrellas.

Tristan could literally feel his spirits rise as Matthew pushed him out into the sunshine. The sky was blue with puffy white clouds. They placed what was left of their coffees on a table on the far side of the patio. There were flowerbeds to his left and right, and they reminded him of Sam. Sam liked to garden and trim trees into animal shapes. It was all quite stunning.

Tristan couldn't help but think about Vincent's offer: a house of their own. He could decorate and garden to his heart's content. He could have his own office and maybe even a library and a separate place for his shoes. However, he still couldn't get over how quickly everything between them had happened, and he worried that something would burst his bubble and he'd lose Vincent. At least he was willing to admit to himself how close he was to saying yes.

"I'm going to get us a few cinnamon rolls. Sound good?" Matthew asked as he eyed the little bakery on the other side of the patio.

"Sounds perfect. Coffee and cinnamon rolls, couldn't get any better than that," Tristan agreed, and Matthew took off.

Tristan sat back and basked in the sunlight; even though he was exhausted, and in pain, he felt at peace for a moment. The first time in days and he couldn't help but smile as he soaked it in.

"Well, isn't that a gorgeous sight," a deep voice said, and Tristan smiled even wider.

He opened his eyes to find the man he loved standing in front of his table with a flower in his hands. "Is that a blue orchid?"

"Yes. It's a gift from my friends Gabe and Johnny. You met them at the barbeque last month," Vincent explained as he set the potted flower on the table and took the seat next to Tristan before kissing him deeply.

"Please thank them for me. It's beautiful. I've never seen quite this color before." Again, Tristan reached out with his right hand only to pull it back at the last moment. He'd have to get used to using his left hand from now on until this damage worked itself out, if it ever did.

Vincent noticed but was astute enough not to say anything. Tristan was still a little touchy about it and his love knew it. His whole career was based around him using his hands to write his stories.

Tristan noticed Vincent had a duffle bag with him. "What's all in there, *nizhóní*?"

"I brought a few pieces of clothing for you. I thought you'd feel more comfortable getting treatment in anything other than a hospital gown. I also packed a few things for myself while I'm staying here with you."

"I've told you, you need to sleep in a bed. You're a big guy. You can't sleep in a recliner. Well. Unless they're the recliners at home, but nothing is that big."

"You let me worry about that," Vincent said. "There's also a surprise in there for you."

That got Tristan's attention. "A gift? What is it? Can I have it?" He loved surprises and Vincent knew it. Which was odd considering all the bad surprises he'd had recently.

"I'll give it to you when we get back up to your room," Vincent stated, which tempted Tristan to peek into the bag.

"Is it something *private* for the two of us?" Now that was something he could get behind. Since he'd gotten sick, Vincent had restricted their amorous adventures to blowjobs and even then, it was only Tristan who received the mind-blowing experience every shower they had.

"I'll show you when we get back to your room. You'll have to be patient."

Before Tristan could dig any further, Matthew returned with three giant cinnamon rolls. He must have seen Vincent join them. "Hey, guys, look at the size of these things, they're massive."

Tristan agreed and knew he'd never get through all that. It had only been little more than a day since he finally got his nausea under control. He didn't want to risk it. "I'll eat a few bites but I think I should take my time with the rest of it."

"Good idea," Matthew agreed. "That's why I got the to-go containers."

"Smart man," Tristan agreed before he took a small bite of the baked goodness before him. Yeah, he liked bakeries and visited them often.

Vincent reached over and held Tristan's right hand, surprising him and making him almost choke on his cinnamon roll. He got himself under control and tried to pull his numb, unusable hand away, but Vincent refused to let go. He wasn't holding him too tightly as to hurt him but was holding firm so that there was no question he wasn't letting go.

"Vincent, please."

He finally let go but moved his chair until he was sitting facing Tristan. "Sparrow, I love every part of you and not only when you're healthy. Your hand, like the rest of you, is beautiful to me. I understand you may not be ready, and I don't want to do anything that makes you uncomfortable. So I'll wait until you're ready."

Tristan didn't know what to say. "Thank you" didn't seem appropriate. "I love you, Vincent." For someone who could barely say the words not long ago, Tristan was certainly making up for lost time.

The three sat enjoying the gorgeous day for another few minutes, but soon enough he could feel his fatigue pulling him down once again. "I think we need to go back to my room."

"Are you okay?" Vincent asked in a rush, concern evident on his face.

"Yeah, I'm getting a bit tired though and could probably lie down," Tristan explained as he placed his roll into the to-go container.

Vincent gathered up his bag and their leftovers and walked alongside Tristan's wheelchair. Tristan's eyes were closing by the time he was rolled into his room. Before he knew it, he was being lifted from the wheelchair and onto his bed. The fog was closing in around him. *I didn't even get my surprise* was the last thing he said to himself before he gave up the fight and fell asleep.

Chapter Eight

Vincent watched as his sparrow slept. It had been two weeks since they'd admitted Tristan into Brighton General and today was the day his love had been waiting for: he was being discharged from the hospital. He could continue his recovery at home as long as he came in for his daily intravenous antibiotic regimen for at least two more weeks. After that, they would reassess and start physiotherapy on his right hand.

Tristan had been through a battle with Lyme disease. He'd come from vomiting, fever, and sleeping over twenty hours a day to fever free, eating, and getting by with only a couple naps during the day. The one thing Vincent had hoped would come around but never did was Tristan's ability to use his right hand. His joints were still swollen and painful. They'd already packed everything and Vincent had taken all Tristan's stuff out to his truck while they waited for Dr. Green to come sign the release papers.

Tristan got his surprise when he'd woken up later that day. Vincent had gotten him voice recognition software with a headset and microphone combo. It wasn't run-of-the-mill, out-of-the-box software; Vincent had given the program to Shannon, who'd worked her magic. Now the entire system could be run by simple voice commands. His sparrow had loved it and gotten back to writing almost immediately.

After the first couple of days, he asked if Vincent could ask Shannon to get the microphone to pick up whispering. Apparently, Tristan was getting a following. People stood outside his room and listened to him "write" his latest book. Flattering but disconcerting Tristan could handle. But creepy made an appearance when über-fan Shawn showed up at the hospital. Dante had been visiting and Tristan was asleep, so Shawn was escorted out of the hospital without incident. Dante and Vincent directed him to Tristan's publicist and asked him to respect Tristan's privacy.

Vincent knew Tristan loved his fans, and from what he'd seen most of them were normal people who worked normal jobs and enjoyed spending their downtime with one of his books. So, even though he wanted to take a different tact, he'd been polite to Shawn and thanked him for his concern before shutting the door and contacting hospital security.

The next day he'd mentioned the incident to Tristan, who was shocked by Shawn's audacity, but let it go as Tristan lost himself in the story he was writing. Vincent had to admit, he liked watching his love work; there was passion in his eyes and Tristan had even shed a tear when he had to kill off one of his main characters. If he was this passionate about writing his books, no wonder his fans were equally as passionate about reading them.

Dr. Green stuck his head into Tristan's room and motioned for Vincent to join him in the hallway. Vincent took one final look at Tristan to confirm he was still asleep then followed the doctor out.

"Is something wrong?" Vincent asked as he joined him and Nurse June.

"Tristan is still fine to go home; I don't want you to worry about that. We have all his medication ready to go and I'll be still seeing him daily when you bring him in," Dr. Green explained.

Vincent knew there had to be more. "You could have told me all of this in the room. What aren't you saying?"

Nurse June replied, "There's been a few phone calls regarding Mr. Michaels, or better said, checking in on him."

"Do you know who it was? Did they tell you their name?"

"That's the thing, he would never leave it. We repeatedly told him that we couldn't release any information, but he was persistent."

"When was the last call?" Vincent asked.

"This morning."

Vincent didn't like the sound of this. He could be overreacting or it could be Stavros. There was no way in hell he'd risk Tristan to find out. He pulled out his cellphone and hit speed dial.

"Hey, aren't you two supposed to be home by now?"

"Spider, we may have a problem."

***

Tristan could feel Vincent's lips on his forehead, then his cheek before stopping at his lips. He'd recognize those lips anywhere and his lover's scent always reminded him of leather so he dove into the kiss without reservation. Vincent moaned his approval as he slowed the kiss; they were still in the hospital—propriety and all that.

He opened his eyes and looked up at the man who'd brought so much happiness into his life. "Hi, you sexy devil."

Vincent's cheeks turned a nice shade of red. *So handsome.* "It's time for us to go home, sparrow."

Tristan couldn't help himself: he cheered, and he would have leapt out of the bed if he wasn't sure he'd fall flat on his ass. Instead, he opened his arms wide and said, "Take me home, love, and have your way with me."

He could hear laughter coming from the hallway a moment before Nurse June walked in with a small bag. "Here are your meds and we'll see you bright and early tomorrow morning for your IV antibiotics."

"Thank you for everything," Tristan said as Vincent lifted him and set him in his wheelchair. It was going to take a while before he'd be able to convince his love that he could walk on his own—slowly, but on his own.

"Don't overdo it because you're out of the hospital," Nurse June warned.

Before he could answer, Vincent piped up, “He won’t, I promise.”

Tristan shook his head at his overprotective partner, grabbed the bag off the bed, and ordered, “Let’s go home.”

Nurse June laughed and waved them off as Vincent pushed Tristan out of the room he was so anxious to leave behind. He felt like he was on top of the world until he saw other members of the team waiting in the hallway. Coop and Dante stood leaning against the wall as if they didn’t have a care in the world, but Tristan knew better.

“What’s wrong?” he asked as he looked up at Vincent.

Vincent answered quickly, too quickly. “Nothing. The team wanted to be here to take you home.”

“And to that I say ‘bullshit.’ Have we learned nothing from the whole Grady and Ben mix-up?” Tristan asked and calmly waited for the truth. He knew Vincent wasn’t trying to deceive him and probably thought he was protecting him.

Vincent came around to the front of his wheelchair and crouched down until they were eye to eye. He looked worried and that put Tristan on alert. “Sparrow, there have been calls coming into the hospital searching for information about you. It seemed to be the same man every time and we want to make sure you’re safe.”

Tristan let that sink in for a moment. “It might have been Shawn again.” Even though that thought was starting to give him the creeps, it was the better alternative to his ex.

“The staff began recording the calls in case we could identify him. I listened to them and I’m positive it wasn’t Shawn. We’re going to keep looking into it to try to identify the person.”

“You think it’s Stavros, don’t you?” Tristan figured he might as well cut to the chase.

Vincent never broke eye contact. “Yes.”

Decision time. He wasn’t going to allow Stavros to force him into hiding and not live his life. Tristan remembered the man’s anger and penchant for violence; the thought of him anywhere near them was terrifying, but he couldn't let that fear rule him.

"I refuse to live in fear. I've gone through far too much to allow that to happen. Of course I'm not crazy so I'll be alert to my surroundings, but I want to start my new life with you." In that moment Tristan had his answer to the question of where home would be. "I want to live with you and have a little place of our own."

His lover's face lit up so quickly Tristan almost laughed. "You're sure?"

"Positive."

Tristan was pulled into Vincent's strong arms and hugged to within an inch of his life. Further confirming he'd made the right choice.

"Let's get you out of here," Vincent stated, and he stood to take up his position at Tristan's back pushing his wheelchair.

"I'm all for that," Tristan replied as Dante took up position in front and Coop behind. He thought it was a bit of overkill, but this was their area of expertise. "I'll need a big closet for my shoes and an office that can double as a library or den."

"We'll get an architect and start drawing up plans as soon as possible," Vincent replied.

"We'll deed the land over to you once you two decide where you want to build," Dante added.

"We'll go for a tour around the property and see what you like, sparrow."

"What *we* like, *nizhóní*." They would be making decisions together.

Vincent ran his hand up and down Tristan's neck and shoulder. He couldn't stop the goosebumps from rising; Vincent's touch did that to him every time. They took the elevator down to the ground level and made their way through staff and visitors to the sliding front doors of the hospital. Tristan could see one of the team's SUVs waiting by the curb with Matthew in the driver's seat. Tristan had the feeling the rest of the team was here somewhere watching from a distance to make sure he was safe.

"Guys, I really don't think—" Tristan began but was cut off.

"Northeast end of the parking lot," Dante ground out.

"Gray sedan," Coop confirmed.

"Got it," Vincent replied as he started to push Tristan a little bit faster.

Tristan glanced at the parking lot where Dante had been looking and saw Shannon approaching a gray, four-door sedan from the front and Spider from the back; there was one person with a camera in the driver's seat. Tristan's sight line was cut off by the SUV's open door just as they were reaching the vehicle.

Slowly he climbed into the backseat and by the time he'd settled and turned back to see what Spider and Shannon were doing, Grady was pulling up in his police cruiser. Things were getting real way too fast, and he was thankful when Matthew pulled away from the curb and headed toward the compound.

"We'll be home in a few minutes, sparrow," Vincent assured him as he gathered Tristan close.

He noticed Dante was on a call and waited until he hung up before asking. "Who was in the car in the parking lot?"

Dante turned around in his seat and faced Tristan before answering. "So far all we have is that the guy is a private detective out of Dallas. We'll dig up more information once we get back to the house and after they have a chance to question him."

"A private detective? Who would send a private investigator after me?" Even as he was saying the words, he knew the answer: Stavros. "Stupid question."

"Nothing you say is stupid," Vincent admonished. "We don't know for sure it was Stavros."

If it wasn't Stavros, who then? He couldn't have that many people looking for him. *Maybe I should have stayed in the hospital. No, I'm not going to crawl away and hide.* Tristan straightened his spine and looked at his lover. "We both know it's likely it's him, but we'll be ready for the asshole this time. He won't get away with this anymore."

Vincent nodded his head before saying, "Damn right we will."

"We'll get him," Coop added.

"He won't know what hit him," Matthew called out from the driver's seat.

"You watch where you're driving, mister," Dante complained and pointed toward the road in front of the vehicle before turning and winking at Tristan.

For the first time since the whole Stavros ordeal began, Tristan felt safe. This new family of his would protect him as much as he'd protect each of them. "Thank you."

He was beginning to understand how close a group the Sentinels really were. It made more and more sense now that the team would talk openly about one another, including him. Tristan was beginning to feel guilty for reacting the way he had when he heard them discussing his health. They were trying to help, and they were willing to put themselves in harm's way to protect him.

The group was quiet the remainder of the drive. Tristan's thoughts centered on how to make sure no one got hurt because of him. Stavros was after him, and he still had no idea why, but the one thing he was sure of was that Stavros would never stop hunting him until he was physically forced. One way or another.

***

Hours later Tristan lay back in their tub enjoying the deliciousness of a bubble bath, which he'd missed while in the hospital. But he was home now—well, his new temporary home. He knew he wasn't going back to live by himself in his apartment, and he didn't want to. His world was intertwined with Vincent's and he planned to build a life with his amazing man. To hell with the whole "It's too soon" bullshit. This was his life and he was taking it by the horns.

There was a soft knock on the door before Vincent walked in with a mug in his hand. He set it on the small bench beside the tub before climbing in with Tristan. This had become one of their favorite ways to unwind. They hadn't received any new information about the private investigator yet, and both Spider and Shannon were still out, which had Tristan on edge and how he found himself in the bubble bath in the first place.

"That's chamomile tea. It will help calm your nerves," Vincent explained as he pointed at the mug.

"Thank you, love," Tristan said once he'd settled back against Vincent's chest. "So when do you want to go look at possible sites for our home?" *Full speed ahead.* Once Tristan had his mind made up about something, there was no holding him back.

"We can take the ATV out tomorrow and have a look around. I'll contact the architect who helped us renovate this house. Do you like what she did with this place?"

Though he did love the design of the old Victorian, Tristan was more of a Craftsmen's bungalow type of guy. "I do like what she did, but I was hoping we could have a different style home."

"You tell her what you envision and Ms. Ryley will help you bring it to life."

"But what about you? Don't you want to choose a style you like?" Tristan didn't want to Vincent to agree with him without having input—he had to have a style in mind.

Vincent ran his hand down the side of Tristan's face before cupping his jaw and gently leaning his head back so Vincent could look him in the eyes. "I have everything I want and need right here. I know it sounds corny as hell but it's true. I've lived through situations where I should have died in one hellhole or another. Now I have this team, this family, and you by my side. I feel whole now."

Now how was Tristan supposed to argue with that? Instead, he raised his lips for a kiss, which Vincent seemed eager to give him. When they broke apart, both were breathing heavily and Tristan's cock had turned to stone. Before he could turn around and do something about it there was a knock on their bedroom door.

Both men groaned but knew they had to answer, especially now with so much going on. “We’ll pick this up later,” Vincent promised before stepping out of the tub, wrapping a towel around his waist, and then heading for the door.

Tristan’s took a sip of his tea and lay back in the tub; he knew time was limited and soon he’d be faced with reality once again. Sure enough, Vincent came walking back in with Tristan’s purple bathrobe in his hands.

“Spider and Shannon are back. Everyone’s waiting for us in the living room,” Vincent said as he set the robe down and grabbed a towel. “Let’s get you dried and dressed.”

Not even five minutes later Tristan was dressed in his oversize Cowboys shirt and his plaid sleeping pants. He didn’t know anything about football, but he was completely on board with the tight pants they wore and all that bending over. Vincent took his hand and they walked into the living room to find the rest of the team waiting, including Shadow.

“Shadow, good to see you, man, but what are you doing back? Did you find Grady’s brother, Randy?” Vincent asked as they sat on one of the three couches set in a U shape in the middle of the living room.

Shadow looked tired when he answered, “No, but I have a few feelers out. While I’m waiting on word back, I figured I’d jump into the exciting things happening right here.”

“Exciting wouldn’t be the word I’d use,” Tristan replied.

Shadow smiled wide before saying, “It’s better than chasing down useless leads. Besides, you’re family now.”

Vincent’s arms tightened around Tristan and he leaned his head back against his love’s shoulder. “I don’t want to drag you away from your search.”

“You aren’t. As soon as I get any information about where he might be, I can head out. I’ll find Grady’s brother. I have a promise to keep," Shadow stated with a professional air, but Tristan could see the concern written all over Shadow's face.

"Randy is such an artistic, gentle soul. I can't imagine him out there alone in one of those damn conversion therapy centers." Tristan shivered at the thought. "Grady used to bring Randy over to my condo to hang out to get away from their father."

"Don't worry, I'll find him and bring him back," Shadow said with confidence.

Dante and Spider walked in carrying a few files, and neither looked particularly happy. *Great, what else have I brought to their doorstep?* Tristan couldn't imagine what was coming next.

"Okay, now that we're all here, let's get started on what we now know." Dante began to hand out the files.

Tristan didn't bother to take one; he'd share Vincent's. When his love flipped the cover open, Tristan was stunned to see pictures of him. Actually, there were more than a dozen pictures of him in Vincent's truck, at the book signing, and others of him sitting on the patio at the hospital. *How long has this guy been tagging me?*

"Who is he and why is he following me?" Tristan cut to the chase; he needed answers.

"His name is Roger Winter. He works for a firm out of Dallas sent to keep an eye on you."

"Did Stavros send him?" Tristan assumed that was an easy answer but he was wrong.

"No," Spider answered. "The police chief got on the phone and demanded answers from Winter's boss. As it turns out Stavros's parents, Cathy and Ron Menzotto, hired the private investigator."

"Why would they want to know where Tristan is and how he's doing?" Vincent asked. He seemed as confused as the rest of them appeared to be.

"It appears that Stavros has escaped his parents' house and they thought he would show up here," Dante explained.

"He's missing?" Tristan almost yelled as he tried to get out of his seat. If it weren't for Vincent's firm hold and calming words, Tristan surely would have fallen on his ass if he'd tried to make his sore body move that quickly. "I knew being arrested wouldn't stop him."

"Why didn't the detectives on the case inform us or Dave that Stavros had taken off?" Coop asked as he flipped through the pictures.

"The parents didn't inform the detectives. They were surprised to get our call. He's been missing for weeks," Spider answered.

"Weeks? He could be in Brighton." Matthew echoed exactly what Tristan was thinking. "Wait, Tristan thought he saw Stavros when he was in the hospital."

That got everyone's attention and questions began to fly. Tristan waved his hands to silence the room before saying, "It was my imagination. The infection had me walking around in a fog. Matthew even looked and saw nothing."

"Are you sure?" Vincent asked.

"Positive."

"We have perimeter fencing and motion sensors connected to monitors surrounding the entire property," Dante assured. Tristan had been told about the attack on Sam while he was in his greenhouse. The property had been secured like a military installation from that point forward. "The house has security systems in place and a safe room if needed. We won't let him get anywhere near you."

"Thank you," Tristan said and then he went one step further. "I'd like to thank all of you for everything you've done for me. I'm sorry I got upset when I heard you all talking about my health, but now I get it. You're a family and I'd love to be part of it."

Tristan leaned back into Vincent's embrace. This was his home. Vincent was his home.

"Welcome aboard," Sam cheered, causing the rest of the team to laugh and lighten the mood in the room for a moment.

"We're done waiting around. It's time for us to go hunting," Dante announced.

A few "hell yeahs" and "damn rights" floated around the room in support of the idea. The team began to make plans, but Tristan noticed he was losing track of the conversation and his eyes began to close. It was his first day out of the hospital and his body was reminding him of that right now. He didn't want to fall asleep during such an important meeting, but it soon became clear he had no choice.

Vincent must have sensed Tristan's body was flagging because he gently tucked Tristan's head under his chin and pulled a blanket over them. Tristan kissed the side of his love's neck before giving up and falling asleep in his arms.

***

He watched from the shadows as one by one the lights turned off in the old Victorian monstrosity. He never understood why some people felt the need to hold on to old things that he'd sooner seen torn down or thrown away. It was that sort of sentimentality that held back progress. Maybe he'd burn it down when he was done.

The night vision binoculars he'd ordered online worked perfectly. He'd have to leave a positive review. He looked back at his target. What he wanted was in that house; he had to figure out how to get in. He'd noticed all the security but didn't take a moment to wonder who the other people were and why they needed all this.

It really didn't matter; he'd kill anyone who got in the way of his prize.

Now all he had to do was wait for the right moment to take what was his.

Chapter Nine

The full moon bathed their bedroom in a grayish-blue glow. Vincent hadn't been able to fall asleep since bringing Tristan to bed. He watched the stars through the open window as the evening breeze made the drapes sway. His sparrow had already been through so much; it gutted Vincent that there was more to come. Tristan had been strong through it all, never complaining unless it was in an attempt to be released from the hospital, and he seemed to always have a smile for others.

Vincent thought about his own nightmares, which had started every night since Tristan had gone into the hospital. Was it an omen of what was to come or simply his fear playing tricks on him? Whatever it was, he swore not to let any harm come to his sparrow.

"Why aren't you sleeping?" Tristan asked. His sleep-roughened voice was sexy and made Vincent's cock take notice.

"Not tired I guess." Vincent didn't want to admit he was worrying over Stavros. That would only make Tristan feel guilty.

"I can think of a way we could tire you out," Tristan rasped, and his green eyes sparkled with desire.

"Yeah, you think you could help wear me out? I'd like to see that." Vincent loved Tristan's playful nature. The man had brought so much happiness into Vincent's life.

"Trust me," Tristan crooned as he pulled the covers off the both of them. Luckily, they were already naked; it saved time. His love crawled over and straddled him. "I'll take good care of you."

Vincent noticed a slight tremble in Tristan's right arm and was quickly reminded that he'd gotten out of the hospital only this morning. Tristan must have noticed his concern because he shook his head and murmured, "I'll be fine."

"Of course you will. Now you mentioned something about hot, sweaty sex."

Tristan broke out into laughter as Vincent had hoped. "I don't think I said those exact words, but sounds like a great plan to me." Leaning forward, Tristan took Vincent's lips in a heated kiss full of tongue. He left his arms above his head, giving his sparrow the control he seemed to need tonight. Vincent understood; Tristan's life had been in a constant state of upheaval over the last few months.

Tristan broke the kiss and began nibbling and licking his way down Vincent's neck and chest. He couldn't help but moan as Tristan's soft, wet lips latched on to his nipple, almost making him lift up off the bed. Tristan sucked and nibbled until Vincent's nipples were sensitive to the slightest touch before his man moved on to outline his abdominal muscles with his tongue.

When Tristan looked up, Vincent nearly came at the sight of the man he loved hovering over his hard cock, his face flushed, lips swollen, and his pupils dilated. He was stunning. Vincent dropped his head back onto his pillow as Tristan sucked Vincent's cock to the back of his throat.

"Lube, babe," Tristan requested with his hand extended before he went back to licking Vincent's cock like a lollipop.

He reached over to the side table, grabbed the bottle of lube from the drawer, and squeezed a liberal amount onto the fingers of Tristan's left hand before throwing the bottle on the bed. Tristan reached back to prepare himself for Vincent's cock. He watched, mesmerized, while Tristan moaned as he drove his own fingers deep. His beautiful face was a study in hedonistic pleasure as he stretched himself and Vincent was entranced.

"I need to be inside you, babe." Vincent could hear the yearning in his voice but didn't care.

His love crawled up Vincent's torso, ever mindful of his weak right hand, until his body hovered over Vincent's throbbing cock. Tristan looked like he wanted to ask him a question. "Is there something you want to say, sparrow?"

"You know all my blood work is clean, and considering we are building a home together I thought maybe…"

"You want to go bareback?" he finished Tristan's sentence for him.

"Yes."

"I have my latest medical in my file on the dresser. I'm clean, I can show it to you. We have to have medicals every couple months for the team's insurance." Vincent would get up right now if Tristan wanted to see it. He wanted his love comfortable with such a big step.

"I know you'd never lie to me. I want to make love to you without anything between us." Vincent was humbled by his love's trust.

"I want that too because you're the man I want to spend the rest of my life with. I love you."

"I love you too," Tristan moaned as he slowly lowered himself, impaling his body on Vincent's waiting cock. They both groaned loudly when Vincent's thighs were snug against Tristan's firm ass. Vincent felt like he was barely hanging on, but he didn't want this to end. He'd never been with anyone without wearing a condom and the sensations and intimacy between them was overpowering.

The feeling of the head of his cock splitting Tristan wide without the cover of latex did something to Vincent. He could no longer hold back and allow Tristan to set the pace. He needed more. Vincent placed his hands around Tristan's thin waist and began moving his lover's beautiful body up and down on his cock. He made sure not to move too fast in case Tristan's joints were hurting him again.

"Faster, Vincent, please move faster," Tristan begged.

"I don't want to hurt you, babe."

"I promise to tell you if something hurts. Please, Vincent, I need you so bad."

That was all it took. Vincent brought his body up, wrapped his arms around Tristan, and flipped them until his sparrow was on his back with Vincent hovering over him. Vincent was still buried deep inside the man he would someday make his husband. He'd keep that to himself for now; Tristan had had enough surprises.

Vincent lifted Tristan's body and placed a pillow underneath his hips to make sure he was comfortable. He pulled almost all the way out of his lover's hot embrace, never once losing eye contact before he drove himself back in and repeated the motion with ever-increasing speed, pegging Tristan's gland with every stroke. The bed began to shake in rhythm with his thrusts as Tristan begged him for even more. Soon the only sounds in the room were their heavy breathing and lovemaking accompanied by their moans and groans of passion.

Sweat beaded on his skin before dropping and mingling with Tristan's. Vincent's skin stood in stark contrast to his lover's pale coloring; they complemented each other perfectly. His hips flexed as their bodies began writhing together until you couldn't tell where one began and the other ended.

Vincent knew he was close to coming; his balls had pulled up tight to his body and he felt a tingle at the base of his spine. There was no way he'd come before his love, so he doubled his efforts and wrapped his hand around Tristan's leaking cock. Vincent pumped his hand in time with his hips and watched as his lover's green eyes closed and his back bowed up off the bed a moment before he came in long streams across his own stomach and chest.

Tristan's channel squeezed Vincent's cock so hard he could barely move and several strokes later, he came deep inside his lover while roaring his release to the ceiling. He'd never been so happy to know the rooms were soundproofed or the entire house would have been woken up. Hell, they still might have heard him. That orgasm had literally drained him as he struggled to keep himself from crushing Tristan.

As soon as he had control over his muscles, Vincent gently slipped out of Tristan and rolled to his side before pulling his love close.

"That was amazing," Tristan sighed. "Can we do it again?"

Vincent couldn't help but laugh. "I don't want to break you, sparrow. We'll wait until you've rested before tackling that again."

"Deal," Tristan agreed as he tried to hide a yawn.

"I'll be right back," Vincent said as he threw his legs over the edge of the bed and stood. He walked into the bathroom and quickly cleaned up before bringing a warm washcloth and towel out to Tristan. He crawled onto the bed and began cleaning and drying his lover.

Tristan hadn't moved; he simply sighed and closed his eyes. Before long Vincent heard his lover's soft snores, confirming he'd fallen back to sleep. Vincent threw the towels toward the bathroom and took Tristan into his arms. He erased every worry and negative thought from his mind and focused on what their lives would be like. How it would be building their home and growing old together.

Vincent's eyes finally grew heavy and he fell asleep wondering how many pairs of shoes his partner had to require their own closet.

***

After breakfast the next morning, Tristan and Vincent took one of the side-by-side ATVs for a tour of the property. Up until now, Tristan hadn't been any farther than a few of the outbuildings that stored the team's gear and vehicles. He'd learned that one of the buildings was always locked and secure; this was where Matthew built his latest gadgets for the team and the armed forces. Matthew worked at a level even higher than renowned scientist and engineers, yet he was the most down-to-earth guy Tristan had ever met.

Vincent drove slowly over the uneven ground for Tristan's benefit; he'd had enough of a workout the night before and still had aches and pains from the Lyme disease. He'd brought a pillow along for his sore ass, but you wouldn't catch him complaining; he'd loved every minute of it.

So far, they'd seen a few possible sites, but nothing had spoken to Tristan. He didn't want to be difficult, but this would be the place he called home for the rest of his life; it had to be special.

"Am I being too picky?" Tristan asked before taking a drink from his water bottle. "Those other locations were nice, one even had a pond."

"It's important to pick the right spot. There's a place I'd like to show you before you decide on anything. It's roughly a ten-minute drive from the main house," Vincent said before turning the ATV east.

Tristan sat back and enjoyed the beauty of nature that surrounded him. They'd already seen a few white-tailed deer, a red fox, and an armadillo on their adventure. The closest he'd ever gotten to nature when he lived in Dallas was the park at the end of his street.

Before long the trees and brush began to thin out until it opened up into a clearing that had a stream running through it. Vincent pointed out oak, elm, and pecan trees surrounding the area while wild grasses stood waist high. Tristan got out and slowly walked to the stream, where he could see tiny fish swimming near the rocks in the crystal-clear water.

He closed his eyes, listened to the sounds of water rushing over the rocks, leaves rustling and grass shifting in the breeze, and knew he was home. This was exactly where he pictured their new home being. The beauty, solitude, and peace would only help him and his writing.

Tristan opened his eyes and turned to Vincent, who was now standing behind him. Vincent's eyes were slightly squinted as if he was trying to read Tristan's mind.

"What do you think, sparrow?"

He threw himself into his lover's arms. "I love it. This spot is absolutely perfect."

Vincent caught him and hugged him close. "I'm so happy you do. I like to come here when I need to unwind and relax. You can swim in the stream. It's about five feet deep in the center."

Tristan looked up and asked, "If you love it here so much, why didn't you bring me here first?"

Instead of answering, Vincent carried him over to the bank of the stream and set him down on one of the large rocks.

"Vincent?"

"I wanted you to have the best house money could buy with your library, office, and walk-in closet. Those other plots of land had enough space for a larger house."

"A larger house would be expensive."

Vincent hung his head and said those seven little words that struck fear into any man. "There's something I need to tell you."

"Okay, whatever it is we can work it out," Tristan stated, and he believed every word. He'd been waiting his entire life for Vincent and he wasn't letting anything come between them.

"It's nothing bad. I should have told you by now, but there was never a time to bring it up," Vincent explained. "I can afford to buy you any size house you want and now that we're together we'll share it."

"I don't need your money. I make a good living on my own."

"I didn't mean it that way, sparrow. I've never had anyone to share everything with and it makes me insanely happy to have you."

Tristan couldn't help it; his curiosity got the better of him. "How much are we talking about?"

"As of Friday when the markets closed, roughly eighty-three million. The team has invested well and we're paid handsomely for our work."

Tristan nearly swallowed his tongue but ended up having a coughing fit instead. That was a hell of a lot of money. It put his six hundred thousand to shame. Vincent was rubbing Tristan's back and remained quiet. Tristan could guess why; money had a strange way of screwing up things. Though it may have been shocking at first, the fact that Vincent had *loads* of money didn't change a thing about how Tristan felt. He had loved his man long before today.

"Okay, I can understand not being able to slip that into an ordinary conversation. But I still don't want access to it, and how does all that affect me wanting this land?"

"A large house wouldn't fit here. It would ruin the beauty of the area. I want you to have what you want, babe."

"We really need to sit down and discuss this because I never said I wanted a big house. I'd live anywhere as long as you're there with me."

"What about your shoes and library?"

"Build me under bed storage for my shoes because I keep them in their original boxes anyway and put a bookshelf up in the living room. The only thing I was hoping for was some sort of space to write in, but as for everything else, I'm good. It could be a one-bedroom bungalow for all I care." They sat there wrapped in each other's arms watching the water float by. "This is our home."

"I'll call the architect as soon as we get back to the house," Vincent agreed but didn't seem to be in a hurry to leave this place so soon.

So they stayed, holding each other close, conjuring their home and their lives for the next two hours.

***

A month and a half later, the blueprints for their house were completed, the exact spot was laid out on the property, and the foundation had been poured. They designed a one-bedroom Craftsmen's bungalow, with an open kitchen, living, and dining area, an *en suite* bathroom as well as a half bath off the small hallway leading to Tristan's office. They'd build the house around the beauty of this spot, ensuring not a single tree would be cut down. They'd decided to keep the building to fifteen hundred square feet with large outside living areas. That was all they needed. The team had moved him out of his apartment and stowed all his belongings in one of the large sheds.

Tristan had always wanted a front porch where he could sit and relax or write, and he would have one. A low-pitched roofline would be built to include the porch along with the gabled roof. There would be exposed rafters in parts with deep eaves, and built-in cabinetry. The ceiling in the kitchen would be a highlight with hammered copper, and the beautiful craftsmanship of the builder would be on display throughout. They'd decided on a construction crew based in Brighton so that they knew the people. Even so, Shannon still did a background check on each and every person setting foot on the property.

There hadn't been any further word on Stavros, and Shadow had left when he'd received a lead on a small town in Arkansas where Randy might be held. Tristan hoped and prayed they found Randy soon. He couldn't imagine what they were doing to him in an attempt to "cure" him of being gay. When would people finally understand that being gay isn't a decision or a disease?

Today would be the first day of framing the house and Tristan couldn't contain his excitement. He'd sent off the first draft of his latest book to his publisher, which he was already stoked about, and now the physical representation of his and Vincent's future would take shape; he didn't even try to contain his happiness.

"I'm surprised you're not bouncing off the walls by now," Matthew commented as he walked into the kitchen. "You want to go over and have a look at how far they've gotten since this morning?"

"Do you think I'll be bugging them?" Tristan asked. After all, he'd already been out there first thing this morning.

"It's not like you're going to pick up a hammer or anything, so how could you bug them? We'll take one of the ATVs over there and watch, that's all." Matthew grabbed the keys from the cupboard and headed for the back door. "You coming?"

Tristan shook his head but followed anyway. It took him a minute to catch up because he was still suffering the effects from the Lyme disease. His joints still ached, making movement painful, and he still didn't have much stamina, but he got up every day thankful that the disease didn't attack his heart or other organs. He'd done a lot of research on Lyme since he had been infected and knew he was luckier than some.

As soon as he sat down beside Matthew, they were off. His friend tried to miss as many bumps as he could. They were halfway to the build site when Tristan noticed something running their way. As it got closer Tristan could make out that it was a dog. A malnourished German Shepard dog to be exact.

Matthew stopped their vehicle and the dog kept on coming, tail wagging, tongue hanging out, looking so happy to see them. She came up to the side of the vehicle and jumped in between Tristan's legs.

"She must be a stray," Matthew said.

"Poor girl. Do we have any water?" Tristan asked as he stroked their new friend's head.

Matthew began rifling around the back as Tristan searched her over for any injuries. Other than her skeletal frame, she didn't seem to have any other immediate concerns.

"A-ha, found it," Matthew said as he lifted a half-empty water bottle in victory.

"Perfect. Do we have anything to pour it into so she can drink?"

"No, sorry."

Tristan cupped his hands in front of the dog and said, "Pour a little at a time into my hands."

Matthew began pouring and she caught on quickly and lapped up all the water in no time. Her tail was wagging as she looked up into Tristan's eyes. "We'll get you some more water and some food when we get back to the house."

"Looks like you got yourself a dog." Matthew laughed as he restarted the ATV. "She must be the one that set off those sensors.

We'll have to find the spot where she got in. I'm happy my new system is working properly, though it reported her as a fox." Matthew had created a security system that could identify what had set off the sensors from thousands of images in his database. It then reported back to the team, who would check on anything suspicious. The new system was a godsend with a property this vast.

Tristan looked down at the dirty face of a dog that looked at him like he was her savior; he really had no other choice. "Looks like Vincent and I won't be the only ones getting a new home."

They continued down the lane with their extra passenger glued to Tristan's side. She was a young dog and he wondered how long she'd been on her own. Well, she wouldn't be a stray anymore. He'd take her to the vet and make sure she was healthy before adding some heft to her skinny frame. Tristan could see a bright pink collar around her neck with tags so she'd never get lost again and Buddy would have a friend. He knew he was rushing ahead; the dog might not even want to stick around, or worse, Vincent might not want to keep her.

He had to give her a name; he couldn't keep saying "the dog," but what? "Ms. Barkley?" She didn't respond. "No, that's not it."

"What are you doing?" Matthew asked.

"Trying to think of a name for her. How about Princess?" Nope. Nothing. "I can't give her a name she doesn't like. That'd be cruel."

"How about Bruiser?" Matthew offered, but she looked less than impressed and turned her head to look out the window.

"Yeah, don't think so. She's not going to be an attack dog, she's a sweetheart." Then it came to him, a story his mother would tell him when he was little about a dog and the moon. "Luna." His new dog looked up and licked his hand before laying her head on his knee. "Okay, Luna it is."

A few moments later, they pulled up to the construction site. Tristan could see the frame of the house was taking shape, making this all seem so much more real. The construction crew consisted of ten men; tradespeople would also be coming in to do the electrical and plumbing. Vincent, Dante, Spider, and Coop worked alongside the other men. Tristan wished he could help with the build, but realistically there was no chance of that happening.

Coop and Vincent set down their tools and walked over. His love was smiling even though Tristan was sure he'd seen Luna. As for Luna, she was standing with her front paws up on the dash and her whole back end wagging in excitement as they approached.

"What do you have there, sparrow?" Vincent asked as he ran his big hand down Luna's head and neck.

"This is Luna, we found her on the way over here," Tristan explained.

"The dog's already got a name. Man, I think you have a dog now," Coop told Vincent before kissing Matthew in greeting.

Tristan thought he'd sweeten the deal a little. "I'll take care of her. You won't have to do a thing. I'll bathe her and take her to the vet. I know how busy you are, and this will take up none of your time." Okay, in truth Tristan was going to keep her anyway, but it was best if Vincent saw it his way.

"Easy, sparrow," Vincent murmured as he leaned down for his kiss. "Luna seems like a good dog and I like the idea of you having a dog while I'm away on assignments. She'd be a companion for you if she sticks around. We'll take her to the vet tomorrow if we can get an appointment."

Tristan couldn't contain himself and wrapped his arms around Vincent and held him tight. Luna decided to get in on some affection and somehow wiggled her way between them.

"I see you guys have been busy since we left you this morning," Matthew noted.

"Everything is coming along fine so far," Vincent responded with what sounded like pride, which made Tristan even happier.

A flash of light caught Tristan's eye and he followed it to the far eastern portion of the property. He got the same feeling in his gut that someone was watching him. Both Vincent and Coop turned their heads in the same direction, their demeanors changing instantly.

"What is it?" Tristan asked. He couldn't help the sliver of fear that ran through his body. It would be this way until Stavros was caught or he found Tristan.

"I don't know, but I need you and Matthew to head back to the main house now," Vincent ordered. "We'll go check it out."

Matthew started the ATV and was turning it around before Tristan had the chance to say good-bye. It felt like they were racing to get back; he didn't even know this vehicle could move this fast. Luna had stuck her head out the side; at least one of them was enjoying the ride.

As they neared the house, Tristan could see Shannon standing on the back deck and didn't miss the gun attached to her side. Her eyes never wavered from the horizon as if she expected someone to jump out of the bush at any moment. *Shit, he couldn't have gotten this close, could he?* Tristan knew he was overreacting; there would have been a warning, and alarms would have sounded.

Matthew didn't park where they usually kept the ATVs but kept going until they were inside the multicar garage. "Better safe than sorry."

Tristan had to agree, though he still wished there wasn't a need for all this. He climbed out of the vehicle as Buddy and Shannon rounded the corner and walked into the garage. Luna jumped out of the front seat before Tristan had the chance to grab her. He soon found out he shouldn't have worried. Luna ran to Buddy and began licking the other dog's muzzle before flopping to the floor on her back.

"I see our family is growing once again," Shannon commented as the three of them watched the two dogs play.

Luna seemed to tire quickly, and Tristan knew it was time to take her inside and take care of her. He would borrow some of Buddy's dog food until he had a chance to go into town and buy Luna her own. "Come on, Luna, let's get you something to eat and drink, you have to be hungry."

It didn't take long for Luna to scarf down her bowl of food and water and now it was time to deal with one stinky problem—it was time for a bath. Matthew went back to his work and Shannon was somewhere in the house. If Tristan had to guess, she was patrolling until she received word that there wasn't a threat.

Mrs. Walker gave him Buddy's special dog shampoo that would take care of any fleas Luna might have. Tristan had already checked her over for ticks. Since his run-in with Lyme he'd become a bit paranoid.

Tristan changed out of his clothes and put on a pair of shorts; this was going to get messy. He filled the tub with warm water and went to find Luna, who had booked it out of their bedroom the moment Tristan had turned on the taps. After a five-minute search, he found her hiding under one of the couches in the living room. He had no idea how she managed to get under there.

With Mrs. Walker's help, he managed to get her back into their bathroom and quickly shut the door. Luna gave him her best puppy-eyes, which almost melted him on the spot. Still, he stayed strong, carried her from the far side of the room, and set her in the warm water. His joints ached but she was light, and once Tristan began washing her down, her fluffy coat stuck to her body. It almost made him cry to see her bones sticking out. He used as much care as possible washing her and she seemed to relax after a while.

He didn't have to lift her out when he was done: Tristan simply stood up and opened a towel and Luna jumped out. "You're such a smart girl, aren't you, Luna?"

Five towels later Luna was dry and Tristan was exhausted. He slipped out of his shorts and climbed into bed, knowing there was no use in fighting it; he was still recovering. Luna jumped onto the end of the bed and lay down on Tristan's feet.

He hadn't heard back from Vincent and fell asleep praying everything was all right.

Chapter Ten

Vincent inched closer to the location where he'd seen the reflection. He, Dante, Coop, and Spider had left the crew working on the new house and were now a hundred yards east of their property line on neighboring government land that had been set aside for new campgrounds and a park. That explained why their sensors didn't go off, but it didn't explain why the flashing was still coming from the same spot. Whoever this was should have hightailed it by now if he had any sense. Vincent was sure it had to be Stavros.

Each member of the team was coming in from different directions, that way there was no chance of Stavros getting away. Vincent had his Glock G19 out and at the ready; he wasn't taking any chances with this lunatic. He made sure to stay in the brush and behind several stands of trees that peppered the long grass, which could hide a person.

He was less than fifteen feet away when he stopped and waited for the signal. Seconds later, he heard the piercing cry of an eagle and rushed forward to surprise their target. What they found was not what he expected. All four men had their guns drawn but there was no one there to capture. Each man spun around, checking for traps; there were none.

In front of them was a piece of rebar stuck into the ground with a sheet of silver reflective paper tied to it by a piece of string. A small patch of grass had been cut away and was covered by a small red towel. As Vincent looked closer, he realized the towel wasn't red; it was a white towel stained with what looked like blood. They checked for traps or sensors attached to the cloth; again there were none.

Coop broke a branch off a nearby tree and used it to move the towel while they all stood a few feet away. It wasn't worth the risk of getting closer if it was rigged. All four men stared at what was discovered underneath. Vincent pulled out his phone and called Shannon.

"Lock the house down." Shannon ended the call without uttering a word. There was no need; they all knew what to do.

Dante was the first one to speak—before Vincent placed the call they had worked in complete silence in case Stavros was still in the area. "What the hell are we dealing with?"

"We need to call this in. The police chief is going to want to see this," Coop grumbled.

"Shit, this went south in a hurry." Spider sighed as he took out his phone and made the call to the Brighton PD.

Vincent remained quiet and stared down at the decomposing severed hand. His world narrowed to one thought alone: he'd have to kill this madman before the lunatic got anywhere near his sparrow.

***

Vincent and the team made it back to the main house after midnight. Luna and Buddy met them at the door. He let them out to do their business while the rest of the team headed to bed; they would discuss everything in the morning. Buddy came back quickly and headed toward the bosses' bedroom, but there was no sign of Luna.

Vincent had a moment of fear; if she didn't come back, Tristan would be heartbroken. He took two steps off the back deck when Luna came sprinting around the garage and straight for him. He drew in a deep breath. Having to tell his love that Luna had taken off on top of what they'd found would be too much. Vincent knew Tristan had fallen in love with the dog the moment he saw them together in the ATV.

Luna continued into the house and headed straight for their bedroom while Vincent did a final check of the security system. The day's events kept running through his mind as exhaustion weighed him down. By the time he made it to his bedroom Luna was lying at the foot of the bed below Tristan; obviously she'd chosen her spot. He'd called his love a couple hours ago, urging him to go to bed. The forensic team was still on site gathering evidence, but he hadn't told him that last part. Vincent was happy to see Tristan had listened; he didn't want his love jeopardizing his recovery.

While Vincent felt guilty for not telling Tristan about what they'd found, the justification was sound—one more peaceful night of sleep before the shit hit the fan. Once Tristan knew about the hand, peace of mind would fly out the window. Vincent stripped out of his clothes and slid into bed beside the man who meant everything to him.

Tristan stirred a little before settling into Vincent's arms. "Vincent?"

"Yes, love," he whispered, hoping Tristan would fall back to sleep.

"Are you okay?" Tristan asked, his voice rough from sleep.

"Absolutely."

"Good, because if you think I believe you found nothing out there, you're off your rocker."

"Trust me, sparrow, tomorrow will come soon enough. I want to hold you tonight and sleep knowing you're right here with me."

Tristan remained quiet for a few minutes and at one point Vincent thought he'd fallen back to sleep until he said, "I understand."

"Thank you, babe."

"Love you," Tristan said sleepily.

"Love you," Vincent replied, and he could feel Luna's tail bouncing on the bed. "We love you too, Luna."

Tristan laughed softly before settling back into Vincent's arms. The team may be his family but right here, this was his heart.

***

Tristan sat staring at Vincent, unsure what to say or do. He felt cold all over and began shivering even though he was in his lover's arms. It took him a moment to actually wrap his mind around the fact that someone had left a hand for them to find. If it had been planted there as a message, Tristan didn't know what it could be. *Hell, what happened to the owner of that hand?*

Could Stavros have truly gone insane? Because whoever did this surely was. They hadn't received any updates. Stavros had missed his court dates and a warrant had been issued for his arrest. How could he be eluding the police for this long? He had to be getting help from someone. But who?

"I promise he won't get anywhere near you, sparrow," Vincent swore while pulling him even closer. "I'll kill him before he has the chance."

"I think that's enough talk about death and dismemberment for a while. I'm not used to things like this happening," Tristan explained. "I've lived the life of an author. Quiet, not too much excitement, except for in my books. Now I've been kidnapped, killed a man, found out Stavros is stalking me and that he's a lunatic, not to mention having Lyme disease, and now there's a severed hand meant to be a threatening calling card. Did I miss anything? Maybe I should see Dr. Gordon after all?"

Tristan felt like he was losing it. *What happened to the good old days when my biggest concern was whether to get this season's collection of Louis Vuitton shoes?*

"Everything will calm down as soon as we catch him. I know you've been through a lot recently. If you want to see Dr. Gordon, I'm all for it but I need you to trust me to keep you safe."

Tristan rubbed his medallion between his fingers before saying, "I do trust you. But I can't stop thinking about the poor person that hand belonged to. Are they dead? Did Stavros kill them? What about their family and loved ones? Did they ever see the person again?"

"You have such a caring soul, my sparrow," Vincent murmured into the side of Tristan's head. Luna decided that she'd waited long enough for attention and jumped onto the bed to join them.

There was a soft knock on their door, and since they were both dressed, Vincent hollered, "Come in."

Dante walked in with a purposeful stride. "Good morning."

Vincent returned the greeting and Tristan simply nodded. What else could be wrong to bring Dante to their door this early? Tristan looked over at the alarm clock—it wasn't even seven in the morning yet.

"I'm sorry to disturb you guys, but we have incoming. The police chief, Grady, and a few federal agents should be here within the next thirty minutes," Dante announced while petting Luna, who had gone to greet him. "We'll be meeting in the conference room. I assume, Tristan, that you're up to date on yesterday's events."

"Yes. But why the agents?" Vincent asked, still holding Tristan in his arms. "Sure, it was government land, but usually they let the locals handle something this small. I didn't think they'd send anyone to check it out."

"I'm unsure, but they demanded to come out to meet Tristan."

"Me. Why do they want to see me?" Tristan asked. Dante shook his head and shrugged.

"Don't worry, sparrow, I'll be right beside you the whole time," Vincent assured.

Tristan could feel it coming, struggled to get out of Vincent's arms, and ran to the bathroom where he dry-heaved into the toilet. He hadn't eaten or drunk anything this morning so he had nothing to throw up. The convulsions hurt his joints with every retch until he had tears running down his face.

He knew Vincent was right there, but he couldn't see him through blurry eyes. A cold cloth was placed on the back of his neck, then forehead, cooling him down until the spasms stopped. Vincent lifted him off the floor and took him back to their bed. He ran the cold cloth over Tristan's face and soon enough he felt almost normal again. Dante had left, and who could blame him? Was the reaction one of the side effects of the Lyme infection lingering in his body, or had he reached his final straw with the federal agents?

"You don't have to attend this meeting. You and Luna can stay here and get some rest, or maybe you'd like to work a little on your next book. Either way, those agents won't be coming in here," Vincent declared, causing Tristan to get his back up. He understood that his love was only trying to protect him, and the whole throwing up thing didn't exactly make him look strong, but he was. He may have been in a bit of a downward slide since the kidnapping, but it was time for him to get his shit together.

"I'm going to the meeting," Tristan stated as he got up from the bed and slowly walked over to his dresser. "Would you please help me get out of my sleepwear and into real clothes? It would make me feel better about meeting them if I look put together." At times, his clothes were his armor; everybody had a thing that made them more confident—his happened to be clothes. "I'd like to wear my green jeans with the white hoodie and my black boots."

Tristan began opening drawers in search of his clothes; moments later Vincent stood beside him, opening the drawers on the other side of the dresser. Vincent pulled out Tristan's pants at the same time Tristan found his hoodie. He grabbed a pair of clean underwear and was lifted back into Vincent's arms.

Vincent walked him over to their bed and gently set him down. "I'm sorry I went all alpha male there on you. I want to protect you, that's all. I wasn't trying to tell you what to do, I would never do that."

Tristan lifted his butt off the bed so that Vincent could slide his pants and underwear off him. Some days his joints were so stiff he couldn't bend over to pull up his own pants. Of course, today was one of those days. Shit. The specialists had said he would regain mobility over time; Tristan hoped they were right. Vincent never made him feel weak; he went on about his business and never said a word as if it were completely normal to have to dress your partner.

Vincent slid Tristan's pants to his knees where Tristan could reach them and pull them up the rest of the way. His hoodie was easy to slip over his head, and Vincent took care of putting on and tying his boots. Armor—check.

"I know you want to protect me, and I love you for it, but I'm going to have to face this head on. It's me he wants. I wish I knew why." Tristan sighed. "That doesn't mean I don't want you by my side. You're the only person I trust with my life."

Tristan was pulled into Vincent's arms and held firmly to the big guy's chest. "I love you, my sparrow."

Before Tristan could reply, the alarm sounded, signaling someone was at the front gates. Their visitors had arrived.

"You ready for this?" Vincent asked as he pulled on his jeans.

"Such a shame to cover that gorgeous ass."

"Gorgeous ass, eh?" Vincent laughed as he turned around and pushed those firm cheeks out.

"Did I say that out loud?"

Vincent smiled and gathered Tristan into his arms. "As long as my ass is gorgeous to you, I'm happy."

Tristan could feel his cheeks warming, which made Vincent smile wider. "We need to go to this meeting. Be good," he said as he stood and headed for their bedroom door. "You coming, *nizhóní*?"

Vincent was on him in seconds, his mouth taking possession of Tristan's. He couldn't help the moans that slipped out as he wrapped his arms and legs around Vincent. His love held him tight; he didn't have to exert any energy to hold on. When they parted, neither spoke; they simply held each other until a knock on their bedroom door tore them apart.

"We need to go," Vincent whispered.

"Yes we do," Tristan agreed as he slid down Vincent's muscled body and stood on his own two feet.

Vincent opened the door to see Sam. "Sorry, guys, but everyone's waiting on the two of you." Sam actually looked sorry.

"I'd hoped you wouldn't have to go through anything else, Tristan, but it looks like I was wrong."

Tristan put his hand on his friend's colorfully tattooed arm and said, "It's okay, Sam, there's nothing anyone can do to stop this runaway train." He took Vincent's hand and followed Sam out the door.

***

Tristan could hear Mrs. Walker in the kitchen preparing breakfast, and he'd give anything to be at that table instead of the one to where he was headed. He couldn't put this off any longer, so he squared his shoulders, walked down the hall and into the conference room.

There were two new people at the front of the room talking to Police Chief Graham and Dante. One was an impeccably dressed man and the other, a woman wearing casual jeans. Absently he wondered if the FBI had a dress code. He let that thought go as the entire room turned at his and Vincent's entrance, causing Tristan to lean further into his partner. Vincent wrapped his arm around Tristan's shoulder as the two newcomers, who he presumed were the federal agents, walked up to him.

"It's uncanny, he fits perfectly," the tall man with a thick 80s moustache said as he looked at Tristan as if he was a bug under a magnifying glass. "He could be the original."

Tristan could feel his body tensing as the still-unidentified man kept talking about him as if he wasn't there. He felt Vincent begin to move seconds before Grady placed himself between the agents and Tristan.

"Maybe we should make a few introductions first," Grady suggested as he made a perfect wall between them, giving Tristan a chance to breathe. He would have to thank his best friend later. Vincent pulled him back, increasing the distance from the agents, and began to rub Tristan's back in slow, comforting circles.

The blonde female agent finally spoke up. "Of course, that was rude of us."

Grady moved out of the way, allowing the agents to start again. The woman stepped forward and stretched out her hand to Tristan. "I'm Agent Staton and my partner is Agent Grimes."

Tristan shook both of their hands and replied, "I'm Tristan Michaels and this is my partner, Vincent Greyson."

Although they'd been properly introduced, Tristan still felt like he was on display for the two agents. Vincent took his hand and led him to the other side of the room where they took their seats. The agents were talking amongst themselves, occasionally looking his way and creeping him right out. When he looked away, his gaze caught Dave's and before he could look away the police chief smiled at him. Why would he smile at the man who killed his cousin? Today was turning out to be Tristan's personal hell.

Dante stood at the front and motioned for everyone to take their seats. "Okay, quiet down, everyone. I'd like to introduce Agents Staton and Grimes. By now, everyone knows about what was found outside our property line yesterday. When the fingerprints were run to try to identify the person it belonged to, the FBI was alerted."

Agent Grimes began handing out files as Dante continued talking, but Tristan quickly lost focus. Instead, he sat frozen, staring at the photos that had slipped out of the file. Lifeless eyes stared up at him, body after body missing their right hands, but that wasn't the worst of it. Each of the five male victims resembled him; they all looked to be his age and body type, even sharing the same red hair and, freaking Tristan the fuck out, they even wore the same green eyeliner. What the hell?

Tristan could feel his face heating up before his eyes went blurry with unshed tears. His emotions ranged from sadness for these poor men, and rage that somebody would do this to another human being. The pictures were taken out of his hands as Vincent's voice thundered through the room.

"You just don't hand shit like that out without warning a person. Not all of us gathered here are used to seeing shit like that."

Tristan looked around the table and noticed Matthew didn't look so good. Sam was a bit better probably because he was a nurse, but he too looked a little shaken.

Agent Grimes's eyes turned cold and hard. "I'm sorry about your delicate sensibilities, but I'm dealing with a serial killer and your *boyfriend* is the only link we have." Tristan was shocked that Grimes even used air quotes to emphasize the point.

Vincent was around the table before Tristan even had a chance to stop him. Luckily, Spider and Coop headed him off before he was able to reach the agent. Tristan wasn't sure if it was the "sensibilities" or the "boyfriend" comment that pissed his lover off more. Tristan knew he had to do something before this meeting descended into hell.

He walked over to the arguing group and stood in front of Vincent, who immediately backed off. Tristan put his hand on Vincent's still-heaving chest and said, "I'm okay. I was caught off guard by the photos. As for the other issue, who really cares what Grimes thinks of us? I want to know what's going on so they can leave."

Vincent took a deep breath and visibly calmed. "You're right, sparrow, what we need now is information."

As they returned to their chairs, Tristan noticed Shannon in the back of the room typing away on her computer with the file wide open. The team probably already had all the information they needed with her on the job, but it was still a good idea to hear the agents out. The rest of the team sat down, leaving the agents standing alone at the front of the room. Staton was staring at her partner, her eyes wide, while Grimes straightened his tie and suit jacket.

"Now that everyone's calmed down, maybe we can get this meeting started," Grimes said as he rolled his head around like a prizefighter loosening his neck and shoulder muscles before a fight.

Tristan watched him with interest; his mannerisms and body language spoke volumes. Grimes was a man who believed himself to be superior to the rest of them. He gave out the appearance of calm sophistication that was belied by the constant flicking of his thumb and little finger. He was nervous, but he didn't want anyone to know it. After years of creating believable characters for his books, Tristan had become accustomed to looking deeper than what was shown on the surface.

Staton pushed a few buttons on her laptop and brought up a map of Texas and Arizona. There were six locations circled in red scattered across the screen.

"The first victim was twenty-four-year-old Trent Williams from Dallas." The screen changed to show a picture of a happy young man in what looked like a yearbook photo. "He was reported missing on May eighth of last year." A new picture was brought up showing Trent's dead body; this time Tristan didn't flinch. "His body was found one week later only a mile from his home."

"How did he die?" Tristan asked. He didn't know why but he wanted an answer.

"He was strangled like all the rest," Staton replied.

Grimes continued in the same fashion as he'd done with the first until he got to the sixth circle. The agent enlarged this location until Tristan realized it was circling Brighton. He got a sick feeling in his stomach.

"The sixth one is you, Mr. Michaels. But we're not certain if you are the next victim or if you were supposed to be the original."

"The original? What does that mean?" Shannon asked.

"Mr. Michaels, when did you first meet Stavros Menzotto?" Staton asked, ignoring Shannon's question.

"Early April of last year."

"And what happened?" she asked.

"We went out only a few times. I ended it because he was overbearing and telling me what I was allowed to do."

"Did he accept that and move on?" Grimes asked with what looked an awful lot like disgust. Tristan wasn't sure if it was over the killings or him. "I understand there was an assault."

"I'm led to believe by your questions that you already know the answers. So how about we skip over this game and get to the important stuff." Tristan was tired of Grimes's attitude. "How do you even know it's Stavros?"

Grimes didn't look impressed but carried on. "We are analyzing DNA we collected at the site of each murder with a sample collected at his home to confirm it is him. Answer this then: do you normally wear green eyeliner?"

Tristan was confused about the question but answered it anyway. "Yes."

"And all the victims were found with the same green eyeliner on, but the families and friends of the victims said that none of them had ever worn eyeliner before. Whoever killed them put the eyeliner on, probably postmortem, and we now believe it was so they would look more like you. He couldn't have you so he chose people similar to you."

Tristan's ears were ringing and he felt a strong headache coming on. "So what you're saying is that these men are dead because I turned down one asshole?"

The room erupted with, "You're not responsible for any of this" and "The man's a lunatic," among other things said in support. Vincent pulled him closer, a stern look on his handsome face. "You are not responsible for the actions of a madman, sparrow. He alone must carry that burden, not you."

Tristan nodded his agreement. He knew they were right; he wasn't the one doing the killing. So why was he feeling so damn guilty?

"Where does cutting off the victim's right hand play into this? Did he leave any at the other sites?" Vincent asked., thankfully taking over the questioning. Tristan's brain was too busy trying to process everything he'd been told.

"It's not uncommon for serial killers to keep a trophy from their victims. Now that he's left the first victim's hand here, we're not so sure," Staton explained.

"It's almost as if it were a gift," Grimes threw in.

"If you say he left it as a gift for me, this meeting's over." The thought of that was one step too far.

Police Chief Graham stood up and cleared his throat. "We all have the files with the information in it. If we need further details, we know where to find you. The real question that needs to be answered here is what's your plan to stop him?"

Both agents turned and looked straight at Tristan. *Shit, I'm going to be bait.*

"Hell no," Vincent thundered without even waiting to hear their response.

"Then more men will die," Grimes replied with a calculating look in his eyes. "Do you want to be responsible for that, Mr. Michaels?"

Vincent stood, plucked Tristan from his chair, and stormed out of the room. He could hear yelling coming from behind them, but he couldn't make out the words. Vincent didn't stop until they were back in their rooms behind a locked door. Luna had stuck beside them the entire way and jumped into Tristan's lap once Vincent set him down in one of their recliners. His eyes were a dark shade of blue that Tristan had never seen before, growing stormier as Vincent paced back and forth between their bed and the lounge area.

"I'm sorry that I brought this into our life," Tristan said as he sunk farther into his recliner. He didn't know what else to say to make any of this better.

Vincent's response was instantaneous as he knelt on the carpeted floor in front of Tristan. "Not for one second do I think you're at fault in any of this."

"But maybe I can help stop him."

"You're not going to be used as a target by the FBI."

Tristan understood Vincent's reaction—hell, Tristan didn't want to be anyone's bait—but how else were they going to catch Stavros?

Someone knocked on the door, making Vincent growl. "If they've come to try to talk us into putting your life in more danger, I'm going to lose my shit."

Tristan couldn't help but laugh. "Lose your shit, huh."

Vincent stopped for a second and smiled for the first time since they'd left for the meeting. "Yeah, you don't want to see that." He held Tristan tight to his chest until there was another knock, and then he got up.

Tristan pulled Luna into his arms and buried his face in her fur. His mind raced with all the information he'd learned in the last half hour. *Could all that killing truly be Stavros? Am I the reason he began killing men that looked like me? Are those deaths my fault?*

"Tristan?" Vincent was looking at him oddly.

"What?"

"I've said your name a few times, but you seemed off in your own world. What's up, sparrow?" Vincent asked as he set two plates full of breakfast goodness on the coffee table in front of him.

"Sorry, my head's all over the place at the moment." Honestly, he wasn't sure how he was holding conversations with the images of those poor men floating through his brain.

Vincent looked worried when he said, "It's completely understandable. When Dante brought the plates, he mentioned that Dave Graham wants to talk to you."

"Dave, why?" This was not what he needed right at this moment.

"He didn't say but he's waiting for your answer on the back deck. Do you want me to tell him you're not up to it right now?" Vincent was offering Tristan a way out, but he'd been avoiding this conversation ever since that horrible night. It was time to face what he'd done.

"I'll meet with him."

Vincent picked the two plates up and headed for the door. "I'll leave our breakfasts in the oven to keep them warm while we go see what the good police chief has to say." His love was playing this off to calm Tristan.

"Are the agents gone?"

"Yeah. They'll update us when they receive any news."

Well, at least he didn't have to worry about running into them. Tristan and Luna followed Vincent out of their bedroom to the kitchen, where the rest of the team were sitting down to breakfast. They smiled as he walked by and before he even had a chance to think of what to say, he was walking onto the deck. Dave stood at the far side with Grady; both turned when Tristan and Vincent arrived.

Vincent carried a chair over under the shade of an umbrella and Dave brought over another. Tristan sat down but he still was unable to look Dave in the eyes, so he looked at Grady, who actually appeared to be angry.

He'd never been shy with his best friend before, so he asked, "What's got you looking so grumpy?"

Grady seemed a bit shocked and grumbled, "Sorry, buddy, but those agents rubbed me the wrong way. They're so gung-ho to catch this guy, which is fine, but they don't seem to care how they do it. Trying to make you feel guilty and wanting to turn you into bait is way over the line."

"I can understand them wanting to catch the person responsible," Dave joined in. "But handing the killer his next victim seems a bit suspect."

"Vincent, why don't we give these guys some privacy?" Grady suggested, indicating the picnic table in the yard. Vincent looked down at Tristan before taking a step away.

"It's okay. I'll be fine," Tristan assured. It was time to "pay the piper."

Vincent nodded, gave Dave a look that radiated warning, and walked away. Tristan sat there for a few moments, unsure what to say. He figured he might as well get this over with. "I'm sorry, Dave. I didn't want to kill your cousin. He wouldn't stop coming after me until I had no choice." Tristan could feel his eyes filling with tears. *Shit.* He didn't want to get emotional. "I warned him."

A few silent moments passed, forcing Tristan to look up to find Dave sitting with his mouth hanging open slightly and a shocked expression on his face. Tristan went on, "I know I've hurt you and your family but—"

"Tristan, I'm not upset with you and neither is anyone in my family," Dave cut in. "No one blames you for what you were forced to do. I thought the reason you were avoiding me was because one of my family members tried to kill you."

"You did?" Tristan asked, wanting to make sure he'd heard him right.

"Hell yes. You have every right to be pissed about what happened to you."

"I'm not pissed at you." The thought had never even crossed Tristan's mind.

The two men sat staring at each other. Tristan still had to double-check. "Are you sure?"

"I felt sorry for Ryan's parents because they are good people no matter what their son did. Ryan chose his own fate and no one's responsible for that but him. I have to admit I felt ashamed that someone in my family could do something so heinous. I worried that the town would lose faith in a police chief whose own family member was capable of what he'd done. Never through any of that did I blame you. You were the victim in this and I'm the one who needs your forgiveness."

Dave wanted Tristan's forgiveness? None of this had been his fault either. If anything, he was a victim of his cousin's heinous behavior. "You've done nothing for me to forgive, Dave."

"Thank you, but I brought my cousin here."

"By that same logic, I brought a serial killer here."

Dave thought about that for a moment before saying, "You've got me on that one."

"So we're good?"

"We never weren't good." Dave smiled. "Apparently, the two of us have been worked up for nothing. I know how hard this has been on you, and I wish I could do something to make it easier. Maybe today can be the start of that healing."

Tristan couldn't help himself. He stood and hugged Dave. The man had suffered because of the whole Ryan fiasco, maybe he could start healing too.

Chapter Eleven

It had been almost a week since the meeting with the FBI agents. They had called to inform them that the DNA they collected at each site matched Stavros, confirming him as the prime suspect in the five deaths. Tristan had been restricted to the main house and immediate area until Stavros was caught.

He hadn't even had a chance to go out and buy Luna her collar, toys, food, and doggie bed, so here he sat looking through various pet stores online. Coop had taken Luna to the vet for a checkup and shots. Other than being malnourished, she was fine, which made Tristan happy though he wished he could have been there for her.

His right hand hadn't improved much since his release from the hospital, but he was starting physiotherapy soon and hoped that would help. By far the most infuriating part of his forced confinement was not being allowed to visit the build site. Vincent had taken pictures and videos, but it wasn't the same as being there in person.

"So should we go with straight pink or tiger print pink?" Tristan asked Luna, who was lying at his feet. She looked up and wagged her tail. Tristan couldn't help but smile; she'd been a great addition to the family. "Tiger print pink it is."

"See I knew you'd crack eventually." Sam laughed as he walked into the living room and sat down on one of the other couches. "You're talking to yourself already."

Tristan straightened his back, tilted his head up slightly, and said in the haughtiest voice he could muster, "I'll have you know I was talking to the fair Princess Luna."

Sam laughed at the same time Buddy came walking in. "And here is her prince coming to rescue her from the trappings of Amazon."

Leave it to Sam to make him laugh even when he didn't feel all that happy. He, Matthew, and Sam had grown a lot closer until Tristan felt like they were brothers of sorts. Of course, the team felt like a family now, but he had a bond with these two.

"How you doing being cooped up?" Sam asked.

"I feel like a prisoner. At least you get to go out."

"Yeah, to the hospital to work, but I'm on strict lockdown the remainder of the time. Everyone's on alert," Sam explained as he threw a water bottle into his backpack. He had his scrubs on, ready for work.

"What hours do you work today?"

"I'm on until ten tonight, then I have three days off so we can have some fun."

"But we're still stuck here."

"Oh don't you worry, I have a plan. The three of us could decorate the indoor pool area with palm trees, turn the bar into a cabana, and have our men serve us drinks poolside in tiny speedos. It'd be our island vacation without leaving home."

Tristan thought about Vincent in a black speedo and nothing else but bronze skin over yummy muscles. "I could get behind that idea."

"Thought you might," Sam said with that cheeky smile on his face. "Well, gotta go. See you tonight. While I'm gone, search for those decorations and have them shipped overnight."

"You got it," Tristan replied before Sam walked through the front door and into freedom.

It wasn't as if Tristan didn't understand the importance of staying safe; the images of those victims ran through his head in a continuous loop. He was pissed off that Stavros was still out there somewhere, doing lord knows what, without being stopped. The Sentinels had gone out searching for him; Shannon and Matthew were scouring the private and public files on the family, trying to determine if he had used any aliases in the past that he might be going under now. Still nothing. It felt like he'd fallen off the face of the earth.

Tristan went back to his shopping, buying the pink tiger-striped dog collar, a matching bed, a load of toys, and a twenty-pound bag of dog food. He'd researched all the brands and decided to change Buddy's dog food to the more protein-rich diet Luna would be on. All, of course, with Sam's permission; Buddy had to be careful with his diet because he was diabetic.

The remainder of the day was spent between research for his next book series and playing with Luna and Buddy. He had occasional visits from Matthew and Shannon, but both were busy doing their computer magic to hunt down Stavros. Dante and Spider were out searching for any sign of Stavros, while Coop and Vincent were out at the build site. It was a little eerie having this big house mainly to himself. Tristan sat with Mrs. Walker and helped roll out dough for biscuits. She was a member of the White Hair Crew and gave him his daily dose of gossip. Those ladies were on the pulse of the community, better than any beat reporter could be.

Apparently, the entire town was on the lookout for anyone matching Stavros's description and the police had upped their patrols. It warmed Tristan's heart to know Brighton was looking out for him, but he wished he hadn't brought this chaos to the people of this community.

A little after five in the afternoon a truck screeched to a halt outside the house. Shannon came running out of her office with a gun in her hand and went out the front door before Tristan could ask her what was going on. Matthew came in from the kitchen wearing some sort of contraption on his right arm. Tristan heard an ATV getting closer and looked out the window to see Vincent and Coop pulling up. Something was wrong.

"What do you have on your arm?" Tristan asked.

"A new laser technology I'm working with. I can slice the arm off a dummy from one hundred feet away," Matthew said with pride.

The front door opened and en masse, the team walked in. Vincent came straight to Tristan and took him into his arms.

"This is my fault. I shouldn't have allowed him to go," Dante growled as he headed for the conference room.

Spider stopped him midstride and cupped the side of Dante's face. "This is not your fault, love. We'll get him back."

"Get who back?" Tristan asked, wanting to know what was going on.

Everyone turned to face him and Vincent, who held Tristan even closer before Dante answered. "Sam's missing."

***

Vincent held a shaking Tristan in his arms as Dave, Grady, and Bo joined them in the conference room. Dave spoke to Dante and Spider in private, making Vincent wonder if there was a lead. His poor sparrow hadn't said a word since finding out his friend was missing. His eyes looked distant, leading him to believe Tristan might be in shock. Vincent wrapped him tighter in the blanket Matthew had brought over to help stop his shaking.

The entire team tensed even further as FBI Agents Staton and Grimes walked in. Shannon was busy trying to bring up the security footage from the hospital to try to figure out who took Sam, but the team already knew who was responsible. Stavros couldn't get to Tristan so he took someone Tristan was close to. Vincent was hoping and praying Sam was unharmed.

An argument broke out at the front of the room between the agents and Dave. Even Dante was getting angry with the agents. *What the actual fuck?*

"You have to tell him. It's his choice," Grimes yelled. His face was red and his shirt collar looked like it was choking him it was so tight.

"No," Spider stated firmly with a look on his face that Vincent hadn't seen often. Even Vincent was smart enough to know when to back down.

"The kidnapper asked for him or your partner dies."

Vincent stood up, placed Tristan with Matthew in the seat beside him, and stormed to the front of the room. If this was what Grimes thought was the solution, there was no way in hell it was happening.

He broke into the argument and asked, "What?"

Agent Grimes turned to Tristan and as loudly as he could said, "The kidnapper wants Tristan in exchange for Sam's life." Vincent wanted to rip the bastard's throat out.

"Shit." Vincent rounded the table to get to his sparrow. There was no way he was going to risk his life. However, his lover had other things in mind.

Tristan stood up straight, looked Grimes right in the eyes with what looked like disgust. "I'll trade myself for Sam, but neither of you two will be involved. I don't trust either of you with my life. With the Sentinels and the Brighton police force, Sam and I will at least have a chance of making it out of this alive."

The entire team started talking, but the only thing Vincent heard were the words "trade myself for Sam." Vincent walked over to Tristan, took his hand, and led him out of the noisy conference room. Tristan didn't fight him and simply followed until they were alone in their bedroom. As always, Luna accompanied them.

The second Tristan sat down he began trying to explain, but Vincent waved him off; he was still trying to keep his shit together. He wasn't surprised that his love would volunteer to trade himself for Sam, but it didn't mean Vincent was good with it. He would do anything to save Sam and bring him home, but risk losing his soul mate was beyond the pale.

Vincent finally calmed enough to sit beside Tristan and take hold of his hand. "Sparrow, I understand why you want to do this, but it's too dangerous. Stavros is a sick fuck. He may keep both of you."

"That's why I'm going to have Matthew suit me up beforehand. I'm not crazy or suicidal, but if there's a chance to get Sam home, I have to take it. Besides, I'll have you and the rest of the family to back me up. Stavros will never have a chance to hurt me."

Vincent took a deep breath. He knew Tristan was right: this was the best way to get Sam back unharmed. However, Vincent's heart was telling him something completely different. In the end this wasn't his decision, Tristan was a grown man capable of choosing for himself. Vincent could only keep him safe while it happened.

"Okay, but you will do everything we say."

"Yes, sir."

"Doesn't that have a certain ring to it?" Vincent asked, causing Tristan to laugh and throw himself into Vincent's open arms. "We'd better get back to the meeting before they send someone out searching for us."

Tristan stood and Vincent watched him and Luna walk to the bedroom door. This was his world and he was about to risk losing it. His dream was finally coming true, and he would do everything in his power to ensure the happy ending if it was the last thing he did.

***

Tristan could feel the sweat rolling down his back. It wasn't that hot out, and a few people wore loose sweaters and light jackets. It was his stress that was making him roast in his clothing. He didn't look out of place wearing a jacket, though his was for an entirely different reason than the weather. Matthew had outfitted him with so many gadgets he hoped to remember them all. To look at him, a normal person wouldn't know he was armed to the teeth.

Now Tristan stood waiting on the sidewalk on the corner of Main and John Streets. He looked around and if he didn't know better he'd say no one was watching him or even looking his way. But he knew different; his family was watching. Tristan rubbed his medallion between his fingers, and thoughts of Vincent helped calm him.

They'd made love most of the night until Tristan passed out with a smile on his face. He felt almost desperate to show his man how much he meant to him.

Tristan looked at his watch. Stavros was late. He touched the small silver clip on the side of the watch head. It amazed him to know that if he pulled it out, a long, thin piece of metal slid out from around the band, turning into a solid knife. Matthew was amazing.

A black truck with deeply tinted windows pulled up beside him on the street. It wasn't Stavros's normal vehicle, but it had to be him. The only contact they'd had with him since the initial call into the police station was through Tristan's fan email address. Stavros had made his demands, set the time, and made his warning clear: Sam died if anyone tried anything.

Slowly, Tristan approached the truck but he still couldn't see the driver; he guessed Stavros was trying to hide his identity, which was beyond strange because they all knew it was him. Tristan reached for the handle and opened the passenger door. What he found inside couldn't have shocked him more if he'd been hit by lightning.

Shawn sat in the driver's seat holding a gun trained right at Tristan's heart. The small red dot glowing on the center of his chest was a big clue. "Hurry, get in."

Tristan did as he was told and as soon as he shut the door, Shawn pulled away from the curb and headed out of town. He finally snapped out of his shock and asked, "Why are you doing this?" *And if you're the one who took Sam, where was Stavros*, but he kept that last bit to himself.

Shawn turned to look at him through bloodshot eyes and his hand was shaking. He didn't look good, and then Tristan saw the track marks going up his right arm. Shawn was a junkie.

"I saw all the signs. I knew I had to save you," Shawn said as he checked and rechecked his mirrors.

"Save me from what?" Tristan asked as they passed the town limits.

"They moved you from your condo in Dallas to take you away from me, but I was smarter than them. I saw the advertisement for your book signing and knew it was your cry for help."

"Cry for help?" Tristan was more confused.

"So I came and they were there, surrounding you, keeping you from me. So I waited for the right time. They had you locked up in that big house, but I swore I'd get you out."

"Shawn, I wasn't a prisoner. Those are my friends." He wasn't going to get into the whole boyfriend thing because he doubted it would help.

Shawn looked at him hard before smiling then looked back at the road. "It's okay, Tristan, I'll help you. I worried that they might have had time to brainwash you, but we'll get help to fix it. I won't let anything happen to you."

Tristan had to ask the obvious question. "Then why are you pointing a gun at me?"

"Don't worry, once we have a chance to reprogram you, I'll never have to again. But for right now it has to stay this way, dear."

Dear? Okay, how to play this because sanity left Shawn behind long ago. I have to get Sam free before doing anything else so I'll play along for now.

Knowing that the team could hear every word, he hoped to hell they understood. "Thank you for coming for me."

His kidnapper turned to look at him and Tristan gave him his best smile of adoration. For a second he worried he'd read the situation wrong until Shawn said, "I'd follow you anywhere, baby."

Other than the sick feeling he was getting, it seemed to work as Shawn was now smiling wide. "Where are we going?" he swallowed hard so he wouldn't puke, "sweetheart."

The gun in Shawn's hand lowered slightly. "I have a surprise for you. I know you're going to be so happy."

"What about Sam?"

"Oh, we'll take care of him when we get there," Shawn muttered as if this was another ordinary day and asking about a kidnapped man was an ordinary question.

They turned onto an old dirt road and drove for another fifteen minutes. All the way Tristan kept praying the team was close because it looked like they were the only ones out this way other than a water delivery truck he saw a few miles back. The truck began to slow and Shawn turned into what looked like an old goats' trail into the bush.

The truck bounced and pitched as Shawn drove farther in and the only thing Tristan could focus on was that gun accidentally going off. The trail opened up to reveal an old house tucked away in the woods. The yellow paint was faded, and the windows that didn't have holes in them were cracked. What was even more concerning was the lean of the building; it looked ready to topple over.

Tristan remembered he had to try to get as much information as he could. "Shawn, what if they come after us? Did you set any traps to stop them or warn us?"

Shawn gave him a strange look and Tristan was sure he'd blown it when Shawn said, "Don't worry, honey, they'll never find us here. They wouldn't even know where to look, and no one was following us so we're safe."

Shawn opened his driver's door and stepped out, but when Tristan tried to do the same, Shawn raised his gun and said, "Come out this way."

Tristan slid across the worn leather seat and stepped out beside Shawn, who motioned him ahead toward the house. Tristan's joints didn't like the uneven ground and ached in response. "I know this is all confusing, but once your head is clear again, we can leave here and go wherever we want."

As Tristan made his way to the front door, he was caught off guard by the stench coming from the house. Something smelled like it was decomposing and he prayed to anyone who'd listen that it wasn't Sam. Then his logic finally kicked in and he realized that it couldn't be Sam; he'd only been gone a few hours. This smelled of days and days of decomposition. Once he'd found a dead raccoon in his parents' attic that smelled something like this.

The sun was beginning to set as he reached for the door handle and opened the door. The squeal of old rusted metal sent shivers down his spine. Shawn shoved him forward, and he had no choice but to walk into the dark interior. Hard to believe, but the smell was getting even worse. It took a few seconds for his eyes to adjust and when they did, he wanted to close them.

Blood was splattered against the walls and floor of the old dilapidated kitchen like a child gone wild with finger paint. There were hand- and fingerprint marks in the dried blood. With another shove to his back Tristan walked into what must have once been a living room or den. His heart started beating faster when he saw Sam tied up to a chair in the middle of the room. He didn't look hurt, just pissed. He had tape over his mouth. Out this far nobody would have heard him if he had yelled for help. Shawn turned on a battery-operated camping light but Tristan never took his eyes off Sam.

"You can let Sam go now that I'm here," Tristan said as he took a step toward his friend while letting the team know Sam was here at the same time.

"Not just yet. We may need him to get out of this backwoods town."

"But you said you'd release him if I came to you."

"Plans change."

Shit. Tristan knew Sam was not leaving here alive. In the back of his mind, he still wondered whose blood was all over the kitchen.

"I have a present for you, Tristan."

Christ, he didn't like the sounds of that. Shawn led him away from Sam and to a rusted old chest freezer in the corner of the room. Tristan started to backpedal when Shawn stabbed the gun into his back. That was going to leave a mark and he hoped that was the only injury he'd receive through this messed-up situation. He continued forward when he felt a slight vibration behind his ear. The signal from a tiny receiver he had stuck to him so that the team could tell him when they were near.

They reached the freezer, flies buzzing around it, and the smell told him this wasn't going to be good. He took a quick look at Sam, who no longer looked pissed but as scared as he was.

"This is for you, Tristan. I wanted to show you how much I love you but I didn't know how. That was until I saw the perfect gift completely by accident as I was taking a tour around that property where you were trapped. I remembered him from one of your book signings when he burst through the crowd and started yelling at you."

Tristan remembered that incident quite well; it had taken three police officers to get Stavros out. Tristan knew what was in the freezer, but nothing could have prepared him for what he saw when Shawn opened the lid.

He began retching almost immediately. The dismembered, decomposing body of Stavros Menzotto filled the freezer as his lifeless eyes stared up at Tristan. He turned and took a few steps away while setting the clip on the inside of the ring Matthew made him wear. He now knew that there was no way out of this if he didn't do it. The ring held a small probe that when deployed would send 50,000 volts through Shawn.

"I killed him for you, sweetheart. He wouldn't leave you alone so I had to stop him. Now we can start our new life," Shawn explained as if murdering and dismembering a person was as normal as baking a cake.

Tristan turned and faced Shawn. Tristan's left hand was in a fist with his knuckles pointing at Shawn. Tristan didn't have a second thought as he fired the probe into Shawn's chest before running to Sam. Glass shattered and wood cracked as the room erupted; all he could think to do was protect Sam. He threw himself in front of Sam and took both of them to the ground, chair and all.

Silence fell but Tristan didn't dare look at the carnage. Someone began grabbing at his jacket and on instinct he threw his elbow back to fight off whoever it was.

As he connected with something or something hard, he heard, "Sparrow, it's me. You're safe." Vincent wrapped his arms around Tristan. He turned and clung to Vincent as he took Tristan from the house. The cool night air made him shiver, causing Vincent to tighten his hold.

Tristan knew one thing for sure: he wasn't moving far from his man's embrace for a long, long time.

Chapter Twelve

Tristan was so excited; he hadn't been out to the build site in weeks. He knew that the walls had been put up and that the kitchen had a counter and all the appliances he'd picked out. He held Vincent's hand as his love drove the ATV toward their new home. It would still be a month before they could move in, and Tristan was counting the days.

"Happy, sparrow?" Vincent asked as they neared the site.

In the distance, Tristan could see the river and the outline of part of their house. "Yes." It was as simple as that. No flowery words could describe how happy he was.

Vincent smiled wide as he slowed the vehicle and rounded the last bend, revealing how far they had gotten on the house. Siding was going up, all the windows were in, the roof was shingled, and the big front porch even had a bench swing. It was perfect. Tristan envisioned the two of them sitting out there at night with Luna watching the water float by.

"Oh Vincent. It's beautiful."

Vincent laid his arm across Tristan's shoulders and pulled him close for a kiss before saying, "I have a surprise for you."

However, this time instead of Tristan freaking out at the thought of another surprise, he was excited. It had been a rough couple of weeks since everything had gone down with Shawn. As it turned out, Shawn had done the FBI's job for them by stopping Stavros from killing again, and Shawn was now a resident of a criminal psychiatric prison states away. Tristan hadn't been in a hurry to leave the main house since then, but he did agree to see Dr. Gordon.

Today he'd woken up with a new plan. He couldn't keep blaming himself for everything that had happened. Sam hadn't blamed him. Stavros was gone and the case closed. It was time to move on with his life. So when he asked Vincent to take him to their home after lunch, his love was so happy that he immediately grabbed the keys and carried Tristan to the ATV. He didn't know if Vincent thought he'd change his mind or something, but he went with it.

They parked, got out, and walked hand in hand to what Tristan believed was the symbol of their future. He intended to live his life to the fullest after coming so close to losing it. They waved at the construction team, who had all stopped working so that he and his man could tour the house in silence. Walls were up and he could imagine where the furniture would go.

"It's so beautiful. It's everything I dreamed it would be."

"Come, sparrow, I have something to show you."

Tristan's curiosity was peaked as they walked into the kitchen, where he froze to the spot. He could feel his mouth was hanging open but damned if he could shut it. There covering the sidewall was a mosaic above their built-in seating area made from his grandmother's broken china. He'd thought he'd lost the only thing he had from her forever when Feisty was destroyed. The mosaic was stunning. The image was of their home with the river and the trees surrounding it.

"I was able to save the pieces and have been storing them in one of the empty rooms," Vincent explained, and when Tristan didn't say a word, he added, "I can take them down if—"

Vincent wasn't able to finish his sentence as Tristan jumped into his arms and began crying.

"Please tell me those are tears of joy."

Tristan looked up and through his blurry vision said, "I'm very lucky."

"After everything you've been through in the last few months, I'm not sure lucky fits," Vincent said as he ran his fingers across the side of Tristan's face and through his hair.

"I would go through all of it again, just to be with you."

"I'd be right by your side, sparrow." Vincent leaned down and took Tristan's lips into a heated kiss, not ending it until they needed to breathe.

They sent the contractors home with a paid half day off and sat in their porch swing through the sunset and until the stars shined above them.

SHADOW

Chapter One

Shadow settled into his perch for another long stakeout. This had been the fifth lead he'd chased across the country, until now. He found himself in Arkansas outside a gated compound and what looked like a dozen old cottages. This was the third day he'd hunkered down to watch the comings and goings of the group. As of yet there was no sign of Randy Reynolds.

Shadow was about a quarter mile back in the forest surrounding the area with his binoculars stuck to his face while he lay on wet leaves. He'd done a little checking into the man he was trying to free from what was known as a conversion therapy center. Randy's father had stuck him in one before attempting to kill his other son, Grady. That day Shadow had sworn a promise that he'd find Randy and bring him home.

Different as night and day, Grady was a police officer with Brighton PD while Randy was an artist. He'd had his abstract paintings in galleries, and they were stunning. Each one Shadow had seen evoked strong emotions. After today, if he didn't get a sign that Randy was here, Shadow would make his way to the next location. He'd had a good feeling about this lead, but he figured he was wrong.

The day was sunny and there were several people milling around. Most of them wore beige scrubs while a few others were dressed in black. Shadow could easily see who was in charge. The "guests" would approach each other, or sit in the sun, but they never spoke. He presumed that it was another rule; he'd observed so many already. One was bowing; the people in the beige outfits would bow to anyone in black.

He noticed movement from one of the cottages in the back where there hadn't been any in the last two days. A small figure dressed in beige stepped slowly down the front steps until he reached the bottom and sat down. Shadow quickly focused in on the lone man and he could feel his heartbeat speeding up. From the guy's messy blond hair to his soft amber eyes, Shadow knew he'd found Randy.

Shadow watched as Randy quickly scanned the area before picking up a long stick and rolling it through his hands. Shadow wasn't close enough to read his facial expressions accurately, but he acted scared. Slowly Randy began drawing in the dirt at his feet. After a few minutes, he seemed to lose himself in his drawing; it was beautiful to see the passion come alive on his face.

Suddenly, a man dressed in a black uniform came around the corner. Randy threw the stick away and was desperately trying to wipe away the dirt where he'd been creating. But it was too late. Shadow got to his knees as the larger man approached Randy. The man yelled something and Randy immediately stood straight. Shadow couldn't understand what the asshole continued to yell, but he kept motioning to the ground. It had something to do with Randy's art.

To Shadow's horror the man pulled what looked like a small black leather whip from his belt. Now Shadow was standing; he knew he'd never make it in time, but everything in him demanded he protect the smaller man. He gripped the tree beside him as the first blow hit Randy across his right shoulder and down his chest, the second across the thigh of his left leg. Shadow could see the fabric begin to stain red with blood.

A rage like nothing he'd ever felt before tore through him as he watched the tears running down Randy's pale face. Shadow took a close look at the man who had hit Randy. If Shadow ever had the chance, he'd return the favor tenfold. The man said something and

Randy turned and limped back into what Shadow assumed was his cottage.

Shadow stood there long after everyone had gone back inside and swore that would be the last time anyone would lay a finger on Randy Reynolds. It was time Shadow did what he did best and god help anyone who got in his way. Somehow, he figured god wouldn't be answering the calls of these assholes.

***

Randy lay on a thin mattress that lay directly on the wooden floor in the corner of his room, watching the stars through the bars on the window. In all his twenty-seven years, he'd never imagined he'd find himself in this position. Kidnapped, abandoned, thrown into this awful place, and chained to the wall. When these people spoke of their version of God, Randy found no resemblance to the one he envisioned.

He moved his left leg and hissed out in pain. The open sores caused by the whip still hadn't been seen to, even though the beating had happened two days prior. Randy couldn't say he was surprised he was their prisoner. His crime—being gay, or more specifically, his father learning Randy was gay—had landed him in this hellhole.

It was still a mystery how his asshole father had found out, but that didn't matter now. Initially, Randy had thought someone would come for him, and he'd make his father pay for doing this to him. But after the first month blended into the second, and then third, he knew he was on his own.

Even his big brother—a cop—had left Randy behind to deal with their father. Randy was half the size of his brother, who took after their father, so there was no chance of fending the old man off. Having been born prematurely had ensured Randy was the smallest and relatively fragile for most of his life. Randy had called his brother Grady so many times before he was brought here, left countless messages, and the dick hadn't responded to a single message.

Randy's mom and sister had taken off on *holiday* when dear old Dad started to let his crazy show. Of course, Randy hadn't been invited along. He knew for certain he had no one he could trust.

Gingerly, he rolled to his side trying not to reopen the welts on his arm and chest. His clothing was already stained with his blood; he didn't need to add to it. The wood-planked cottage was old and drafty, and from what he noticed, the other buildings looked much the same. Only the members of the fellowship had rooms in the insulated main building, where he received his daily dose of bigotry, hate, and guilt.

The few shelves in the hut were devoid of extra clothing, books, paper, or pens, let alone his paints. It was all gone. Randy was grateful for a friend's advice to get himself a small storage unit. His father had taken to cutting the canvases he'd found around the house, and Randy had managed to find a place where he could take his art where his family couldn't find it.

But at this rate, he'd never see those paintings again.

Now all he wished for was sleep to take him away from this, even if only for a little while. To get lost in one of his paintings, to feel the strength of the colors, the flow of the paint, the touch of brush to canvas. What he'd give to make that a reality again. For real, Randy would settle for an old worn-out pencil and scrap piece of paper about now.

His eyes began to close as he felt beads of sweat rolling down his forehead. He was running a fever and wondered if anybody actually cared. At the rate he was heating up, Randy was going to need antibiotics, lots of fluids, and some nourishment or else all would be lost.

A few moments later as he began to drift off, he heard it. At first he thought it was his imagination but it continued methodically: "tap, tap, tap-tap, tap." He thought perhaps one of the other "patients" had gotten out of their restraints. The guards didn't bother to patrol at night, considering everyone was chained to the wall every evening.

Randy gathered what was left of his nerve—he was an artist not a fighter, and a small artist at that—and popped his head up to look out the window directly over his mattress. He froze. He was eye to eye with a man dressed all in black. As frightened as he was, he couldn't help but notice that those eyes were mesmerizing—sage green with a rim of rusty copper running around the iris. Utterly stunning.

The man tapped again—yeah, Randy was in a stupor. The guy's face was covered in one of those ski-mask thingies so his eyes were all Randy could make out.

The man placed a piece of paper up to the window. It read, "Here to get you out. Stay quiet." Randy couldn't have been more surprised. Someone was rescuing him. The ninja dude vanished under the cottage and a few seconds later, a barely perceptible whine came from the floorboards. Randy backed into a corner, as a beam of light was followed by what looked like a saw blade cutting through the wood.

The guy was cutting through the two-inch-thick floorboards and was barely making a sound. Maybe those things didn't happen only in movies. Randy tried to pull his leg out of the way but the chain held him tight. The edge of the blade drew ever closer, and he struggled but it was no use. The first nick of the blade made him pull back farther until he couldn't control it, he whimpered. He clasped both hands against his mouth, desperate not to make another sound.

He braced, telling himself it was a small cut compared to the pain he'd already suffered. Honestly, the damage wasn't too bad, and if it meant he was getting out of here, he was okay with the pain. Soon the blade moved farther away from his already damaged limb and he pulled the pant leg of his uniform down and pressed it against the wound to slow the bleeding.

Shortly after the whining stopped, a piece of the floor fell away and a head sprang up out of the hole. Now that the dude was on this side of the bars, Randy wasn't so certain about the whole thing. After all, how could he trust a stranger when he sure as hell couldn't trust his own family?

Randy's rescuer crawled over to him and motioned for him to remain silent. He was okay with that. He could hardly breathe, and what little energy he had left he had to devote to keeping the pain at bay. The huge man slowly reached for the chain attaching Randy to the wall but stopped short when the man noticed the blood on his pant leg.

He couldn't help but rear back when the guy lifted the discolored material aside. The chain shifted and rattled, then those gorgeous eyes looked up at him. Randy knew he was behaving like a coward but after everything he'd seen and been through, he couldn't help his reactions.

Then it struck him that this could be a trap. The fellowship could be testing him to see what he would do. Randy had no idea what was real anymore. What he'd thought his life would be like, and the family he'd believed he could trust had failed him. Monumentally.

The stranger raised his hands in surrender before reaching for his black ski mask and pulling it off. If Randy thought the man's eyes were breathtaking, there were no words to describe the entire reveal. The dude's dark hair was cut high and tight, and his tanned skin seemed to glow in the moonlight. Combine that with his strong jaw and cushion lips, ah, yeah. Perfect. Like Rodin perfect. Randy, who was in no shape to notice anything but the pain he was in and that his world had deteriorated into him being chained to a wall, noticed everything about this gorgeous man, including his bulges straining against his dark clothes.

While Randy's brain had been assessing the magnificence before him, the man had inched closer. By the time Randy noticed the stranger was right by his side and it was too late to control his reaction. A large—like really large—warm, calloused hand covered his mouth, preventing his scream from being heard.

The man brought his lips to Randy's ear, his hot breath sending chills through Randy's body. "My name is Shadow. I'm here to free you," he whispered.

"Why?" Randy asked. He couldn't think of a single person who would have hired someone to bust him out.

Shadow looked confused for a moment before answering. "Because you're a prisoner here."

"Trust me, I know that," Randy replied in a hushed voice while lifting his chained leg. "I have no one who would have sent you. For all I know you could be part of the fellowship."

"Your brother Grady sent me. I made a promise to find you and I never break a promise," Shadow answered, as if this should be enough for Randy to trust him.

"Grady doesn't care about me. You should have done your research," Randy huffed out in disappointment. He wanted to believe the dude, but evidence to the contrary had him believing this too would be a fail. "What game is the fellowship playing this time, torture the gays with dreams of escape? Leave me be. I'm already in enough pain."

Randy turned his head away; he was so tired. Gently, but steadily, Shadow turned his head back so that they were eye to eye. "I understand that you don't know me or trust me yet, but are you willing to give up your chance for freedom because you're scared?"

Scared. Is this guy for real?

All his life, he was the smallest or the weakest in most any group he'd been in, and as such people assumed they had to treat him with kid gloves. Which pissed him off. "Don't you dare assume anything about me and what I've been through. Scared left the camp months ago. Now I'm in survival mode. So forgive me for not jumping at the opportunity to crawl through that hole with you on the mere mention of a brother who abandoned me even after I begged him for help."

That got Shadow's attention. Sweat dripped down the side of Randy's face. He was battered, bleeding and bruised, all of which had become infected.

His evening wasn't looking up.

"I need you to trust me," Shadow stated. "I will get you to safety. You need to see a doctor."

"No doctor," Randy almost screamed, but remembered to whisper at the last second. "There are other people involved in this, no one can be trusted. I've seen the local sheriff in the offices with the fellowship staff on more than one occasion." Too late Randy realized that if this whole breakout scenario was some fellowship plan then he'd sunk himself and good.

"Okay, no doctor or sheriff. But we need to get out of here before we're spotted."

Randy knew he had to take the chance. "Promise me. You said you never break a promise. Look me in the eyes and swear to me you'll get me away from here. No Grady either. I need to figure out who I can trust. For obvious reasons, I'll take you at your word if you swear it."

Shadow's face seemed to soften before he said, "I swear to get you to safety. I will not inform your brother as to where we are until you tell me to. But I must contact my team to give them updates and ensure your continued safety."

Randy didn't break eye contact. He didn't know what he was looking for but something deep inside told him to believe Shadow. "Deal." Randy stuck his hand out and when Shadow took it a rush like an electrical current zinged its way through Randy's body.

His alleged savior worked quickly, pulling a few medical supplies from the many pockets on his clothing. Shadow stopped at the cut Randy had received from the blade. The big man looked up and Randy could see the guilt and felt the need to comfort him. "It was an accident." After a quick moment, Shadow seemed to snap out of it and soon Randy's wounds were wrapped and bandaged, the deft skill telling him this man had medical training.

"What branch of the military are you from?" Randy asked. After all, he was a son and brother to police officers and had met a few active and retired military men in his time. Shadow had found him, gotten into the camp, cut a hole in the floor, and patched him up.

"Marine," Shadow answered easily, giving Randy no reason to doubt him. He placed a cylindrical object against the first link in the chain. The tip of object began to heat and turned red.

Shadow looked up and waited for Randy to give the go-ahead. After a single nod the cutting began. The smell coming from the melting metal wasn't helping his pounding head, but he shoved the queasy feeling aside and concentrated on freedom.

Randy knew he was putting a lot of faith in a man he didn't even know, but he didn't have a choice. Of course he was worried this was a trap, but if he had even the slimmest chance of getting out of this nightmare, he was going to take it.

When he heard the chain fall to the floor, the first real feelings of hope pushed their way through his doubt and fear. He would still have the manacle around his ankle but at least he'd be able to run. Their eyes met and Randy couldn't help the crack in his voice when he begged, "Please, don't betray me."

Shadow leaned in close. "I would never consider it, cutie."

Cutie? The endearment caught him off guard, but it didn't seem as though Shadow was being flippant or intentionally snide. He sounded as if he meant it.

Shadow knelt at the edge of the hole in the floor and held out his hand. This was it. Either Randy took the chance or he died in this horrible place. He pulled in a deep breath and grabbed the outstretched fingers.

His life was now in Shadow's hands.

Chapter Two

Shadow refused to let go of Randy. The man had placed all his trust in him and Shadow would not disappoint. He slowed his pace once they were clear of the barbed wire fences and were well into the forest. Randy hadn't complained or even spoken since they crawled out from under that POS hut. He'd kept up with Shadow, only stumbling a few times over the large tree roots. Shadow was about to stop for a moment to allow Randy a chance to rest when he heard the man's painful grunt before he fell to his knees.

"I'm sorry. I'll keep up," Randy gasped as he struggled to get back to his feet.

Shadow quickly lifted the smaller man into his arms and walked him over to a nearby tree stump. Randy was considerably lighter than Shadow had expected, which made him wonder if those bastards had given him anything more than bread and water.

Shadow set Randy down and knelt in front of him. "What hurts?"

"My lungs," Randy rasped out.

"What can I do to help?" Shadow asked while kicking himself in the ass for not being more thorough in his research of Randy's physical capabilities. Grady had told him that his brother had been born prematurely and had a variety of health problems, along with being small. Shadow should have had his team pull up Randy's medical records.

"I just need to rest for a minute. I'll be fine," Randy tried to reassure him, even going as far as to force out a small smile.

Shadow knew Randy was downplaying how weak he was. Aside from his usual physical ailments, the wounds from the beating Shadow had witnessed hadn't healed, and Randy's skin was hot to the touch. Infection had set in. To make matters worse, Shadow had fucking cut him with the saw.

He rechecked the temporary bandages. Once he had Randy in a safe location, Shadow would clean him up and get antibiotics into him. The injury Shadow had caused had stopped bleeding but would require a few stitches once it was cleaned.

The Marines had trained Shadow well. He'd been a medic in his unit and was grateful for the knowledge he had to care for Randy. Those expressive amber eyes watched his every move and for the first time in decades, Shadow felt self-conscious. There had been a reason he'd earned his moniker, Shadow preferred to blend into the background.

He didn't know what it was about Randy, but the man called out to every part of Shadow. It seemed as though those eyes could see into his very soul, leaving him feeling exposed and vulnerable—two emotions he was unfamiliar with and found not particularly comfortable.

For the first time in decades, Shadow wanted to be *seen*.

This brave, tenacious man had never given in. After being locked up, beaten, and starved for months, they hadn't broke him. Fire still burned in his eyes.

"What's your birth name?" Randy asked.

The question came out of nowhere and threw him. Shadow couldn't remember the last time someone asked him that. "Jake. My name is Jake Kennedy."

Randy held out his hand. "Thank you for coming for me, Jake."

The sound of his name on Randy's lips did things to Shadow's body, things he shouldn't be even considering at this moment. "You're welcome. I know you have no reason to, but I promise you can trust me."

Randy stared at him for a moment and Shadow couldn't help but wonder if he met with the man's approval. When Randy realized he was staring, he turned his head, but not before Shadow saw the red staining his cheeks.

"My truck isn't far from here. It should take us another forty-five minutes or so to get to it. Then I'll get you to a safe house over the state line where you can rest and heal."

"You promised not to tell my family…my brother where I am."

"And I intend to keep that promise until otherwise told. But I refuse to let Grady suffer more by not telling him you are at least safe. I'll contact my team so they know where we are, and I'll have them contact Grady."

Shadow had no idea what was going on between the brothers. Grady had seemed to be a straight-up guy, but for some reason Randy didn't trust him. Randy had said something about his brother abandoning him after he begged for help. Which didn't sound like the Grady Shadow knew. There was a story there, and Shadow meant to get to the bottom of it.

Randy opened his mouth and looked like he was about to say something but stopped himself and turned away.

"You can ask me anything," Shadow reassured. "I'll answer you as honestly as I can."

"Aren't you supposed to say 'I'll answer you honestly,' not 'as honestly as I can'?"

"That would be a lie and I said I wouldn't do that."

Randy dipped his chin. "Well, there is that." He raised he head and took a shallow breath. "How's Grady?"

Clearly, Randy had feelings for his brother, or he wouldn't have asked after him. "Grady's better now that your father has been put away."

"Put away?" Randy looked shocked. "He's in jail?"

"It's a prison for the criminally insane, but yeah. He's never getting out, so he won't hurt you again." Shadow watched the play of emotions on the beautiful man's face. "He will never hurt you again, I swear it."

Tears filled Randy's amber eyes and began to drip down his face. Shadow felt the overwhelming need to comfort him, and for the first time he didn't fight it. He picked the sobbing man up off the tree stump and sat with Randy on his lap. He held the man as he released what had to be years of pent-up emotion, coupled with the trauma he'd suffered these past few months,

Shadow rubbed Randy's back and slowly he began to calm. His face was buried against Shadow's chest and he wasn't surprised when he heard a soft snore. The poor guy had passed out from physical and emotional exhaustion. Shadow stood with the man still in his arms and began walking in the direction of his truck.

He'd made up time by increasing his pace now that he no longer had to compensate for Randy's injuries and got to the hidden vehicle in under thirty minutes. Randy was tucked into the backseat of the quad cab and hadn't woken up. Shadow was beginning to worry, given Randy's injuries and infection. He knew he had to get Randy to the safe house and dose him as soon as possible.

There was no way in hell he was losing what he'd only just found.

***

Randy struggled to open his eyes, but they felt like they'd been glued shut. He couldn't decide which was worse, the throbbing pain or unbearable heat radiating through his body. The sheets underneath him were wet and he was naked. Panic like he'd never felt before raced into his thoughts when he realized there was something attached to his right arm.

Without conscious thought he began to struggle, prying his eyes open no matter how much the light was hurting them. His world was blurry because his eyes were watering and he didn't recognize anything.

Damn. Shadow had taken him to the hospital after he promised he wouldn't. Randy should have never trusted him. Knowing he'd been betrayed yet again felt like a knife to his stomach.

"Easy, easy, buddy. You're safe. No one is going to hurt you."

The sound of Shadow's voice calmed Randy a bit, allowing the time needed for his sight to clear. When he finally was able to focus on his surroundings, he was surprised to see he wasn't in the hospital, though he did have an IV in his arm. He was lying in the middle of a large bed in a good-size bedroom. A large bay window filled the room with light as he slowly looked around until he was staring into those expressive green eyes once again.

Shadow was kneeling on the mattress beside him, holding both of Randy's hands. "Where are we?"

The big man released Randy and told him, "Near Tulsa, Oklahoma." Shadow then brought a glass of water to Randy's parched lips for him to take a much-needed drink.

"Thank you," he said after he drank a small amount. His stomach felt sour and he didn't want to risk throwing up. The sheet covering him felt cool against his overheated skin and he was about back to calm when there was a knock on the bedroom door. "We're not alone?"

Shadow cupped Randy's cheeks so that he looked straight at him. "I promised I'd take care of you and keep you safe. The person on the other side of that door would no sooner hurt you than I would, and she loves me."

Great. Randy knew Shadow would have a wife or girlfriend, and Randy couldn't help the disappointment he was desperately trying to hide. The handsome man looked at him closely, as if reading Randy's thoughts. He tried to look away but that gaze had captured him. The knock came again, bringing both of them back to the here and now.

Shadow grinned slightly before releasing Randy, walked over and opened the door allowing an older woman to enter. Her dark hair had one strip of white tucked behind her left ear and her tanned skin hinted at a love for the outdoors. She smiled brightly at him and brought the tray she was carrying over to the side table and set it down.

"It's good to see you awake, dear. You had my Jake worried. We'll get you on the mend in no time at all."

Shadow came to her side and wrapped his arm around her shoulders. Randy could see the love and pride all over the big guy's face. "Randy, I would like you to meet a special lady, Joanne Kennedy, my mother."

The relief Randy felt was immeasurable. He had no idea why he cared so much that the guy was straight.

"It's nice to meet you, Mrs. Kennedy. Thank you for taking care of me." Randy raised his hand and that was when he realized how weak he was. He could barely raise it a few inches off the bed.

Mrs. Kennedy reached down to take it. "Call me Jo. I've been helping but my son is the one who has been your main caregiver. And don't you worry. You are welcome in my home. How those people get away with doing things like this I will never understand."

"They won't be getting away with it much longer if the Sentinels have anything to say about it," Shadow stated before touching the sheets around Randy's body. "We need to change your bedding before we try to get you to eat some beef broth."

"Thank you," Randy replied before asking the question he was most concerned about. "Why am I so weak? The walk in the forest shouldn't have knocked me out like this."

"It was the perfect storm of being starved, beaten, and the conditions you were living in when the infection set in. Your immune system couldn't fight it off. It spread and turned into a systemic infection, which is why," he glanced at Randy's arm, "you have intravenous antibiotics." Shadow checked over the multiple bandages covering Randy's body. "You've been asleep for almost two days."

The realization that he could have died if Shadow hadn't come for him had Randy stuttering his, "Thank you." He had thought it could happen given what they had done to him and his living conditions, but to realize how close he really came was shattering.

"You'll never have to go through anything like that ever again. You're safe," Shadow promised in a voice slightly above a whisper. "Now let's get your sheets changed."

Randy wanted to believe him, but he needed time to believe he was safe and would stay that way. He knew he was still in survival mode and would be for a long time.

Jo brought over a set of dry linens and Shadow gently lifted Randy from the bed. Thankfully, he still had the one top sheet covering his body or else he'd have been naked. Then it hit him, how did he get naked? Randy understood he was being dramatic, but his body was nowhere near the way it usually looked. Besides the many wounds and bruises, he'd been given little to eat, and the other day he'd realized he could count his ribs—visually. Not sexy.

"Um, Shadow, do you have something I can wear until I can get a few outfits of my own?" It occurred to him that he had no money or belongings. He'd have to figure something out. Like where was he going to go, where would he live, how would he pay rent and for the food and medicine he would need, and how would he get around. He had no family or friends he could depend on. Maybe a shelter once he was healed and found a job, but the thought of that was terrifying.

"We'll figure everything out in time. All I want you to do now is to concentrate on healing." Shadow seemed to have a direct line to Randy's thoughts. It was weird and sort of intrusive, but right now he was too weak to mind. "I'll bring you a shirt, which should cover you to your knees, allowing me to care for your wounds."

Randy nodded his head before laying it against Shadow's chest, feeling worn out. He didn't like feeling feeble and incapacitated, and swore he'd be back on his feet as soon as possible. He had fought his entire life for his independence. As early as he could remember adults would treat him as if he were made of spun glass that was about to shatter at any moment. He'd be the first to admit he'd had a few health concerns, but it had never been enough to stop him.

He watched as Jo stripped the bed and remade it; her years of motherly experience making the process seem simple. As he was watching Jo's economical movements, it happened. Shadow rubbed his lips across the top of Randy's head at the same time his mother turned around.

Jo didn't miss a beat. "Sweetheart, put Randy back in bed so that you can feed him before he falls asleep in your arms," she ordered with a smile, not giving a sign she'd seen what her son had done.

Okay, he must be hallucinating. Or dreaming. Or losing his freakin' mind.

Then it happened again.

Shadow brushed his lips again across Randy's forehead before returning him to the bed. Then Shadow turned to a dresser on the far wall where he pulled out a large gray t-shirt that said "MARINE" on the front in big black letters. Still stunned, Randy lay back in silence as everything carried on around him. Like it was normal.

What the hell?

"I'm running to the grocery store, dear." Jo bent toward him. "What are some of your favorite foods?" she asked as she gathered up the dirty sheets.

Answer her so they won't figure out I'm losing it. "I'm happy with whatever you make, ma'am." There was no way he would ask the woman who had opened her home to him to make him special meals.

"Call me Jo. Ma'am makes me sound old," she corrected him with a wink. "I'll let Jake get it out of you. Be back in a couple hours, boys."

"Thanks, Mom," Shadow said before returning to Randy with the shirt. "I'll help you get this on, and then we'll try the broth."

Everything was so matter of fact that Randy lay there sort of paralyzed while Shadow began pulling the sheet down. He snapped out of it and grabbed the sheet before it cleared his hips.

"I can do it myself," Randy snapped.

Shadow looked at him closely before saying, "I've already seen you naked. There's nothing for you to be embarrassed about."

"You're entitled to your opinion, but it's my body. Right now I'm a skin-covered skeleton with bruises and injuries that make me look hideous," Randy argued while holding on to the sheet with the little strength he had.

Shadow's response was instantaneous. He cupped Randy's jaw and looked him straight in the eye. "You are beautiful. Now let's get you dressed and fed."

Randy was stunned. Again. Shadow was gay. Right? Randy had to know and couldn't stop the question from leaving his lips. "Jake, are you gay?"

Shadow smiled wide, those distinctive eyes seemed to flash in the sunlight. "You bet your cute ass I am."

With the word *beautiful* whispering through his mind, Randy released his hold on the sheet and allowed Shadow to dress him. His eyes were beginning to droop and he knew he'd be asleep in less than a minute.

"No. No sleeping until we get a bit of food into you," Shadow ordered before propping Randy up with a few pillows and reaching for a bowl that was on the nearby tray. Randy had to admit the broth smelled wonderful and caused his stomach to growl. "We'll work you up to more solid food as you heal, but for now this shouldn't upset your stomach."

Shadow held the spoon to Randy's mouth and he took his first sip. The flavors exploded across his taste buds. This wasn't beef broth you bought in a can or a box; this was the real deal. Compared to the bland slop he had been fed for the last several months, this was heaven and he couldn't help but moan.

Shadow smiled wide as he scooped up another spoonful. "You like it."

"Oh god yes. It's been so long since I've had real food with actual taste." Randy took another sip and closed his eyes to savor it. When he opened them, Shadow was watching him.

"What?"

Shadow seemed to snap out of it and quickly refilled the spoon. "Sorry, I must be a bit tired myself. I didn't mean to stare or make you feel uncomfortable."

"You didn't. Maybe you should have a nap while I'm sleeping. This bed is more than big enough if you want to crawl in." Randy had no idea why he'd said that, but he wasn't about to take it back.

He took another sip of the broth before giving in to his need to sleep. Shadow placed the bowl back on the tray and took the extra pillows from behind Randy's back so that he could lie down. Randy was nearly asleep when he felt the bed dip and Shadow crawl in beside him.

Shadow lay with his arms under his head and Randy couldn't fight the impulse to put his head on the big man's chest. He told himself that due to his deteriorated state he needed comfort and warmth, and Shadow was the only person he could trust to give that to him.

When he felt a strong, muscled arm wrap around him, all rational thought faded away.

"Rest. I'll keep you safe."

"Thanks, Jake. You have no idea how much this means to me." Randy wasn't blowing smoke. He was a man alone in the world with nothing of his own. Those bastards who'd tortured him were probably searching everywhere to bring him back and chain him back to the wall or worse. With what he'd come to learn, they would never stop looking for him. "They'll come for me."

Shadow held him a bit tighter but not so much as to cause him any pain from his injuries. "They'll never get near you. I promise."

Randy's eyes fluttered closed no matter how much he tried to fight it. "I know things…too many things…for them to let me go."

The last few words were a mere whisper as his world faded back to black.

Chapter Three

As he'd done for the past several days, Shadow watched over Randy while he slept. Having him in his arms appealed to Shadow's protective nature, but it also brought emotions to the surface that were better left buried. Turning his mind to questions left unanswered, he wondered what Randy had meant when he said "he knew things" about the fellowship.

He glanced over at the box sitting on his bookshelf that contained an American flag folded thirteen times. The lone sound of a bugler playing "Taps" echoed in his head as the memories flooded his mind. Over twenty years of never-forgotten pain tried to surface but he fought it back with everything he had. There was no use in dwelling in the past; too many years had been lost to giving in to the dark spaces in his brain.

Shadow concentrated on the sound of Randy's breathing, the feel of his body, and the warm hand lying against Shadow's left pec, which helped to shove his demons back into that triangular, wooden box.

Coop and Spider were stationed around the property, doing what they did best—keeping Randy safe. Shadow had honored his promise; Grady knew his brother was safe and that was all. Until Shadow figured out what the hell was going on, that's the way it would stay. He'd relayed to the team what Randy had said about his brother abandoning him and ignoring his calls for help. Before even considering allowing Grady anywhere near his brother, he would have to give them answers that contradicted Randy's take on the situation. Shannon was already checking into Randy's assertions, along with Matthew. If it was true, and if there were a cause for Grady's behavior, they'd find it.

Having Randy in Shadow's family home and his childhood bedroom should have felt odd, but in truth, it calmed him. Something settled inside of him even if he didn't want to examine it too closely.

His amazing mother hadn't even batted an eye when he'd showed up at her door with Randy in his arms. Instead, she'd worked tirelessly by Shadow's side to clean Randy's wounds and stitch them up before getting him settled and on the road to recovery.

Shadow had explained his mission to find Randy and what had been done at that fucking camp. Of course, his mom wanted to call in the authorities, but he'd explained why that wasn't the best option at this time.

His mother had been a single parent who worked two jobs to make ends meet. When Shadow had come out to her, her only concern was over how other people would treat him. She loved him and supported him, and he knew he was one of the lucky ones.

As soon as he'd graduated high school, he'd enlisted in the Marines and sent his pay home to his mom. Years later, he'd discovered that she'd been putting all his money into a savings account for when he returned home.

Ever since signing up with the Sentinels, he'd done everything he could to make sure his mom never had to work another day in her life if she didn't want to. He'd paid off the mortgage on the old farmhouse and had it renovated exactly the way she'd wanted. Her retirement was well planned, and although she'd fought him tooth and nail, she'd acquiesced when he told her she had access to all his accounts, and that she'd take whatever she needed. Now every time she used her bankcard it made him happy, but she still worked even though she didn't have to.

Shadow had expected nothing less.

He felt his cellphone vibrate in his pocket; he pulled it out and read the text message on the screen.

Lots of movement inside the camp. Looks like they increased security and the local sheriff has been out multiple times today. Dante.

The team had been keeping an eye on the camp after finding a small GPS tracker sewn into Randy's uniform. Thankfully, Shadow had found it before reaching his mother's house and disabled it, but it proved Randy's theory that they wouldn't let him go easily.

Shadow relayed what Randy had said about "knowing things" to Dante, but they'd all have to wait until Randy was stronger to get their answers. Tristan had offered to come to Oklahoma since he'd known Randy for years. The Sentinels had discussed whether it would help calm Randy and make him trust giving them the information by having a familiar face around. They decided Shadow would share the offer and would allow Randy to decide if he wanted Tristan there. Randy would be making his own decisions from this point onward. Enough people had taken that option away from him for far too long.

There was a soft knock on the bedroom door before his mother peeked in. She smiled wide as she neared the bed to take the tray of food away; it had been hardly touched.

"Did Randy fall asleep before he ate?" she asked in a whisper.

Shadow nodded.

"Poor dear. I'll have something fresh ready for him when he wakes up," she murmured before quietly leaving the room.

Every time Randy stirred, Shadow would hold him close and whisper, "You're safe," and each time the man would fall back to sleep. Shadow's heart constricted each time even as his chest expanded; knowing that he could provide him with comfort made him feel valued.

During the many years of war and missions from one hellhole to another, somewhere along the line he'd lost sight of how it felt to be normal—to be a man caring for someone instead of a trained hunter waiting for his next call to suit up.

His mind was filled with what-ifs he'd buried long ago in Arlington, Virginia, before he became a Sentinel. Shadow closed his eyes and savored this quiet time before it was inevitably taken away once again. Soon his eyes grew heavy after days of watching over Randy, and Shadow allowed himself the simple pleasure of falling to sleep with this man, who'd become something more than an assignment, in his arms.

***

Randy remembered waking a few times, but Shadow had soothed him back to sleep, making Randy feel safe and protected. Now, he didn't want to move an inch because the handsome Marine was dead asleep and Randy didn't want to wake him up. But Randy needed to go to the bathroom. Bad.

He'd been staring at his rescuer for the past ten minutes, unable to look away. Shadow's strong jaw had several days' worth of stubble, and it looked good on him. He seemed to be in his late thirties or early forties, and the one tattoo that was partially visible ran up his right arm and under his shirt. Honestly, the man was drop-dead gorgeous and Randy knew he was out of his league. He didn't fool himself into thinking that this "rescue" would go beyond Shadow keeping his promise to Randy's brother. Why Grady would even bother was still a mystery.

Randy couldn't wait any longer; his bladder was set to explode. "Shadow."

Those beautiful sage green eyes flew open and Shadow propped himself up on his elbows and scanned the room before his laser gaze focused on Randy.

"Are you okay?" were the first words out of Shadow's mouth, making Randy feel warm all over. He couldn't remember a time in his life when anyone had been solely concerned about him.

"I'm sorry to wake you but I need to go to the bathroom," Randy explained. He knew he didn't have enough strength to get himself out of the bed let alone walk to the bathroom, and he hated to ask, but had to. “I don’t think I can make it on my own.”

Shadow caressed Randy’s jaw before gently sliding his arm around his neck. “No problem, I want you to reach out to me for anything at any time.”

Ummm…the whole caress thing was too delicious to take seriously, and the offer was kind and generous, but Randy knew better than to get too used to it. And he saw it for what it was, a good man committed to his job who could read that Randy was still freaking out. “Thank you.”

Shadow sat up, dipped his body, and brought his strong, muscled arm under Randy’s legs. Then Shadow swung his body to the side of the bed. He glanced down a moment, gave a short chin jerk, and then stood, holding Randy close to that hard chest.

Tilting his head toward the IV pole, he asked, "Can you reach?”

Randy nodded, grabbed the pole, then Shadow walked across the room as if he were carrying a box of feathers. They turned to the right, and Randy was treated to his first view of the house. Brightly colored flowered wallpaper made the long hallway cheerful, and the large window at the far end flooded it with light. Right before the window, Shadow turned left—Randy bumped the pole against the wall and Shadow backed up. Randy shrugged, tugged the pole around the doorjamb, and saw they were in a white tiled bathroom with dark blue accents that had a large whirlpool tub.

While Randy took in the room, his next problem reared its ugly head. In his weakened state, he wasn’t going to be able to stand on his own while relieving himself. Before he had to voice this mortifying concern, Shadow provided the answer.

“I’ll set you on the toilet and turn my back to give you some privacy. You have only my shirt on so there won’t be much we have to navigate.” It wasn’t his solution that calmed Randy as much as it was Shadow’s warm smile. “I won’t be far if you need me.”

“Okay,” he agreed as Shadow turned him toward the toilet in a bathroom that looked more like a spa. The limestone-topped vanity had two sinks, and an antique armoire stood in the corner. Randy would love to spend some time in that large whirlpool bathtub and couldn't help but stare at it.

Of course, Shadow noticed. "Once you're a little further along in your healing, I'll make sure you two have some time together. For now we'll get you set up in the shower later on."

Randy looked over at the huge glassed-in shower with its rainfall showerhead and multiple body sprayers and almost melted right there. But… "I won't be able to stand in the shower."

"Don't worry. I'll be in there with you so you don't fall," Shadow said casually.

Ummm… The images Randy conjured froze his brain. By the time he was able to get his mouth to work, he was already being set down on the toilet.

As promised, Shadow turned his back and allowed Randy as much privacy as he could without being too far away. Which came in handy when he leaned on the vanity and tried to stand, but managed instead to tip himself over. Shadow caught him before he hit the floor, but only barely.

"New rule," Shadow ordered. "You'll tell me before you try anything like that again. I understand it might be hard for you to accept your limitations, but I will not risk you being reinjured because of your pride."

As far as scoldings went, Shadow hadn't changed his tone of voice or its volume, but it still caused Randy to bristle. "I'm not a child. I misjudged my ability. I won't repeat the mistake. I don't need your *rules*."

Shadow stopped in front of the vanity, his green eyes unreadable. "Trust me. I know you are all man." Then he turned Randy, leaned him forward so he could wash his hands.

The return trip was tense and Randy felt like a fool. He knew Shadow was trying to keep him safe and he went and bit the guy's head off.

Shadow laid him on the bed, covered Randy with a blanket, positioned the IV pole then sat on the bed beside him. "I'm piecing together that the people in your life have not treated you as an equal. That's not me. When you began falling, it scared me and I reacted to that fear. I wasn't implying that you have the mentality of a child, and I promise I will never treat you any other way than my equal."

Well, hell. Slowly, Randy reached out and Shadow took his hand. "Thank you for understanding. I can't tell you the last time I felt someone actually consider me their equal. Not even Grady."

A sharp knock on the bedroom door sent a spike of fear through him and he tried to jerk his hand out of Shadow's. Damn it. How could he expect to be treated as an equal if he jumped at every noise?

Randy tried again to pull his hand back, but Shadow refused to let go. "Don't misinterpret the fear you feel as weakness. Everyone feels fear. It kept you on guard, and as you said, you were in survival mode because of it. You're alive and safe. Over time your fear will lessen."

Shadow lifted Randy's hand and lightly kissed it before standing and walking to the door. Randy dug his nails into his palm to confirm he wasn't still asleep and all this was a dream.

Randy heard another male voice talking to Shadow on the other side of the door. He couldn't make out what was being said, but for the first time he didn't get that anxious feeling. Randy was starting to believe that Shadow wouldn't betray him. Yeah, his mind was getting there, but his body, not so much. As he reached for the glass of water on the side table, he used both of his hands but they were shaking so badly, he pulled them back and made fists to keep them still.

Shadow came back into the bedroom with a bag in his hand. He set it down beside Randy then brought over a chair and sat beside the bed. In truth he preferred Shadow on the bed.

"I'd like a drink of water." Randy had barely gotten the words out and the glass was pressed to his lips. The water strafed his dry throat, making him cough, but he managed to get a bit down without choking, then took one last sip.

Shadow rechecked the IV, turned and sat down again before he nudged the bright red bag closer to Randy. He couldn't imagine what might be in the bag but whatever it was seemed to bring a smile to Shadow's face, so Randy figured he'd play along. "I might need a little help."

Shadow looked like he was opening a Christmas present as he reached into the bag and began pulling out things Randy never dreamed he'd ever see again. A thick sketchbook bound by metal rings, pencils, a tray of paints with a few brushes in different sizes, colored pencils and pens, everything important that had been taken away from him. There was even a leather case to store it in that he could carry with him.

Randy could feel his heart rate speeding up as he ghosted his hands over the precious objects. His face was heating up and his vision blurred. Shadow moved the art supplies aside and sat on the bed, leaning in to take Randy in his arms. He couldn't hold his emotions back and he didn't care if it made him seem weak. The things he'd longed for the most had been returned to him. Shadow had given him this.

Randy could barely speak when he whispered, "Thank you, Jake."

Chapter Four

Shadow's mom was in the corner chair reading a book when he walked out of his bedroom, leaving Randy asleep. The past forty-eight hours had forever changed Shadow and he was reeling. Without trying, or intending to, Randy had demolished each and every one of the fortifications Shadow had painstakingly erected around himself for the past two decades.

The second step on the stairs from the bottom squeaked, as it had always done since he could remember, even before his father left. Shadow walked into his mom's chef's kitchen, where everything she could ever want or need was at her fingertips. With Shannon's help he'd outfitted the place with an active AI system connected to an independent power supply under the house guaranteed to run twenty-five years without renewal. The AI was set to assist and protect the people in this farmhouse.

"Good afternoon, Shadow. How may I assist?" a voice modeled after his asked. His mom had wanted it to sound like him, she'd said if she couldn't have him around at least she could hear his voice.

"Where are Coop and Spider?"

"Coop is twenty-two meters to the south and Spider is on the front porch."

Shadow walked through the kitchen and down the hallway leading out onto the spacious front porch. Spider stood on the far east side looking out onto the acres of cornfields surrounding the house. Large wheat fields could be seen in the distance, as well as old Mr. Thompson's cattle farm.

"How is Randy?" Spider asked without turning around.

"He's gaining strength every day."

Spider turned and looked Shadow in the eyes. "How long do you think we can keep Grady from his brother?"

"Until we have answers for Randy's fears," Shadow answered.

Spider looked at him closely, too closely. Shadow turned away and looked out onto the fields. He knew his Sentinel brother would be able to read him like a book, and he'd hoped to keep the knowledge to himself, for now.

No such luck.

"You want him."

Shadow wasn't sure what about that statement ticked him off more, the casual way in which Spider had said it, as if Randy were nothing more than a one-night stand, or the fact that Spider was right. "Don't you dare belittle this. He is an amazing man who through no fault of his own has been treated like baggage, something to be stowed away until he was useful or finally remembered. That man has more compassion in his baby finger than all of us," Shadow waved his hand to encompass the farm, "have in our entire bodies and all he asked was to be loved and treated like an equal. That man has managed to mean more to me in the few days I've known him than anyone. Don't assume this is a quick fuck I'll forget before I finish tying up my boots."

Shadow would have preferred to have this conversation with Randy first, but ocean-size emotions were running too close to the surface and Shadow couldn't find his cool for the life of him.

Spider blinked and took a step back with his hands raised. "I have your back, brother."

Shadow dragged in a deep breath and tried to bring his body down from combat ready. He shook out his arms and rolled his neck, loosening as he scanned their surroundings for any threats.

"Look, man, I didn't mean to belittle what you're feeling, but shit, I've never seen you interested in anyone past a quick lay, and even then that was once in a blue moon. Hell, I've never even heard you talk so much at once. I respect what you're saying and your decision. Question, though—does Randy know that you've claimed him?"

And therein lay his concern. What if Randy didn't want him? What if he was simply grateful and didn't feel the same connection as Shadow did? What if he decided to put this all behind him once he was safe? There were too many "what-ifs."

"I see. Well, we'll have to make sure Randy gets to see all your finest qualities," Spider explained. "Now if we could only figure out what those were."

Shadow couldn't help his bark of laughter; leave it to Spider to deescalate with a joke. "Thanks, boss man."

Spider grabbed hold of Shadow's shoulder and gave it a firm squeeze. "Things have a way of working themselves out. The team's here for you."

Shadow nodded before turning and heading for the porch's back stairs. "Going to take a look around, clear my head."

He walked down the well-worn path toward the barns to visit with Meg, his mom's twelve-year-old Appaloosa. As soon as he neared the fence, Meg whinnied from inside the shade-covered barn. Moments later the majestic beauty came prancing out with Oliver, her young billy goat friend, trailing behind.

Meg broke out into a gallop as soon as she saw Shadow and headed straight for him. He and his mom were there the day Meg was born and they'd been family ever since. Meg's mother had passed away a few years before and that was when Oliver joined them. When she was only a few feet away Meg slowed, allowing Oliver to catch up. She lifted her head up over the top of the fence and nuzzled the side of Shadow's face with her soft muzzle.

"Hello, darlin', have you been a good girl?" Shadow crooned as he scratched behind her ears just the way she liked.

Bleating alerted him to another friend who demanded his share of Shadow's attention. He climbed through the rails of the fence and knelt down next to the chubby black-and-white goat. Oliver took advantage of the opportunity and pretty much glued himself to Shadow's side.

As he scratched both four-legged family members, his mind wandered, as it had been doing often, to the man lying in his bed. Now that Randy was recovering, Shadow knew his first order of business should be assuring his continued safety. However, he hadn't even begun questioning him about the camp and what he meant about knowing things. And then, there was the whole issue of Grady.

Shadow knew all his excuses for holding off on moving forward with the investigation part of this "rescue" were little more than deflections. In truth, he believed once everything was settled Randy would return to his life. With no oppressive father to control him, he was free to live as he wished, and would have no desire to take on a worn-out shell of a man who had lived in the shadows for the past twenty years.

Meg's head reared up and her full attention was on the house when Shadow heard the first scream. He vaulted over the fence and sprinted toward the sounds of Randy's terrified yelling.

He saw Coop racing in from the opposite direction before Shadow rounded the house and ran straight through the back. The screen door crashed to the ground behind him after he'd ripped it from its hinges when opening it. He took the stairs two at a time, rushing to get to Randy. Spider was waiting for him on the second-story landing, repeating a single word, "Sorry."

Before Shadow could even acknowledge him, he was through his bedroom door and beside his bed. His mom sat holding Randy in the center of the bed and most of the blankets were scattered across the floor. Shadow climbed onto the bed, took Randy from his mom's arms, and carried him across the room to a cushioned window bench seat. He clung to Shadow and gasped for breath.

"I've got you, you're safe. I won't let anything happen to you."

"Y-you were gone and there…was a huge man hovering over me," Randy managed to say with a shaky voice.

Shadow looked across the room at his mom for answers. He could see Spider, who hadn't followed Shadow in, waiting with Coop in the hallway.

Mom sat on the edge of the bed and spoke in a soft voice as if trying to calm a scared animal. "I'd stepped out of the room to use the bathroom. I was on my way back when I heard him scream and ran in to find Spider setting a tray of food on the side table. It must have been a shock when Randy opened his eyes and found a strange man in the room."

"Terrified. Not shocked, terrified," Shadow growled, and Spider looked up at him through the open doorway. It was plain to see his boss was beside himself with guilt and that served to ratchet Shadow's anger down a few bars.

He looked at his mom, hoping she understood his anger wasn't directed at her. She gifted him with a small smile, letting him know everything was fine. "I believe it's best if we leave these two alone for a while. Perhaps it's time for Randy to meet your friends once this is all settled."

Once he heard the bedroom door close behind her, Shadow stood, removed his boots, and carried Randy back to bed. Shadow would have to recheck all the bandages to make sure nothing had been torn open, but he would wait until he calmed down. Thankfully, Randy was no longer on an IV drip or he surely would have pulled that out. Shadow laid Randy down on the mattress and crawled in beside him before pulling one of the blankets over both of them.

Randy had been quiet since he'd calmed from his initial panic and Shadow hoped all the progress they'd made over the past few days hadn't been lost due to one person's misstep.

***

Randy wished a hole would open up in the earth and swallow him up; he'd hand in his man card on the way down. *When faced with danger what does he do? He screams for help.* No thought of defending himself or even finding out who the hell the guy was. Nope, he screamed and cried like a frightened child. All hope that Shadow would see him for the man he truly was was long forgotten.

"Please look up at me." Shadow didn't sound disappointed but how could he not be. Randy had made a fool of himself in front of Shadow's teammates. People important to him. People who were there to protect him.

Slowly he raised his head. His cheeks were still damp and he was sure he looked as bad as he felt. When their eyes met, Randy froze. Shadow's compassion held no censure and his guilt was almost palpable.

"I'm so sorry. This should have never happened," Shadow apologized. "You trusted me to protect you and the first time I leave you you're confronted by a strange man in our room."

"It's not your fault," Randy was quick to say. After all, Jake couldn't be expected to stay by Randy's side twenty-four seven. And the bastards responsible for the insurmountable fear surging through every thought he had were not the people in this house. *Yeah, but tell my brain that.*

Shadow pulled him closer. "I should have introduced the guys to you, instead of keeping you tucked away up here."

"I like being tucked up here. It wasn't as if I was up for visitors the last couple days. Hell, most of the time I was asleep." Randy sighed. "No one in this house is at fault. The people who've taught me to be afraid are out there," he flicked his fingers, "somewhere."

Shadow closed his eyes and Randy hoped he took what he'd said to heart. His father and the people running that camp were to blame, the ones who sat by while it happened in their own backyards, and the people pounding the "good book" with their fists in indignation whenever asked why they looked the other way.

After a moment, Shadow opened those sage green beauties and looked down at Randy. "Since when do you comfort me? It should be the other way around."

"We all need to be comforted now and again, no matter how big and strong you are."

Shadow smiled and slowly released Randy so that he could lean back against the pillows. He went around the room and picked up a stray pillow and blankets he'd kicked off in his attempt at getting away.

"I think it's time to get you out of this room. I'll get you a pair of drawstring shorts and we'll go down and make the introductions I should have done yesterday. Then we can eat out on the covered porch before your shower."

Several things excited Randy about that statement. Going outside into the fresh air, being able to apologize to Spider when they were introduced, and best of all, his upcoming shower. So far, he'd been having sponge baths, but now he'd progressed to standing for short periods, and he had a special leaning post. And in the shower meant an almost naked Shadow. Almost, only because the big guy had said he'd keep his underwear on. *Why bother?*

Come on, who in their right mind wouldn't want to see Shadow naked? There was only so much willpower a man could be expected to have when coming face-to-face with everything he'd ever wanted.

Shadow rechecked Randy's injuries before he dressed in a red t-shirt with gold letters that read "Semper Fi." The drawstring shorts, with a Marine logo, were several sizes too big. Randy looked down at the writing across his chest. "Do all your t-shirts have Marine sayings or logos on them?"

Shadow laughed, making Randy smile even wider. "Well, you can say I don't stray much from what I know."

"I could take you shopping for a few new things…I mean…um." Brilliant. Insinuate yourself into Shadow's life much?

Before Randy could get too carried away, Shadow said, "Sounds like a perfect plan. We can go over to Houston." Randy waited for the punch line but it never came. "Deal?"

He nodded, his head bobbling like one of those stupid toys people put on the dashboards of their cars.

Shadow carried Randy down the staircase and into an airy country kitchen complete with raw beams, milk glass lighting, and what looked like white oak built-ins. The oversize white porcelain sink matched the white six-burner stove and the huge double-door refrigerator. This was what a real *home* looked like. "It's beautiful."

"Well, thank you," Jo responded from the large island where she sat drinking what smelled like coffee. "Jake and I designed it." Randy wasn't surprised that Shadow had a hand in this.

"Where are Spider and Coop?" Shadow asked.

"Out on the porch."

"Thanks."

Shadow carried Randy down the hallway and out an open doorway. A screen door lay on the ground a few feet away. The man who had scared the crap out of him was busy attaching a new hinge as a second man kept watch in the far corner.

"You have anything to do with that?" Randy asked and then watched in fascination as Jake blushed.

"I was in kind of a hurry," he said by way of explanation.

Hearing their voices, the other men turned and the one named Spider straightened away from the doorjamb. Randy wasn't sure what to say. Shadow spoke up, "Randy, I would like to introduce you to Spider, one of our team's leaders and Coop, the blond-haired used-to-be manwhore."

"Hey, don't go spreading my secrets, man." Coop laughed as he walked toward them, and Randy could see why. Those blue eyes sparkled, while his sharp cheek and jawbones gave him a young Cary Grant kind of masculinity. Gorgeous, no doubt, but no one could compare to Shadow.

After Coop shook his hand, Randy turned to Spider and said, "I'm sorry."

Spider's mouth hung open for a second before he asked, "Why are you sorry? I'm the one who screwed up."

"You were trying to do something nice for me. I overreacted."

"I should have never gone in without checking first."

"No, you're here to help protect me and I screamed at you."

"Well…"

"That's enough," Shadow cut in. "Now let's try this again. Randy, I would like you to meet Spider."

Randy got the hint and simply held out his hand for the other man to shake. "It's nice to meet you."

Spider breathed deep and took Randy's hand. "It's good to meet you as well, Randy." And in that moment on the porch they started over again, which made him happy.

Over the next two hours, Randy, bundled into an oversize patio chair, ate lunch—he'd graduated to mushy things from liquid—and listened to the teammates try to out-danger each other by reliving a few of their missions.

It felt normal and homey; even Jo got in some jabs with stories about Shadow when he was a child. It didn't come as much of a shock to find out his teenage years were spent racing around the farm in anything with an engine he could find and fix. One thing that struck Randy as odd was that neither of them mentioned Shadow's father.

Randy was flagging, but he didn't want to leave the comfort of decent people and easy conversation. But nothing got by Shadow. "Ready to go back inside?" Shadow asked him what he wanted, and didn't order him around.

"Yeah. I guess I'm a bit wiped."

Shadow helped Randy stand on his shaky legs, giving him the boost he needed before being lifted into Shadow's arms. Bit by bit, Randy's strength was returning and each day brought him closer to his independence.

Hard-won, and getting there was not without scars. Yet, he wondered, could he be independent and still share his life with someone?

All musings fled at the next four words out of Shadow's mouth. "Time for your shower."

Chapter Five

Randy felt as though he were in a fog as Shadow walked past their bedroom and into the bathroom. He set Randy on top of the long vanity between the two sinks before turning to shut the door. Randy's heart was racing at the thought of Shadow in the shower, and other parts of Randy's body perked up at that idea in an obvious way. *Damn.*

"Huh?" Shadow asked.

"What?"

"Damn."

"Did I say that out loud?"

"Yep, I've noticed you sometimes voice your personal thoughts."

This was news to Randy. "I do?" How much had he said?

"You've done it three times now. Not complete phrases, just a word here and there."

Oh thank god, he'd only said the word "damn" and hadn't voiced what he was really thinking about. "I'm used to being alone…"

"Shit." Shadowed dropped his head. "Sorry, man. Really. Total idiot here."

Randy wanted to reach out and lay his hand on Shadow's shoulder. "Jake." Shadow's head jerked up and he locked his gaze on Randy. "I'm not made of glass, and I don't need you to tiptoe around me. Yeah, I have my moments, and if I need you to back off, I think you get by now, I'll tell you. 'Kay?"

Shadow drew in a deep breath. "'Kay." He waited a beat and seemed to map Randy's face, then pulled his shirt over his head.

Randy bit his tongue. He sure as hell wasn't going to blurt out what was going through his mind.

Shadow's muscles flexed, emphasizing the tattoo covering his arm and half his chest. An American eagle with a streamer in its mouth proclaiming "Semper Fidelis" flew in front of the flag. Over his strong shoulder and down his bicep were pieces of medieval armor that seemed so lifelike that Randy wanted to trace the outline with his tongue. And, upon closer inspection, he could make out an odd scar under the dark ink.

He knew Shadow had asked him something but for the life of him, he didn't catch what it was. "Huh?"

Shadow chuckled. "Can you take off your shirt or do you need my help?"

Randy reached back and grabbed the neck of his shirt and then pulled it over his head.

Shadow smiled and pulled down his jeans then stepped out of them. *Gulp.* All that was Shadow was bared to Randy except what was covered by his white boxer briefs, but there wasn't much left to the imagination. His pronounced bulge commanded all of Randy's attention.

Until that moment, Randy hadn't believed physical attraction could make the air charge with electricity.

Shadow didn't move and Randy couldn't breathe.

Spider's voice yelling something to Coop broke the spell. Shadow moved forward. His long fingers made easy work of the drawstring on Randy's shorts and in the work of a moment he found himself naked while still sitting on the vanity.

Randy tried to hide his hard-on from Shadow, but knew it was a futile exercise. He turned his head away and tried to think of baseball, but then he imagined Shadow in those tight pants. Randy changed the scenario—he was watering a garden, which turned into Shadow wetting his body down with the hose. Those tiny droplets of water glistening as they caressed every muscle while skimming down his hard body. *I'm doomed.*

When he turned back, that spectacularly muscled chest was directly in front of him. Randy hadn't even heard him move. Shadow gently pulled Randy's hands to his side, causing him to look up into eyes that were several shades darker than before.

"Don't hide from me," Shadow whispered. "You're beautiful and I'm relieved to see this isn't one-sided."

"This?"

"Attraction," Shadow said before rubbing the hard bulge in his underwear against Randy's uninjured leg.

"You're attracted to me?" Randy asked, wanting to clarify he hadn't misunderstood.

"Oh yeah," Shadow confirmed before running his hand along Randy's thigh. "But…." There was always a "but" in there somewhere. He knew it couldn't be that simple, at least not for him. His shoulders sagged. Shadow grinned before continuing, "But I won't act on it until you've had more time to heal and give me the go-ahead."

Randy waited for the other shoe to fall, and then waited some more, surprised when it didn't. All right. This was a sympathy fuck thing. Poor Randy, kidnapped and sent to a hell camp. "Me?"

"Why not you? You're compassionate, kind, caring, strong, and beautiful. You make me feel happier and *lighter* than I have in more years than I'd like to admit. You've reminded me of the man I used to be." Shadow's expression changed. "Unless I have this wrong."

"What? Are you crazy?" Randy shouted, making that sexy smile return to Shadow's face. He didn't want there to be any question about it. Randy had never imagined the man he found himself drawn to would be drawn to him. Experiences had taught him not to count on reciprocated feelings.

Shadow was honorable and genuine. What you saw was what you got. Which was so refreshing. He treated him as an equal and had gained Randy's trust, which was not an easy thing normally, after everything he had been through these past few months, near impossible,

"Let's get you in the shower," Shadow said before walking over and turning on the water. He placed a slanted wood bench under the rainfall stream then came back for Randy. "Ready to give it a shot?"

Shadow stood with his arm out and Randy knew what was about to happen meant a whole lot more than a shower. He drew in a deep breath, then said, "Right by your side, Jake."

As he bent forward, Shadow's jaw jumped and he seemed to be tense. Catching Randy under his knee, Shadow lifted him and Randy had no choice but to throw his arms around Shadow's broad shoulders. The warmth of his skin caused every nerve ending in Randy's body to spark. Shadow rechecked the temperature and then stepped into the steam-filled shower.

The hot water pulsed over him with soothing relief and his stress was slowly washed away. He couldn't help but close his eyes and moan in relief. An answering groan had him opening his eyes and he found himself caught in Shadow's heated gaze. In that moment all he wanted was Shadow's mouth covering his, and for the first time in his life, Randy took what he wanted.

When their lips met, the world melted away and this magnificent, deep wet kiss was the only thing that mattered. The warmth of Shadow's tongue as he took control made Randy's knees weak. When Shadow nibbled across Randy's jaw and followed with more kisses to ease the sting, Randy couldn't help but rub his hard cock against Shadow.

"Touch me," Randy moaned in desperation. "Please, I need…"

"I've got you," Shadow assured as he leaned Randy against the tiled wall. The body sprayers were brushing over his sensitive skin, heightening his need. Randy wondered if he'd ever felt this out of control while knowing he had nothing to fear.

Shadow supported Randy's body with one arm while wrapping his hand around Randy's aching cock as the water and mist engulfed them. Each stroke of his work-roughened hands sent Randy higher. His mouth was captured in Shadow's devouring kiss and his balls pulled up tight as his legs fell open while fire raced down his spine, through his balls and out the end of his cock.

Before he could catch his breath, Shadow scooped him up and cradled him as they sat on the wooden bench under a slower stream of water. Randy wanted to yell at the top of his lungs at the same time he wanted to be anywhere but in Shadow's lap, a reminder of how he wasn't strong enough to be a whole man. Again.

He watched as Shadow poured body wash onto a cloth before soaping up Randy's legs. The tender way in which he avoided Randy's injuries made him fall a bit deeper, while reinforcing his invalid status. He hated being weak around Shadow, and Randy cursed that he couldn't do more. "Wish I could repay the favor."

Shadow's chest rumbled when he laughed. "Don't worry about me, babe, I received as much pleasure watching you fall apart in my arms."

***

Shadow rechecked the cushions behind Randy's back as everyone gathered in the living room. Shadow knew he was way off the scale when it came to overprotectiveness, but Randy had just had the last of his stitches removed.

"I'm much stronger now, Jake. You don't have to worry about me." Randy tried to reason with him, but Shadow would have none of it.

"Let him fuss. It looks good on him." His mom laughed as she sat down on a nearby couch, joined by Spider, Coop, Dante, and Police Chief Dave Graham. The last two had arrived early this morning with Dave dressed in his street clothes. Files were open on a nearby coffee table. He already knew everything that was in them, but it was time to involve Randy in the investigation.

Shadow sat down in a chair right beside the man who'd come to be one of the most important people in his life. It had been almost two weeks since they'd first met, and some would say that it was too soon to feel the way he felt. He didn't give a damn what anyone else thought. He knew all too well the pain of regret, the evil that lurks beneath the surface, the stench of death and the cries of suffering from mothers burying their children. No one had the right to tell him he didn't know what love felt like, when to feel it, or what to feel when those amber eyes looked into his soul and still found him worthy. If someone didn't understand their connection, then they could go fuck themselves.

"As Shadow has explained, Randy, we're building a case against the Fellowship so that we can bring in the state police and FBI. The local authorities have been compromised; therefore, they will be of no assistance. There hasn't been much movement at the camp. It's as if they carried on after you escaped without concern you might go to the police. They had to have known you had help. It was pretty obvious."

"That peace won't be lasting for much longer," Randy remarked and seemed to catch himself at the last minute before carrying on.

"What do you know?" Dave asked. "We need your help to shut them down."

Randy reached for Shadow's hand, which he gave immediately.

"Would you prefer to talk alone?" Dave asked.

Randy shook his head. "They are part of my family. I trust them with my life."

He looked over to Shadow's mom, who was nodding her agreement. "These are members of the Sentinels and they are family to us."

Randy seemed to weigh his options before asking, "If I go to jail, will you still want me?"

The question was so far off-the-wall that it was in another building. Shadow sat dumbfounded until Spider spoke. "Whatever happened, you were a prisoner at the time and whatever you were forced to do was under duress."

What Spider said was the truth, but Randy still hadn't looked away from Shadow. Thankfully, he managed to get his shit together. "I would stand by your side through hell and back."

Randy turned to look at the men in front of him. The team knew all of Randy's details and understood that even though he had been healing, the physical repercussions of having been a prisoner were healing far faster than the emotional manifestations ever could. In the end, it was up to Randy how much he chose to share and when. Shadow wasn't lying; he'd stand with Randy no matter what he decided and where it led them.

"I've been thinking about allowing Tristan to be here. Is it still okay for him to come?" Randy asked Dante.

"Of course," Dante assured, his posture relaxed and open. Shadow knew his boss was trying to be less intimidating. "Tristan will want to bring Vincent, his partner. He is part of our team as well."

"It's nice to know Tristan has someone to look out for him now. Shadow explained that Tristan's crazy ex and a fan had been stalking him. I'm happy he's finally safe." Randy's tone seemed even, but Shadow could tell he was nervous.

"We were considering bringing the entire team here until this is settled and those responsible are behind bars. What do you think?" Spider asked.

Shadow appreciated his team involving Randy in the decision-making process. He knew how much it meant to him.

"I don't know. Is it okay for you, Jo? I don't want to make you more inconvenienced than you already are." Shadow couldn't help but smile. Randy's first thought was for someone else. Yep, Shadow loved that man. He hadn't told Randy that though. Shadow didn't want to scare him off.

"Oh, don't worry, honey. These boys know how to clean up after themselves," mom assured with a wink.

"Okay," Randy answered Spider. "But not Grady. Not yet."

That was the first time Randy had mentioned his brother's name without being provoked since his first days of freedom. Grady had admitted to not calling Randy after moving to Brighton. Grady explained he'd meant to before the incident with Travis and his disciplinary hearing. Then there was the shooting and his father's attack, but he swore he never received any of Randy's phone calls for help.

Earlier today, Randy had listened as Dante repeated what Grady had told them and answered with one word, "Tristan." It took Shadow and the others a few moments to make the connection. Grady had been shot in the line of duty, not seriously but he had a few days off on medical leave. He'd called Tristan, who was living in Dallas at the time, and the two went on a small holiday to the coast. Not once thinking of the brother he'd left behind to deal with a lunatic.

The room grew quiet yet again. The tension grew to the point that Shadow was ready to call an end to it, but Randy finally spoke. "It's always confused me when people assume artists can't possibly be good at anything else or they'd be doing that instead." Shadow knew a rhetorical statement when he heard one and stayed silent. "See, I have this gift, or curse, depending on your point of view. How much has Grady told you about me?"

Shadow could hear the pain in Randy's voice when he said his brother's name. Everyone in the room had to feel it.

"We know the basics, age, career, and, uh, family concerns," Coop stated.

Randy broke out laughing, dispelling the seriousness hanging over the room. "Concerns is a delicate way to put it. Thank you, Coop. Unfortunately, the truth is much harsher. My dad didn't start out resembling the monster he turned into. There was a time that we were a happy family."

Shadow watched as Randy's eyes fixed on a spot on the coffee table as he relived the past. "When I was a toddler I excelled in math. Years later, I was pushed forward grade after grade until my parents took me to be tested. In the end the doctors claimed I had an eidetic memory with an affinity for numbers."

Randy turned to Shadow, who nodded for him to continue.

"Soon after that I found my passion in the arts, and with my paintings I gained my freedom. Needless to say, my parents weren't pleased by my choice in careers and fought me at every turn. Once my paintings began bringing in an income, as well as giving dear old Dad a few pointers on his investments, they backed off. But I knew my father was disappointed I didn't use my *ability* to make buckets of money in investments or become a CEO of some faceless corporation. I heard the depth of it when he was in a drunken rage on my twenty-fifth birthday. Over the years my father turned into someone I didn't even recognize, but after Grady left,

the old man really let his crazy out." Randy shivered and Shadow rubbed his arm.

"No one talked about it after he lost it. My mother and sister walked on eggshells in the house and spent as much time away from the house as they could. I didn't have much of a relationship with my father by then, but I had no idea what he had planned, and what my mother and sister allowed. Not until the sack was pulled off my head on my first day at the camp and I knew my family had sold me out."

The air in the room was still and everyone seemed to be holding their breath.

"It didn't take long to realize that after the Fellowship doled out their fair share of hate and bible-thumping bigotry that I had a purpose. They knew I could make them money and set about doing that."

"How did they want you to make money for them?" Jo asked.

"The Fellowship goes by many different names with dozens of branches across the US and overseas. Now imagine that each one of those has a minimum of three accounts, one legal and ready for anything the IRS could throw at it, and the others are all accounts in banks in the Caymans."

"How many accounts do they have?" Dave asked, pen at the ready.

"One hundred forty-eight separate numbered accounts, from twenty-six different Fellowship branches," Randy answered before tapping the side of head. "This is where my eidetic memory comes in. Once I see something, I remember it. I'm able to scan through countless pages of statistics, rumors, facts, history, trends, hype, and multiple other resources in the time it takes for a typical person to get ready in the morning."

"So they were having you investing money for them?" Coop asked.

"That and much more. As they began seeing returns on their money, the head of the camp, Mr. Bowen, gave me greater access until eventually, I was moving millions of dollars daily between branches and the various numbered accounts. That's when I knew I had them."

"Mr. Bowen?" Dante asked as he wrote on his notepad.

Shadow could feel another tremor work its way down Randy's hand before he turned to look at him. "He's the one you saw giving me these." Randy pointed to the whip marks.

Shadow couldn't stop the angry growl that worked its way up from his chest. Randy had worked so hard to convince everyone he was dealing with all the abuse he had suffered, but Shadow knew differently. And it pissed him off. He couldn't help his reaction. "Out," he shouted before standing and taking Randy in his arms. The team filed out without another word. His mom softly closed the large pocket doors between the kitchen and the living room.

"We don't have to continue if you want to stop," Shadow offered as he felt Randy bury his face further into Shadow's chest. "I'll tell them we're done for now."

He turned with the intention of taking Randy upstairs when he said, "No, I have to tell them everything. You'll need to know before things start to happen."

Shadow didn't like the sound of that, but he'd try to make this as comfortable for Randy as possible. "You seemed to like sitting out on the porch, do you want to talk out there?"

Randy's amber eyes were glassy with unshed tears. "I'd like that."

Shadow held Randy close before heading for the doors and out into the kitchen. Everyone was sitting around the kitchen island when they walked in. More than one of them hadn't had time to hide their anger, leading to Randy misinterpreting their behavior.

"Sorry. I didn't mean to make anyone angry."

The men stood and got themselves back in check. "They're not angry with you," Shadow explained. He knew his team as well as he knew himself. "They're angry at the people who did this to you."

"I'd love to have the opportunity to snap the asshole in half." Coop even went as far as miming the action as he spoke.

"This Bowen person had better hope there's enough left of him to give to the police." Spider clenched his hands into fists.

Shadow wondered if the mention of more violence might set Randy off, but he laughed, and shook his head. "I wished I'd met all of you earlier; things would have turned out so differently. You would have noticed if I went missing."

"You won't be going missing ever again. They'd have to get through me first," Shadow stated.

"Us," Dante was quick to say.

Chapter Six

Randy sat down in his favorite oversize chair and sank into the plush blue cushions. He gathered all the strength he could muster and knew he had to tell them the rest no matter if it led to his arrest or, worse, if he lost Shadow's regard. Randy wasn't fooled by the intensity of the situation. He knew once they returned to their lives that the likelihood he and Shadow could be anything more than friends was slim to none. But Randy would take what he could get—he couldn't fathom not having Shadow in his life.

With a deep breath he continued. "Bowen gave me access, assuming the beatings had made me docile." Various grumbles broke out, which he ignored before carrying on. "With each passing day I was watched less and less, until I would go for hours without anyone else in the office. I used my time to track down every penny and every person involved. The conversion therapy camps were used as a front for gun and drug running, with a side of prostitution and money laundering. Really, who would look into these good ol' boys out here in the middle of nowhere trying to reform the gays? These organizations are spread across multiple states and international borders intentionally."

"You can remember all of this down to the last person and account number?" Dave asked, unable to hold back his excitement. This was a multi-jurisdictional criminal organization, which would require the FBI and CIA's participation.

"Yes." It was as simple as that and equally as complicated. "You might not like where that leads. It's not only the local authorities involved."

"If they're involved, they'll get what's coming to them, but I think it might be a good idea to get those names before we decide who to involve in our investigation." Randy agreed with Dave's logic.

"I can have it written out for you by tomorrow night, but there's always the chance I didn't find them all."

"We'll get as many as we can."

"There is something else you should know." Randy searched out Shadow's hand and held on tight. "Bowen will come looking for me soon. I'm not sure why he hasn't already. Perhaps he doesn't realize how big a threat I am."

"Why are you sure he'll come?" Coop asked from his spot on the porch railing.

"Because I set him up. My fascination with numbers leaked over into computer programming. Add in a few hacker buddies and let's say I developed skills. I employed those skills on the Fellowship's computers." Randy gave the group a small grin. "If I don't log into a file I buried deep inside their network within a certain number of days, it will begin an unstoppable chain of events. Branch by branch, accounts will start emptying. The money will be redirected into an account I opened in Bowen's name. In case they killed me I wasn't going down alone." Randy didn't care what it said about him that Bowen would suffer an untimely death at the Fellowship's hands.

"I don't understand. Why would you want to give that horrible man any money?" Jo asked, but before Randy could answer, Shadow spoke.

"He doesn't know about it?" Shadow's eyes lit up.

"Nope," Randy answered.

"He has no access to it," Dante stated and Randy was relieved they'd caught on.

"None."

"It will appear as if Bowen stole the money from the others," Spider added.

"Exactly. One by one, accounts will drain and no one will be able to stop it. The paper trail will lead back to Bowen while the money will be safely tucked away in another part of the world. I even threw in a couple dead ends so when his colleagues start looking for their money, it will seem as if Bowen had tried to hide it."

"How?" Coop asked, looking stunned. "That's some serious hacker ability you got there. I know you're making it seem so easy, but I'm guessing it's not."

"It's good to have a hobby," Randy said by way of an explanation. The technical explanation was his to know. "I had months of access, and as long as the investments showed a return they didn't bother with me. Until I'd become distracted." Randy turned to Shadow. "Like that day you said you saw me through your binoculars. Sometimes I become lost when creating."

"You are an artist. It's to be expected," Shadow declared as if this were common knowledge. Randy wished more people understood that.

"Shannon and Matthew are going to love you," Coop said with an evil grin. "With the three of you we could take over a small country, but it has to be tropical. I'm done with sand without palm trees and drinks with those little umbrellas in them."

Randy couldn't help but like Coop. He never held anything back. Plus, Shannon and Matthew sounded like people he wanted to meet.

"When does the chain reaction start?" Dante asked. Randy had noticed that Dante was always focused on the facts.

"Midnight tonight."

That got everyone's attention.

"Tonight?" Shadow asked.

"Yes, and there's no way to stop it now. You have to understand, I did all this under the assumption I'd be dead." Randy then looked at Dave. "I realize what I've done is a criminal act. I accept that."

Randy knew Shadow was on edge, but he wasn't sure if it was because of what he did, or the danger he had put them in. "I'm sorry."

Shadow turned to Randy. "Don't apologize. You did what you had to do."

Randy tilted his head. "They even had a file on which public officials were bought off or blackmailed. They don't have it now. I buried it so deep that whatever scandal they had proof of is long gone. Saved where no one would think to look."

"You managed to get a lot done," Dave stated, and Randy could hear a touch of disbelief in his voice.

Randy looked him straight in the eyes and said. "Police Chief David Edward Graham, born June sixth, nineteen eighty, married to Kate Rose Mason Graham, pediatric nurse with Brighton General. One daughter named Kimberly Elizabeth, but everyone calls her Kimmy. Your babysitter is Jessica Fowler, aged seventeen, lives four doors down from that big, beautiful Victorian house of yours. Do you wish me to continue, perhaps reveal your salary, social security number, or the rate you received when you renegotiated your mortgage? By the way, you were smart to lock that in."

Dave's brows were in the middle of his forehead.

Randy smiled. "I did that with a borrowed smartphone in under thirty minutes. Imagine what I could do with months of single-minded hatred. Every beat of my heart drove me forward." Randy had spent his life proving himself to other people, and guessed this was no different. He couldn't help but be a touch disappointed.

Everyone was quiet until Dave finally spoke. "I need to apologize. I shouldn't have doubted you. I'm sorry."

Randy could tell that Dave meant it. "That's okay, you're a police officer. You need to question to get to the truth."

"Thanks." Dave nodded and got right back to business. "You'll have those names for me by tomorrow night and then we can come up with a game plan."

Dante flipped over the page on his notepad and asked, "Where is the money going?"

"Into a secure bank account."

"Can you be more specific?"

"No."

Shadow looked at him. "Why won't you share the account information?"

"Because this is my load to carry. I'm the only person who knows the account number and its location. If I were to share that information with you, then Bowen would come after you. Right now, I'm the only target and I prefer to keep it that way. Besides, I put a fail-safe on it that will trigger an order to distribute all the money as anonymous donations to over twenty different charitable organizations."

"You've been busy," Jo noted with a smirk on her face.

"I had a lot of time to devote to it," Randy replied. Dante's phone rang. When he stood to answer it, Randy turned to Shadow, who was watching him closely. "Are you upset with me?"

Shadow's eyebrows furrowed before he asked, "Why would I be upset with you?"

"Because I didn't tell you. Because I signed the death warrant on another man." Randy had no idea what came over him or where this overwhelming feeling of guilt was coming from. "It's not as if that was the end result I was looking for, but it was the only logical way to shut these people down. And why shouldn't he pay for what he's done?"

Shadow was up and out of the chair before Randy could even realize he had tears streaming down his cheeks. When had he started crying? He closed his eyes, suddenly feeling more tired than he had in days.

Doors opened and closed, but he barely noticed as he questioned his motives, his actions, and their repercussions. By the time his back touched the mattress, he'd worked himself up so much he was gasping for air. Some tough cyber warrior he was, crying at the thought of someone being hurt because of something he did. Even though that someone was a cruel, murdering drug trafficker.

Shadow lay down beside him before he pulled the blankets up to cover them. Randy berated himself as Shadow lay silently holding him. This was nobody else's weight to bear. He'd made his choice many months ago and he would stand by it.

"Shadow?"

"Yes, love."

"Am I a horrible person?" Randy asked before it hit him that Shadow had called him love. "Love?"

Shadow chuckled. "You are not a horrible person, Randy. I've met and disposed of truly evil people. People who have killed hundreds and thousands of innocent people for no better reason than worshipping differently than themselves. Evil people who burn down schoolhouses with the children still inside, or kidnap people to sell to the highest bidder. Those are the kinds of horrible, evil people who I try to protect the world from. You, Randy, are not even a touch evil or horrible, proven by what you're feeling right now."

"What do you mean?"

Shadow rolled onto his side, never once losing contact with him, and looked down into Randy's eyes. "Do you think that truly evil and horrible people care if someone is hurt? I can tell you with absolute certainty that their only concern is getting what they want and terrorizing people into doing it. Bowen never stopped to care about the people he was hurting in that camp, or from his drugs and guns. He wouldn't have and that's what makes you one of the good guys. You didn't steal the money for your own gain. The only people getting hurt are the criminals themselves and those helping them. I don't want you to feel any guilt for this. You did what you had to do, and I would have done the same thing if I had anything beyond a basic operating knowledge of computer systems."

Randy looked up into Shadow's expressive green eyes, the rust-colored ridge around his irises seemed to stand out in stark contrast.

He understood what Shadow was saying and imagined in time he would be able to live with it. However, at the moment he felt unsure.

"Oh, and yes 'love.'" Shadow finished and rolled back onto his back.

Randy's head popped up so fast that it swam a little. After blinking a few times to clear away the fuzzy feeling, he crawled on top of Shadow's chest. "What do you mean, Jake?"

Shadow cupped Randy's face, looked him straight in the eye, and said, "I love you, Randy. I know it's early on in this relationship, but if you'll have this old Marine I'd be mighty thankful."

Randy couldn't help but break out into a smile. He was happy for the first time in a long while. Even before his mother, sister, and brother abandoned him to his father's designs. He was about to throw caution to the wind to share how he felt when someone began banging on their bedroom door.

He lowered his head to Shadow's chest and let out a frustrated huff. "I think that's for you," Randy groaned.

Shadow reached up and kissed him softly. Randy had learned how affectionate the big guy could be. They kissed, cuddled, held hands, and all Randy wanted to do now was melt into Shadow and tell him he'd fallen in love with him as well, but the knocking continued.

Randy rolled off Shadow, allowing him to stand to answer the door. Dante stood on the other side, said a few words, and handed Shadow a writing pad. Randy understood they needed the information stuck in his head to ensure the safety of everyone. He stood and reached for his new messenger bag and walked over to the window seat built into the window facing the back of the house and the barns.

After he sat down, he pulled out all his belongings, which consisted of the art supplies Shadow had given him and a few new sketches he'd been working on. Shadow had already arranged for his storage locker to be emptied out and what was left of his paintings were safely delivered to the Sentinels' compound. He heard the door shut and looked up to watch the gorgeous man who had captured his heart walk toward him.

Shadow sat down and picked up one of his rough sketches. "This is bold and vibrant. Are you trying something new? Because it's stunning. I can't wait to see it on a canvas."

"You don't think it's too bold, the forms and colors? My prior pieces were more representative of a different time in my life. Creating an atmosphere, concepts, and feelings that are new to me have come out in my recent work."

"You're reinventing yourself."

"I think it's time."

"It's beautiful. It feels as if it was, or should be, accompanied by music. The shapes feel almost heavy or daunting, while the colors bring in a sense of hope."

Randy sat back in awe. The man had no formal knowledge of Randy's art form but picked up on all the minute details behind his emotion. He slid his supplies out of the way and knelt on the bench in front of Shadow before wrapping his arms around his neck.

"You are awe-inspiring. You actually get me and my craziness. I love you, Jake."

Shadow's face lit up and he pulled Randy onto his lap. No words, but Shadow's mouth did all the talking he needed when he slanted his head and laid his lips on Randy's. The all-encompassing kiss was everything. Shadow's tongue explored and commanded him easily, while passionate moans filled the air and his body. Randy wrapped his legs around Shadow's waist and arched his neck back as Shadow nibbled his way down Randy's neck. He couldn't help rubbing his hard cock against Shadow's rippled abdomen.

Randy hadn't ever felt a need for someone this encompassing in his entire life. The world could be exploding outside their door and he would have never known. Well, up until Shadow's phone began to ring. They pulled back. Shadow's pupils were dilated, his nostrils flared, and his face was flushed. Hot, sticky sex screamed from his chiseled face, and Randy could do nothing about it.

The phone rang again and slowly Randy backed down and returned to his original seat on the window-bench while Shadow looked at his cell. He didn't look pleased about having to stop, and Randy commiserated.

"I have to go. There's been some recent movement back at the camp, and considering I've been studying it for the longest, I need to check it out."

"I understand. Go protect people."

"You are not people to me. You are the man I love and want to spend my life with. There are no limits to what I'd do for you."

Randy felt that punch through his chest. "I love you too, Jake. Be careful."

"I will. I have you to come back to now. Coop and Dave will be staying here while Spider, Dante, and I go back. The rest of the team will be arriving by tomorrow afternoon so you'll have lots of people to get to know."

Randy couldn't help but feel anxious about that, but he buried it. Shadow didn't need another thing to worry about. "That'll be exciting."

"They are my team, my friends, and my family. I trust them with your life. If something happens, listen to them, they'll protect you."

"I will." Randy agreed as he picked up the blank notepad. "Besides, I'm going to be busy. It'll help keep me out of trouble."

Shadow stood and after one last kiss, he left the bedroom. Randy pulled his knees up to his chest and stared out of his window and onto the endless fields of green. He couldn't help but smile at the realization that the person he loved, loved him back. Had he ever felt his love reflected back to him in equal measure?

Chapter Seven

Shadow watched as the last of the trucks were loaded with filing cabinets and office equipment. Five other trucks had already left with GPS trackers attached to their frames. It had taken the three team members hours to get close enough to pull that off without being seen. Even then Shadow was the one with the most skill when it came to remaining unseen, so he'd placed the devices. Now there was no chance they couldn't find these people again, unless they found the devices, and Shadow made sure that wasn't going to happen. The team had spread out into the surrounding forest, but he lay hidden only ten feet away from the last cube van. He didn't care that the staff, including Bowen, had already left. What he was after was in this innocuous white van.

He heard various beeps in his earpiece confirming the team had gotten into position. The full moon shone through the passing clouds, bathing everything in its silver glow. It would be more difficult for him to go unseen in these conditions, but it wasn't impossible. He slowed his breathing and cleared his mind. His vision sharpened as he took his first steps out into the clearing less than five feet behind a guard with "US ARMY" tattooed on his left forearm and a dagger wrapped in an American flag on his other.

The sight made Shadow furious. This fuckwit dishonored his pledge and instead used his knowledge and training to hurt innocent people. Shadow noted the handguns holstered to the guard's hips and an AK-47 leaning against the front driver's wheel.

One by one, the guards led their prisoners to the back of the van, never once spotting the danger only a few feet away. He could feel his team's eyes on him and was positive that two or more sights were honed in on the last two remaining guards, but the team knew they needed them alive to get answers.

This was the first time Shadow was able to get a good look at the remaining camp prisoners. Each of the men had visible bruising and were extremely thin, much like Randy had been. They were all fairly young-looking, and so far he hadn't seen anyone above the age of thirty. Shadow slid under the van and positioned himself beside the open driver's door. When he heard their retreating steps, he slid out of his hiding place, pulled the keys from the ignition, grabbed the AK, and vanished back into the trees.

From his perch halfway up a leafy oak tree, Shadow watched as they returned carrying a stretcher. The man on it didn't look like the rest; he had to be in his late thirties with a muscular frame. His right leg didn't look right. It appeared to bend forward, which made Shadow suspect the man's knee was broken. While all the prisoners were handcuffed, whoever his guy was had been tied to the stretcher, telling Shadow that the guards viewed him as the biggest threat. Interesting.

They slid the stretcher into the back of the van, and one of the other four prisoners knelt down and wrapped his arms, which were still handcuffed, around the bigger man's neck before breaking into tears. The same guard with the tattoos laughed before shutting the back of the van.

"The asshole is mine," Shadow whispered into the tiny microphone built into his collar. The responding beeps confirmed he'd been heard.

The two Fellowship guards turned and walked to the cab of the panel van, jumped into the front seats, and were about to shut their doors when the second guard stopped. "Where are the keys, man?"

The first guard hopped out of the driver's seat and walked around to the front tire. "Where's my gun?"

Shadow watched as the realization dawned on the asshole's face and he reached for his handgun. Before he had the chance to pull it out three red dots appeared on the guy's chest and he froze. He knew he was fucked.

The second guard came around the front of the truck at the same time his partner was slowly raising his hands. "What the hell are you doing?"

Shadow targeted the second man over his heart, which shut him up as he raised his hands along with the first guy.

"Use the thumb and index finger of your left hand to remove your guns from their holsters and throw them away from you." Dante's voice seemed to roar in the silence of the forest.

The guards threw their guns away and Shadow jumped down from the tree, never once taking his eyes off them. Spider emerged from under a nearby cottage while Dante walked down the hill overlooking the main building. Shadow kicked the guns on the ground farther away before picking them up, emptying them and stuffing them into a pack he'd been carrying.

Spider had both men sitting on the ground with their hands tied, and Shadow couldn't help but be disappointed. He'd hoped to get a crack at that one asshole, but the guy had given up easily.

Shadow joined Dante at the back of the van where the door was open. Shadow pulled the keys he'd removed from the ignition out of his pocket and looked for the one to the handcuffs. Once he found the key, he began setting the five of them free. Dante cut the ropes binding the larger man to his stretcher, but as of yet none of them had spoken.

"You're safe now," Dante said, but still no one made a sound. All of them looked at Dante and Shadow with suspicion. He'd seen that look before, when he'd come to rescue Randy.

"This isn't some sort of Fellowship setup. We're real and we're here to get all of you out," Shadow assured.

One of the younger men inched forward and Shadow stepped back, not wanting to crowd him. He took a quick peek around the edge of open door and said, “There’s only one other man out there and the guards are tied up.”

“How did you know about the Fellowship and us being set up as games for their enjoyment?” the big guy asked while the smaller man who had been hugging him now hid behind him.

“We know they do fucked-up shit and we’re here to get you to a safe place to recover.” Shadow tilted up his chin. “What’s your name, man?”

“I’m Ricky,” the smaller man said before pointing toward the bigger man, and told them, “and this is my brother, Tony. Did you guys rescue Randy? I was afraid they’d killed him. He wasn’t around anymore and I didn’t dare ask what happened to him.”

Shadow slid his gaze to Spider then Dante. Both men gave him a slight nod. “Randy is safe and healing, as you will be soon.” Shadow could see the hope in the young man’s eyes.

“I remember Bowen talking about a Randy, but I wasn’t paying attention at the time. I’d been captured by the damn sheriff trying to find a way into this hellhole. I was desperate to get to my brother when they began questioning me about Randy. I guess they finally believed I didn’t know who Randy was after they busted my kneecap and I still hadn’t confessed to knowing him,” Tony ground out between clenched teeth. The man had to be in some serious pain but he refused to show it.

“Okay, let’s get out of here before anyone notices a missing van. I’ll need everyone to check their clothing for anything out of the ordinary. Shadow, where did you find the tracking device on Randy’s clothes?” Dante asked before beginning the search.

For the next ten minutes they searched each other’s clothing and sure enough all five men had one or two tracking devices embedded in their clothing. The stretcher had one, and both guards had one each. Once everything was clean, Tony was medicated and his leg was stabilized, Dante called in the SUVs that were waiting for the all-clear. They also had drones sweeping the area for any type of movement. They weren't taking any chance that the Fellowship might turn back.

Spider brought the two guards over to the side of the cabins. One was smart enough to look scared, but the man with the tattoos was pissed. "Bunch of fucking faggots. It'd be better to kill each and every last one of those deviants."

Spider snickered. "Yo, asshole. We're all 'deviants' here."

Shadow walked over and looked at the tattooed man with disgust. "Tell me which part bugs you most, that we don't want you or that you desperately want us."

"I'm not gay. I'm a soldier."

"Saw your tats, but I'm guessing you were dishonorably discharged."

"I served three tours of duty. I'm a proud American," he blustered.

"I know a few decorated Army heroes," Shadow couldn't help but look up at his bosses, "who wouldn't want your ass watching their backs when it counted."

Tat man looked between Shadow, Spider, and Dante. "You guys can't be soldiers, you're gay."

"You're right, I can't be a soldier, but they the sure as hell are. I'm a Marine, you insignificant bullet stopper."

"Fucking gay jarhead."

Shadow wanted to beat this asshole into the ground.

Mouthy tried to stand, but with his hands tied behind his back, he ended up falling down on his butt. "If my hands weren't tied, I'd kick your dick-filled Marine ass."

Shadow looked at Dante and Spider, who were shaking their heads. "But it'll be over before the SUVs arrive, I promise."

"Five minutes he's on the ground or you've missed your chance."

Dante gave in, but the asshole mistook whom the boss was talking too. "This jarhead will be on the ground in under a minute."

Shadow turned to the five survivors to make sure they were okay with the sight of more violence. That would be the only reason Shadow would call it off. This bigot needed his ass handed to him in the worst way. Thankfully, all of them seemed fine and a few looked excited at the prospect of seeing the man who had tortured them get some payback.

Shadow handed his weapons to Dante. This would be a fair fight. He stretched his arms out wide and loosened his neck. One thought burned bright in his mind, this was one of the men who'd beaten his Randy. Shadow could picture every bruise and cut, every stitch and painful cry. This asshole had no idea what and who was coming for him.

Spider released tat man, who came charging at him the moment he was free. Full of rage and self-righteousness, fists up at the ready, and a grin firmly in place. Shadow almost felt sorry for the guy…almost. As soon as he was within striking distance, his opponent threw a punch, which Shadow avoided with a sway. "Lesson one," he taunted. "Never leave yourself open to your opponent. Lesson two. Use the heel of your hand to ensure you don't break one or more of the twenty-seven bones in your hand." Then he brought the heel of his hand down on the moron's nose, which imploded exactly as Shadow had intended, sending the now screaming man to the ground. "Less than ten seconds. Oorah, motherfucker."

***

Randy had written pages and pages of information until his hand was so sore he couldn't write any longer then Jo took over as he dictated. Everything he'd learned, the names, locations, money trails, all of which he regurgitated onto those pages, releasing the weight he'd been carrying. By the time he was finished, he was exhausted. When Jo took all the information down to Dave, Randy pulled a warm, knitted blanket over himself and curled up on the window seat, staring at the stars.

He'd seen Coop walking the yard and out into the cornfields. Trucks had arrived but Shadow wasn't back yet so Randy remained in his room. He had always been awkward in social situations and felt if he went down he'd say or do something embarrassing.

That was one of the main reasons Randy had had so few exhibitions of his work. Typically opening night he would be expected to make an appearance and schmooze with patrons and critics alike. It never worked out well for him. The last one Randy had accidentally called one of the gallery's largest benefactors "sir." She wasn't amused. But in his defense, she did have more hair on her chin than he had.

Jake had been gone since yesterday morning and Randy hadn't heard a word. Of course the team had reported in and he knew they were okay, but he wished he could hear Jake's voice. Probably help if he had a cell phone, but other than Jake, he had no one else to call.

Randy's wake-up call of this near-death experience had him reexamining his life in every way. People he'd thought were friends hadn't even reported him missing. Randy had asked Jake to look into it and he hadn't found one report.

While his family had never been close, he'd never expected his mother and sister to actively abandon him to his crazy father. Randy remembered a time when he and Grady were young and their father was still a dad. He would read to "his boys" every night before bed when Randy and Grady had shared a room. Grady wanted him around back then.

Things changed when the apple of their father's eye joined the police academy. Grady would be the one to make the old man proud. His mother and sister would be out doing girl stuff while Dad and Grady went to the shooting range to practice. Grady began talking to Randy less and less, up until he moved out.

He understood he was the little "little" brother and didn't quite fit in, but he still would call Grady every Sunday evening. They would run down the week's events, giving Randy at least some semblance of closeness to his brother.

He had suspected Grady was gay much earlier than anyone else. When his father would ask about any of his brother's possible girlfriends, Randy would cover and weave a tail of Grady's escapades with girls. Even though he knew for a fact his brother hadn't ever done any of those things. When Grady found out, instead of thanking Randy for backing him up, he blew up, declaring that he wasn't gay, and stormed away. Of course, back then Grady was still figuring it out and he didn't need his little brother shoving it in his face. Randy had brushed it off as he'd done so many times in his life.

Years later, when Grady came out to the family, Randy was so proud of him. Even if that meant their father knew Randy had been lying to him for years. Randy had paid for that mistake. When Grady had finally had enough of their father's abuse, he broke free and moved away. Randy had been so happy for him, even after their father directed all his anger at Randy.

Back then he'd had a cell phone and would call Grady every Sunday evening as he'd always done. All he got was a prerecorded voice telling Randy to leave a message. That voice had been the only one he'd heard month after month. He would pour himself into those messages, hoping to get a reply from Grady. Which never happened.

After a while, he accepted the writing on the wall. Shortly afterward, he was dragged into a van, a bag was placed over his head, and life as he knew it had ended.

Jake had said that Randy was reinventing himself through his art, but it was much more than that. He didn't have to live in fear anymore. He didn't have to beg for someone's love. Amazingly, Jake gave that to him freely. Finally he had that one person he could count on, that one person who loved him and would miss him should anything ever happen to him again.

Randy fell asleep on the window seat under the stars, comforted by the fact that for the first time in his life, he wasn't alone.

Chapter Eight

The sunlight began to trickle through the room as birds chattered outside the window. Randy slowly opened his eyes and the first thing he noticed was that he was now in bed, the second was the muscled arm around his waist. Jake was home. Randy couldn't help but wiggle around to look at the gorgeous man's face.

Jake's green eyes held Randy in their spell as he murmured, "I missed you."

"I missed you too." Jake smiled.

"It feels good to be missed," Randy said before asking, "Did you get what you needed from the camp?"

"We managed to free the remaining five prisoners. They're all safe and resting comfortably in the bedrooms in the basement," Jake explained as he rubbed his nose against Randy's.

"Are you okay? Was anyone hurt?" The last thing Randy wanted was for someone to be injured.

That brought a wide smile to Jake's lips. "One of the two guards was injured."

"Guards? Are they here?" Randy couldn't help the fear that raced through his body.

Shadow pulled him closer and nuzzled the side of his neck. "I would never bring them anywhere near you. They're tucked away in a jail cell in a nearby county awaiting a visit from the feds. The local sheriff's a friend of Dave's."

"Are these people you can trust?" Randy knew there were more than a few public figures involved with the Fellowship's dirty business.

"Yes. Dave has been in constant contact with trustworthy agents he personally has had contact with in the past. You don't need to worry. The investigations are already under way."

"By now several branches of the Fellowship will be penniless. The heat should be on Bowen within the next few days. Once they start searching for the money." Randy couldn't help but remind Shadow because soon Bowen would be coming after him.

"Yes, babe, we're aware and we're tracking Bowen as we speak," Shadow told him as he nibbled his way down the other side of Randy's neck.

"Really?"

"Really, really." Shadow stopped his exploration and looked Randy in the eyes. "I will do whatever it takes to protect you."

Randy couldn't help but hug the big guy. This was the beginning of the end for Bowen and every other person belonging to the Fellowship. Jake rolled onto his back, taking Randy with him until he now lay on top of the sexy man. Jake's eyes were soft and his hands gentle as they skimmed over Randy's sensitive body. All he wanted to do was get closer to the man he loved.

"I love you, Jake. I want to have a life with you after this is over." There it was, out in the open. He would have never been so bold as to lay his cards out like that, but this was a step forward into his new life.

Randy must have said the right thing because Jake looked as if he were about to shout with excitement. "I want you to return with me to Brighton. We have a large plot of land there and we could build whatever we want. Alternatively, I have a large suite we could stay in if you preferred to live in the main house. Whatever, we can figure it out."

"It doesn't matter to me, as long as you're there," Randy answered. He'd live in a cave as long as Jake was on the slab of rock beside him.

Jake weaved his fingers through Randy's hair, sending a tingle through his body. He brought his head down so he could capture Jake's mouth. His lips were soft and warm, enticing Randy further into the pleasure-filled haze surrounding them. Jake's tongue dove deep, commanding the kiss as he mapped Randy's mouth. His large hands slid under Randy's track pants and cupped his ass cheeks. He couldn't help but moan.

Randy's hands drifted down Jake's naked body, tracing every peak and valley. His lover was built like a Greek god and Randy felt like a kid in a toy store, needing to touch everything. The thin material of his track pants was the only barrier left between them and Randy wanted it gone. He was desperate to feel Jake against him, inside him, everywhere.

"Make love to me," Randy groaned as Jake's index finger tapped his eager hole.

He flipped them over again with Randy's back against the mattress. He went to the end of the bed and pulled Randy's pants free in one quick movement. His dick stood tall as evidence of his arousal and matched Jake's beautiful cock. It had a thick base and girth, only slightly veined and smooth, a nicely rounded head in proportion with his shaft, and was about eight inches long. What more could he ask for, well, other than to have that handsome man inside him.

The quick intake of breath alerted him that his lover had noticed Randy's surprise—he'd done a little manscaping while Jake was away. Randy had never liked the feel of hair on his body…having it rubbed against him by another body, yes, on himself, no.

"You're hairless," Jake almost purred. "You are absolutely breathtaking." He splayed his large hand over Randy's groin, sliding his fingertips over Randy's sensitive balls and up his shaft. A whimper escaped from his throat, but at the moment, Randy didn't care.

As Jake crawled up the bed, he took his time, stopping to kiss and lick as he went. It seemed like his new mission was to lick and kiss every part of Randy's body. Either that or drive him crazy with this sensual torture. Jake's tongue traced the inside of Randy's right thigh with a warm, wet slide while Jake's hands trailed across Randy's pounding chest.

Jake continued his upward journey, stopping only to suck up the odd mark onto Randy's pale skin. Each touch was making him more sensitive than the last. With his head thrown back he cried out when Jake slowly licked his cock from base to tip. A steady stream of moans filled the room. Jake was merciless in his attention, leaving Randy desperate to feel that thick cock buried deep inside him. He wanted to be joined to the man he loved.

When Jake reached Randy's lips, he slowed the kiss. His lips coaxed Randy's to open, allowing Jake to trace them with his tongue. The reverence in which Jake took exploring every inch of him made Randy feel cherished, loved, and most of all seen for the man he was. Jake was making love to Randy body and soul.

Randy's heart beat faster when Jake reached over to the side table and pulled out a new bottle of lube and a condom. Randy wanted to share everything with Jake, and for the first time in his life, Randy did not want to hold anything back.

Jake held the bottle near Randy's face. "Are you sure this is what you want?" How could he not love the man? Even now Jake's sole concern was for him.

"Yes." If there was only one thing that Randy knew for certain, it was he wanted to have this connection with Jake. He didn't care what anyone thought about the speed in which they fell in love. When it was right, it was right, and he'd never give that up. "I've never been surer of anything. I love you, Jake, and I want to spend the rest of my life with you. If that's okay?"

"That's more than okay with me, love," Jake answered before capturing Randy in a passion-filled kiss, leaving them both breathless. "I don't ever want to be without you."

Randy heard the snap of a cap and seconds later, he felt Shadow's slick fingers brush up against his hole. He spread his legs wider as Shadow circled his aching hole before sliding his thick finger in deep.

"Yes, oh yes, yes, yes." Randy loved the initial stretch and burn. Jake's husky growl was his only response before he slid in the second finger.

The moment those talented fingers found Randy's prostate the world melted away and he was left floating in bliss. With unerring accuracy, Jake rubbed against Randy's gland with every thrust. He could feel the telltale signs as pressure built deep within his body and his balls pulled up tight.

"Jake, I'm going to come if you don't slow down." However, instead of slowing his thrusts, Jake began to pump even faster.

"Come for me, beautiful," Jake ordered as he took Randy's hard shaft into his hot, wet mouth, swallowing him down his throat.

A rush washed through Randy with every contraction until the electrical storm of his orgasm broke free. Pump after pump wrung Randy out until only his spent body remained slack against the pillows. Jake licked him clean, even going as far as dipping the tip of his tongue into Randy's slit, causing one final contraction and pulse.

His ears were ringing as he struggled to catch his breath. He could hear Jake's deep voice telling him how much he was loved as he floated on a wave of indescribable pleasure. Jake thrust three fingers inside him, heightening his already acute need to have his lover's cock there.

Jake's fingers disappeared and Randy was about to protest when he heard the rip of the condom wrapper. He opened his eyes, unsure when he'd closed them, and watched as Jake rolled the latex over his girth. The look in his eyes surprised Randy. He'd expected to see raw need but saw love.

Slowly Jake raised both of Randy's legs over his shoulders, kissing each ankle as he went. He could feel the head of Jake's cock nudging him as if waiting for permission. Their eyes met and held as Randy's body opened to accept Jake into him. Inch by inch he was filled, every ridge exciting new nerves as he went until Jake was fully seated inside him.

Both were panting but neither had taken theirs eyes off the other. Every emotion was there, plain to see. Jake's hips began to flex and set a rhythm that brought Randy's cock back to life. Groans took over speech, as everything seemed to silence around them. As his sensitive shaft hardened, Jake increased his pace until Randy was forced to hold on tight. Jake released his legs and pulled Randy up onto his lap, all while remaining balls deep inside him.

Randy's legs wrapped around the strong man as he lifted him easily by his hips before plunging him back down onto Jake's thick cock over and over. Randy couldn't believe that he felt the flames of his orgasm come over him once again. He'd known it was possible, but it had never happened to him before.

"Jake, yes…don't stop, I'm—" Jake bit down on Randy's shoulder, pushing him over the edge for a second time.

Between the sound of his own heartbeat and the roar of his release, Randy felt Jake lift him off his cock, placing him on his hands and knees. How his lover was still going strong was a mystery that Randy intended to research thoroughly. He could feel all those chest muscles pressing against his back as Jake blanketed him. Moments later his thrusts began to lose their rhythm as Jake lost control as he neared his release. With one final thrust, he buried himself deep inside Randy and growled deep as he came. Randy had never heard anything so sexy.

As he felt his arms and legs give out, Jake held him to his body with one muscled arm. Slowly Jake lowered them to their sides and Randy let out a sigh of contentment. He closed his eyes and fell asleep wrapped safely in Jake's arms.

***

"No, I don't fucking know where your money is. Threaten me again and they'll never find your body," Stone Bowen yelled into his cell phone before hurling it against the bricks of his fireplace. His men stood nearby, unfazed. They would slit his throat as easily as work for him when it came down to the right price. That's why he kept them well paid. There was no loyalty in this business anymore. Maybe it was time to retire.

"Another inquiry, *boss*?" Jackson asked as he walked through the open glass doors leading out onto a large balcony overlooking the Arkansas River outside Fort Smith.

Bowen would have thrown the phone at Jackson's head if he'd walked in earlier. The prick was getting his rocks off watching Bowen field angry calls from the other Fellowship branches. "I'd like to remind you that this is none of your business."

"Well, if that's the case, why am I receiving inquiries as well? Is there something I can assist you with?" Jackson asked.

"That will be the fucking day, little brother. Everyone's well aware of your inability to handle decision making," Bowen jeered as he'd done on multiple occasions. "Don't embarrass yourself any further."

"That wasn't my fault," Jackson said with a little more heat, and Bowen reveled in his brother's pain.

"Your 'fault' was an over twelve-million-dollar loss to our father."

"That was a strong investment. I couldn't predict that a hostile takeover would put the company out of business." Which in all honesty was true, but Bowen wouldn't allow it to heal, ripping off the scab every chance he got.

"And therein lies the problem. You can't see the big picture," Bowen gloated. Little did his dear brother know he was the financial backer for the takeover that had destroyed their father's faith in

Jackson. Which was one of the deciding factors their father had used when choosing which son should head Bowen Industries.

"Oh, and joining this group and then loosing Fellowship money is part of the big picture?"

"You chose to stay out of any dealings with the Fellowship, so your shit isn't needed here. Why don't you run along and leave the big boys to take care of business?" Bowen couldn't help but twist the blade a little deeper. Jackson was such an easy target.

"Yes, you're the one who decided to get involved with them in the first place. So it's fitting you go down with the ship, but I won't be joining you. Have a nice day, brother." Jackson smiled at Bowen before turning around and walking away.

For the first time, Bowen wasn't completely satisfied he'd won that exchange. Odd, Jackson used to be much easier to rile up, which Bowen loved to do as often as possible. He'd have to do a bit of digging to find out where his brother was getting his balls.

The phone on his desk rang and he was about to rip it out of the wall when he recognized the number on the screen. "Where the hell have you been?" Bowen growled by way of a hello. "You were supposed to check in two days ago."

"Sorry, boss. It's not easy to move around unnoticed in this Mayberry town. Everybody's up in my business, asking questions, but my cover's holding so far," Nigel explained.

"Have you found him?" That was all that mattered. The need to reclaim his prize driving him on.

"Yeah, boss, he's sittin' in his cop car across from the diner."

"Any sign of Randy?"

"Nothin' yet, boss. The guy looks pretty tore up about something. You sure this guy ain't dead?"

He will wish he was, once I get ahold of him. "Keep sitting on Grady, I'm positive his brother will show up." He had to. It was the only lead he had. Randy's tracker had stopped working a couple miles into Oklahoma, and his father, the detective, was tucked away in a state medical facility for the criminally insane. So he'd be of no help.

"Of course, boss, but we ain't never chased after any of the other fags that got away. Does this Randy guy have somethin' on ya?"

"The reason is unimportant. Don't fuck this up, understand?" Bowen's voice lowered until it became almost a growl. He didn't appreciate having his orders questioned.

Nigel was quick to answer knowing that his life may depend on it. "Yeah, boss, whatever you say, it'll get done."

"Much better," Bowen hissed before slamming the phone back down onto its base.

Bowen stormed out of his office and onto the balcony, taking a deep lungful of air into his body in search of calm. However, he knew calm had vanished days ago along with the 1.2 million dollars in the first Fellowship account. So far, three accounts had been emptied with everyone wondering which branch would be next.

Though two branches in nearby states had been cleaned out, his remained untouched. Bowen had his best guys trying to track the money and find out who was behind this. It had been a difficult couple of weeks since someone broke his cash cow out, and now with money going missing. Bowen couldn't help but be concerned that the two things were related.

The question remained: where was Randy Reynolds?

Chapter Nine

Randy had finished dressing and stood staring out of their bedroom window at the newly arrived vehicles. He knew Tristan, and the rest of Jake's team, had come to help him and the five other camp survivors who were recovering downstairs. By the murmurs of several conversations he'd overheard, he knew the house would be busy.

After their shower, Shadow had wanted to wait to escort him down so that it wouldn't be overwhelming. Randy was quick to nix that idea, though he loved the fact that Jake wanted to protect him. His new life deserved better than existing in the background hoping someone might notice him, and fearing it, all at the same time.

Randy gathered himself, straightened his back, and headed for the door. He had it open and was walking through it before he could talk himself out of it. The hallway was empty and he heard the odd word floating up the staircase. Bowls clanged and the soft thud of plates being set on the long, rectangular wooden kitchen table sounded. House noise. Normal. Regular. He could deal with that.

With a final scan of his surroundings, Randy took hold of the railing and began descending the stairs, one shaky foot at a time. As he neared the bottom, the ambient noise disappeared, but he kept moving forward until he walked into the bright, airy kitchen and into a room full of people.

He recognized Jo, Dante, Spider, Dave, Coop, and, of course Jake, but there were many new faces and one he hadn't seen in over a year, Tristan. His brother's best friend had been MIA after Grady moved out and now Randy was second-guessing having him here. He could feel his cheeks begin to heat up, but he didn't turn away. From now on he would face the world around him head on.

Jake began to make his way across the kitchen toward him, those eyes holding him and giving him strength. Randy stepped into Jake's embrace as soon as he was close. "I'm so proud of you," he whispered, and in the background Jo could be heard asking everyone why they were standing around and that they needed to get moving. He loved Jo.

Randy couldn't hide the smile on his face. Every step, no matter how small, was leading him where he wanted to go, and into the life he was determined to have. "Thank you."

"I'll introduce you to the people you haven't met, okay?" Jake asked as he always did, never telling Randy what to do but allowing him to decide. As an equal. Randy understood there might be a time when Jake would have to tell him what to do in order to protect him, and while he hoped that day never came, he knew it was a possibility.

Two dogs wandered into the kitchen and up to Randy. One was a gorgeous golden retriever and the other a happy and chubby German Shepherd. Both looked up at him with doggie happiness. He crouched down and gave them a good scratch behind their ears.

"These two are important members of the family. This hairy fellow is Buddy and the glowing Luna, who's expecting their first litter in the next few weeks."

"They are beautiful," Randy couldn't help but gush. He'd never had a pet. He ruffled Buddy's long neck fur and asked, "You're the proud daddy, aren't you?" Then he turned to Luna, who was waiting patiently. "You're such a good girl. You'll be a fabulous mom."

"I'd like to meet the rest of your *family*," Randy said, bringing a smile to Jake's face.

When they turned, many of the new arrivals were looking at Jake as if he had two heads. A smaller man with one green eye and one hazel, along with an array of striking freckles sprinkled across his face, stepped forward.

"Don't worry about them. They're a bit shocked that Shadow has a soft side. I'm Matthew, Coop's hotter partner." Matthew winked and Randy couldn't help but laugh. "It's nice to finally meet you," Matthew said before taking Randy into a hug. Not a fake hug but one his whole body got involved in.

Randy wrapped his arms around Matthew and hugged him in return. "It's wonderful to meet you. Coop has been doing a good job keeping me safe."

Matthew stepped back and said, "You are a sweetie, just like these guys keep saying."

Randy wasn't sure if he wanted to be known as a "sweetie," but if it made Matthew happy, Randy was good with it. Another man stepped forward who had curly red hair and a stunning patchwork of vibrant tattoos. "I'm Sam. Dante and Spider are my partners."

"You're the one with all the topiaries." Jake had explained that the house was surrounded by creatures made out of trees and hedges. Randy went on to explain, "I would love the opportunity to paint while you're creating one of your artworks. To feel the energy and shapes that appear through living art would transfer wonderfully on canvas."

Sam's face lit up so fast Randy was afraid the man might faint. "I'd love to work together with you," Sam said before hugging Randy tight. Then Sam turned and went back to sit between Dante and Spider.

As Sam sat, a tall, fit woman with flowing blonde hair and the most amazing crystal-clear blue eyes stepped forward. "Hi, I'm Shannon. I keep an eye on these idiots out in the field and have been known to bring down assholes using my computer. I hear you're quite the hacker."

"I'm fascinated by the entire system, from basic command lines, console tools and networking, to cryptography and reverse engineering," Randy explained and watched Shannon's eyes light up.

"Welcome aboard," Shannon said before taking him into another hug. He couldn't help but wonder, other than Jo, when was the last time a woman had hugged him? It certainly hadn't been his mother, who had centered all her attention on his sister, Rachel.

Jake led Randy to a quiet corner where Tristan stood with a tall, handsome man with long black hair. Instead of introductions, Jake and the man who, based on Jake's stories, Randy guessed was Vincent, walked away, leaving Tristan and Randy alone. For the life of him, he didn't know what to say when suddenly Tristan engulfed him in a strong hug and began crying.

"Let's go outside for some privacy," Randy suggested before leading Tristan out the garden doors and onto the porch.

This wasn't how Randy saw this playing out. He'd thought that he'd be the one melting down. Randy directed Tristan to the far corner where two cushioned Adirondack chairs sat. Once he got Tristan seated and sat himself, Jake and Vincent reappeared, one with a box of tissues, the other cups of coffee.

Randy took the opportunity to introduce himself to Vincent. "Hello, I'm Randy." He held out his hand.

"Vincent," he replied and didn't hesitate to take Randy's hand. "It's good to meet you."

Jake crouched down beside Randy and asked, "Are you fine with doing this alone?

Randy ran his fingers through Jake's short hair, loving the feel of the soft bristles against his palm. "Yeah, I'm fine." Jake nodded before standing, then walked to the other end of the porch along with Vincent. Randy knew the two of them would still be able to hear their conversation, but he didn't have anything to hide.

Tristan balled up the tissue in his hands. For the life of him Randy couldn't figure out what he was so nervous about. "What's wrong?"

Tristan looked up, making the first lengthy eye-to-eye contact with him since meeting again after such a long time. "I'm sorry I wasn't there for you when you needed me." Tristan had stayed in Dallas for months after Grady moved away, and in all that time, he'd never kept up with Randy.

Instead of feeling angry, Randy felt numb. "I'm not your responsibility. It's not your fault." No matter how much it hurt to say it, he was beginning to accept it. Perhaps lacking parental figures, or at least positive ones, made him put a disproportionate emphasis on his other relationships. Randy's head was spinning, as things suddenly became clearer.

"Not my responsibility? It should have been," Tristan declared before resting his head on the table in what looked like exhaustion. "All the years you were the only one who had welcomed me into your family's house when the rest of your family thought I was the Prince of Darkness."

Randy couldn't help the laugh that burst out, making not only Tristan, but Jake and Vincent, look at him strangely. "I'm sorry. I was remembering the Halloween you showed up at our door dressed like Prince with the white ruffled blouse and deep purple suit. You almost gave the old man a heart attack." Tristan began to laugh, making Randy feel more optimistic about this conversation.

"You see, right there. You're trying to make me feel better, you always have. When your parents wouldn't let me sit at the family table with them, you brought Grady and me supper out on the patio. Or the time I got drunk because I was upset at being dumped again. You were the one who came and got me. You picked me up and drove me to your house, cleaned me up, held my head up when I puked, and told me over and over again that I'd find the right guy someday." Tristan stopped and looked over at Vincent. "And I did."

"Grady would have done the same thing if he wasn't out of town," Randy told him.

"That's not the point. You did it. I wasn't your responsibility, but time and time again, you went out of your way to help me. Hell, Randy, you demanded your father treat me with dignity and respect."

"Yeah, a lot of good that did. Had to have my jaw wired shut the next morning," Randy remarked. Jake's growl from across the porch was angry enough for the both of them. Randy calmed his lover with a smile and mouthed the words, "I love you."

"Don't belittle all that you've done," Tristan admonished while shaking his head.

"Why shouldn't I?" Randy snapped. "Everyone else did. You, and my brother. Do you know how many times I had to cover for the two of you?" he asked rhetorically. "Then Grady came out and I was so proud of him. Even if it meant me spending a couple days in pain when Father realized I'd been lying to him for years. But nobody saw that or bothered to look.

"You two went off to your own lives without looking back. Don't get me wrong, I understand you had concerns about your ex, and I'm relieved you're safe and happy. But I had hoped not to be so easily forgotten by everyone in my life. You and Grady moved on, my mother and sister left without even telling me where they were going, and I was alone, left to deal with the crazy man who had a gun."

"We should have never done that. We all knew what your father was capable of. I can't explain why it never struck me to check in with you. You were always in my thoughts," Tristan tried to explain.

"Huh," Randy grunted. "I was first to get a call if I was needed, but the last to get the call any other time. And while that is on you, it seemed as if I could fade away into the wallpaper, never to be seen again. I did that to myself," Randy admitted. "Now, I'm starting over and I'm not upset with you anymore."

Tristan sat stunned for a moment. "You might not be, but I am with myself. You've always been a kind, generous, and reliable friend, and I promise to do better if you give me the chance." Tristan was tearing a tissue into confetti-size pieces.

Randy knew Tristan was a good person, but he hadn't been a great friend. Conversely, Randy had never reached out, and he was starting to realize that maybe he had played a role in his isolation. The kidnapping and the camp belonged to his evil father and complicit mother and sister, but Randy had expected other people to act. To save him. Now, he wanted to move on with his life, and if Tristan wanted to remain a part of it, that was up to him. Thanks to Jake, Randy finally understood he deserved to be loved, respected, and remembered.

"Of course, I don't want to lose your friendship." The moment the words left Randy's mouth Tristan leapt out of his chair and pounced on him. Randy couldn't help but hug him back.

He'd missed Tristan. At least now, they were on the right path.

***

Shadow sat at one end of the kitchen table with Randy by his side. The team had called an impromptu meeting after everyone had been fed. Laptops and maps covered the century-old reclaimed wood table, leaving only glimpses of the aged beauty underneath. Each and every day of the six months it took him to painstakingly bring it to life was seared into his memory. With the remaining pieces, he made that triangular box sitting upstairs on his shelf. Shadow ran his thumb over a shallow groove made by decades of use before he even had his hands on the lumber. He couldn't bear to bring himself to sand away a physical reminder that time keeps marching on.

His gaze drifted over to his mom, who was watching him closely. She knew to where his thoughts had wandered—never a safe road to travel down. Randy's hand tightened on Shadow's thigh, making him notice his lover had been watching him.

"Something wrong?" Randy asked as he looked between Shadow and his mom.

"No, I'm fine." His go-to answer was out of his mouth before he even realized it. Shadow had been using that response every time his mind wandered to the past.

Then he saw it, that brief moment of hurt that flitted across Randy's face before he turned away and concentrated on Matthew and Shannon, who were working away. Every so often either one would look up at Randy and smirk. The lie tasted sour on Shadow's tongue, but this was neither the time nor the place to come clean.

"What's going on?" Shadow asked after the fourth glance their way.

Randy smiled wide and said, "They're trying to hack into the program I created, if they've even found it yet."

Shadow didn't know how to take the fact that members of his team were essentially trying to force their way into Randy's program. "This doesn't bother you?"

"No, I'm actually flattered," Randy explained. "To have people of their caliber trying to break in to something I've created is a ringing endorsement of my skills."

Watching Randy come out of his shell and challenge himself gave Shadow pleasure. And Randy had blown him away with how he'd handled the situation with Tristan. He'd been kind but firm. Setting out what he'd expected, which wasn't more than Tristan deserved, given that Randy was willing to allow their friendship to continue.

In getting to know Randy, Shadow was able to fill in the blanks about the man before he'd been taken by the Fellowship. He'd been the "odd person out" since the beginning of his life because he was born prematurely with a few health concerns. As the years went on his mother and sister had distanced themselves from him, then his father, and, ultimately, Grady when his brother had decided to join the force.

When Randy had decided not to use his talents to pursue the almighty dollar, it put the last nail in the proverbial coffin as far as his parents were concerned. The two concentrated on their other children and left Randy to his own devices. He was quiet and reserved, not wanting to draw attention to himself, but had been screaming for someone to see him for the person he was. He'd put a great deal of love and effort into the remaining relationships he'd had left, his brother and Tristan.

That's what made their lack of concern all the more difficult to swallow, then months after he'd been imprisoned Randy accepted the truth as he knew it—no one remembered him and no one was looking for him.

"After this is all over you'll have to explain to me how you hid it." Shannon eyed Randy as she threw up her hands in defeat and leaned back in her chair.

"I'm not giving up, I'll find it," Matthew muttered as he continued typing away. "I can find the money and trace it back to the different branches with the information you've given us. But whatever you did froze all their accounts while systematically emptying them one by one."

Randy grinned. "I didn't want them to have a chance to move it once other accounts were hit. I froze them all while the program released into their network. Once started there's no way to turn it off." Randy leaned back into Shadow and he gathered the brilliant man close.

"So far over fifty percent of all the accounts have been cleared out and exactly as you'd intended, it all leads to Stone Bowen. But the account is inaccessible," Dante reviewed as he rifled through a thick file.

"I like your style, kid," Coop joked, bringing a smile to Randy's face.

"Why didn't you build in a fail-safe?" Dave asked.

"Truthfully, I thought I'd be dead. Even after Shadow found me, I barely made it through the infection. Why would I have wanted to stop it?" That declaration silenced everyone in the room. "You have to understand that I'd intended to set it off myself if given enough time. The fail-safe was buried into the code for the original program, ensuring its takeover, whether or not I died, the Fellowship wouldn't be able to hurt more people, or at least I could slow them down."

"I see 'signatures' all over this," Shannon stated. "The branches have had their guys searching for the money. I doubt there's any question among them now where the money is going." Shannon's smile was still glued to her face.

"It appears Grady's got himself a new friend," Spider said as he handed a picture to them. "Do you recognize this guy?"

Randy reached for the picture and flipped it over. His face went white before he muttered, "Nigel. He's vicious."

Shadow pulled him closer and said, "You're safe. He can't get to you."

Randy seemed frantic and turned to Shadow. "You have to warn Grady. He isn't safe. Nigel works for Stone Bowen, and he'll do whatever he's told, even kill people."

"We will. Grady's already wary of him," Dante assured before Shadow had a chance.

Randy grabbed Shadow's cell off the table and handed it to him. "Call and warn him."

Shadow pulled Grady's number up from "Contacts" and pressed.

"Grady here." Shadow knew Randy could hear his brother's deep voice.

"Shadow."

"Is Randy okay?"

Shadow watched as Randy looked away, trying to hide his eyes. No one doubted that the brothers loved each other, it was plain to see, but Randy couldn't get past the betrayal. "He's fine, getting stronger every day."

"Good, good."

"Randy wanted me to call you. He recognized the guy who's following you. His name is Nigel and he works for Bowen. A soldier who'll do anything he's told. Got me?"

Grady grunted, "Yeah."

"Right. Randy wanted you to know so that you were safe." Shadow ignored Randy's angry glare.

"He did?"

"Yeah."

"Thank him for me," Grady's voice deepened. "Is this Nigel guy responsible for any of my brother's pain?"

Randy wouldn't look him in the eye, and Shadow had his answer. "Probably." Grady was quiet on the other end of the line. Too quiet. "Be cool, man. This shit has to play out. Revenge'll have to wait. Got me?"

On a raised voice, Dave ordered, "We might need to use this Nigel. Tell Grady to carry on as usual until we can think it over."

"You hear that?"

"Yeah," Grady acknowledged.

"I'll keep you in the loop."

"I'd appreciate that, man," Grady grumbled before disconnecting.

Shadow placed his phone on the table in front of Randy and felt the subtle change in Randy moments before he lifted the phone and looked at the screen. His body went from relaxed to rigid, but he remained silent. Everyone carried on with what they were doing as Randy browsed through Shadow's calls.

Slowly, Randy held up the screen so Shadow could see what he was looking at. "Is this the last number you called?" he asked while pointing at his outbound call list.

Shadow was confused but answered what should have been obvious. "Yeah."

"And that was my brother's cell?"

"Yeah." Shadow felt like he was missing a piece of information.

Randy sat staring at the screen until it turned dark. His body began to tremble and Shadow was about to take him out of the room but Randy held up his hand. He turned to Tristan, who was looking on with interest, and repeated the number to Grady's cell phone.

"Is this the number you have for Grady?"

"Yep," Tristan answered, looking as unsure as Shadow felt.

"Damn." Randy shook his head.

"What's wrong?" Shadow asked, pulling Randy closer as his body molded to Shadow's chest.

"He changed his number," Randy mumbled.

Shadow ran what he knew about Randy's attempts to contact his brother. Shit. "Grady didn't give you his new number."

Randy shook his head but said nothing. The room went silent and Shadow began grasping at straws. "Maybe he forgot to tell everyone back home?"

"Tristan has the correct one." What the fuck? Grady sounded like he missed and loved his brother, but then this. "It's okay, it explains a lot. I'm getting tired. I think I'll go up and get some rest."

Randy stood and Shadow went to follow, but Randy held him in place. "I'm going to sleep. You stay here and work with your team so we can go home soon. No offense, Jo."

"None taken, sweetheart. Can I get you anything?"

"No, thank you. I'll come back and help you later with supper." Randy bent and kissed Shadow softly before turning and leaving the room. Buddy and Luna were on his heels.

No one said a word until they heard the bedroom door close and even then they spoke in hushed tones. "What the hell is going on? One minute he's the loving brother, the next he couldn't be bothered to tell Randy his new phone number."

"I don't get it. Grady changed it when he moved to Brighton. I understand why he wouldn't give his father the number but Randy?" Tristan agreed, looking as confused as everyone else. The team knew about the reasons Randy didn't feel comfortable seeing Grady. This was insult to injury.

"Maybe he did and Randy forgot?" Coop offered.

"Super memory?" Vincent answered. "Randy wouldn't have forgotten."

"Besides, even if Randy forgot the number, one phone call from Grady to check in on his brother would have corrected any misunderstandings," Tristan stated, his tone angry. "I admit, I was an asshole for not checking in on Randy. We can make excuses like I've been through a lot, but it was one lousy phone call." Vincent stood, tugged Tristan's hand and they walked out of the room.

"Things don't add up. Grady has always struck me as a solid guy," Shannon stated as she tried to put the pieces together. "I can see him screwing up and forgetting to or putting off calling Randy, but not to give him the new number doesn't fit the man I've come to know."

"Let's get Grady on the line and have him explain," Spider suggested. There were more twists and turns in this than Shadow had ever expected when he'd sworn to find Randy Reynolds.

"I'm going to head out and walk the perimeter for a bit, clear my head," Shadow explained as he stood, holstered his gun, and headed for the door.

"Shadow," Shannon called. "Randy said he'd left voice messages, right?"

"Yeah. Spider, keep an eye on Randy," Shadow requested.

"Of course, man."

Shadow nodded then walked out onto the porch. He took a moment to suck in some fresh air and swore to do everything in his power to never let Randy down.

He'd had enough people doing that already.

Chapter Ten

Randy watched as Jake walked out into the backyard. He made a handsome silhouette with the sun as a backdrop as he stepped into the twelve-foot-high cornfield and vanished. For the first time since meeting him, Randy felt that Jake had lied to him. There were moments when he seemed distant and he couldn't hide the sadness on his face.

At the moment though, that worry paled in comparison to the discovery that Grady hadn't shared his new phone number with Randy. He'd been shocked at first when he saw the number on the screen. Then, of course, came denial: "That had to be the number at the police station where he worked." But when Jake confirmed it was indeed Grady's personal number, Randy went numb.

He couldn't help but remember the old saying, "The straw that broke the camel's back." This was no simple piece of straw but the whole hayloft. He looked down at Buddy and Luna who had followed him into the bedroom. He didn't have the heart to send them away. He hoped no one minded, they were going to keep him company for a little while.

He gathered his art supplies and crawled into the center of the bed. He had no idea how he was going to pay Jake back for the supplies, the clothes, and all the other expenses he was racking up. Randy knew he had to get a job, and thought that maybe he could sell a few of his paintings to get by until he was back on his feet.

You honestly think you can have an ordinary life after what you did to the type of people you screwed over? His conscience was laying the guilt on thick, as it had been doing for the past couple days. *They'll come for you and kill anyone in their way.*

He pulled out his sketchbook and colored pencils, desperate to silence his maddening thoughts. He poured the set of pencils across the patchwork comforter and reached for the first one that caught his eye, cobalt blue. The first bold, brash sweep of the pigment across the crisp white paper brought his world into perspective. The second, his heart rate slowed and by the third, all thought drifted away.

He felt both Buddy and Luna climb up onto the bed and lie down, but his world was narrowing. The clean lines appeared to glow, bringing shapes and designs into focus and allowing Randy to once again get lost inside his art.

***

Shadow returned hours later to find Dante and Spider waiting for him on the back patio. No one else seemed to be around, making him wonder what was going on. The warm midday sun did nothing to dissipate the feeling of foreboding that shrouded Shadow's body.

He walked up to them and a pair of headphones on the table that was connected to Dante's cell phone. "What did you find?"

"With Grady's old number, Shannon and Matthew were able to dig up Randy's phone messages and the reason Grady never received them. Grady's old number was still activated even though he'd stayed with the same company."

"The number was reassigned, that's not unusual. Most cell companies do that after ninety days." Shadow took a moment to think about it. "You mean someone else was receiving Randy's voice messages?"

"Not someone else as in an unknown—Richard Reynolds was receiving the messages."

"How the hell did their father end up with Grady's old number? Randy told me he got Grady's same voice message as always."

"It appears Detective Reynolds pulled a few illegal strings. The team is still trying to track down the details," Spider explained before looking down at the headset. "We have a few of the messages taped. That asshole saved them."

Shadow sat and looked at the headphones as if they were going to strike at any second. "Those are private messages. Have you forwarded them to Grady?"

"Yep. We asked Randy before we did anything."

"Randy knows?"

"Of course. We didn't want to do anything without his permission. He came down for a bottle of water and we spoke with him. He gave us the go-ahead to listen as well."

"Why wouldn't you wait for me to come back before you approached him? And why the hell would he do that?" Shadow would imagine Randy would want to keep that private between him and his brother.

"We didn't approach him. When Randy came down, he asked us if we'd found anything and I refused to lie to him. It seems to me he's had enough of that from people already," Dante stated with a bit of a bite.

"Right." Shadow's shoulders were bunched around his neck. "You know I trust that you'd never do anything to hurt Randy, but I…." He shook his head, unable to explain how he wanted to shield Randy from any more pain while trying to give him the space he needed to trust Shadow's intentions.

Dante's jaw muscles relaxed. "The reason he wanted us to listen was because Randy gave Grady information on the comings and goings of their father, and the names and dates of certain visitors that was more crucial than we'd expected. High-ranking officials, CEOs of corporations, and several mob bosses."

Spider continued where Dante left off. "Randy gave the information to Grady thinking his brother would know if it was important or not."

"But Grady wasn't getting the messages, their father was." Shadow let that sink in for a moment. Richard Reynolds knew his son was keeping tabs on him and his associates. "Randy wasn't kidnapped and thrown into that conversion camp because he was gay, or even for his abilities. Richard Reynolds needed Randy to disappear."

"Exactly, the POS probably used Randy's gift as an incentive for Bowen to take him, which seemed to do the trick. With Randy tucked away, Richard went after Grady."

Shadow looked at the headphones. "If you left that there for me to listen to, I'm not interested in hearing that shit."

"You haven't got a choice, buddy. Randy wants you to. He was adamant," Dante explained as he held the headphones out to Shadow. "Sam said it was as if Randy wants you to see all his 'sides' so that you have a clearer vision of the whole. Don't quite understand what he meant by that, but it seemed important."

He knew exactly what it meant. Randy had spent his life feeling cut off from the people who were supposed to love him. He'd hidden himself away hoping someone he loved would eventually see him. Now that he had someone he loved, Randy wanted to make sure there were no secrets between them. He'd given so much of himself already, and probably believed this last bit of information would complete the picture of who he was.

Shadow took the headphones from Dante and put them on. Twelve minutes later, he took them off. He'd heard enough. Randy trying to reach out to his brother, hope waning in every message, cut Shadow to the core. "I haven't heard from you in a couple months. I know you must be busy," "I hope you're safe"; "I miss you. Maybe I can come down for a visit." The messages changed as fear began to creep in. "Dad's really beginning to worry me," "I'm alone with him now. I need your help," "I think he's planning something." Until one of the last messages was Randy begging for his brother to call him, promising Grady that he wouldn't be any trouble if he'd come get him.

Shadow stood from the table and headed into the house without saying a word. He passed his mom, Matthew, and Sam, who were preparing food around the kitchen island. All three turned to him with the same look in their eyes. They knew.

"Wipe those looks off your faces. Randy does not want pity from anyone."

Mom replaced her long face with a smile. "Absolutely. I'll pass it along."

Shadow softened his voice. "Thank you," he muttered, before leaving the room to go up the stairs.

When he opened the door to the bedroom, the sight that met him calmed his frayed nerves. Randy lay in the center of the bed on top of the blankets, fast asleep, his face serene and free from the stress he'd been carrying around. Buddy and Luna were lying on either side of him like bookends. Sometimes Shadow forgot it hadn't been so long ago that Randy couldn't even walk on his own, and that he needed his rest to continue healing.

Randy's sketchbook and colored pencils lay scattered around him. Carefully, Shadow removed all of Randy's supplies under the watchful eyes of the dogs. Shadow softly tapped his thigh with the palm of his hand and both Buddy and Luna jumped off the bed and headed out the door before he shut it.

He took off his boots and shirt. He wanted to hold Randy against his skin, and crawled in beside him. Shadow wrapped himself around his lover and held him tight.

After a few minutes, Randy spoke with a sexy, sleep-roughened voice, "Love you, Jake."

"I'll love you forever, Randy."

***

The sound of pure joy echoed through the yard as Randy laughed without restraint, not only catching Shadow's attention but many of his team members as well. With every circle around the ring, his laughter grew. Meg was taking Randy for his first horseback ride and it seemed to be a hit as Sam, Matthew, and Tristan watched.

It had been four days since discovering what Randy's father had done with Grady's phone number. Grady had explained that he'd given his new number to their mother before leaving town, and asked her to give it to Randy because he was away the day Grady left. That didn't excuse him for not calling Randy, but it seemed to quell his feeling his brother had abandoned him, so Shadow was fine with it.

Shadow watched as Meg threw her head back and whinnied, showing off for her new rider, and Randy looked like he was loving every minute of it. Jo had Meg on a long lead and stood in the center of the ring, as she would have done with all first-time riders.

Dante, Dave, and Vincent were sitting with Shadow out on the patio while Spider, Coop, and Shannon were out on patrol. They were talking, but it was background noise as Shadow watched Randy suck back some happy.

"Yo, man, you with us?" Vincent laughed as he threw something at Shadow's head, which he dodged.

"Yeah. Asshat. What?"

Dave shook his head before saying, "The five survivors you freed from the camp will be taken to Brighton tomorrow. Jesse should have their rooms ready at Haven even though they're not scheduled to open the doors to the shelter for another couple months. Most of the construction is finished and I figure these guys can help out with the painting or gardening."

"Are they okay with staying in the apartments even though the rest of the complex will be empty?" Shadow asked. He was glad that Jesse and Royce were opening the doors to the new community center and LGBTQ outreach program for these men.

"They understand it's for their safety. Once we have all this sorted out, we can concentrate on what is best for them. It's not as if they can go back to their families," Dave explained.

"Originally the big guy, Tony, wanted to take his younger brother, Ricky, home to his own apartment. But after we explained that that might be the first place the Fellowship looked, he agreed to the arrangements," Dante said as he removed his sunglasses now that the sun had set behind the barn.

"Tristan and I will set out after breakfast. Once we get them settled, we'll check in at home with Mrs. Walker, spend the night, and be back here by the following afternoon," Vincent mapped out their plan.

"I've heard back from a few informants. Apparently, Bowen has gone underground," Dave spat out with undisguised disgust. "There's a price on his head. The rest of the Fellowship branches are too busy fighting with each other to realize a federal task force is bearing down on them."

"So basically Randy's plan to stop the Fellowship is working way better than even he expected. He should be proud of himself. Without him none of this would have been possible," Dante said with a healthy dose of respect.

Shadow turned around in time to see Randy leading Meg back into the barn. "Do we have any idea where Bowen is now?"

"None. He dropped his tail outside Fort Smith and no one has seen him since," Dave answered.

Shadow's mind raced with possible outcomes. He wished he could take Randy away to where no one could harm him. Not feasible, but it felt like a compulsion since the threat wouldn't be erased until Bowen was caught.

"We'll keep patrols rotating every twelve hours until Bowen turns up. His man, Nigel, is still in Brighton expecting Randy to show up there. He'll be safest here," Dante assured. Unfortunately, Shadow didn't share his boss's confidence.

"That everything?" Shadow asked.

"Yeah, for now."

The words had barely gotten out of Dave's mouth before Shadow was up out of his chair and walking across the yard toward the barn.

He had to be near Randy, assure himself Randy was safe and make sure he stayed that way. Nothing else mattered at this point. Shadow had failed to keep a promise years ago, and it wouldn't happen this time.

His crappy mood cleared the moment he walked into the barn. Meg stood without her saddle and her eyes were half shut while Sam, Matthew, Tristan, and Randy huddled around her, brushing and curry combing her. Randy was speaking animatedly as he stroked the brush across Meg's neck.

"I thought I'd bounce right off Meg's back. But I know, she's such a good girl she'd never do that. No you wouldn't, sweetie," Randy's voice lowered as cooed into the side of Meg's head.

"You did a great job," Matthew said as he reached to brush Meg's back. "She sure is a long way up."

"Next time you should give it a try."

"Oh no. Coop may have improved my ability to protect myself, but there isn't a magic pill to take away clumsy. I'd end up breaking my neck."

"You should be proud of how far you've come," Sam said.

"Was it that bad?" Randy asked.

"The first time I met Coop I fell out of a tree and busted my ankle," Matthew explained.

"Ouch."

The four laughed while Meg's eyes remained closed, basking in the attention she was getting. It was all so *normal* that Shadow could almost forget that Randy's life was in danger.

His mom came out of the barn to stand beside him as he continued to watch the four carry on. "Looks like Randy's having a great time," Shadow told her. He knew his mom had something on her mind. She'd been holding it in for days.

"Yes, he is. Randy's a wonderful man. You'll be lucky to keep him," she stated in a low voice.

Shadow hadn't looked away from Randy, who was now smiling at him. "Yeah, he is wonderful," Shadow agreed. "Now, care to explain why I will be lucky to keep him?"

"That man loves you."

"And I love him."

"I know you do, son. But how long do you think he'll wait for you to be as open with him as he's been with you?"

Shadow looked down to his mom. He should have known she'd bring it up eventually. Hell, he'd had it on his mind for days. "I'll think about it."

She huffed. "While you're thinking, Randy already suspects that something's wrong. He's going to begin assuming it's him. That's why he keeps asking if you're okay every time you drift off. I don't want to make light of your pain, but it's been almost twenty years. I'm not telling you to forget what happened, but you need to live in the here and now. You may be a Shadow to the rest of the world, but you must allow Randy the chance to see all of you."

Randy turned to look at him again and Shadow could see his concern even though he was still smiling. Shadow had sworn to never do anything that might hurt Randy, and he was breaking that oath by withholding the thing that made him the man he was today.

"Please consider it." Mom laid a hand on his forearm before she headed back into the barn.

Randy was headed Shadow's way and he knew what he had to do, but dredging up a series of events that had taken place in what felt like a lifetime time ago had him wondering how he'd handle doing what he needed to do.

Randy wrapped his arms around Shadow the moment he was within reach and kissed him lightly before asking, "Are you okay?"

For the first time Shadow answered honestly, "No. I'm not."

Chapter Eleven

Randy thought he'd misheard Jake. For a while now, Randy had thought there was something Jake wasn't telling him, but he didn't know how far he should push it. Instead of looking behind the statement and twisting himself with imagined motive, he asked, "What?"

Shadow looked down at him with that sexy grin on his face and said, "Don't take this the wrong way, but we should talk."

Alarm bells began sounding, and Randy thought they were in his head. Then he realized he was being pulled toward the house, and Jake was yelling, "Run," when Randy recognized the noise was coming from the security system. He tried to catch a glimpse of what was going on, but Jake was yanking him up the porch stairs. It wasn't until they stood in the center of kitchen that his head finally stopped spinning.

"I need you to stay here while we figure out what's tripped the sensors."

"Do you think Bowen found me?" Randy asked. "What about the other survivors and your mom?"

"They're safe. Mom probably has her twelve gauge loaded," Shadow told him. "Don't worry. I promise I won't let him get anywhere near you."

After one quick kiss, Jake was gone and Randy stood alone in the room. He quickly ran upstairs to the bedroom and locked the door behind him, knowing it was foolish to believe that the small lock would stop anyone. He went to the window seat to try to get a better look at what was going on.

The moment he sat down, Coop and Vincent signaled from the backyard for him to move away from the window. It dawned on Randy that Bowen could be out there with a gun waiting for a chance to pick him off. He backed away from the window as if it were on fire. He couldn't believe he hadn't thought of that possibility before he sat down.

The back of his legs hit the bed, causing him to fall back onto the mattress, and he lay there staring at the ceiling, trying to get his breathing under control. He knew that there had always been a chance of being found, but the reality of it scared the crap out of him.

Randy hoped no one else would be hurt because of him and what he'd done. He'd never forgive himself.

***

Half of the team was making their way toward the front gate at the end of the long lane that led to the farm, while the other half stayed behind to protect the house and everyone in it. Shadow watched as Dave and Dante walked straight down the center of the lane toward the two dark SUVs waiting on the other side of the gate.

Coop was working his way in from the side while Shadow did what he did best: he lurked in the background. He was roughly twenty feet away from the vehicles before he stopped and hunkered down, his rifle at the ready. No one had seen or heard him, which wasn't a shock, but the Arkansas license plates were. How did the Fellowship find them, and why would they wait at the front gate instead of attacking?

Each team member was wearing an earpiece to hear what was being said and coordinate with everyone back at the house. Coop radioed that he was in position and Shadow counted heads in the vehicles.

"Six, three and three," he said, indicating three persons in each vehicle.

"Got it," Dante answered through the thin flexible band around their necks that picked up on the slightest sound.

As Dave and Dante neared the gate, neither bothered to hide the fact that they were armed. In fact, Dante held his AK47 across his chest.

"The license plates belong to Bowen Industries. Repeat Bowen Industries." Shannon's voice in their ears confirmed what he'd already suspected: Bowen had found Randy.

The passenger door of the first vehicle began to open and Shadow set his sights on the man who stepped out. He took a quick picture and sent it back to Shannon for her to identify. In a few seconds they'd have all his information even down to if he flossed this morning.

The unidentified man took a few steps away from the truck with his hands raised. The other five men stayed seated inside the vehicles. When Dante and Dave were roughly ten feet from the man, they stopped and raised their weapons.

"I don't remember sending out any invitations, so you all must be at the wrong farm," Dave said as he uncovered his badge from under the jacket he was wearing.

"That is Jackson Bowen, Stone Bowen's brother and silent co-owner of Bowen Industries, which specializes in aviation," Shannon reported. "No criminal record, head of multiple charities and founder of Flight for Life. Get this, the guy flies doctors and nurses around the world to help wherever it is needed."

"You sure he's a Bowen?" Coop asked.

Before Shannon could answer, the man spoke. "By now you know who I am, but I'll still introduce myself. I'm Jackson Bowen and my brother is hunting someone you know, Randy Reynolds."

Shadow could feel his senses sharpening. Two drones hovered over the two SUVs. Matthew was getting a look-see and scanning the vehicles for weapons. The man was brilliant.

"And what are you exactly? Your brother's messenger boy?" Dante asked.

Shadow could see Jackson Bowen twitch; Dante had hit a nerve. "No. I am not associated with anything my brother has done or will do. But I find that you and I have a similar interest."

"Is that so?" Dave asked.

"You want my brother behind bars and so do I."

"Jackson has no weapons. The five remaining each have side arms," Matthew reported.

"So you came here to *talk?*" Dante questioned, knowing this was bullshit. "Your friends slowly get out of their vehicles, remove their guns, and drop them on the ground. Now."

Jackson's eyes darted around and he became a little less confident. He turned to the driver of his car and said, "Do it. All of you." As instructed, his men got out of the vehicles but only four of them placed their guns on the ground.

Before either Dave or Dante could say a word, Matthew ran out of patience. One of the drones came down and hovered a foot away from the asshole's face. Shadow painted the guy's chest with a red dot and took aim.

The fifth man slowly removed his gun and laid it on the ground. The drone moved away.

"Seems you share more attributes with your brother than you profess. Lies and deceit from the beginning." Dante shook his head.

Slowly Shadow and Coop came out and revealed themselves, causing a few of the men to jump. Shadow never took his sights off Jackson Bowen. Coop gathered the guns, dropped their clips then pocketed them, and then circled the SUVs and shut then locked the doors after pocketing the keys.

"I apologize for my bodyguard's actions." Jackson Bowen bowed his head. "He's been protecting me since I was young and is more like a member of my family."

Coop brought the briefcase one of the men had been carrying over to Dante. Shadow lowered his weapon but kept it at the ready.

In his experience, no one this powerful did anything without it benefitting them.

Dante riffled through the papers in the case while Dave instructed Bowen to, "Talk."

Jackson and his men lowered their arms. Then the brother of the asshole who wanted the man Shadow loved dead laid out his plan.

***

"Not a fucking chance," Shadow growled as he stormed past Spider and out into the cool night air. Their visitors' vehicles were at the gate, and the men were locked into the bunkhouse far from the main house.

"I know it's not the best option, but that's why it's called the last resort," Dave said as he followed Shadow and the rest of his team outside.

"You want me to sacrifice Randy to catch Bowen. Are you insane?" There was no way he was allowing that. He'd grab Randy and take off before that would happen. Shadow had enough money to take care of Randy anywhere he wanted to go.

"No, I don't want to see anything happen to Randy. If the other measures don't work, we need to have a backup plan. Randy would be protected," Dave explained.

"It may not even come to that. We will exhaust every option before ever taking that step." Dante weighed in with his own assurances.

"Shannon has checked Jackson out top to bottom, and other than a few speeding tickets he came out clean. Using their IDs, she even dug into the five other people. Other than a few petty crimes committed over a decade ago, there's nothing on them."

"It's bullshit, and you know it. Plenty of bastards skate because they keep a clean profile. No way am I'm buying the good man philanthropy angle. Even if the brothers aren't cut from the same cloth, what's in it for him? I haven't heard one good reason other than him taking a bigger piece of his family's money."

When they had questioned Jackson Bowen's motives, he'd told them, "I have to save my father's legacy."

"You want to endanger an innocent man to save a legacy?" Shadow questioned.

"No. I would rather die than have that happen, and if it came down to it, I would," Jackson declared. "My brother and I have been opposites our entire lives, and when it comes down to it, we hate each other. My father chose Stone to be the COO of Bowen Industries after my brother assured my failure in another venture. Now that Stone has almost driven the business into the ground, my father regrets his decision. He attempted to reverse it since he was still acting CEO, but as always Stone seemed to be one step ahead. He'd been gathering and fabricating evidence that questioned our father's sanity. So now, it's for the courts to decide. My father worked his entire life to build that company from nothing, and because of that I am able to help the people I do through Flight for Life and my other charities."

Shadow didn't know if he believed Jackson Bowen, but if he was true, this could help them turn the corner to finding Stone Bowen, which would put an end to the nightmare Randy had been living.

"We'll search every safe house that Jackson's been able to locate over the years. He has to be at one of them," Dave said with conviction. "Randy will never be safe until Bowen is caught." There it was, the final nail.

Shadow raked his hand through his hair. He knew Dave was right; Bowen would never stop. He looked at the house to see the light was still on in their bedroom. He imagined Randy was waiting for him. Shadow visited Randy earlier to assure him that everyone was safe. Now all he wanted to do was return to him.

"I'll discuss everything with Randy," Shadow stated. "We'll have a decision for you in the morning."

He walked away from the group and headed straight for the house. Sam, Matthew, Tristan, and his mom were sitting in rockers on the porch as he approached. His mind was a storm of conflicting emotions and thoughts, which must have shown on his face because no one said a word as he passed by them.

He took the stairs two at a time but had to slow himself before he ran headlong through the door and scared Randy. Once he thought he had himself under control he turned the knob and walked in.

Randy sat on the floor surrounded by pages he'd torn out of his sketchbook. Each one covered in different colored designs that seemed to jump off the page. Randy looked so lost in the middle of a sea of colors.

Carefully, Shadow began collecting the papers until he had a clear pathway to Randy, who was concentrating on what he was working on. He had spent many hours watching the brilliant man create, pouring his soul out onto his pages and canvases. Shadow knelt down and he began rubbing his love's tense neck.

The pencil Randy was using slowed until he finally looked up at Shadow with those warm amber eyes. "Hi."

Shadow could feel himself falling deeper in love, if that were even possible. The absolute joy, love, and acceptance that Randy continually gave to him was commanding in its strength.

"Hi. You ready for bed, love?" Shadow asked while cupping Randy's soft cheek.

"Yeah," Randy replied as he attempted to stand, but it was obvious his legs were cramped from sitting cross-legged on the floor.

Shadow plucked him out from between his artworks and set him on the bed before returning to pick up the rest of the pages and pencils. He understood how important Randy's belongings were to him. Shadow and Randy had spent plenty of time over the past weeks purchasing things online. They had been delivered to the Sentinel compound for when they were able to return to Brighton.

Initially, Randy had been reluctant until Shadow promised to keep track of everything so that he could pay him back. He knew Randy was determined to make a new start and regain control over his life. Shadow would never stand in Randy's way. If that was what he needed, Shadow would give it to him.

Once everything had been cleared away, Shadow began to take off his clothes and turned to find his lover already naked. Randy's head was resting on his arms, the sheets were pulled back, and he wore a sexy smile on his face. Shadow had a good idea what was running through his mind.

"We should talk." Shadow didn't want to talk. He wanted to get into bed and fall into his man's arms. But he had to tell him what was going on since Jackson Bowen had arrived.

Randy's smile was still in place. "Okay, and then after that you're mine."

Shadow was surprised by the forceful way Randy had said that, but he was nervous.

Once Shadow's last piece of clothing hit the floor, he crawled up the bottom of the bed and over to his love. "I'll always be yours. You can do whatever you want with me."

Randy's eyes lit up as he ran his hands over Shadow's body, making his skin burn with need. He wanted to take Randy into his arms and make him scream with passion, but that would have to wait. Instead of covering Randy's body with his own, Shadow shifted and lay down beside him.

"Is this the same talk we were supposed to have before the alarms went off?" Randy asked.

"No, love. We still need to talk about that, but something has come up that we need to deal with first."

"Sounds important. Does it have anything to do with Jackson?"

"Yeah. He has a plan to find his brother. Jackson has been compiling locations of safe houses that Bowen has been using over the years. His team is willing to work with us so that we can organize a task force to hit each location until we find him."

"Okay, but what part of that did we need to discuss?" Randy asked as he ran his fingers over Shadow's tattoo.

Shadow took a deep breath. "If they don't find him at any of those locations, they have another suggestion."

"Why do I get the feeling I'm not going to like this?"

"Because you are perceptive," Shadow said truthfully before kissing the side of Randy's head. "Nigel is still in Brighton keeping tabs on Grady. They want to have your brother come here so Nigel reports your location back to Bowen. When he comes to find you, we would be ready for him."

Shadow remained quiet while giving Randy the time to think the plan over. He had half expected Randy to tell him where to go. The idea of using him as bait felt all kinds of wrong, not to mention this maneuver would force Randy to face Grady.

"Do you trust him?" Randy asked, catching Shadow off guard. He'd expected him to ask more questions about how they would ensure he stayed safe.

He had no choice but to tell him the truth, no matter how much he didn't like it. "Mostly. I believe we all want the same result. Stone Bowen behind bars."

"Okay."

"Okay?"

"Yeah, okay. If you 'mostly' trust him, then so do I. Let's hope they find him at one of the other locations first."

Shadow pushed himself up onto his elbow and looked down at Randy. "Best-case scenario. But are you sure?"

"It's simple. I love you and I know you love me. If you thought for one moment that this wouldn't have a good result, you wouldn't have asked me. One way or another this is going to come to an end, and I'd rather have it happen in the place of our choosing."

"You're supposed to be the emotional artist, not the logical one," Shadow teased as he rolled over onto his back, taking Randy with him. "You amaze me with your strength every day."

Randy's eyes turned fiery before he said, "How about I amaze you in a more tactile way."

Shadow threw his arms up over his head and relaxed back onto the bed. "I'm all yours."

Chapter Twelve

Randy had Jake right where he wanted him, and he intended to savor every inch of his lover's hot body. He began with Jake's ear, nibbling and licking as he went. When he reached his lover's neck, Jake moaned long and loud, which went straight to Randy's hardening cock.

The mark he left behind on that strong neck would be visible for days, giving Randy a strange sense of pride. He wanted his marks on Jake's body. Randy had never been this possessive in his life. With the tip of his tongue, Randy traced the outline of Jake's intricate tattoo and the buried scars underneath before sucking Jake's nipple into his mouth. Jake's muscled chest arched up from the mattress, meeting every lick and nibble as Randy worked his way down some fantastic rippled abdominal muscles.

Jake's moans were getting progressively louder the closer Randy came to his prize. That thick, beautiful cock stood waiting for Randy's attention and he wasted no time before taking what he desired down his throat and swallowing. Jake's response was instantaneous. He brought his hands down and placed them on Randy's head while opening his legs even wider.

Randy massaged Jake's balls as he began humming with his lover's cock in his mouth. The slight vibration was enough to make Jake's entire body shake, giving Randy even more reason to do it over and over again.

He soon realized that Jake had reached his breaking point when Randy was lifted away and flipped onto his stomach. Two lubed fingers circled his hole before sliding in deep, making Randy whine with need as his sensitive nerve endings lit up.

"More please, more, Jake." His lover took him at his word and added a third finger. Every thrust rubbed against his prostate, increasing his pleasure as the pressure grew.

The rip of the condom wrapper heralded the main event and Randy couldn't wait to have Jake inside him. A muscled arm slid under his stomach, lifting Randy to his hands and knees before he felt the head of Jake's cock pressing against his hole.

"Love you, baby," Jake groaned as he pushed forward until he was fully seated inside Randy.

Pressure was building deep inside him and he was becoming desperate to feel the friction that came from the slide of Jake's cock. "Move. I need you to move, love."

Jake did not disappoint. The feel of his chest against Randy's back felt both comforting and commanding. Jake pulled out, then slid back in and the dance began. The feel of their sweat-covered skin rubbing against each other only heightened the building pleasure.

Randy allowed himself to be engulfed by the sensations running through his body and he soon found himself on the verge of climax. Jake must have noticed the change in Randy's body and sped up until he was pistoning in and out.

There was no stopping it. A thrilling sensation raced down his spine and his balls pulled up tight moments before the first contraction hit and soon after, he came in long streams. Jake's hips bucked Randy upward several more times before he too came on a deep growl.

He collapsed on top of Randy, who felt his whole body melt into the bed. When he woke up hours later, the room was dark, his body cleaned, and he was wrapped in Jake's arms. This was exactly where he wanted to wake up, exactly like this for the rest of his life, and he was determined to do whatever it took to make that a reality.

***

The next morning, thunder and lightning rattled the windows. A severe storm had moved in and would be hanging around for a few days. Randy had finished dressing and waited for Jake to come back to their room after he'd shaved. Randy glanced over at the shelves and zeroed in on a folded flag that looked like it was from a military member's funeral. But whose? Randy had seen Jake glance at it on several occasions, and a sad look crossed his face each and every time. Randy knew that Jake's father had left him and his mom when Jake was young and he'd never been in the military. Perhaps the flag belonged to another family member or close friend who had died.

Randy ran the tip of his finger over the wooden case. It reminded him of the wood table in the kitchen, and both brought out something in Jake. Randy wondered if this had anything to do with what Jake had wanted to talk about before Jackson Bowen drove up to the gate.

"Randy. Did you hear me?" Jake's voice made him pull his hand away like a child caught where he wasn't supposed to be.

"What?"

"I asked what you were doing," Jake stated without any censure in his voice.

Randy couldn't help but glance back at the case and decided to go with the truth. "I was wondering who this belonged to and why you're so sad when you look at it."

Jake walked across the room until he stood beside Randy. Jake reached for the case and brushed away a bit of dust before picking up the flag and handing it to Randy.

"Let's sit," Jake suggested as he led Randy over to the window seat.

"Does this have something to do with the talk we were supposed to have yesterday?"

"It has everything to do with that."

Randy sat as a brilliant streak of lighting raced across the dark, menacing sky and hoped that wasn't an omen of what was to come.

"I want to share something with you that might help explain why I'm the way I am. The team wasn't far off when they joked about being shocked I showed emotions. You brought that out in me. I'm going to try to get through this in one shot. It's been a long time so you'll have to bear with me."

"I'm right here if you need me, Jake," Randy assured as he rested the case on his lap.

Jake turned his head to look out the window and Randy couldn't help but compare the storm raging outside to the vibe he felt coming from Jake. Randy swore to himself that no matter what his partner revealed, he would stay calm and support him.

"I'm responsible for the death of my sergeant, best friend, and lover." Randy could feel those cold fingers of shock wrap around his throat. "His name was Daniel, Dan, and we'd been together over four years. We used to talk about when we got out, what we'd do and where we'd go. I loved him and I killed him. We'd been deployed to Afghanistan for a couple years and our unit had seen its fair share of action.

"We were in one of the northern provinces out on patrol when our unit was hit. I was operating one of the turret-mounted fifty caliber machine guns as the rebels closed in around us. Dan was in the vehicle in front of mine when a single al-Qaeda fighter broke free from the rest. With explosives taped to his body, he was running straight for the lead vehicle and Dan. I swung my gun around to stop the suicide bomber, but as I squeezed the trigger something slammed into my left side and I couldn't move," Jake explained, and Randy knew by the far-off look in his eyes that Jake was reliving it. Randy wondered how often he went through this in a day.

"I was forced to watch as everything within a ten-foot radius of Dan's armored vehicle was obliterated before I passed out. Every part of me died that day along with him. When I woke up, I was in a hospital in Germany. Two weeks had passed and Dan had already been buried back home. The VA therapist tried to explain away my feelings by telling me it was normal to have survivor's guilt. I knew different. When I was released from the hospital and was sent home, Dan's parents came to see me. I was dreading the visit, but figured I'd finally have someone else to agree that it was my fault Dan was dead.

"They didn't blame me but wanted to thank me for making their son so happy before he died. No matter how many times I explained what happened, they remained confident that I'd done everything I could have. I was messed up for a long time after all that happened, and I hid down here on the farm, trying to figure out how to go on. His parents had given me the flag from Dan's casket and I spent days creating the case. Then I went on to use the same wood for the kitchen table before I redid the stables inside the barn and the ring. Hell, at that point, I would have built anything to keep my mind busy."

After everything he'd lived through, the pain and guilt must have been suffocating. Randy reached across the bench and took his man's hand before Jake continued.

"My mom, the angel that she is, stood by me the entire year. Then on the first anniversary of Dan's death she kicked my ass to the curb. She told me I had my time to grieve and it was now time to start living again."

"Sounds like her."

"Yeah, it does. And it was the smartest thing she could have done to save me. I had a truck and an offer of employment from Dante and Spider. They'd worked with my unit many times in Afghanistan and asked if I'd be interested in joining the Sentinels. If Mom hadn't done what she did, I might have stayed here and wallowed in my guilt until I killed myself."

Those words made a chill travel up Randy's spine.

"Like you are doing, I reinvented myself, deciding that aloof was how I'd hold myself together. No more wearing my damn heart on my sleeve. I'd blend in, go unnoticed, I wouldn't get emotionally involved again. I would become unseen."

"Become a shadow," Randy murmured.

Jake smiled sadly. "Yeah, love. I became a shadow of who I used to be. In the end it turned out I had a talent that the team could use. Slowly, over the years I was able to settle what happened in my mind and carry on as a productive member of the team. I made friends and lived a quiet life."

"In the shadows," Randy whispered.

Jake gave him a small smile. "Right. Then you showed up." His smile widened. "You swept into my carefully structured life and made every one of my walls crumble to the ground. Now I find myself in the same situation. Someone I love is in danger and depending on me to keep him safe."

Randy watched as Jake removed the folded flag from the case, uncovering a military dog tag and a picture. He reached inside and pulled out the photo. His face softened when he looked down at the picture, and Randy knew Jake would always love Dan. No jealousy. Relief. Randy now knew that when Jake loved someone, he was all in. It felt right that a part of his heart would always remain with Dan.

Jake handed the worn picture over to Randy. Two young men stood hand in hand at what looked like a barbeque. "That was taken out in the backyard when Dan and I were on leave. Back then there were few places where we were safe enough to show any affection toward each other."

"He was handsome," Randy muttered as he looked at the blond man with huge dimples and a killer smile. Dan reminded him of a gorgeous surfer without a care in the world.

"Yeah, he was. I know it might be difficult for you to see my sadness when I think of him, especially considering it's another man. It's not fair to you and I promise to try to get it under control."

"Don't you dare," Randy demanded as he took the case out of Shadow's hands and set it on the desk before climbing into his arms. "You loved Dan, and I know the two of you would have built a life together. Dan deserves to have a special place in your heart because you will always love him and he loved you." Randy held the photo out for Shadow to look at. "You can see it in his eyes. He has that goofy, over-the-moon look of love and it's directed at you."

"In my experience people don't like to share, especially when it comes to someone's love."

Randy wrapped his arms around Jake's neck and let everything he was feeling shine through. "Because I love you and no matter how hard you try to hide, I see you. A man who doesn't break a promise, agrees to save a friend's brother without even knowing him, and risks his life on countless missions to save people he doesn't even know is brave. A man who holds nothing back when he loves someone and suffered through a terrible loss that wasn't his fault only to carry on helping others is strong. I have no concerns about sharing your love with Dan, who, by all rights, was there first." Randy smiled, hoping to assure Jake he meant what he said.

Jake looked at him for long moments and Randy was becoming worried he'd said the wrong thing until Jake wrapped his arms around him and held him tight. "Thank you, baby. I promise to make you happy and love you without end."

"That sounds absolutely perfect to me."

Chapter Thirteen

Six days after the Feds began raiding the safe houses on Jackson's list, Dave received word that the last address was a bust. The decision was made, and Grady was on his way to the farm with Nigel tailing not far behind. Randy had decided to spend the day with the guys painting while Sam brought one of Shadow's mom's old hedges back to life.

Vincent and Tristan had brought a few canvases back with them when they took the survivors to Haven in Brighton. Randy had been so excited when he saw them that he hugged them before dancing around with them in his arms. Matthew decided to work on the blueprints for another gadget and Tristan broke out his laptop to write a few chapters.

It felt so normal that to the naked eye they looked like they didn't have a care in the world, when in reality Grady was leading a known killer directly to Randy. Everyone was on edge. Five days ago, Jackson and his men had been allowed to leave since everyone agreed they didn't pose a threat. They'd be returning before Grady arrived.

The team didn't know if Bowen would come alone or bring anyone with him, and they knew they'd have to deal with Nigel. Jake didn't like all the unknowns. Every one meant there was a chance Randy could be hurt. That was unacceptable.

"Well, all Fellowship accounts have been emptied and the one Randy set up in Bowen's name has disappeared," Shannon announced as she entered the kitchen and set her laptop down on the table.

"Jackson and his men are coming up the drive," Dante stated after putting down his cell.

No one could miss how Shannon's face lit up. Shadow didn't have time to think on that new development. All of his attention needed to be on Randy.

"So do we know where all the money went?" Dave asked while looking pointedly at Shadow.

"Dave, even if I knew I wouldn't tell you. The only thing you need to know is that Randy didn't keep a cent. It was divvied up among numerous charities as anonymous gifts."

Dave leaned back in his chair and said, "I imagine it will go to good use instead of sitting in the federal coffers. I can live with that."

"Well, Police Chief, you're going to have to." Spider laughed. "There's no trace of it now."

"I'm glad you guys work on the good side of the law, ahem…most of the time," Dave shot back before laughing.

Shadow knew his friends were looking for ways to keep the heavy from suffocating the room.

"We have all the sensors set around the property. No one will be able to wipe their butt without us knowing it. The basement has been converted into our command center where we'll keep an eye on everything through the cameras and the drones," Shannon explained. "We can protect Jo, Randy, Sam, Tristan, and Matthew down there while you guys protect the house. "Besides Matthew is the only one who knows how to operate the P three forty-five B."

"Which is?" Dave asked.

"Matthew's latest toy. Imagine one of those RC dune buggies but about three times the size and loaded with offensive and defensive capabilities," Shannon explained.

"Don't forget about Buddy and Luna," Coop said. "Luna's about ready to have those puppies."

"We'll have everyone tucked away downstairs in the rec room."

"Why didn't you take your partners back to Brighton until this was over?" Jo asked, and the guys started looking around at one another before breaking into fits of laughter. "What'd I say?"

"My balls would be hanging on the wall as a trophy if I even suggested that," Dante explained. "All our men are trained to defend themselves and how to use a firearm."

"Hell, Tristan had two center mass shots at four hundred meters the other day," Vincent boasted.

One of the sensors sounded an alarm and Shannon brought up the corresponding camera. Grady's truck appeared on the screen and Dante pressed the release on the front gate. It would be all coming to a head soon, and Shadow knew they were prepared for it. But it didn't stop his heart from beating double time.

"I'll go let Randy know his brother is here," Shadow said as he stood and walked out onto the back patio.

When he rounded the corner, he was surprised to see everyone standing around Randy's easel. The hedge had been trimmed and shaped into a stunning fountain. Clearly, Sam was branching out from creating animals. Matthew's blueprints and Tristan's laptop lay forgotten on a nearby table, and Randy knelt on the ground cleaning paint from his hands and arms in a bucket of water.

Shadow passed the easel and everyone surrounding it was smiling wide when he approached. He wished he didn't have to give him news that would take that away.

"Hi, Jake," Randy said as he stood, dried his hands on a small towel, and turned to wrap his arms around Shadow, squeezing him tight.

"Hey, love. Having fun?" Shadow asked as he nuzzled Randy's ear.

"I was able to get a large part of this piece started. Would you like to see?"

"Of course."

Randy took Shadow's hand and led him over to the canvas. Everyone else had backed away and he got his first look at what Randy had been working on. The delicate green circles seemed to cascade down one side of the canvas. Each circle a slightly different variation than the one before. The background of vertical gold lines shone in the sunlight and made the circles jump off the page.

"It's stunning."

"Well, maybe not yet, but it could be. It's not complete." Randy blushed.

"It's still stunning, babe," Shadow restated as he looked Randy in his eyes, driving the point home.

"I agree," Sam added.

"Me too," Matthew said.

Along with Tristan's, "Yeah, it is."

Randy blushed even brighter at the praise.

"There's something you should know," Shadow said, hating that Randy's smile disappeared from his face. "Your brother is here."

The stress and anger he expected never appeared. Instead, a calm seemed to settle over him. "It's okay. I've come to terms with everything that's happened. Now we'll find out if there's ever going to be a chance of a relationship between the two of us." Randy cuddled into Shadow. "I refuse to live in the past any longer. I have so much to look forward to now that I have you."

The two of them stood in the garden holding each other for a few minutes, basking in the warm sun and enjoying each other's company. When they finally parted, everyone and everything was gone, including Randy's art supplies. The guys were giving them some alone time before reentering the house.

Shadow heard Grady's truck pull up, park, and the door slam shut. "I'm not leaving your side."

"I wouldn't want you any other place," Randy responded before standing on his tiptoes and demanding a kiss that Shadow gave gladly.

***

Hand in hand, they walked around to the back of the house and in through the patio doors. The buzz of everyone talking cut off like a knife when they entered. *Great.* As if there wasn't enough pressure already.

Randy took a deep breath, searching for his calm before looking Grady in the eyes. "Hey, Grady."

His brother looked exhausted. The dark circles under his eyes were deep and the scruff covering his jaw was messy. Grady looked as if he hadn't slept in days and Randy's first impulse was to run over to him and tell him everything would be all right, but he stood his ground. Randy knew his brother was a good man and thought perhaps that they could figure out a way to be friends because obviously being brothers hadn't worked out.

"How are you?" Grady asked.

This was so awkward, and that was the last thing he wanted their reunion to be. Looking around the room, he thought a less crowded location might help.

"I'm healing up and feeling much better. Would you like to go sit in the living room where we can talk?" Randy did not intend to allow this tension to drag out. He had enough to worry about simply staying alive.

"I'd like that," his brother agreed and flashed a smile.

"I'll bring coffee," Jo said before heading to the coffee machine. Randy had never once seen that pot empty. There had to be a storeroom around here stuffed full of coffee beans.

He led the way through the kitchen, down the hall, and into the cozy living room, never once releasing Jake's hand. He no longer had to face the world alone. Jake had his back and was by his side. They sat down on either side of the coffee table and Jo brought their coffees. She gave him an encouraging smile before retreating. Randy was unsure how to proceed, but Grady took that concern right out of his hands.

"I'm an idiot, and I'm sorry for taking you for granted. I have no explanation for my actions other than the driving need to get away. That's no excuse for leaving you behind like I did. During the move and settling in, I screwed up at work and had to go before the review board, then after being shot, and having to deal with a stalker who turned out to be our father, and Ben being hurt had me pretty messed up. I don't want to blame any of those events for my failing you, it is my fault."

Randy had questions, but at the moment, he could only think of one. "Did you think about me or miss me?" To him that was the only part that mattered. If Grady said no, there was no hope at ever rebuilding their relationship.

"Of course I did. I thought our mother was trustworthy, that she would give you the number, but she sold you out to our father. The first week I waited for your Sunday night call, had my cell phone sitting right on top of my cruiser's computer terminal, but it never came."

"I called your old number."

"I know that now. At the time, I thought that you might be pissed at me for moving away so I decided to wait until you called. I know it sounds insane, but I was dealing with some pretty insane circumstances."

Randy felt his body heat rising as the anger he thought he had a grip on boiled over. "Insane circumstances? You all left me with the king of insane. You have no idea what our father put me through after you left. I was in that camp being beaten every day for months, and nobody knew because I had no family left." He looked around, and realized he'd stood up. "Every part that made me the person I used to be was ripped away, and I don't want that näive, weak man back."

"You were none of those things." Now Grady was standing only a few feet away from him. "I was the asshole who assumed you'd always be there. I was wrong, everything I did was wrong. I should have given you the new number myself. I should have called you.

Hell, I should have taken you with me. I was selfish and angry at our father and couldn't see past my own survival."

"We can't ever go back to the way we used to be, and honestly I really wouldn't want to."

"I understand," Grady said, looking and sounding dejected.

Randy moved a bit closer. "Maybe we can start over without our family in the way. Who knows what could happen in time."

Grady's face lit up like someone had thrown a switch, and Randy knew in his heart he could never be without his brother. He loved the idiot. Randy closed the distance and wrapped his arms around his big brother. Grady's body began to shake slightly and Randy heard his muffled sobs, which made him hold his brother even tighter. Nothing would come between them again. He turned his head to look at Jake, who was standing several feet away. Randy mouthed, "I love you" to the man who gave him the strength and helped make this possible.

***

Two days later, Randy had been lounging on the couch with Sam and Tristan when the alarms started blaring. All three of them jumped up and headed for the basement door. Randy ran into Jake and the others as they entered the kitchen. Randy had never seen so many guns in one place. Before he realized it, Jake had placed a gun in his hand that reminded him of his father's Glock.

"You know how to use this, don't hesitate," he ordered before taking Randy's mouth in a deep kiss. "I love you, babe. Stay safe for me."

"I love you too, Jake. Please be careful," Randy begged.

He gave Jake one more kiss before he was led to the basement. Jake disappeared and Randy was left praying he'd see him again. The basement was a hive of activity. Shannon and Matthew were sitting at a table surrounded by screens, keyboards, and what looked like game controllers.

Sam and Tristan were rounding up Buddy and Luna into a room farther back and out of the way. Randy slid his gun into the holster he'd buckled onto his waist and noticed that everyone was armed. The alarms were silenced and the lights blinked off. For the longest two seconds of his life, Randy stood in complete darkness.

The next moment the screens lit back up as well as all of Shannon's and Matthew's equipment. "Like I didn't expect them to cut off the juice." She laughed. "Rent-a-thug wannabes."

Randy looked over at Jo, who handed him a flashlight and replied to his unasked question. "They have backup power cells set up all over the house. Don't worry, hon, they're all well-trained professionals. Shadow will be fine." She was being strong for him, but she had to be worried about her son.

"Um, guys. I think we have a problem," Sam said as he stood holding a flashlight to the front of himself only a few feet away. No one could miss the bright red spots on Sam's yellow shirt.

Chapter Fourteen

The farm was dark but that made no difference to the team, they could work effectively in any situation. They'd trained for it. Shadow knew Shannon would have her backups in the basement to keep the systems running. Dave, Grady, Jackson, and his men were stationed around the house to keep anyone out while Shadow and his team went hunting.

"Six targets, sending image." Matthew's voice was calm as it came over their earpieces. He knew the drones were hovering above them.

Shadow hunkered down behind an old cement silo that hadn't been used in years and had begun crumbling on one side. He slid his left sleeve up to reveal his tracker, which had six tiny red dots on it. All the other men assisting them and the team were wearing tiny transponders that showed them as white dots. When Bowen and his men crossed onto the property, the sensors would have picked them up and released a clear mist into the air that covered their clothing, making them bright red to all sensors and drones. Shadow couldn't help but think one of those red dots was Bowen and how much he hoped to meet him face-to-face.

He stuck to the plan, chose the dot closest to him, and cleared his mind and began flowing from one shadow to the next, never quite seen. The howling wind was all they heard. Not a single misplaced step, not a sound. His world narrowed to one specific target that had walked by him unaware of the danger he was in.

Without missing a step, Shadow materialized from his hiding place as the hired thug turned. He didn't stand a chance. Within seconds, Shadow was pulling the unconscious body into the underbrush so as not to alert anyone else of his fate.

Once he had him tied up and tucked away, Shadow reemerged, rechecked his tracker, and was about to carry on to the next closest target when gunfire erupted near the house. His first instinct was to race back to make sure Randy was safe, but he fought it, knowing that they'd prepared for that. There were trained men watching the house. He had to carry on with the mission.

Again, he zeroed onto the next trespasser on his screen. He noticed another white dot headed that way, but something inside Shadow told him to follow. He never questioned that little voice. It had saved his life on more than one occasion.

He blended back into the shadows and followed them across the farm and up to the bunkhouse. Shadow looked at his tracker and noticed the other red dots were no longer moving except for the one two hundred yards ahead of him past the corner of the bunkhouse.

Hoping that meant all the others had been captured, Shadow carried on toward his target. When he eased around the corner, he was surprised by what he saw, but he remained hidden, moving in the shadows. Bowen stood over Jackson, who was kneeling on the ground with his hands behind his head.

Shadow had no idea why Jackson was out here, but that could be settled later. The anger on Jackson's face told him enough. If given a chance, Jackson would kill his brother where he stood. It was poignant how Randy and Grady's love for each other saved them, while Bowen and Jackson would assuredly leave here with the other one dead.

"You're helping them destroy me," Bowen screamed. "You bastard. You think you can take over for me while I'm rotting in some jail cell?"

"You're nothing but a thug, Stone. You bribe, blackmail, hurt, and kill people on a daily basis. It's time for that to end."

"Oh and you're the one to stop me? After I put a bullet in your head, I'm going to find that little faggot and tear strips of his flesh off until he tells me where my money is," Bowen snarled, making it difficult for Shadow not to react by ending his existence.

"Don't you mean Fellowship money, brother? I'm sure they're hunting you as we speak," Jackson fired back with undisguised disgust.

"Once I have the money, I'll disappear. They'll never catch me and there's nothing your do-gooder ass can do to stop me," Bowen sneered even though Jackson was looking the other way.

"Oh, you poor, overconfident bastard. You've already been caught," Jackson said, and he did the strangest thing, he looked straight at Shadow. No one could uncover him when he was in the field. He wondered how Jackson knew he was there.

"What are you talking about? There's no one here but you and me, asshole." Bowen scanned the area, his eyes flicking right over Shadow without seeing him. "It's time for you to die. I'll make sure dear old Dad follows you shortly."

Before Bowen lifted to aim his gun at the back of Jackson's head, Shadow used the red dot on his sight to paint Bowen's chest before walking out of the shadows.

"Put the gun down," Shadow ordered, but Bowen didn't move.

He looked up at Shadow, his eyes wild with rage. Shadow glanced at Jackson and that's when they both realized Bowen was going to fire his gun. Without hesitation, Shadow pulled the trigger and eliminated the threat.

Bowen's body crumpled to the ground alongside his brother, who was down on his hands and knees throwing up. It was never easy seeing a dead body but was made worse since it was Jackson's brother.

Moments later members of his team emerged from the cornfield and around the side of the bunkhouse. Dante went into assessment mode immediately. "We whole?"

The team looked around at each other and everyone seemed fine, but Shadow remembered the gunfire near the house. "There was an incident near the house," he stated and was ready to run in that direction until Vincent stopped him.

"It's okay, brother. The one who tried to get near the house is no longer a concern."

"Thank you, brother."

Shadow was anxious to return to Randy but knew he had to stay and help. He went to collect the unconscious man he'd hidden and once Shadow carried the guy and deposited him on the ground, Dante motioned for him to go to the house. He didn't have to be told twice and took off at a run.

As he neared he announced himself through their earpieces. He didn't need to be accidentally shot. A body lay in the laneway as he came around from the back of the house. Nigel, that POS. Shadow remembered what the guy looked like from the picture Randy used to identify him.

When he reached the porch, Grady was waiting for him and asked, "Is Randy safe?"

"The threat no longer exists," Shadow told him before slapping him on the shoulder and walking into the house.

He headed straight for the basement door and opened it, careful not to break another set of hinges. His mom would have his hide if he kept doing that. His joy was short-lived when he saw Sam and his mom cleaning their bloody hands off on towels. When his mom saw him, she didn't even try to explain, knowing that Shadow was beyond logic, and pointed to the spare bedroom.

Without missing a beat, he turned and headed straight for the room. The door was open so he walked right in, ready to handle any possible situation except the one in front of him. Randy sat on the floor beside Luna, Buddy, and a pile of blankets. It wasn't until he saw one of the blankets move that he realized what was going on.

"Puppies." Randy gaped with all the awe of a child who'd seen his first Christmas tree.

Shadow set his rifle down and slid to the floor beside his man. The doggie parents fussed over their babies as Randy looked on in amazement. Shadow had gone from death to birth in the span of minutes. It felt almost surreal until Randy laid his head against Shadow's shoulder, bringing him back to reality.

Sitting by the light of a single flashlight, Shadow held Randy as the new family bonded. For once, he didn't want to disappear into the shadows.

"Love you, Jake," Randy whispered.

Shadow ran his fingers through Randy's blond hair, thanking everyone and anyone who may have had anything to do with their meeting. "I love you, Randy. You are the light to my shadow."

Epilogue

Randy cleaned his brushes as he thought about the next steps in his creation. The murmuring of people in the background didn't bother him in the least, he'd become accustomed to it over the past couple weeks.

He stretched his stiff back and stared at his work in progress. It was much bigger than anything he'd ever done before, but he thought it was coming along well. The sound of a circular saw blasted into his space when the exterior door was opened. He looked up to find Jesse, Royce, and Jake walking into the building.

Randy packed away his supplies. He had a date tonight and he wasn't going to miss one minute of it.

"Wow…I still can't believe you're doing this for us," Jesse gushed.

"It's breathtaking," Royce agreed as he wrapped his arm around Jesse's waist.

Randy looked up at the mural he was creating for the new Haven center. It would be the first thing people saw when they walked into the building, and Randy wanted it to be perfect.

"A mural from Randy Reynolds." Jesse sighed. "Are you sure you don't want to be paid for this?"

Randy gathered up his messenger bag containing his sketches and designs and joined Jake, who was holding his arms open for him to walk straight into. He loved that his partner knew exactly what he needed.

"I don't want payment. I want it to be my contribution to this special place. What you're doing here is beyond anything I ever imagined possible. There was a time I could have used a place like this."

When he glanced outside, he saw a few of the survivors from the camp working on one of the gardens. It had been months since the terror that Bowen had created was ended. With his death went the mystery of the missing money and over two hundred individuals were waiting behind bars for their trials.

However, at the moment all that mattered was Jake. The man who'd saved him not only by breaking him out of the camp but through his unwavering support and love.

"You ready to go, baby?" Jake asked as he took the bag from Randy and threw it over his own shoulder.

"Yep. Grady and Ben are going to meet us at the restaurant. When is Mom due to arrive?" Randy had begun calling Jo Mom.

"She should be in by Wednesday," Shadow answered before turning to Jesse and Royce. "Good night, guys."

"Wait, we forgot to give you the good news," Jesse told them. "We received a large anonymous donation. Now we can finish the pool area before we open the doors."

"That's great news," Jake said as he hugged Randy closer. Jake knew better than to ask if Randy had anything to do with it. He'd shared that multiple charities benefitted and never said anything more.

Jake walked out to his truck with his arm around Randy's shoulders. When they were a few feet away the head of one of Luna's pups popped up in the back window of the quad cab. The puppies were over ten weeks old and were almost ready for adoption by their new owners all over Brighton. It had been hard for Randy since he'd become attached to the runt of the litter. The little guy had fought so hard to live and flourish even though he was half the size of his brothers and sisters. They had struck up a sort of kinship.

"What's Bits doing here? I thought his new owner was coming to get him today."

"His owner is about to take possession," Shadow stated as he held out a white, bone-shaped dog tag with Bits written across it in big black letters.

Randy looked between the tag and the happy puppy bouncing up on the seat trying to get a glimpse of them.

"He's mine?" This wasn't making sense. "But you told me we weren't ready to take on a puppy. That it would be too much work."

"After seeing the connection you two have, there was no way I could break that up."

Randy's heart began to race as he jumped into Shadow's arms and kissed him deeply before sliding down and running for the truck. He opened the back door and Bits flew across the seat and into Randy's arms.

As Bits licked his cheek, Randy brought him over to Jake. His man wrapped both of them in his big arms and one word kept echoing through Randy's mind.

Family.

THE HOLIDAYS

Brighton, Texas. Population 6,293 (and counting) – est. 1895

A town founded on the one guiding belief that families have the right to take any form, shape, or size. All are welcome, and anyone can find their place here.

Chapter One

Gabe and Johnny

Johnny ran the tips of his scarred fingers across the raised lettering of his and Gabe's wedding invitation. The gold calligraphy seemed to dance across the page as his heart sped up at the thought that in less than thirty days he'd be marrying the man who'd literally saved his life, and then had shown him what real love felt like. The date was set for December twenty-fourth, Christmas Eve, and Johnny knew that no other present could ever compare to the vows they planned to say to one another.

The invitations had been sent out weeks ago, and now Johnny was busy creating a wedding scrapbook that they could show their children someday. Yes, that's right, children. Over a year ago they'd filled out copious amount of paperwork, had been visited by social workers a number of times, and then they were told to wait. Gabe and Johnny had been placed on an adoption waiting list, and it had been almost a year before they finally received word that a three-year-old girl from Costa Rica needed a loving home.

They'd been given the news two months ago. Gabe had been so excited that he'd called four times, texted eight times, and when he burst through the door of their home, Johnny would never forget Gabe's whooping and hollering when he tore down the hall and launched himself into Johnny's arms.

Lucy would be arriving in less than a week, and thanks to the help of the Mason clan—he loved those Masons—who worked by Gabe's and Johnny's sides, the guys believed they were ready. Well, as ready as anybody can be when a child was coming into their home.

On numerous occasions since they'd received the news, Johnny had been brought to tears at the thought of their daughter being with them on their wedding day. Of course, Lucy would be part of the event since they were a family. He wondered how overwhelmed she'd feel, but hoped by that time she'd know how much she was loved and wanted, and would see the wedding as a big party. Thankfully, the wedding had been planned down to the last napkin, so he and Gabe could spend their time with their daughter, making sure she felt she was home and loved.

The weather had cooled, with highs in the sixties and lows in the forties, but he was nice and warm. He'd set up a secondary office space in the corner of Gabe's greenhouse, among his love's stunning orchids. With his specially modified computer system, Johnny had been able to carry on after the fire damaged his hands and body. His clientele didn't care that he'd lost the full range of motion in a few of his fingers due to the nerve damage caused by the flames. As long as they received sound marketing advice and moneymaking advertisements, they were happy. However, with the pending arrival of their daughter, Johnny had scaled back his client roster so he could concentrate his time on Lucy.

Gabe would be home any minute from his shift at the fire station, the last one for a few months. He was taking parental leave so their family could bond. Since they'd begun submitting their paperwork, Gabe had been banking his leave time—no vacations this past year—to cover bonding leave when their child arrived.

Johnny heard Gabe's truck pull into their driveway and set his project aside for later; his man was home. Johnny pulled his jacket around himself and left the greenhouse. He went into the house through the patio doors and heard knocking on the front door. He was sure that had been Gabe's truck pulling up the drive, so why would he knock?

Johnny rushed to the door and opened it wide. What he found on the other side was a bit shocking. He was face-to-face with a bear. A stuffed bear almost the same size as he was with plush pink fur, big brown eyes, and a rainbow bowtie. He stepped back as the bear entered followed by his overjoyed fiancé.

"Honey, we have a lot of toys for Lucy already." Johnny didn't want to sound stern since Gabe's joy filled the room. There was no doubt who of the two of them would be the one spoiling their daughter.

"I couldn't say no to Ms. Snuffle Van Bearstein when I saw her in the window over at Marie's toy shop."

"Who?" Johnny asked. Gabe held out a framed birth certificate with gold and pink curlicues around the edges. Sure enough, Ms. Van Bearstein's name was on it. "Well, as long as it's all legal, I guess it's okay," Johnny joked as he took Gabe's duffle bag and set it on the couch. The sight of Johnny's large, muscled firefighter holding a giant pink teddy bear made him melt. The strong, dominant man who thrived on control and taking care of others was completely blown away, and undone, by their daughter's impending arrival.

Years ago, Gabe had pulled Johnny out of a burning building, sat with him for days on end in the hospital, and then brought him home, opening his world to unconditional love. He could imagine what his loving man would do for his child.

Gabe set the new bear on the chair and pulled Johnny into his arms. "I love you, Johnny."

He couldn't help but sink into Gabe's arms; the man was irresistible. "I love you too, honey. Should we go find a home for the new arrival?"

"Definitely." Gabe smiled. "But first, I've been dreaming of doing this all day." Johnny was swept up into Gabe's arms, and turned until his back was pressed against the living room wall.

Gabe didn't give Johnny a chance to catch his breath. He was being kissed by a man enflamed. Gabe thoroughly mapped Johnny's mouth with an eager tongue before releasing him, leaving him hard and needy. Johnny held on to his fiancé's hand for a few seconds. He needed to allow his head to stop spinning while adjusting his jeans.

Gabe had a way of taking over, leaving Johnny dizzy from the onslaught, but he wouldn't have it any other way.

Once he regained the ability to walk, Johnny followed Gabe down the hallway with Lucy's big pink bear in tow. As soon as they got the news, they'd rushed out and bought paint and furniture to convert one of the guestrooms into their daughter's bedroom. Johnny had designed the room to be airy and calm by suggesting they paint it a soft muted blue with an occasional cloud or bird in the sky. Gabe had painted the blue and Johnny painted the clouds, birds, and tree on the far side of the longest wall. A small play table sat under the painted leaves, and Lucy's hand-crafted wooden bed, sat a few feet away. A gift from Gabe's aunts, who knew many local artists through their shop, Hidden Treasures. They'd had the bed commissioned.

The closet was full of clothing in their daughter's size and bigger. The adoption agency had provided Lucy's measurements as well as a few precious photographs. The child's toy box was filled to the brim as Gabe proudly set Ms. Van Bearstein in the center of the white duvet covering the bed.

"Perfect," Gabe announced with pride before pulling Johnny close. "Absolutely perfect."

Johnny knew he wasn't only commenting about the room. It had been a hard road getting to this place, but now that they'd arrived at this point, Johnny could be philosophical about what they'd been through. The fire had brought him Gabe, and the time he'd spent healing gave them time to get to know one another, to explore their deep feelings, wants, and desires. The physical trauma of losing the full use of his hands had taught Johnny patience while he worked through physiotherapy. And while he would have been all too happy not to have experienced the pain knowing this about himself, Chris, Gabe's ex, had taught Johnny to fight for what he wanted.

His life had completely changed compared to when he lived under his father's rule. He hadn't heard from his father in over three years, which was odd, given his father thrived on controlling his sons.

That thought reminded him. "Frank sent me another email today. He received the invitation to our wedding." His brother still lived in the same Manhattan condominium for the past eight years, making it easy to track him down.

"What did your brother have to say?" Gabe asked, unable to conceal his concern.

Johnny understood the trepidation. He and Frank had lost touch for what felt like a lifetime. Johnny had assumed his brother had been living the life of a celebrity plastic surgeon and had no time for him. About the same time his father had thankfully decided to lose interest in Johnny, unfortunately, so did Frank. Which made sense since the communication stopped a little before his brother and father became partners in their own practice.

"That he may be able to come to our wedding." Even though they'd lost touch, Johnny still wanted his brother there when he married Gabe.

"Really?" Gabe sounded shocked.

"Yes. What do you think?" Johnny asked, because at the moment he didn't even have a clue as to how he felt about it. He'd asked figuring he'd receive no response or a no. The "maybe" yes had surprised him.

"Honestly, that he wants something," Gabe stated bluntly.

"Why? I don't have anything."

"You haven't talked to your brother in years and then suddenly he's free for our wedding. It's suspicious." Gabe shook his head.

Johnny couldn't disagree. The sudden "warming" was odd. Now that Gabe knew Frank might come to the wedding, he'd be in protection mode if Frank showed, which meant he'd be keeping an eye on the man.

"I know it's out of character for him to say yes, and we talked about me sending the invitation, but I need to know why he stepped out of my life like that."

"You may not like the answer, baby." Gabe held him close. "But I'll be right by your side."

Johnny never doubted that for a second.

***

Five days later, Gabe was sitting next to Johnny in one of the adoption agency's offices, which they had decorated to look more like a living room. They were waiting for their daughter to arrive. Gabe was excited and terrified at the same time, but he had to be strong for Johnny, who looked two seconds away from an emotional breakdown. His love had such a soft and caring heart, Gabe knew he was lucky to have him, and little Lucy was about to learn how special a daddy Johnny would be.

"What if she's afraid of us?" Johnny asked, squeezing Gabe's hand tight.

"This is all new to her, baby. She's bound to be afraid of a lot of things until she becomes accustomed to our home and to us." Gabe went with logic to try to calm his fiancé.

"What if I screw up?"

"All new parents feel that way."

"If we have to wait much longer, I think I might pass out," Johnny admitted. Gabe was unsure if he was joking or not, so he pulled his chair closer in case.

Gabe had been dreaming of this moment for many years and it was finally here. He was finally getting the family he'd dreamed of, and he couldn't be happier. Of course, he and Johnny were a family already but with so much love to give, it made sense to share it. Providing a child with a safe, loving home where they could grow in peace was natural to him.

He thought he'd try to take Johnny's mind off the waiting. "Jesse called to say Randy finished the mural in Haven so everything is moving as planned and should be ready for the wedding and reception."

Jesse and Royce were almost at the end of construction on the new Safe Haven Center for the LGBTQ+ community's teenagers and adults in crisis. Everyone called it Haven for short. It combined housing, schooling, and counseling for anyone in need. Many of the homeless youths were escaping violence, and/or were kicked out of their family homes because of their sexual orientation or gender identity. The Haven was open to anyone who needed a safe place until they could get back on their feet.

Gabe and Johnny had decided to have their wedding there on Christmas Eve in celebration of new beginnings. For them, for Haven, and for all the people who would be helped in the coming years.

Before Johnny could respond to Gabe's comment, the door to the room opened and Mrs. Connor, the representative from the adoption agency, walked in carrying an adorable toddler in her arms. Lucy Rose Mason. Her brown hair was up in a ponytail, her beautiful dark eyes looked around the room, and her chubby cheeks showcased the cutest dimples.

Their daughter Lucy was perfect.

They both stood, unsure if they should approach her or wait for her to come to them. Thankfully, Mrs. Connor took that decision out of their hands.

"Why don't the two of you sit down in the play area and we'll join you," she suggested.

"Thank you," Gabe said in relief.

"It's normal for parents to be cautious, not wanting the first time they meet their child to be stressful. I've seen children leave here in tears and others in laughter. Neither reaction has any effect on the bond that will grow weeks and months into the future. Please don't worry."

Gabe led Johnny to the thick rug in the play area and they sat cross-legged on the floor. Mrs. Connor brought Lucy over; her tiny head was turning left and right trying to see everything in the room.

Gabe's heart was racing as his daughter was placed on the floor, among the toys, a foot away from them.

At first, she looked a bit unsure until Johnny got down on his belly and began playing with the toys. Leave it to him to break the ice. Lucy joined right in as if she'd done this a thousand times. Gabe lay down on the other side of their daughter, picked up a plush stuffed puppy, and began to play with it. The three of them carried on like this, playing with and talking to Lucy, who seemed to accept their presence.

"I see the scar from her surgery is healing well," Johnny whispered to Mrs. Connor.

Gabe had noticed the scar on his daughter's top lip. Lucy had had surgery to repair her cleft lip and palate.

"Yes, the surgeon with Doctors Without Borders has helped children from the orphanage before and, apparently, is well known in his field. He did an amazing job and her speech has improved because of it," Mrs. Connor explained.

"How delayed is her speech?" Gabe asked.

"I was told six months. On occasion she will repeat a small word but hasn't managed to put two words together quite yet."

Gabe's heart skipped a beat when Lucy crawled over to him and handed Gabe a block before taking the stuffed puppy he was holding. His cheeks hurt, he was smiling so wide. "Do you like the puppy, Lucy? He's soft, isn't he?" She probably had no idea what he was saying, but her toothy smile was all the response he needed.

"Pu…pup," Lucy said as she bounced the stuffed animal on the ground.

"Yes, puppy. You have a puppy," Johnny's voice cracked slightly as he spoke, his emotions riding close to the surface.

Gabe knew those were happy tears gathering in those stunning green eyes, but apparently Lucy didn't. She scooted herself closer to Johnny before handing him the puppy. In all honesty, she sort of mushed it into Johnny's face, but it produced the same result. Johnny held the stuffed puppy as if it were the most precious gift he'd ever received.

That was how their new family began their life together.

Years later, when their daughter would surely ask why a raggedy stuffed puppy was tucked away in the safe, Gabe would explain how it was her Pop's most prized possession.

Chapter Two

Sam, Dante, and Spider

Dante backed the final trailer up to the garage of a colorful bungalow located pretty much in the center of Brighton. An American flag attached to the front porch blew in the wind of the cool December afternoon, but Dante couldn't have felt warmer or happier than he was at this moment. Sam, the man responsible for this day, walked out the front door and up to the rear of the trailer. Other team members had already returned to the main house in their compound to get things ready for the barbeque celebration.

He shut the truck off and stepped out onto the newly mowed lawn, which they had cut yesterday when they had gotten back from another mission. The house hadn't been lived in for a little while and would need to have a few things repaired and refreshed, but his mom had loved it the first time she'd laid her eyes on it.

Yes, Joanne and Frank Phillips had moved to Brighton, and Dante was ecstatic along with his partners Sam and Spider. Truthfully, if it hadn't been for Sam's digging, and his huge, unrelenting heart, none of this would be happening. Dante tried not to think of the many years wasted due to a stupid misunderstanding, and while he wished he could get them back, he knew he couldn't undo the past. Now, he had a chance to rebuild his relationship with his foster parents, who had been "real" parents, and it was full steam ahead.

"Are you going to help with these boxes or are you going to stand there all day looking at the lawn?" Sam asked while juggling two boxes in his arms.

"Yes, Trouble, I'm coming," Dante huffed good-naturedly, receiving a glowing smile from his fiery redheaded lover before he walked back into the house.

A lot had happened since he and Spider first met Sam. Between houses blowing up, and adding Randy, Shadow's partner, the latest member to the Sentinel's ranks of significant others, it had been a nonstop several months. However, now they were taking some time off, the whole team, to enjoy the holidays, and the New Year with the people they loved.

Spider came out the open garage door and he immediately wrapped his arms around Dante. "Happy, love?"

"Yes, and I'll be much happier when we get this couch in the house," Dante grumbled before nibbling the side of Spider's thick neck. "Then I can get you and Sam home and start the real fun."

"That's sounds perfect," Spider moaned as Dante continued to explore.

"Sounds good to me too," Sam laughed as he popped up in between them exactly where they liked him. Spider kissed the side of Sam's head while Dante mapped his mouth with his tongue. His men meant the world to him, and the love the three of them shared was forever growing.

"You three can't help yourselves, can you?" his mom asked from somewhere behind them. His parents supported the fact that they'd become a triad, and seemed to fit in well with the Brighton philosophy of accepting families of all shapes and sizes.

"Spider's the one who started it," Dante threw his love right under the bus—figuratively.

"You little shit," Spider growled before laughing along with Sam and his parents.

The three broke up their impromptu love-fest of sorts and attacked the rest of the boxes and furniture. Once they had everything placed where his mom wanted it, for the fourth or fifth time, the four men collapsed onto the couch they'd just moved…again. Dad took a drink from his water bottle before calling an end to the day's activities.

"Joanne, sweetheart, stop before I gain a hernia along with this money pit," Dad joked as he stretched out his back. "I'm getting too old for this."

"First, it's a beautiful house, and second, you were told not to lift anything heavy by the entire team, your son, Spider, and Sam. So don't be whining about it now."

Leave it to Mom to cut straight through the bullshit. It was her gift. Dante couldn't help but laugh. He'd missed this. Hell, he'd missed everything about the two people who had saved his life. Without Frank and Joanne Phillips, Dante seriously doubted whether he'd be alive today. When he was young, after his father had taken off and his mother drank herself to death, he was left in the care of his sadistic uncle. After one beating, he'd gone to the Phillipses' house for help after not being able to stop his nosebleed by himself. He never returned to his uncle's "care."

Sometimes, Dante questioned his good fortune after finding Spider. Then the two of them found Sam, and now having his parents back in his life it all seemed too good to be true. It was overwhelming and exhilarating at the same time.

This year he'd be counting his blessings with his family.

***

Spider drove their truck back to their big old Victorian. On the way, they stopped to admire the holiday decorations making their appearance all over town. It seemed everywhere you looked there were menorahs or Kwanza baskets in windows, tinkling multicolored lights, flowers, tinsel, ribbon, and sparkling bulbs hanging from trees and bushes. He hadn't had the chance to enjoy a real Christmas in a long time. Of course, he, Dante, and their team had celebrated one way or another, but they'd usually been on missions at the time.

This year they'd be home with their loved ones without having to dodge any incoming rounds, or burrow in some hellhole tunnel.

The Sentinels' house had been decorated with the help of the entire team and their partners. At night, it shone like a beacon with all the lights they had strung up on it. The one time he'd mentioned that they might have overdone it, he was banished to the garage to untangle four more boxes of the twinkling bastards. Spider never made that mistake again.

Both Dante and Sam were lost in thought, but both had smiles on their faces, which made Spider happy. His parents had died a long time ago, while he was still in the military, but between the Masons and Dante's parents, and their team family, Spider never felt lonely. Of course, he missed his folks, but the pain was a bit lighter having all the people he cared about and who cared about him around.

As they pulled up to the house, all that cheery goodness was out on display for Dante's parents' arrival. Their car pulled up right behind Spider's truck and everyone jumped out. The wind blew colder as night had fallen, but at least he wasn't shoveling snow. There were benefits to this milder weather they were having.

"Sons, it's beautiful," Joanne's voice cracked, and Sam wrapped his arms around her as Frank stood between Dante and Spider. Sam's heart knew no bounds, and all Spider could say was that he was blessed to have his love.

"You've done good, boys," Frank said as he placed his arms over their shoulders and gave them a hug. "We're so proud to be a part of your family."

Dante and Spider hugged him back and the five of them walked up the blinking walkway into the shiny house. Once they opened the doors, two excited dogs and a pack of puppies greeted them with licks and barks. Buddy was wearing reindeer antlers and Luna had on a candy cane collar while their puppies, all six of them, had miniature collars with Christmas colors on display.

"It's like Christmas blew up in here." Spider could hear the disbelief in his own voice.

The team had been busy while the five of them finished off the Phillipses's new house. Garland was strung across the wide living room from all points on the ceiling. The furniture was covered in themed pillows, and the tables were covered with beautiful red and green linens. Several sconces now had themed light bulbs, and everywhere he looked, stars, Christmas trees, angels, reindeer, and snowmen covered every flat surface in the house. The big Christmas tree they'd set up a few days ago was now covered with even more lights, and a large fluffy white tree skirt was wrapped around its base with wrapped presents loaded beneath it.

"How long have we been gone?" Dante asked, sounding as shocked as he felt.

"This team rocks," Sam cheered as he ran around looking at the decorations and checking out the tags on each of the presents.

A heavenly smell was coming from the back of the house, so they followed their noses to the screened-in back patio. There were space heaters to assure everyone stayed warm while the barbeques flamed away at the far end. Once they stepped over the threshold, the team cheered, raising their drinks in celebration.

"It isn't Christmas yet?" Dante asked as he held on to Spider's and Sam's hands.

"We don't need an occasion to celebrate being together, we're a family," Shannon explained before she wrapped her arm around Jackson Bowen. They'd been dating since meeting on their last mission to protect Randy from Jackson's brother.

Spider could feel the slight tremble in Dante's hand before he spoke. "I want to thank all of you, every single one. I…I remember the child I was, wishing for this, and you've all given that to me. It's a gift I can never repay."

Both he and Sam were quick to gather Dante into their arms. Their triad and their extended family could never be replaced. He looked out to see every member of his team, with their partners, along with Frank and Joanne, holding a glass up. Matthew quickly brought over three glasses of beer for them.

Dante raised his glass and shouted, "To family."

"To family," everyone cheered in unison with a few barks from the puppies added in to round out the joy.

It wasn't fancy, there was no champagne, and there were more than a few ripped jeans in the group, but he couldn't have been in finer company.

It was his and it was perfect.

***

Sam set the last plate into the dishwasher, closed the door, and turned it on. He didn't want to leave a mess for Mrs. Walker. Frank and Joanne had gone home, a few of the team members were still hanging out in the living room while others had already said their good nights and were off to bed. Spider walked into the kitchen with the lasts bits of trash, deposited them in the garbage, and took Sam into his arms.

He loved the feeling of being in his lovers' tattooed, muscled arms. His men were gods and he was a lucky and happy man. They loved him so completely that Sam never had any doubts since they'd sorted out their bumps in the road to forever.

"Are Dante's parents okay with going to Gabe and Johnny's wedding?" They were new to town and told Sam they didn't want to impose even though Johnny had invited them.

"Yeah, they're good once we explained that most of the town would be there at some point during the day," Spider assured as he nibbled down the side of Sam's neck. "I've sent Dante to have a shower, baby. Do you want to go and help scrub his back?" Spider asked before lifting Sam off the floor and into his arms. "I'll scrub yours."

Sam couldn't help the small moan that escaped as Spider kissed and nuzzled the side of his neck. He basked in the attention Spider was giving him. The three of them had fought tooth and nail for their happy ending, and he'd never take any of this for granted.

He could feel they were moving down the hallway toward their suite of rooms, but chose to concentrate on Spider's glorious lips instead. Spider's teeth scraped against his sensitive skin, causing goosebumps to rise all over his overheated body.

As soon as they closed the door to their private realm, they began stripping at a frantic pace, desperate to get back in each other's arms. The second his boxers hit the floor, Sam jumped up into his lover's waiting embrace and dove in for a deep kiss full of tongues and teeth. He could hear the water running in their walk-in shower and Spider turned in that direction.

Sam knew Dante would already know they were there. No one could sneak up on the man. Spider carried Sam straight into the shower and into Dante's open arms.

"There you are, beautiful. I've been waiting for my men to join me," Dante said in a way that felt like he was claiming them all over again.

Sam felt Spider cover his back and he found himself back in his favorite place, cuddled between his men. The brilliantly colored tattoos on his arms stood in contrast to Dante and Spider's black and gray military designs. He loved that about himself and his men, the differences, which only made them a stronger triad.

His men's hands ghosted across his sensitive skin as they explored his body while Sam chased the beads of water running down Dante's neck with his tongue.

"God I love the two of you so much," Dante growled, taking Spider's lips in a demanding kiss before turning and doing the same to Sam.

Once he could breathe again Sam replied, "I love you too, Dante." Then turning his head he looked Spider in the eyes. "I love you, Jack. I don't know how I ever lived without the two of you."

"You'll never have to find that out, baby. I love you and Dante, and plan to spend the rest of my life like this," Spider explained before he reached for the waterproof lube they kept in the shower. "Now, I need to be balls deep inside you."

Soon Sam felt Spider's thick finger circling his hole, loosening the tight muscles. Then a second finger joined it from the opposite side. Dante. His two lovers worked together until Sam was a writhing mess whimpering between them. His hard cock felt like it was ready to explode, but he fought off his orgasm with everything he had, this wasn't ending so soon.

Spider took him into his arms and pressed his back against the cool tile wall. Sam wrapped his legs around his lover's muscled waist and began sucking marks up on his neck, Sam's cock finding much needed friction against Spider's rippled abdomen.

"Hold on, baby, no coming yet," Spider groaned loudly, and Sam felt the large, spongy head of Spider's cock at his entrance.

"I need—" Whatever he was about to say was cut off by his own deep moan as Spider sank his thick cock deep in one slow stroke.

Sam felt full as every nerve ending in his body screamed to life while he held on to his lover's shoulders and watched as Dante approached Spider from behind. Spider's body shook as he waited for Dante to prepare him for his cock. Sam couldn't hold still no matter how hard he tried and began pushing himself farther down on Spider's throbbing shaft.

"Dante, sweetheart. You'd better make this quick. I need you inside me before Sam has me pounding him into the tile."

Dante must have taken Spider at his word because in under a minute Dante was stepping up behind Spider to slide himself in. Spider moaned in Sam's ear, every hitch in Spider's breath and tremble in his body sent Sam further into a world of pure pleasure.

Spider moved Sam up and down on his cock while Sam took the opportunity to rub his needy shaft against Spider's abs. Dante hissed as he pulled out of Spider and slammed right back in, causing Sam to slide even farther down on Spider's cock. All three moaned as their triad joined, and soon the sound of skin meeting skin and men groaning filled their *en suite*.

Dante leaned forward and took Sam's lips in a demanding kiss as he pounded into Spider while Spider did the same to Sam. He ran his hands over both of his men. Their pupils were blown wide open as both of his lovers looked at Sam with raw, passionate love. That was Sam's tipping point, without one more rub against Spider's tight abs, Sam came in long, pulsing streams against Spider.

He felt Spider's cock pulse as Sam's own muscles squeezed his lover tight until he too came with a loud roar. Sam's eyes were fuzzy as he watched Dante's face transformed from almost pain and need into unadulterated joy and pleasure. It was beautiful to witness his men at their most vulnerable.

Dante leaned his head on Spider's back as Sam leaned back against the now warm tile wall. Spider stood supporting both of them without a single complaint. Sam felt his men washing his body and heard their murmuring voices, but all the day's activity had caught up with him, and all he could do was enjoy the ride.

The next thing he knew he was dried and cuddled in the middle of the bed as Dante and Spider turned off the lights. His lovers climbed into bed on either side of him, each wrapping one of their arms over him, loving and protecting him, as was their nature.

"You know I think there's a saying somewhere that you never really meet the ones you were meant to love, because a part of them has been with you all along." Sam spoke just above a whisper. "A part of each of you has been with me from the beginning. I like the sound of that."

Dante leaned over and softly kissed Sam. "I like the sound of that too, beautiful."

Spider kissed his way up from Sam's shoulder until he took control of his lips. Once they parted he said, "When we met, it felt like a part of me recognized you the same way it recognized Dante when we first met."

Sam looked up at his men. "This is exactly where I want to be. No doubts, no regrets, only love."

Dante and Spider looked at each other then back down at Sam. Every emotion was plain to see on their faces: joy, desire, contentment, awe, and profound love.

There wasn't really a need for more words, was there?

Chapter Three

Rick, Bear, and Josh

Rick gathered up the parade of action figures, dolls, blocks, and books from the living room floor for the second time today, knowing he'd be doing it all over again soon enough. The thought brought a smile to his face. He would have never believed it if someone had told him sixteen months ago that he'd be clearing a path through his nephew's toys so his partner could bring in boxes of Christmas decorations from the garage.

Josh was down for his afternoon nap after his play date with Lucy, Gabe and Johnny's newly adopted daughter. The toddler was such a joy, and the pride Rick saw on her parents' faces was unmistakable. Lucy was adjusting well, but didn't wander far away from her dads too often quite yet. She would only allow Johnny and Gabe to lift and carry her, which was completely understandable. After all, everything was all new to her, including the language.

But the one thing she seemed to understand was that she was loved.

This quiet time while Josh was napping would give Rick and Bear the chance to set up the tree by the bay window in their living room. As he went along, Rick couldn't help but look at the pictures that now covered the walls. Front and center was a large picture of Jenny, Josh's mother and Bear's sister, the same dark blue eyes as her brother seemed to watch him as he cleaned. Their new family had done so much since Jenny's death it was sometimes hard to believe that Rick, the anxiety-ridden librarian, was a part of his own family now—toddler included.

Most of the photographs strewn around the house he'd taken. Trips to Dallas and South Padre Island, Kemah Boardwalk, the Children's Museum in Houston, and even a two-day getaway for him and Bear in Galveston Beach were displayed in a variety of frames. Josh had been in the loving care of the White Hair Crew while they were gone. After all, they were the mothers to the whole town.

His life had changed so significantly. It wasn't that his anxiety had magically disappeared, but due to the amazing man who was carrying two boxes through the doorway, Rick had found a way to enjoy life one day at a time.

He jumped out of the way as Bear set the boxes down. The larger of the two contained their big, bushy artificial tree. After hearing the stats on how many fires live trees caused, there was no way he was bringing one into their house. *An average of two hundred structural fires annually in the U.S. caused by Christmas trees.* Now Rick couldn't help but smile at his info-drop, when before Bear, Rick would have chastised himself for his idiosyncrasies. Bear had helped Rick accept that it was part of him and not to feel ashamed when he did it in front of people. Rick was still working on that.

The tree they'd purchased last year before Jenny's death looked like a Virginia pine so there wasn't really a difference if it was alive or not in Rick's mind. Besides, they had a few trees decorated and lit in their yard if anyone wanted to see a living tree sparkle and shine.

Bear turned to Rick and wrapped him in his big arms. "Excited, baby?"

"Yep. You know I love Christmas." Rick had been passionate about Christmas for as long as he could remember. "I enjoy the closeness everyone feels toward each other, the love they share and gifts they give. It's perfect."

"And so are you," Bear softly growled before taking Rick's lips in a deep, exploring kiss. Though Rick wasn't so sure about that, his boyfriend was convinced and stated it often.

It was always a boost knowing that Bear saw him that way. No one else had ever suggested anything even close to perfect in the same sentence as Rick Johansson. It had taken him a while to accept that, but he no longer argued when his lover said it.

"I have three more boxes in the garage plus all the new decorations you've been ordering over the last year." Bear rolled his eyes in mock exasperation.

"Isn't it amazing? You can buy Christmas stuff all year long," Rick gushed, as if that was Christmas magic all by itself.

"I don't know about amazing but I do know it's heavy. Are you sure there isn't too much?" Bear asked for what had to be the tenth time.

"You said the same thing about Easter, July Fourth, and Thanksgiving, but didn't they turn out to be amazing holidays?"

"Yeah, they did," Bear agreed before pulling Rick close and nuzzling the side of his head with a wild beard that tickled. He loved that his big, burly biker was unafraid to show his love. "You've outdone yourself every time. I'm positive that everything you put into it helped Josh through it without his mother. I know it helped me cope without Jenny. You are an incredible man. I love you beyond what I ever thought was possible."

Rick had wanted to make the holidays easier on his family and was happy to hear that it had worked. It had been a year of ups and downs, both emotionally and physically, but they'd survived and flourished together. Rick ran his hand over the scars on his abdomen left by a piece of the engine, which had impaled him after he'd run the car he'd been forced to drive by Josh's attempted kidnapper off the road.

"I love you too, Bear. I love Josh, and I love our new life together. I wouldn't change it for the world," Rick said before giving his love a quick kiss and then a slap to his muscled ass. "Now back to work. My master plan requires time to assemble."

Bear laughed softly, trying not to wake Josh before releasing Rick and heading back to the garage for another load. Rick turned and dug into the first box, his mind awhirl with decor ideas. He pulled out strand after strand of colorful lights, as well as garland and ribbon. He'd always liked colored Christmas lights because it had been his mother's favorite. Carefully he set his mom's nativity scene aside. He would construct the tableau with porcelain figurines on the fireplace mantel to keep it safe. He would never leave Josh out of the fun of putting everything together, so the painted, wooden nativity scene would be assembled lower within Josh's reach.

Smaller boxes containing the different bulbs were placed on the end of their large sectional couch until they put up the tree. Everything was moving along quickly as he emptied box after box of Christmas decorations until the living room was full. He couldn't imagine being happier than he was at that moment.

"Rick, baby, why don't you come sit down on the couch with me for a moment," Bear asked, and Rick turned to find his man sitting in his usual spot in the corner of the sectional. He always said the corner was his because he could hold Rick and Josh on either side of him.

Rick set the tinsel down and walked over to his lover, who had a package wrapped in brown shipping paper on his lap. When they were first getting to know each other, Bear would bring Rick first editions from his favorite author, Tom Clancy. The memory brought a huge smile to his face. The little things his man would do for him only reinforced the rock-solid love they shared.

"What's this?" Rick asked as he cuddled into Bear's waiting arms.

"It's a surprise," Bear replied before biting his lip. "I wanted to give you this not as a Christmas gift but as something from me to the man I love."

Rick hugged Bear close before taking the package in his hands. He opened it, careful not to damage anything beneath the paper. Sure enough, there was a book under the wrapping but it wasn't a novel but a hardcover picture book. Rick looked up at Bear, who only smiled in return.

He opened the first page and found a picture of the four of them, Rick, Bear, Josh, and Jenny before she was hospitalized. The next was a picture of him asleep on Bear's chest, and then one of him sitting at Josh's bedside reading him a book, playing in the backyard in their new sandbox. The next was Josh asleep in Rick's arms as they lay on the couch, and another of Rick covered in sticky marshmallow the day they decided to make s'mores.

The pictures went on and on until Rick came to the end and found a small velvet bag attached to the binding. He looked up at Bear once again.

"Open it, sweetheart," Bear whispered.

Rick could feel his heart racing as he undid the knot with his shaky fingers and reached inside. The metal was warm against his skin and Rick couldn't stop the tears from falling while he removed the gold band from the bag. There were three square-cut diamonds set in the band and engraved on the inside the words "*Simply Perfect.*"

***

Bear could feel his heart doing a drum solo in his chest. He hoped it was excitement and not that he might be having a heart attack.

Rick twisted around until he was facing him. "Bear, it's beautiful."

"Not nearly as much as you are to me," Bear admitted honestly. "The book are pictures of you when you weren't looking. I wanted to show you what I see when I look at you. The love, the bravery, the beauty that is all you, Rick, and I'm the lucky one to have you. I never dreamed I'd have this life, never thought it was possible for me. Who'd think an enforcer with an MC out of Chicago would be given this chance. And I can tell ya, I'm not going to blow it. Marry me, baby. Make an honest man out of me."

Bear brushed the tears off his love's red cheeks. He knew Rick was having a hard time getting himself together, but was surprised when he shoved the ring into Bear's hands. However, at the same moment, Rick extended his left hand and he knew what his love wanted. Bear decided to go all the way. He carried Rick to the center of the living room, surrounded by toys, boxes, and Christmas decorations, and Bear dropped to one knee in front of the man he loved.

"Rick, will you marry me?" Words Bear never thought would come from his mouth now flowed freely to the man who'd changed his world so completely. "Make me the luckiest man on this planet."

"Y-yes. I…I love you, Bear," Rick answered as his voice cracked with emotion.

Bear slid the band onto the third finger of Rick's left hand and then kissed it to seal the deal. Rick clung to him and slid down onto the ground and into Bear's lap. Though Rick was still in tears, Bear knew they were happy tears and shed a few of his own.

There they sat, in each other's arms in a sea of tinsel. It was exactly how Bear wanted it. Real life, not some make-believe moment achieved by spending exorbitant amounts of money. He wasn't saying Rick wasn't worth that, because he was, but that wasn't them. This was real, right here.

"We'll pick a date once the holidays and Gabe and Johnny's wedding are over. I know it will be hard to keep it small, being in Brighton and all, but maybe we could have the ceremony outside." Rick was making plans and Bear's heart sang.

"You can plan it any way you want it, baby. I'm sure the White Hair Crew would love to help us."

"I bet they would. That would be great," Rick near shouted with excitement. Bear had to shake himself that he was the one giving Rick this. Bear was the cause of Rick's happiness and intended to keep doing it until Bear breathed his last breath. "We should get back to it. We should at least have the tree up for Josh to help decorate when he wakes up."

"He will be the ring bearer, and maybe Lucy would like to be the flower girl….wait, stop. One thing at a time, Christmas first, right."

Bear couldn't help but be excited. It wasn't like him to run ahead of himself, but hell, he was marrying Rick. "You're my fiancé now."

"Fiancé," Rick whispered before breaking out into one of his full-on beautiful smiles. "You're my fiancé too."

"I can tell you honestly, I never thought I'd have one," Bear said in awe. "Never thought I'd be this lucky."

"Same here," Rick agreed, never once losing his smile.

Bear stood and helped Rick to his feet. While Rick continued emptying boxes, Bear got busy setting up the tree. They were never more than a few feet away from each other as they worked. Kisses and soft touches seemed to further solidify their bond, and their new path.

Soon Josh woke from his nap and Rick went to get him while Bear continued to wrap lights around the tree. They'd gotten most of the decorations up around the house, and, of course, his fiancé had been correct, it looked amazing. They'd not decorated the tree further than lights and garland. They'd agreed the rest would be done together as a family.

Ten minutes later his family appeared at the bottom of the stairs. Josh's eyes were wide, as he took in the decorations from his perch on his Rick's hip.

"Unk…unk, Christmas," Josh cheered while waving his stuffed dragon in the air.

"Yeah, big guy, Christmas," Bear agreed as he walked over, picked Josh out of Rick's arms, and showed Josh everything.

The three of them did a lap around the house because there wasn't a room untouched by an elf named Rick. Josh seemed to get more and more excited as the tour carried on. They wrapped up beside their Christmas tree. The only boxes left out contained the ornaments.

Bear set Josh down among the boxes. The breakable ornaments were all safely on the dining room table so that Josh could investigate without fear of demolishing anything. Rick and Bear intended that they would finish the tree together every year until

Josh had a family of his own, and then they'd be included in the annual ritual.

The little guy began digging in, pulling one ornament out after the next until he was surrounded. Both Bear and Rick were down on their hands and knees making sure Josh saw every one of them.

"These go on the Christmas tree, Josh," Rick instructed, then picked up a wooden angel and placed it on the tree.

Josh was bright and got the hang of what to do quickly. After the boy had put all "his" ornaments around the tree, they lifted him to the top of the tree to put on more ornaments. Their laughter filled the room as Josh talked their ears off about reindeer as he made one jump from branch to branch.

They stopped decorating to eat dinner as the light outside slowly faded to night. Once the dishes were placed in the dishwasher they came back out to finish, Josh ready to go all over again. Part way through Rick returned to the kitchen to make them all hot chocolate with little marshmallows.

Finally, Rick opened the last box. It contained the angel Bear's sister Jenny had given them for their last Christmas together. Bear could feel the weight pressing down on his chest. He missed his sister. He held Josh a bit closer and took the angel from his fiancé's hands, his grief easy to see no matter how much Rick tried to hide it. Bear loved him so completely and times like this only reinforced that.

Josh touched the golden feathers with the tips of his chubby little fingers. Bear never wanted his nephew to forget Jenny and he would spend the rest of his life reminding her son what a wonderful woman she was. "This is Mommy's angel. Mommy gave this to us." Bear wasn't sure how Josh would react, if at all. It had been months since he'd woken up at night calling for her.

Bear could almost see his toddler brain trying to figure it out. Then suddenly he said, "Mommy loves me," before pointing to the picture Rick had framed and hung on the wall.

Every day he'd hear Rick talking about Jenny to Josh and point at the picture. Bear did it as well, but considering Rick was home full time, he had more of an impact on Josh. It did something to Bear knowing his love was doing everything to keep Jenny's memory alive for Josh.

"Yes, Mommy loves you very much," Rick was quick to say as Bear fought back tears.

He mouthed the words "thank you" to Rick before turning to Josh, saying, "Mommy gave that to us so that she would be with us every Christmas. But you know what I think, big guy?"

Josh looked up at Bear with the same blue eyes as Jenny and Bear had. "I think Mommy is here with us every day, not just Christmas, and she watches over you."

He knew Josh didn't completely understand what Bear was trying to explain but someday he would, and that's what mattered. Bear lifted Josh toward the top of the tree as Rick helped direct Josh what to do. Between the three of them, the angel managed to reach its perch for another season and they turned on the Christmas lights.

The effect was magical, exactly as Rick had intended. The tiny lights glowed cheerfully as the three sank onto the sectional in their normal positions, Bear in the middle with Rick and Josh on either side. Exactly where they belonged and where he could take care of them.

Then he turned on the TV to a Christmas special with Burl Ives narrating as a snowman, the show a classic Bear had grown up watching. He leaned back with his arms around his family and let himself fall into the Christmas magic his love had created.

Chapter Four

Jesse and Royce

"I think it's stunning, absolutely gorgeous. Johnny and Gabe will love it as the backdrop to their wedding," Nardo said before shooting another picture for the *Brighton Bugler*.

Jesse watched on as the young man shined. Nardo had come to Haven with his brother Tony and three more young men when they were rescued from a conversion therapy center in another state. When they'd arrived, Nardo had barely said a word. His older brother, Tony, spoke for him and Nardo had refused to leave his brother's side.

The mural renowned artist Randy Reynolds had painted on the wall in the large community center exuded joy. Jesse wasn't sure how Randy could make paint produce such strong emotions, but it was the man's innate talent, which he shared freely. The mural had been a gift from Shadow and Randy to celebrate The Safe Haven Center's Grand Opening.

"That should do it," Nardo said as he handed the camera back over to Mr. Weaver, the owner of the *Bugler*. He'd come in initially to take the shots himself, noticed Nardo's interest, showed him how the camera worked, and let the young man free.

Nardo looked nervous as Mr. Weaver reviewed the photos on the camera screen. A few moments passed until he looked up at Nardo and said, "You have an eye for this, son. These shots are well done." Then Mr. Weaver reached into his bag, pulled out a business card, and handed it to Nardo. "You give me a call after Christmas and we'll see where you might fit at the *Bugler*."

The young man held the card like it was the most precious thing he'd ever received. "Thank you, Mr. Weaver." Nardo looked over and smiled at Jesse before running to his brother, who was watching from the doors to the small café that they'd built. God he loved Brighton and the people that called it home.

It was these moments that drove Jesse to work harder to ensure as many people as possible had a safe place to go and a place to thrive.

"Have I told you yet how proud I am of you today?" Royce asked as he wrapped his arms around Jesse's waist from behind. His strong arms always made Jesse feel safe and loved even though he outweighed his partner by over sixty-five pounds and stood a few inches taller. Royce was his rock.

"Only once or twice, but I like hearing it. Along with 'I love you,'" Jesse teased as he turned around to face his amazing boyfriend—the man who had stood right beside him through everything that had been thrown at them, even when his family had tried to make Jesse disappear.

"Well then, I must rectify this immediately. I love you, Jesse, and I'm proud of you." Royce's voice was strong and sure, guaranteeing that Jesse never had to worry about his man's feelings.

"Proud of us. We did this together, don't you forget that." Jesse leaned forward and kissed the person who meant everything to him. "Without you, none of this would have ever been possible. Without you, everything could have been taken from me…even my life."

"We're in this together. We're a team, a family." Royce kept his voice low so that their conversation wouldn't be overheard. "Your old family is locked away for a long time. No one will ever hurt you again."

Jesse laid his head against Royce's and simply enjoyed the moment in his partner's arms before the next Haven issue required their attention. As if he'd portended it, a heavy can crashed to the floor somewhere behind him. When Jesse and Royce turned to see what had happened, they found Simon, one of the other young men who'd been brought to Haven from the conversion center, standing over a spilt can of white paint on their newly polished concrete floor. He still had the brush in his hand. He had been helping paint the trim around the doors and windows of the offices.

Simon looked ready to break down or run, either was possible, and Jesse was quick to respond. "It's okay, man. No worries. It was an accident."

Unfortunately, that didn't seem to help and sadly Jesse completely understood. The people coming here for help and safety had been through so much trauma already that they could have fear responses and flashbacks at any time. Simon's hand was shaking so hard that Jesse wasn't sure how he was still holding the brush.

The few people in the large room had stopped what they were doing, and were now staring at Simon. *Not helping*. "Simon, it's okay. Everyone else, please step out for a moment."

As the room cleared, Jesse approached Simon slowly with his hands out in front of him. He tried to make himself as small as possible, which was a feat in itself considering how big he was. He and Simon had spent a fair bit of time talking since he'd arrived and Jesse hoped that would be enough for the scared man to give him a chance.

"No one is upset with you. No one is going to hurt you. I promise you I would never let that happen. It was an accident. We'll clean it up and start over." Jesse kept up the one-sided conversation as he got closer, and it seemed to be working. At least, Simon's hand had stopped shaking.

"B-but I ruined it. It's all my fault. I have to be severely punished or how will you know that I'm sorry?" Simon asked in such a sad voice it nearly broke Jesse's heart. What this poor young man must have gone through.

"I know you're sorry, Simon. It was an accident. You didn't do it on purpose, did you?"

Simon was quick to answer. "No. I would never do that. You've given me so much."

Jesse knelt down beside the puddle of white paint and righted the can. “See, I knew you didn’t. You’ve been such an asset to me since you’ve arrived here. You’re always helping out, showing how much you care about Haven.”

The abject fear in Simon’s eyes finally melted away and he looked at the mess on the floor with new eyes. “How will we clean this up?” Jesse let out a breath he hadn’t known he was holding.

“With these,” Jesse said as he got up, went to the back room and then came out with an arm full of paper towels and a garbage can. “They’ll do the trick, no worries, and we’ll help you.”

Simon looked back and forth between Jesse, who was still kneeling on the floor and Royce, who was standing at the ready. “O-okay,” he agreed, still looking unsure, as if waiting for the other shoe to fall.

Royce handed out the towels and both he and Simon knelt down and joined Jesse as they wiped up the paint. Simon seemed like he was starting to believe nothing bad would happen to him, and one by one, people began returning inside the building and joined in the cleanup. Nardo and Tony brought out cleaning supplies to use on the floor after the paint had been cleared away. Jesse wasn’t one hundred percent sure if the oil-based paint would mar the flooring and didn’t care if it did. It could be replaced. Providing Simon with the safety and security he needed was more important.

With everyone’s help, the mess was cleaned away in no time, and surprisingly with very little damage to the floor. Jesse took the paintbrush out of Simon’s hand, went to the storage room, and got a new can of paint and a brush. When he returned Simon was back to looking unsure even though Royce was talking to him calmly.

Jesse handed the can of paint and new brush to Simon without saying a word. Simon would have to decide if he wanted to pick himself up and try again. Jesse stood silently for a few moments before he put the can and brush down on the floor. He hoped Simon would take that next step and as he was getting ready to walk away, he was shocked when Simon wrapped his arms around him and said, "Thank you."

As quickly as he'd grabbed him, Simon released Jesse, picked up his supplies, and walked back to where he originally had been painting. Jesse watched on with pride. Simon had made it over another hurdle.

A sense of belonging washed over Jesse, He was convinced that this was the path his grandfather had wanted him to take when he'd left Jesse the farm.

He could feel Royce's presence beside him, his rock, always and forever.

***

Hours later Royce was in his home office staring at the nondescript cardboard box at his feet. Hesitating wasn't in his character, and right at that moment he felt unsure, making him even more frustrated.

"How long are you going to stare at it?" Jesse asked from the open doorway. "Tell me what has you so bothered, love, and I'll try to help."

Jesse walked into the room and sat in the chair opposite Royce, placing the box between them. He leaned back in his old leather high-back chair and noted the concern and confusion on his lover's face. That wouldn't do. It was time to man up. He got out of his chair and sat on the carpeted floor before motioning Jesse to join him.

"Come sit with me, love."

The big man could move fast when he wanted to. Jesse was on the floor by Royce's side almost immediately. He wrapped his arm around Jesse and pulled him close. He preferred having his partner as near to him as possible. He didn't know how Jesse would respond to what Royce wanted to do. Would he become angry or defensive? Would he be hurt by it and see it as a slap in his face? Even though

Jesse had been accepting of Royce's past before, it did not mean there wasn't a chance of Royce pushing him too hard.

"Jesse, I have something I'd like to ask you and I want you to answer me honestly. If you have a concern about it, then I will never bring it up again. I won't have you upset and I don't want to hurt you in any way."

As he expected, that got Jesse's full attention. "Is something wrong?"

"No, no, love. It has something to do with my past," Royce tried to explain but wasn't sure where to start.

Jesse cupped Royce's cheek, sending warmth throughout his body. "Whatever it is, Royce, know that I love you. Ask me and we can figure it out together."

"Maybe I should show you first." Royce said before opening the box and pulling the first wrapped figure out of safekeeping, where he'd placed them a lifetime ago.

One by one, he removed the bubble wrap surrounding the figures and buildings until a small town began to take shape. He touched every carved piece with the same care he'd used to pack it away for what he thought would be forever. Now, things had changed. His life was filled with love and purpose again.

"Is that Bear's diner?" Jesse asked in what sounded like awe.

"Yeah," Royce answered as he placed the gazebo down beside the park swings.

"The firehouse and town hall, too. It looks like the entire main street is here," Jesse gushed at the discovery. "It's beautiful. Who made these?"

"Daniel." One word, yet so many emotions. Royce's first husband and high school sweetheart had died many years ago in an automobile accident. That was when he'd packed a large part of his life away along with any hope for the future. That had changed the day Royce had walked into the diner and saw Jesse behind the counter for the first time.

"They're stunning. He was really talented," Jesse said as he reached for the diner, but stopping short. "Is it okay if I touch them?"

"Of course." Royce watched as the man he intended to spend the rest of his life with carefully examined the creations made by the man with whom Royce had begun his life. He watched Jesse closely for any sign of discomfort or concern, but saw none.

"There's the Brighton Christmas Tree, and there are Christmas decorations in the shop windows. This is the whole town decked out for Christmas," Jesse said as he became more excited.

"That's what I wanted to ask you. We used to put this up on the mantel every Christmas and Daniel would always make a new one every year. Don't feel as though you have to say yes, truly, but I was hoping we could display them again."

Jesse set the town hall down and took Royce into his arms. "Sweetheart, of course we can. I know you still love Daniel."

Royce didn't want to upset Jesse but he couldn't lie. "I do."

"That's the way it's supposed to be. You and Daniel loved each other for many years and probably would still be together now if it hadn't been for the accident. I know this, but that doesn't mean you love me any less. I want you to remember and celebrate the love the two of you shared. He will always be a part of you, the same as I am. Your heart is certainly big enough, and I don't mind sharing it with your first love."

Royce could only stare at the smiling man in front of him. How had he been afraid of Jesse's response? He should have known better and now he felt a touch of shame for thinking the worse. "I'm sorry, honey."

"There's nothing to be sorry about. You were worried because you didn't want to hurt me or make me feel bad. I'm lucky to have someone as thoughtful as you," Jesse explained before giving him a kiss that Royce quickly dominated, causing his man to moan. "None of that until we get the Brighton Christmas Town set up."

The two of them placed the figures back into the box and headed for their living room. Jesse began to clear off the mantel as Royce continued to unwrap the remaining figures of the town.

"Oh wait, I have something that will work perfectly," Jesse announced before leaving the room and heading down the hallway to their spare bedroom.

Royce couldn't wipe the smile from his face even if he wanted to, which he didn't. Most of the town's people liked to refer to Jesse as the gentle giant, and for good reason. The scope of the man's love and understanding never ceased to amaze Royce.

"Here it is," Jesse hollered before he came racing back down the hall with something that looked like sparkling cotton pressed into thick sheets. "I was out buying more wrapping paper and I saw this and had to have it. I didn't know what the hell I was going to do with it but now I know. It was meant to be."

Jesse spread the cotton over the top of their wooden mantel before reaching for the diner and placing it on top. "Snow."

"You're brilliant. It looks perfect and at least one of the Brightons will have a white Christmas," Royce said as he set out the firehouse and police station.

For the next forty minutes, they set up the town. They even went so far as to take pieces of the cotton and drape them over rooftops, making it looked like it had recently snowed. They turned off all the house lights, and sat on the plush area rug with only the glow of the Christmas tree lights to see the replica town.

"I bet I could make small streetlights that actually light for up and down main street," Jesse offered before he began biting his lip. "That is if it's okay with you. I don't want to…."

Whatever else his man was about to say was cut off when Royce took Jesse's lips in a blistering kiss full of teeth and tongues. Royce pushed Jesse onto his back and followed him down without breaking their kiss. So many emotions were racing through Royce's body, from joy to a newfound peace. But more than anything, at that moment Royce *needed* to make love to his partner.

"I would love it if you made streetlights for the town. I want a part of you involved with that piece of Daniel I carry in my heart," Royce assured him before diving back in for an even deeper kiss as he began unbuttoning Jesse's shirt.

Royce could feel his lover's hard cock through the denim of Jesse's jeans and had the intense urge to taste his smooth, salty skin. "Clothes off, babe," Royce said as he stood and began stripping.

He watched as Jesse shimmied out of his jeans and boxers, his shirt and socks soon joined the growing pile of clothing. Royce couldn't help but groan at the delectable sight in front of him.

Jesse's sandy blond hair stood out in all directions from running his hands through it, while his dark brown eyes pulled Royce even deeper into whatever spell the man had over him. His tanned muscular body was a work of art, and Royce crawled over his man, intent on getting his taste.

Royce began licking and sucking his way up Jesse's inner thighs, tormenting him by getting close to the prize, but heading back down to start all over again. The big man shook with need. Jesse reached for his cock but Royce had other things in mind. "Don't touch yourself. You belong to me and will not come until I allow you."

Royce had always been the dominant man in their relationship, and today was no exception as he watched Jesse's hands rise above his head to lie flat on the floor. His lover's breathing sped up as he moaned his agreement. Because of his size people always mistook him as the dominant partner, especially in bed, but it couldn't be further from the truth. Jesse thrived and was happiest in a more submissive role and Royce was more than happy to oblige.

"That's it, Jesse, I'll give you what you need," Royce said, and without warning, he took Jesse's hard cock down his throat and swallowed. His throat muscles squeezed and massaged Jesse's shaft repeatedly as he cried out. But he didn't come, which made Royce happy. He intended to give his amazing man an earth-shaking orgasm.

Jesse was babbling in between moans, exactly where Royce wanted him. He took the bottle of lube they kept hidden under the couch cushions and began circling Jesse's hole with slippery fingers. Not once did he release his hold on Jesse's cock as he continued licking and sucking him down.

One finger than another slid in and out of his lover, giving Jesse a prostate massage like nothing he'd ever had before. Royce took his time stretching and rubbing, every moan driving him forward.

"Honey, please…please, I need you inside me," Jesse begged as he pulled his legs back.

Royce released his prize with one final lick and brought his body over the top of his needy partner. Jesse watched every move he made. His pupils were blown wide and his face flushed, heightening his incredible beauty. Royce lined his cock up with Jesse's hole, allowing the head to enter his lover before leaning down and taking Jesse in a slow, passionate kiss. He released all of his emotions to run freely through that kiss before pushing himself farther in until his balls touched Jesse's ass.

They both groaned at the intense pleasure they were sharing, and neither had looked away from the other the entire time. "You are so beautiful, Jesse. Every part of you deserves to be cherished, and I intend to do that for the rest of my life."

Jesse reached up and ran his fingers through Royce's hair. "I love you so much."

Royce couldn't hold back any longer and flexed his hips before pulling back and driving forward again. They set a furious pace, both lost to their passion. The colorful Christmas lights bathed them in a warm glow while their bodies joined together as their hearts already had.

Jesse's moans and gasps told Royce that his lover was close to losing control, and his fight not to come without permission. He would never do anything cruel to his man. Sex play was supposed to enhance the experience, not diminish it or denigrate his lover.

"Come for me," Royce commanded as he wrapped his hand around Jesse's hard cock and pumped him at the same speed as his own cock was driving in and out of his lover.

Jesse froze for a fraction of a second before roaring his release to the ceiling as pulse after pulse of come splashed onto his muscled stomach. His channel squeezed Royce tight and he fought to slide as deeply as possible before being overcome by his own release.

His ears were still ringing for several moments as they both gasped for air while tangled in each other's arms. Royce gently pulled out and lay beside his lover before reaching up to the couch and pulling a knitted blanket over the both of them. Jesse had a peaceful smile on his face and Royce couldn't look away from the sight.

"Royce?"

"Yes, babe."

"You know how much you mean to me, right?" Jesse asked before opening his eyes to look up at him. His eyes said it all without him uttering a word. The powerful love in those brown depths was unmistakable.

Royce ran his fingers through Jesse's hair and answered, "Yes. You don't have to worry that anything was ever left unsaid. As I hope it is the same when I look at you."

Jesse's smile lit up his face. "Yeah, I know."

Royce leaned down and slowly kissed the man who had shown him he could still live even after tragedy. He lay back onto the carpeting, tucked a throw pillow under his head while Jesse settled his head on Royce's chest, and covered him with his leg. Soon Jesse's breathing evened out, his handsome face aglow with the reds, yellows, and oranges of the Christmas tree lights.

For the first time in a very long time, Royce looked upon the Christmas town as a work in progress. Ever evolving, ever changing, and simply because one great love had begun it didn't mean another couldn't join in and help it grow.

The town would look amazing with streetlights.

Chapter Five

Coop and Matthew

"Move it two inches to the east," Matthew repeated into his walkie-talkie.

The view on his monitor changed ever so slightly but now it included the rear entrance and the entire northeast side of the building.

"Perfect," he confirmed. "Bolt it in."

Matthew flipped to another screen before rechecking if the camera was in the right position. Out of the over one hundred cameras they were installing, they'd had to adjust only two. He'd take that as a victory. Months of preparation to secure Haven was finally coming to fruition, and Matthew couldn't have been happier with the results.

It meant something knowing that in any small way he had helped to make the people coming to the Haven safe. He rubbed the small scar on his right cheek, a constant reminder that evil did exist. Matthew pushed those thoughts far away and concentrated on the systems in front of him. He clicked to the cameras in the pool area, which were still being positioned, to find the sexiest man Matthew had ever seen, Coop.

His man was helping move bags of concrete over to the mixer as the crew worked on the finishing details of the pool. When they weren't away on missions, the Sentinel team had been pitching in around the new center. Matthew couldn't help himself and zoomed in on his partner. He watched as Coop's muscles flexed and bulged with every move he made. Matthew liked to joke that Coop was built like a Greek god, but in truth he absolutely was, no joke.

Matthew picked up his cellphone and pushed the button with Coop's handsome face on it. He watched as Coop pulled out his phone and smiled wide, giving Matthew a bird's-eye view into how happy Coop was when Matthew called. That left a warm feeling in his chest, and while he knew the big guy loved him, there was no harm in being reassured.

"Hi, beautiful. What's up?" Coop's deep voice touched him like an actual caress.

"Finishing confirming the cameras are in the correct locations and then I found something I couldn't take my eyes off of," Matthew teased as Coop began looking around until he found the camera and stared straight at him.

"You little peeping Tom you." Coop laughed as he waved at the camera Matthew was using.

"You can't blame me when the view is this good."

The system was so accurate that Matthew could see Coop's cheeks turning red. "You almost done up there?"

"I'll be another hour tops."

"Okay, we can stop at the diner on our way home," Coop suggested. "I heard some of the contractors mentioning that Travis had fried chicken on the menu as today's special."

Travis made the best chicken in town. Matthew didn't know what it was that the man did differently, but whatever it was he, like the rest of the town, hoped Travis kept doing it. "Can we take it to go?"

Matthew watched as Coop's smile widened. "You want to have a picnic?"

"Definitely. I'll come find you when I'm done, but can you do me one favor?"

"Of course, beautiful. What do you need?"

"For you to turn around slowly and show me that gorgeous ass of yours." Matthew would not forego the opportunity to zoom into that perfect peach-shaped tush. "Oh yeah, that's the stuff."

Coop laughed as he turned around anyway and gave Matthew a little shake before saying, "Love you, you pervert."

"Love you too, Coop," Matthew replied before hanging up and switching to another camera.

As he continued his triple check of the completed systems, Matthew couldn't help but think how much his life had changed. Without Coop, he'd still be in his one-bedroom condo in San Diego working behind the scenes on whatever mission he'd chosen, or working on munitions he was busy creating. Never out in the open or part of a team.

Now he was a Sentinel, contract and all, and not simply because he was with Coop. He'd travelled further than he ever thought he'd go, learned how to defend himself and to get control over his clumsy self. Although, on occasion he was known to trip over air, those instances were now rare. Well, if you didn't count the lip of the shower on Tuesday, or the potted plant on Friday.

Once he was done with his camera check, he left and locked the security room before heading in search of the man who'd laid claim to his heart, not to mention body. He walked along a path surrounded by flowers and trees. Jesse had said he wanted this place to feel homey and loved, so now gardens could be found everywhere. A noise caught his attention, causing Matthew to stop and listen more closely.

Snip…snip… Matthew followed the sound down a side path until he came face-to-back with Tommy. Tommy was one of the three young men freed from the conversion therapy center and had been brought to Haven. He was using small pruning shears on a shrub that stood about three feet tall. Even from where Matthew was standing, he could make out the shape of a birdbath.

"Hello, Tommy, what are you up to today?" Matthew asked, causing the poor man to jump in surprise. At least he hadn't screamed. That would have brought the cavalry running. "It's okay, it's only me."

"I'm sorry, Mr. Whitton, I didn't hear you coming." Tommy hid the shears behind his leg as if what he was doing could get him into trouble.

"Tommy, what's up? Is something wrong?" 'Cause if there was Matthew would fix it or have Coop do it. Since his arrival, Tommy had been kind and courteous to everyone.

The young man brought the shears back out and showed Matthew. "I promise I didn't steal them."

"Of course you haven't," Matthew assured.

"I borrowed them from the garden shed. I would have put them right back."

Matthew's heart broke for what this poor man had been through to fear everything and everyone. "Come sit with me, let's talk," he said before leading Tommy to a nearby concrete bench.

"I know you wouldn't steal them. I believe you."

Tommy looked shocked but he did his best to hide it. "You believe me?"

"Yeah, sure."

"But you don't even really know me."

"From what I have seen so far, I have no reason not to trust you," Matthew explained. "Now, tell me what you're creating?"

Tommy lowered his head before answering. "A mess."

"I don't know about that. Is it going to be a birdbath?"

Tommy's eyes lit up. "It is."

"Were you always interested in art?"

"Art?"

"Yeah, topiary. Living sculpture."

"I didn't know it was a form of art, but I used to do it with my mother when I was small, before she left."

Matthew refused to let the sadness he felt inside for the young man show. Poor guy, working alone to keep his memories of his mother alive was heartbreaking. "Well, I have a good friend named Sam who does this as well. Here, I'll show you some pictures." He reached into his pocket, pulled out his cell, and opened his phone's photo file. One by one, he flipped through the pictures of the topiaries surrounding the old Victorian house at the compound. Tommy looked on in complete fascination.

There was no way Matthew could simply let this go, that wasn't his style. "I could bring you out sometime to see them if you want."

"Really?" Tommy couldn't hide his excitement, making Matthew smile.

"Sure, and maybe I could ask Sam to be there when you visit. It would be good to get two artists together to talk over things. Me, I don't have a clue other than they're beautiful." Matthew's heart went out to Tommy, alone in the world, knowing he was tossed aside without a care for his safety. Matthew knew what that felt like. He had no doubt Sam would want to help as well.

"That would be awesome. Thank you." The change from when Matthew first saw Tommy to now would make someone believe he'd given him something priceless. All Matthew wanted to do was make the young man smile.

"Okay. I'll be here at Haven often and we'll work out a good time for everyone to visit." He stood and turned to the soon to be birdbath and said, "You can show him this when you're finished. Have a good day, Tommy."

"Thank you, Mr. Whitton."

Matthew retraced his steps until he was back on the original path and found Coop waiting there for him. His lover wrapped those muscled arms around him and lifted Matthew into the air. "There you are," he muttered before taking Matthew's lips in a passionate kiss, wiping away any residual sadness he was still carrying.

Matthew knew how lucky he was to have a life with this amazing man.

***

Coop knew how lucky he was to have a life with this beautiful man.

They stopped by the diner on their way home and picked up two fried chicken dinners. Mrs. Walker had the evening off so the team had to fend for themselves. The moment they walked through the door Matthew ran to find Sam. Coop had heard about Tommy, and was sure Matthew wouldn't let the young man down. Coop's man always kept his promises. After Matthew had shared, he shut it down. Coop had learned his partner preferred doing things without praise. Matthew had told him a ton of times that what Matthew did was simple acts of kindness that everyone should engage in, nothing to be thanked for.

Matthew was one of a kind, like his multicolored eyes, and Coop had no idea what he did before this man had come into his life. Well, other than the fact that he'd been a love 'em and leave 'em kinda guy, but once he met Matthew, those days were over.

Coop had placed their food into an insulated bag to keep it warm while he quickly stripped and jumped into the shower. The steam floated around him, fogging up the glass. He sensed the moment he was no longer alone and waited for his man to join him. He didn't have to wait long.

Matthew's hands explored Coop's back before wrapping around him from behind. Coop loved having Matthew close and twisted in his arms so that he was now facing his man.

"Hi there, lover. Want me to scrub your back?" Coop asked.

"And my sides and we can't forget about my front. I need your personal attention." Matthew played along.

"Hmmm, I'll have to see what I can do for you, beautiful," Coop teased as he pulled Matthew even closer before claiming his lips.

After a few moments, he had Matthew moaning into the kiss while rubbing his hard cock against Coop's leg. This was how he loved to see his partner, wet and needy. Coop could definitely work with this. He reached down, covered Matthew's ass cheeks with large hands, and squeezed before lifting his love so that they were now eye-to-eye.

Matthew wiggled, desperately trying to find any friction on his cock. Coop worked his way down his lover's neck, licking and sucking hard enough to leave marks as he went. The feel of Matthew's hard cock and balls rubbing up and down his abdomen made his own swollen balls throb with need.

"That's it, beautiful, take what you need from me," Coop groaned as he reached for the waterproof lube.

Moments later, he was circling Matthew's tight hole, loosening the muscles enough to allow him in. His first finger slid in deep and Matthew's moans grew louder in the tiled enclosure. Coop pressed Matthew's back against the wall and sunk another finger in beside the first.

The stunning man in his arms began to cry out and soon Coop had three fingers in, making sure his lover was stretched.

"Ready, baby?" Coop growled. He was barely holding on at this point and needed to bury himself deep inside Matthew.

"Please hurry."

That was all the assurance Coop needed as he lined the sensitive head of his cock up with Matthew's waiting hole. Slowly and with great care he pushed forward until his balls were snug to his lover's ass. He groaned at the tight heat squeezing his cock as muscles spasmed around him.

Coop took Matthew's red, swollen lips in another deep kiss, desperate to show his man how much he loved him. Wanting to give him everything, wanting him to know every part of Coop belonged to Matthew. He no longer feared love, now he felt more secure and solid with it than without. Matthew had given this to him.

He flexed his hips, driving a bit deeper before pulling out. On his way back in he made sure to rub Matthew's prostate until his lover began babbling between moans. Coop loved it when he was able to drive Matthew to the point of pure bliss.

"I-I'm… come," Matthew moaned.

Coop immediately took hold of his partner's cock and began pumping him long and hard. With a dip of his nail into his lover's slit, Coop felt Matthew's muscles tighten before he cried out and painted Coop's stomach in warm come. The feel of Matthew coming apart in Coop's arms did nothing for his stamina, but he pushed on until several moments later Coop came deep inside the man who had made his life whole.

Matthew clung to him as they both fought to catch their breath. Coop had braced himself against the tile, never wanting his beauty to slip out of his arms. Once he was sure Matthew could stand on his own two feet again, Coop set him down and began washing him. The dreamy smile on his partner's face never ceased to fill Coop with a smug pride. He'd put that smile there.

"How are you feeling?" Coop asked as he began rinsing off Matthew.

"Happy, relaxed, loved…there's more but you get the gist." Matthew punctuated every emotion with a kiss to Coop's chest.

"Perfect. Right where I want you." Coop finished washing himself before leading his partner out of the shower and drying him off.

They put on their matching robes, a gift from Matthew, and headed back into the bedroom to unpack their picnic. Shadow laid a blanket on the floor in front of the gas fireplace before turning it on. The glow from the flames made everything more intimate. Matthew set out the plates and cutlery while he dug the takeout containers from the insulated bag. Thankfully, everything was still warm.

Matthew pulled a bottle of wine out of their new wine fridge they'd installed in their bedroom. Private picnics had been their thing since the beginning. The two would sit cuddled together on their ever growing stack of pillows in front of the fire with a glass of wine a few times a week to wind down and share the day's events. Coop reached into the bottom dresser drawer for the last and most important piece of what he wanted to discuss with Matthew this evening. He hoped he wasn't pushing their relationship too quickly, but couldn't help wanting to move forward.

"What do you have there?" Matthew asked as Coop set the cardboard tube on the floor beside his plate.

"A question."

That got Matthew's interest. "A question in a tube?"

"Yeah, but I thought we should wait until after we've eaten."

"Not a chance, big guy. I'm not waiting. What's your question?"

Coop thought about it for a moment before agreeing it might be best to get this out of the way first. He opened the lid on the tube and slid the rolled-up paper out and onto the floor in front of Matthew. With one final curious look at Coop, Matthew unrolled the papers and got his first look at a dream close to Coop's heart.

He didn't say a word, he simply allowed Matthew to look through the pages without his commentary. His lover took his time reviewing each page until he came to the end and looked up at Coop.

"How long have you had these drawings?"

"Years. I drew them up quite a while ago."

"And what do you wish to do with them?"

"What I want *us* to do with these blueprints is build it. You know, once you've had a chance to look over it and make any changes you want."

"You want to build a house with me?"

"No, I want to build a home with you. More than anything. There's a beautiful plot of land I want to take you to see and—"

Whatever else he was going to say was cut off when Matthew dove into Coop's arms, repeating the same word over and over again between kisses.

"Yes."

Chapter Six

Gabe and Johnny

Johnny held his phone closer to his ear so that he could hear over Gabe and Lucy's playtime in the center of their living room. The two were having a tea party, and for the life of him, he couldn't figure out how tea could be so loud. But he loved every minute of it.

"Hold on, Saint. I'm walking outside onto the patio," Johnny said to his brother, Frank, better known as Saint, who was waiting on the other end of the line. He didn't know why his brother was reaching out to him after being absent from his life for years. This sounded like he wanted to talk about more than coming to the wedding.

"It's okay, Johnny, I don't mind holding," Saint replied happily, which was even more puzzling.

He closed the patio door behind him and stepped out into the cool night breeze. "Okay, I'm outside now. What were you saying?"

"I was letting you know that I'm going to be in Brighton next week and I'm hoping we could get together," Saint explained.

Johnny could hear the uncertainty in his brother's voice. "Is something wrong? Are you okay?" Johnny may have lost track of his brother for a few years, but Saint was still his older brother. He loved him even if he had followed their father into medicine, plastic surgery particularly, for money, not healing.

"Nothing's wrong, little brother. I would really like to see you and your family." Saint hesitated. "I've missed you."

Johnny couldn't hear any dissembling in his voice, which surprised him. Giving a mental shrug, he replied, "Okay, when will you be getting in?"

He heard his brother let out a breath before answering. "I'll be in town on the fifteenth before I continue on out to Los Angeles after your wedding."

"What's in Los Angeles?" Johnny asked, considering the medical practice was based in New York.

"I'll catch you up with the whole of it when I see you, little brother. Thank you for agreeing to see me and inviting me to your wedding."

"You're my brother. Of course I want you there." He'd always wanted his brother there, even when Saint had pulled away.

"I know we haven't been close over the last few years, but I'd like to change that if I can."

"I'd like that as well, Saint."

"Good. I'll call you when I get into town." Saint sounded much happier than he had at the beginning of their conversation. "Love you, bro," he said before the line went dead.

Johnny stood there for several minutes, staring at the phone in his hand. He couldn't remember the last time his brother said that he loved him.

Something was seriously wrong.

Chapter Seven

Travis and Bo

The flow of charcoal from his pencil made the lines darker than the softest graphite pencil ever could. There was always something about that first stroke of pencil to paper, or paint to canvas, that sent excitement rushing through his veins. Add to that the fact that this wasn't some ordinary drawing. This one was special. Travis had drawn and redrawn this design over twenty times by now and he wouldn't stop until it was perfect.

Late afternoon sunshine streamed into his studio that Bo had created for him in the house they now shared. His boyfriend was out back working in his gardens, giving Travis the time he needed to perfect what he was creating, then scanning it, and sending it on over to Olivia to trace for her stencil. The design incorporated Bo's work life as a police officer and Travis's as an artist, combining both passions as they had done in their private lives.

Bo's badge stood proudly in the center of the piece with different aspects of their lives together peeking out from behind it. Travis's sable paintbrush, flowers from Bo's garden, the badge number of Bo's first partner on the force who was killed in a shootout, the name of the soup kitchen where Travis and his dad had helped before his father's death, and the Mason family crest. If Travis had to say so himself, the piece was beautiful. There were to be two versions of the drawing, one larger than the other, otherwise, they were identical.

His mind wandered as he worked, which happened often when he was creating. Many months had passed since he'd moved in with Bo, and every day he woke up in that wonderful man's arms. Travis reached back and scratched at the small rash he'd gotten rolling around in the grass in their backyard without his shirt on. Bo had a picnic set up for them when he'd gotten off shift at the diner, and it was a good thing they had a tall fence and mature trees.

Amazing to begin with was Travis had taken off his shirt while outside. He'd never have considered doing it in the past even though they were alone and away from prying eyes. It was yet another step forward. As he scratched, he was careful not to push too hard on the raised scars left behind when his skin had burned in the fire. Sometimes they could become sensitive.

For the first time in Travis's life, his appearance wasn't his defining feature. His scars didn't rule his thoughts as they used to, and with Bo, family and friends, and with the help of Dr. Gordon, Travis was rebuilding his life, and for the first time planning for the future.

Hours passed before he was finally satisfied. Travis scanned the final work and sent it off. It was time to find the man he loved. Travis stepped out onto the back patio in time to see Bo closing the garden shed before walking toward him. The blinding smile on Bo's face did wonders for Travis. He was the one who made Bo smile like that, and he would do anything to keep it that way. Travis watched transfixed as Bo's muscles flexed as he moved. *Yep, all mine.*

"Hey, babe, all done?" Bo asked as he stepped onto the patio and took Travis into his arms.

Travis snaked his hands over Bo's wide chest and up around his neck. "Yep, already sent it off."

"Excited?"

"Definitely. You?"

"Oh yeah, I've been wanting to do this for a while now," Bo replied before he began kissing his way down Travis's neck, almost distracting him.

"None of that quite yet. We still have to take a drive out to Haven to okay the installation," Travis reminded his insistent partner.

Bo playfully growled but pulled back. "But I want to get you naked."

"And you will, later," Travis assured.

Funny how such a big man could pout as effectively as his goddaughter, who was only two. "Come on, it won't take long, and then you can play when we soak in the tub."

That brought Bo's smile back and soon enough they were in the truck and on the road to the new addition to Brighton, Safe Haven. In only a few more weeks they'd all be celebrating Bo's cousin, Gabe, and Johnny's wedding at the Center. With all the anticipation leading up to the event, it felt like the whole town would be there to celebrate.

Bo held his hand as Travis drove them out to the site that would be officially dedicated in seven days. Along with a phalanx of Brighton residents, Jesse and Royce had worked hard to make this happen. In all his years spent on the streets, Travis had never seen anything like Brighton. The town reminded him of what everyone imagined the ideal small town in America looked like, with the bonus of everyday technology and convenience, and an overall attitude of acceptance and tolerance.

They pulled into the recently paved parking lot with fresh yellow lines marking each parking spot. Everything was so new, and every attention to detail had been employed. It was an exciting time for the town. Bo walked around the truck and came to the driver's side to retake Travis's hand and lead him toward the main building. He couldn't help rub his shoulder against Bo as they walked. If he could, he'd be in constant contact with his man. Bo smiled down at him before pulling Travis even closer. *Yeah, I'm a lucky man.*

They walked into the foyer of Haven, and Travis was overwhelmed by what stood dead center in a place of honor. Three pieces of his artwork, large, medium, and small, hung behind glass with lights artfully arranged to highlight his paintings. Travis had donated the set of three images he'd painted of downtown Brighton to the Haven, but he never thought they'd be hung here like this. In all honesty, Travis thought they might be put up in the offices not displayed like actual artwork.

"It is artwork, sweetheart," Bo said, and Travis realized he must have said that last part aloud. "You are talented, and I'll keep saying it until it gets through."

The large painting depicted downtown, with its shops and flowers, street signs and lights. The image had been ingrained in his mind since the day he'd walked to Keith's art store for the first time. The medium-size painting was of the diner, the first place he'd called home since he turned eighteen. The smallest painting was of the flowers in Bo's gardens where they'd had their first date.

Below the paintings was a picture of Travis they must have gotten from Bo. Above the paintings was Travis's name in bold gold lettering. Underneath it, written in quotation was, "Dedicated to all those starting over and finding their own path. You will always find a home here."

Travis felt tears rolling down his cheeks but he was powerless to stop them. As Bo took him into his arms, Travis knew that his father was looking down on him with pride.

***

Bo sat back in the leather chair and laid his head against the headrest. The buzzing sound coming from another room confirmed that they were busy in the shop today. He wasn't nervous. He was overjoyed to be doing this with the man he loved. While Olivia prepared herself, Travis sat in the chair right by Bo's side, staring down at his own forearm with a wide smile. Bo heard someone groan from down the hall but nothing could pierce the happiness going on in this room.

Olivia pulled on her black latex gloves and smiled down at Bo. "Ready?"

"Definitely." Bo couldn't help his excitement.

Travis took hold of his hand and stared straight into Bo's eyes as Olivia leaned over to ink the first line. The pain from the needle was instantaneous but nothing he couldn't tolerate. The design Travis had drawn was breathtaking, and seeing a part of him inked onto his lover's body was almost perfect. Perfect would be after his own larger version of the tattoo was completed on his left pectoral muscle.

Bo had remembered Travis telling him that he used to design a new tattoo whenever he made it through another surgery. He stopped the day his mother had kicked him out after his father died. Bo had wanted to celebrate their union and asked Travis to create something for the two of them to share. The joy he'd seen today when Travis sat for his tattoo was worth anything and everything Bo had.

"You okay?" Travis asked as they stared at one another, never breaking contact.

"I'm doing fine, sweetheart. Are you happy with yours?" Bo thought he'd change the subject because for some odd reason Travis was great at getting a tattoo, but watching Bo get one was another matter. He looked ready to faint.

Travis looked down at his arm before gushing, "It's perfect."

"It is. Absolutely perfect, just like you."

Travis blushed as Bo had hoped he would before continuing with a conversation that he hoped was distracting Travis. Even when a particularly dark spot became tender, Bo didn't change his tone or facial expression. By the time Olivia was finished, they'd pretty much talked about and decided their entire holiday schedule. He looked down to see his new tattoo but Olivia wasn't done.

She cleaned the area and motioned for Bo to stand so he could get his first look at his chest. The tattoo spanned the width of his left pectoral muscle. Its bold lines flowed throughout the design, tying everything together in one stunning piece of art.

"Do you like it?" Travis asked, and Bo could hear the uncertainty in his lover's voice.

"It's breathtaking." Bo wasn't simply saying that to make Travis happy. It was one hundred percent truth. "You're amazing."

Bo pulled Travis close to his side and both stood looking into the mirror at their matching tattoos. He couldn't help the feeling of pride it gave him to have one of Travis's artworks over his heart. This was another step forward in their relationship while building their lives together, and he couldn't have been happier.

They held hands as they walked out of the shop and headed toward the diner. Bo wished he could walk around shirtless to show off his tattoo but that wouldn't do for a public servant of the community. He looked down at Travis who was beaming with happiness, and Bo knew he'd do everything to keep him that way as often as possible.

"You didn't even squirm," Travis said proudly. "You're amazing."

"I don't know. I hear getting a tattoo on a fleshy part of skin is less painful than boney areas like your forearm." Bo was quick to mention not wanting Travis to feel less for moving a bit.

"Yeah, I've heard that before too," Travis agreed. "Maybe they're right."

"I'm guessing they are. Now for our celebratory dinner. Are you sure you don't want to go to one of the fancier restaurants in the town one over?" Bo wanted this to be special. And since Travis worked at the diner, Bo thought his man might like the change.

"I wouldn't want to be anywhere else. This is where I met you, made new friends, gained a family and my life back." Travis stopped and wrapped his arms around Bo but held himself away to keep from smushing his chest. "This is the perfect place to celebrate."

Bo had to admit, his lover was right. They walked through the glass doors and listened to the hum of conversations carrying on around them as they found their seats. They slid into a booth, both on the same side, and perused a menu they already had memorized from front to back.

One of the two high school kids Bear had hired to help in the dining room came over with two glasses of water. She took their order, which was the special, roast beef dinner, because Bear was cooking and Bo's partner's favorite meal was roast beef. Anytime now Rick and Josh would be walking through those doors to visit and have dinner. Things like that were what made Brighton special—family, familiarity, the people.

Travis cuddled into Bo's side as they waited for their meal and Bo noticed a new person sitting in a booth in the back corner. He was a big man with curly blond hair and blue eyes, and reminded Bo of someone.

"Love, have you seen that guy before?"

Travis looked up to see where Bo was looking before answering. "Yeah. He got into town this morning before the end of my shift. He's a doctor."

"How do you know that?"

"He has the caduceus on his necklace."

"I'm sorry, what?"

"You know that medical symbol you see. The one with two snakes wrapped around a rod. It's supposed to be the rod wielded by a Greek god of healing and medicine," Travis explained. "When I was going through all my surgeries several of the doctors and nurses had some form of that symbol somewhere, like a necklace, bracelet, or pin. I asked him why he was wearing it."

"You up and asked him?" Bo questioned, knowing how shy Travis was.

"Okay, I got Sarah to ask him. She was already having a conversation with him so I had her throw that in out of curiosity. He's a plastic surgeon, that's all I know."

Bo had no idea why he couldn't let it go but there was something so familiar about the guy. That could be good or bad in his line of work. "I'll be right back, sweetheart. I'll go introduce myself in case he needs anything."

"Sure, in case he needs anything, right." Travis nodded. He knew Bo was going to check the stranger out.

A few people noticed him approach the table where the man was reading what looked like a thick textbook. The spine read "Refurbishing an Old Building." Bo waited until the man noticed him.

"Hello, I'm Bo," he said when the guy looked up. The feeling that he knew this man grew even stronger. Bo held out his hand for him to shake but the stranger stood instead, displaying his bandaged hands. Bo had been so consumed by trying to figure out why he felt he knew the man that he didn't notice the man's hands. "I'm Saint, nice to meet you. Care to join me?"

Bo noticed two other things right off the bat, the man was favoring his right side and he was huge. Taller than Bo's six foot five, and this guy had muscles to spare. The man's eyes read nothing but welcome so Bo thought he'd sit for a moment.

"I wanted to introduce myself, I'm Bo Mason and I'm a police officer here in Brighton. If you need anything, give me a call at the station." Bo smiled hoping he didn't look like a complete busybody.

Saint grinned before saying, "Officer Mason, my name is Dr. Frank Jeffrey but I don't go by that anymore."

"That's okay. I don't need your full name."

Saint smiled even wider. "I'd be disappointed if you didn't take it. My little brother told me Brighton was a close-knit community that looked out for him."

"Your brother?"

"Johnny Jeffrey. He's going to marry, I'm guessing, a relative of yours named Gabe Mason. Please correct me if I'm presuming."

"That's it, that's why I thought I recognized you. You and your brother look alike. Well other than the size difference," Bo muttered. "And yeah, he's marrying my cousin."

At that, Saint laughed, which made the big man hold his side as if trying to ease a pain. Bo could see his and Travis's food being delivered to their table and decided the man wasn't a threat and no he hadn't seen him from one of their mug shots. "Well, I'll leave you in peace. I imagine we'll see you at the wedding." Bo wanted to ask about his injuries but decided that was one step too far.

"If everything works out I intend to be there."

That was an odd thing to say, but Bo let it go, and walked back to his amazing boyfriend who looked at him through hooded eyes. Bo knew exactly what Travis was dreaming about and intended to fill those desires as soon as they got home. For now, he sat beside his lover in a diner full of friends, family, and neighbors, in a town he was proud to call home.

He was a fortunate man.

Chapter Eight

Dr. Frank Jeffrey - Saint

Saint concentrated harder than he'd ever had to before as he tried to get back to his motel room without alerting anyone. He didn't need these people to waste their time worrying about him. He smiled and waved to people as they passed by on the sidewalk and made sure his happy mask was firmly in place at least until he passed the threshold of his motel room. The weather had turned colder, but at least there wasn't any snow to navigate. If he was at his cabin in upstate New York, he'd be shoveling piles of it, not as if he could shovel *shit* now anyway.

He took the last hundred feet at an almost jog, which didn't help his pain, but he'd made it inside with no one the wiser. He tamped down his need to rage and scream at the injustice of it all, but what the hell was the use. Nothing would change. And he'd gotten the best opinions New York's finest doctors could offer.

With the limited mobility he had left in his hands, Saint removed his boots and jeans before sliding his shirt over his head. He looked down at the bandages wrapped around his waist and checked for blood. He'd thought for sure he'd busted a stitch, but there wasn't a red spot to be found.

He picked up his pain medication, which the pharmacist had placed in an easy open container for people with arthritis that Saint wanted to chuck across the room. He wasn't an invalid. Once his tantrum faded he took his time wrapping his fingers around the bottle of water, not wanting to drop it, and swallowed a pill down. He didn't like taking them, but had to admit at times like these they were necessary. The pain became too much to bear.

In the blink of an eye he was transported back to the chilling scene where he was lying in the dirt surrounded by puddles of his blood. He shook his head, pushing that memory deep, where no one would see it.

Using both hands, he set the water bottle down on the bedside table and slowly crawled onto the bed and used his legs to get his body under the covers. It had been nice to hear that he and his brother resembled one another. In the past, everyone had always been overly concerned about their differences. Saint loved his brother more than Johnny knew. That's why he'd done what was necessary to ensure his brother's peace.

Saint looked around his room. His home for the next little while wasn't anything like the typical small-town motel. This place could rival any five-star hotel he'd stayed in. He even had a patio with potted plants and a longue jutting out of the back of his room. The bed was a California king, the room was spotless, the décor upscale, the furniture was newish, and a large flat-screen TV hung on the wall. The room was equipped with a single-serve coffeemaker and a mini-fridge. Waiting on his doorstep this morning, along with his continental basket of fresh baked muffins, croissant, a ramekin of butter, and individual bottles of British jellies, he had two newspapers rolled up standing against the wall next to the door—the small local paper and *The Wall Street Journal.* This place provided superior accommodations for a vacation, even though that was the last thing he was here to do.

His medication began to kick in as his eyes slowly closed. Tomorrow would be another day. A gift he'd almost lost while simultaneously being his own personal hell.

Chapter Nine

Grady and Ben

Ben pulled their new SUV up to the side of the cottage, put it in park, and turned off the ignition. He turned to look at the gorgeous man sleeping soundly in the reclined bucket seat beside him. Grady had worked the night shift before they'd loaded up and headed out, and Ben was reluctant to wake him. However, there was no way he would leave his boyfriend crammed in the seat when spacious beds were only feet away.

"Babe, we're here. Wake up," he whispered, not wanting to startle him.

Grady began to move and stretched his arms above his head before opening his big brown eyes and gazing at Ben. "Hey, we're here already? That was fast."

"No comments about my driving, you were asleep."

"Sure, Andretti." Grady smiled before leaning over for a kiss Ben was happy to give.

The touch of his soft lips never failed to excite Ben, but he held himself in check. Grady needed rest after a long shift protecting Brighton. "Let's get you inside, sweetheart."

"I like the sound of that," Grady playfully growled, pulling Ben in for another kiss. Several moments later both were breathing heavily, and the windows began to fog.

"Come on, you need to get some more rest, there's plenty of time for that later."

Grady frowned, but whatever complaint he was going to level lost its effectiveness when he yawned. Ben laughed and opened the driver's door, walked to the back and retrieved their bags, and headed to the front door behind his drowsy lover. Ben still had the occasional twinge of pain in his shoulder from the gunshot wound he'd sustained, but other than that, he was back to full strength.

The Mason family's light blue cottage stood with its wood shutters closed and door locked tight. No one had been here since his mom and aunts had come up to set everything to right after the mess with Grady's father. Ben had brought along new bedding, food, drinks, and whatever else they might need for their little getaway.

Ben noticed Grady pause before putting the key into the lock on the door. There were a lot of not-so-happy memories here, and Ben hoped they had made the right decision to create new memories.

Grady squared his shoulders and turned to look at Ben. "Are you okay with all of this?"

Ben should have known that while he was worried how this would affect Grady, his man would do the same for him. Ben set their bags down and took his amazing man into his arms.

"I want us to be able to come here. I've always loved this place." Ben had enjoyed staying at the lake as often as possible, and he refused to let some asshole take that away from him.

Grady looked at him for a few seconds, nodded, and turned to unlock the door. Of course, it opened with a squeal of disuse, and the interior was dark. However, as soon as he had a chance, he'd open the shutters and let the light and fresh air flow in. He and Grady took their bedding and bags to one of the bedrooms before bringing in the cooler of food. Ben insisted they head back into the bedroom and make the bed. He knew Grady was going to crash soon.

Sure enough, ten minutes after they'd gotten the bedroom squared away, Grady was fading fast. He was fighting to keep his eyes open. "Go to sleep," Ben ordered. "I can take care of everything and I'll wake you for supper."

"I can't leave you to do everything by yourself, babe."

"You're not leaving me to do anything. I'm telling you to go get some rest because I intend to take advantage of being out in the middle of nowhere. Once the room airs out, I'm gonna get this fire started, and then I'll declare this a clothes-free cottage."

Grady's eyes turned fiery as he reached out for Ben, only to come up empty when he backed away. "Sleep now, play later, love. That's the deal."

"You drive a hard bargain, babe. But okay, I'll go get some shut-eye but if you need anything you wake me up."

It felt wonderful to have a partner to share everything, especially the responsibilities. Typically, Ben had always been the one to provide everything and take responsibility for the same. The big, muscled firefighter. Now, it wasn't all on him.

"I will wake you if necessary," he promised. *Never going to happen.*

Grady shook his head as if he'd read Ben's mind but acquiesced before giving him a kiss and walking to their bedroom. Once he heard the door close Ben went to work. He planned to have this place comfy-cozy by the time Grady woke up. Ben wanted them to have good memories here in one of his favorite places.

He understood that Grady's first impression of the cottage had been skewed by the former threat of a stalker hovering over them. When the stalker turned out to be Grady's father, it was a shock, and Ben wasn't sure if his lover had fully recovered. But for the next three days it would be love and laughter that filled their time here, not fear or pain. They'd be back to Brighton a couple days before Gabe and Johnny's wedding. Ben would never miss his cousin and fellow firefighter's big day.

One by one, he opened the old wooden shutters as he'd done hundreds of times before. The cottage immediately filled with light, dispelling any trace of gloom. He opened a couple of windows, then went to the back of the house, or the front as some people called it because of its aspect. He stopped to look out onto the quiet lake. Birds took flight from the surface, leaving trails in the water after they were long gone. Tall trees stood guard around the cottage, but most of the flowers had gone with the cooler weather.

It was an honor to be allowed to stand among this beauty. Trees hundreds of years old a constant reminder of how fleeting his time was on earth. After everything he'd gone through and how close he'd come to death, it was even more poignant.

Ben shook himself, freeing the melancholy feelings that kept trying to cling to him. His brush with death reinforced his need to live life to the fullest, and he intended to do just that. He went back to work on the shutters, closed the windows, and then turned on the electricity and the water from the well. They had everything they needed right here, and family and friends knew not to call unless it was an emergency. This was their private time and he didn't want anything or anyone to mess with it.

Life had been hectic since he'd been released from the hospital for the second time. Between doctors and physio appointments, moving Grady into their home, searching for and finding Grady's brother Randy, work and recovery… time had been rushing by and neither of them had had a chance to celebrate their union, and simply enjoy the moment, until now.

Ben brought five loads of dried wood into the cottage and set it in the bin near the large stone fireplace. On either side of the fireplace were garden doors leading out to the patio overlooking the water. He had special plans for the spot on the rug in front of the roaring fire he was busy building. Everything would be ready for him to lavish love and attention onto the man who meant everything to him.

***

Grady arched his back, desperate to feel the work-roughened hands of his lover as they ghosted over his chest. He hadn't opened his eyes yet, basking in the loving attention he was receiving from Ben.

"Open your eyes, love, dinner is almost ready. There's enough time for you to have a shower and join me in the living room," Ben whispered in Grady's ear. The deep timbre of Ben's voice seemed to vibrate through Grady's suddenly overheated body.

He opened his eyes to find the man of his dreams sitting beside him on the bed wearing a dark blue bathrobe. His hair was wet from what Grady presumed was Ben's shower.

"Why didn't you wait for me? We could have taken a shower together." Grady tried for his best pout but by the smile on Ben's face, it wasn't working.

"If I had done that, dinner would have been ruined by the time we made it out of this room. Now, get up and put this on after your shower." Ben held up another robe identical to his own. "This is the only piece of clothing we wear while inside the cottage."

Oh hell yes, things were looking up. Grady reached for the robe, imagining all the fun to be had in wearing only that. At the last moment, Ben swooped in and pulled Grady into his arms before taking Grady's mouth in an all-consuming kiss. By the time Ben released him, Grady had been well and truly snogged. His heart was racing and his dick was hard.

"Don't take too long, babe," Ben told him as he stood and walked out of the room with a noticeable tent in the front of his robe.

Grady wasted no time in jumping into the shower, his man was waiting for him one room away. He was surprised by how relaxed he felt while being back in the place where he'd almost lost Ben. Initially, Grady wasn't certain about coming back to this place, but he realized how much the cottage meant to Ben and there was no way Grady would keep him from it. However, everywhere Grady looked he was reminded of what his father had tried to do to the man Grady loved.

He showered quickly, shaved, and donned his robe, ready for the evening alone with Ben. It felt as though they'd been constantly moving since they'd first met and had never had the chance to enjoy one another. Now was that time.

Grady walked out the bedroom door and down the short hallway on his way to the main room. He wasn't prepared for what he found waiting for him. All the windows were now uncovered and a stunning sunset could be seen dipping into the lake. A fire roared in the hearth, and the coffee table had been removed and in its place were plush-looking blankets and pillows surrounding what appeared to be a short stump, but without the bark. It was, in essence, a nest. The main overhead lights had been turned off, leaving the fire to paint everything in its golden glow.

Ben came from the kitchen area carrying two plates. "There you are. Right on time, babe."

Grady couldn't help but smile wide. Ben had done all this for him. He joined Ben in the center of their blanket-buffeted nest and helped Ben set the plates down beside a dented silver bucket full of ice chilling a bottle of wine. Grady took the opportunity to pull Ben into his arms and held him tight.

"Thank you, babe."

Ben cupped Grady's cheek and murmured, "Anything for you." Ben's soft lips felt like heaven against Grady's skin as his lover kissed the side of his neck. "I've been waiting for this all day. Naked time."

Grady reached for his belt holding his robe closed as Ben did the same. Inch by inch, Ben's tanned skin revealed itself to Grady's appreciative gaze. Neither looked away from the other, enjoying the freedom they had being here together. Both lowered to the floor after a few explorative caresses and Grady looked at his plate sitting on one side of the wide piece of wood of the stump. He knew he shouldn't be surprised about finding his favorite meal of lasagna on the menu, but the care Ben had taken to prepare all this was humbling. Grady was a lucky man.

"Everything is perfect." Grady voice cracked slightly. "I love you so much."

Ben took Grady's hand and kissed his palm. "I love you just as much."

Sometimes Grady thought all this was too good to be true, but then he remembered what they'd been through to be together and knew it was real. He dug into his meal, moaning as the sweet tomatoes, gooey cheese, and perfectly cooked noodles hit his tongue. This was heaven. Sitting in the glow of the fireplace eating an amazing meal with the sexiest man he'd ever seen was the stuff dreams were made of. Ben poured two glasses of wine before digging into his own plate of food with a moan of his own.

"You made all this while I was sleeping?" Grady asked, duly impressed.

"Well, I prepared a lot of it ahead of time while you were on shift last night. The rest I did when we got here. Do you like it?"

"Oh babe, it's phenomenal. All the more special because you made it for me."

Ben smiled, making Grady's heart skip a beat at how breathtaking his partner was. It wasn't simply his appearance, though that would be godlike stature; it was the whole package. Ben's bravery, compassion, strength, love, and kindness rounded out the total picture of Grady's man.

They continued eating with the occasional touch or caress, and by the end of the meal, their legs were intertwined to one side of the stump they were using as a table. Ben took Grady's empty plate, untangled himself before standing, and deposited the dishes in the sink. Grady watched Ben's beautiful ass flex as he walked away, but the return journey held him mesmerized. He could feel his own cock hardening by the second.

"Before dessert I have something for you," Ben announced as he sat down and reached between the couch cushions to retrieve a long slender box.

Grady didn't know what to say. Ben had made this evening so memorable to begin with he had no idea what else there could be. Ben held the box out and Grady's hand shook as he took it. His love remained quiet as Grady unwrapped the bow around the box and opened it. What he found inside made him gasp.

The gold shined in the firelight as he pulled the necklace from the box. The chain wasn't overly thick, but was substantial enough he wouldn't worry wearing it. On the end was a small medallion with the image of Saint Michael the Archangel, the patron saint of police officers. It was more than decorative and beautiful—it had strong meaning.

"I know we haven't talked about religion before, and I hope this doesn't upset you, but I had Father John bless it before I brought it here." Ben blushed but continued, "I figured it couldn't hurt to have the big guy on our side. Now, when I'm not with you I feel a bit better knowing that someone's looking out for you." Ben looked away.

Grady would have none of that. There was no reason for his partner to be embarrassed. This was the most significant and stunning gift he'd ever received. He lifted the stump and placed it off to the side before crawling over to his lover.

He cupped Ben's cheek and said with a slight tremble in his voice, "Thank you. No one has ever given me something this special. I'll treasure it forever." Grady held out the necklace. "Will you put it on me?"

Ben took the necklace before motioning for Grady to turn around. He complied and moments later felt the chain lying against his skin. He looked down at the medallion that now sat in the center of his chest and traced it with his fingertip.

Strong arms wrapped around him from behind. "I'll do anything to keep you safe. I want to spend the rest of my life with you."

Had he ever been loved so thoroughly? Grady leaned back onto Ben's chest and soaked in the love and care his partner was lavishing on him. Ben's hands roamed over Grady's chest, making his nipples harden before pinching them between his fingers and sending a jolt of need straight to his hardening cock. The groan that escaped his lips seemed to bounce off the walls in the quiet room.

"Make love to me, Ben." Grady didn't want to wait another minute. He craved his lover who was currently kissing his ear. Ben brought every need Grady had storming to the surface, begging to be satisfied.

"Oh, I will, but I want to love on you for a while first," Ben purred, his voice like warm honey flowing over Grady's hot skin. With every lick and suck, goose bumps appeared and excitement surged through his veins.

Ben lowered Grady to the soft blankets covering the floor and began mapping Grady's body with his hot, wet tongue. His breathing sped up as his lover explored every inch. The one time he tried to reach for Ben, his hands were caught and placed above his head.

"I want this to be all about you, sweetheart," Ben explained before taking Grady's cock in his mouth and swallowing him down his throat.

Grady cried out at the sudden intense pleasure flooding through him. Ben played his body like a finely tuned instrument, bringing him close to the edge before backing off, never allowing him to fall over. By the time Ben slid his finger into him, Grady was trembling with need. One quickly became two, then three. It seemed as though Ben needed him as much as Grady wanted Ben.

"Ready, babe?" Ben asked as he lined himself up with Grady's hole.

"More than ready. I need you inside me."

The slight burn was quickly replaced with desire as Ben brushed against his prostate, sending Grady flying. By the time Ben was fully seated inside him, Grady was a panting, moaning mess begging for more. Ben was the only man with this much power over him. But, no matter how lost he became in the throes of passion, Ben was there to guide him home. It was freeing being able to completely let go without fear.

His world narrowed to the sensations running through his body and Ben's hooded green eyes. Soon he felt his balls pull up tight and the pressure building and knew he'd not be able to stop this time.

"Ben, I'm…" His voice was lost as his orgasm overtook him. Pulse after pulse was pulled from his body until he had nothing left to give.

Ben's roar filled the room moments before he collapsed onto Grady. It was a good thing they were the same size so that he could hold Ben's weight. He ran his hands over Ben's sweaty skin, tracing his muscles as well as the scar left behind by Grady's father's bullet.

"Love you," Ben said, and kissed Grady gently before rolling onto his side. "You're everything to me, babe."

Grady held him tight and after a couple minutes, Ben began to snore. Considering everything he'd done today, driving up here, and preparing all this for Grady, he understood completely. He reached over and pulled a blanket over the two of them. The fire was still going strong as he took a good look around the room.

Before today, he would have not seen the appeal to a place that held so many bad memories. Now, looking at the thick timbers, mismatched rugs, old family photos covering every wall, and fishing trophies that sat proudly on the mantel, Grady could see the draw. Ben's love of the place made Grady look at it through different eyes, ones that did not include his father.

He reached for his medallion and held it between his fingers. This was what love was meant to be. This was the all-encompassing feeling he never thought he'd have, and the man he never dreamed he'd be fortunate enough to be loved by.

He looked down at the engraving of Saint Michael and smiled. Every bad memory he'd had in this cottage was being replaced with love. Now, as Ben had wished, this cottage had transformed back into a place the two of them could escape to as often as possible. Ben had given him this peace and Grady loved him for it.

Now he had to wait for round two as he looked at the tasty man lying on his chest. With this level of temptation, Grady definitely needed the patience of a saint.

Chapter Ten

The White Hair Crew

Rose, Jackie, Betty, Bertha, and Joan, grandmas all, watched as the latest arrival in town walked down Main Street on his way from the Brighton Motel. His name was Saint, and according to the Brighton grapevine, he was Johnny's brother. Which made sense considering the wedding coming up. However, Rose recognized a lost soul when she saw one.

"So what's the plan?" Joan asked.

"What do you mean?" Rose asked, knowing full well the other four already knew who she was thinking about.

"Really, we're way too old to play that game, Rose." Bertha laughed as she stirred her cup of wild berry tea. "Out with it."

"Do any of you get the feeling that Dr. Saint Jeffrey is struggling?" she asked.

"He looks like he's been through something awful. There is so much pain in his eyes and it's not all the physical kind. Although that boy does look like he's been hurt, with those bandages and all," Jackie stated.

"The question is, what are we going to do about it, ladies?" Betty asked as she pulled a notepad from her bedazzled purse. Her granddaughter had made it for her as a birthday gift and she never went anywhere without it.

Rose thought about it for a moment before asking, "He's here for Johnny's wedding, right?"

"Yep, that's what Travis said," Bertha told them.

"So we have ten days to figure it out. I say we start by getting to know him, and that can start right now," Rose said as she motioned toward the front doors of the diner. Saint was walking in with the same book he carried under his arm everywhere she'd seen him.

Joan stood and called out, "Saint. Come sit with us, young man." Mrs. Walker wasn't known for her subtlety.

Saint looked ready to bolt but Rose had to give him credit, he squared his shoulders and walked over to their table. "Good morning, ladies."

"Good morning, Saint," the Crew said in unison, and the man took a half step back.

"Yep, we're giving off the cult vibe, girls, and scaring the poor young man. Tone it down a touch," Rose admonished before pulling an extra chair over from the next table and motioning for him to sit. "Join us for a coffee, Dr. Jeffrey." It wasn't a question.

"Saint. I don't go by doctor any longer," he explained a bit gruffly. "I'm sorry but I won't be able to join you ladies, my brother wanted to meet me for coffee."

"That's fine, young man, we'll keep you company until Johnny arrives," Jackie said as she waved down Katie, one of the high school girls who was waitressing. Rose would have to thank her for her quick thinking later.

"I hope Johnny brings Lucy with him. She's such a sweet child and she's starting to come out of her shell. But she still won't go to anyone other than Gabe and Johnny," Betty commented before stuffing her knitting back into her patchwork bag.

Saint scanned the diner as if looking for a way out. When he saw none his shoulders drooped and he sat. "How are you ladies this morning?" She and the other women knew the poor man wanted to be anywhere other than here, but at least he was polite.

For the next five minutes, the Crew chatted about various aches and pains each woke up with as Rose watched him navigate his coffee with the palms of both bandaged hands. It reminded her of how boxers tape their hands before putting boxing gloves on. The more the women talked the calmer Saint became until he began leaning back in his chair, releasing some of the anxiety he was carrying around. Rose imagined him to be quite a nice fellow if he weren't carrying around so much sorrow.

"So, are you going to be buying a place here in Brighton to refurbish?" Rose asked while pointing to the big book he'd been hauling around since arriving.

Saint ran his finger across the spine before answering. "No ma'am, I'm not buying in Brighton. I have a place in LA that I'll be heading to after the wedding."

"Los Angeles, how exciting," Bertha said while waving her right hand and almost knocking Rose in the face if she hadn't ducked. Saint smiled but it quickly melted away.

"I don't know about exciting, but from what I've heard and seen, it's going to take a lot of work bringing the building back to its former glory."

"Do you have a contractor set up yet?" Rose asked, her mind already working.

"No. I haven't found the right person for the job. I need someone who has extensive knowledge about refurbishing old buildings in DTLA, and has contacts in the city. The permitting process is a nightmare." Well, that question had gotten him in high dungeon.

"Now, don't you worry," Rose told him, "my nephew's son is a contractor out that way. I'll give him a call and see if he can recommend someone."

"Kind of you. But I'm…picky. I couldn't ask you to put yourself out," Saint said with a fair amount of starch in his voice.

"You didn't ask, I offered. This is Brighton after all." Rose patted his arm and waved away any further discussion even though she could tell he wasn't cottoning to the suggestion one bit.

Saint looked ready to continue arguing the point, but a loud gasp had them all turning their heads to find Johnny with Gabe, who was holding Lucy, a few feet away from their table.

"Frank, my god, what happened to your hands?"

Simultaneously, Lucy squirmed to get out of Gabe's arms and ran to a man who should have been a stranger yelling, "Saint, Saint."

Chapter Eleven

Saint

Saint was stunned as Lucy bounced up and down beside his chair, looking so much happier than the last time they'd been together. The table had fallen silent, and both his brother and the guy he assumed was Gabe stared at him and Lucy as if they had four heads. He knew explanations would be expected, but he didn't know if he was up to reliving the entire nightmare for public consumption.

"Perhaps we should discuss this someplace else," Saint suggested. Even though the situation sucked, he couldn't help the genuine smile on his face at seeing his younger brother after such a long time.

The shock in Johnny's eyes faded to concern. Saint could no longer keep Lucy at bay and picked her up onto his lap with the unmistakable hiss of pain.

"Where else are you hurt?" Johnny asked, but thankfully, the man with his brother stepped in.

"Sweetheart, we should take your brother to the house where he'd be more comfortable."

Saint found that a bit forward considering he hadn't been invited to their home before. They'd wanted to meet him here at the diner, and who could blame them, he was essentially a stranger now.

Johnny seemed to snap out of it and looked around the diner. "Absolutely. Of course. You can come with us and we'll bring you back to the motel later. Do you need any help standing?"

Throughout this, Lucy sat as happy as a clam on his lap. Saint was positive the entire diner was wondering how a plastic surgeon from New York knew an orphaned toddler from Costa Rica.

That question opened a Pandora's box he'd fought to keep closed for many years. Nevertheless, with the complete joy only a child could give, the box had been blown wide open leaving him without protection to face his brother, whom he hadn't spoken to in years.

Chapter Twelve

Vincent and Tristan

Tristan opened the box that had been delivered to the main house that morning, excited to be able to get his hands on the hard copies. Packing paper went flying into the air as he dug to get to his prize, and there it was, all shiny and new, *Protected*, the first novel from his new series. It followed the lives of a group of military men finding their way after getting out of the service. *Yeah, yeah, where would I come up with that idea?*

The words of his grade eight English teacher floated through his head: write what you know. After everything he'd seen and been through, Tristan had a wealth of information to call upon. He took one book out before setting the box on the kitchen floor, and then he reached for his mug of coffee. Sitting at the large table, his hand on his book, his gaze was drawn to the wall mosaic that his lover had made for him out of his grandmother's smashed dishes. That gift spoke volumes. He remembered the pain he had felt when he'd learned the china had been smashed, that the last physical remnant of his beloved grans had been destroyed. But Vincent had put everything to rights by creating this incredible mosaic.

Luna came running in through her doggie-door followed by two of her puppies. Tristan couldn't believe how much time had flown by—the pups were old enough to roam on their own and freely moved between the main house and Tristan and Vincent's home.

"Hello, pretty girl. What are you all up to today?" Tristan asked as Luna and her pups jumped onto the couch and got comfortable. "Ah, I see, nap time."

The Sentinels had gotten a routine of sorts down since the puppies came along and Tristan was sharing visitation rights with Sam. The doggie family went where they pleased, begging treats and spreading love wherever they went. Soon though one of those balls of fluff would be leaving them behind to start a new life with a different owner.

If he'd thought the Sentinels were protective of their family and friends, he'd marveled at their downright obsession over a defenseless puppy. Before they would consider letting one of their doggie family go, the adopters had to fill out a detailed, and rather intrusive, questionnaire, which Shannon and Matthew would dissect. Then there was a home visit to make sure the puppy would be safe and cared for. Last was the contract that allowed the team members to retrieve the puppy if they felt it was in danger.

The first female puppy was going to Gabe and Johnny's adopted daughter, Lucy. Yep, they had to go through all the steps. Tristan smiled remembering the day the whole team showed up at Gabe and Johnny's house for inspection. Apparently, the whole time the Sentinels clomped through the house and yard, Johnny watched them, looking nervous, while Gabe sat back watching a princess movie with Lucy. By the end of the "home inspection," the whole team had ended up on the couch or floor watching the movie right along with them.

Family. You had to love 'em.

Speaking of family, Tristan's mom and dad came down for a visit to meet everyone and scolded him for not telling them about his Lyme infection. Somehow, the fact that he didn't want to worry them wasn't a good enough reason. Vincent couldn't contain his "told ya so" and sat back to watch the fireworks. Eventually they'd calmed down and were happy Tristan was on the mend. Lord knows what they would have done if they ever found out about his ex and his stalker.

Tristan lifted his right hand and flexed the fingers out before bringing them in to make a fist. His thumb and little finger did as he wanted but the other three could make it only halfway. He'd been in physiotherapy for months, but recovery was slow and his joints still ached. Funny how having to fight for his own and Sam's lives put a completely new spin on things. His damaged hand wasn't that much of an issue in the grand scheme of things.

Working through his issues with Dr. Gordon had been amazing so far. Now Tristan understood why everyone had recommended the doc so highly. Tristan was still processing his guilt over killing Ryan Graham, but at least it no longer felt as though he was suffocating when he thought of it.

Vincent had been gone for two days and wasn't due back for another. Though they were essentially on their holiday vacation, a call had come in from an old friend who needed his help. Vincent and his friend were protecting a man scheduled to testify against two members of the Sorrel crime family in Chicago.

Though Tristan missed Vincent, he understood that this was a part of his life, and it was his calling. Vincent had fought to protect people his entire life, through his military service and as a member of the Sentinel team. Tristan would never do anything to stop him from following his calling, even if he missed him like crazy.

Tristan walked out onto his front porch with his coffee and sat on the pillow-covered swing that faced the gently flowing river running beside their house. They'd chosen this spot to make their home. This was their idea of paradise.

The box of Christmas decoration his parents had sent was waiting patiently by the fireplace alongside the ones Vincent's parents had given them when they had visited them in Arizona. Both boxes held new ornaments, some handmade, and a few heirloom pieces. Before Vincent had left, he and Tristan had gone to the local garden center and picked out a small loblolly pine tree. It was still in its own pot, and after Christmas, they intended to plant it somewhere on their property.

Everything was sitting, waiting, ready to go for when the man who owned Tristan's heart came home.

Tristan pushed his foot against the wood decking and sent the porch swing into motion. Even though the wind had turned a bit colder these past couple of days, he still loved to sit on the porch. Besides, the new sweater Mrs. Walker had made for him kept him nice and toasty. It was bright red to match his hair, and Tristan loved it.

He was busy getting his laptop set up when he heard an engine. He wondered if one of the guys was coming out for another visit. Tristan, Matthew, Sam, and Randy had become each other's support group when any of their men were away on assignments. It helped make the time more bearable, and they enjoyed each other's company.

Concerned, he noted this engine sounded more powerful than his friends' ATVs. He set his laptop down and stood looking toward the spot where their laneway broke through the tree line. The moment he saw it, his heart started pounding in his throat. Vincent was home.

Tristan jumped off the porch and ran toward their garage as Vincent parked his big truck beside Tristan's new feisty Fiesta, in hot pepper metallic red.

Tristan didn't stop running until he jumped into Vincent's open arms. The feel of those strong arms wrapping around his body gave Tristan a peace he felt only when his partner was near.

"I've missed you, sparrow," Vincent groaned as he crushed Tristan to his muscled chest.

"Same here, babe." Tristan's voice was muffled by Vincent's shirt.

The two stood in the driveway for several minutes, neither seemed able to let go of the other. Funny how everything felt as though it was in its right place when they were together.

"You weren't due back for another day. What happened? Was anyone hurt?" Tristan asked before pulling away to get a good look at his man. "I told you not to come back with a scratch." His lover knew he was joking…sort of.

"No, sparrow, I'm not hurt. As it turns out, the two Sorrel crime bosses he was set to testify against turned up dead," Vincent explained. "So since there wasn't a trial, the witness was sent off to his new life in the witness protection program." He lowered his head to take Tristan's lips in a hungry kiss.

Vincent bent and then picked up Tristan, pulling him into that massive chest, and headed for the house. Tristan was on the same page. He needed to be as close to his lover as he could get and that required a lot less clothing.

For someone who thought he'd never know what real love felt like, Tristan was making up for lost time.

***

Vincent stirred the cream into his coffee, grabbed the two mugs, and headed for the living room. The main lights had been dimmed, and the Christmas lights were glowing, making the living room feel cozy. It was a stark difference to his last two days stuck in a cheap hotel in downtown Chicago. The Windy City was way too crowded for his liking. He looked out their front window at the stars hanging low in the sky. This was his idea of heaven, and his angel was currently sitting in front of their first Christmas tree wearing only his boxers, waiting for him.

"Here you go, sparrow," Vincent said as he handed over one of the mugs before sitting down beside Tristan on the floor.

"Thank you." His beauty's smile never ceased to make Vincent's heart skip a beat. His old life couldn't compare to this and the love they shared. "I've been dying to go through these boxes."

Vincent sat back and watched as one by one, Tristan removed and unwrapped ornament after ornament. His face aglow as each was revealed, as if each was a Christmas gift on their own.

"I made this in second grade," he announced while holding up a colorful clay handprint. It had sparkles and feathers glued all along the edges. "I had style even back then."

Vincent couldn't help but laugh and pulled his love even closer. After a quick kiss, Tristan continued to sort through all the ornaments when he held up one of Vincent's, looking confused.

Vincent raised a brow. "It was supposed to be a horse from our ranch." He shrugged at the lump. "I was five."

Tristan tilted his chin down, doing a poor job of concealing his grin. "It's adorable." He reached into the box and grabbed another item. "Oh my god, is this your cowboy hat?"

Sure enough, he pulled out a pint-size straw Stetson from the box. It had been Vincent's first. "I didn't even know my mom had saved this."

Tristan reached up and placed it on his head. Vincent was sure that the brim that hadn't even fit his small head as a child was no more than the size of a small saucer now. But it brought back fond memories. New memories with the man with whom he'd spend the rest of his life was Vincent's mission.

"I can imagine you running wild with the ranch as your playground. Sounds like paradise," Tristan said wistfully.

Vincent gathered his sparrow close. "It was. I've been fortunate to have had a wonderful childhood, but nothing compares to my life now, with you."

Tristan wrapped his arms around Vincent's neck. "You sweet talker, you. Keep that up and I just might keep you."

"Might keep me, huh?" Vincent began tickling his sassy boyfriend's sides until he was out of breath from laughing so much. "You're stuck with me, brat."

"I'm completely on board with that," Tristan said once he could breathe properly again.

Vincent pulled over the box Tristan's parents had given them and pulled out a Santa covered in various shades of blue.

"That was my blue phase," Tristan answered without skipping a beat.

His sparrow, an original, and all his.

Vincent remembered the moment he first laid eyes on Tristan at the Brighton Police Station. Tristan had stood ready to defend his friend Grady that day, not concerned in the least that he was the smallest person in the room. His curly fire-red hair was messed from running his fingers through it, and Tristan's striking green eyes caught Vincent's attention within seconds of entering the room. He hadn't been able to look away since. Nor did he wish to.

The rest of the evening played out with nostalgia and laughter. Old memories relived and new memories made. By the end of the night they sat together on the floor, Tristan leaning back against Vincent's chest, both admiring the fully decorated tree with a child's cowboy hat as its star.

Tristan had added light to Vincent's life much like the Christmas tree they were sitting beside. Tristan was Vincent's light, leading him home after each mission, after every time he risked his life to save a life, and he knew he was blessed to have it.

This complete joy he never saw coming would be his greatest gift this year, and for many more to come.

Chapter Thirteen

Gabe and Johnny

Johnny helped his brother out of the truck and onto the walkway leading to their home. Gabe held a sleeping Lucy close to his chest, and headed for her bedroom to lay her down for her nap. Saint looked ashen and weak. Nothing like what Johnny remembered of his brother's movie-star good looks. He was still huge but it seemed as if the life had been drained out of him, painfully.

"Do you want anything to eat or drink, Saint?" Johnny asked as he helped him sit in one of the chairs in the living room.

'Yes, water, please," he replied in the same monotone voice Johnny had noted he'd used when they spoke at the diner.

Saint's eyes were another story. Flat and void of emotion, the only time Johnny saw any happiness there was when his brother looked at him.

Johnny left the living room quickly, eager to get back to his brother as fast as possible. By the time he pulled a bottle of water from the fridge, Gabe was at his side in the kitchen.

He pulled Johnny into a much-needed hug and said, "Don't worry, we'll find out what happened to him."

"No matter what, he's still my brother. If he's in trouble, we have to help him," Johnny stated firmly. It didn't matter that he hadn't seen him in years, Saint was his brother.

"We will figure it out, I promise."

Together they walked back into the living room to find Saint in exactly the same position, as if he was afraid to move. "Here you go," Johnny said as he handed over the bottle of water.

Saint smiled but remained silent. By the time, they sat down on the opposite couch, Johnny's mind was a jumble of questions but thankfully, Gabe took over.

"Can you tell us what happened to you and how you know our daughter?" Gabe cut to the big questions first.

Saint reached into his jacket pocket and pulled out a prescription bottle, but couldn't manage to open it. Stubbornly, he continued to try until Johnny stood and took the bottle and opened it for him.

"Thank you," Saint huffed out in defeat as Gabe opened his bottle of water as well.

"When I first came here, Gabe had to do those same things for me because my hands were burned," Johnny said while holding up his scarred hands. He'd already explained to his brother what had happened over the phone.

Saint looked at them closely before saying, "I'm glad they're healed nicely and that you had someone there for you. I'm sorry that it wasn't me."

That statement shocked Johnny considering he hadn't heard a peep from his brother in years, but he let it go. The man was in enough pain. He watched as Saint took his pill and shoved the bottle back into his pocket.

"If something's wrong or someone's after you, we can help," Gabe spoke up. "But you need to tell us everything first."

Saint looked at Johnny and Gabe. "I guess I should start at the beginning. I'll do my best to filter it down to the 'highlights.'" There was anger and frustration in his voice, but he sat a bit straighter. "I'm sorry I was such an asshole brother to you the past several years."

"You weren't an asshole. You stopped talking to me, and I never knew why," Johnny replied at the same time Gabe wrapped his arm around him in support. "It hurt not having you in my life."

"I'm sorry," Saint stated. He sounded genuine but Johnny could be hoping he was without knowing. "You were picking out your major for college and Dad was all over you to choose something in the medical field. We both knew that wasn't your calling, but the old man was relentless."

"I remember it was hell, and you were already away at school for a couple years by then."

"Yeah, I was aiming to be a general practitioner. I loved it. The thought of having a small practice of my own. However, Father didn't think it was prestigious enough. Big shock, huh, little brother?"

Johnny couldn't help but smile at "little brother." He'd missed that.

"By then Mom had died and Dad seemed to be on a mission to erase her from our lives. I was home one weekend from school and he was particularly cruel to you."

"I remember. It was the last weekend you ever came home." Johnny knew the date well.

"Yeah, that was the day I signed my deal with the devil," Saint admitted, and Gabe held Johnny closer. "I'd had enough. I couldn't tolerate the way he was treating you, and I told him as much when I cornered him in his study."

"You told him that. What did he do?" Johnny knew his father could be violent when provoked.

"I expected him to flip like he always did. Maybe knock me into the wall again, but he had something more heinous in mind. You know, it wasn't until that day that I realized how evil and manipulative he could be."

Chapter Fourteen

Saint

He felt the chill run through his body exactly as it had that day years ago. He didn't want to have this conversation, but Johnny deserved the truth and to know the danger their father could pose. "Now that I look back on it, I realize the bastard had it all planned out. I'm convinced he'd upped the abuse that weekend for my benefit."

"For your benefit? I was the one who'd been threatened with the possibility of no college. Even though Mom left us enough money to attend, the old man had hold of the strings. If I didn't change my major, he'd not release a cent."

"You're right. He wouldn't have, and mine as well. It was his endgame of sorts. Neither one of us were doing what he wanted, and without Mom there to rein him in, he did whatever he wanted." Memories of that evening flooded back, and Saint felt the same anger, fear, and helplessness he had all those years ago. "I was a college kid, not a strategic general. When I confronted him, I gave him his chance to strike. He'd had the damned contract written up, all ready for my signature."

Johnny looked at his brother, even more confused, and Saint understood this would be a lot to take in. Saint pulled two items from his pocket that were tucked behind the medicine bottle and set them on the coffee table. One was a few old pieces of paper stapled together. The other was a key.

"The contract." Saint nodded at the papers while trying to point with his bandaged hand. "It's kind of surreal that those few pieces of paper could destroy so much."

Gabe reached across the table and picked them up. “How old were you when you signed these?” he asked.

“Over eighteen. Old enough for the contract to be legal. The choice he gave me was clear and exacting. If I didn’t sign, both of us would have been left without an education or a future.”

“What did the contract say?” Johnny asked.

Saint leaned back in his chair. The pain was finally easing, but he was getting tired. He’d have to rest soon, but not until this was all out in the open. He looked over at Gabe, who had the contract in his hand. “Would you mind reading out the main points for me please, Gabe.”

Gabe nodded his agreement and began where all great tragedies began, with shock and doubt. “This can’t be legal.”

“Oh I assure you it is, even though I was forced to sign it. Which, I learned later, was coercion and would have voided the agreement. I didn’t know that then. But that wasn’t the reason I adhered to it,” Saint explained, giving Gabe a moment to figure it out.

“I understand.” Gabe nodded

“You understand what?” Johnny insisted.

“First item agreed upon was that you would change your major to plastic surgery,” Gabe began.

“Just like dear old Dad,” Saint sighed and sank deeper into the comfortable chair.

“You would complete your education and join your father’s practice. You were to cease all contact with Johnny from that day forward. Your father agreed to not encumber or prevent Johnny from completing his marketing degree. He would ensure Johnny received all the money his mother bequeathed to him. But you wouldn’t go along with any of it unless he never insinuated himself into Johnny’s life or attempted to intimidate him in any way.” Gabe looked up. “The last part must have been penned in after the original agreement was typed up. I see it was initialed by both of you.”

"I wouldn't allow him to continue to terrorize Johnny. I had to make sure he would stick to the deal so I wrote it in," Shadow explained as he laid his head back against the soft cushions. "With his inheritance, he could do what he wanted. He was free." His voice sounded as groggy as he felt.

He must have drifted off because somehow his body was going back. He realized Johnny was pulling the chair out into a recliner. A moment later a blanket was being tucked in around him.

He was too tired to care that he wasn't done with his story, but Saint needed Johnny to be prepared. He didn't know if or when the danger would come.

Chapter Fifteen

Gabe and Johnny

"Careful if Dad turns up," were the last words Saint muttered before he fell into a deep sleep.

Gabe held Johnny tight. Neither of them had expected what they had learned today.

Initially, when he'd heard Saint was coming to the wedding, Gabe had believed Saint wanted something from Johnny. Hell, he still could, but Gabe wasn't so sure of that any longer. He led his soon-to-be husband to the kitchen so they could talk without disturbing Saint.

They sat at the kitchen island and Johnny took the contract out of Gabe's hands. "Could this be fake?"

"Sure, it could. Anything could be faked given today's technology."

Johnny looked at him closely. "But you don't think it is."

"It doesn't matter what I think, sweetheart."

"Please."

"No. I don't believe it's fake." He had to be honest, even if it hurt. This was a deep, dark family secret that had needed to see the light of day years ago. "But we still don't know how he knows Lucy. I can guess he was her surgeon, but there's a lot of missing information that we'll have to wait to learn. Your brother needs to recuperate from whatever was done to him. I'm surprised he made it to Brighton given his condition."

Johnny shook his head. "I remember that weekend so well. I tried to stay off Dad's radar because he was in a horrible mood. Saint had come home from school and everything seemed normal between us. Then the next morning he was gone without a word and I never spoke to him again other than in passing. I thought he didn't have time for me anymore because he was too busy following in our dad's footsteps. Shit, how did I not suspect something was up? I was wrapped up in my own world and didn't even stop to consider that this wasn't the way my brother behaved. Selfish of me not to have seen that."

"You were young, and you didn't have anyone to help you. The blame lies with your father alone." Gabe tried to ease Johnny's growing guilt. If this turned out to be a scam, Gabe swore Saint would be even more damaged before he left Brighton for putting Johnny through this.

There was a knock on their front door and Gabe stood, gave Johnny a kiss, and went to answer it. He opened the door to find Vincent with a box in his hand, and his lover Tristan waiting on the other side. Gabe brought his finger up to his mouth and made a barely there "shush."

"We brought some of the pup's toys over and her bed so that you can be all ready for tomorrow. Are we being quiet because Lucy's napping?" Tristan asked in a whisper.

"That, and because Johnny's brother is sleeping as well," Gabe answered quietly while pointing to Saint, who was asleep in the recliner.

Gabe knew something was wrong almost immediately as Vincent's face changed from curiosity to shock. "That's Johnny's brother?"

Johnny came over to the group and said, "Yeah. His name is Saint… Frank Jeffrey officially."

Tristan had turned to look at Vincent. "What's wrong?"

"That's the same man I pulled out of Venezuela four weeks back. He was among a team of doctors and nurses taken hostage while offering medical aid in-country. We were sent over to get them back. He was in rough shape when we found him. It's good to see he's recovered." Vincent turned toward Johnny, "If I had known, I swear

I would have told you. I didn't know who he was other than a hostage."

"My brother was on an aid mission to another country?" Johnny looked ready to pass out. "How did I not know this? I don't know my own brother."

Gabe gathered him into his arms. "Maybe you both have been given this chance to change that."

Chapter Sixteen

Saint

He could smell food cooking, its aroma heavenly. His stomach growled in agreement. When Saint opened his eyes, he was aware of two things, he wasn't in his motel room, and the little cutie he'd operated on in Costa Rica was peeking over the edge of the chair he had been sleeping in. He wondered what the odds were that this was the child his brother had adopted, and was the same one he'd helped.

"Hello, Lucy," he whispered, not wanting to scare her. Lucy's smile was instantaneous and warmed some of the cold deep inside him.

"Saint play?" She held up two dolls and looked hopeful.

Who can say no to that? When he pushed on the chair to bring it back into an upright position, he'd momentarily forgotten about the healing wound on his stomach. The first cry brought his brother and Gabe running from the kitchen.

How can I forget about the damn hole in my side?

Johnny picked up Lucy as Gabe said, "I'm a medic with the fire department, let me have a look." Saint nodded, and Gabe raised his shirt. Shit. Saint felt weaker than he had yesterday and knew he was overtaxing himself, but things needed to be done before he headed to LA.

"Okay, it doesn't look as if you've pulled anything open, but I'd have a better idea if I knew what I'm working with," Gabe stated pointedly.

"Three gunshot wounds, stomach and both hands," Saint explained, hearing his brother's gasp in the background. "It should be okay, I have an appointment for a checkup with a Dr. Green tomorrow morning."

"How did you get shot?" Johnny asked, looking shocked.

"Some people didn't want me in their country any longer." Saint knew that oversimplified explanation wouldn't stand.

Gabe covered Saint's heavily bandaged abdomen and helped set the chair upright. The minute Gabe stepped back, Lucy decided her path was clear and insisted, "Saint play."

"Why don't you bring your dollies over to show Saint? He still has a tummy ache," Johnny suggested, and Lucy thought it over for a minute. It was amazing to see how far the little girl had come. She toddled toward the big toy box against the wall chanting, "Dolly, dolly."

When Saint looked back up, he could see the questions in Gabe's and Johnny's eyes and decided to get the rest over with as quickly as possible.

"Lucy was a patient of mine. I repaired her cleft palate and lip. She had a hard time settling down in the strange environment of the clinic so I sat with her and rocked her until she fell asleep. Over the course of the next several days she figured out my name and has been saying it ever since."

Saint waited for the questions he'd expected to come, but both Johnny and Gabe didn't say a word. Something was up.

"Saint, while you were sleeping a couple of our friends came by to drop things off for our new puppy that's arriving tomorrow. One of the men works as a Sentinel, his name is Vincent," Johnny explained, and light bulbs starting going off in Saint's head. Things kept getting stranger and stranger. Coincidence is rarely that, but in this case…

"Then you know," Saint stated, happy not to have to relive it, but wished that he'd been the one to explain.

"Not all of it. Vincent told us you were taken as a hostage in Venezuela,"

"That's where they found me. Our father had control of my professional life but he couldn't do anything about my free time. On my 'vacations' I volunteered my time with Flight for Life all over the world. I could finally put this medical training to good use, not for only increasing someone's breast size or sucking fat from their asses. I was helping people who truly needed it." Saint got lost in his thoughts for a moment, the taste of blood, the burn of bullets ripping through his flesh, the cruel laughter surrounding him…he wondered if it would ever leave him.

"Easy, Saint. You're safe, big brother." Johnny's voice broke through the haze of those dire memories, bringing Saint back to the here and now. He knew what was happening to him; he was, or used to be, a doctor and knew the signs. Post traumatic stress disorder, and he'd be damned if he'd surrender one more thing. His sanity was not up for grabs like his life's passion was.

"I'm okay. Sorting through the memories. Anyway, that's how I met Lucy and why I look the way I do," Saint explained, not wanting to delve any deeper than necessary. He noticed the key was still on the table and could use that to redirect the conversation. "That key is for you, Johnny."

Johnny turned to the coffee table and picked it up, flipping it through his fingers. "What's the key open?"

"A lock box I've brought with me. I couldn't carry it to the diner so I figured you could come back to my room and get it when you have time," Saint explained, realizing that soon he'd have his answer after years of wondering whether he did the right thing in saving it.

"What's inside the box?" Johnny asked.

"As much of Mom's jewelry as I could save."

Johnny sat with a thump onto the floor and Gabe was at his side in seconds. It would be a long time before he'd be able to move that fast again.

"You have them?" Johnny asked in disbelief.

"Well, originally Dad had them. I liberated them before he could sell them. I've been holding on to them for years, trying to figure out a way to get them to you. I know how much they meant to you, so I thought you'd like to have them." He remembered all the times Johnny could be found playing with the pieces when Mom got ready to go out.

Johnny looked at the key in his hand wistfully. Saint had wanted to give that to his brother for so long.

"Thank you, Saint," Johnny said as Lucy brought over three dolls and laid them on Saint's arm before returning to the box.

"Wait, why are you doing all this now?" Gabe asked, seemingly realizing where this conversation was going. "If it wasn't safe before, then why now?"

Saint raised his hands and looked Gabe in the eyes. "Because I'm no longer useful to him." He ground his teeth together. "I'll never be able to operate again."

"Oh, Saint. I'm so sorry," Johnny said as he stood and gave him a hug around his neck, mindful of Saint's injuries. He couldn't even remember the last time someone hugged him for no other reason but to support him. Of course, people hugged him when he'd fixed something on them or one of their relatives, but never just for him. It felt nice.

"Thank you, but lots of plans ahead. New things to learn and see." *That's it, give 'em the brave face.*

Johnny looked at him as if he wasn't buying it for a minute, but thankfully let it go. "I'm happy to have you back in our lives."

"Me too, and I'm happy you found someone who can protect you in case Dad comes calling."

"You think he will?" Gabe questioned in a voice Saint called the first responder tone.

"I hope not, but I've learned he's capable of anything," Saint answered with absolute seriousness.

Chapter Seventeen

Shadow (Jake) and Randy

Randy stood in the living room of the big old Victorian he now called home, staring at the huge, heavily decorated Christmas tree, of all things. If someone walked in on him now, they would think he'd lost his mind. Perhaps he had. Randy hadn't had a full-blown Christmas in over ten years. His parents decided to skip the "hoopla" long ago in favor of sunny vacations in tropical locations without him or Grady. After Grady had moved out, Randy had spent the holidays alone.

He wasn't sure how he should feel about the change. Overwhelmed was the first emotion that came to mind. This Christmas he'd be celebrating with a town and house full of people, and for some reason that had him unsettled. Randy had never belonged to anything. It wasn't that he didn't want to have his new friends around him during the holidays, quite the opposite. He even had a healthy relationship with his brother, Grady, again. But it had been a long time since Randy had trusted anyone, and even longer since strangers became friends. He imagined he'd be able to handle what was coming because he had Jake. The strong, kind, courageous man he loved. Randy had a lot to be thankful for this year. He hoped he could handle it without making a fool of himself.

For a long time now, all he'd wanted was a normal family, especially around the holidays, and he was frustrated that doubt and trepidation clung to him like the tinsel on the tree. Everything was perfect and he still wasn't settled. He huffed and ran the palm of his hand down his face before he turned and walked to the kitchen where Mrs. Walker was busy baking Christmas cookies. He couldn't remember a time he'd ever seen his own mother baking anything, let alone cookies. Randy had to admit he'd never eaten so well in his life. Mrs. Walker was a cooking goddess.

"Hi, Mrs. Walker," Randy murmured. His voice sounded flat and he knew it.

"Well, hello there, Randy," she replied before giving him a shrewd look. "Why don't you come over here and help me for a bit. I could use another pair of hands."

Jake was busy in town, and everyone else was off working on personal projects. Randy had thought he might finish a painting he was working on, but helping Mrs. Walker seemed a better distraction. All he was doing was making himself feel worse, so why not help out. "Sure. But I warn you, I've never baked cookies. This could turn out badly."

"No worries, hon. You sit right there and I'll get you an apron."

Apron?

Randy took his seat at the large kitchen island and waited for Mrs. Walker to return. The room smelled like a bakery, and the counters were covered in flour, cookie cutters, bins, bowls, icing, and candy. After a quick look around, he helped himself to a mini candy cane. He was a sucker for these little buggers. He used to buy a bag of them and stash it away in his dresser to have throughout the year.

He popped it into his mouth as Mrs. Walker came back into the kitchen with a bright red and green reindeer apron decorated with "XMAS" in big white letters across the front. The nose of the reindeer sparkled with red glitter, proclaiming him as the one and only Rudolf.

"Here you go, young man," she said as she handed the apron over. "I'll get a bowl set up for you to mix."

She looked so delighted with the ridiculous apron that Randy put it on. Jake had explained about the White Hair Crew, and somehow Randy wasn't surprised that in a town like Brighton there was a gang of do-gooding grandmas. As he'd explored his new hometown on his daily bike rides, people would wave at him and say hello. One day when the chain fell off the temporary bike he was using, so many vehicles stopped to help that they created a mini traffic jam on the normally quite country road.

Mrs. Walker placed a bowl full of dry ingredients and one that had wet and fluffy ingredients in front of him. She handed over a big wooden spoon and instructed, "Now you need to add the dry mix slowly to the wet until it's blended."

Randy looked at both bowls with the spoon in this hand. "Are you sure I can't mess this up?" He imagined the guys biting into a cookie and spitting it out in disgust.

"I trust you will do fine." Mrs. Walker smiled. "Now get to it. We've got lots of people to feed."

He couldn't help but smile back and got to work. Over the next several hours they mixed, rolled, cut out various Christmas shapes, baked, and then decorated, once the cookies were cooled. As time went by, and with Mrs. Walker's commentary and knowledge, he began to feel a certain calm settle over him. As members of the household dropped in for a cookie or three, they praised Mrs. Walker and him on their cookie-making skills.

His fingers were stained red from icing, he had flour on his face and in his hair, and his fancy apron was covered with a little bit of everything, but he felt happy. Slowly, Randy allowed himself to feel connected to the people and rhythm of the house as they joked, ate cookies, and downed hot chocolate like it was going to disappear.

Randy was laughing along with everyone else when he noticed the man of his dreams hanging back and watching him with a smile on his face. Jake stood leaning against the back wall, arms crossed, biceps bulging. Randy wasn't sure how long Jake had been standing there watching him, but he had the need for a little Jake time.

His lover crooked his finger. It seemed as if Jake needed a little Randy time as well. He wiped his hands on the dishtowel lying on the counter, picked up a Santa cookie, and joined Jake, who now stood with his arms open wide.

Randy looked down at the front of himself. “I’m a mess.”

“Don’t care,” Jake said before pulling him close. “Having fun, babe?”

“Believe it or not, this is the first time I’ve ever baked cookies,” Randy said proudly as he presented Jake with his Santa.

Jake brushed flour off Randy’s cheek and forehead. “You look like you’re an old pro at it.”

Randy knew Jake was teasing him and loved him all the more for it. Jake took a bite of his cookie and his eyes went wide. “This is really good.”

“Don’t look so surprised. Mrs. Walker taught me. I’m thinking of trying my hand at baking every so often.”

“I’m all for it. I love Christmas,” Coop cheered before stuffing his mouth with another candy cane cookie.

***

Shadow led his talented boyfriend back to their suite of rooms that was much the same setup as the other guys’ rooms. He had a large bedroom, *en suite*, and a lounge space with a television and couch. He could hear Bits, Randy’s puppy, trailing behind them. The two of them had a special bond. Bits was the runt of the litter, and was so small, but he was a fighter just like Shadow’s Randy.

They’d been able to move all of Randy’s artwork, at least the ones he’d managed to save after his father destroyed so many beautiful pieces, to the room next door because it had the best light, according to his partner. It was set up as his studio for now until they decided if they were going to build a home of their own. Shadow wasn’t in any hurry to undertake a big project quite yet; he wanted to enjoy the gift he’d been given and let Randy become acclimated to their lives.

It had been only three and a half months since he’d found this special man chained to a wall, and it had been crazy busy ever since. Between protecting Randy while he healed, and getting his life back together with everything from identification to underwear, the poor guy hadn't had a chance to slow down and ease into the new and different world Shadow had brought him into

Shadow had noticed the lost, unsure look in his lover's eyes on several occasions, and he hoped to address that right now. He opened their bedroom door and Randy bent to scoop up Bits before smiling at him and walking in. His gasp was instantaneous, and Shadow was unsure if that was good or bad. He shut the door behind them and followed Randy to the center of their suite.

"Jake, it's…beautiful." Randy's voice was filled with awe.

Shadow looked around at the hideaway he'd created for Randy with the help of his friends. While his man had been busy baking cookies, a few of the guys hung out in the kitchen to keep him distracted while the rest were in here. Their plain king-size bed had been replaced with a stylish, rosewood four-poster bed. The dark, reddish brown wood complemented the thick, dark red drapes that flowed from around the bed and covered the windows. He'd enlisted his mom as well as the team and their partners to make sure he got it right. Shadow was the first to admit he didn't know a thing about decorating or romance.

Battery-operated candles that were incredibly real-looking glowed around the room without the fear of causing a fire. After all, they had a puppy. Thick plush pillows and a blanket covered their bed, and potted poinsettias dotted the room. In the lounge area, two stockings hung above the gas fireplace, and a smaller, personal Christmas tree stood proudly in the corner with presents already wrapped stuffed underneath it. The room was decked out to be warm, cozy, and Christmassy. Exactly as Shadow had planned. All that was left was to explain.

Randy set Bits down so their puppy could explore. Shadow took his partner's hand before leading him to the Christmas tree. "I know that everything is strange and different for you. You haven't really had a chance to relax and take it all in."

"I'm okay, Jake," Randy said with a smile, but Shadow knew his man was trying to keep him from worrying. The one thing Shadow had learned about his boyfriend, Randy always thought of others first.

"You're more than okay, you're fantastic, but this hasn't been easy on you. So, I've made us our very own hideaway. The mini fridge and cabinet are stocked, microwave and Tassimo stand at the ready, and whatever we don't have we can sneak into the kitchen and liberate." Shadow took Randy into his arms and held him tight. "We're going to slow down now, me and you. I've even downloaded a lengthy list of Christmas movies for us to watch while we cuddle by the fire. Christmas Eve after the wedding ceremony, we'll stay for dinner, wish them our best, and sneak away back to our hideaway. Christmas morning, we'll open up our presents in here, only the two of us, before joining the rest of the team. I don't want you to feel rushed or uncomfortable."

Randy's eyes were still wide but he had a big smile on his face, so Shadow took that as a good sign. Until the tears started. After the first drop fell, he quickly gathered Randy into his arms and sat down on the couch. Shadow wasn't sure what was wrong, but he had to fix it.

"I can take it all down if you want me to."

"Don't you dare, it's perfect," Randy muttered as he sniffled. "How did you know this is what I needed when I didn't even know?"

Shadow could feel the weight of worry being lifted from his shoulders. Randy wasn't upset, he was happy. He looked up at Shadow with those warm amber eyes and Shadow could read every emotion: relief, happiness, surprise, all went flittering across Randy's handsome face, but most importantly, love.

"Because I know how hard you try to make other people happy without any thought for yourself. The mural that took you weeks to complete, the decorations, always smiling and meeting all the new people who live and work in Brighton, and then helping around here in between working on your art and baking cookies. You haven't slowed down since getting free of that hellhole. So, from now until after the New Year, we're hiding out in here. We'll go out when and if we want, and for no other reason. Oh, except to take out Bits to do his business, but then that's it."

Randy wrapped his arms around Shadow's neck and hugged him tight. "It's perfect. Thank you, Jake."

"Your welcome, sweetheart," Shadow replied before realizing he'd forgotten one of his surprises. "I've got something for you for Christmas, but I'd like to give it to you now, okay?"

"Jake, you've already given me so much."

"You'll need this, and it's for your safety."

That got Randy's attention. "I think I'm the safest I've ever been in my entire life already."

"You'll understand when you see it." Shadow stood, leaving Randy to wait on the couch.

He went to their en suite and opened the door. It only took him a couple moments before he called out, "Close your eyes." His lover complied and Shadow wheeled out his surprise in front of the Christmas tree. "Okay, open them."

"Jake…" Randy stood and joined him in front of the tree. "It's… I don't want to keep saying perfect, but it's the only word that fits." Randy ran his fingertips over the frame of his new bike. Shadow knew how much his man liked to go biking even though he couldn't go long distances because of his weak lungs. This bike was one of the lightest Shadow could find, and it was made by hand and guaranteed to not leave Randy stranded anywhere.

"This one won't leave you stuck on the side of the road, like that other one did."

Randy picked it up and said, "It's so light. How much did this cost you?"

"You can't know or argue because it's a Christmas present," Shadow stated matter-of-factly.

"Christmas present, huh?"

"Yep, those are the Christmas rules, honey. I didn't make them, but I'm not going to piss off the big, bearded guy by breaking them." Randy laughed as Shadow had hoped. "Want to try it on for size?"

Instead of throwing his leg over the bike as Shadow had expected, Randy put the kickstand down and said, "I can think of something else I'd prefer to do."

"Yeah, and what's that?" Shadow asked as he rounded the bike and pulled Randy into his arms.

"I think I need to get all this flour off me with a soak in a deep bubble bath. Would you be interested in joining me?" Randy asked as he kissed the side of Shadow's neck, making his body perk right up.

"Oh yeah, you bet your cute ass I do. Go start the water and I'll pour us two glasses of wine."

Randy's eyes were truly windows to his soul, and Shadow could see his future in their depths. With one final kiss, Randy turned and walked into the en suite. Shadow couldn't look away until the door shut, his man was that mesmerizing.

Finally, he forced himself to the fridge, pulled out a bottle of Chardonnay, and uncorked it. Shadow looked around his personal space, for years it had been empty and soulless. Suddenly, colors were flooding his world again, bringing back emotions he'd thought all but lost. His room was like a mirror to his soul, now filled with life and light. All thanks to the amazing man waiting for him in a tub full of hot, soapy water.

Shadow reached out and grabbed two wine glasses along with the bottle. He had some new memories to make.

Chapter Eighteen

Rick, Bear, and Josh

Five days before the wedding

Bear looked out at the heavily decorated dining room from the kitchen's serving window. Rick had outdone himself. He swept the booths and counter, confirming the dinner crowd had finally slowed enough for him to go over the new stock that had been delivered earlier in the day.

"Hey, Jesse. I'm headed to the back to check out the order."

"I got it covered, boss man," Jesse replied, making Bear grin. The guy was more family than employee, but he still called Bear boss man. Bear would miss having Jesse around after Haven opened, but understood that running the center would take his full attention and time. Of course, the diner had hired more cooks, and between Jesse and Travis's training they were ready for the changeover, but Bear would miss seeing his friend daily.

He left Jesse in charge and walked to the back of the diner and the storeroom. He flicked on the single light hanging by its cord in the middle of the room and grabbed his clipboard from the top of one of several skids of product. There was triple the amount of food in this order to account for Johnny and Gabe's wedding. He still had to go through the freezers and fridges after this. It was a huge undertaking, but he'd prepared for that. The diner would be closed Christmas Eve day and Christmas day so that he and the White Hair Crew could do final preparations.

Johnny had asked for the food to be set up buffet style so that people could go for more food any time they wanted. There were quite a few big men who lived in town who'd be in attendance and they could pack away a ton of food. It would be like serving almost everything on the menu all at once, as well as a few new dishes Rick had convinced him to serve. His lover was always his biggest supporter, and especially Rick loved it when Bear was working on new recipes. With all the planning done, he'd been prepping for days. The entire twelfth grade would be working at the event to ensure everyone had lots to eat and drink during the course of the evening. It was a good way for them to earn some volunteer hours.

Bear was roughly halfway down his list when he felt a pair of warm hands sliding around his waist. Bear knew those hands. He looked down at the ring he'd put on that finger sparkle in the light. Everything was right with the world once again.

"Hey, babe, come for a visit?" Bear asked as he turned around to face Rick, his lover and partner in everything. He took Rick's lips in a deep kiss that had him completely forgetting about stock, orders, and the countless preparations that needed to be done. Instead, his body was acutely aware of the handsome man in his arms.

When he finally let Rick up for air, he answered, "Yep, I came to visit. You've been working so much lately with Christmas and the wedding coming up that we haven't had much alone time." Rick tried for his best pout, and Bear had to admit, his man was adorable. "Josh is with the gang of grandmas, and Jessie is in the kitchen. We have a solid fifteen minutes, baby, let's not waste them."

Bear chuckled as he closed the stockroom door and placed a heavy box in front of it so that no one could walk in on them. He remembered when they first met, Rick was the quiet librarian. He was still that in some ways, but sex wasn't one of them. Rick knew what he wanted and wasn't afraid to ask for it.

"There isn't enough time for me to prepare you properly and I refuse to hurt you no matter how much we want each other," Bear explained as he rubbed his hands down Rick's back on his way to squeezing his ass. He liked to take his time and make sure Rick was ready and comfortable.

"I've already taken care of that, Bear," Rick said while wiggling that cute ass of his.

"You're not teasing me, are you?" Bear reached down and unzipped his lover's pants before pushing them to the floor and off Rick's socked feet. Bear took only a moment to wonder where Rick's shoes were before he reached around and found what he was looking for. "A butt plug, you smart, horny, sexy man. Thank God."

Bear didn't think he had the patience left to wait now that he knew his lover was ready. Rick had been telling the truth, Bear had been working long hours lately and they hadn't made love in over a week. That changed today. Bear flipped Rick around and braced him against a skid full of bagged linens wrapped in packing plastic. He licked and sucked his way down his lover's neck, making Rick moan and push his ass out invitingly.

He couldn't resist playing with the butt plug and aiming for Rick's prostate, when his love went off, he knew he'd found it. Over and over again, he pulled the plug out before sliding it back into his lover's ass, taking him a bit higher with every move. Rick used his own arm to muffle his moans in an attempt at not alerting anyone to what they were doing.

Bear reached for one of the stacks of clean linens and pulled out a couple of towels, placing one on the floor. He'd gladly pay for a few missing towels. Rick's body was shaking in Bear's arms as he removed the plug and set it on the towel, then he handed the other one to Rick for better muffling. Quickly, Bear undid his jeans, hissing when he pulled his boxers over his hard cock. He blanketed Rick, and with one more kiss he pushed deep inside Rick's hot, tight ass.

They both groaned out their pleasure when Bear's balls touched Rick's cheeks. Every time the two of them made love, Bear lost himself to the feel of his fiancé's body. His soft skin begged to be touched and worshiped. With his arms wrapped tight around Rick, he lifted him off the floor to get the right angle in order to send his lover even further into a world of sensations and pleasure.

Rick arched his back, allowing Bear to go a touch deeper and driving him on even faster. His hips pistoned back and forth as the sounds of flesh slapping and moans of pleasure filled the room. Bear mastered Rick's body, exactly as his lover liked it, leaving nothing untouched.

Moments later he felt Rick stiffen before his body clamped down on Bear's cock. Spasms rocked through his man and into Bear, pulling his orgasm from his body without warning. He buried his face in Rick's soft hair and groaned as he came deep inside his lover.

Bear held on to Rick's limp body as they both recovered in a haze of gasping breaths and aftershocks. Their stolen moment was slowly coming to an end and he was loath to release Rick quite yet.

"Love you, Bear," Rick murmured as he rubbed the side of his face against Bear's chest.

"Love you so much, Rick," Bear replied while letting out a deep breath. "We are never waiting that long again. I swear."

"Hallelujah."

Chapter Nineteen

Dante, Spider, and Sam

The emergency room was unusually quite that morning and it gave Sam the time he needed to catch up on the never-ending pile of work growing wild on in his computer. He loved being a nurse and helping people, but could do with a touch less processing work. He was in the back office surrounded by Christmas cookies when he looked up through one of the interior windows and saw Johnny and a man, who had to be his brother, approaching the admissions desk. The family, hell, most of Brighton had heard of Johnny's brother already, and a few knew what he'd been through.

Sam stood up, walked out of the office, and approached them as they were checking in with the admissions clerk. "Hello, Johnny."

Johnny looked up and smiled. The guy was one of the happiest men Sam had ever met. "Hi, Sam." Then he pointed to the other man. "This is my brother, Frank Jeffrey, but he goes by Saint. He has an appointment with Dr. Green," Johnny said and went on to explain to his brother, "Sam is one of Gabe's cousins."

Sam could see the bandages and noted the exhaustion in Saint's eyes. "Nice to meet you. How are you feeling today?" *Awful, by the looks of you.*

"Holding strong," Saint stated before taking his information back from the clerk. "Thank you for all you did for my brother."

"No thanks needed, we're family," Sam assured, but he saw Saint cringe at the word "family." He also looked like he was ready to fall over. "Why don't you guys follow me and I'll get you settled in a room."

On his tablet, Sam looked up Saint's file, and then led them to a quiet room in the back to give them as much privacy as possible for an ER. Sam chose a space without a window so that the big man could rest without the daylight bothering him.

"You didn't have to come with me, little brother. I'm capable of bringing myself where I need to go. I don't want to take you away from all your wedding plans so close to the event," Saint grumbled as they entered the patient assessment room.

"You're my brother and you look like you're ready to pass out. There's no way in hell I'm leaving you to your own devices. I love you, and I don't want to see anything else happening to you," Johnny argued, which had Saint smirking.

"What happened to the kid who couldn't stand up for himself?" Saint asked.

"He grew up and had a family. Now, lay your ass down on that gurney and rest until the doctor gets here," Johnny ordered. Sam couldn't help but smile. Johnny was the sweetest guy you'd ever want to meet, but when it came to the health of someone he loved, he was a pit bull. Okay, maybe not a pit bull, maybe a French bulldog, but those pipsqueaks could take you down with the right motivation.

Saint lay down on the gurney without another complaint. Well, he certainly grumbled but didn't say a word. Sam took Saint's blood pressure and temperature, both were a bit high, and he noted everything in the exam screen on Saint's chart. With gunshot wounds, medical staff had to watch out for any possible infections, and an increased temperature could be a sign that Saint was fighting one. Sam wrapped rubber tubing around Saint's arm so he could draw blood, but the band wouldn't stay on. The man's bicep was huge.

"I'll have to get a longer one of these, be right back." Sam left the room and went to search the shelves of medical supplies in the back room. He found what he was looking for, pulled out a longer piece of tubing from the roll, and cut it.

When he walked back into the room, Saint was nearly asleep but Sam needed him awake for the blood draw. “Saint, you need to stay awake for me while I take your blood.”

His eyes popped open so fast that Sam doubted Saint realized he was falling asleep. Johnny had been quiet since he’d gotten his brother onto the bed, watching everything going on. Once Sam had finished drawing two vials, he placed a small gauze square over the small hole the needle had made, then wrapped mesh adhesive over the gauze.

“I’ll take these to the lab and alert Dr. Green that you’re here, Dr. Jeffrey,” Sam told Saint as he gathered up his tablet and the vials of blood.

“Not doctor. Call me Saint,” he responded before laying his head back down.

Sam looked over at Johnny, who seemed heartbroken, before saying, “Okay, Saint it is.” On his way out, he squeezed Johnny’s shoulder. This had to be difficult for both of them. Sam put a rush on the blood work and headed to Dr. Green’s office.

The doctor’s door was closed so Sam knocked and waited. It didn’t take long for Dr. Green to answer. “Hey, Sam, what do you have?”

“Frank Jeffrey is in exam room ten for his appointment. I’ve noted his blood pressure and temperature are both high and took his blood to be tested and have a CBC and panel done up.”

“How does he present?” the doctor asked.

“He appears to be exhausted and in pain. I won’t be surprised if he’s sleeping by the time we go back in. Also, don’t call him doctor, he doesn’t like that.” Sam didn’t want to upset the man a second time by using the word.

“Okay, the blood work will give us a better insight into whether he’s fighting an infection. Go grab the supplies to clean and redress his wounds while I go introduce myself.”

“On it.” Sam returned to the back room and gathered everything they might need: sterile instruments, dressings and tape, along with sterile saline to clean the wounds. He stopped by the meds room and prepared a syringe of pain reliever in case it became necessary. By the time he returned to the room, Dr. Green was waking Saint and introducing himself. It seemed that the patient was having a hard time waking up. When he finally did, Saint looked confused.

"Mr. Jeffrey, how are you feeling?" Dr. Green asked.

"Tired, but I'll fix that with a couple hours' rest." Saint's voice was gruff before he cleared his throat.

Dr. Green listened to Saint's heart and lungs before lifting his shirt and examining the dressings. "We'll get these changed for you, Mr. Jeffrey, and have a look at how you're healing."

"Saint, please. They call me Saint."

"Okay, Saint. Sam, will you start with the left hand while I begin with the stomach wound," Dr. Green stated. "Have you taken you pain medication today?"

"I try not to use them."

Dr. Green picked up the syringe from the tray. "I'm afraid this will be far too painful without some sort of pain medication."

Saint agreed with a nod. He was giving the shot before Sam would begin removing the bandages from his left hand. Sam would have hated trying to clean these wounds with the man feeling one hundred percent of the pain. Sam never liked causing anyone pain, although it was inevitable in his profession. He and the doc donned their gloves and went to work.

Johnny stood by the head of the bed and laid his hand on Saint's bicep while Sam revealed more and more damage with each layer of removed gauze. Saint never flinched. Not when the gauze stuck to one of his sutures or when Sam cleaned the pitted wound running through the center of his heavily sutured hand.

Dr. Green cleaned and bandaged the wound on Saint's stomach and was moving on to his right hand, and still not a peep out of their patient. Sam had to look up on several occasions to make sure Saint was okay, but the man was staring at the ceiling. The only indication of pain came from the beads of sweat on his forehead. Sam tried to be quick but careful to make sure the wound was thoroughly cleaned and healing.

Care and precision meant it took a while before they finished, but the wounds were completely cleaned and bandaged. By now Johnny was the one who looked like he was ready to pass out, and Saint was drifting back to sleep. The exhaustion and medication finally caught up with the poor guy.

Dr. Green stepped to the rolling computer outside of Saint's room to check the status of his blood work. Sam came around the table and took Johnny into his arms. "He'll be okay, he's healing. I promise."

"What kind of person would do that to another human being?" Johnny's voice cracked as he spoke, his emotions getting the best of him.

"Animals, plain and simple. No one with a conscience could do that." Sam could feel the anger coming off his friend. "Don't waste your energy on anger. There is nothing you can do to change it. Your brother needs you to be strong for him."

Johnny seemed to consider what Sam had said as Saint began to snore, loudly. Dr. Green came back in the room with a concerned expression on his face.

"I see our patient is asleep but he did sign the release to discuss his healthcare with you, Johnny. Do you want to sit down?" Dr. Green asked.

Johnny stood tall and squared his shoulders. "I'm fine, thank you. Can you tell me if my brother is going to be okay?"

"The wounds are severe, as you saw, but they are healing. He is fighting a small infection and to be on the safe side I'd like to hook him up to some fluids and antibiotics. He needs to remain in the hospital for a couple days until he's stronger. I don't feel comfortable releasing him given the shape he's in currently." Dr. Green looked Johnny straight in the eyes. "Can you convince him of that? I had a look at the original hospital records and found he'd checked himself out against doctor's orders after his last surgery to repair the damage."

Johnny's eyes opened wide. "He didn't mention anything about that. Don't you worry, Dr. Green, he'll be staying right here until you feel it's safe for him to leave." Johnny crossed his arms and looked down at the sleeping man with conviction and affection.

Sam couldn't imagine what Johnny or Saint were going through. Being apart for so many years only to come together under the stress of everything that had caused these severe health concerns. There was nothing Sam could do to change what happened, and listening to his own advice, he stood strong.

Sam wrapped his arms around Johnny and said, "I'll be right by your side, buddy."

Chapter Twenty

Jesse and Royce

Jesse wandered through Haven in the early hours of December twenty-third. In the predawn light, he walked the halls of this place where his dreams had come to life. He couldn't stop the goose bumps from rising when the oranges and yellows danced across the walls from the sunrise peeking over the trees. He ran his hand across the solid walls as he passed, strong walls to protect all who would come here.

He knew that soon enough these halls and rooms would be filled with people from all over connected by a single thread of hope. Hope that this time, in this place, they'd find what they were looking for and the help they needed.

The trained staff he'd hired would ensure that the people were safe and cared for, giving each of them the one thing they'd been denied: a chance. Everyone needed a chance to build a future for themselves, to learn, and to grow without fear and pain, and then to go on to help others. Yes, this was his dream, and he'd do anything to see it succeed.

Jesse sat in one of the new desks at the back of one of the many classrooms. This would be where Mrs. Connor would teach English. More rooms down the halls were set aside for science and math, as well as rooms that would be devoted to budgeting, taught by a retired CPA, and the ever-important cooking, and how to do laundry taught by the White Hair Crew. These young people would be coming here lacking basic and complex knowledge and skills that Jesse wanted to provide for them so they were able to learn how to cope with the world, and have the choice to move on to higher education, if they so desired.

He understood that the core classes were essential, and they wanted to assist those who were missing their GED to get it. The life classes would change and grow as needs were discovered. They were working with Shannon from the Sentinels to teach a self-defense course, and an art class led by Travis. There was also a chance for horticulture, which had been thrown into the ring by Sam, first aid led by Royce, and creative writing led by Tristan. Many others in the town wanted to help. Even a few ranchers had offered to teach whoever was interested how to work on a farm, and with animals.

Things were coming along better than Jesse could have ever imagined, and he recognized that without the townspeople's help, none of this would have ever happened. Brighton had accepted and protected him. It had given him his first real home and a way to support himself. It brought him Royce, a gift that had changed his life and filled his heart.

Jesse headed back to the main offices, passing the pool, first aid station, computer room, and cafeteria. The front of the building had sweeping, wide steps to welcome people in, and a wall of glass adorned the front of Haven. Once inside, comfortable couches and chairs were dotted every few feet, making sure everyone had room to study, chat, or sprawl. The front desk was well lit and cheerful. People standing at the desk waiting for assistance would be able to see Randy's inspiring artwork on the far wall.

The storage rooms were filled with clothing, shoes, toiletries, and school supplies. The cupboards, fridges, and freezers were full of nutritious food and drinks. The whole building was standing at the ready for the day they opened at the beginning of the New Year. Jesse had been fielding calls from schools and other shelters as word of Haven spread.

The sun rose above the trees, bathing the front of Haven and Jesse in its warm glow. He walked over to the metal plaque he'd had commissioned from one of the local artisans. As he ran his fingers over the letters and words, one thought remained centered in his mind. His grandpa would have been proud.

Welcome to Safe HAVEN

To All the Souls that Enter, May You Find

Peace and Safety Here.

Dedicated to the Town and People of Brighton, Texas

And in the Loving Memory of Grandpa Roy Tribalt

As a single tear rolled down Jesse's cheek, he could hear his grandpa and what he'd written in his will for Jesse to read.

Believe me when I say you will find a love that will fill all the empty places in your heart just like your grandma did for me. Be a smart man, and hold on to it as hard as you can because if anyone deserves to be happy it's you.

And Jesse was truly happy.

Chapter Twenty-One

Gabe and Johnny

The heavenly sound of steak sizzling on the barbeque filled the backyard of Gabe's best friend's house. Gabe could hear his stomach growling at the thought of a thick, juicy steak. It was the evening before his and Johnny's wedding, and they were having a barbeque at their best men's house. Royce was standing up for Gabe and Jesse was doing the same for Johnny.

Gabe was positive their family and friends were knee deep in bows by now, and busy decorating Haven for the wedding and reception. Johnny and Gabe had been warned to stay away under pain of a tongue lashing from the White Hair Crew. Taking the admonition seriously, the four of them were having a quiet night before tomorrow's ceremony and festivities. Johnny had settled down now that his brother was out of the hospital and resting comfortably in the spare bedroom at their house.

Thankfully, most of the wedding preparations had either been completed or assigned, so they had this night to relax. They'd picked up their suits today, the last thing on their list, and had chosen not to be separated before the wedding. Traditions were made to be broken, and there was no way they would be apart. And in keeping with doing things their way, they'd decided to walk down the aisle together.

Lucy was already asleep in Royce's spare bedroom, having had her dinner before everybody else. Of course, the trusty baby monitor was never too far away, in case she needed them. Gabe pulled his soon-to-be husband closer as the two of them cuddled under a blanket on the deck swing. Their friends had set up outdoor heaters so that the area would be comfortable, which helped, but they still would be eating inside.

Jesse was manning the grill as Royce handed out another round of beers and asked, “So any nerves, you two?”

Gabe was quick to answer. “Not a one.” He couldn’t wait to make Johnny his husband.

Johnny, on the other hand, had a different take on the upcoming nuptials. “Of course.”

“What do you have nerves about, babe?” Gabe asked out of curiosity. Maybe he could help.

Johnny was quick to look up at him. “Not about marrying you, that’s the best part of tomorrow. Everything else is what’s worrying me. What if there’s a problem with the food, or the flowers? What if we don’t have enough chairs or tables, or if there’s a freak snowstorm?”

Freak snowstorm. Gabe nearly laughed, but knew his man was stuck in worst-case scenario mode, worrying everything wouldn’t be perfect.

He reached out and cupped his fiancé’s face in his hands, humbled by the love and trust in those brilliant green eyes. “Babe, as long as you become my husband, the day will be a success. The rest can work itself out. It’s time to relax and enjoy this moment together.” He took Johnny’s lips in a deep kiss, expressing his emotions through his touch.

Every word was the absolute truth, and them getting married was what mattered. As far as Gabe was concerned, the rest was for everyone else.

From the moment Johnny had come into Gabe’s life, he knew he’d been blessed. The quiet, unassuming man, who’d saved two lives in the fire that brought them together, was a gift. The love they had for each other was so strong that they’d decided they needed to share it, and now they had their daughter. There had been a time when Gabe had pretty much given up on his own happily-ever-after.

Now he had his soon-to-be husband and a beautiful daughter, his family to love and care for.

Gabe had everything he'd ever dreamt of, and it was all due to the man in his arms.

Chapter Twenty-Two

December 24th

Wedding Day

Johnny was losing his mind and no one seemed to care. Okay, maybe a bit overdramatic, but his kitchen was flooded. The dishwasher had decided today of all days would be the perfect day to have a crisis mid-cycle. Every towel they owned lay covering the kitchen tile in an attempt to soak up the soapy water.

Saint stood looking from the safety of the dining room with Lucy in his arms as their new puppy came around the corner and slid through the bubbles. Gabe had left in search of some sort of part they needed to fix the traitorous machine, and Johnny stood front and center of his own nightmare. Today was supposed to be calm and joyous, not soggy and soapy.

"Chill, bro, it'll be fine. The wedding is still hours away. I've got Lucy. You don't need to worry about her. She'll be ready to go." Johnny knew his brother was trying to calm him, "trying" being the operative word. The good news, Saint looked much better now that he'd spent a few extra days under medical care, relieving some of Johnny's worry.

"You're hurt, you need to be resting and recuperating, not chasing a toddler around." Johnny wanted to crawl back into bed and start over. He knew he was already strung tight, but this wasn't helping, and now his brother risked his recovery to help him. Not going to happen.

"No worries, a young woman named Josie called to say she'd come help me today. She said she's Gabe's cousin. Is that the one you told me about in the fire, the one you grabbed onto outside the window?"

"Yep, that's Josie. She called you? How did she get your phone number?" The home phone hadn't rung.

Saint squinted before he began to grin. "I don't know. I didn't even think about it. Could this be one of those Brighton things you told me about?"

Johnny couldn't help but smile. "That would be it. Once the town's people decide you're family they swoop right in."

"Not entirely a bad thing, little brother," Saint observed, and Johnny understood the draw that kind of life had to each of them. Even before their mother had died, life was less than ideal for them under their father's rule.

Johnny heard a truck pull in and assumed it was Gabe back from the store, until there was a knock on the front door. He dried his wet feet and went to answer it. When he opened the door, he was confused as to why Mr. Tucker, from down the street, was standing there with a Santa hat on and his toolbox in his hand.

"Hello, Mr. Tucker. How can I help you?"

"You've got that the wrong way around, young man. It's what we can do to help you. We heard you had a bit of an issue this morning and we've come to help," he told Johnny while holding up the toolbox.

"We've?" Johnny looked behind the older man to find his wife and Mrs. Walker, from across the street, carrying mops and pails. "I can't ask you to do that."

"Who asked?" he inquired before walking in and headed to the kitchen followed by his smiling wife.

"Don't you worry, we'll get things to right in no time. You go sit down and rest. You have a big day ahead of you," Mrs. Walker ordered before following the first two "helpers" into the other room.

Johnny stood there staring at her retreating figure, unsure what just happened. Saint came over with a strange look on his face, but said nothing.

Johnny looked at his big brother and said, “Yep, it’s a Brighton thing.”

***

Hours later, Johnny was doing his final tour of Haven, taking in that all the decorations were up, the flowers were delivered, and seats were all set for the ceremony. In a nearby room, tables had been pushed together against the far wall, and covered in lovely tablecloths to hold the buffet dinner. After that the room would become their dance hall.

Everything looked even better than he had imagined. The decorations, in rainbow shades, were spectacular. Ribbons and bows hung around the room and on the chairs, while small twinkling lights shined in various spots along the walls. They intended to have the overhead lights muted during the ceremony, giving the room a more intimate feel.

A twelve-foot, fully decorated Christmas tree glowed from the front of the room where they’d be exchanging their vows, with Father John officiating. Poinsettias bloomed from hand-decorated pots, and orchids stood tall in their elegant beauty. Johnny had insisted on having orchids from Gabe’s greenhouse at the ceremony. His love had labored over them especially for today. His mom would have loved that.

“How you doing, sweetheart?” Gabe asked as he came up behind Johnny and hugged him to his broad chest. Johnny couldn’t help but melt into Gabe’s arms.

“It’s all so beautiful,” Johnny’s voice cracked as he spoke. “I’m overwhelmed that so many people came together to give us this. I just…” He wasn’t sure what was happening. He felt like he was having an emotional breakdown.

Gabe spun Johnny around and gathered him in his arms. Johnny couldn’t help but reach for the comfort his love was offering. Everything was so real, and yet he felt he was drowning at the same time. He needed a minute to come up for air. Gabe reached down and picked him up, then carried him out of the room.

He heard a door shut and looked up to see where Gabe had taken him. They were in their assigned consultation office/change room. A desk and chairs were set up to the right while an orange couch stood against the back wall. The bathroom door was open revealing a mirror, sink, and toilet. The sparkle from the rubies and emeralds of his mother's vintage brooch, pinned to the lapel of his suit jacket, caught his eye.

"Why did you bring me here?" Johnny asked.

Gabe sat down on the couch before rearranging Johnny, turning and lying down with him on top of Gabe's chest. "Because this is where you and I are going to hide out until the ceremony."

"But there's so much to do." Johnny's mind was racing. "What about Lucy?"

"Lucy is completely happy with her Uncle Saint and Cousin Josie. As for everything else, there are a lot of family and friends out there to take care of it. Right now, all I want is to be alone with you before you become my husband." Gabe kissed Johnny's forehead.

Johnny got comfortable on Gabe's chest and concentrated on his lover's strong heartbeat. Gentle fingers began running through his hair, helping him settle even further.

"When we first met, I knew you were special. The one person just for me," Gabe murmured, his voice vibrating through his chest as he spoke. "The person who would teach me how to trust again and open my heart to a future. Never having to live with doubt or fear again. Without you, Johnny Jeffrey, I am nothing."

"I thought you were crazy," Johnny deadpanned, making Gabe laugh, as he'd hoped. "However, after the initial shock wore off, I realized I'd found my home and my family. At first, I worried that you were too perfect and my dreams would be taken away from me at any moment, but we stood strong together. You helped me gain back my independence and a career I love. You're my anchor, my love, and my life. Without you, Gabe Mason, I am nothing."

They spent a few moments holding each other in silence, the air thick with emotion. "Why do I feel like we just exchanged our vows," Gabe teased as he snuggled Johnny closer. "We couldn't have said it any better."

***

Later that evening the two lovers walked hand in hand down the aisle with their special flower girl at their side. They made their heartfelt vows before their family and friends, new and old, in the small town of Brighton, Texas.

What began in the flames of a fire was now completed in the glow of holiday lights. The community gathered to share their love and joy with the happy new family in the season that embodied the mandate of peace, love, and joy. Laughter and songs could be heard late into the evening and early the next morning.

Thank you from everyone in the town of Brighton for joining us as we watched the trials and tribulations on the road to love between people who deserved a happily-ever-after.

ABOUT THE AUTHOR

M. Tasia is a M/M romance author who lives in Ontario, Canada. She's is a dedicated people watcher, lover of romance novels, 80's rock, and happily-ever-afters (once the MCs are put through their paces, of course), who grew up with a love of reading.

She's a firm believer that everyone deserves to have love, excitement, and crazy hot romance in their lives. Love should be celebrated and shared.

Connect with M.:
mtasiabooks.com
FB: mtasiabooks
twitter: @mtasiaauthor
IG: @m.tasia.author
TikTok: @mtasiauthor

www.BOROUGHSPUBLISHINGGROUP.com

If you enjoyed this book, please write a review. Our authors appreciate the feedback, and it helps future readers find books they love. We welcome your comments and invite you to send them to info@boroughspublishinggroup.com.

Follow us on TikTok and Instagram, and be sure to sign up for our newsletter for surprises and new releases from your favorite authors.

Are you an aspiring writer? Check out www.boroughspublishinggroup.com/submit and see if we can help you make your dreams come true.

Love podcasts? Enjoy ours at www.boroughspublishinggroup.com/podcast

www.ingramcontent.com/pod-product-compliance
Lightning Source LLC
LaVergne TN
LVHW050908080826
845145LV00001B/11